W9-BRB-662

WORLD'S END

BY THE SAME AUTHOR

NOVELS

Budding Prospects
Water Music

SHORT STORIES

Descent of Man
Greasy Lake

T. CORAGHESSAN BOYLE

WORLD'S END

A NOVEL

VIKING

VIKING
Viking Penguin Inc., 40 West 23rd Street,
New York, New York 10010, U.S.A.
Penguin Books Ltd, 27 Wrights Lane, London W8 5TZ
(Publishing & Editorial) and Harmondsworth, Middlesex,
England (Distribution & Warehouse)
Penguin Books Australia Ltd, Ringwood,
Victoria, Australia
Penguin Books Canada Limited, 2801 John Street,
Markham, Ontario, Canada L3R 1B4
Penguin Books (N.Z.) Ltd, 182-190 Wairau Road,
Auckland 10, New Zealand

First published in 1987 by Viking Penguin Inc.
Published simultaneously in Canada

AUTHOR'S NOTE:

The following is an historical fugue. It bears small relation to actual places and events, and none whatever to people living or dead. It is pure fiction.

Grateful acknowledgment is made for permission to reprint excerpts from the following copyrighted works:

"Gerontion," from *Collected Poems 1909–1962* by T. S. Eliot. Copyright 1936 by Harcourt Brace Jovanovich, Inc.; copyright © 1963, 1964 by T. S. Eliot. Reprinted by permission of Harcourt Brace Jovanovich, Inc. and Faber and Faber Limited.

Desire Under the Elms, from *The Plays of Eugene O'Neill*. Copyright © 1924, renewed 1952 by Eugene O'Neill. Reprinted by permission of Random House, Inc.

LIBRARY OF CONGRESS CATALOGING IN PUBLICATION DATA
Boyle, T. Coraghessan.
World's end.
I. Title.
PS3552.0932W67 1987 813'.54 87-40023
ISBN 0-670-81489-X

Printed in the United States of America by
Haddon Craftsmen, Scranton, Pennsylvania
Set in Sabon
Designed by Francesca Belanger

In memory of my own lost father

After such knowledge, what forgiveness?

—T. S. Eliot,
"Gerontion"

ACKNOWLEDGMENTS

The author would like to thank the following people for their assistance in gathering material for this book: Alan and Seymour Arkawy, Mitchell Burgess, Richard Chambers, Chuck Fadel, Ken Fortgang, Rick Miles, Jack and Jerry Miller and the crew of the *Clearwater*.

CONTENTS

Part II
WORLD'S END

PRINCIPAL CHARACTERS

IN THE SEVENTEENTH CENTURY

At Nysen's Roost

HARMANUS VAN BRUNT, a tenant farmer
AGATHA VAN BRUNT, his wife
JEREMIAS VAN BRUNT, their son
KATRINCHEE VAN BRUNT, their daughter
WOUTER VAN BRUNT, their son

<table><tr><td>WOUTER VAN BRUNT
HARMANUS VAN BRUNT
STAATS VAN BRUNT
GEESJE VAN BRUNT
AGATHA VAN BRUNT
GERTRUYD VAN BRUNT</td><td>children of Jeremias Van Brunt and Neeltje Cats Van Brunt</td></tr></table>

Among the Kitchawanks

SACHOES, *sachem* of the Kitchawanks
WAHWAHTAYSEE, his wife
MINEWA, their daughter
MOHONK (MOHEWONECK), their son
JEREMY MOHONK (SQUAGGANEEK), son of Katrinchee Van Brunt and Mohonk

At Van Wartwyck

OLOFFE STEPHANUS VAN WART, a Dutch patroon
GERTRUYD VAN WART, his wife
STEPHANUS OLOFFE ROMBOUT VAN WART, their son
HESTER LOVELACE VAN WART, his wife
ROMBOUT VAN WART, their son and heir
OLOFFE VAN WART } their sons
PIETER VAN WART }
SASKIA VAN WART, their daughter

JOOST CATS, the *schout*
GEESJE CATS, his wife
NEELTJE CATS } their daughters
ANS CATS }
TRIJINTJE CATS }
STAATS VAN DER MEULEN, a tenant farmer
MEINTJE VAN DER MEULEN, his wife
DOUW VAN DER MEULEN } their children
JANNETJE VAN DER MEULEN }
KLAES VAN DER MEULEN }
BARENT VAN DER MEULEN }
HACKALIAH CRANE
CADWALLADER CRANE, his son
JAN PIETERSE
DOMINIE VAN SCHAIK
JAN THE KITCHAWANK
WOLF NYSEN
ALBREGT VAN DEN POST

IN THE TWENTIETH CENTURY

At Kitchawank Colony

TRUMAN VAN BRUNT
CHRISTINA ALVING VAN BRUNT, his wife
WALTER TRUMAN VAN BRUNT, their son
JESSICA CONKLIN WING VAN BRUNT, Walter's wife
LOLA SOLOVAY } Walter's adoptive parents
HESH SOLOVAY }

At the Shawangunk Reservation

JEREMY MOHONK *père*
MILDRED TANTAQUIDGEON, his wife
JEREMY MOHONK, their son and last of the Kitchawanks
HORACE TANTAQUIDGEON, Mildred's brother

In Van Wartville

ROMBOUT VAN WART, eleventh heir to Van Wart Manor
CATHERINE DEPEYSTER VAN WART, his wife
DEPEYSTER VAN WART, their son and heir
JOANNA VAN WART, Depeyster's wife
MARDI VAN WART, their daughter

PELETIAH CRANE
STANDARD CRANE, son of Peletiah
TOM CRANE, son of Standard
PIET AUKEMA

Part I

MARTYR'S REACH

He began to doubt
whether both he and the world around him
were not bewitched.

—Washington Irving,
"Rip Van Winkle"

A Collision with History

ON THE day he lost his right foot, Walter Van Brunt had been haunted, however haphazardly, by ghosts of the past. It began in the morning, when he woke to the smell of potato pancakes, a smell that reminded him of his mother, dead of sorrow after the Peterskill riots of 1949, and it carried through the miserable lunch break he divided between nostalgic recollections of his paternal grandmother and a liverwurst sandwich that tasted of dead flesh and chemicals. Over the whine of the lathe that afternoon he was surprised by a waking dream of his grandfather, a morose, big-bellied man so covered with hair he could have been an ogre out of a children's tale, and then, just before five, he had a vague rippling vision of a leering Dutchman in sugarloaf hat and pantaloons.

The first ghost, the ghost of the pancakes, was conjured by the deft culinary hand of Lola Solovay, his adoptive mother. Though Walter was only midway through his fourth year when his natural mother succumbed to the forces of bigotry and misguided patriotism, he remembered her chiefly for her eyes, which were like souls made flesh, and her potato pancakes, which were light, toothsome, and drowned in sour cream and homemade applesauce. Lying abed, waiting in the limbo between dreaming and consciousness for the alarm to summon him to his hellish job at Depeyster Manufacturing, he caught the scent of those ethereal pancakes, and for just a moment his mother was there with him.

The ghost of his grandmother, Elsa Van Brunt, was also mixed up with the scent of food. He unwrapped the liverwurst on white Lola had concocted for him in the penumbral dawn, and suddenly he was ten years old, spending the summer on the river with his grandparents, the day as dark as December with the storm sitting atop Dunderberg Mountain. His grandmother had got up from her potter's wheel to fix his lunch and tell him the story of Sachoes' daughter. Sachoes, as Walter knew from previous episodes, was chief of the Kitchawanks, the tribe that was flimflammed out of its land by the founders of Peterskill-on-the-Hudson back in the days of the Colony. At that time, the Kitchawanks, who were, generally speaking, a lethargic, peace-loving, oyster-eating clan of layabouts and bark-hut builders, owed fealty to the fierce Mohawk to the north. Indeed, so fierce, so savage, so warlike and predatory were these Mohawk that a single brave could be sent down to collect tribute, and Manitou have mercy on the tribe that failed to feast him like a god and laden him with *wampumpeak* and *seawant*. *Kanyengahaga*, the Mohawk called themselves, people of the place of flint; the Kitchawanks and their Mohican cousins called them *Mohawk*, people who eat people, a reference to their propensity for roasting and devouring those who failed to please them.

Well. White bread was laid out on the plate, tomatoes were sliced, a cellophane-wrapped tube of liverwurst produced from the refrigerator. He had a daughter, Walter's grandmother said, and her name was Minewa, after the goddess of the river who hurled thunderbolts. She pointed out the window and across the broad back of the Hudson to where lightning sprang like nerve endings from the crown of Dunderberg. Like those.

One lazy August afternoon, a Mohawk brave strode into the village, naked but for his breechclout and painted like death and the devil. Tribute, he demanded, in a tongue that sounded like the thrashing of adders, and then he fell down in a swoon, blood pouring from his mouth and ears, and the pockmarks standing out on his face. Minewa nursed him. If he died, there would be no more oyster eating, no fooling around in bark canoes and plucking the sweet white meat from the cavities of blueclaw crabs: there would be no more Kitchawanks. The Mohawk would see to that.

For a month he lay prostrate in Sachoes' hut, his head cradled in Minewa's lap while she assuaged his fever with otter musk and fed him herbs and wild onion. Gradually he began to regain his strength, until one day he was able to stand without support and repeat his demand for tribute. But this time it wasn't beaverskins or *wampumpeak* he wanted: it was Minewa. Sachoes was reluctant, but the Mohawk blustered and threatened and cut open his chest in three places to show his sincerity. He would take her to the north country and make her a queen. Of course, if Sachoes preferred, the brave would go home empty-handed and then return one starless night with a raiding party and cut up the Kitchawanks like dogs. Sachoes, who was shortly thereafter to be hoodwinked by the Dutch trader who founded Peterskill on the sacred rock where the chief's forefathers had watched Manitou's big woman descend to earth, said "Sure, take her."

Two weeks later a party of Kitchawanks was combing the adjoining valley for acorns, chestnuts and rose hips when they came across the smoke of a cooking fire. With stealth, with courage and curiosity and not a little audacity—Manitou knows, it could have been the devil himself cooking up a plague—they approached the clearing from which the smoke rose into the sky like a capnomancer's dream. What they saw, Walter's grandmother said, spreading mayonnaise, was betrayal. What they saw was the Mohawk and Minewa, what was left of her. She was nothing from the waist down, his grandmother said, setting the sandwich before him—liverwurst, the texture and color, the very smell of flesh—nothing but bone.

If the images of mother and grandmother had been summoned by a tickle of the olfactory lobe, the ghost of his grandfather was more problematic. Perhaps it was a matter of association: once the pattern is established, one thing gives rise to another and the mind plays out memories like beads on a string. At any rate, in the heat of the afternoon, old Harmanus Van Brunt had materialized just to the left of the lathe, big-boned, big-bellied, and big-headed, hairy as a hog, with cutting oil and aluminum shavings caught in the hair of his forearms and a clay pipe clenched between his teeth. All his life he'd been a fisherman, hauling nets with the strength of his shoulders and the counterbalance of his belly, and he'd died as he'd been born: on the river. Walter had been twelve or thirteen at the time. His grandfather, too old at that point to handle the big gill nets weighted down with stripers or sturgeon, had kept his hand in by netting killifish and keeping them in pens for sale as bait. One afternoon—and for Walter the recollection was like a hot cautery—the old man's face went numb and the stroke folded him up like a jackknife and pitched him into the bait pen, where the mass of killifish closed over him. By the time Walter could get help, the old man had drowned.

The Dutchman was something else. Something Walter had seen in a gallery in Amsterdam when the Solovays had taken him to Europe. Or maybe on a cigar box. He puzzled over it a minute, then chalked it up to genetic memory and indigestion, in equal parts. When the five o'clock whistle blew, he shook his head twice, as if to clear it, and then ran his bike down to the Throbbing Elbow to drain a sad pitcher of beer in honor of his twenty-second birthday.

But even here in the shrine of the present, with its neon glare, its thumping woofers and black lights, he suffered an attack of history. Clumping through the door in his new Dingo boots with the imitation spur straps, he could have sworn he saw his father standing at the bar with a girl whose dress was so short as to expose the nether curve of her buttocks. He was wrong. About his father, that is; for their part, the girl's buttocks were incontrovertible. She was wearing a paper miniskirt hand-dyed by the Shawangunk Indians on their reservation south of Jamestown, with matching panties. The man beside her turned out to be Hector Mantequilla, with ragged wild hair and eight-inch collar points. "Van," he said, swinging around, "what's happening?" The girl turned around now too, hair in her eyes, a pout of makeup, nothing wrong and nothing right. Walter hadn't seen his father in eleven years.

Walter shrugged. He was feeling sorry for himself, feeling orphaned and martyred and strung out, full of the merde of human existence and sick with the idea of decay: feeling old. It was 1968. Sartre was front-page news, *Saturday Review* was asking "Can We Survive Nihilism?" and *Life* had photographed Jack Gelber adrift on an ice flow. Walter knew all about it. He was an alienated hero himself, he was a Meursault, a Rocquentin, a man of iron and tears facing the world in unhope and as riddled with the nausea as a Jarlsberg is with holes. There was no way, for instance, he was going home to the chicken cordon bleu, asparagus vinaigrette, and glittering chocolate mousse his adoptive mother had prepared for him. No way he was going to thankfully tear open his sweetheart Jessica's gift—a new helmet, bronze like the sun and decorated with daisy decals that spelled out his name—and then tenderly undress her beneath the azalea bush out back with the night like a sleeper's breath whispering in his ear. No way. At least for a while yet.

"What you drinking, man?" Hector said, leaning into the bar for support. His shirt, which seemed to be fashioned from a synthetic fabric composed of Handi-Wrap and styrofoam, featured a pair of bleeding eyeballs and a slick pink tongue that plunged into the depths of his waistband.

Walter didn't answer right away, and when he did it was with a non sequitur. "It's my birthday," he said. Though he was looking at the girl, he was seeing his grandmother again, the flesh of her heavy arms trembling over a mound of turnip peels, the look on her face when she told him she'd had the phone disconnected because her neighbor—a notorious witch—was sending witch lice over the wire. Superstitious in a way that connected her to the past as firmly as the gravestones rooted in the cemetery on the hill, she'd spent the last twenty years of her life making ceramic ashtrays in the shape of the trash fish her husband extracted from his nets and tossed on the riverbank to rot. They're the dispossessed, she used to say, glaring at Walter's hairy grandfather. God's creatures. I can see them in my sleep. Fish, fish, fish.

"Yes, yes!" Hector shouted. "Your birthday, man!" And then roared for Benny Settembre, the bartender, to set them up. Hector was a native of Muchas Vacas, P.R., the son of slaves and Indians who became slaves. The son of something else too: his eyes were as green as the Statue of Liberty. "I got something for you, man—something special," he said, taking Walter's arm. "In the men's room, you know?"

Walter nodded. The jukebox started up with the sound of shattering glass and rocks against the flanks of buses. Hector took hold of his arm and started toward the bathroom, then stopped cold. "Oh yeah," he said, indicating the girl. "This is Mardi."

Six hours later, Walter found himself thinking about water sports. But only fleetingly and because the occasion suggested it. He was on the far side of the river from Peterskill, a mile and a half from home as the fish swims, eleven or twelve by car, and up to his neck in the greasy Stygian drift of the nighttime Hudson. Swimming. Or about to swim. At the moment he was feeling his way through the bottom muck, planted firmly against the current, the rich organic scent of the river in his nostrils, a perfume that managed to combine the essences of aquatic devolution, orange peels, diesel fuel and, yes, merde. Ahead of him, in the dark, he could hear Mardi's laughter and the soft gentle swirl of her scissor kick. "Come on," she whispered. "It's nice, really." And then she giggled, a sound so natural it could have come from one of the lovelorn insects in the trees that rose up from the shore in a black unfathomable wall.

"Shit!" Hector cursed softly behind them, and there was a terrific splash—the sound of disporting porpoises, depth charges, beer kegs dropped from a pier—and then his high wild laugh.

"Shhhh!" Walter hissed. He didn't like this, didn't like it at all. But he was drunk—worse, he was stoned off his feet on the pills Hector had been feeding him all night—and past the point of caring. He felt the buoyancy of the water like the hands of the river nymphs as he lifted off and dug into the surface in a stealthy breaststroke.

They'd left the Elbow at ten to sit out back in Hector's bumper-blasted '55 Pontiac and pass a pipe. Walter hadn't called home—hadn't done much of anything for that matter except pin beer bottles to his lips—and he thought of Jessica, of Hesh and Lola and his aunt Katrina, with a sort of perverse pleasure. They were missing him now, that was for sure. The chicken Cordon Bleu had dried up in the oven, the asparagus gone limp, the mousse fallen. He pictured them huddled glumly around the redwood picnic table, cocktails going weak with melted ice, toothpicks congealing in a puddle of grease on the platter long since denuded of Swedish meatballs. He pictured them—his family, his girlfriend—waiting for him, Walter Truman Van Brunt, creature of his own destiny, soulless, hard, free from convention and the twin burdens of love and duty, and took the pipe from the hand of a stranger. They were missing him now, oh yes indeed.

But then he felt a stab of guilt, the curse of the apostate, and saw his father again. This time the old man was crossing the parking lot alone, hands thrust deep in the pockets of his striped bell-bottoms, a mauve scarf trailing down his chest. He stopped even with the car window, bent from the waist, and peered in with that mad, tortured look he'd brought with him when he appeared out of nowhere for Walter's eleventh birthday.

Out of nowhere. Like an apparition. Huge, his head cropped to a reddish stubble, pants torn and greasy, jacket too small, he'd looked like a cross between the Wandering Jew and the Ghost of Christmas Past, he'd looked like an ecstatic who's lost the ecstasy, a man with no future, a bum. So insubstantial Walter would have missed him altogether if it weren't for the shouting. Eleven years old, glutted on pink-frosted cake, root beer, chocolate marshmallow supreme and Mars Bars, Walter was up in his room knocking around with his new set of Presidents, Regents and Ministers of the World when he heard a tumult of voices from the front of the house. Hesh's voice. Lola's. And another, a voice that sounded as if it were inside his head, as if it were thinking for him, strange, magnetic and familiar all at once.

The front door was open. Hesh stood in the doorway like a colossus, Lola at his side. Beyond them, on the front lawn, was a man with a head like a pumpkin and colorless, rinsed-out eyes. He was wrought up, this man, nearly amuck, dancing on one foot with anger and chanting like a shaman, the litany of his hurts pouring out of him like vinegar. "Flesh of my flesh!" the man yelled, over and over.

Hesh, big Hesh, with his bald honest head and his forearms that were like hammers, was shouting at this man who looked like a bum—at Walter's father—as if he wanted to kill him. "Son of a bitch!" Hesh raged in a high agitated voice, each word cut clear and distinct. "Liar, thief, murderer! Get out. Get out of here!"

"Kidnappers!" the man bawled back at him, bending to pound the earth in his rage. But then all of a sudden Walter edged into view, puzzled and frightened, and the man fell silent. A change came over his face—it had been ugly and vehement and now suddenly it was as composed as a priest's—and he went down on one knee and spread his arms. "Walter," he said, and the tone of it was the most seductive thing the boy had ever heard. "Don't you know who I am?"

"Truman," Hesh said, and it was both a plea and a warning.

Walter knew.

And then he saw it. Behind his father, behind the pale, shorn, washed-out man in the bum's suit of clothes, stood a motorcycle. A little pony Parilla, 98cc, red paint and chrome, gleaming like a puddle in the desert. "Come here, Walter," his father said. "Come to your father."

Walter glanced up at the man he knew as his daddy, the man who'd fed and clothed him, who'd stood by him through his traumas, there to throw the ball and catch it, to cow his teachers and subdue his enemies with a glance, to anchor and protect him. And then he looked out at the man on the lawn, the father he barely knew, and the motorcycle that stood behind him. "Come on, I won't bite."

Walter went.

And now here he was again, come back after eleven years, come back the second time that day. Only now he was black, a solid presence, with a pair of red-rimmed eyes and a nose that looked as if it had been stepped on. Now he was leaning through the window of the Pontiac and lighting a cigarette off Hector's joint and reaching out to take Walter's hand in a soul clasp and inquire as to how the fuck he was doing, man. Now he was Herbert Pompey, denizen of South Street bars, poet, player of the cornet and nose flute, part-time *Man of La Mancha* hoofer, weekend doper.

Sick with history, the past coming at him like a succession of screaming fire trucks, Walter could only tug weakly at Pompey's hand and murmur something to the effect that he was doing okay but that he had a headache, he was feeling pretty stoned and thought he might be having a little trouble with his eyes. And his ears. And come to think of it, maybe his brain too.

There followed an interval during which Pompey joined them in the big airship of the Pontiac's interior—Hector, Mardi and Walter in front, Pompey stretched out across the back seat with a pint of Spañada that had appeared in his hand as if through the intercession of spirits—an interval during which they communed with the tinny rattle of the radio, the texture of the night, a greenish blur in the sky that might have been a UFO but was probably a weather balloon and the great starry firmament that stretched out over the hood of the Pontiac like a sea of felt. Gravity tugged at Walter's lower lip. The neck of the Spañada bottle loomed up on his right, the joint on his left. He was numb as a corpse. The attack of history was over.

It was Mardi who came up with the idea of swimming out to the ghost ships. An idea that had sounded far better in the conception than the execution. "It's fantastic," she insisted, "no, no, it's really fantastic," as if someone were contradicting her. And so they were, Walter, Mardi and Hector (Pompey had wisely chosen to stay with the car), swimming out to the black silent shapes that lay anchored in thirty feet of water off Dunderberg Mountain.

Stroke, kick, stroke, kick, Walter chanted under his breath, trying to remember if he was supposed to breathe with his head above the surface or beneath it. He was thinking about water sports. Scuba. Water polo. Jackknife. Dead man's float. He was no slouch: he'd done them all at one time or another, had dunked heads and hammered goals with the best of them, swum rivers, lakes, inlets, murky primeval ponds and chloraseptic pools, a marvel of windmilling arms and slashing feet. But this, this was different. He was too far gone for this. The water was like heavy cream, his arms like spars. Where was she?

She was nowhere. The night fell on him from the recesses of space, shearing past the immemorial mountains, the oaks and tamaracks and hickories, melding finally in a black pool with the chill, imp-haunted river that tugged at him from below. Stroke, kick: he could see nothing. Might as well have his eyes closed. But wait—there, against the flat black keel of the near ship, wasn't that her? That spot of white? Yes, there she was, the little tease, the bulb of her face like a night-blooming flower, a beacon, a flag of truce or capitulation. The keel rose behind her like a precipice, bats skittered over the water's surface, insects chirred and somewhere, lost in obscurity, Hector floundered like a fish in a net, his soft curses softened by the night until they fell away into infinity.

Walter was thinking of how Mardi had shucked the paper dress in the gloom of the shore as casually as if she were undressing in her own bedroom, thinking of the thrill that had lit his groin as she steadied herself against him to perch first on one leg and then the other as she slipped off the paper panties and dropped them in the mud. Ghostly, a pale presence against the backdrop of the night, she'd disappeared into the grip of the water before he'd had a chance to yank his shirt off. Now he concentrated on the milky blur of her face and paddled toward her.

"Hector?" she called as he glided up to her. She was trying to shimmy up the anchor chain, gripping the cold pitted steel with naked flesh, hugging it to her, swaying above the surface like the carved figurehead that comes to life in legends.

"No," he whispered, "it's me, Walter."

She seemed to find this funny, and giggled yet again. Then she dropped back into the water with a splash that could have alerted all the specter sailors of all the ships of the fleet—or, at the very least, the watchman she'd been jabbering about all the way over in the car. Walter clutched the anchor chain and peered up at the ship that loomed above him. It was a merchantman from the Second World War like the others beyond it, ships of the mothball fleet that had risen and fallen with the tide twice a day since Walter was born. Their holds were full of the grain the government bought up to keep free enterprise from strangling the farmers of Iowa, Nebraska and Kansas. Below them, somewhere in a pocket off Jones Point, lay the wreck of the *Quedah Merchant,* scuttled there by William Kidd's men in 1699. Legend had it that you could still see her when the river cleared, full-rigged and ready to sail, still laden with treasure from Hispaniola and the Barbary Coast.

But Walter wasn't after treasure. Or rotting wheat germ strewn with rat turds, or even some good clean healthy exercise. In fact, until he brushed against Mardi in the water beneath the taut and rusted anchor chain, he wasn't sure what he was after. "Surprise," she gushed, bobbing up beside him, one arm on the chain, the other flung around his neck. And then, pressing her body to him—no, rubbing against him as if she'd suddenly developed some sort of subaqueous itch—she murmured, "Is it really your birthday?"

He'd almost forgotten. The sad censorious faces of Jessica, Lola and Hesh passed in quick review, a sudden manifestation of a larger affliction, and then he was grabbing for her, seeking orifices, trying to kiss, nuzzle, grip the anchor chain, tread water and copulate all at once. He got a mouthful of river and came up coughing.

Mardi made a soft, moaning, lip-smacking noise, as if she were tasting soup or sherbet. Wavelets lapped around them. Walter was still coughing.

"Listen, birthday boy," she whispered, breaking away and then pulling close again, "I could be real nice to you if you'd do something for me."

Walter was electrified. Hot, eager, bereft of judgment. The chill, fishy current was as warm suddenly as a palm-fringed Jacuzzi. "Huh?" he said.

What she wanted, bobbing there like a naiad in the turbid ancient Hudson in the late hours of the night and with the great high monumental V-shaped prow of the ship hanging over her, was derring-do. Heroics. Feats of strength and agility. What she wanted was to see Walter hoist himself up the anchor chain like a naked buccaneer and vanish into the fastness of the mystery ship, there to unravel the skein of its secrets, absorb the feel of its artifacts and memorize the lay of its decks. Or something like that. "My arms are too weak," she said. "I can't do it myself."

A tug moved by in the distance, towing a barge. Beyond it, Walter could make out the dim lights of Peterskill, hazy with distance and the pall of mist that hung over the river's middle reaches.

"Come on," she prodded. "Just take a peek."

Walter thought about the presumptive watchman, the penalties for trespassing on federal property, his fear of heights, the crapulous, narcotized, soporific state of his mind and body that made every movement a risk, and said, "Why not?"

Hand over hand, foot over foot, he ascended the chain like a true nihilist and existential hero. What did danger matter? Life had neither meaning nor value, one lived only for personal extinction, for the void, for nothingness. It was dangerous to sit on a sofa, lift a fork to your mouth, brush your teeth. Danger. Walter laughed in the face of it. Of course, for all that, he was terrified.

Two-thirds of the way up he lost his grip and snatched at the chain like a madman, twelve pints of blood suddenly pounding in his ears. Below, blackness; above, the shadowy outline of the ship's rail. Walter caught his breath, and then continued upward, dangling high above the water like a big pale spider. When finally he reached the top, when finally he could snake out a tentative hand and touch skin to the great cold fastness of the ship's hull, he found that the anchor chain plunged into an evil-looking porthole sort of thing that might have been the monstrous, staved-in, piratical eye of the entire ghostly fleet. He leaned back to take in the huge block letters that identified the old hulk—U.S.S. *Anima*—hesitated a moment, then twisted his way through the porthole.

He was inside now, in an undefined space of utter, impossible, unalloyed darkness. Bare feet gripped bare steel, his fingers played along the walls. There was a smell of metal in decay, of oil sludge and dead paint. He worked his way forward, inch by inch, until shadows began to emerge from the obscurity and he found himself on the main deck. A covered hatch stood before him; above rose the mainmast and cargo booms. The rest of the ship—cabins, boats, masts and cranes—fell off into darkness. He had the feeling of perching on a great height, of flying, as if he were strolling the aisles of a jetliner high above the clouds. There was nothing here but shadows. And the thousand creaks and groans of the inanimate in faint, rhythmic motion.

But something was wrong. Something about the place seemed to rekindle the flames of nostalgia that had licked at him throughout the day. He stood stock-still. He drew in his breath. When he turned around he was only mildly surprised to see his grandmother perched on the rail behind him. "Walter," she said, and her voice crackled with static as if she were talking on a bad long-distance connection. "Walter, you've got no clothes on."

"But Gram," he said, "I've been swimming."

She was wearing a big sack dress and she was as fat as she'd been in life. "No matter," she said, waving a dimpled wrist in dismissal, "I wanted to tell you about your father, I wanted to explain. . . . I—"

"I don't need any explanation," a voice growled behind him.

Walter whirled around. It had been going on all day—yes, from the moment he'd opened his eyes—and he was sick of it. "You," he said.

His father grunted. "Me," he said.

The eleven years had wrought their changes. The old man seemed even bigger now, his head swollen like something you'd find carved into the cornice of a building or standing watch over an ancient tomb. And his hair had grown out, greasy dark fangs of it jabbing at his face and trailing down his neck. The suit—it seemed to be the same one he'd been wearing on Walter's eleventh birthday—hung in tatters, blasted by the years. There was something else too. A crutch. Hacked like a witching stick from some roadside tree, still mottled with bark, it propped him up as if he were damaged goods. Walter glanced down, expecting a gouty toe or a foot bound in rags, but could see nothing in the puddle of shadow that swallowed up the lower half of his father's body like a shroud.

"But Truman," Walter's grandmother said, "I was just trying to explain to the boy what I told him all my life. . . . I was trying to tell him it wasn't your fault, it was the circumstances and what you believed in your heart. God knows—"

"Quiet down, Mama. I tell you, I don't need any explanations. I'd do it again tomorrow."

It was at this point that Walter realized his father was not alone. There were others behind him—a whole audience. He could hear them snuffling and groaning, and now—all of a sudden—he could see them. Bums. There must have been thirty of them, ragged, red-eyed, drooling and stinking. Oh yes: he could smell them now too, a smell of stockyards, foot fungus, piss-stained underwear. "America for Americans!" Walter's father shouted, and the phantom crowd took it up with a gibber and wheeze that wound down finally to a crazed muttering in the dark.

"You're drunk!" Walter said, and he didn't know why he'd said it. Perhaps it was some recollection of the early years, after his mother died and before his father disappeared for good, of the summers at his grandparents' when his father would be around for weeks at a time. Always—whether the old man was asleep on the couch, helping his own father with the nets, taking Walter out to the Acquasinnick trestle for crabs or to the Polo Grounds for a ballgame—there had been the smell of alcohol. Maybe that's what had done it tonight, at the Elbow. The smell of alcohol. It was the cipher to his father as surely as the potato pancakes and liverwurst were ciphers to his sad-eyed mother and the big-armed, superstitious woman who'd tried to fill the gap she left.

"What of it," his father said.

Just then a little man with a gargoyle's face stepped out of the shadows. He wasn't wearing the sugarloaf hat or pantaloons—no, he was dressed in a blue work shirt and baggy pleated trousers with side pockets—but Walter recognized him. "No drunker than you," the man said.

Walter ignored him. "You deserted me," he said, turning on his father.

"The boy's right, Truman," his grandmother crackled, her voice frying like grease in a skillet.

The old man seemed to break down then, and the words caught in his throat. "You think I've had it easy?" he asked. "I mean, living with these bums and all?" He paused a moment, as if to collect himself. "You know what we eat, Walter? Shit, that's what. A handful of this spoiled wheat, maybe a mud carp somebody catches over the side or a rat they got lucky and skewered. Christ, if it wasn't for the still Piet set up—" He never finished the thought, just spread his hand and let it fall like a severed head. "A long absurd drop," he muttered, "from the womb to the tomb."

And then the little man—Walter saw with a jolt that he reached no higher than his father's waist—was tugging at the old man's elbow; Truman bent low to hold a whispered colloquy with him. "Got to go, Walter," the old man said, turning to leave.

"Wait!" Walter gasped, desperate all of a sudden. There was unfinished business here, something he had to ask, had to know. "Dad!" It was then that it happened: the atmosphere brightened just perceptibly, and only for an instant. Perhaps it was the effect of the moon, tumbled out from behind the clouds, or maybe it was swampfire, or the entire population of the Bronx staggering from their beds to switch on their bathroom lights in unison—but whatever it was, it gave Walter a single evanescent glimpse of his father's left leg as the old man swayed off into the darkness. Walter went cold: the cuff was empty.

Before he could react, the shadows closed up again like a fist, and the little man was at his side, leering up at him like something twisted and unclean, like the imp that prods the ogre. "Now don't you go following in your father's footsteps, hear?"

Next thing Walter knew he was on his bike (bike: it was a horse, a fire-breathing, shit-kicking terror, a big top-of-the-line Norton Commando that could jerk the fillings out of your molars), the washed-out, bird-bedeviled dawn flashing by on either side of him like the picture on a black-and-white portable with a bad horizontal hold. He was invincible, immortal, impervious to the hurts and surprises of the universe, coming out of Peterskill at ninety-five. The road cut left, and he cut with it; there was a dip, a rise—he clung to the machine like a new coat of paint. One hundred. One-oh-five. One-ten. He was heading home, the night a blur—had he passed out in the back of Hector's car on the way back from Dunderberg?—heading home to the bed of an existential hero above the kitchen in his adoptive parents' clapboard bungalow. There was dew on the road. It wasn't quite light yet.

And then all at once, as if a switch had been thrown inside his head, he was slowing down—whatever it was that had got him up to a hundred and ten had suddenly left him. He let off on the throttle, took it down—ninety, eighty, seventy—only mortal after all. Up ahead on the right (he barely noticed it, had been by it a thousand times, ten thousand) was a historical marker, blue and yellow, a rectangle cut out of the gloom. What was it—iron? Raised letters, yellow—or gold—against the blue background. Poor suckers probably made them down at Sing Sing or something. There was a lot of history in the area, he supposed, George Washington and Benedict Arnold and all of that, but history really didn't do much for him. Fact is, he'd never even read the inscription on the thing.

Never even read it. For all he knew, it could have commemorated one of Lafayette's bowel movements or the discovery of the onion; it was nothing to him. Something along the side of the road, that's all: Slow Down, Bad Curve, oak tree, billboard, historical marker, driveway. Even now he wouldn't have given it a second glance if it weren't for the shadow that suddenly shot across the road in front of him. That shadow (it was nothing recognizable—no rabbit, opossum, coon or skunk—just a shadow) caused him to jerk the handlebars. And that jerk caused him to lose control. Yes. And that loss of control put him down for an instant on the right side, down on the new Dingo boot with the imitation spur strap, put him down before he could straighten up and made him hit that blue-and-yellow sign with a jolt that was worthy of a major god.

Next afternoon, when he woke to the avocado walls, crackling intercom and astringent reek of the Peterskill Hospital's East Wing, he was feeling no pain. It was a puzzle: he should have been. He examined his forearms, wrapped in gauze, felt something tugging at his ribs. For a moment he panicked—Hesh and Lola were there, murmuring blandishments and words of amelioration, and Jessica too, tears in her eyes. Was he dead? Was that it? But then the drugs took over and his eyelids fell to of their own accord.

"Walter," Lola was whispering as if from a great distance. "Walter—are you all right?"

He tried to pin it down, put it all together again. Mardi. Hector. Pompey. The ghost ships. Had he climbed the anchor chain? Had he actually done that? He remembered the car, Pompey's wasted face, the way Mardi's paper dress had begun to dissolve from contact with her wet skin. He had his hands on her breasts and Hector's were moving between her legs. She was giggling. And then it was dawn. Birds going at it. The parking lot out back of the Elbow. "Yeah," he croaked, opening his eyes again, "I'm all right."

Lola was biting her lip. Hesh wouldn't look him in the eye. And Jessica—soft, powdered, sweet-smelling Jessica—looked as if she'd just run back-to-back marathons and finished last. Both times.

"What happened?" Walter asked, stirring his legs.

"It's okay," Hesh said.

"It's okay," Lola said. "It's okay."

It was then that he looked down at the base of the bed, looked down at the sheet where his left foot poked up like the centerpole of a tent, and at the sad collapsed puddle of linen where his right foot should have been.

O Pioneers!

Some three hundred years before Walter dodged a shadow and made his mark on the cutting edge of history, the first of the Peterskill Van Brunts set foot in the Hudson Valley. Harmanus Jochem Van Brunt, a novice farmer from Zeeland, was a descendant of herring fishermen in whose hands the nets had gone rotten. He arrived in New Amsterdam on the schooner *De Vergulde Bever* in March of 1663, seeking to place as great a distance as possible between himself and the ancestral nets, which he left in the care of his younger brother. His passage had been underwritten by the son of a Haarlem brewer, one Oloffe Stephanus Van Wart, who, under the authority of Their High Mightinesses of the States General of Holland, had been granted a patroonship in what is now northern Westchester. Van Wart's agent in Rotterdam had paid out the princely sum of two hundred fifty guilders to cover the transoceanic fare for Harmanus and his family. In return, Harmanus, his wife (the *goude vrouw* Agatha, née Hooghboom) and their *kinderen,* Katrinchee, Jeremias and Wouter, would be indentured servants to the Van Warts for all their days on earth.

The family was settled on a five-morgen farm a mile or so beyond Jan Pieterse's trading post at the mouth of Acquasinnick Creek, on land that had lately been the tribal legacy of the Kitchawanks. A crude timber-and-thatch hut awaited them. The patroon, old Van Wart, provided them with an axe, a plow, half a dozen scabious fowl, a cachexic ox, and two milch cows, both within a dribble of running dry, as well as a selection of staved-in, battered and cast-off kitchen implements. As a return on his investment, he would expect five hundred guilders in rent, two fathoms of firewood (split, delivered and reverently stacked in the cavernous woodshed at the upper manor house), two bushels of wheat, two pair of fowl, and twenty-five pounds of butter. Due and payable in six months' time.

A lesser soul might have been discouraged. But Harmanus, known in his native village of Schobbejacken as Ham Bones, in deference to his strength, agility and gustatory prowess, was no man to give in easily. With his two young sons at his side (Jeremias was thirteen, Wouter nine), he was able to clear and sow two and a half acres of rich but stony soil by the end of May. Katrinchee, a fifteen-year-old with blooming breasts and expanding bottom, dreamed of cabbages. By midsummer, she and her mother had established a flourishing kitchen garden of peas, haricots verts, carrots, cabbages, turnips and cauliflower, as well as a double row of Indian corn and pumpkin squash, the seeds of which she'd obtained from the late Sachoes' degenerate son, Mohonk.* Under Katrinchee's patient tutelage, the ancient, long-faced cows—*Kaas* and *Boter,* as they were hopefully christened by little Wouter—gradually came to take on the silky svelteness of adolescence. Each morning she tugged at their shrunken teats; each evening she fed them a mash of hackberry and snakewort, serenading them in a wavering contralto that drifted out over the fields like something snatched from a dream. The turning point came when, with Mohonk's contrivance, she obtained the newly tanned hides of a pair of calves, which she stuffed with straw and propped up on sticks in the cows' pen—within a week the old bossies were nuzzling the forgeries in maternal bliss and filling the milk pails as fast as Katrinchee could empty them. And as if that weren't enough, the hens too seemed rejuvenated. Inspired by their bovine counterparts, they began to lay like blue-ribbon winners, and the tattered cock sprouted a magnificent new spray of tail feathers.

The land was fat, and the Van Brunts tumbled into the expansive embrace of it like orphans into a mother's lap. If sugar was dear, honey was theirs for the taking. So too blueberries, crab apples,

* Shortened from *Mohewoneck,* or raccoon skin coat, a reference to the only garment he was seen to wear, winter or summer. Apart, of course, from his breechclout.

chickory and dandelion greens. And game! It practically fell from the heavens. A blast of the blunderbuss brought down a rain of gobblers or scattered coneys like grain, deer peered in at the open windows, geese and canvasbacks tangled themselves in the wash as it hung out to dry. No sooner would Jeremias shove off onto the Hudson—or North River, as it was called then—than a sturgeon or rockfish would leap into the canoe.

Even the house was beginning to shape up under the rigorous regime of Vrouw Van Brunt. She expanded the cellar, scoured the floors with sand, fashioned furniture from wicker and wood, put up shutters to keep out deerflies and the fierce sudden thunderstorms that emanated like afterthoughts from the crown of Dunderberg on a muggy afternoon. She even planted tulips out front—in two rows so straight they could have been laid out by a surveyor.

Then, in mid-August, things began to go sour. Outwardly, life had never been better: trees were falling, the woodpile growing, the fields knee-high with wheat and the smokehouse full. Katrinchee was turning into a woman, the boys were tanned and hard and healthy as frogs, Agatha hummed over her dustmop and broom. And Harmanus, liberated from the patrimonial nets, worked like five men. But slowly, imperceptibly, like the first whispering nibble of the first termite at the floor joists, suffering and privation crept into their lives.

It began with Harmanus. He came in from the fields one night and sat down at the table with an appetite so keen it cut at him like a sword. While Agatha busied herself with a *hutspot* of turnips, onions and venison, she set out a five-pound wheel of milk cheese and a loaf of day-old *bruinbrod*, hard as stone. Flies and mosquitoes hung in the air; the children, playing at tag, shouted from the yard. When she turned around, bread and cheese were gone and her husband sat contemplating the crumbs with a strange vacant gaze, the hard muscles working in his jaw. "My God, Harmanus," she laughed, "save something for the children."

It wasn't till supper that she became alarmed. Besides the stew—it was enough for the next three days, at least—there was a game pie, another loaf, two pounds of butter, garden salad and a stone jar of creamed fish. The children barely had time to fill their plates. Harmanus lashed into the eatables as if he were sitting down to the annual *Pinkster* eating contest at the Schobbejacken tavern. Jeremias and Wouter ran off to kick a ball in the fading light, but Katrinchee, who'd stayed behind to clear up, watched in awe as her father attacked the pie, shoveled up the creamed fish with a wedge of bread, scraped the stewpot clean. He sat at the table for nearly two hours, and in all that time not a word escaped his lips but for the occasional mumbled request for water, cider or bread.

In the morning it was no different. He was up at first light, as usual, but instead of taking a loaf from the table and heading out with axe or plow, he lingered in the kitchen. "What is it, Harmanus?" Agatha asked, a trace of apprehension creeping into her voice.

He sat at the crude table, big hands folded before him, and looked up at her, and she thought for a moment she was looking into the eyes of a stranger. "I'm hungry," he said.

She was sweeping the floorboards, her elbows jumping like mice. "Shall I make some eggs?"

He nodded. "And meat."

Just then Katrinchee stepped through the door with a pail of fresh milk. Harmanus nearly kicked the table over. "Milk," he said, as if associating word and object for the first time; his voice was flat, dead, without intonation, the voice of a phantom. He snatched the pail from her hands, lifted it to his lips and drank without pause till it was empty. Then he threw it to the floor, belched, and looked around the room as if he'd never seen it before. "Eggs," he repeated. "Meat."

By this point, the whole family was frightened. Jeremias looked on with a pale face as his father ate his way through the larder, wrestled sturgeon from the smokehouse, plucked a pair of hens for the pot. Katrinchee and Agatha flew around the kitchen, chopping, kneading, frying and baking. Wouter was sent for wood, steam rose from the kettle. There was no work in the fields that day. Harmanus ate till early afternoon, ate till he'd ravaged the garden, emptied the cellar, threatened the livestock. His shirt was a patchwork of grease, egg yolk, sauce and cider. He looked drunk, like one of the genever-soaked beggars on the Heerengracht in Amsterdam. Then all at once he staggered up from the table as if he'd been wounded and fell on a pallet in the corner: he was asleep before he hit the straw.

The kitchen was devastated, the pots blackened; spatters of food maculated the floorboards, the table, the fieldstone of the hearth. The smokehouse was empty—no venison, no sturgeon, no rabbit or turkey—and the grain and condiments they'd bartered from the van der Meulens were gone too. Agatha could as well have been cooking for the whole village of Schobbejacken, for a wedding feast that had gone on for days. Exhausted, she sank into a chair and held her head in her hands.

"What's wrong with *vader?*" Wouter asked. Jeremias stood at his side. They both looked scared.

Agatha stared at them in bewilderment. She'd barely had time to puzzle over it herself. What *had* come over him? She remembered something like it when she was a child in Twistzoekeren. One day, Dries Herpertz, the village baker, had declared that cherry tarts were the perfect food and that he would eat nothing else till the day he died. Soup, at least, you must have soup, people said. Milk. Cabbage. Meat. He turned his nose to the air, disdaining them as if they were a coven of sinners, devils set out to tempt him. For a year he ate nothing but cherry tarts. He became fat, enormous, soft as raw dough. He lost his hair, his teeth fell out. A bit of fish, his wife pleaded. Some nice *braadwurst.* Cheese? Grapes? Waffles? Salmon? He waved her off. She spent all day preparing fabulous meals, combed the markets for exotic fruits, dishes from Araby and the Orient, snails, truffles, the swollen livers of force-fed geese, but nothing would tempt him. Finally, after five years of trying, she dropped dead of exhaustion, face down in a *filosoof* casserole. Dries was unmoved. Toothless, fat as a sow, he lived on into his eighties, sitting out in front of his bakeshop and sucking the sweet red goo from thumbs the size of spatulas. But this, this was something different. "I don't know," she said, and her voice was a whisper.

Around nightfall, Harmanus began to toss on his pallet. He cried out in his sleep, moaning something over and over. Agatha gently shook him. "Harmanus," she whispered. "It's all right. Wake up."

Suddenly his eyes snapped open. His lips began to move.

"Yes?" she said, leaning over him. "Yes, what is it?"

He was trying to say something—a single word—but couldn't get it out.

Agatha turned to her daughter. "Quick, a glass of water."

He sat up, drank off the water in a gulp. His lips began to quiver.

"Harmanus, what is it?"

"Pie," he croaked.

"Pie? You want pie?"

"Pie."

It was then that she felt herself slipping. In all their years of marriage, through all the time he'd sat helpless over his torn nets or had to be coaxed from bed to take his dory out on the windswept Scheldt, through all the tension and uncertainty of the move to the New World and the hardships they'd faced, she'd barely raised her voice to him. But now, suddenly, she felt something give way. "Pie?" she echoed. "Pie?" And then she was clawing at the shelf beside the hearth, tearing open sacks and boxes, flinging kettles, wooden bowls, porringers and spoons to the floor as if they were dross. "Pie!" she shrieked, turning on him, the cast-iron pan shielding her breast. "And what am I supposed to make it out of—nimbleweed and river sand? You've eaten everything else—shortening, flour, fatback, eggs, cheese, even the dried marigolds I brought with me all the way from Twistzoekeren." She was breathing hard. "Pie! Pie! Pie!" she suddenly cried, and it was like the call of a great hysterical bird flushed from its roost; a second later she collapsed in the corner, heaving with sobs.

Katrinchee and her brothers were pressed flat against the wall, their faces small and white. Harmanus didn't seem to notice them. He shoved himself up from the bed and began rummaging around the room for something to eat. After a moment, he came up with a bag of acorns Katrinchee had collected to make paste; crunching them between his teeth, shells and all, he wandered out into the night and disappeared.

It was past four in the morning by the time they found him. Guided by a faint glow from Van Wart Ridge, Agatha and her daughter forded Acquasinnick Creek, stumbled up the sheer bank that rose on the far side, and fought their way through a morass of briars, nettles and branches hung with nightdrift. They were terrified. Not only for husband and father, but for themselves. Lowlanders, accustomed to polder and dike and a prospect that went on and on until it faded into the indefinite blue reaches of the sea, here they were in a barbaric new world that teemed with demons and imps, with strange creatures and half-naked savages, hemmed in by the trees. They fought back panic, bit their lips and pressed on. Finally, exhausted, they found themselves in a clearing lit by the unsteady flicker of a campfire.

There he was. Harmanus. His big head and torso throwing macabre shadows against the ghostly twisted trunks of the white birches behind him, a joint the size of a thighbone pressed to his face. They stepped closer. His shirt was torn, stained with blood and grease; gobs of meat—flesh as pink and fat-ribbed as a baby's—crackled above the flames on a crude spit. And then they saw it, lying there at his feet: the head and shoulders, the very eyes and ears, the face with its squint of death. No baby. A pig. A very particular pig. Old Volckert Varken, Van Wart's prize boar.

Harmanus was docile, a babe himself, as Agatha drew his wrists behind him and cinched the hemp cords she'd stuffed into her apron half an hour earlier amid the wreckage of the kitchen. Then she looped a halter around his neck and guided him home like a stray calf. It was nearly dawn when they reached the cabin. Agatha led her husband through the door while the hushed boys looked on, and laid him out on the pallet like a corpse. Then she bound his feet. "Katrinchee," she choked, her voice wound tight as the knotted cords. "Go fetch Mohonk."

Since she was at so great a remove from the centers of learning and quackery, and since the only physician in New Amsterdam at the time was a one-eyed Walloon named Huysterkarkus who lived on the isle of the Manhattoes, some six hours away by sloop, Agatha had no recourse to the accepted modes of diagnosis and treatment. Indeed, had the great physicians of Utrecht or Padua been present, they wouldn't have been able to do much more than cut and pray or prescribe plucked axillary hairs in a glass of cinchona wine or the menses of the dormouse packed in cow dung. But the great physicians weren't present—it would be some five or six years before Nipperhausen himself would draw his first breath, and that in the Palatine—and so the colonists had come to rely in extreme cases on the arts and exorcisms of the Kitchawanks, Canarsees and Wappingers. Hence, Mohonk.

Half an hour later, Katrinchee stepped through the doorway, shadowed by Sachoes' youngest son. Mohonk was twenty-two, addicted to sangarees, genever and tobacco, tall as the roof and thin as a stork. Hunched there in the doorway, the raccoon coat bristling around him, he looked like a dandelion gone to seed. "Ah," he said, and then ran through his entire Dutch vocabulary: *"Alstublieft, dank u, niet te danken."* He shuffled forward, the heavy musk of raccoon around him, and hung over the patient.

Harmanus gazed up at him like a chastened child, utterly docile and contrite. His voice was barely audible. "Pie," he moaned.

Mohonk looked at Agatha. "Too much eat," she said, pantomiming the act. *"Eten. Te veel."*

For a moment, the Kitchawank seemed puzzled. *"Eten?"* he repeated. But when Agatha snatched up a wooden spoon and began furiously jabbing it at her mouth, a look first of enlightenment, then of horror, invaded the Indian's features. He jumped back from Harmanus as if he'd been stung, his long coppery hands fumbling vaguely with the belt of his coat.

Agatha let out a gasp, little Wouter began to snuffle, Jeremias studied his feet. The Indian was backing out the door when Katrinchee stepped forward and took hold of his arm. "What is it?" she asked. "What's the matter?" She spoke in the language of his ancestors, the language he'd taught her over the backs of the cows. But he wouldn't answer—he just licked at his lips and tightened the belt of his coat, though it was ninety degrees already and getting hotter. "My mother," he said finally. "I've got to get my mother."

The birds had settled in the trees and the mosquitoes risen from the swamps in all their powers and dominions when he returned with a withered old squaw in dirty leggings and apron. Dried up like an ear of seed corn, stooped and palsied, her face a sinkhole, she looked as if she'd been unearthed in a peat bog or hoisted down from a hook in the Catacombs. When she was six years old and smooth as a salamander, she'd stood waist-deep in the river with the rest of the tribe and watched as the *Half Moon* silently beat its way up against the current. The ship was a wonder, a vision, a token from the reclusive gods who'd buckled up the mountains to preserve their doings from the eyes of mortal men. Some said it was a gift from Manitou, a great white bird come to sanctify their lives; others, less sanguine, identified it as a devilfish, come to annihilate them. Since that time she'd seen her husband hoodwinked by Jan Pieterse and Oloffe Van Wart, her daughter cannibalized, her youngest son besotted by drink and the third part of her tribe wiped out by smallpox, green sickness and various genital disorders attributed by the Walloons to the Dutch, the Dutch to the English and the English to the French. Her name was Wahwahtaysee.

Mohonk said something in his language that Agatha didn't catch, and his mother, Wahwahtaysee the Firefly, stepped cautiously into the room. She brought with her a string bag of devil-driving appurtenances (the canine teeth of opossum and she-wolf, the notochord of the sturgeon, various feathers, dried leaves and several discolored lumps of organic matter so esoteric that even she had forgotten their use or origin) and a rank wild odor that reminded Agatha of low tide at Twistzoekeren. Barely glancing at Harmanus, who had begun to thrash on his pallet and call out for pie once again, she shuffled to the table and unceremoniously dumped out the contents of the string bag. Then she called to her son in short angry syllables that shot from her lips like wasps swarming from the hive. Mohonk, in turn, said something to Katrinchee, who swung around on Jeremias and Wouter. "She wants the fire built up—a real blaze. Now run quick to the woodpile!"

Soon the room was infernally hot—hot as a Finnish sauna—and the old squaw, her sweat tinged with the rancid mink oil with which she smeared herself for health and vigor, began tossing her amulets into the flames one by one. All the while, she kept up a rasping singsong chant effective against *pukwidjinnies,* the ghost spirit *Jeebi* and devils of all stripes. As Katrinchee was later to learn from Mohonk, she was attempting to exorcise the noxious spirits that had gathered around the place and somehow infected Harmanus. For the cabin, built some six years before by Wolf Nysen, a Swede from Pavonia, had been erected at precisely the spot where the hunting party had found Minewa.

After an hour or so, the old woman thrust her hand into the fire—and held it there until Agatha thought she could smell the flesh roasting. Flames licked up through the spread fingers, played over the swollen veins that stood out on the back of her hand, yet Wahwahtaysee never flinched. The seconds bled by, Harmanus lay quiet, the children watched in horror. When finally the squaw withdrew her hand from the flames, it was unscathed. She held it up and examined it for a long while, as if she'd never before seen flesh and blood, sinew and bone; then she heaved herself up, shambled across the room and laid her palm flat against Harmanus' brow. There was no reaction; he just lay there looking up at her without interest or animation, precisely as he had when she'd walked in the door an hour earlier. About the only difference was that he didn't ask for pie.

But in the morning he seemed his old self. He was up at dawn, joking with the boys. Meintje van der Meulen, hearing of their plight, had sent over half a dozen little round loaves, and Harmanus selected the smallest of them, tucked it into his pouch, shouldered his axe and headed off across the fields. At noon, he returned and took a bit of pease pottage—"Have just a spoonful more, won't you, Harmanus?" Agatha pleaded, but to no avail—and in the evening he ate a rockfish fillet, a bit of lettuce and two ears of Indian corn before drifting off into a contented sleep. Agatha felt as if an immeasurable burden had been lifted from her shoulders; she felt relieved and thankful. Yes, the garden was decimated and the smokehouse empty, and old Van Wart wanted seventy-five guilders in reparation for his boar, but at least she had her husband back, at least the family was whole once again. That night she said a prayer to Saint Nicholas.

The prayer fell on deaf ears. Or perhaps it was intercepted by Knecht Ruprecht, the saint's malicious servant. Or perhaps, given the mysteries of the New World and its multifarious and competing divinities, the notion of prayer as Agatha had known it in Twistzoekeren didn't hold much water. In any case, the tempo of disintegration began to accelerate: on the very day following Harmanus' return to the realm of moderation, an accident befell Jeremias.

Picture the day: hot, cloudless, the air so thick you couldn't fall down in a swoon if you wanted to. Jeremias was helping his father clear brush on a bristling hillock that abutted Van Wart Pond, a.k.a. Wapatoosik Water, working mechanically, oblivious alike to nip of mosquito and bite of deerfly. He must have humped past the dun-colored pond twenty times—arms laden, eyes stung with sweat—

before it occurred to him to shuck his clothes and refresh himself. Naked, he waded into the muck at the pond's edge. He was feeling his way gingerly, the mud tugging at him as if it were alive, when suddenly the bottom of the pond fell away and something seized his right ankle with a grip as fiery and indomitable as Death. It wasn't Death. It was a snapping turtle, *Chelydra serpentina,* big as a wagonwheel. By the time Harmanus got there with his axe, the water had gone red with blood and he had to wade in up to his knees to locate the creature's evil, horny, antediluvian head and cleave it off at the carapace. The head stayed put. The rest of the thing, claws still churning, slid back into the murk.

At home, Harmanus pried open the locked jaws with a blacksmith's tongs, and Agatha dressed the wound as best she could. Of course, it would be some two hundred years before the agents of sepsis were identified (invisible little animalcules indeed—any fool knew that night vapors turned a wound black and that either the presence or absence of comets made it draw), and so Jeremias' ankle was bound in dirty rags and left to itself. Five days later the boy's lower leg was the color of rotten summer squash and oozing a pale wheylike fluid from beneath the bandages. Fever set in. Mohonk prescribed beaver water fresh from the bladder, but each beaver he shot perversely loosed its bowels before it could be drawn ashore. The fever worsened. On the seventh day, Harmanus appeared in the doorway with the crosscut saw from the woodpile. Half a mile away, perched on the lip of the Blue Rock with Jan Pieterse and a cask of Barbados rum, Mohonk, Katrinchee and little Wouter tried to shut their ears to the maddening, startled, breathless screams that silenced the birds like the coming of night.

Miraculously, Jeremias survived. Harmanus didn't. When bone separated from bone and his son's pallet became a froth of flesh and churning fluids, he threw down the saw and bolted headlong for the woods, moaning like a gutshot horse. He ran for nearly two miles and then flung himself face down in the bushes, where he lay in shock till after sundown. The next day his skin began to itch, and then finally to erupt in pustules; by the end of the week he lay stretched out supine on the pallet next to his son's, eyes swollen closed, his face like something out of a leper's nightmare. Again, Mohonk was called in, this time to lay poultices of sassafras over the sores; when these proved ineffective, Agatha appealed to the patroon, begging him to send downriver for Huysterkarkus. Van Wart was sorry, but he couldn't help her.

It wasn't Katrinchee's fault. All right, perhaps she was dreaming of Mohonk and the way he'd touched her the week before as they emerged from a frolic in the icy waters of Acquasinnick Creek, and perhaps she *had* sprained her wrist hoeing up a new cabbage patch, but it could have happened to anyone. The stewed haunch of venison, that is. She was moving toward the table with it, the place cramped anyway, tiny, unlivable, the size of the outhouse they'd had in Zeeland, when she banged up against the milkpail, skated across the floor in her wooden shoes and dumped the whole mess—hot enough to repel invaders at the castle wall—down her father's shirt.

It was the end of Harmanus. He rose from the straw pallet in one astonishing leap that left him hanging in the air like a puppet for a full five seconds before he burst through the new shutters without so much as a whimper and ran off into the trees, flailing blindly from one trunk to another as the family gave chase. They found him amongst the jagged stones at the base of Van Wart Ridge, a sheer drop of some one hundred fifty feet. Jeremias had trouble with the chronology of events that year, but as near as he could recall, it was about a month later that lightning struck the house and burned it to the ground, taking his mother and Wouter with it. The next day, Katrinchee consigned herself to the fires of hell by running off to Indian Point with the heathen Mohonk.

When November came around and the rents fell due, Van Wart's agent rode up from the lower manor house in Croton, a saddle pouch crammed with accounts ledgers flapping at his rear. He'd expected trouble at the Van Brunt farm—they were delinquent both with regard to firewood and produce delivery—but when he found himself at the end of the cart track that gave onto the property, he was stupefied. Where the cabin had once stood, there were only ashes. The grain had parched in the field, and then, beaten down by the first winter storm, it had frozen to the ground in scattered clumps. As for the livestock, it had disappeared altogether: the far-flung heaps of feathers gave testimony to the fate of the poultry, but the ox and milch cows were nowhere to be seen. Now the agent was a practical man, a scrupulous man, big of bottom and gut. Though he would have liked nothing better than to hie himself to Jan Pieterse's trading post and sit before the fire with a mug of lager, he nonetheless chucked the cold flanks of his mount and trundled forward to pursue the matter further.

He circumnavigated the white oak that stood in the front yard, turned up a rusted plow by the half-finished fence, peered down the well. Just as he was about to give it up, he spotted a wisp of smoke rising from the bristle of woods before him. Pausing only to relight his pipe and shift his buttocks in the icy saddle, Van Wart's agent traversed the clearing and plunged into the winter-stripped undergrowth on the far side. The first thing he saw was the ox, or rather what was left of it, hide frozen to bone, eyes, ears and lips picked away to nothing by woodland scavengers. Beyond it, a crude lean-to. "Hallo!" he called. There was no response.

Then he saw the boy. Swathed in rags and depilitated furs, crouched atop a cowhide in the shadow of the lean-to. Watching him.

The agent maneuvered the horse forward and cleared his throat. "Van Brunt?" he asked.

Jeremias nodded. The temperature was in the teens, the wind from the northwest, out of Canada. He shifted his good leg beneath him. The other one, the one that ended in a wooden peg like the pugnacious Pieter Stuyvesant's, lay exposed, insensitive to the cold. He watched in silence as the fat man above him twisted in the saddle to reach behind him and produce a big leather-bound book. The fat man thumbed through this book, marked the place with the stem of his pipe and looked down at him. "For the use and increase of this land under the patroonship of Oloffe Stephanus Van Wart in the Van Wartwyck Patent, you now stand in arrears of two fathoms of firewood, two bushels of wheat, two pair of fowl, twenty-five pounds of butter and five hundred guilders annual rent. Plus a special assessment of seventy-five guilders in the case of one misappropriated boar."

Jeremias said nothing. He leaned forward to rake up the coals of the fire, the smoke stinging his eyes. The fat man was wearing shoes with silver buckles, flannel hose, a fur cloak and rabbit-skin earmuffs beneath his high-peaked hat. "I say, Van Brunt: have you heard me?" the agent asked.

A long moment ticked by, the winter woods as silent as a tomb. "I'm just a boy," Jeremias said finally, his voice choked with the weight of all he'd been through. "*Vader* and *moeder* are dead, and everybody else too."

The agent shifted in his saddle, cleared his throat a second time, then drew on his pipe. A gust tore the smoke from his lips. "You mean you haven't got it, then?"

Jeremias looked away.

"Well, sir," the agent said after a moment, "I must inform you that you are in default of the conditions of your agreement with the patroon. I'm afraid you'll have to vacate the premises."

Ancestral Dirt

DEPEYSTER Van Wart, twelfth heir to Van Wart Manor, the late seventeenth-century country house that lay just outside Peterskill on Van Wart Ridge where it commanded a sweeping view of the town dump and the rushing, refuse-clogged waters of Van Wart Creek, was a terraphage. That is, he ate dirt. Nothing so common as leaf mold or carpet dust, but a very particular species of dirt, bone-dry and smelling faintly of the deaths of the trillions of microscopic creatures that gave it body and substance, dirt that hadn't seen the light of day in three hundred years and sifted cool and sterile through the fingers, as rarefied in its way as the stuff trapped beneath the temple at Angkor Wat or moldering in Grant's Tomb. No, what he ate was ancestral dirt, scooped with a garden digger from the cool weatherless caverns beneath the house. Even now, as he sat idly at his ceremonial desk behind the frosted glass door at Depeyster Manufacturing, thinking of lunch, the afternoon paper and the acquisition of property, the business envelope in his breast pocket was half-filled with it. From time to time, ruminative, he would wet the tip of his forefinger and dip it furtively into the envelope before bringing it to his lips.

Some smoked; others drank, cheated at cards or abused their wives. But Depeyster indulged only this one harmless eccentricity, his sole vice. He was a toddler, no more than two, when he first wandered away from his nurse (an ancient black woman named Ismailia Pompey who'd been with the family so long she was able to overlook the fact that Lincoln had freed the slaves), found the bleached and paint-stripped door ajar and pushed his way into the comforting cool depths of the cellar. Silently, he pulled the door to and sat down to his first repast. While he squatted there in the dark, grinding dirt between his milk teeth, shaping it with his tongue, relishing the faint fecal taste of it, a search that became part of the family legend raged on above him. Edging back into that nurturing ancestral darkness, he must have heard his name called a thousand times while he listened to the beat of frantic footsteps overhead, his mother's voice on the telephone, his father, summoned home from the office, raging, angrily clacking decanter and glass. How many times had the door to his sanctuary been flung back so that he could see framed in a rectangle of light the face of one worry-worn adult after another? How many times had they propelled his name into that consuming darkness before finally, when the sun had set and they were dragging the pond, he had emerged, lips smeared with his secret? His mother had pressed him to her bosom in a nimbus of body heat and perfume, and his father, that humorless and profligate man, dissolved in tears: the wayward child had come home.

He was no child now. Fifty years old—fifty-one come October—smooth and handsome and with an accent rich with the patrician emphases of the Roosevelts, Schuylers, Depeysters and Van Rensselaers who'd preceded him, scion of the Van Wart dynasty and nominal head of Depeyster Manufacturing, he was a man in the prime of life, tanned, graceful and athletic, the cynosure of the community. He was also a man who carried his sorrow around with him like that hidden envelope of dust. That sorrow was an ache in the loins, a stutter-shot to the heart—to think of it was to think of extinction, the black and uncaring universe, the futility of human existence and endeavor: he was the last of the Van Warts.

Married twenty-three years to a woman who had given him one child—a daughter—and then redirected her sexual energies toward shopping, facials, ethnic cooking and Indian relief, he had tried everything conceivable to produce a legitimate heir. In the early days, when they were still conjugal, he tried ointments, unguents and evil-smelling concoctions he'd purchased from sideways-glancing clerks in Chinatown. He dressed in costume, read his wife lubricious passages from *Lolita, The Carpetbaggers* and the *Old Testament,* consulted therapists, counselors, physicians, technicians, quacks and horse breeders, but all to no avail. Not only did Joanna fail to become pregnant again, she began dodging him at bedtime, in the morning, at lunch and in the immediate vicinity of any of the six bathrooms. He was putting too much pressure on her, she said. Sex had become an obligation, a duty, alternately clinical and perverse, like being in a laboratory one day and a witchdoctor's hut the next. What did he think she was, a prize bitch or something? It was not long after that she'd discovered the Indians.

Anyone else might have petitioned for divorce, but not Depeyster. No Van Wart had ever divorced, and he wasn't about to set a precedent. He loved her, too, in his way. She was a striking woman, with her startled eyes, her fine bones and the way she carried herself like a gift on a tray, and sometimes he found himself longing for her as she used to be. There were times, though, when he let his mind wander and pictured her fatally injured in an auto accident or the victim of a malignant virus. There would be a funeral. He would grieve. Wear a black armband. And then go out and find himself a strong-legged fecund young equestrian or acrobat. Or one of the barefooted, brassiereless, vacant-eyed college girls who slipped in and out of the house under his daughter's tutelage. Fertile ground. That's what he needed. And if the time should come when he himself was at fault, when the mechanism failed to respond as it should, well, there was always the subzero vault at Trilby, Inc., where a dozen packets of his seed lay sequestered in perpetual readiness.

Depeyster sighed, and had another pinch of dirt. It was too hot for golf—ninety-five already and with the humidity up around the breaking point—and the thought of rigging up the *Catherine Depeyster* was enough to prostrate him. He glanced at his watch: 1:15. Too early to go home yet, but then who was he fooling? Every last worker at the plant, right on down to the pimply fat girl they'd taken on in the packing room two days ago, knew that he couldn't tell a muffin from an aximax and couldn't have cared less. So to hell with them. What he would do, he thought, standing and meditatively stroking the envelope in his breast pocket, was go home for a bite of lunch, an iced tea and the afternoon edition of the *Peterskill Post Dispatch Herald Star Reporter,* have a nap and then, if it cooled off later in the day, drive by the Crane property and dream that old man Crane had sold it to him.

At home, in the kitchen, slicing a tomato on the mahogany sideboard presented to Pierre Van Wart by the Marquis de Lafayette in 1778 as an expression of heartfelt gratitude for nursing him through a six-week illness, Depeyster glanced down at the headlines of the paper, which lay, still folded, beside him. SCHOOL BOARD MEETS, he read. MURIEL MOTT BACK FROM TANZANIA TREK. The tomato was still warm from the garden. He cut it in thick slabs, peeled a Bermuda onion and dug into the refrigerator for the ham, white cheddar and mayonnaise. RUSSIANS INVADE CZECHOSLOVAKIA. The ancient planks groaned beneath his feet, Virginia ham and pungent white cheese mounted on a piece of corn rye; he sliced the onion, spread mayonnaise and carried plate and newspaper to the cherrywood table that had been in the family for better than two hundred years. DOGS ALLOWED TO RUN WILD. FAGNOLI GARBAGE HIT BY STRIKE. There were salt and pepper on the table in Delft shakers molded in the shape of wooden clogs. He sprinkled the tomato faces with both, and then, glancing over his shoulder, he slipped a hand into his breast pocket for a pinch of dirt. When dusted on the sandwich, it was barely distinguishable from the other condiments.

He unfolded the paper with a snort of contempt. The school board was a joke, he'd always detested Muriel Mott and in fact had hoped she'd be torn to pieces by hyenas at some remote blistering outpost, Fagnoli didn't affect him and he routinely shot any dog he encountered on the property. As for the Russians, he'd always sided with his old commander, General George S. Patton, on that issue. But down toward the bottom of the page, a lesser headline caught his eye:

LOCAL MAN INJURED IN DAWN ACCIDENT

> Walter Truman Van Brunt, 22, of 1777 Baron de Hirsch Road, Kitchawank Colony, was injured early this morning when he lost con trol of his motorcycle on Van Wart Road, just east of Peterskill. Van Brunt suffered a fractured rib and facial confusions in adition the to loss of his right foot. Burleigh Strang, of Strang Ferilizer, came upon the scene of the accident moments after blood all over the place," Strang said, "and it was so

foggy I darn near run him over myself." Strang is crdited with saving Van Brunt's life, who doctors at Peterskill Community Hospital say would have bled to
twelve people present. Dr. Rausch, Superintendent of Schools, addressed the problem of individual lockers for members of the girls' field hockey
quick-thinking and laying him in the bed of his pickup truck and also remembering to bring the detached foot along in the hope that doc tors could save it. Van Brunt is listed in guarded condition.

Van Brunt. Truman Van Brunt. It had been years since he'd heard that name. Years. What was it, fifteen? Twenty? He looked up from the paper, and there in the kitchen, over the onion, the ham and the pinch of tribal dirt, Truman's face suddenly materialized, just as it had been in 1949, on the night of the riot. The reddish dark hair freighted with sweat and clinging to his brow like a crown of thorns, blood dried at the corner of his mouth, his pale washed-out eyes—eyes the color of river ice—numb with shock. I've come for my thirty pieces of silver, he said, and then Joanna was there too, at the door, her smile wilting like a cut flower. She was young, her legs smooth and firm, the kimono clasped across her breast; she didn't need any makeup. I beg your pardon? she said, and Depeyster was already rising from his chair. Ask him, Truman said, stepping through the doorway to point a finger stained with blood, and then he was gone.

Depeyster shook his head as if to clear it, and then, lifting the sandwich to his lips, fastened on the article again. Truman Van Brunt, he thought. Bad luck and trouble, nothing but. And now here was his son—just a kid—mutilated for life.

He read the article through a second time, then set the sandwich down and peeled back the top slice of bread. Bits of onion clung to the mayonnaise, which had begun to take on a pinkish cast through contact with the tomato. He peppered the whole thing with a talismanic sprinkle of cellar dust, glancing up just as his daughter, Mardi, sauntered into the room.

If she'd seen anything, she gave no indication of it—just slouched toward the refrigerator in a dirty housecoat, last night's makeup ringing her eyes like greasepaint. She looked haggard, looked like a Harpie, a dope user, a wino. He supposed she'd been out all night again. He had an urge to say something, something sharp and wounding, critical, bitter. But he softened, remembering the little girl, and then, as she bent to peer into the bright depths of the refrigerator, marveling at this creature, with her bare feet and ropes of dark frizzed hippie hair, this bewildering adult, this woman, only fruit of his loins.

"Morning," he said finally, giving it an ironic lift.

"You seen the orange juice?"

He considered this a moment, taking a judicious bite of his sandwich and patting his lips with a paper napkin. For a moment he caught the shrewd eyes and faintly bemused smile of General Philip Van Wart (1749–1831), whose portrait, by Ezra Ames, had hung beside the kitchen window since his death. "What about in the freezer?"

Mardi swung back the plastic door to the freezer compartment without comment. As he watched her snatch the garish container from the shelf and fumble with the electric can opener, he was suddenly seized with the desire to shake her, shake her till she woke up, cut her hair, stuffed her miniskirts and fishnet stockings in the trash can where they belonged and rejoined the community of man. So far as he could see, all she ever did was chase after a bunch of characters who looked as if they'd crawled out of some cave in New Guinea, espouse sexual liberation and freedom for the oppressed peoples of Asia at the dinner table and sleep till noon. She'd graduated from Bard in June and the closest she'd come to a career move since was an offhand comment about some bar in Peterskill: in the fall, when so-and-so left for Maui, she might be able to get a gig tending bar two nights a week. Nothing definite yet, of course.

Shake her! a voice raged in his head. Shake the piss out of her!

"You seen mom?" she murmured, overfilling the English scratched-ware pitcher. A vaguely yellowish liquid seeped from pitcher to counter, from counter to floor: drip—drip—drip.

"What?" he asked, though he'd heard her perfectly clearly.

"Mom."

"What about her?"

"You seen her?"

He'd seen her all right. At dawn. Backing the station wagon out of the driveway for the trip up to Jamestown and the Indian reservation. The wagon was so overloaded with old shirts, rags, staved-in hats and odd-sized, out-of-fashion shoes that it had listed dangerously, like a foreign-registered freighter coming into port with a load of ball bearings. Joanna, her hair in curlers, had given a stiff, humorless wave and indicated that she'd be home the following day, as usual. He waved back, numbly. Anyone who'd seen them—he in his grandfather's silk Jakarta dressing gown, standing there in the birdy hush of dawn; she, grim, makeupless and bland, wheeling out of the driveway atop her mound of trash—might have thought he'd just fired the maid or struck up a nefarious bargain with the Salvation Army. He glanced up at his daughter. "No," he said. "I haven't seen her."

This information didn't seem to have much effect on Mardi one way or the other. She drained a glass of juice, poured another and lurched toward the table, where she collapsed in the chair, glass clutched desperately in her hand, and made a peremptive snatch for the paper. "Christ," she muttered, "I feel like shit." It was the most communicative she'd been in recent memory.

He was about to inquire as to the cause and root of this feeling, as a way perhaps of drawing closer to her, commiserating with her, bridging the gap between the generations, when she lit a cigarette, and exhaling in his face, said: "Anything in this rag today?"

Suddenly he felt humbled, weary, a lip-speller in the presence of the Great Enigma. In his most inoffensive tone, generally reserved for fellow members of the Van Wartville Historical Society, he said, "As a matter of fact, there is. Down at the bottom there. A thing about the son of a man I used to know—a real hard-luck case—who had an accident last night. Funny, because—"

"Oh, who cares?" she snarled, pushing herself up from the table and crumpling the paper in her free hand. "Who gives a good goddamn about you and your old cronies—they're just a bunch of Birchers and rednecks anyway."

Now she'd done it. That urge to shake her, to slap some awareness into those smug lifeless eyes, seized him like a set of claws. He jumped to his feet. "Don't you talk to me like that, you, you. . . . Look at yourself," he sputtered, flying into a denunciatory harangue that savaged every aspect of her hippie credo, behavior and habits, from her grinding moronic music to her unwashed, unshorn tribal cohorts, and ending with a philippic on one of those cohorts in particular, the Crane kid. "Skinniest, dirtiest, unhealthiest-looking—"

"You're just mad because his grandfather won't sell you the precious property, aren't you?" She sliced the air with the edge of her hand, as absolute and immovable as a hanging judge. "Is that all you can think about, huh? History and money?"

"Hippie," he hissed. "Tramp."

"Snob. Dirt-eater."

"Christ!" he roared. "I was only trying to make conversation, be nice for a change. That's all. I used to know his father, this Van Brunt kid, that's all. We're two human beings, right? Father and daughter. Communicating, right? Well, I used to know this man, that's all. And I thought it was ironic, interesting in a kind of morbid way, when I saw that his son had lost his foot."

Mardi's expression had changed. "What'd you say his name was?" she asked, bending for the paper.

"Van Brunt. Truman. Or, no, the son's named something else. William or Walter or something."

She was on her knees, smoothing out the newspaper on the three-hundred-year-old planks of the kitchen floor. "Walter," she murmured, reading aloud. "Walter Truman Van Brunt."

"You know him?"

The look she gave him was like a sword thrust. "Not in the biblical sense," she said. "Not yet, anyway."

Prosthesis

WALTER was lucky.

Two weeks after his collision with history, he left Peterskill Community Hospital with a new plastic flesh-colored foot, courtesy of Drs. Ziss and Huysterkark, the Insurance Underwriters of Pensacola Corporation, and Hesh and Lola. Dr. Ziss, after three vigorous sets of early-morning tennis, had been called in to the emergency room to ensure safe closure of the wound. He debrided the damaged tissue, recessed tibia and fibula, brought down two flaps of skin and muscle for cushioning and sutured them together over the bone in a fishmouth closure. Dr. Huysterkark had appeared the following afternoon to provide hope and demonstrate the prosthesis. The Insurance Underwriters, in collaboration with Hesh and Lola, footed the bill.

Walter had been dozing when Huysterkark turned up; he woke to find the doctor perched on the edge of the visitor's chair, the plastic foot in his lap. Walter's eyes went instantly from the doctor's patchy hair and fixed smile to the prosthesis, with its bulge of ankle and indentations meant to delineate toes. It looked like something wrenched from a department store mannequin.

"You're awake," the doctor said, barely moving his thin, salmon lips. He wore a scrub coat and two-tone shoes, and he had the air of a man who could sell ice to the Eskimos. "Sleep well?"

Walter nodded automatically. In fact, he'd slept like a prisoner awaiting execution, beset by irrational fears and the demons of the unconscious.

"I've brought along the prosthesis," Huysterkark said, "and

some"—he'd begun to fumble through a manila folder—"supporting materials."

Though Walter had graduated from the state university, where he'd studied the liberal arts (a patchy overview of world literature, a seminar on circumcision rites in the Trobriand Islands and courses in the history of agriculture, medieval lute-making and contemporary philosophy with emphasis on death obsession and existentialist thought, to mention a few of the highlights), he was unfamiliar with the term. "Prosthesis?" he echoed, his eyes fixed on the plastic foot. All at once he was seized with panic. This obscene lump of plastic, this doll's foot, was going to be grafted in some unspeakable way to his own torn and wanting self. He thought of Ahab, Long John Silver, old Joe Crudwell up the block who'd lost both legs and his right forearm to a German grenade in Belleau Wood.

Intent on the folder, Huysterkark barely glanced up. "A replacement part. From the Greek: a putting to, an addition."

"Is that it?"

Huysterkark ignored the question, but he lifted his eyes to pin Walter with a look of shrewd appraisal. "Think of it this way," he said after a moment. "What if your body was a machine, Walter—an automobile, let's say? What if you were a Cutlass convertible? Hm? Shiny, sleek, right off the showroom floor?" Walter didn't know what to say. He didn't want to talk about cars—he wanted to talk about feet, about mobility, he wanted to talk about the rest of his life. "Chances are you'd run trouble-free for years, Walter, but as you accumulate mileage something's bound to give out sooner or later, you follow me?" Huysterkark leaned forward. "In your case, let's say one of the wheels goes bad."

Walter tried to hold the doctor's gaze, but he couldn't. He studied his hands, the sleeves of his hospital gown, the crease of the sheets.

"Well, what do you do? Hm?" Huysterkark paused. The foot sat like a stone in his lap. "You go down to the parts store and get yourself a new one, that's what." The doctor looked pleased with himself, looked as if he'd just announced a single cure for cancer, heart disease and yaws. "We've got it all here, Walter," he said with a sweep of his arm that took in the whole hospital. "Eyes, legs, kneecaps, plastic heart valves and steel vertebrae. We've got mechanical hands that can peel a grape, Walter. In a few years we'll have artificial kidneys, livers, hearts. Maybe someday we'll even be able to replace faulty circuits in the brain."

There was no breath in Walter's body. He could barely form the question and he felt almost reprehensible for asking it, but really, he had to know. "Can I—I mean, will I—will I ever be able to walk again?"

The doctor found this hilarious. His head shot back and his smile widened to expose a triad of stained teeth and gums the color of mayonnaise. "Walk?" he hooted. "Before you know it you'll be dancing." Then he dropped his head, crossed his legs and began reshuffling the papers; in the process, the foot slid from the lap, fell to the floor with a dull thump and skittered under the chair. He didn't seem to notice. "Ah, here," he said, holding up a photograph of a man in gym shorts and sneakers jogging along a macadam road. The man's leg was abbreviated some six inches below the knee, and a steel post descended from that point to a plastic, flesh-colored ankle. The whole business was held in place by means of straps attached to the upper thigh. "The Ia Drang Valley," the doctor said. "An unfortunate encounter with one of the enemy's, uh, antipersonnel mines, I believe they call them. I fitted him myself."

Walter didn't know whether to feel relieved or sickened. His first impulse was to leap from the bed, hop howling down the corridor and throw himself from the window. His second impulse was to lean forward and slap the therapeutic smile from the doctor's face. His third impulse, the one he ultimately obeyed, was to sit rigid and clench his teeth like a catatonic.

The doctor was oblivious. He was busy fishing under the chair for Walter's foot, all the while lecturing him on the use and care of the thing as if it were a hothouse plant instead of an inert lump of plastic manufactured in Weehawken, New Jersey. "Of course," he said, as he straightened up, the recovered foot in hand, "it's no use fooling yourself. You are now deficient"—he paused—"and will experience some loss of mobility. Still, as things stand, I believe you'll find yourself capable of just about the full range of your previous activities."

Walter wasn't listening. He was staring at the foot in Huysterkark's lap (the doctor unconsciously juggled it from one hand to the other as he spoke), a sense of hopelessness and irremediable doom working its way through his veins like some sort of infection, feeling judged and condemned and at the same time revolting against the unfairness of it all. Old Joe had the Huns to excoriate, Ahab the whale. Walter had a shadow, and the image of his father.

Why me? he kept thinking as the doctor played with the alien foot as if it were a curio or paperweight. Why me?

"No, no, Walter," Huysterkark was saying, "in point of fact you're actually very lucky. Very lucky indeed. Had you hit that sign a bit higher and lost the leg above the knee, well—" His hands finished the thought.

The sun was sitting in the treetops beyond the window. Out there, along the highway, people were going off to play tennis, shop for groceries, swim, golf, rig up sailboats at the Peterskill Marina or stop in for a cold one at the Elbow. Walter lay amidst the stiff white sheets, frozen with self-pity, beyond repair. But lucky. Oh, yes indeed. Lucky, lucky, lucky.

The night before, after Hesh and Lola and Jessica had left and the anesthesia had begun to let go of him, Walter had a dream. The pale glow of the corridor faded into mist, the whisper of the intercom was translated to the lap of dirty water at the pilings, the tide running out, the smell as keen as everything that has ever lived and died upon the earth. He was crabbing. With his father. With Truman. Up at dawn, traps flung in the trunk of the Studebaker, bait wrapped in newspaper, walking out along the Acquasinnick trestle where the river opens up at high tide to flow all the way up Van Wart Creek. Stay off the tracks, his father warned him, and Walter stared into the mist, half-expecting the 6:20 from Albany to break free of the morning and tear him in two. But that would have been too easy. This dream was subtler, the payoff more sinister.

The bait? What was it? Fish gone high, covered with flies. Bones. Marrow. Chicken backs so rotten your hand would stink for a week if you touched them. When people drowned in the river, when they lay pale and bloated in the muck, pinned beneath a downed tree or the skeleton of a car, when they began to go soft, the crabs got them. His father never talked of it. But the neighborhood kids did, the river rats did, the bums who lived in the waterfront shanties you could see from here—they did. Anyway, maybe the 6:20 went by with an apocalyptic roar that felt as if it would rip the trestle from the pilings, maybe it didn't. But Walter pulled at the line and the net was stuck, wouldn't budge. His father, smelling of alcohol, a cigarette clenched between his lips and eyes squinted against the smoke, set down his beer to help him. Work it easy, he grunted. Don't want to snap the line. Then it was free, rising toward him, as heavy as if it were filled with bricks.

There were no bricks. There was no trap. Just Walter's mother, she of the soulful eyes, her hair in a cloud and the crabs all over her, nothing from the waist down. Nothing but bone.

Next thing he knew the nurse was there. A big woman, middle-aged, with something extra stuffed into her uniform about the hips and thighs, she took the room by storm, hitting the overhead light, the blinds, flourishing bedpan and syringe, plying the rectal thermometer like a saber. Sunlight screamed through the windows, she was whistling some martial tune—was that Sousa or the "Marine Corps Hymn"?—and he felt a brief fluctuation in the calculus of pain as the IV was jerked from his arm and clumsily reinserted.

The dream—horrible enough—was letting go its grip and Walter was waking to an insupportable reality. Everything came on him in a rush, the voice of waking rationality hissing in his ear like a bulletin from the front: *You're in the hospital, your ribs on fire, your arm a scab. And what about this: you've got no foot. None. Nothing at all. You're a cripple. A freak. A freak for life.*

Next came breakfast. Reconstituted orange juice, powdered eggs, simulated bacon. Brought by a nurse so incommunicative she might have taken a vow of silence, and a lush sixteen-year-old candy striper who discovered a bird on the far windowsill and cooed to it the entire time she was in the room: "Oooh, the wittle widgeon, oooh the wittle wittle." Walter wasn't hungry.

When they left, he sat up and tentatively examined his leg. There was a dull throb in his kneecap, a slice of pain where he'd taken twenty stitches in his calf. His fingers roamed lower, creeping down his shin, reluctant, skirting disclosure. He felt bandages—gauze and tape—and then, touching it as he might have touched a hot iron, the flat hewn stump of his leg. He threw back the sheets. There it was. His leg. Or no, this was somebody else's leg, truncated and ravaged, obscene, alien, inert as a log. He thought of bread, French bread, hacked across the beam. He thought of liverwurst.

Then he was asleep again. Out cold. Tugged down by the morphia and Demerol, he substituted one nightmare for another. Sleeping, he relived the accident. There was the shadow, the marker, the feeling of helplessness and predestination. And then he was an old man, stooped, white-haired, beslobbered with his own spittle, selling pencils on a street corner in the Bowery or stretched out on a pallet in some charity ward with a hundred other cripples and half-wits. Sleeping, he saw his grandfather's corpse and the cloud of killifish closing over it. Sleeping, he saw his father.

The old man was sitting in a chair beside the bed. His hair was cut, parted and freshly combed; he was wearing a mohair suit and silk tie, and his eyes were serene. But here was the odd part: he wasn't wearing any shoes. Or socks. And as Walter turned his head to gaze at him, Truman made a point of lifting first one foot, then the other, and depositing them on the edge of the bed as if they were on exhibit. Then he wriggled his bare toes and held Walter's gaze.

"But, but I thought—" Walter sputtered.

"Thought what?" the old man said. "That I was a cripple too?" He flexed his toes, then dropped both feet to the floor. "But I am, Walter, I am," he said, shutting his eyes and rubbing the bridge of his nose, "—you just can't see it, that's all."

"On the boat, the ship—" Walter began.

Truman waved his hand as if he were deflecting smoke. "An illusion," he said. "A warning." He leaned forward, elbows pressed to his knees. "Watch your step, Walter."

It was then that Walter was seized with inspiration, then that he understood what it was he'd meant to ask on the ghost ship. All his life he'd bought the story handed down by Hesh and Lola as if it were chiseled in granite on Anthony's Nose—his father was a traitor, a conscienceless fiend who'd betrayed them, sold them out, and his mother had died because of it. And yet no one, not even Hesh, knew for sure. "Nineteen forty-nine," Walter said. "The riots. Tell me, what did you do to her? What was it?"

Truman said nothing.

"It killed her, didn't it?"

His father's eyes had hardened, the look of the mad prophet come to dwell there once again. After a moment, he said: "Yeah, I guess it did."

"Hesh says you're no better than a murderer—"

"Hesh." Truman spat out the name as if he'd bitten into something rotten. "You want to know?" He paused. "Go back and take a look at that sign."

"Sign? What sign?"

The old man was standing now, an odd composite of what he'd been eleven years earlier and the man who'd made his way in the world since. He almost looked dapper. "You tell me," he said, glancing down at Walter's leg, and then he swung around and strode out the door.

It was the ghost ship all over again. "Come back here!" Walter shouted. "Come back, you son of a bitch!"

"I'm right here, Walter."

He opened his eyes. At first he didn't know where he was, couldn't focus on the pale white field hanging over him, but then the smell of her—creme rinse, My Sin, tutti-frutti gum—brought him back. "Jessica," he murmured.

"You were dreaming, that's all." Her hand was on his brow, her breast in his face. He reached up, still groggy, and as if it were the most natural thing in the world under the circumstances, began to fumble with the buttons of her blouse. She didn't seem to mind. He fumbled some more, his brain numb, fingers like breadsticks, and then he had her breasts in his hands, weighing and kneading them, pulling them to his lips as if he were an infant in the cradle. But no, wait: he *was* an infant, his mother leaning over him with her depthless eyes, the world as pure and uncomplicated as a dapple of mid-morning sun on the nursery walls. . . .

Jessica pressed her lips to his forehead, whispered his name. In that instant, the whole great busy chattering institution fell silent—the TVs were dead, the intercom mute, the hallways under a spell. Every doctor, every nurse, orderly, newborn babe and jittery blood donor held his breath. No hypodermic slid into arm or buttock, no dog-bitten child cried out. There were no footsteps in the corridor, no birds in the trees, no recalcitrant engines in the parking lot. Only silence. And at the very hub and center of that silence that was like an ocean deep lay Walter, with his abridged leg, and Jessica. In his fear, his solitude, his abandonment to grief and despair, he clutched gratefully at her, fastening himself to her like something half-drowned clinging to a rock in the midst of a torrent. Had he been crazy that night? To be hard, soulless and free was one thing, to be cut adrift from comfort and the community of man was another. He was a cripple, a pariah. And here she was, Joan of Arc, Calypso and Florence Nightingale all rolled into one. What more could he want?

"Jessica," he whispered as she swayed above him, the gently undulating blond arras of her hair shielding him from the oppressive walls, the intolerable flowers, the bedside table with its tattered copies of *Argosy* and *Reader's Digest,* the sickness and the hurt, "Jessica, I think . . . I mean . . . do you think we ought to get married?"

The silence held. A fairy silence, oneiric, magical, the moment suspended and refined out of all proportion to the myriad moments that comprise a life. It held until she broke it—with a murmur of assent.

Lucky, lucky, lucky.

Neeltje Waved Back

Jeremias was not so lucky. He withdrew into himself, gathered the meager skins about him and sat rigid as an ice sculpture while Van Wart's agent fidgeted in the saddle, blustered, cajoled and threatened. The agent tried to reason with him, tried to beat him down and strike fear into his heart—he even tried appealing to the boy's better nature, singing "Plead my cause, O Lord, with them that strive with me" in a high reedy tenor that belied his bulk. The wind howled down out of the mountains. Jeremias wouldn't even look at him. Finally the agent swung his horse around and thundered off to fetch the law.

By the time he returned with the *schout*, the weather had worsened. For one thing, it was snowing—big feathery flakes torn from the breast of the sky and mounting against the downed trees and bracken like the sign of some cumulate cosmic wrath; for another, the temperature had dropped to six degrees above zero. The *schout*, whose duty it was to enforce the law for the patroon, of the patroon and by the patroon, was a lean ferrety fellow by the name of Joost Cats. He came armed with an eviction notice bearing the mark of his employer (a V wedded to a W, VW, the logo utilized by Oloffe Stephanus to authenticate his edicts, identify his goods and chattels and decorate his undergarments), and the rapier, baldric and silver-plumed hat that were the perquisites of his office.

"Young layabout," the agent was saying as the snow played around his jowls. "Slaughtered the livestock and let the place fall to wrack and ruin. I'd as soon see him hung as evicted."

Joost didn't answer, his black staring eyes masked by the brim of his hat, the sharp little beard clinging like a stain to his chin. Erratic posture bowed his back like a sickle and he sat so low in the saddle you wouldn't know he was coming but for the exuberant plume jogging between his horse's ears. He didn't answer because he was in a vicious mood. Here he was out in the hind end of nowhere, the sky like a cracked pitcher and snow powdering his black cloak till he looked like an *olykoek* dusted with sugar, and for what? To listen to the yabbering of the fat, red-faced, pompous ass beside him and bully a one-legged boy out into the maw of the great barren uncivilized world. He cleared his throat noisily and spat in disgust.

By the time they reached the naked white oak that in better times had shaded the Van Brunt household, the snow had begun to taper off and the temperature had dropped another five degrees. To their left, against the fastness of the trees, was the half-finished fieldstone wall begun by Wolf Nysen before he went mad, butchered his family and took to the hills. He'd cut their throats as they lay sleeping—sister, wife and two teenaged daughters—and left them to rot. When Joost's predecessor, old Hoogstraten, had finally found them, they were so far gone they might have been molded of porridge. People said that the Swede was still up there somewhere, living like a red Indian, swathing himself in skins and killing rabbits with his bare hands. Joost glanced uneasily about him. Dead ahead lay the charred bones of the cabin poking through the skin of snow like a compound fracture.

"Here," puffed the agent, "see what they've done to the place."

Joost gave it a minute, his horse picking through the drifted snow like an old man stepping into a bath, before he responded. "Looks like the patroon ought to give up on this place. It's nothing but bad luck."

The agent ignored him. "Over there," he said, pointing a thick finger in the direction of Jeremias' lean-to. Joost dropped the reins and thrust his numbed hands into his pockets while his horse—a one-eyed nag with an overactive appetite and dropsical mien—bobbed stupidly after the agent's mare.

"Van Brunt!" the agent called as they hovered over the empty lean-to and the snowy hummock that represented the corpse of the unhappy ox. "Show yourself this instant!"

There was no response.

The agent was blowing up a regular hurricane of exasperated breath, summoning up terms like brass, effrontery and cheek, when Joost pointed to a half-filled track in the snow at the rear of the lean-to. Beyond it was a similar print, and beyond that another. Upon closer examination, and after a full sixty seconds given over to reasoning in the deductive mode, the agent determined that these were young Van Brunt's footprints; viz., the mark of one shoe—the left—roughly paralleled by a shallow trough connecting a pair of pegholes.

Though the snow had stopped, the wind had begun to kick up and the sky was darkening toward evening. Joost was of the opinion that they should leave well enough alone—the boy was gone, that's all that mattered. But the agent, scrupulous as he was, felt obliged to make sure. After an exchange of opinion on the subject—Where do you expect him to go, Joost asked at one point, back to Zeeland?—the two set off at a slow plod to track the boy down and evict him properly.

The trail wound like a tattered ribbon through the forest and into a dense copse where grouse chuckled and turkeys roosted in the lower branches of the trees. Beyond the copse were hills uncountable, balled up like hedgehogs and bristling with timber, home to heath hen, pigeon, deer, pheasant, moose, and the lynx, catamount and wolf that preyed on them. And beyond the hills were the violent shadowy mountains—Dunderberg, Suycker Broodt, Klinkersberg—that swallowed up the river and gave rise to the Kaaterskill range and the unnamed territories that stretched out behind it all the way to the sun's furthest decline. Looking into all that wild territory with its unknown terrors, with darkness coming on and his toes gone numb in his boots, Joost spurred his horse forward and prayed the trail would take them toward the glowing lights and commodious hearth of the upper house.

It didn't. Jeremias had headed south and east, skirting the big house and making instead toward the van der Meulen farm. Joost and the agent saw where he'd stopped to make water in the snow or nibble a few last withered berries and chew a bit of bark; they saw how the pegleg had grown heavier and dug deeper into the snow. And finally, to their everlasting relief, they saw that the tracks would indeed lead them across the Meulen Brook, past the great plank doors of Staats van der Meulen's barn and into the warm, taper-lit, bread-smelling kitchen of Vrouw van der Meulen herself, a woman renowned all the way to Croton for her *honingkoek* and *appelbeignet.*

If they expected hospitality, if they sought the warmth of Meintje van der Meulen's kitchen and smile too, they were disappointed. She greeted them at the door with an expression every bit as cold as the night at their backs. *"Goedenavend,"* said the agent, doffing his hat with a flourish.

Vrouw van der Meulen's eyes shot suspiciously from agent to *schout* and then back again. Behind them they could hear the muffled lowing of the van der Meulen cattle as Staats forked down hay from the barn's rafters. Meintje didn't return the agent's greeting, but merely stepped back and pulled the door open for them to enter.

Inside, it was heaven. The front room, which ran the length of the house and occupied the lion's share of its space—there were smaller sleeping quarters in back—was warm as a featherbed with a good wife and two dogs in it. Flickering coals glowed in the huge hearth and the big blackened pot that hung over them gave off the most intoxicating aroma of meat broth. There were loaves in the beehive oven—Joost could smell them, ambrosia and manna—and a little spider pot of corn mush crouched over a handful of coals on the hearthstone. The *kas* doors were open and the table half set. In the far corner, an old water dog wearily lifted its head and two white-haired van der Meulen children gazed up at them with the look of cherubim.

"Well," Meintje said finally, closing the door behind them, "whatever could bring the honorable *commis* and his colleague the *schout* to our lonely farm on such a night?"

Joost's back was not nearly so bowed as when he was mounted, yet he still slumped badly. Working the plumed hat in his hands, he slouched against the doorframe and attempted an explanation. "Van Brunt," he began, but was cut off by the officious agent, who laid out the patroon's case against Harmanus' sad and solitary heir as if he were pleading before a court of the accused's peers (though of course there was neither need nor precedent for such a court, as the patroon was judge, jury and prosecutor on his own lands, and paid the *schout* and hangman to take care of the rest). He ended, having in the process managed to edge closer to the hearth and its paradisaic aromas, by attesting that they'd followed the malefactor's trail right on up to the *goude vrouw's* doorstep.

Meintje waited until he'd finished and then she plucked a wooden spoon from the cupboard and began to curse him—curse *them*—Joost, to his horror, equally indicted in her wrath. *They* were the criminals—no, worse, they were fiends, cloven-hoofed *duyvils,* followers of Beelzebub and his unholy tribe. How could they even think to hound the poor orphaned child from the only home he knew? How could they? Were they Christians? Were they men? Human beings even? For a full five minutes Meintje excoriated them, all the while brandishing the wooden spoon like the sword of righteousness. With each emphatic gesture she backed the agent up till he'd given over his hard-won place at the hearth and found himself pressing his buttocks to the cold unyielding planks of the door as if he would melt into them, while Joost slumped so low in shame and mortification he could have unbuckled his boots with his teeth.

It was at this juncture that Staats, bringing with him a stale whiff of the barn and a jacket of cold, slammed through the door. In doing so, he relocated the agent's center of gravity and sent him reeling halfway across the room, where he fetched up against the birch rocker with a look of wounded dignity. Staats was a powerful, big-nosed, raw-skinned man with eyes so intense they were like twin slaps in the face. He seemed utterly bewildered by the presence of *commis* and *schout,* though he must have seen their blanketed horses tied outside the door. "Holy *Moeder* in heaven," he rumbled. "What's this?"

"Staats," Meintje cried, rushing to him and repeating his name twice more in a plaintive wail, "they've come for the boy."

"Boy?" he repeated, as if the word were new to him. His eyes roved about the room, searching for a clue, and he lifted his mink cap to scratch a head as hard and hairless as a chestnut.

"Little Jeremias," his wife whispered in clarification.

Joost watched them uneasily. As he would later learn, the boy had turned up some two hours earlier begging for shelter and a bit to eat. Vrouw van der Meulen had at first shut the door on him in horror—a haunt had appeared on her *stoep,* withered and mutilated, one of the undead—but when she took a second look, she saw only the half-starved child, motherless in the snow. She'd held him to her, bundled him up in front of the fire, fed him soup, hot chocolate and honey cake while her own curious brood pressed around. Why hadn't he come sooner? she asked. Where had he been all this time? Didn't he know that she and Staats and the Oothouses too thought he'd perished in the blaze that took his poor *moeder?*

No, he'd said, shaking his head, no, and she'd wondered whether he was responding to her question or denying some horror she couldn't know. The fire, he murmured, and his voice was slow and halting, the voice of the hermit, the pariah, the anchorite who spoke only to trees and birds. They'd all been out in the fields that fateful afternoon, hoeing up weeds and clattering pans to keep the *maes dieven* out of the corn and wheat—all except for Katrinchee, that is, who was off somewhere with Mohonk the Kitchawank. Jeremias had regained his strength by then and was able to get around pretty well on the strut he'd carved from a piece of cherrywood, but his solicitous mother had sent him off to drive away the birds while she and Wouter did the heavier work. When the storm broke, he lost sight of them; next thing he knew the cabin was in flames. When Staats and the Oothouse man had come around he'd hidden in the woods with his cattle, hidden in shock and fear and shame. But now he could hide no longer.

"Jeremias?" Staats repeated, comprehension trickling into his features like water dripping through a hole in the roof. "I'll kill them first," he said, glaring at Joost and the agent.

It was then that the subject of the controversy appeared in the doorway to the back room—a thin boy, but big-boned and tall for his age. He was wearing a woolen shirt, knee breeches and a single heavy stocking borrowed from the van der Meulen's eldest boy, and he stood wide-legged, cocked defiantly on his wooden peg. The look on his face was something Joost would never forget. It was a look of hatred, a look of defiance, of contempt for authority, for rapiers, baldrics, silver plumes and accounts ledgers alike, a look that would have challenged the patroon himself had he been there to confront it. His voice was low, soft, the voice of a child, but the scorn in it was unmistakable. "You looking for me?" he asked.

The following summer, a dramatic and sweeping change was to come to New Amsterdam and the sleepy settlements along the North River. It was a hot still morning in late August when Klaes Swits, a Breucklyn clam-digger, looked up from his rake to see five British men-o'-war bobbing at anchor in the very neck of the Narrows. In his haste to apprise the governor and his council of this extraordinary discovery, he unhappily lost his anchor, splintered both his oars and his rake in the bargain, and was finally reduced to paddling Indian-style all the way from the South Breucklyn Bight to the Battery. As it turned out, the clamdigger's mission was superfluous—as all of New Amsterdam would know three hours later, the ships were commanded by Colonel Richard Nicolls of the Royal Navy, who was demanding immediate capitulation and surrender of the entire province to Charles II, king of England. Charles laid claim to all territory on the coast of North America from Cape Fear River in the south to the Bay of Fundy in the north, on the basis of English exploration that antedated the Dutch cozening of the Manhattoes Indians. John Smith had been there before any cheese-eating Dutchmen, Charles insisted, and Sebastian Cabot too. And as if that weren't enough, the very isle of the Manhattoes and the river that washed it had been discovered by an Englishman, even if he was sailing for the Nederlanders.

Pieter Stuyvesant didn't like it. He was a rough, tough, bellicose, fighting Frisian who'd lost a leg to the Portuguese and would yield to no man. He hurled defiance in Nicolls' teeth: come what may, he would fight the Englishers to the death. Unfortunately, the good burghers of New Amsterdam, who resented the West India Company's monopoly, eschewed taxation without representation and hated the despotic governor as if he were the devil himself, refused to back him. And so, on September 9, 1664, after fifty-five years of Dutch rule, New Amsterdam became New York—after Charles' brother, James the duke of York—and the great, green, roiled, broad-backed North River became the Hudson, after the true-blue Englishman who'd discovered it.

Yes, the changes were dramatic—suddenly there was new currency to handle, a new language to learn, suddenly there were Connecticut Yankees swarming into the Valley like gnats—but none of these changes had much effect on life in Van Wartwyck. If Oloffe Stephanus throve under Dutch rule, he throve and multiplied and throve again under the English. The new rulers, hardly known as a nation for an affinity to radical change, preserved the status quo—i.e., the landlord on top and the yeoman on bottom. Oloffe's wealth and political power grew. His eldest son and heir, Stephanus, who was twenty-one when Stuyvesant capitulated, would see the original 10,000-acre Dutch patent expanded more than eightfold when William and Mary chartered Van Wart Manor in the declining years of the century.

As for Joost, he performed his duties as before, answerable to no one but old Van Wart, who continued to exercise feudal dominion over his lands. The *schout* worked his little farm on the Croton River that lay within hollering distance of the lower manor house, harvested in season, went a-hunting, a-fishing and a-crabbing according to the calendar, raised his three daughters to be mindful of the laws of God and man, and satisfied his employer with the promptness and efficiency with which he settled disputes among the tenants, tracked down malefactors and collected past-due rents. For the most part, things were pretty quiet in the period following the English takeover. A few Yankees threw up shacks in the vicinity of Jan Pieterse's place, where they would later draw up a charter for the town of Peterskill, and Reinier Oothouse got drunk and burned down his own barn, but aside from that nothing out of the ordinary cropped up. Lulled by the tranquillity of those years, Joost had nearly forgotten Jeremias, when one afternoon, in the company of his eldest, little Neeltje, he ran into him at the Blue Rock.

It was late May, the planting was done and the mornings were as gentle as a kiss on the cheek. Joost had left the lower manor house at dawn with a bundle of things for the patroon's wife, Gertruyd, who was in the midst of a religious retreat at the upper manor house, and with instructions from the patroon to arbitrate a dispute between Hackaliah Crane, the new Yankee tenant, and Reinier Oothouse. Neeltje, who'd turned fifteen the month before, had begged to come along, ostensibly to keep her father company, but in truth to buy a bit of ribbon or hard candy at Pieterse's with the stivers she'd earned dipping sacramental candles for Vrouw Van Wart.

The weather was clear and fair, and the sun had dried up the bogs and quagmires that had made the road practically impassable a month before. They covered the eight miles from Croton to the upper manor house in good time, and were able to meet with both Crane and Oothouse before noon. (Reinier, who was drunk as usual, claimed that the long-nosed Yankee had called him an "old dog" after he, Reinier, had boxed the ears of the Yankee's youngest boy, one Cadwallader, for chasing a brood of setting hens off their nests. Reinier had responded to the insult by "twisting the Yankee's great flapping ears and giving him a flathand across the bridge of his broomstick nose," immediately following which the Yankee had "treacherously thrown [him] to the ground and kicked [him] in a tender spot." Crane, a learned scion of the Connecticut Cranes, a family destined to furnish the Colonies with a limitless supply of itinerant pedants, potmakers and nostrum peddlers, denied everything. The *schout,* attesting Reinier's drunkenness and perhaps a bit cowed by the Yankee's learning, found for Crane and fined Oothouse five guilders, payable in fresh eggs, to be delivered to Vrouw Van Wart at the upper manor house—raw eggs being the only foodstuff she would consume while suffering the throes of religious abnegation—at the rate of four per day.) Afterward, father and daughter dined on eels, shad roe and perch with pickled cabbage in the great cool thick-walled kitchen at the upper manor house. Then they stopped at Jan Pieterse's.

The trading post comprised a rude corral, a haphazardly fenced chicken coop and a long dark hut illuminated only by a pair of slit windows at front and back and the light from the door, which stood open from May to September. Jan Pieterse, who was said to be among the richest men in the valley, slept on a corn husk mattress in back. His principal trade had originally been with the Indians—*wampumpeak,* knives, axes and iron cookpots in exchange for furs—but as beaver and Indian alike had been on the decline and Boers and Yankees on the upswing, he'd begun to stock bits of imported cloth, farm implements, fish hooks, pipes of wine and kegs of soused pigs' feet to appeal to his changing clientele. But there was more to the place than trade alone—along with the mill Van Wart had erected up the creek, the trading post was a great gathering spot for the community. There you might see half a dozen skulking Kitchawanks or Nochpeems (it was strictly verboten to sell rum to the Indians, but they wanted nothing more, and with a nod to necessity and a wink for the law, Jan Pieterse provided it), or Dominie Van Schaik taking up a collection for the construction of a yellow-brick church on the

Verplanck road. Then too there might be any number of farmers in homespun *paltroks,* steeple hats and wooden shoes accompanied by their *vrouwen* and grimly linking arms with their ripe young daughters who made the fashions of the previous century seem au courant, and, of course, the horny-handed, red-faced, grinning young country louts who stood off in a corner thumping one another in the chest.

On this particular day, as Joost helped his daughter down from her mount, he saw only Jan Pieterse and Heyndrick Ten Haer sharing a pipe on the porch while a Wappinger brave lay spread-eagled in a patch of poison ivy up the lane, drunk as a lord and with his genitals exposed for all the world to see. Beyond the Indian, the river was as flat and still as hammered pewter, and Dunderberg rose up, a deep shadowed blue, to tilt at the horizon.

"Vader," Neeltje said before she'd touched ground, "please, may I go right in?" She'd spoken of nothing but ribbon, broadcloth and velvet since they'd left Croton that morning. Mariken Van Wart had the prettiest silk petticoats and blue satin skirt, and she was only thirteen, even if she was the patroon's niece. And armozine ribbon—you should have seen it!

Joost handed her down, straightened up briefly and then fell again into his habitual slump. "Yes," he whispered, "yes, of course, go ahead," and then he ambled up to shoot the breeze with Jan Pieterse and Farmer Ten Haer.

He'd been slouching there on the *stoep* some ten minutes or so, puffing fraternally at his clay pipe and relishing the rich westering sun in those few moments before he would ask Jan Pieterse to join him in a pint of ale, when he became aware that his daughter was talking to someone inside the store. He remarked it only because he'd assumed the store was empty. There were only two horses in the lot—his own sorry, one-eyed nag and the sleek tawny mare he'd conscripted from the Van Wart stable for his daughter—and Farmer Ten Haer's wagon stood alone beneath the chestnut tree. Whoever could she be talking to? he wondered, but Heyndrick Ten Haer was in the middle of a story about Wolf Nysen—whether or not he was even alive still, the renegade Swede had become the bogey of the neighborhood, blamed for everything from a missing hen to some *huis vrouw*'s shin splints—and Joost momentarily forgot about it.

"Oh, ja, ja," Farmer Ten Haer said, nodding vigorously. "He come up out of the swamp near that turtle pond where his farm used to be, black as the devil, not a stitch on him and covered head to toe with mud, and he had this terrific big axe with him, the blade all crusted over with blood—"

Joost was picturing this monster, this Nysen, when he quite distinctly heard his daughter giggle from inside the dim storehouse. He craned his neck to peer through the gloomy doorway, but could see nothing aside from the pile of ragged furs and the gray-whiskered snout of Jan Pieterse's retriever, asleep in their midst. "Is someone in there?" he asked, turning to the trader.

"She was gathering mushrooms out there, my Maria was, when he come for her without warning, howling like a beast—"

"Yes, and I suppose his hoofs were cloven and he smelled of brimstone too," Jan said, and then, leaning toward Joost and lowering his voice: "Oh, ja—the pegleg, you know, the Van Brunt boy."

It came back to him in a rush—the night at the van der Meulen farm, the look of unquenchable hatred on the boy's face, his own shame and uneasiness—and his first reaction was fear for his daughter. He'd actually turned away from the others and squared his shoulders for action when he checked himself. This was only a boy, an orphan, one of the afflicted and downtrodden of the earth—not some sort of ogre. He'd been overwrought that night, that was all.

"It's the God's honest truth," Farmer Ten Haer declared, clamping his arms across his chest.

It was then that Neeltje appeared in the doorway, a pretty girl in petticoats and tight-waisted skirt, smiling still, as if at some private joke. Behind her, dwarfing her, was a man six feet tall at least, with shoulders that had burst the seams of his woolen *hemdrok*. He guided her through the doorway and then stepped out into the sunlight himself, the pegleg knocking at the floorboards like a fist at the door. Joost saw the same unyielding expression, the same arrogance, he'd seen in the boy. If Jeremias recognized him, he gave no sign of it.

"Well, *younker,*" Jan Pieterse said, drawing the pipe from his mouth, "have you decided on anything?"

Jeremias nodded and replied that yes, sir, he had. He held out a big work-hardened palm in which there were five fish hooks and two glossy cubes of rock candy, and paid with a coin that looked as if it had been buried and dug up six times already. And then, ignoring Joost, he pressed a cube of candy into Neeltje's palm as if it were a jewel from Africa, tucked the other inside his cheek, and thumped off, the wooden strut stabbing rhythmically at the earth with each thrust of his leg.

They watched in silence—Joost, Neeltje, Farmer Ten Haer and Jan Pieterse—as he swayed off across the lot, awkward and graceful at the same time. His right arm swung out like a baton, his shoulders were thrust back and the dark long blades of his hair cut at the collar of his shirt. They watched as he skirted a rotten stump and passed between a pair of lichen-encrusted boulders, watched as he entered the shadows at the edge of the wood and turned to wave.

Joost's hands were in his pockets. Farmer Ten Haer and Jan Pieterse lifted their arms half-heartedly, as if afraid to break the spell. Neeltje—only Neeltje—waved back.

The Last of the Kitchawanks

WHEN the market crashed in the fall of 1929, Rombout Van Wart, sire of Depeyster, husband to Catherine Depeyster and eleventh heir to Van Wart Manor, did not jump from the roof of the Stock Exchange or hang himself beneath the stately gables of the upper manor house. He did take a beating, though—in both the literal and figurative senses. Figuratively speaking, he lost a fortune. The family timber business went under; the foundry—which at that time produced iron cookware, but had, during the war, turned out breeches for artillery guns—fell on hard times; he lost an unspecified sum in stock holdings purchased on margin and dropped two thousand dollars in one grim afternoon at Belmont Park. The other beating, the literal one, was administered by a transient with a hawk's nose and burnt-umber complexion who called himself Jeremy Mohonk and claimed to be the last of the Kitchawanks, a tribe no one in the Peterskill/Van Wartville area had ever heard of. Asserting his right to tribal lands, he threw up a tar-paper shack at Nysen's Roost, an untenanted sector of the Van Wart estate on which Rombout had recently reintroduced the wild turkey after an attack of feudal nostalgia.

It was Rombout himself who discovered the squatter's presence. Mounted on Pierre, a bay gelding with blood lines nearly as rich as his own, the lord of the manor was taking his exercise in the bracing autumn air (and at the same time attempting to exorcise the demon of his financial woes with the aid of a silver flask inscribed with the time-honored logo of the Van Wart clan) when he came upon the interloper's shack. He was appalled. Beneath the venerable white oak in which his great grandfather, Oloffe III, had carved his initials, there now stood a sort of gypsy outhouse, a peeling, unsightly, tumble-down shanty such as one might expect to see at the far end of a hog pen in Alabama or Mississippi. Drawing closer, he spotted a ragged figure crouched over a cookfire, and then, galloping into the miserable, garbage-strewn yard, he recognized the plucked and decapitated carcass of a turkey sizzling on the spit.

It was too much. He sprang down from his horse, the riding crop clenched in his fist, as the tattered beggar lurched to his feet in alarm. "What in hell do you think you're doing here?" Rombout raged, shaking the whip in the trespasser's face.

The Indian—for Indian he was—backpedaled, watching for sudden movement.

"This . . . this is trespassing!" Rombout shouted. "Vandalism. Poaching, for God's sake. These are private lands!"

The Indian had stopped backpedaling. He was dressed in a cheap flannel shirt, torn working pants and a crushed bowler hat he might have fished out of a public urinal; he was barefoot despite the incipient cold. "Private lands, my ass," he said, folding his arms across his chest and fixing the lord of the manor with a cold, challenging, green-eyed glare. (*Indian?* Rombout would later snort in disbelief. Whoever heard of an *Indian* with green eyes?)

Rombout was beside himself with rage. It should be said too that he was fairly well inebriated, having consumed cognac in proportion to the magnitude of the anxiety it was meant to soothe—and that anxiety, pecuniary in nature, was monumental, blocklike and impervious as marble. In fact, two days earlier he'd confided to a fellow member of the Yale Club that financially speaking he was going to hell in a handbasket. Now he suddenly roared at the Indian, "Do you know who I am?" punctuating each stentorian syllable with a flourish of the whip.

Unutterably calm, as if he were the property owner and Rombout the trespasser, the Indian nodded his head gravely. "A criminal," he said.

Rombout was struck dumb. No man had insulted him to his face in twenty-five years—not since a brash upperclassman at college had called him "a starched-up ass" and taken a concussive blow to the right ear in swift retribution. And here was this trespasser, this swarthy hook-nosed bum in a ragpicker's suit of clothes, bearding him on his own property.

"A criminal and an expropriator," the Indian continued. "A pauperizer of the working classes, a pander to the twin whores of privilege and capital, and a polluter of the land my ancestors lived in harmony with for seven thousand years." The Indian paused. "You want to hear more? Huh?" He was pointing his index finger now. "You're the trespasser, friend, not me. I've come to reclaim my birthright."

It was then that Rombout struck him—once only—a vicious swipe of the riding crop aimed at those chilly, hateful, incongruous green eyes. The sound of it, like a single burst of brutal applause, faded quickly on the antiseptic air, till in an instant only the memory of it remained.

For his part, the Indian seemed almost to welcome the blow. He barely flinched, though Rombout had put everything he had into it. Which admittedly wasn't much, considering the fact that he was in his mid-forties and given to a sedentary life relieved only by the occasional round of golf or canter across the property. By contrast, the Indian appeared to be in his early twenties; he was tall and fine-whittled, hardened by work and indigence. Dew drops of blood began to appear in a band that rimmed his eyes and traced the bridge of his nose like the blueprint for a pair of spectacles.

"Damn you," Rombout cursed, trembling with the chemical emissions his anger had released in his blood. He didn't have a chance to say more, because the Indian bent to snatch up a stick of firewood the length and breadth of a baseball bat and laid into the side of his head like the immortal Bambino going for the stands. It later came out—at the Indian's trial—that the attacker landed several other blows as well, including kicks, punches and knee drops, but Rombout was aware only of the first and of the blackness that followed precipitately on its heels.

He wasn't dead—no, he would live to recover his health and vigor, only to fatally inhale a raw oyster at Delmonico's some ten years later—but he might as well have been. He never stirred. For three hours he lay there, bleeding and clotting, clotting and bleeding.

He came to briefly once or twice, saw a world that looked as if it were ten fathoms beneath the ocean, tasted his own blood and descended again into the penumbral depths of unconsciousness. In all that time the Indian did nothing—he didn't renew his attack, didn't attempt to aid his victim, lift his wallet or abscond with Pierre, the magnificent bay gelding. He merely sat there at the doorway of his shanty, rolling and smoking cigarettes, a self-righteous look on his face.

It was Herbert Pompey—chauffeur, stable hand, gardener, factotum, jack-of-all-trades, major domo and son of Ismailia the nurse—who ultimately rescued the lord of the manor. When after several hours Rombout hadn't returned, Herbert went to his mother to ask her advice. "He drunk is what he is," she opined. "Pass out against some tree, or maybe he just fell off that animal and broke his head." Then she told him to put one foot in front of the other and go have a look for him.

Pompey tried the dairy farm first. Rombout would sometimes ride out there to drink black coffee and grappa with Enzo Fagnoli, whose family had been milking cows for the Van Warts for eighty years. (The Fagnolis had taken over for the van der Mules or Meulens, tenants at Van Wart Manor since the world began. Apprised that the state legislature was about to put an end to the manorial system in the Hudson Valley, giving leaseholders title to the farms they'd worked for generations, Rombout's great grandfather, Oloffe III, had evicted the Dutchmen in favor of the intrepid Italians, who converted the farm to dairy production and worked for an annual wage. It was hard on Oloffe, having to adjust to paying his tenants rather than vice versa, but the unquenchable hordes of New York City clamored for his milk, butter and cheese, his herds multiplied till they darkened the hills and in time he was able to admit that it was all for the best.) Enzo, in overalls and porkpie hat, greeted Pompey with enthusiasm and offered him a swig of apple wine from a green jug, but regretted to say that he hadn't seen Rombout in nearly a week.

Next it was the Blue Rock Inn, where the lord of the manor was wont to take a hiatus from the rigors of equestrian exercise in order to share a cup of bootleg bourbon with the proprietor, Charlie Outhouse, who more typically regaled his guests with soda water and orange pekoe tea. Pompey retraced his steps, passing within hailing distance of the manor house—still no Rombout—and hiked down to where the inn perched over Van Wart Creek as it debouched in the Hudson. Charlie was out back, plucking hens for dinner. He hadn't seen Rombout either. Pompey kept walking, skirting Acquasinnick Ridge and following the bank of the creek until finally he swung north for Nysen's Roost.

He struck the stony path that traversed Blood Creek (so named because Wolf Nysen had incarnadined its waters in trying to wash the blood of his daughters from his hands), his legs heavy with fatigue as he pumped up the steep hill. His mother, a gossipy, superstitious woman, repository of local legend and guardian of the Van Wart family history, had told him tales of Wolf Nysen, the mad murdering Swede. And of the loup-garou, the *pukwidjinnies* and the wailing woman of the Blue Rock, who'd perished in a snowstorm and whose voice could still be heard on nights when the snow fell thick. The woods were dense here—never lumbered—and the shadows gathered in clots around the bones of fallen trees. It was an unlucky place, strangely silent even in summer, and as boy and man, Pompey had avoided it. But now, though the leaves were ankle deep on the trail, he could see that a horse had passed this way recently, and he felt nothing but relief.

When he emerged from the woods at the top of the rise, he was as surprised as his employer had been to find a crude habitation of notched saplings and tar paper huddled beneath the big old white oak that stood sentinel over the place. The next thing he noticed was Pierre, still saddled, grazing quietly beneath the tree. Then, as he drew closer, he became aware of a stranger sitting in the doorway of the shack—a bum, from the look of him—and beyond him, something like a heap of rags cast off in the stiff high grass. But where was Rombout?

Never hesitating, though his gut was clenched with foreboding, Pompey strode right on up to the shack to confront this stranger. He halted five feet from him, hands on hips. *Who the devil are you?*—the words were on his lips when he glanced down at that heap of rags. Rombout looked as if he were sleeping, but there was blood on the side of his head. His riding boots—Pompey had put a shine on them that very morning—glinted in the pale autumn light.

"What happen here?" Pompey demanded of the Indian, who'd barely raised his head to watch him stride up to the shack. A great lowering ancestral fear gripped Pompey as he looked down at the white man sprawled in the grass.

The Indian said nothing.

"You do this?" Pompey was scared. Scared and angry. "Huh?"

Still the Indian held his silence.

"Who you, anyway? What you want?" Pompey was glancing distractedly from the Indian to the horse and from the horse to the terrible inert bundle of clothing on the ground.

"Me?" the Indian said finally, raising his head slowly to pin him with those fanatic's eyes. "I'm the last of the Kitchawanks."

The trial didn't last an hour. The Indian was accused of criminal trespass, assault with a deadly weapon and attempted murder. His attorney, appointed by the court, had gone to school with Rombout. The sheriff, the court recorder, the district attorney and the district attorney's assistant had also gone to school with Rombout. The judge had gone to school with Rombout's father.

"Clearly, your honor," the Indian's attorney pleaded, "my client is not in possession of his faculties."

"Yes?" returned the judge, who was a big, harsh, reactionary man, known for his impatience with hoboes, panhandlers, gypsies and the like. "And just how is that?"

"He claims to be an Indian, your honor."

"An Indian?" The judge lifted his eyebrows while everyone in the courtroom stole a glance at the Kitchawank, who sat erect as a pillar in the witness box.

The judge now turned to him. "Jeremy Mohonk," he began, and then glanced at the court recorder. "Mohonk? Is that right?" The recorder nodded, and the judge turned back to the accused. "Do you understand the nature of the charges against you?"

"I was defending my person and my property," the Indian growled, his eyes sweeping the room. Rombout, his head still bandaged and the left side of his face swollen and discolored, looked away.

"*Your* property?" the judge asked.

The Indian's attorney was on his feet. "Your honor," he began, but the judge waved him off.

"Are you aware, sir, that the property you claim as your own has been in the Van Wart family since before this country, as we know it, even came into existence?"

"And before that?" the Indian countered. His eyes were like claws, tearing at every face in the courtroom. "Before that it belonged to *my* family—until we were cheated out of it. And if you want to know something, so did the land this courtroom stands on."

"You do then claim to be an Indian?"

"Part Indian. My blood has been polluted."

The judge gazed at him for a long moment, smacking his lips from time to time and twice removing his glasses to wipe them on the sleeve of his robe. Finally he spoke. "Nonsense. There are Indians in Montana, Oklahoma, the Black Hills. There are no Indians here." Then he dismissed the defense attorney and asked the D.A. if he had any further questions to put to the accused.

The jury, eight of whom had gone to school with Rombout, was out for five minutes. Their verdict: guilty as charged. The judge sentenced Jeremy Mohonk to twenty years at Sing Sing, a place named, ironically enough, for the Sint Sinks, a long extinct tribe that had been second cousin to the Kitchawanks.

Rombout had seen justice done, and yet that piece of property—disputed by a madman and never much good for anything anyway—proved too great a burden to bear. Six months after Jeremy Mohonk had been shunted off to prison and his shack razed, Rombout was forced to put the place up for sale. Over the years, through legislation, population pressure, division among heirs and other forms of attrition, the original Van Wart estate had shrunk from 86,000 acres to fewer than two hundred. Now it would be deprived of fifty more.

Times were hard all over. For two years the plot remained on the market and not a single bid was forthcoming, until finally Rombout put an ad in the *Peterskill Post Dispatch* (soon to merge with both the *Herald* and the *Star Reporter*). The day after the ad appeared, a gleaming late-model Packard sedan made its slow, flatulent way up the drive to the manor house. Inside was Peletiah Crane, principal of the Van Wartville school and descendant of the legendary pedagogue–

legislator. He was dressed in his principal's pinstripes, replete with bow tie, celluloid collar and straw boater, and he carried with him a black satchel similar to those employed by doctors making their rounds.

Pompey led the educator into the brightly lit back parlor, where Rombout and his thirteen-year-old son, Depeyster, sat over a game of chess. "Peletiah?" Rombout exclaimed in surprise, rising and extending his hand.

The principal was smiling—no, grinning—till he looked like a walnut about to split open. Depeyster ducked his head. He knew that grin. It was a variant of the one Old Stone Beak, as they called him, employed just prior to lifting his cane down from the wall and applying it to some miscreant's backside. Wider, gummier and more compressed about the lips than the caning grin, this one was reserved for special occasions of triumph, as when Dr. Crane had assembled the student body to announce that his own son had won the essay contest commemorating the founding of Peterskill, or when he'd curtailed athletics for a month because Anthony Fagnoli had desecrated the shower stall with an anatomical diagram. Thirteen years old and mortified in the face of that smile, Depeyster felt like slipping down to the cellar for a pinch of dirt. Instead, he concentrated on the chessboard.

The principal pumped his father's hand joyously and then took a seat. "Mr. Van Wart," he said, "Rombout," and he was tapping the black bag in his lap with a knowing and proprietary air, as if it contained the philosopher's stone or the first draft of Roosevelt's New Deal speech, "I've come to make an offer on the property."

The Finger

IT WAS February, grim and cold and gray. Walter, a young man with two feet like anyone else, was still in school, sitting down to his desk with a jar of wheat germ and a carton of prune-whip yogurt, trying to make sense of Heidegger. His motorcycle was in the garage out back of the rooming house in which he ate, slept, shat and ruminated over questions pertaining to man's fate in an indifferent universe, where it stood forlornly amidst a clutter of three-legged tables, disemboweled armchairs and lamps with mismatched shades. He wouldn't be needing it for a while. The outside temperature was twenty below, he was three hundred fifty miles and a whole universe away from the clapboard bungalow in Kitchawank Colony and the hissing inferno of Depeyster Manufacturing and he had three more interminable months to endure before he could accept his diploma from the liver-spotted hands of President Crumley and tear the pages from Heidegger with the same slow malicious pleasure with which he'd torn the wings from flies as a child.

Jessica was at school too. In Albany. She hadn't seen Walter since Christmas break and had written him three times without reply in the past week. She'd also written to graduate schools. Scripps, Miami, N.Y.U., Mayaguez. What she wanted from Walter was love, fidelity and an enduring relationship; what she wanted from Scripps, Miami, N.Y.U. and Mayaguez was a chance to study marine biology. At the moment, she was contemplating the typescript of her senior thesis, which lay on the desk beside yet another letter to Walter. Her legs were crossed, and a furry slipper, shaped like a rabbit but made of cotton, dangled from her pink-frosted toes. The title gave her a little thrill of pleasure: *The Effect of Temperature Fluctuation on Vanadium Concentration in Tunicates of the Intertidal Zone,* by Jessica Conklin Wing. She weathered the thrill, turned the page and began to read.

Tom Crane, grandson to Peletiah, friend and father confessor to Jessica and lifelong boon companion to Walter, was not in school. Not as of two weeks ago, anyway. Nope. Not he. He was a dropout, and proud of it. Cornell, as far as he was concerned, was strictly a bourgeois institution, repressive, reactionary and stultifyingly dull. He'd dissected his last frog, tortured his last rat and struggled for the last time to heft twenty-five-pound textbooks crammed with illustrations, diagrams and appendices. He'd cleaned up his room and sold the whole business—desk, chair, tensor lamp, slide rule, texts, dictionaries, his fieldbook of natural history and a two-year-old calendar featuring the wildflowers of the Northeast as displayed against the wet vulvae of naked, black-nippled Puerto Rican girls—for twenty-six dollars, stuffed his underwear in a rucksack and hitchhiked home.

"What are you going to do now?" his grandfather asked him when he got there.

Hunched and dirty, the eight-foot canary-yellow scarf wrapped around his neck like an anaconda and his World War I German aviator's coat hanging open to the waist, he merely shrugged. "Don't know," he said. "Might get a job, I guess."

His grandfather, former guiding light of the Van Wartville and Peterskill schools and a firm believer in the dignity of work and the principles of John Dewey, gave a snort of contempt. He was seventy-seven years old and his eyebrows rose and fell again like great white swooping owls.

"I wanted to ask you if I could live in the shack."

For a moment the old man was speechless. "The Indian's shack?" he said finally, a fine trembling crusty incredulity oscillating his voice. "Way out there in the hind end of nowhere? Good Christ, you'll freeze to death."

Oh no, he wouldn't freeze. Last summer he'd equipped the place with a new wood stove, replaced the windows and patched the chinks in the walls with scrap lumber and wood putty. And the summer before he'd put up a porch, installed a chemical toilet and dragged enough crapped-over discarded furniture up there to make the place habitable. Besides, he had a good down bag and fifty acres of firewood.

His grandfather, he of the sharp Crane beak and devouring Crane eyes, had doted on him since he lay kicking in the cradle, and now that his own son was gone, the old man clung to him with a fierceness that had all the desperate love of dying blood in it. That is, he was a pushover. "If that's what you want," he said at last, heaving a sigh that might have raised the curtains.

And so here he was, living like a hermit, a man of the mountains, a saint of the forest and hero of the people, free of the petty pecuniary worries that nag shop owner and working stiff alike. Sure it was nippy, and yes, necessity forced him to trudge out to Van Wart Road and hitch the two miles to his grandfather's for a hot meal and the occasional ritual peeling of the long johns and immersion in a steaming tub, but he was doing it. Independence was his! Self-direction! The joy of sloth! He lay in bed all morning, wrapped in his sleeping bag, his arms pinned beneath the weight of Indian blankets uncountable and an old reeking raccoon coat he'd found in his grandmother's closet, watching his breath hang in the air. Sometimes he'd get up to open a can of creamed corn and set it on the kerosene stove or maybe make himself a cup of herb tea or hot chocolate, but mostly he just lay there, listening to his beard grow and relishing his freedom. About ten or eleven—he couldn't tell which, didn't have a clock or watch—he'd begin reading. Typically, he'd start out light, with some elfin fantasy or sci fi, with Tolkien or Vonnegut or Salmón. After lunch—chick peas mashed into brown rice with lentil gravy, out of the five-gallon pot—he'd get into the heavy stuff. Lenin, Trotsky, Bakunin, cheap pamphlets with gray or green covers, the paper no better than newsprint. What did he care for leather bindings and rag content?—he was studying for the revolution.

But now, on this grim winter's night, while Walter lucubrated and Jessica turned her thoughts to Holothurians, Tom Crane was pulling on his pink suede lace-up boots (with the unfortunate smirches of motor oil he'd tried to remove by applying a solution of carbon tetrachloride and high-test gasoline) and slipping into the houndstooth bellbottoms that hugged his bony knees and made racing chocks of his feet. He was grabbing for the aviator's coat and mummy-wrapping the scarf around his neck, heading out the door, suffused with an excitement that made his long bony feet tap across the porch as if they'd come loose: he was going to a concert. A rock concert. A wild, joyous, jungle-thumping celebration of nubility, rebelliousness, draft resistance, drug indulgence, sexual liberation and libidinous release. He'd been waiting three whole days for it.

The sky was low, black, rippled with cloud, and the warming trend of the past few days had pushed the mercury all the way up to fifteen above. He had to feel his way out to the road, the thin jerky beam of the flashlight so weak it could do little more than satisfy his curiosity as to which quivering, low-hanging branch had poked him in the eye or grabbed hold of the frayed tail of his scarf. It was half a mile down the stony, concave path to Van Wart Creek and the wooden footbridge erected by some altruist in times gone by, and then another quarter mile or so across a marshy pasture that was home to grazing cows and dotted like a minefield with their skillet-sized puddles of excrement. The path then wound through a copse of naked beech and thick-clustered fir, ascended a short rise and finally emerged on the motionless black river of macadam that was Van Wart Road.

(So what if it was a regular and tedious trek out to or in from the road, made all the more tedious when the trekker was laden with bursting sacks of lentil flakes, pinto beans or bran pellets? The remoteness of the place had its advantages. A hero of the people and saint of the forest could expect few visitors, for example, or representatives of the duly constituted authorities of the county and township, like the assessor, inspectors from the Department of Building and Safety or the sheriff and his minions. Nor would he be much bothered by drummers, panhandlers, Avon ladies and Jehovah's Witnesses, as these, passing by on the road, would see only an infinity of trees, each one adumbrating the next. For the initiated, however, for his privileged guests, Tom Crane had provided the Packard hubcap. If you slowed in the vicinity of a certain diseased-looking elm that was one-tenth of a mile beyond a certain breached guardrail, and you recognized the hubcap depending from a nail driven into the trunk of that certain elm, you would park and walk in: Tom was at home. If the hubcap was on the ground, you needn't bother.)

Out on the road, Tom removed his deerskin gloves—one of sixteen pairs his father had inadvertently bequeathed him. He'd found them, some still wrapped in gift paper that featured snowmen and candy canes, while poking around in his father's bureau the week after his parents' first vacation in twenty years had been terminated by pilot error somewhere over San Juan. He stuffed the gloves inside the belt loop of his aviator's coat, slipped the all-but-useless flashlight in the back pocket of his bellbottoms, and removed the Packard hubcup from the tree. Then he blew on his hands and turned to address the long black shadow that stretched along the side of the road like the mouth of an unfathomable cave.

This was the Packard itself, a relic of the distant past, painted the color of sleep and forgetfulness and pitted with rust. Its windows were jammed open, the brakes were a memory and the floorboards had dissolved in a delicate tracery that left the pedals floating in space while the road moved beneath them like a conveyor belt. A genuine artifact, as revealing in its way of previous civilization as the arrowhead or potsherd, the old hulk had been unearthed the previous year in the shed out back of his grandfather's place. The elder Crane had owned a succession of Packards, and this, dating from the late forties, was the last of them. ("They went bad after the War," the old man insisted, real vehemence inflating the flanges of his magnificent nose. "Junk. Nothing but junk.") Now it was Tom's.

Working by rote, he struggled to lift and brace the hood and then remove the air filter. He was in the act of spraying ether into what he took in the darkness to be the carburetor when he first spotted the flying saucer. Trembling and luminous, it jerked violently across the sky, coming to an abrupt halt directly above him, where it hovered tentatively, as if looking for a place to land. Tom froze. He watched the thing without apprehension and with a keen sciential eye (it was saucer-shaped, all right, and emitting a pale, rinsed-out light), surprised, but only mildly. He believed in clairvoyance, reincarnation, astrology and the economic theories of Karl Marx, and as he stood there, he could feel his belief system opening up to include an unshakable faith in the existence of extraterrestrial life as well. Still, after ten minutes or so his neck began to go stiff, and he found himself wishing that this marvelous apparition would do something—spit flames, open up like an eye, turn to mud or jelly—anything but hover interminably over his head. It was then that he reached surreptitiously for the flashlight he'd tucked in his back pocket, thinking in a vague way of signaling to the aliens in Morse code or something.

No sooner did he touch the flashlight, however, than the shadow of a great hand obliterated the alien spacecraft; when he released it, the wily aliens returned, hovering as before. He began to feel a little foolish. He stood there playing with the flashlight a minute more, then sent the saucer hurtling to its doom in the inky black reaches of space and turned back to the car. The old hulk started up with a volcanic roar and a brilliant explosion of blue flame from the carburetor; the saint of the forest hustled out to replace the air filter and slam the hood shut. And then he was off with a shriek of the steering wheel and a groan of the tires, off to pour his soul into the Dionysian frenzy of the concert.

The concert, which featured a well-known underground band whose members invested every nickel of their take in preferred stock, was held in Poughkeepsie, in the Vassar College gymnasium. Tom presented his ticket and shuffled through the doors with the rest of the sloe-eyed, hirsute, bead-rattling crowd, glad to get in out of the cold. He was unaware that Poughkeepsie was an Algonquin term meaning "safe harbor," but then no one else in the crowd was aware of it either. In fact, there were few who had any grasp at all of the notion that history had preceded them. They knew, in an abstract way, about Thanksgiving and the pilgrims, about Washington, Lincoln, Hitler and John F. Kennedy, about the Depression—could their parents ever let them forget it?—and they dimly recalled the construction of the local shopping center in some distant formative epoch of their lives. But it was all disconnected, trivial, the sort of knowledge useful in the sixth grade for multiple-choice tests or for scoring the odd answer on a TV quiz show. What was real, what mattered, was the present. And in the present, they and they alone were ascendant—they'd invented sex, hair, marijuana and the electric guitar, and civilization began and ended with them.

Be that as it may, the saint of the forest entered the auditorium that night like a sloop coming in off a choppy sea. The cold wind at his back blew the scarf up around his ears like a luffing sail and a full-body shiver shook him to the gunwales. He stamped and shuddered and quaked, his elbows flying out like quivering booms, as he inched forward, boxed in by shoulders and heads, by greatcoats, army jackets and fringed vests. There was the scent of cold air on upturned collars, trailing from scarves, caught in the vegetal explosion of hair, but it faded quickly, absorbed in the warmth of the crowd. A moment later he was in, the mob dispersing, the big electric heaters wafting tropical breezes, soft lights overhead, a murmur of voices rippling about him like wavelets lapping the pier.

All at once he felt it welling up in him, a sense of exhilaration, of love as pure as Himalayan snow, of brotherhood and communal joy akin to what Gandhi must have felt among the unwashed hordes of Delhi or Lahore. He'd been a hermit too long (it was almost two weeks now), too long out of contact with the energy of the people and the élan vital of the age. Besides, he hadn't been within two feet of a girl since September, when Amy Clutterbuck had let him hold her hand in a darkened movie house in Ithaca. And now he was surrounded by them.

Here a blonde, there a blonde, everywhere a blonde, blonde, he clucked to himself as he made his way to the bleachers and mounted the levels with big, pumping, awkward strides. God, this was great! The smells alone! Perfume, incense, pot, tobacco, Sen-Sen! He was nearly dizzy with excitement as he appropriated a seat midway up the near bleacher, flung himself onto the cold hard plank and coincidentally thrust his knees into the back of the girl in front of him. But it wasn't merely a thrust—the long shanks of his legs may as well have been spring-coiled, the fierce whittled bones of his kneecaps could have been knives—no, it was a savage piercing stab to the victim's kidneys that made her jerk upright in shock and swing around on him like a Harpy.

He saw a small white face devoured by hair, eyes like violets under glass, a crease of rage between a pair of perfect unplucked eyebrows. "What the fuck's the idea?" she spat, the force of the fricative stirring the very roots of his beard.

"I—I—I—" he began, as if he were about to sneeze. But then he got hold of himself and launched into an apology so profound, so heartfelt, fawning and all-reaching that it might have mollified Ho

Chi Minh himself. He concluded by offering a stick of gum. Which she accepted.

"Long legs, huh?" she said, showing her teeth in a rich little smile.

He nodded, the sharp Crane beak stabbing at the air and the ratty braid of his hair flapping at his collar. Was he from around here? she wanted to know. No, he was from Peterskill, just quit school at Cornell—it was a real drag, did she know what he meant?—and had his own place now, really cool, out in the woods.

"Peterskill?" she yelped. "No kidding?" She was from Van Wartville herself. Yup, born and raised. Went to private school. She was at Bard now. Did he have a car?

He did.

She wouldn't mind going home for the weekend, maybe blowing off her Monday classes and getting her father to drive her back up. Would that be okay with him—a ride maybe?

He nodded till his neck began to ache, grinned so hard the corners of his mouth went numb. Sure, of course, no problem, any time. "I'm Tom Crane," he said, holding out his hand.

She shook, and her hand was as cold as one of the innumerable, dumb-staring perch he'd cut open in Bio lab. "I'm Mardi," she said.

He was about to say something inane, just to keep the conversation going, something like "I'm a Libra," but just then the lights went down and the emcee announced the band. That was when things began to get peculiar. Because instead of the band, with their ragged hair and sneers, suddenly there was another character at the microphone—a dean or something, in suit and tie—announcing in a voice that was almost a yelp that there'd been an accident and asking for the crowd's cooperation. People began to look around them. A murmur went up. It seemed that someone—a gatecrasher—had attempted to slip in through one of the great long windows that ran the length of each wall and stood about twenty feet above the floor. The gatecrasher had climbed in, hung for a moment from the ledge and then dropped down into the crowd. Or so the dean explained.

The murmur became louder. Was he—a representative of the warmongering elite—asking them, the audience, the people, to turn in one of their own? To fink, rat, betray? Tom was thunderstruck. He studied the crown of Mardi's head, the part of her hair, the slope of her shoulders, in growing outrage. But no. That wasn't it at all. The gatecrasher had been hurt. His ring had hung up on the window catch when he dropped to the floor: the ring, along with the finger it had encircled, had been torn from his hand. Would the audience take a minute to search for the finger so that it might be saved?

The murmur rose to a shout. They were on their feet now, and a great sound of shuffling and groaning pervaded the place, as of a vast herd in migratory movement; panic was writ on their faces. Somewhere out there, in a lap or handbag or ground beneath somebody's heel, was a bleeding finger, still-living flesh: it was enough to make you get down on all fours and bay like a hound. Tom felt sick, all the joy and exhilaration gone out of him like wind from a balloon. There was a general moaning and gnashing of teeth. "There's no cause for panic!" the dean was shouting through the microphone, but no one seemed to hear him.

Mardi had stood fixedly through all of this, one step down from the saint of the forest, her eyes scanning the crowd. Now she turned to him, fanning out her hair with a reflexive jerk of her neck, and there it was, the finger. It fell, like a pale grub, from the snarled web of her hair and dropped to the seat beside her. "There!" Tom shouted, pointing at the seat in horror and fascination. "There it is!" She glanced down. And up at him. The expression on her face—she wasn't appalled, disgusted, panicked, didn't scream or dance on her toes—was like nothing Tom had ever seen. Or no: it was feral. She was a cat and this bit of flesh was something she'd prized from a nest or a hole in a tree. A smile began to make its slow way across her lips, until amidst the confusion, the howls and the uneasy fits and starts of laughter with which the place reverberated like some chamber of doom, she was beaming at him. "We cannot start the concert," the dean was shouting, but Mardi paid no attention. Still beaming, still holding Tom's eyes, she bent ever so slightly from the waist and flicked the finger into the shadowy maw of the bleacher.

Patrimony

It was as if Walter had awakened from a long sleep, as if the past twenty-odd years were the illusion, and this—the dreams and visions, history and its pertinacity—the reality. He couldn't be sure of anything any more. All the empirical underpinnings of the world—Boyle's Law, Newtonian physics, doctrines of evolution and genetic inheritence, TV, gravity, the social contract, merde—had suddenly become suspect. His grandmother had been right all along. His grandmother—the fisherman's wife, with the stockings fallen down around her ankles and her faintly mustachioed upper lip rising and falling in ceaseless incantation—had perceived the world more keenly than philosophers and presidents, pharmacists and ad men. She'd seen through the veil of Maya—seen the world for what it was—a haunted place, where anything could happen and nothing was as it seemed, where shadows had fangs and doom festered in the blood. Walter felt he might float off into space, explode like a sweet potato left too long in the oven, grow hair on his palms or turn to grape jelly. Why not? If there were apparitions, shadows on dark roadways, voices speaking in the rootless night, why not imps and goblins, God, St. Nick, UFOs and *pukwidjinnies* too?

He left the hospital on a sunstruck morning in August, and the first thing he did—before he had a beer or monster burger with pickle, relish, mayonnaise, mustard and three-star chili sauce, before he hustled Jessica up to his room above the kitchen to finish what he'd begun on the hard flat institutional bed in the East Wing—was this: he went back and read the inscription on the road sign, as the barefoot specter of his father had advised him. Jessica drove. She wore a shift that was made of the filmy stuff of lingerie, she wore sandals, jewelry, makeup, perfume. Walter watched the trees flit by the window, one after another, in endless unbroken succession, a green so intense he had to shield his eyes; Jessica hummed along with the radio. She was effusive, lighthearted, gay and unconstrained; he was subdued and withdrawn. She prattled on about wedding plans, told jokes, fumbled with the gilt foil on the neck of the bottle of Möet et Chandon clenched between her thighs and filled him in on people they knew—Hector, Tom Crane, Susie Cats—as if he'd been gone a year. He didn't have much to say.

The sign—the historical marker, that is—had barely been damaged by Walter's assault on it. The stanchion was gouged where the footpeg had hit it and the whole thing was tilted back a degree or two so that the legend could most comfortably be perused from the lower branches of the maple across the street, but basically Walter was much more the worse for wear than the instrument of his mutilation. That much he could see from the car window as they pulled up on the shoulder. Emerging from the passenger side of Jessica's VW like a crab shrugging off its shell, he braced himself on his crutches—every time he put his weight on the still-tender stump of his right leg it felt as if it were on fire—and hobbled up to decipher the sign that had become for him as momentous and mysterious as the Sinai tablets must have been for the tribes of Israel. He could have asked Jessica or Lola or Tom Crane to go have a look at it while he lay helpless in bed, tormented by the image of his father and the brutal commingling of dream and reality, but he preferred it this way. After all, he hadn't hit a tree, mailbox, fireplug or lamppost, but a sign—symbol, token and signifier—yes, a sign, and it might as well have been inscribed with hieroglyphs for all the attention he'd paid it in the past. There was a message here. He yearned for enlightenment.

It was hot. The end of summer. Cars shot past with a suck of air. There was no blood, no oil slick on the road—just the sign, with its gouge. He read:

> On this spot in 1693, Cadwallader Crane, leader of an armed uprising on Van Wart Manor, surrendered to authorities. He

was hanged, along with co-conspirator Jeremy Mohonk, at Gallows Hill, Van Wartville, in 1694.

He read, but he was not enlightened. He stood there like a man of stone, conning it over, word by word. And then, after a long moment during which he cursed his dreams, his father and the state historical society, he swung around on his crutches and stumped back to the car.

At home—the world had shifted beneath his feet, changed as surely and irrevocably as if it had been hit by a comet or visited by a delegation of three-headed aliens from Alpha Centauri, and yet here all was the same, right down to the muted bands of sunlight that fell across the Turkish carpet like a benediction and the twin lamps with shades the color and texture of ancient parchment—Walter stood awkwardly in the middle of the cluttered den and gave himself up to Lola's sinewy embrace. The paneled walls were still hung with the dim sepia photos of Lola's parents in their Moldavian overcoats, galoshes and fur hats; the black-and-whites of Walter in his Little League uniform; the overexposed snapshot of Lola and Walter's mother as high school girls, their hair long, arms entwined; and the turgid official portrait of Lenin that occupied the place of honor over the mantelpiece. The cane plant in the corner was still dead and the empty aquarium still crusted with a jagged layer of petrified sludge. On the bookshelves, amidst the faded spines and crumbling dust jackets of books that hadn't been moved for as long as Walter could remember, crouched the ceramic tigers and elephants, the ivory rooks and knights and pawns he'd played with as a boy, all exactly as he'd left them on that distant morning of the potato pancakes. He'd been gone two weeks to the day. Everything was the same, and everything was changed. "Well," Lola said. "Well. You're back."

Jessica stood beside him, fidgeting with her purse. She was wearing an embarrassed smile. Lola was smiling too, but her smile was worn and rueful. Walter, despite himself, found that he was smiling back at her. His wasn't a comforting smile, though. He was too disoriented, too crushed by the ghost of the familiar that screamed like something choked in the bushes each time he glanced down at his right foot, to smile like an unconstrained and doting son. No, his smile was more a baring of the teeth.

Did he want something to eat? Lola wanted to know. A little borscht maybe? With some rye bread? Tea? Cookies? Did he want to sit down? Was it too warm? Should she turn on the fan? Hesh would be thrilled when he got home from work.

Walter didn't want any borscht. Nor rye bread, tea or cookies either. It wasn't too warm. The fan could rest. He looked forward to seeing Hesh. But for now—and here he gave Jessica a significant look—he just wanted to go up to bed. To rest, that is. He would not drink the champagne, he would not have a beer or monster burger and he would not engage in an act of love and affirmation with his fiancée. Instead, he would mount the stairs to his boyhood room like a soldier returned from battle, like a martyr, and he would draw the shades, stretch out on the bed and watch the shadows deepen toward night.

Next morning he awoke to the smell of potato pancakes, a smell that roused him like a slap in the face. He sat up in bed, seized with fear and loathing. The cycle was beginning again. Already his mother's sorrowful eyes had begun to detach themselves from the gloom in the corner behind the bureau. A minute more and his grandmother would be looking over his shoulder and his father poking fun at him or delivering yet another cryptic message. It was intolerable. How many pounds of flesh did he have to sacrifice? How many limbs? He fumbled with the straps of the prosthesis, jerked on his clothes, seized the crutches and flung himself down the stairs like a hunted man.

It was 7:00 A.M. Hesh and Lola were in the kitchen, their voices soft and murmurous. The house ticked with the small comfortable sounds he'd missed in the hospital—water trickling through the pipes, the hum of dishwasher and refrigerator. Outside, the sun slanted through elms and maples and spilled across the lawn and into the garden. Walter stood at the window a moment to collect himself. He saw corn. Tomatoes. Pumpkins, cucumbers, squash. Hesh had planted them. In May. Before Walter had gone to work at Depeyster Manufacturing, before he'd reconditioned the Norton and discovered a ghost in the scent of a pancake. And now here they were, rooted in the ground.

In the kitchen, he braced his crutches against the wall and sat down at the table across from Hesh. Lola stood at the gas range, flipping pancakes. "I made your favorite, Walter," she said.

The smell was intolerable. It was death. He'd rather have snuffed the fumes of burning plastic, nerve gas, blood and offal and shit. A glass of milk stood beside his plate. He took a sip. It was warm. "I'm not hungry," he said.

"Not hungry?" Hesh echoed. He was perched over his muffin like an eagle masking its kill. His forearms swelled against the edge of the table. "Come on, kid, snap out of it. You lost your foot. Okay. It's not the end of the world."

Walter set down the glass of milk. "Please, Lola," he said, craning his neck to look over his shoulder, "not now. I just can't eat." And then, turning back to Hesh, who was licking butter from the tips of his fingers and chewing with a rhythmic roll of his great, clean-shaven jaws, he said, "It's not that. Really. It's"—he didn't know how to tell him—"I've been thinking about my father lately."

Hesh had stopped chewing. "Your father?" he repeated, as if he hadn't heard properly. He picked up the butter knife and laid it down again. "You know how I feel about your father."

Walter knew. But whatever had gone wrong with him had its roots here—in the riots, on the ghost ships, in the conundrum of the marker and the burden of heredity. "Yeah, I know. But things are different now and I have a right to know what he did to you and Lola and my mother that was so awful, and I have a right to know where he is now. I have a right to ask him myself."

Hesh's eyes had changed. They were open—fixed on Walter's—but they might as well have been shut fast. He'd begun chewing again, but more slowly, and, it seemed, without relish. "Sure," he said finally, while Lola rattled pans at the stove. "You've got all the right in the world. But your mother made us your legal guardians, not him. He deserted you, Walter. And even after he came back, those summers, you think he was about to take on the responsibility of raising a kid even though he caused a big stink all the time? Huh? Do you?"

Walter shrugged. The pancakes were killing him. He felt as if he were about to cry.

"Look him up, go ahead. Where you'll look, God only knows.

But as far as I'm concerned, he's a bum. A Judas. Persona non grata. As far as I'm concerned, the book is closed."

But the book is never closed.

Hesh went off to his glazier's shop on Houston Street and Lola sat at the table and told Walter the story of the riots for the thousandth time. He knew every nuance, anticipated her every pause and change of inflection as if he were speaking himself, but he listened now as if he'd never heard the story before, listened as he had the day after his eleventh birthday when Lola sat him down and tried to explain why Hesh and his father had nearly come to blows over so marvelous and inoffensive a thing as an Italian motorbike with red fenders and chrome-plated handlebars. He listened.

She hadn't been able to get near the place—the concert grounds, that is. But Hesh had. And Walter's father and mother too. The organizing committee had asked them to come early to set up the chairs and see to the lights and loudspeakers. After that, Christina would be in charge of programs and literature, and Hesh and Truman were supposed to mingle with the crowd and keep an eye out for trouble. It was going to be quite a night: the warmth of the summer evening like a big communal blanket, the stars overhead, a thousand voices joined in song. They'd talked about nothing else for weeks.

Will Connell was going to be there, to strum his guitar and sing his songs about the working people of America (later, when the whole country had caught the sickness of the riots, he would be blacklisted by every record company, every music publisher, booking agent and theater owner from Maine to California). A woman from the New York stage was going to sing too. And there were two speakers, one from the Garment Workers' Union, the other a party member who'd fought in the Abraham Lincoln Brigade. The big attraction, though—the man everyone was coming to see—was Paul Robeson. Paul Robeson was a Negro and a Communist, he was an actor and a civil libertarian, he was a great huge lion of a man who could sing the old spirituals till you could feel them in the marrow of your bones.

Lola had seen him at the pavilion in Kitchawank Colony just the year before. Two hundred or so had turned out to hear him that time, local people from the Colony mostly, the graying Anarchists and Socialists who'd founded the community back in the twenties because they wanted to free themselves from the diseases of city life and give their children a libertarian education, and the party-line Communists who'd begun to supplant them. People brought sandwiches and sat on the grass—old couples, children, pregnant women. There was no trouble. Just a nice time for everyone. A little culture in the hinterlands.

But the following year—in August, late August—it was a different story. Lola was working then, a half-day shift at the counter in the old van der Meulen bakeshop in Peterskill, and so she couldn't go in early with Hesh and Truman. Walter's mother went, though. Christina made up some sandwiches and a thermos of iced tea, dropped Walter at his grandmother's—he'd just turned three, did he remember?—and then climbed into Hesh's 1940 Plymouth with her husband and his buddy Piet.

Lola tilted her head back and glanced around the room. A cup of black coffee sat before her on the table, going cold. She lit a cigarette, shook out the match and exhaled. "He was quite a character, Piet," she said. "Short little guy, no higher than my chin. And always playing practical jokes—you know, your father was a great one for jokes." She took a sip of cold coffee. "The two of them were always at it. Silly stuff. Palm buzzers and squirting carnations and whatnot. I wonder what ever became of him?—Piet, I mean. Your father thought he was really something else."

There were no jokes that night. Hesh drove. Christina sat up front, with the thermos and sandwiches and the box of programs and party literature; Truman and Piet were in back, boxed in by sound equipment. Lola was planning to join them later, as soon as she got out of work. There'd be plenty of time—she got off at seven and the concert wasn't scheduled to start until seven-thirty. She hoped they'd save her a seat.

Anyway, they were going to hold the concert down near the river, just off Van Wart Road, on some property owned by Peletiah Crane, who was then superintendent of the Peterskill schools. (*Yes, that's right,* Lola had said when she'd first told him the story, *Tom's grandpa.*) Peletiah wasn't a party member himself, but he was sympathetic to the cause and he'd been a supporter of cultural events in the Colony for years. When it became apparent that the concert and rally would be much bigger than the last—a show of solidarity for progressives that would attract perhaps two and a half thousand from the City—the Kitchawank Colony Association realized it wouldn't have the space or facilities to handle such a crowd and dropped its sponsorship of the event. That's when Peletiah stepped in. He offered the Robeson people the use of his property for nothing, and this encouraged one of the trade unions to put up the money to rent chairs, sound equipment and floodlights. Sasha Freeman, the novelist, and Morton Blum, the builder, were the chief organizers. They didn't expect any trouble, but you never knew. They asked Hesh and Truman, both of them party members and big men, toughened by war and adversity, to be in charge of security.

Hesh had his hair then, and for all his gruffness he was a teddy bear inside. Truman was the best-looking man in Peterskill, wild, a daredevil who rented a plane and flew it under the Bear Mountain Bridge—upside down, yet—and had his license taken away by the C.A.A. He and Hesh were best friends (*Yes,* she'd told him that first time, *like you and Tom*)—they were all friends. Lola and Christina had gone through school together, first at the Colony Free School and then later at Peterskill High. After the war, when Christina brought Walter's father around, everybody fell for him. (Almost a local boy, but not quite, he'd grown up in Verplanck and gone to school at Hendrick Hudson. Hesh had played opposite him in football, and Lola recognized him at once as the vanquisher of Peterskill's best, the triple threat who'd so many times made her heart sink as he poked a baseball over the fence, dribbled downcourt in his silken shorts or burst through a gap in the line with his muddied calves and the angry black slashes of greasepaint masking his eyes.) He was working in the old Van Wart iron foundry, which had gone out of business during the Depression and been revived and retooled by a one-armed war veteran from Brooklyn, and he was going to night school at City College to earn a B.A. degree in American history. "History," Lola said, lingering over the syllables, "that was his passion.

"Your mother's father—he was a president of the Colony Association and a party member—he gave Truman some literature and talked to him about the dignity of the worker, surplus value and the fetishism of commodities—we all did, we all talked to him—and before long, he'd joined us. Of course, it was your mother who really won him over, but that's another story. That fall they were married, and they rented a little two-room bungalow out back of the Rosenberg place—you remember it, don't you?"

Lola paused to snub out her cigarette. "In the summer, Walter, summer of forty-six, you were born."

Walter knew when he was born. He'd learned the date when he was three or four, and if it should ever happen to slip his mind, he could always consult his driver's license. He knew that bungalow too, his home through the first dim years of his life, just as he knew what was coming next. He leaned forward all the same.

So Truman joined the party. Truman got married. Truman spent two nights a week at City College, studying the American Revolution, and five nights a week at the card table in Hesh and Lola's front room. One night Christina would make up a pan of stuffed cabbage or a *hutspot* stew she'd learned from her mother, or her crisp potato pancakes; the next night, Lola would bake a cheese-and-noodle kugel. That was the way it was. Lola couldn't have children of her own. But when Walter was born, Truman came to her and asked if she and Hesh would consent to be the boy's godparents, and the evenings went on as before, only now little Walter's crib stood in the corner.

And then it was 1949. August. And the party wanted Paul Robeson to give a concert in Peterskill, and Sasha Freeman and Morton Blum came to Hesh and to Truman. For security. There wouldn't be any violence. No, they didn't think so. It was going to be a peaceful affair, Negroes and whites together, working people, women and children and old folks, enjoying a concert and maybe a couple of political speeches, exercising their right to assemble and to express unpopular ideas. But Sasha Freeman and Morton Blum came to Hesh and Truman. Just in case.

Hesh swung off a dirt lane onto Van Wart Road, not a mile from the concert grounds, and the first thing he noticed was the number of people gathered along the road. Some were headed in the direction of the Crane property, in groups of four and five, ambling and desultory, beer bottles in hand; others just stood at the side of the road, waiting, as if for a parade. A moment later he encountered the cars. Scores of them, parked alongside the road, drawn up on the shoulders on both sides, so that only a narrow one-way lane remained between them. It was only half past six.

Hesh was mystified. Peletiah had set aside a pasture the size of three football fields expressly for parking, and here they were lined up along the road like cabbies at the airport, practically choking off access to the place. Buses had to get through here, buses from the City, and camp trucks and more buses from the summer colonies in Rockland County and the Catskills. Not to mention hundreds upon hundreds of private cars. What was going on here? Why hadn't they parked on the concert grounds?

He got his answer soon enough.

No one had even glanced at them until they reached the gauntlet of parked cars, but now, once they'd entered the single lane heading for the entrance to the concert grounds, heads began to turn. A man in an overseas cap shouted an obscenity and then something glanced off the side of the car. These people hadn't come to see the concert—they'd come to prevent it.

Sasha Freeman and Morton Blum didn't think there would be any violence—though the Peterskill paper had seethed with anti-Communist, anti-Jew and anti-Negro invective for the past month, though the local chapter of the VFW had threatened to hold a "loyalty rally" to protest against the concert, though flags had been waving aggressively from every porch in town and placards reviling Robeson had begun to appear in shop windows—but here it was. At the entrance, Hesh was confronted with a larger and denser crowd—two hundred or more—that erupted in jeers and insults when it became clear that he and his passengers were concertgoers rather than kindred spirits. They rolled up the windows, though it was eighty-five degrees outside, and Hesh shifted down as he approached the mouth of the narrow dirt road that gave onto Peletiah's property.

"Nigger lovers!" someone shouted.

"Kikes!"

"Commie Jew bastards!"

A teenager with slicked-back hair and a face red with hate loomed out of the crowd to spit across the windshield, and suddenly Hesh had had enough and put his foot to the floor. The Plymouth leapt forward and the crowd parted with a shout, there was the thump-thump-

thump of angry fists and feet against fenders and doors, and then they were in and the crowd was receding in the rearview mirror.

Shaken, Hesh pulled into the lot beside a rented bus. Three other buses, a truck bearing the legend "Camp Wahwahtaysee" and perhaps twelve or fifteen cars were already there. Christina's face was white. Truman and Piet were silent. "Trouble," Hesh muttered, "son of a bitch. We're in for it now."

Seven o'clock came and went. There was no Robeson, no Freeman, no Blum. Out on the road, nothing moved. The access routes were either blocked or jammed with the cars and buses of frustrated concertgoers, and no one could get in or out. Except for the patriots, that is, who fingered brass knuckles and tire irons or tore up fence posts and tried the heft of them, ambling along the blacktop road as if they owned it. Which they did, for some four hours that night. The unlucky few who did actually make it to Van Wart Road, thinking to sit on a blanket, sip a Coke or beer and enjoy a concert, were routed past the blockaded concert grounds, pulled from their cars and beaten. No one, from Peterskill to Kitchawank Colony and back again, saw a single policeman.

There were maybe a hundred and fifty people gathered in front of the stage when Hesh and the others arrived. Most were women and children who'd turned out early to enjoy an evening in the sylvan glades of northern Westchester. Besides Hesh, Truman and Piet, there were about forty men among them; up above, beyond the line of trees that marked the boundary of Peletiah's property, five hundred patriots stormed up and down the road, looking for Communists.

Hesh took charge. He sent five teenagers—three boys and two girls who'd come up from Staten Island to serve as ushers—to keep an eye on the crowd at the entrance. "If they set foot on the property, you let me know," he said. "Right away. Understand?" He asked Truman and Piet to take six of the men, arm themselves with anything they could find and fan out across the field to make sure none of the zealots came at them from the rear. Then he organized the rest of the men in ranks, eight across, their arms linked, and marched them up the road. The women and children—Walter's mother amongst them—gathered around the empty stage. In the distance, they could hear the sound of shattering glass, truncated cries, the roar of the mob.

Walter knew the old road into the Crane place, didn't he? It was no more than a footpath now, walled off since the riots, but in those days it was a pretty well-worn dirt road with a hummock of grass in the middle. Narrow though, and with steep shoulders and impenetrable brush—sticker bushes and poison ivy and whatnot—on either side. The road wound down into the meadow and then turned into a path when it crossed the stream on the far side and climbed up the ridge. People would drive down there for a little privacy—to play their car radios, neck and drink beer. Some nights there'd be ten cars parked in the meadow. Anyway, there was but one other way in and that was by foot only—at the far end of the meadow, where Van Wart Road swung back on it half a mile up. Hesh figured if he could hold the road, they'd be all right. If real trouble started, that is. He hoped the police would show up before then.

They didn't.

The first fracas broke out about seven-thirty. Hesh and his men had stationed themselves just out of sight of the mob, at the road's narrowest point, and they'd backed the camp truck up against their flank to further obstruct the way. If the patriots got worked up enough to attack—with odds something like fifteen to one—they had to be held here; if they reached the stage, and the women and children, anything could happen. And so they stood there, arms linked, waiting. Thirty-two strangers. A black stevedore in sweatshirt and jeans, a handful of men in merchant marine uniform, pot-bellied car dealers and liquor store owners and shipping clerks, an encyclopedia salesman from Yonkers and three scared black seminary students, who, like the kids at the gate, had come early to serve as ushers. They stood there and listened to the howls and curses of the mob and waited for the police to come and break it up. No one wanted a concert any more, no one wanted speeches or even the inalienable rights guaranteed under the Constitution: all they wanted, to a man, was to be out of there.

And then it started. There was a roar from the crowd, succeeded by a prolonged hiss and clatter that might have been the blast of a tropical storm thrashing the trees, and then the five ushers suddenly appeared around the bend—the three boys and two girls—running for their lives in a hail of rocks and bottles. The look in their eyes was something Hesh had seen before—at Omaha Beach, at Isigny, St. Lo and Nantes. Both girls were sobbing and one of the boys—he couldn't have been more than fifteen—was bleeding from a gash over his right eye. They passed through the lines and then Hesh and his recruits locked arms once again.

A moment later the mob was on them. Five hundred or more strong now, but funneled into the narrow road like cattle in a chute, they burst against the defenders in a frenzied, stick-wielding rush. Hesh was struck across the face, slashed just behind the ear and battered on both forearms. "Kill the commies!" the mob chanted. "Lynch the niggers!"

It lasted no more than two or three minutes. Hesh's men were bruised and bleeding, but they'd repulsed the first wave. Rabid, shrieking insults and flinging sticks and stones and whatever else they could lay their hands on, the mob withdrew a hundred feet to regroup. The better part of them were drunk, whipped to a frenzy by irrational hates and prejudices that were like open wounds, but others—there was a knot of them, the ones in dress shirts and ties and Legionnaire's caps—were as cool as field marshals. Depeyster Van Wart was among this latter group, stiff and formal, his face composed, but with a pair of eyes that could have eaten holes in the camp truck. He was conferring with his brother—the one who was killed in Korea—and LeClerc Outhouse, who'd made all that money in the restaurant business. Did Walter remember him?

Walter nodded.

"Go back to Russia!" a man screamed, shaking his fist, and the whole crowd took it up. They were about to break ranks and charge again when the three policemen showed up. These were local cops, not state police, and the patriots knew them by name.

"Now boys," Hesh could hear one of them saying, "we don't like this any better than you do, but let's keep it legal, huh?" And then, while his partners placated the mob with more of the same—"If it was up to me I'd shoot 'em down like dogs, right here and now, but you know we can't do that; not in America, anyways"—the one who'd spoken first hitched up his trousers, squared his crotch and sauntered down to where Hesh and his battered recruits stood with folded arms and lacerated flesh.

"Who's in charge here?" he demanded.

Hesh recognized him in that instant: Anthony Fagnoli. They'd gone to school together. Fagnoli had been two years younger, a criminal type with greased hair who was forever being suspended for smoking in the boys' room or coming to class drunk. He'd dropped out of school as a sophomore to drive one of his uncle's garbage trucks. Now he was a cop.

Hesh glanced around. Sasha Freeman hadn't made it. Nor Morton Blum either. "I guess I am," he said.

"You are, huh?" Fagnoli gave no sign of recognition.

"Kike!" screamed a patriot. "Hitler didn't get you, but we will!"

"So just what in the fuck do you think you're trying to do here, Mister?" Fagnoli said.

"You know damn well what we're doing." Hesh looked him hard in the eye. "We're exercising our right of peaceful assembly—on private property, I might add."

"Peaceful?" Fagnoli practically howled the word. "Peaceful?" he repeated, and then jerked a thumb over his shoulder in the direction of the crowd. "You call that peaceful?"

Hesh gave it up. "Look," he said, "we don't want any part of this. The concert is done. Off. It's over. All we want is out."

Fagnoli was smirking now. "Out?" he said, shrugging his shoulders. "You made this mess, clean it up yourself." And then he turned his back and started to walk off.

"Officer. Please. If you tell them to disperse, they'll listen."

Fagnoli swung around as if he'd been hit from behind. His face was like a clenched fist. "Up yours," he hissed.

Hesh watched him swagger back up the road and push his way into the mob, where he stopped a moment to confer with Van Wart and Outhouse and the other ringleaders. Then he turned to his two compatriots and said, in a voice that carried all the way back to Hesh and his men, "They want out, boys. What do you think of that?"

A man in an overseas cap suddenly bawled, "Out! You never get out! Every nigger bastard dies here tonight! Every Jew bastard dies here tonight!" And the crowd began to roar. Fagnoli and the two other cops had disappeared.

The second charge came a moment later. The patriots screamed down the narrow roadway, swinging fence posts and tire irons, flinging rocks and bottles, slamming with all the weight and fury of those behind them into Hesh's lines. Hesh stood firm, grappled with a man swinging a fence post and ground his fist into the center of the man's face till he felt something give. Again, the melee lasted no more than three or four minutes, and the attackers fell back. But Hesh was hurt. And so were his men. Hurt and scared. They had to get word out to the world at large, had to phone the police, the governor, *The New York Times*—they had to have help. And quick. If it didn't come soon, there was no doubt in anyone's mind that some of them would die there on the road before the night was out.

It was at that point that Truman came into the picture. Like Hesh, he'd been out of the service for nearly four years now—but unlike Hesh and most other veterans, he'd never abandoned the habit of regular physical exercise. He kept himself in trim with the daily regimen of calisthenics, cross-country running and weight-lifting he'd begun when he was with Army Intelligence in England. At thirty-one, he'd barely lost a step on the eighteen-year-old dynamo who'd led Hendrick Hudson to the county championship in two sports. When Hesh realized that someone had to get out, he knew Truman was his man.

Instructing his troops to hold out at all costs, he doubled back down the road to the meadow, passing the forlorn cars and buses of the concertgoers and skirting the stage where a thousand folding chairs stood unoccupied. Hurrying, he caught a glimpse of Christina, white-faced and glum, sitting at the table with her pamphlets, and of the other women gathered in clusters before the empty stage. Here and there children were playing, but in hushed voices and with movements that might have been choreographed for an underwater ballet. One of the unlucky ushers—a girl of sixteen—sat alone beneath the stage, a bright carnation of blood flowering at the neck of her blouse.

He found Truman leaning against a tree that commanded a view of the meadow all the way out to the road at the far end of the property. Piet was with him, and they were conferring in low tones like a pair of military strategists surveying a battlefield—which wasn't far from the truth of the matter. Their squad had caught two of the patriots out in the open and driven them back, but otherwise things were quiet. Hesh explained the situation and asked Truman if he would try to slip out and get to a phone. It would be dangerous, and he'd have to leave Christina behind, but if he didn't get through it looked as if the worst was going to happen.

Truman shrugged. Sure, he'd give it a try.

"Good," Hesh said. "Good. If the troopers know we've called out, if they know we've got to the papers, they'll have no excuse—they'll have to bail us out."

Truman was staring down at his feet. He glanced up at Hesh and then away again. In the distance, they could hear the mob roaring. "Yeah," he said, "I'll go. But I want to take Piet with me."

Hesh glanced at Piet. His face was expressionless and pale, and his ears seemed unnaturally large in proportion to the rest of him. He couldn't have been taller than four-eight or -nine, and if he weighed eighty-five pounds, half of it must have been in the funny old-fashioned buckled boots he always wore. "What the hell," Hesh murmured. "Take him." Piet wasn't in this anyway—he'd come on a lark—and he probably couldn't have held back one of the rednecks' grandmothers if he'd wanted to. "You sure he won't slow you down?"

Truman replied that Piet could take care of himself, and then he turned and started off across the field, the little man jogging to keep up with him, all but lost in the high stiff grass. It was the last Hesh—or anyone else—would see of them that night.

Lola paused. She'd lit another cigarette and let it burn itself out. The coffee cup was empty. The first time Walter had heard the story he'd interrupted here to ask what had happened to them; now he wanted to hear it again. "So what happened?"

No one knew for sure. It was as if he and Piet had simply vanished. There was no record of any call to the police or newspapers, Hesh's knock sounded hollowly on the Dutch door of Piet's furnished room in Peterskill next morning, and none of the injured at the local hospitals answered to their descriptions. Hesh was afraid they'd been killed, beaten to death by the mob and dumped in a gully along the road. Though he had a headache that was like a mallet inside his skull, though he'd taken ten stitches in his forearms and half a dozen over his right ear, and though he was haggard from stress and lack of sleep, he was up at first light on the morning following the riot, beating the bushes on either side of Van Wart Road. He found nothing. Little did he realize it at the time, but it would be nearly fifteen months before either he or Lola would lay eyes on Truman again. And Piet—Piet was gone for good.

Two days after the riot, Truman turned up at the bungalow out back of the Rosenberg place. By that point, Christina was in shock. Walter was three. He clung to his father's knees, chanting "Daddy, Daddy," but Truman ignored him. Truman gave Christina a weak grin and began to pack his things. "We thought you were dead," she said. "What happened? What are you doing?" He wouldn't answer her. Just kept packing. Sweaters, underwear, books—his precious books. Walter was crying. "Did they hurt you, is that it?" Christina screamed. "Truman, answer me!"

A car stood in the driveway. It was a Buick, and they say it belonged to Depeyster Van Wart. Piet, barely visible over the dash, was sitting in the passenger seat. "I'm sorry," Truman said, and then he was gone.

It was nearly a year after the funeral when he turned up again. Unshaven, drunk, sorrowful-looking, in clothes that hung from him like a beggar's rags, he showed up at Lola's door, demanding to see his son. "He was abusive, Walter," Lola said. "A changed man. He called me names." This wasn't the man she knew—this was some crazy on a street corner in Times Square, some bum. When Hesh came up from the basement to see what the commotion was about, Truman tried to shove past him and Hesh hit him, hit him in the face and then in the gut. Truman went down on his hands and knees on the front porch, gasping till the tears came to his eyes. Hesh shut the door.

By then, people were certain that Truman had betrayed them, that his sympathies had always been with the "patriots" and that he'd turned his back on family and friends in the most calculating and callous way. Rose Pollack, who hadn't been able to get into the concert grounds that night, had seen him on the road with Depeyster Van Wart and LeClerc Outhouse just before a criminal put a brick through her windshield, and the day he turned up in the Colony to break the heart of Walter's mother and pack up his books and underwear, Lorelee Shapiro had seen him driving Van Wart's car. Or so she said. Lola didn't know what to think—or Hesh either. They'd loved him, this jubilant and quick-smiling man, their comrade and friend, husband of Christina Alving, father of their godson. After the riots people were hysterical—they were looking for scapegoats. Lola—and Hesh too, Hesh too—had wanted to believe in him, but the evidence was against him. There was the way he'd disappeared, for one thing. And then there was that terrible fateful night of the riot itself.

Truman never called the state police; he never called the *Times*. And twenty minutes after he started off across the field, a hundred patriots swarmed in from the same direction—unchecked, and shouting filth. "Was it a coincidence, Walter? Was it?" Lola was asking the questions now. Walter said nothing.

It was getting dark, and out on the road the mob had begun to pelt Hesh and his defenders with rocks—fist-sized and bigger, hundreds upon hundreds of them, thudding against the flank of the camp truck, striking men in the face, in the chest and legs and groin. One of the seminary students was knocked flat, his nose smashed to pulp; the stevedore, a huge black man who made a conspicuous target, was already bleeding from a scalp wound when a barrage of stones brought him to his knees.

The patriots were thirty feet away now and closing. Their arms whipped forward, stones boomed off the truck, skittered across the road, hit home with a dull wet thump. Hesh heard that sound, the sound of the butcher's mallet on a slab of meat—thump, thump, thump—and knew they were finished. He saw the stevedore go down, and then felt himself hit in both legs; in the same instant a stone glanced off his cheek, and when he raised an arm to shield his face, a beer bottle caught him in the ribs. This was ridiculous. Useless. Suicidal. He was no martyr. "Break!" he suddenly roared. "Break and run!" Bleeding, battered, their suits and sportshirts torn to rags, the defenders dropped back, skirted the truck and flung themselves headlong down the darkened road. Behind them, the patriots surged forward with a shout.

At first, Hesh and the others retreated in panic, without direction, every man for himself. All that changed when they came upon the arena. The field was brightly lit—one of the women had started up the generator and flashed on the stage lights as night fell—and Hesh and his dazed comrades were suddenly confronted by the spectacle of a hundred wild-eyed men running amuck amidst their wives and children. It was unendurable. Without hesitation—without even breaking stride—they came together again, charging into the melee in a wedge, swinging sticks and fists, sick and maddened and ready to die. The patriots fell back under the fury of the assault, and the women and children who'd been caught out in the open made for the stage as if it were a life raft in a churning sea. Hesh and his men grappled with their adversaries for a moment and then broke for the stage themselves as the patriots from above roared down on them. It was then that an unknown hand let loose the bottle that laid Hesh low. One moment he was handing a child up to the stage, and the next he was stretched out on the ground.

Hesh never knew how long he was out—half an hour? Forty-five minutes? But when he woke, the night was black, lit only by a bonfire in front of the stage, and the patriots were gone. They'd spent their rage on the folding chairs, on the pamphlets and tables and sound equipment. One of them had cut the lights and then they'd rampaged through the field, smashing chairs, burning books and pamphlets, putting stones through the windows of the buses and cars in the lot. They were like Indians in a movie, Christina said later. Savages. Whooping, screaming like animals. They destroyed everything they could get their hands on, and then, as if by a prearranged signal, they vanished. A few of the women had been hurt in the scuffle, a dozen others were hysterical (Christina included, who couldn't locate either Truman or Hesh and feared the worst), and several of the men had broken bones and gashes that required stitches, but no one had been lynched, no one died.

Just after Hesh regained his senses, six pairs of headlights appeared on the dirt road above them, which the patriots had obligingly cleared by overturning the camp truck in the weeds and opening a path through the barrier at Van Wart Road. Frozen, expecting some new treachery, the concertgoers huddled on the stage and watched the cold beams approach. Then, suddenly, the red lights began to flash and a woman cried out, "Thank God, they're finally here!"

Walter didn't want to hear the rest. Didn't want to hear how

Lorelee Shapiro had got through to the state police, who'd known about the situation all along but took their own sweet time getting there, or how his mother was in a state of shock, or how Lola had helped organize the second concert, held a week later on the same bloodied ground, a concert at which Paul Robeson and Will Connell actually did sing and which was attended by 20,000 people and went off without a hitch—until the concertgoers tried to get out. He didn't want to hear about the second riot, about the cars and buses stoned all the way out Van Wart Road to the parkway, didn't want to hear about police collusion and the redneck veterans of the first riot sporting armbands that read WAKE UP, AMERICA: PETERSKILL DID! It was history. All he wanted to hear was that his father wasn't a traitor, a turncoat, a backstabber and a fink.

"Next week it was worse, Walter," Lola was saying, caught up in her own story now, a freshly lighted cigarette in the ashtray before her, but Walter was no longer listening. He remembered that scene in the kitchen of the bungalow as he might have remembered a distant nightmare, remembered clinging to his father's legs while his mother raged, remembered the smell of him, the sweat like a tomcat's musk, the sweet corrupt odor of alcohol. No! his mother shrieked. No! No! No!

"But we had to do it, Walter—we couldn't let them get away with it. We had to show them that this was America, that we could say and think and do what we wanted. Twenty thousand turned out, Walter. Twenty thousand."

Scum. His father was scum. A man who'd sold out his friends and deserted his wife and son. Why fight it? That's what Walter was thinking when he looked up from the table and saw his father standing there by the stove, framed between Lola's head and the rigid declamatory index finger of her right hand. He looked as he had in the hospital—neat, in suit and tie and with his hair cut and combed, but barefoot still. *Don't you believe it,* Truman growled.

Lola didn't see him, didn't hear him. "Animals, Walter. They were animals. Filth. Nazis."

Two sides, Walter, his father said. *Two sides to every story.*

Suddenly Walter cut her off. "Lola, okay. Thanks. I've heard enough." He pushed himself up from the table and grappled with his crutches. Outside, birds sat motionless in the trees and pale yellow moths tumbled like confetti through cathedrals of sunlight. Truman was gone. "He had to have a reason," Walter said. "My father, I mean. Nobody knows what really happened, right? You weren't even there, and my mother's dead. I mean, nobody knows for sure."

Lola took a long slow drag at her cigarette before she answered. Her eyes were distant and strange, her features masked in smoke. "Go ask Van Wart," she said.

Among the Savages

She was living in a bark hut on the outskirts of a Weckquaesgeek village, ostracized by Boer and redman alike, and she'd shaved her head with an oyster shell as a token of abnegation and penance. On that fateful day three years back when God's wrath had spared the oak tree only to strike at her home and abolish her family, Katrinchee, who should have been out in the fields with them, should have been huddled with them in the cabin when the thunderbolt struck, was instead sequestered in a shady bower with Mohonk, son of Sachoes, and a stone bottle of gin. She stroked his chest, his thighs and his groin, as he stroked her, and she sipped gin to assuage the guilt she felt over her father's death. (Oh yes: that guilt haunted her night and day. She couldn't look at a stewpot without seeing her father, and the thought of venison in any of its incarnations was so inadmissible that even the sight of a startled doe on some woodland path was enough to make her go dizzy and feel the nausea creeping up her throat.) When a Kitchawank boy came to them in the wigwam where they'd gone to seek shelter from the storm, breathless, his eyes wild, a tale of destruction rained from the heavens on his lips, the guilt rose up to suffocate her. *Moeder,* she choked, and then collapsed as if her legs had been shot out from under her. Sitting there in a daze, staring numbly at Mohonk, at Wahwahtaysee and the faces of the savage painted strangers hovering over her, she felt a new and insupportable knowledge festering in her veins: she'd killed them all. Yes. Killed them as surely as if she'd lined them up and shot them. First her father and now this: she'd lain with a heathen, and here was God's vengeance. In grief, in despair, she took a honed shell to her scalp and buried herself in Mohonk.

Her son Squagganeek* was born a year later. His eyes were green, like Agatha's, and this peculiarity caused a good deal of consternation among the Kitchawanks. They were the eyes of greed, argued one faction, the eyes of a devil, a sorcerer, a white man, and the infant should be cast out to wander the waste places of the earth. But another faction, Wahwahtaysee among them, argued that he was the son of the son of a chief and that he had his place in the tribe. As things turned out, none of it really mattered. It was Mohonk, and Mohonk alone, who would decide the fate of his son.

But Mohonk had turned strange. Ever since she'd cut her hair, Katrinchee had noticed the change in him. He was testy. He was morose. He launched interminable thick-tongued diatribes against the least offensive objects—stones, dirt clods, fallen leaves. He drank gin and it made him crazy. Snow owl, he called her and pointed derisively to her cropped head. Her hair had been the color of the hawk's underbelly, copper red, sacred and unattainable. Now, with her smooth white skull that looked like the bulb of an onion and the eyes that stared out of her face in their huge riveting grief, she looked like the snow owl. One night, three days drunk on the Hollands he'd filched from Jan Pieterse, he rose shakily to his feet and stood over her as she suckled the infant. "Snow owl," he said, the light of the fire elongating his cheekbones and masking his eyes in shadow, "go catch a mouse." Then he pulled the raccoon coat tight around him and lurched off into the night on spindle legs. She never saw him again.

To the Weckquaesgeeks, she was a holy fool, one of the mad wandering ones to whom visions are granted. (And she did have her visions. Shivering in the hut, Squagganeek at her breast, she saw Harmanus, his limbs twisted from the fall, dancing a macabre shuffle; she saw Agatha with her broom raised in anger; she saw Jeremias and the terrible annealed scar that terminated his leg.) The day after Mohonk walked out on her she'd gathered up her things, strapped Squagganeek to her back and followed the river north; two days later she stumbled across the Weckquaesgeek camp on a miserable wind-

* Leaf-eye.

swept beach below Suycker Broodt mountain. With her shorn head, tattered dress and the trembling lips that never ceased their muttering, she came on them like an apparition, a pale ghost, and they gathered around to stare at her and the freak of an infant she held in her arms. Exhausted, she fell back against a tree and slumped to the ground; within minutes, she was asleep.

In the morning she woke to find that someone had thrown a bearskin over her legs and set a bowl of corn mush on the stump beside her. The Weckquaesgeeks—an unlucky tribe, losers of fingers, toes and eyes, disease-ridden and unkempt—watched her at a respectful distance. Slowly, with trembling hands and wild eyes, she brought the bowl to her lips and ate. Then, after making gestures of thanksgiving and suckling Squagganeek at her breast, she got up and built herself a crude hut against the base of a tree. From then on, each morning, she found a bowl of squash or sturgeon or acorn meal on her doorstep, or perhaps a pigeon or rabbit (but no venison—no, never venison). The seasons changed. Squagganeek grew. She squatted in the hut and chewed hides till they were soft, wore moccasins and a leather apron like a squaw and shaved her head to the quick whenever she happened to reach up and feel the bristle sprouting there. Cramped, dirty, a breeding ground for ticks, chiggers, gnats and no-see-ums, the hut was no better than an animal's den. But what could she expect? This was her due.

At one point, for her son's sake, she thought of returning to Van Wartwyck, of throwing herself on the mercy of the patroon and begging for shelter and employment, but she knew there would be no mercy for her. She was a miscegenator, a renegade, a whore: there were penalties for what she'd done. The Dutch laws, now superseded by as yet undefined English ones, called for a fine of twenty-five guilders for cohabiting with a squaw, escalating to fifty if she conceived and to a hundred if she gave birth; the concept of a white woman fornicating with a greasy musk-smeared savage was so utterly unthinkable that the good burghers and Boers hadn't bothered with a law—bodily mutilation and banishment would suffice in a pinch.

And so it was—life like a succession of wounds, no joy but for the child, the seasons giving way in null repetition—until one day in early summer a waking vision took on flesh and came to redeem her.

She was crouched in the hut, chewing hides, Squagganeek's cries drifting faintly to her as the Weckquaesgeek boys tormented him for his green eyes and mad white mother, when a face appeared in the doorway. It was a face she'd seen a thousand times in her sleep or in the embers of the fire, but now it was changed somehow, no longer the face of a boy—no, it was fuller, harder, better defined. She squeezed her eyes shut and murmured an incantation. Nothing happened. The face hung there in that doorway so low even a dog would have to stoop to enter, hung there as if disembodied, the features that were so familiar and yet so alien to her creased with shock and bewilderment. She was about to cry out, shriek his name—anything to break the spell—but Jeremias spoke first. He uttered a single word, his voice quavering with shock and disbelief: "Katrinchee?"

They'd taken him to their bosom, Staats and Meintje, fed and clothed him and treated him as one of their own. He worked in the fields alongside Staats and his eldest boy Douw, wielding scythe and mathook like a full-grown man, though he was just sixteen and laboring under his handicap. When they sat down to table, Meintje always managed to find him a choice cut of meat or a lump of sugar for his hot chocolate, and she was always urging more on him, as if to make up for his time of affliction and want when there was no hand to feed him. They gave him affection and they gave him hope, and Jeremias never forgot it. But when he thought of Van Wart, growing fat off the labor of others, when he thought of the bow-backed *schout* and that lard-ass of an agent who'd driven him from the farm where his father had died, he felt the resentment seethe in him like pus in a wound.

He'd lived at peace with himself for two and a half years, thinking neither of past nor future, whittling a new strut for his leg every few months as he grew up and away from the old one, picking at the acne that sprouted like bread mold on his face and neck, hunting the woods and fishing the river. But then one afternoon he walked down to Jan Pieterse's—for some fish hooks, he told himself, but in truth because he was feeling restless, stifled, dissatisfied in a new and indefinable way, and he just wanted to get away from the farm for a bit—and all that suddenly changed. He was in the back of the store, savoring the smells, the quiet, the rich immovable shadows that were like the background of a painting he'd seen once in the nave of a church in Schobbejacken, lingering amongst the furs that whispered of secret wild places, the hogsheads of ale and salt herring, the sacks of spices, the bolts of cloth and kegs of spirits. From outside, beyond the open door, the voices of Jan Pieterse and Farmer Ten Haer drifted lazily across the sunstruck afternoon. Jeremias leaned back against a shelf of furs, the fish hooks gone warm in his hand, and closed his eyes.

When he opened them, a girl was standing there, her back against the wall, looking as if she'd just discovered a toad in the butter dish. "Oh," she said, glancing away, catching his eye and then glancing away again, "I didn't know anyone was back here." She was holding a length of ribbon in her hand, and she was dressed in homespun skirts, linen cap and a white blouse that pinched her arms just above the elbow.

"I'm back here, I guess," Jeremias said. He felt stupid; there were cobwebs in his brain. "Um, I mean, I was just buying some hooks." He opened his palm and held out his hand to show her.

"Ja," she said, "and I was buying ribbon." She dangled a length of black armozine and smiled.

He smiled back and said he'd never seen her here before.

She shrugged as if to say so much the worse for you, and then found it necessary to balance on one foot and twist a finger in her hair while she told him she lived in Croton, near the Van Wart house. As an afterthought, she added, "Sometime *vader* brings me up this way when he has business."

Then they both fell silent and Jeremias became aware of a new voice outside the door—a voice he'd heard before, cadences summoned from some deep recess of memory. He heard Farmer Ten Haer blustering about Wolf Nysen, heard Jan Pieterse's scoffing retort, and then that other voice, and it made him go cold.

"And you?" she said finally.

Jan Pieterse's dog changed his position among the furs with a sybaritic grunt. Jeremias found himself staring into a pair of eyes that were like the blueware of the rich, a sheen of glaze and a color as deep as the Scheldt. "Me?" he said. "I live up on the van der Meulen farm, but I'm a Van Brunt. Jeremias Van Brunt. I'll be seventeen this summer."

"I'm Neeltje Cats," she said. "I just turned fifteen." And then, with pride: "My father's the *schout*."

Yes. Of course. The *schout*. Jeremias' eyes went hard and he gritted his teeth.

"What—?" she began, and then faltered. She was staring at the loose cuff of his pantaloons. "What happened to you?"

He looked down at his wooden leg as if he were seeing it for the first time. Suddenly the atmosphere had changed. He couldn't see the pelts for the claws that dully glinted in the light filtering through the open door. "I had an accident," he said. "When I was fourteen."

She nodded as if to say yes, it doesn't matter, the world's a harsh place—or so her parents had told her. "My father says Pieter Stuyvesant was a great man."

"He was," Jeremias said. "He is." And then all at once he felt something go loose in him, some cord that had been wound too tight, and suddenly he was playing the fool, skating across the floor on his wooden strut, hair in his eyes and his face frozen in a scowl, leveling an imaginary sword at the Englishers like the great man himself.

Neeltje laughed. Pure, untroubled, as marvelous a thing as the music of the spheres, that laugh was what hooked him. No, he didn't prick his finger on one of the barbs or fall face forward into the barrel of soused pig's feet, but he was hooked all the same. That laugh was a revelation. He looked at her, laughing himself now, studied her as she stood there grinning with a piece of ribbon in her hand, and saw his future.

The first thing he did when he got back to the farm was ask Staats about her. His stepfather was around the side of the house, standing on a chair and painting the wall with a whitewash made of pulverized oyster shells. "Cats?" he said, pausing to shove back his wide-brimmed hat and rub a palm over his bare skull. "I knew a Cats once back in Volendam. Nasty beggar. Full of piss and vinegar."

Jeremias stood in the gathering dusk and listened politely as his stepfather gave a detailed account of the petty crimes and scandals fomented by this nefarious Cats—Staats couldn't recall the *duyvil*'s first name—some twenty years earlier in the town of Volendam, halfway around the world. When Staats paused for breath, Jeremias gently steered him back to the here and now. "But what about the *schout*—Joost Cats?"

Staats paused again. "Joost?" he said, groping for the connection. "Ja, Ja, Joost. He doesn't have a daughter, does he?"

Meintje was no more helpful. A militant look came into her eyes at the mention of the *schout* and she advised Jeremias to let bygones be bygones. "If I was you," she said, "I woudn't go near him or his daughter either."

A month dragged by. Jeremias cleared land, burned stumps, built walls of fieldstone, milked and fed the cows, weeded the barley field and shoveled shit. He ate fish, fowl and game, ate corn cakes, porridge and *bruinbrod,* drank cider and 'Sopus ale. He slept on a cornhusk mattress with Douw van der Meulen, pinched tobacco and tried it behind the barn, swam naked in Van Wart Creek. And there were long hot afternoons when all he did was wander over to the old farm and stare at the ashes. Through it all though, he never shook the image of Neeltje Cats.

Then came the day when a pock-marked Kitchawank in a pair of expansive pantaloons knocked at the door. It was mid-June, the light like a fine wash, and Jeremias had just sat down with the family to the evening meal. Meintje opened the door partway, as she might have opened it on a peddler back in Volendam. "Yes?" she said.

But Staats was already on his feet, Jeremias, Douw and the three younger children staring up at him in surprise. "Why, it's old Jan," he said, and Meintje pulled back the door.

The Kitchawank was shirtless, his torso a topography of scars, abrasions and infected insect bites, his moccasins torn and mud-spattered. He was known as old Jan in the neighborhood and he made his living doing odd jobs and drifting from village to village, carrying messages for a doit or a stein of beer. He'd survived the smallpox that had ravaged his tribe some thirty years earlier, only to find that the fever had coddled his brain. Staats knew him from Jan Pieterse's. Meintje had never laid eyes on him before.

"What is it, Jan?" Staats said. "Have you got a message for us?"

The Indian stood there in the doorway, impassive, his face as blasted and worn as bedrock. "Ja, I have a message," he said in his halting, rudimentary Dutch. "For him," and he pointed to Jeremias.

"Me?" Jeremias rose from the table in confusion. Who would send him a message? He didn't know a soul in the great wide world but for the boys of the neighborhood and the people gathered around the table.

Old Jan nodded. Then he turned to point at a gap in the trees beyond the barn, and Jeremias, standing at the door now with Staats and Meintje, with Douw and Barent, Klaes and little Jannetje, saw a gaunt figure wrapped in a raccoon coat emerge from the shadows. "Your sister," old Jan began, turning back to him, and all at once Jeremias could feel the blood beating in his ears. Katrinchee. He hadn't given her a thought in ages. For all he knew she might have been dead, so completely had she vanished from the community. "Your sister," the Indian repeated, but his voice trailed off. He looked at Jeremias and his eyes were asleep.

"Yes? What about her?" Staats said.

From across the field came the sound of Mohonk's voice, urgent and nagging, and old Jan's head jerked up as if he'd been caught napping. "She thinks," he murmured, "you are burned up and dead. "She's—" and his voice gave out.

"Jan, Jan—snap out of it," Staats growled, taking the Indian by the arm, but it was the sound of Mohonk's voice that brought him around again. Mohonk cupped his hands to his mouth and shouted a second time, and old Jan's eyes cleared momentarily. He swept their faces with a distant gaze and said, "A glass of beer."

"Yes, yes, beer," Staats said. "But first the message."

He looked at them as if he'd just come into the world. "Your sister," he repeated for the third time, "she's a Weckquaesgeek whore."

Staats van der Meulen was a compassionate man. There was no room for her in the house, but he fixed up a pallet in the barrack of the barn and Katrinchee crept into the straw with her child like some shorn and abandoned madonna. Oxen snorted, cows lowed, swallows flitted among the shadows. Meintje bit her lip and sent a basket of day-old bread and a bit of milk cheese out to her. "This is only temporary," she warned Staats, leveling her wooden spoon at him. "Tomorrow—and here she might have been talking of a matricide or leper—"she goes."

Tomorrow became the next day and then the next. "We can't just turn her out to go back to the savages," Staats argued, but Meintje was adamant. The girl was fallen, she was subversive and unrepentant, a miscegenator, and they couldn't have her around the children. "I give you to the end of the week," she warned.

For his part, Jeremias knew nothing of the conflict broiling around him. He was spending most of his time out in the barn with Katrinchee and Squagganeek, relearning the past, and he was too elated to notice much of anything. A week before he'd been fatherless, motherless, bereft of siblings, his nearest blood relation an uncle in Schobbejacken he hardly knew. And now, not only had his sister been restored to him, but wonder of wonders, he'd become an uncle himself. He sat for hours with Squagganeek, playing at cards or Trock, staring into the child's eyes and seeing his father, his mother, seeing little Wouter. There was never any doubt in his mind: of course Staats and Meintje would take them in. Of course they would.

But when the week was up, Meintje took matters into her own hands. There were no tears, no fits, no raised voices or recriminations. When Staats and the children awoke at first light to the bleating of unmilked goats and the petulant squabbling of unfed chickens, they found the hearth cold, and Meintje, still in her nightgown, seated in her rocker on the far side of the room. What's more, her hands were clasped together, as if in prayer, and she was facing the wall. "Meintje—what is it?" Staats cried, rushing to her. "Are you all right? Is it the grippe?" She said nothing. He took hold of her hands. They were lifeless, they were dead. She was staring at the wall.

Within minutes, the house was in an uproar. Meintje, who'd never before sat down in her life except to shuck peas or darn stockings and whose hands had never been idle, had been stricken by some terrible and enervating affliction—she'd become one of the living dead, unhearing, unseeing, unmoving. "*Moeder!*" cried little Jannetje, flinging herself at her mother's feet, while the baby, little Klaes, howled as if all the world's dole had suddenly been revealed to him. Meintje never even turned her head. Jeremias hovered uneasily in the background, exchanging looks with Douw. Then he went out to see to his sister.

Meintje sat there for six days. No one saw her move, not even to get up and relieve herself. Sometimes her eyes were closed; sometimes they were fixed on the wall in an unblinking stare. Talking to her—asking if she wanted to eat, sleep, see a doctor, send back to Volendam for her aged mother—was like talking to a stone. Meanwhile, the family managed as best it could. Douw and Barent tried their hands at cooking, Staats did the wash, and once, in desperation, Jeremias attempted a batch of corn cakes that looked and tasted like the residue of a chimney fire. Before long, Meintje's kitchen—the envy of the neighborhood, refulgent as an ice pond and scoured right on down to the cracks of the floorboards—was a festering quagmire of food scraps, barnyard muck and shattered crockery. Finally, on the eve of the seventh day, she spoke.

The family was startled. They'd got so used to her silence and immobility they'd forgotten she was there at all. This was not the wife and mother they'd known a week ago, this was a piece of furniture, a footstool, a coatrack. Odds and ends had begun to accumulate around her like detritus: socks, vegetable peels, a half-chewed carrot. Jannetje's doll lay nose down in her lap, Klaes' cap was flung over the back of the chair and the Trock board had somehow become wedged between her shoulder and the chair arm. Now, as she spoke, the entire family started up in fright, as if the floorboards had shouted "You're trampling me!" or the kettle had shrieked as the kindling caught fire beneath it. For all that, her message was pretty straightforward. Staats slapped his forehead, Jeremias went cold. Meintje spoke to the wall, four words only, each one bitten off as if it cost a thousand guilders: "Is she gone yet?"

For Jeremias, the choice was clear. He wheeled around, thumped through the door, stalked across the yard and into the barn. Five minutes later he emerged with Squagganeek on his back and the shorn and wild-eyed Katrinchee at his side. He took nothing with him: no clothes, no tools, no food. He didn't look back.

It took Staats nearly a week to find him. He traveled as far south as the Sint Sink village, went north to Cold Spring and east to Crom's Pond. He knocked at farmhouse doors, poked his head into shanties, wigwams and taverns, and got the same answer everywhere he went: no one had seen a one-legged boy, nor a shorn *meisje* or half-breed toddler either—it was almost as if they'd vanished from the face of the earth. But Staats persisted. He had to find them, had to tell Jeremias how he felt, had to explain and absolve himself. It was Meintje—he couldn't do anything with her. If it was up to him he would have found room under his roof for Katrinchee and her bastard too. He would have. Jeremias knew that. It was just that Meintje was a strong-willed woman, that's all, a woman who stuck to her principles. . . .

Staats wasn't a man for words, but he rehearsed his speech like a practiced orator as he plodded through the woods or walked his horse along the glittering mud banks of the river. If it weren't for Douw, though, he might never have had the chance to deliver it. Jeremias wasn't in Croton or Crom's Pond or Beverwyck or Poughkeepsie either. Douw could have told him that. After all, they'd slept in the same bed for two and a half years, they'd roamed the hills together, sat over hornbooks in the Crane parlor, filched pumpkins and crept up side by side on nesting quail and dozing frogs—Douw knew him as well as he knew himself. When finally his father thought to ask, and Douw let him know where Jeremias would almost certainly have gone, Staats stared at him dumbfounded for a moment, then cursed himself. Of course: the old farm.

That evening Staats ate a hurried supper of bread and porridge, and then made his way on foot out to the Van Brunt place. It was dusk when he got there, fireflies cutting holes in the shadows, the boles of the trees slipping in and out of rank, cicadas chattering, mosquitoes on the wing. At first he saw nothing—or rather, he saw leaves and trees, the ruins of the cabin, the white oak in its full vigor—but then, as he edged closer, he saw that Jeremias' rotting lean-to, the lean-to of his exile and abandonment, was freshly covered with sheets of elm bark. And there was a sound he picked up now too, a scraping or rasping that could have come from no animal he knew.

He found Jeremias crouched over the carcass of a rabbit, skinning it with a sharpened stone. Katrinchee and Squagganeek, who'd been gathering kindling, looked up with startled faces. "Jeremias," Staats said, and when the boy shot him a glance over his shoulder, his eyes were feral and cold.

Staats repeated the name twice more, then delivered his halting speech. He'd brought along an axe and a knife, and he held them out now to Jeremias, along with the basket of food—bread, smoked shad and cabbage—Meintje had packed for him. Jeremias said nothing. "Won't you come home?" Staats asked him, and it was almost a whisper.

"This is my home," Jeremias said.

It was crazy. Hopeless. Irresponsible. June already, and the crops in the ground, and Jeremias wanted to make a go of it. A cripple with a half-mad sister and her little shit-pants bastard, and he wanted to rebuild the cabin, reclaim the fields, put in a tardy crop and harvest for winter. Meintje clucked her tongue over it, Douw stared down into his cup of cider. But the following morning, Staats, Douw and ten-year-old Barent were there with their tools and a hamper of food that could have provisioned the English fleet. Jeremias embraced them solemnly, one by one. Then they started plowing.

Over the weeks, the entire community pitched in. Reinier Oothouse lent a hand with the carpentry, Hackaliah Crane stopped by with his team, Oom Egthuysen pledged a milk cow that properly belonged to the patroon and Meintje took up a collection among the *huis vrouwen* for the odd cup and saucer, bedding and cookware. Even Jan Pieterse got into the act, donating two barrels of 'Sopus ale, a sack of seed onions and a new plowshare and moldboard. It wasn't much, but it was enough to get them on their feet. By early July, Jeremias had wheat and corn in the ground and a patch of pumpkin, calabash and turnip sprouting outside the door, and Katrinchee, now nearly nineteen, was presiding over her own kitchen for the first time in her young life. The cabin had gone up in two weeks, right over the charred remnants of the old one, and though it was crude, musty, close and dank, it would keep them alive through the winter. Things were looking up.

How the patroon got wind of it was a mystery to Staats (old Van Wart was afflicted in knuckle and toe by a virulent eruption of the gout, and hadn't been up from Croton in six months or more), but get wind of it he did. The patroon was incensed. He was being taken advantage of while he lay on his sickbed. There were squatters at Nysen's Roost, freeloaders, vagrants who'd moved in like skulking savages and laid claim to his land without bothering to acknowledge his sovereignty or make arrangements to pay him rent. It was intolerable. An outrage to the laws of man and God, and a thumbing of the nose at the very lineaments of a just society. He sent the *schout* to investigate.

Joost didn't relish the job. And he didn't want to bring Neeltje along either. He really didn't. It wasn't that he expected trouble—not at this stage, at any rate—but that he was afraid she might see something she shouldn't. Who knew who these people were? They could be drunk and depraved, living in sin, eating offal and sucking oyster shells; they could be half-breeds or Yankees or runaway slaves. All he knew was that a family—man, woman and child—had taken up residence on the Nysen place and that it was his job either to settle them in properly as tenants of the patroon or evict them. No, he definitely didn't want to bring his daughter along. But then Neeltje had other ideas. "*Vader,*" she pleaded, giving him a look that would have stripped the feathers from an angel's wing, "won't you take me along with you? Please?" It would be so easy, she argued. He could leave her at Jan Pieterse's while he saw to his business and then come for her afterward. *Moeder* had a whole list of things she needed, and why shouldn't he save himself some time and let her get them? She could pick up little presents for the *younkers* too. "Oh, please, please?" she begged, and Ans and Trijintje, nine and ten respectively, looked on with hopeful faces. "There's so much we need."

So he'd saddled the one-eyed nag and gone up to the patroon's stable for the mare, and they set out for the upper manor house for the first time since spring and the Crane/Oothouse dispute. Joost was miserable. The day was hot, the deerflies were a plague and a menace, the baldric tugged at his shoulder and the silver plume hung in his eyes, and with each lurching step the nag took he swore he'd rather be out on the bay dipping for crabs, but he went on anyway, ever responsive to the call of duty. Neeltje, on the other hand, didn't mind the heat a bit. Or the deerflies either. She was going to Jan Pieterse's, and her sisters weren't. That was enough for her.

They stopped in at the upper manor house for a bite to eat, and the place was as cool as a cellar with its great three-foot-thick walls. Vrouw van Bilevelt, who, along with Cubit the slave and his wife, looked after the place, served them a cold cream soup and crabcakes. They paid their respects to Gerrit Jacobzoon de Vries and his family, who'd managed the upper farm and overseen the mill since the death of the patroon's brother, and then made their way down to the Blue Rock so that Neeltje could do her shopping while Joost saw to the interlopers at Nysen's Roost. But when they got there, they found the trading post deserted and the door barred. Neeltje, biting her lip in frustration, tried the latch sixteen times and knocked at the door till Joost thought her knuckles would crack open. Then she discovered Jan Pieterse's note. In the dirt. *Dipping crabs,* she read aloud. *Back at six.* Joost shook his head. It was barely two-thirty. There was nothing to do but take Neeltje along with him.

On the way up the hill from Acquasinnick Creek, through the woods that were haunted by the phantoms of murdered Kitchawanks and the unhappy daughters of Wolf Nysen, he told her that he didn't expect any trouble, but that for her own safety she should come no nearer than the edge of the clearing and under no circumstances should she attempt to interfere or to speak with these people. Was that clear? Neeltje looked glumly at the splintered rock and rotting trunks that lay around her, at the shadows that were like pools in the belly of a cave, and nodded her head. She had no interest in this place or these people, no interest in her father's affairs, for that matter. All she cared about was Jan Pieterse's, and Jan Pieterse's, of all days of the year, had to be closed today. She was so frustrated she felt like shrieking till her lungs turned inside out. And she would have done it too if her father weren't there—and if the place weren't quite so hushed and gloomy.

Before long they'd reached the top of the rise and emerged on a clearing dominated by a single high-crowned tree. On the left was a tumbledown wall and to the right a crude cabin of notched green logs. There was no barn, no pond, no orchard and no animals but for a sickly cow tethered beneath the tree. The place seemed deserted. "Stay here," her father said, and he straightened up in his saddle and jogged forward into the dooryard. "Hello!" he called. "Anybody home?"

Not a sound.

Her father called out again, and the cow gave him a baleful look before dropping its head to crop a tuft of grass at the perimeter of its tether. It was then that a woman appeared from around the corner of the house, a bucket in her hand. The first thing Neeltje noticed was her feet. They were shoeless and filthy, gleaming with fresh muck as if she'd just waded out of a bog or something. And her dress—it was an obvious hand-me-down, patched, faded and stained, and so worn the flesh showed through. But that wasn't the worst of it. As the woman drew closer to her father, Neeltje saw with a jolt that what she'd taken to be a cap was no cap at all—this wasn't linen, but flesh. The woman was bald! Scalped, plucked, denuded, her head as smooth and pale and barren as Dominie Van Schaik's. Neeltje felt something tighten in her stomach. How could a woman do that to herself? she wondered. It was so . . . so ugly. Was it lice, was that it? Was she a harlot cast out of Connecticut? A Roman nun? Had the Indians got hold of her and . . . and *violated* her?

"I'm the sheriff here," she heard her father say, "Joost Cats. I've been sent by the lawful owner and proprietor of these lands to inquire as to your presence here."

The woman looked bewildered, lost, as if it were she who'd arrived at this place for the first time in her life and not Neeltje. Did she speak Dutch even?

"You have no right here," Joost said. "Who are you and where have you come from?"

"Katrinchee," the woman said finally, setting down the bucket. "I'm Katrinchee."

But then two more figures appeared around the corner of the house—a child, pale eyes in a dark face—and a man swaying awkwardly over a muddy wooden peg. It took her a moment—everything so different, the place so strange—before she recognized him. *Jeremias.* The name had been on her lips before. In the spring. For a month or so after the last trip it had been with her at the oddest moments—in the early hours of the morning, at prayers, as she sat at the loom or butterchurn. *Jeremias.* But what was he doing here?

She was no more surprised than her father. The *schout* jerked his head back as if he'd been snatched by the collar, springing up out of his customary slouch like a jack-in-the-box. "Van Brunt?" he gasped, his voice breaking with incredulity. "Jeremias Van Brunt?"

Jeremias crossed the yard to where the *schout* perched atop the one-eyed nag. He stopped directly in front of him, no more than a yard away, measuring him with a steady gaze. "That's right," he said. "I've come back home."

"But you can't. . . . These are private lands."

"Private lands, my ass," Jeremias said, and he bent to pluck a stick of firewood from the ground. The woman drew back and pressed the child to her.

Joost snatched angrily at the reins and the nag shivered and showed its teeth in protest. The boy was impossible. A renegade. A loser. He had no respect for authority, no knowledge of the world and nothing to sustain him but his self-righteous smirk. Joost remembered the defiant little face in the van der Meulens' doorway, the cocky thrust of the shoulders at Jan Pieterse's, his daughter's laughter and the gift of sugar candy that was like a violation of his fatherhood. He was beside himself. "You owe the patroon," he snarled.

"Screw the patroon," Jeremias said, and it was more than Joost could bear. Before he could think, he was on him, the sword of office jerked from its scabbard like a sudden slashing beam of light, the woman clutching the child and Jeremias falling back before the stagger of the horse. "No!" Neeltje screamed, and Jeremias, holding up the stick to defend himself, glanced at her—she saw him, he glanced at her—at the moment the sword fell. The woman screamed too. Then there was silence.

Chiefly Nuptial

So Walter sought out the twelfth heir to Van Wart Manor, as the smoke-wreathed figure of his adoptive mother had challenged him to, and then, six weeks later, he married Jessica beneath the ancient twisted white oak that loomed over Tom Crane's cabin like a great cupped hand.

Actually, he didn't so much seek out Depeyster Van Wart as blunder across him, as if their meeting had somehow been preordained. He got up from the table that morning in the kitchen that still reeked of potato pancakes, groped for his crutches and told Lola that that was exactly what he intended to do: ask Depeyster Van Wart. He borrowed her beat-up Volvo—was he sure? Shouldn't he rest, just out of the hospital and all?—and backed down the narrow gravel drive, past the trees lit with birds, past the chin-high cornstalks, staked tomatoes and random swelling pumpkins of Hesh's garden, and out onto the molten blacktop of Baron de Hirsch Road.

If he'd been asleep all these years, unconscious of the impact of history and the myths that shaped him, he still wasn't fully awake. Thus, he had never connected this Depeyster Van Wart with the eponym of the infernal tool-and-die company that had employed him at minimum wage for the past two months, never connected this figure of dim legend with the dinning caliginous hole where he'd learned to dread the keen of the lathe as he might have dreaded the screech of some carrion bird come each day to tear out his liver anew. No: Depeyster Manufacturing was just a name, that was all. Like Kitchawank Colony, Otis Elevator, Fleischmann's Yeast. Like Peterskill or Poughkeepsie. It meant nothing to him.

He shifted into first and lurched off down the road, the new foot dead on the gas pedal, and he'd actually reached the first intersection before he realized he had no idea where he was going. Van Wart. Where would he find Van Wart? There were probably thirty Van Warts in Peterskill alone. Leaning on the brake and casting around him for inspiration, he suddenly focused on Skip's Texaco, with its twin pumps and phone booth, sitting directly across the road from him. He pulled in, lifted himself from the car, and consulted the white pages.

VAN WART, he read, DEPEYSTER R. 16 VAN WART RD., VAN WARTVILLE.

He'd lost a foot, been haunted by ghosts of the past, listened in silence to the story of his father's perfidy and desertion: he was numb. Van Wartville. It meant nothing to him. Just an address.

He took the Mohican Parkway to the upper end of Van Wart Road, uncertain which way the numbers ran, and discovered to his irritation that here they were in the five-thousand range. The first mailbox he came across told him that much. Rusted, battered, the victim of innumerable scrapes and vehicular miscues, it read, in a script that might have been adapted from the Aztec: FAGNOLI, 5120. Swinging southwest, toward Peterskill, Walter looked neither right nor left, the roadside scenery so familiar he hadn't given it a second glance since he was an eighth-grader on his way to music lessons. He was in no hurry—it had taken him all these years to begin pursuing the specter of his father, so what was the rush?—and yet before he knew it he was speeding, the alien foot dead on the accelerator, hydrants and mailboxes flashing by like pages in a leafing book. He shot past banks of elm, oak and sycamore, past junked cars, startled pedestrians and scratching dogs. He took the warning light at Cats' Corners at sixty, downshifted for the *S* curve beyond it and came out of the chute doing seventy-five. It wasn't until he blew past Tom Crane's place, with its hubcap on the tree and the fateful pasture below, that he began to locate the brake.

The houses were clustered more thickly now, falling back from both sides of the road on lawns that were like coves and inlets of green; there was a church, a cemetery, another blinking yellow light. He saw a station wagon backing out of a driveway on his right, and up ahead on the opposite side, like the residue of a nightmare, the cryptic marker that had set the whole thing in motion. Jeremy Mohonk, he muttered to himself. Cadwallader Crane. For one inspired instant he envisioned himself swerving wide, out across the opposite lane and onto the shoulder, bearing down on that insidious road sign in a cloud of dust and obliterating it with a ton and a half of vengeful Swedish steel. But then he was dodging the station wagon—downshifting, stabbing at the brake pedal—and the sign, still canted heavenward, still mocking, was behind him. A moment later, just before he reached the Peterskill town line, he found what he was looking for, Number 18, the numerals cut into the stone pillar outside the gates to the old manor house on the hill. Van Wart Manor. Van Wartville. Van Wart Road. He began to understand.

The woman who answered the door was middle-aged, black, in a cotton shift and apron, and she looked so familiar he thought he'd begun to hallucinate again. "Ye—ess?" she said, drawing it out to two rich clarion syllables, almost yodeling it. "Can I help you?"

Walter was standing on a porch the size of the quarterdeck of one of the ghost ships anchored off Dunderberg. The house to which it was attached rose over him, fell away beneath him, stretched out on both sides of him like some great living presence, some diluvian monster arisen from the deep to devour him. He saw naked rock, black with age and dug from the earth in some distant epoch; he saw beams of oak that had stood as trees in centuries past; he saw scalloped shingles, wooden shutters, gables, chimneys, a slate roof the color of the morning sky in winter. How many times had he passed by on the road and glanced up at the place without a glimmer of recognition? Now he was here, on the porch, at the door, and he felt as he had on the morning of the potato pancakes. "Uh, yeah," he said. "I'd like to speak to Mr. Van Wart?"

He'd rehearsed the scene all the way over in the car. There he would be, son of the father, hunched forward on his crutches. Van Wart would open the door, Van Wart himself. The monster, the bogey, the unenlightened Nazi Bircher fiend who'd fomented the riots that shamed his father and broke his mother's heart. Van Wart. The man who could once and for all damn or vindicate the name of Truman Van Brunt. *Hi,* Walter would say, *I'm Truman Van Brunt's son*. Or no. *Hello, my name's Walter Van Brunt. I think you knew my father?* But now he was on the steps of a mansion, a great big gingerbread thing that might have been drawn from the pages of Hawthorne or Poe, talking with a maid who looked like . . . like . . . like Herbert Pompey, and he'd begun to feel dislocated and unsure of himself.

"I'm sorry," she said, looking hard at his crutches, the hair gone long down his neck and creeping over his ears, the twenty-seven black specks above his upper lip that might have been a mustache and then again might not have been, "he's not in right now." The maid had stopped yodeling, and her face was set with suspicion. "What you want with him?"

"Nothing," Walter mumbled, and he was about to mumble further and in an even lower and less audible tone that he'd be back later, already thinking about the Peterskill library and the handprinted card catalogue he'd used for high school reports on the state of Alaska, John Steinbeck and the B.&O. Railroad, wondering if there would be any reference to Mohonk or Crane, when a voice called out from deep inside the house: "Lula? Lula, who is it?"

Through the open door Walter could see heavy dark pieces of furniture, a worn strip of Oriental carpet and a gloomy portrait on the wall. "Nobody," the maid called over her shoulder, and then she turned back to Walter. He could have taken this as his dismissal, he could have swung around on his crutches and thumped down the stairs, across the drive and into his car, but he didn't. Instead he just stood there, propped up under the armpits, and waited until the footsteps stopped at the door and he was looking up into the tanned inquisitive face of a woman who looked so familiar she might have come to him in a dream.

The woman seemed to be about Lola's age—or no, younger. Forty or so. She was wearing corduroy pants and moccasins, and some sort of Indian headband encrusted with plastic beads. She gave him a puzzled look, shot a glance at the maid and then turned back to him. "May I help you?" she said.

He was hallucinating, no doubt about it. If the maid had Pompey's bridgeless nose and bulging eyes, then this woman, with her icy violet stare, her high cheekbones and strong jaw, reminded him uncannily of someone too. But who? He had a sense of déjà vu, felt the flesh tearing as he went down on the hard cold pavement, heard the derisive laughter of the bums ranged along the deck of the U.S.S. *Anima*. He was almost there—he'd almost got it, that face—when her voice came back at him again, softened now, alarmed even. "Are you all right?"

"I'm Truman Van Brunt's son," he said.

"Whose son?"

"Truman Van Brunt's. My name's Walter. I wanted to maybe talk with Mr. Van Wart . . . about my father."

She didn't flinch at the name, didn't raise a hand up to mask her face or fall dead away in a faint. But her eyes, which had begun ever so slightly to defrost, went gelid again. "I'm sorry," she said. "I can't help you."

So much for the seeking.

Next day, after spending a futile hour in the library (he found references to Mo-ho, Mohole, Moholy-Nagy, the Mohr Diagram and Mohsin-ul Mulk, but no Mohonk, while the Cranes were represented by the juridical reminiscences, circa 1800, of one I. C. Crane), he drove down to Depeyster Manufacturing to pick up his check and tell Doug, the foreman, that he'd be coming back to work in a week or so but couldn't stand at the lathe anymore on account of his foot. The factory was housed in an ancient brick building on Water Street in Peterskill, amid the derelict warehouses and the tottering ruins of the stove works, wire, hat and oilcloth factories that harkened back to Peterskill's boom days at the end of the last century. The industries had grown up here along the river's edge to take advantage of both the fresh water for cooling and waste disposal and easy access to shipping and railways. But the semi-truck had come to supersede barge and boxcar, oilcloth had given way to Formica, pot-bellied stoves to gas and electric ranges, the demand for hoopskirt wire wasn't what it was and no one wore hats anymore. To Walter, of course, the ruins along Water Street were as incomprehensible as Stonehenge or the Great Pyramid at Giza. Someone had made something there once. What it was or who made it or for what purpose couldn't have interested him less.

He parked the Volvo in the employees' lot next to Peter O'Reilly's primer-splotched '55 Chevy, exchanged a mumbled greeting with the sullen, bullet-headed brother who worked the loading dock and wore T-shirts imprinted with uplifting slogans like "Off Pigs" and "Free Huey," and then shoved his way through the big steel door marked EMPLOYEES ONLY. Unfortunately, the weight of the door threw him off balance, and he lurched into the raging din of the shop like a drunken pencil peddler, fouling his crutches and snatching wildly at the time clock to keep from pitching face forward on the concrete floor. In the next moment he came within an ace of being run down by some idiot on a forklift, and then Doug had him by the arm, leading him along the pocked and faded brick wall to his office.

Walter had been absent for almost three weeks now, and during that time he'd begun to forget just how dismal the place really was. Cavernous and dim, lit at intervals by flickering fluorescent lights that descended from the ceiling on aluminum stalks, reeking of cutting oil and degreasing fluid and vibrating with the ceaseless racket of machinery, it could have been one of the subterranean sweatshops of *Metropolis*. People ran about in filthy green smocks, dodging in and out of clouds of vapor the color of ginger ale, shouting at one another over the clamor like pale frantic drones. Walter didn't like it, didn't like it a bit. As he swung along beside Doug, nodding at his coworkers—they looked up blearily, in a pall of smoke, from their lathes—he knew all at once that he wasn't coming back. Ever. Even if they offered him a sit-down job in the inspection room, even if they made him foreman, president, chairman of the board. The job had been Hesh's idea in the first place. Something temporary, something to hold him till he decided what he wanted to do with his degree. All that had changed now.

"So," Doug said, once he'd pulled Walter into a grimy office decorated with oil-soaked rags and trays of rejected muffins and aximaxes that rose in tottering array to the ceiling, "we heard about your foot."

In here, behind the smudged glass door, the noise was muted to a dull insistent drone, the sound of a distant phalanx of dentists gearing up their drills. Walter shrugged. He was leaning heavily on his crutches, and the stump of his leg ached. "Yeah," he said.

Doug was about thirty, a Depeyster Company lifer whose salient physical feature was an upper lip as broad, hairless and mobile as a chimpanzee's. Once, when Walter had questioned his lathe settings, Doug had reminded him that he wasn't paid to think, and then, in an offhand and edifying way, had mentioned the key to his own success. "I'm different than the rest of you guys around here, you know," he'd said, nodding significantly. "And you better believe it—I got a hundred and five I.Q." Now, pausing to light a cigarette, he glanced down at Walter's foot and asked, "Does it hurt?"

Walter gave him another shrug. "Look, Doug," he said, "I don't know if I'll be able to work anymore. I just came in to pick up my check."

Doug had begun to cough. He hacked for a moment, took another drag of his cigarette, and then leaned over to spit in the wastebasket. His eyes had watered, and he looked bewildered, as if Walter had just asked him to dance or name the square root of 256. "I don't got it," he said finally. "You got to go up to the front office for that."

A moment later Walter found himself gliding along a carpeted hallway, looking for Miss Egthuysen's office, while cooling breezes wafted around him and the mellifluous strains of violin, cello and viola poured forth from hidden speakers to massage his ears. There were potted plants, framed watercolors; the walls looked as if they'd been painted yesterday and the skylights glowed with sunlight that was like a shower of gold. The contrast wasn't lost on him. No more than a hundred feet from where he'd sweated over the lathe and counted the interminable minutes until the five o'clock whistle blew, there was this. Walter felt cheated.

Miss Egthuysen was the secretary. Doug had scrawled her name and the number of her office on a soiled scrap of paper—#1, or maybe it was #7, Walter couldn't tell which—and escorted him through the door at the far end of the shop and into the inner sanctum. Then he'd swung around without a word and faded back into the gloom of the shop. Walter was cursing under his breath—cursing Doug, cursing the hours he'd wasted in the pit behind him, cursing Huysterkark and Mrs. Van Wart, cursing the meanness and perfidy of a world every bit as rotten as Sartre had made it out to be in Philosophy 451—when he found it, #1, a frosted-glass door with nothing but the single numeral painted on its face. He tried the door. It was locked. No one answered his knock.

Cursing still—cursing Miss Egthuysen and the bosses who'd hired her, cursing the eggheads in lab coats and ties who strolled out of this very hallway and into the shop once a month to make notations in loose-leaf binders—he swung around and considered the slip of paper in his hand. What he'd taken to be a one could actually have been a seven. Or a nine, for that matter. Doug's scrawl was just about undecipherable—but then, with his soaring I.Q., Doug couldn't really be expected to waste his precious mental resources on so tedious a consideration as penmanship. Walter trudged back up the hall, located #7, and tried the door.

It was open.

Manning his crutches with a clatter, he leaned against the corrugated glass and pushed his way in. He saw a desk, a chair, a filing cabinet. Plants. Framed pictures. But wait a minute: something was wrong here. This wasn't Miss Egthuysen gaping up at him in alarm, slipping an envelope into the desk and slamming the drawer with a report like the blast of a shotgun, this was the man in the tan summer suit, the one he'd glimpsed now and again probing among the eggheads at the door to the shop. "I, uh—" Walter began.

The man was glaring at him now, boring into him with a look of such ferocity that Walter suddenly began to wish he were out in the shop breathing fumes, back in the hospital, anywhere but here. "Uh, I was looking for Miss—" Walter murmured, but then stopped cold. There was a nameplate on the man's desk. Of course.

"What are you doing here?" Van Wart demanded. He was on his feet now, and he looked alarmed. He looked angry. Threatened. "You were at the house yesterday, weren't you?"

"Yes, but"—guilty, guilty, why did he always feel guilty?—"I . . . I work here."

Van Wart's face went blank. "*You* work for *me*?"

"Just since the end of May, but I didn't know. . . . I mean, I didn't realize—"

But the eponym of Depeyster Manufacturing wasn't listening. "Well, that's rich," he said, dropping into his swivel chair as if the news had somehow weakened his legs. "Out on the floor?"

"Uh-huh. I run one of the lathes?"

"That's really rich," Van Wart repeated, and suddenly he cracked a grin that was like a crevasse leaping across an ice field. "Truman Van Brunt's son." Then he glanced down at Walter's foot and the smile faded. "I was sorry to hear about your accident." There was silence. "Your name's Walter, right?"

Walter nodded.

"I read about it in the paper."

Walter nodded again.

"I knew your father."

Walter said nothing. He was waiting.

"Years ago."

"I know." Walter's voice was hushed, almost a whisper. There was another moment of silence, during which Van Wart slid back the desk drawer and began to fumble through his papers. "That's why I went out to your house," Walter confessed. "That's what I wanted to ask you about. My father."

Van Wart looked distracted. He looked old, and in that moment, vulnerable. Without lifting the envelope from the drawer, he slipped a pinch of something into his mouth. "Truman?" he said finally. "What, he hasn't turned up, has he?"

When Walter answered in the negative, Van Wart seemed relieved. He helped himself to another pinch of whatever it was he kept in that precious envelope and then stared down at his impeccable shirt cuffs and manicured hands. So this was the ogre, Walter thought, the bogeyman, the Fascist who'd masterminded the slaughter of the innocents and haunted the bedtime tales of a generation of Colony children. Somehow he didn't look the part. With his fine, clean, razor-cut hair, his strong teeth and even tan, with his air of well-being and the precise hieratic tones of his speech, he could have been the saintly and forebearing father of TV legend, he could have been a judge, a professor, a pianist or conductor.

But all that was dispelled in the next instant. Van Wart looked up and said suddenly, "Don't you believe them, Walter. Don't listen to them. Your father was all right. He was somebody who could stand up to the lot of them and their stinking vicious lies." His eyes had taken hold of Walter's now and there was nothing genial about them.

Those eyes were outraged, formidable, those eyes were capable of anything. "Your father," he said, leaning forward and making an effort to control his voice, "your father was a patriot."

Then there was the wedding.

If life had begun to peel away from Walter, layer by layer, like some great unfathomable onion, if all its mysterious manifestations—the accident, the marker, the ghosts and pancakes, the face in the doorway at Van Wart Manor, Van Wart himself—were pieces of a puzzle, the wedding was a breath of fresh air: the wedding, at least, was unequivocal. Walter, former brooding and alienated hero to whom commitment and marriage were as death, loved Jessica, and she loved him. But no, it was more than that. Or maybe less. Walter needed her—he had but one foot on the ground now—and she needed to be needed.

The ceremony was performed in a field of lush, knee-deep grass amidst the sleepy drone of Tom Crane's bees and within a stone's throw of his shack. Jessica's family had pushed for a traditional wedding, with organ music, garter tossing and a seven-tiered cake, to be held at the Episcopal church in Peterskill, but both bride and groom had rejected it outright. They were no slaves to tradition. They were originals, free spirits, flamboyant and daring, and it took them no more than five minutes to hit on Tom Crane's place as the ideal site of their nuptials.

What could be better, after all? No corrupt institution would cast its gloom over the ceremony, and nature itself would become a celebrant. It would be an outdoor wedding, irreverent and unconstrained, with a barbecue—and tofu sandwiches for the vegetarians. And they would have readings from Gurdjieff or Kahlil Gibran instead of the dreary maunderings of the civil and religious ceremonies, and music from Herbert Pompey and his nose flute rather than the tedium of Mendelssohn. The bride would wear flowers in her hair. The groom would wear flowers in his hair. The guests, in serapes and boots and fringed suede, would wear flowers in their hair. And then of course, for Walter, the pasture below had its own special significance.

Walter arrived early. His bachelor party, which had begun at the Elbow with several rounds of boilermakers and ended with cooking sherry and kif at the apartment of one of his old high school compatriots—he couldn't remember which—had left him feeling drained and hung over. He'd finally got to bed around four, but a steady procession of historical markers began marching around his room to the beat of "Yankee Doodle Dandy" as soon as he closed his eyes, and his dreams were the dreams of a man who has left his youth behind. He woke at seven, shagged and unrefreshed, to an intense itching in his missing foot. That was when he decided to pull on his wedding outfit and head over to Tom Crane's.

It was late September, the morning warm and hazy, the light held out to him in a bundle above the treetops. He looked up into the web of branches that fell back from the windshield and saw that the maples had turned, and though it was early yet, he could detect the faint caustic odor of burning leaves on the air. When he'd had his accident, now almost two months ago, he'd stopped shaving, and as he drove, he stroked the patchy stubble that had sprouted beneath his nose and along the plane of his sideburns. He was dressed in white, like a guru or Paschal Lamb, wearing the Nehru shirt and cotton bells Jessica had chosen for his wedding ensemble. His hair, after the fashion of the day, trailed down his neck. He wore the familiar Dingo boots, and for color and good luck both, he'd slipped on a belt that his soulful, sorrowful mother had braided from pink and blue plastic lanyards when she was a girl at summer camp.

He negotiated the hill down from the road without much trouble—he was getting used to the prosthesis in the way he'd got used to his first pair of skates, and he'd been lifting weights to strengthen the long muscles of his thighs for added support. It wasn't his leg that bothered him, it was his head. The cooking sherry had been a mistake, no doubt about it. As he wound his way down the trail that roughly followed the course of the old road, sidestepping the odd cow pie, he found himself envying Tom Crane, who'd left after two beers, pleading pronubial responsibilities. He paused for a moment in the mist-shrouded meadow that gave on to the creek, thinking *Here was the stage, and there the parking lot,* then turned and clumped over the footbridge, startling the swallows that nested beneath it. He was going to be married. Here. Here of all places. The choice of it, he understood, hadn't been so whimsical as he might have led himself to believe.

Walter was climbing the steep trail up from Van Wart Creek, the nervous little tributary known as Blood Creek on his left, Tom Crane's beehives and the still-burgeoning vegetable patch with its fat zucchini, pumpkins and late tomato on his right, when he ran across the first of the uninvited guests. Her back was to him, the heavy stockings were rolled down over the tops of her shoes and he could see the veins standing out in her legs. He recognized her with the first skip of his heart. She was bent over, searching for something—or no, she was pulling weeds, her knees stiff and her big backside waving in the breeze like a target at the fair. He remembered the day he'd found that target so irresistible and pelted her with dirt clods as she stooped over the tulip bed out front of the house in Verplanck, and he remembered the retribution that had followed when his grandfather came home from his nets and introduced him to the bitter end of an old ship's halyard. Pulling weeds. It was just like her. He remembered how each hairy taproot or cluster of crabgrass would merit an incantation in the Low Dutch that people had forgotten a century before, as she wished it on the swinish Mrs. Collins across the street or on Nettie Nysen, the witch who'd forced her to disconnect the phone. In the spring, she buried the frozen deadman of a crab—eyestalks and brain—with each new packet of seed. "Gram," he said, and she whirled around as if he'd startled her.

So what if he had?—he was angry. He thought he was done with all this, thought he'd left the dreams and visions in the hospital or along the road, thought the sacrifice of a foot was enough. But he was wrong.

She was smiling now, fat and glowing with the health of the indiscriminate eater, the woman who'd breakfasted every morning of her life on kippered herring, jelly doughnuts and sugared coffee as thick and black as motor oil. "Walter," she murmured in her crackling voice, "I just wanted to wish you the best on your wedding day." And then, with all the finesse of a backyard gossip: "So how's the foot?"

The foot? Suddenly he wanted to scream at her: *Did you have anything to do with that? Did you?* But he was staring at the stump of a tree taken down by Jeremy Mohonk on his release from prison in 1946. His grandmother was gone. More history. All at once he felt weary. Nostalgia filled him, wine turned to vinegar, and the birds railed at him from the trees that crowded in on him like a mob. He'd tried to put it all out of his mind, tried to remember that he hated his father and didn't give a damn where he was, that he had a life and being of his own that transcended that of the abandoned boy, the motherless boy, the boy who'd grown up among strangers. He'd tried to concentrate on Jessica, on the union that would redeem him and make him whole. And now here it was again: more history.

He plodded up the hill and his incorporeal grandmother was whispering in his ear, retelling one of his favorite stories—one he liked better than the betrayal of Minewa or the hoodwinking of Sachoes—the story of his parents' wedding. What did they wear? he would ask her. What was my mother like? Tell me about the lake.

Your mother was like royalty, she told him. And your father was the handsomest man in the county. An athlete, a prankster, full of jokes and high spirits. He was married in his uniform, with the medals on his chest and the sergeant's stripes on his shoulder. Your mother was an Alving. Swedish. Her father was Magnus Alving, the architect—he drew up the plans for the free school in the Colony, did you know that?—and her mother was of Dutch descent, an Opdycke. She wore her mother's gown—peau de soie, trimmed with seed pearls and Madeira lace. Her hair was up and she was wearing white heels like she just stepped out of a fairy tale. They held the ceremony outdoors, on the beach at Kitchawank Lake, though it was late in the year and turning cold, and when the justice said "You may kiss the bride" and your father took your mother in his arms, all the geese around the lake started honking and the fish threw themselves up on shore like pieces of tinfoil. Hesh was best man.

He'd almost reached the top of the hill when another voice began to intrude on his consciousness. He looked up. There before him, pale, bowlegged and naked as a wood sprite, stood Tom Crane. The saint of the forest clutched a bottle of baby shampoo in one hand, and in the other, a towel as stiff as a sheet of cardboard. He was grinning and saying something about getting cold feet, but Walter couldn't quite make it out, the buzz of his grandmother's voice murmuring in his ears still. *Walter, Walter,* she said, her voice dolorous and fading now, *don't blame him. He loved her. He did. It's just that in his heart . . . he loved his country . . . more. . . .*

"Hey, Walter—Van—snap out of it." The naked saint was two feet from him now, peering into his eyes as if into the far end of a telescope. "You still zonked from last night or what?"

He was. Yes. That was it. He focused on Tom Crane for the first time and saw that the saint's skinny frame was maculated with boils, blemishes and insect bites. Tom was scratching his beard. His ribs were slats in a fence, his feet so white and long and flat they might have been molded of dough that wouldn't rise. His lips were moving now and he was saying something about waking up, a dip in the creek and hot coffee and bourbon up at the shack. Walter allowed himself to be led back down the hill, across the footbridge and into the ferns at water's edge.

The stream was low this time of year, but the saint of the forest, looking to his toilet, had dammed it up under the bridge—the resulting pool was about as deep as a bathtub and three times as wide. Pausing only to wedge his towel in the crotch of a tree, Tom stepped into the pool, exposing the flat pale nates that hadn't felt the embrace of cotton briefs since his mother had stopped doing his laundry when he went off to Cornell four years earlier. He eased himself into the creek like a mutant water strider, ass first, hooting with the shock of it.

Walter was slower. Fumbling back down the path had left him winded and sweat-soaked. His leg suddenly felt as if it had been rubbed with jalapeño oil from the knee down and his eyes were still playing tricks on him. It was nothing major—the trees didn't transform themselves into claws or lollipops and his grandmother was nowhere in sight—yet everything seemed skewed and out of focus, the visible world in intricate motion, as if he were examining a drop of pond water under a microscope. The leaves that overhung them, the peeling footbridge, the bark of the trees and the grain of the rock: they'd all been reduced to their components, to a grid of minuscule dancing dots. It was last night, he figured. The cooking sherry. That had to be it. He lowered himself down on a rock and began to tug at his left boot.

Tom was thrashing his limbs spastically and deep-breathing like a seal coming up for air.

"Cold?" Walter asked.

"No, no," Tom said, too quickly. "Just right." He averted his eyes as Walter removed the boot from his other foot.

Walter pulled the Nehru shirt up over his head, dropped his pants and undershorts and stood there naked among the ferns and saplings. He could feel the mud of the bank between the toes of his left foot; the right foot, the inert one, planted itself like a stone. No one had seen him like this, not even Jessica. And Tom Crane, his oldest friend and intellectual mentor, wasn't looking.

"You know something?" Tom said, glancing at Walter as he lowered himself into the water, and then looking away again. "Cars. Automobiles. They were originally going to call them electrobats." He was snickering with the idea of it. "Electrobats," he repeated.

The water was cold as glacial runoff. Walter didn't cry out, didn't catch his breath, didn't curse or thrash. He just settled there on his back, the current lifting his genitals and subtly reconstituting itself to accommodate his neck and shoulders. After a moment he lifted his right leg from the water and propped the plastic foot on a rock at the edge of the pool.

"Oleo locomotives," Tom said. "That one was in the running too." But the levity had gone out of his voice. "That's it, huh?" he said. And then: "How does it feel?"

"Right now it hurts like a son of a bitch." Walter paused, contemplating the plastic sculpture at the nether end of his leg. "The doctor says I'll learn to live with it."

The sun was climbing through the trees now, firming up the shadows and suffusing the undergrowth with a rich golden light that clung to the leaves like batter. Walter counted the fronds of the fern beside him, watched the minnows drop down with the current and settle between his legs, listened to the rap of woodpecker and the call of vireo. For a moment he felt a part of it all, creature of the forest primeval that antedated macadam, case-hardened steel and the plastic prosthesis, but then the stutter of a motorcycle out on Van Wart Road brought him back. "All right," he said, rising from the pool in the slow groping way of an octogenarian. "Okay. I'm all right now."

"Use my towel if you want," Tom said. He was sitting up, blowing and puffing still, the long wet queue of his hair trailing down his pimply back like something that had clung to him and drowned.

Walter flayed himself with the stiff stinking towel while mosquitoes whined around him and mud worked between his toes. He was feeling better, no doubt about it. The headache had receded, the leaves and twigs that reached out to him seemed to have consolidated once again, and the pain had gone out of his numbed leg. It was then, standing there on the mud bank and shivering in the early morning light, that he had a revelation. All at once he realized that the whole business of daily life was irrelevant to him, that he didn't want to make small talk, didn't want to discuss electrobats, last night's party, drugs, nerve gas or revolution in Latin America. No: what he really wanted to talk about was his father. He wanted to open himself up to the quivering, abject, bony mass of gooseflesh that now stood dripping beside him and tell him that he'd been fooling himself, tell him that now and always he did give a damn where his father was and wanted nothing more—nothing, not Jessica, not the flesh and bone that had been torn from him—than to find him, confront him, wave the bloody rag of the past in his face and reclaim himself in the process. He didn't want to talk about his wedding or about music or health food or UFOs. He wanted to talk about the mothball fleet and genealogy, about his grandmother, about a ghost in the scent of a pancake and the trouble with his eyes that made the past come alive in the present.

But he never got the chance.

Because the saint of the forest, blue in the face and chattering with the cold in every molar and ratcheting joint, the ratty towel working furiously at his splayed shoulders and bald scrotum, suddenly said, "What did you do to Mardi, anyway?"

Mardi. She was a shadow, a fragment of memory, a stain on his consciousness—she was another ghost. "Who?"

"You know: Mardi. Mardi Van Wart."

Walter didn't know. Didn't want to know. There was a screaming in his ears, a terrible unquenchable din that all at once rose up from the bloodied ground before him. He could hear the cries of the victims, his mother's caressing voice stretched taut, the rabid raging curses of the men with sticks and tire irons and fence posts in their hands. Kike, nigger, Commie: he was in the eye of the storm. *Van Wart?* Mardi *Van Wart?*

"She says she was with you and Hector the night you, uh, had your accident, you know? Says she really needs to see you."

He felt it tugging at him, something obscene, unholy, irresistible. "You . . . you know her?"

Tom Crane was ridiculous. Naked, dripping, the reeking towel clamped under one arm and a toothbrush nonchalantly dangling from his lip, he paused to give Walter a big meaningful goat-toothed grin. "Oh, yeah," he said, the cries of the innocents echoing around him, "I know her."

Jessica wore a lace dress laboriously tatted by underfed peasants on the far side of the world, a pair of unadorned white sandals and her grandmother's ivory cameo brooch. In her hair, which shone with a blonde brilliance that might have blinded the Vikings themselves, there were glimmers of baby's breath and primrose. Walter stood beside her in the late morning with its insouciant bees and butterflies, flanked by Hesh and Lola and Jessica's pink-faced parents, while Tom Crane read a passage from a science fiction novel about extraterrestrial propagation and Herbert Pompey danced around under the weight of the flowers in his hair and rendered the serpentine melodies of the Indian snake charmers on his nose flute. Then Jessica recited a couple of verses by an obscure scribbler on the subject of love and fish, and Hesh stepped forward to read the climactic lines from the civil ceremony ("Do you, Walter Truman Van Brunt, take this woman . . . till death do you part?"). "I do," said Walter, and he kissed the bride in a surge of emotion—in love and gratitude and the fullest apprehension of life and youth—that lifted him for the moment from the trough of confusion into which the accident had thrust him. It was then that Hector Mantequilla set off a string of Arecibo firecrackers and the celebration began in earnest.

Jessica's family, Conklins and Wings alike, left early. Grandmother Conklin, a starchy old patrician with dead white skin, pendulous nose and tortoise eyes, had been carried up the hill in a blanket. She sat on a folding chair in the shade of the oak tree, surrounded by aged nieces from Connecticut, a conspicuous smear of cowshit on her black patent leather pumps, glaring her disapproval of the proceedings. Half an hour after the punch was served and the cake cut, she was gone. The aged nieces soon followed, and then John Wing himself—as bland and awkwardly handsome as the star of a sitcom about the wisdom of fathers—was shaking Walter's hand in parting and telling him to take care of his little girl. By late afternoon, all the representatives of the elder generations had departed, scratching insect bites and dabbing handkerchiefs at sun-blistered faces. Hesh, Lola and Walter's aunt Katrina (three sheets to the wind and fighting back tears) were the last of them.

The storm began to kick up around four. Jessica, bright-eyed and thick-tongued, was giving Nancy Fagnoli an exhaustive biographical account of Herbert Axelrod, patron saint of tropical fish, Walter was swilling rotgut champagne and smoking a joint with Herbert Pompey out by the bee tenements, and Tom Crane was squatting on the porch in a cloud of smoke with Hector and half a dozen other epithalamial celebrants. Susie Cats, a big overwrought girl with soft-boiled eyes, had passed out on Tom Crane's cot after drinking fourteen cups of tequila punch and crying without remit for two hours. She lay there now, her faint rhythmic snores drifting across the clearing to where Walter stood with Herbert Pompey. Someone was strumming a guitar somewhere up in the woods.

Walter watched the low belly of the sky as it edged over the treetops, sank into the cleft of the hill behind him and billowed up to snuff out the sun. Within minutes, the sky was dark. Squinting against the smoke, Herbert Pompey handed him the yellowed nub of a joint. "Looks like it's going to rain on your party."

Walter shrugged. He was feeling pretty numb. Champagne, pot, a hit of this and a hit of that, the bourbon in his coffee that morning and the excesses of the night before: the cumulative effect was leveling. He was married, and over there by the oak tree stood his bride, that much he knew. He knew too that in a few hours they would take the train up to Rhinebeck and check into a quaint hotel full of gloomy nooks and dusty bric-a-brac and that afterward they'd make love and fall asleep in each other's arms. As for the weather, he could give a shit. "What'd you expect?" he said, dropping the bottle in the grass. Then he took Pompey by the arm and went looking for another.

The storm didn't break until nearly an hour later, and by then the second uninvited guest had shown up. Though he'd been fighting it,

Walter understood just how susceptible he was at this moment to history, nostalgia and the patterns of the past, and throughout the day he'd half-expected to glance up and see his father perched on the edge of the porch between Tom Crane and Hector Mantequilla or picking his way through the high grass with a bottle of cheap champagne clamped in his big iron hand. But it wasn't his father who emerged from the shadow of the trees as Walter stood urinating against the side of the shack—it was Mardi.

She made straight for him, half a smile caught on her lips, a package wrapped in tissue paper in her hand. He tried to be nonchalant, but as it turned out he was too hasty with the business of micturition, with stowing away his equipment and zipping up, and he turned to face her with warm urine on his thigh and in the crotch of his pants. "Hi," she said. "Remember me?"

She was barefoot, wearing a miniskirt (not paper this time, not anything that might dissolve in his wet hands, but leather) and a shimmering low-cut blouse that matched the color of her eyes. There were Indian beads around her neck and she wore earrings fashioned from tiny shells and feathers. She looked like her mother. She looked like her father. "Sure, yeah," Walter said, "I remember you," and they both glanced down at his foot.

"I brought this for you," she said, handing him the package.

"Oh, hey, you didn't have to—" he began, looking reflexively over his shoulder for Jessica, but no one was there. They stood alone at the rear of the shack; the birds had gone quiet suddenly and the sky was like the underside of a dream. The package was small and heavy. He tore back the paper. Brass and wood, the heft of metal: he held a telescope in his hand. Or no, it was a telescope with something else grafted to it, a dull brass quarter-circle ticked out with calibrations and festooned with clamps, screws and mirrors. She was watching him. He caught her eye and then glanced down at the thing in his hand, trying to look knowledgeable and appreciative. "It's, uh . . . nice. Really nice."

"You know what it is?"

He shook his head slowly. "Not really." The brass was green with age, the wood of the telescope chipped and gouged as if gnawed by some marooned mariner in times gone by. "Looks old," he offered.

Mardi was grinning at him. She wasn't wearing any makeup—or maybe just a trace. Her legs were naked and strong, and her feet—uniformly tan, fine-boned, with perfect arches and a tracery of rich blue veins—were beautiful. "It's a sextant," she said. "They used to use them for navigation in the old days. My father had it lying around."

"Oh," said Walter, as if it should have been obvious to him all along. He'd just been married, he was stoned and exalted, the sky was splitting open and lightning sat in the trees. He was holding a sextant in his hand, and he wondered why.

"It's kind of a joke," she said. "So you can find your way to me, you know?" He didn't know, but the words stirred him. "Don't you remember? That night down at the river?"

He gave her a numb look: maybe he remembered and maybe he didn't. A lot had happened that night. Suddenly, maddeningly, he felt a terrific itch in his missing foot.

She was fishing for something in a leather pouch: Walter saw a comb, a mirror, a tube of lipstick. "I mean our date." She found what she was looking for—cigarettes—and she shook one from the pack and lit it. Walter said nothing, but he watched her as if he'd never seen match or cigarette before. "My father's sailboat," she said. "I'm taking you out to the ghost ships." She glanced up at him and her eyes were cold and hard as marbles. He felt the first few heavy drops of rain through the back of his shirt. There was a rumble of thunder. "You didn't forget?"

"No," he lied. "No, no," and he knew in that moment he would take her up on it, knew he would go back and walk the barren rusted decks as he'd gone back to stand yearning and bewildered before the road marker, knew he was bound to her in some frightening and unfathomable way.

"How does it feel?" she asked suddenly.

"What?" he said, but he didn't have to ask.

"You know: your foot."

The rain was coming harder now, big pregnant drops that tickled his scalp and wet his cheeks. He shrugged. "Like nothing," he said. "It feels dead."

And then, just as he was about to turn and jog around the corner to huddle with the others beneath the leaky roof of Tom Crane's shack, she took his arm and pulled him toward her. Her voice was a whisper, a rasp. "Can I see it?"

Thunder crashed in the trees, a bolt of lightning lit the branches of the big white oak that snaked over them. He didn't know what he must have looked like at that moment, but his face showed what he felt. She let go of him. "Not now," he heard her say as he turned and plunged through the quickening rain, seeing the pall of mist, the road marker and the swift glancing shadow all over again, "I don't mean now." He kept going. "Walter!" she called. "Walter!" He'd reached the corner of the shack and could see Jessica, Tom and Hector huddled under the eaves before him by the time he stopped to look over his shoulder. Mardi was standing there, indifferent to the rain. Wet hair clung to her face, her hands were outstretched in supplication. "Not now," she repeated, and the skies broke open above her.

With the Patroon's Blessing

Dominie Van Schaik, as yet churchless, had to hike all the way out to the Van Brunt farm for the christening. He'd spent the previous night on a pallet at the upper manor house and had breakfasted on hard biscuit and water before conducting a dawn service for Vrouw Van Wart, a service followed by two rigorous hours of prayer and meditation (rigorous, to say the least—the woman was a fanatic). He could feel every amen in the crook of his knee as he shambled over the crude footbridge and struggled up the steep stony path to the farm.

It was late September, overcast but warm—oppressively warm—and by the time he was halfway up the hill he found he had to sit a moment and refresh himself beside the stream that chattered along the path in a ribbon of fern and skunk cabbage. The local farmers, he recalled, referred to the runlet as Blood Creek for some superstitious reason, something about a filicide who supposedly stalked these woods. Rustic superstitions had little effect on the Dominie, a man who followed Gomarus and walked the path of righteousness, but still he had to admit that these woods were particularly gloomy and ominous. What was it? The trees were thicker here, he supposed, the light more tenuous. And there seemed to be a disproportionate number of rotting trunks among the healthy trees, big Cretaceous giants that leaned precariously against their still vital neighbors or stretched out prone—their bark gone in patches and covered all over with earlike growths of fungus—until they were swallowed up in the shadows of the forest floor.

The Dominie had just cupped his hands and bent forward to drink from a limpid stony pool, when he glanced up and spotted the figure of a man poised amidst the scrub oak and mountain laurel. It was a shock, and for all his certainty, for all his contempt for the bogeys that haunt the primitive mind, he felt his heart turn over in him. But the shock was momentary: this was no red-bearded Swede with a dripping axe, this was . . . nothing. The figure, if it had been there at all, had faded into the undergrowth like a phantom. Had his eyes been playing tricks on him? No. He'd seen it clear as day. A man of flesh and blood, gaunt, tall, with the facial features of an aborigine and wrapped in a coat of animal fur. Shaken, the Dominie rose cautiously to his feet. "Hello?" he called. "Is anyone there?"

Not a leaf stirred. From an invisible perch, high above him, a crow called out in its harsh mocking tones. All at once the Dominie was angry with himself—he'd fallen prey to superstition, if only for an instant. But then anger gave way to fear: rational, cold, self-serving fear. If what he'd seen out there wasn't an apparition, it occurred to him that a painted savage was even then lurking amidst the bushes, stalking him—the Dominie—as he might have stalked a turkey or quail. Recollections of the Indian massacres of the forties succeeded this revelation, and the Dominie, picturing splayed limbs and tomahawked scalps, gathered himself up and hurried on his way.

He was winded by the time he reached the crest of the hill, and he took a moment to catch his breath and survey the untidy little farm that lay before him. The place was even worse than he'd imagined. A recent thunderstorm had made a quagmire of the yard out front of the house (if you could call it a house), the stone fences were in disrepair and there was a pervasive reek of human slops about the place. The woman, with her shaved head and dumb-staring eyes, came out to greet him. She was wearing a dress that might have been scavenged from a corpse, and the half-breed child—he looked to be about two or so—trailed behind her, naked as the day he was born. The Dominie made his greetings and sat out front on the chopping block, drinking more water—didn't anyone serve ale any more?—and nibbling at a sourish corn cake while the child ran to fetch his uncle, and a Canada goose with clipped wings looked on expectantly.

Young Van Brunt came in from the fields and extended a callused hand. "Pleased to see you again, Dominie," he said. "We're thankful you could make it."

The pastor had meant to be severe, to give the boy a piece of his mind with regard to raising half-breed bastards, defying the patroon's authority and running afoul of the *schout,* but Jeremias' humble greeting softened him. He took the proferred hand, looked past the angry reddened welt the *schout*'s sword had left like a surveyor's plumb line on the boy's face, and into the shifting deeps of his eyes. "It's more than God's duty," he murmured. "It's a pleasure too."

The ceremony was nothing—a saying of words and a sprinkling of water the woman fetched from the creek—a ceremony he'd performed a hundred times and more, but what gave him trouble was the name. He actually stumbled over it, twice, before Jeremias' soft assured tones corrected him. Jeremy—the Englishers' version of Jeremias—was no problem; it was the patronym that made his tongue cleave to his palate like a half-baked honeycake. "Mohonk?" he said. "Is that right?"

Two months before, on that stifling July afternoon when Jan Pieterse left his store to dip crabs on Acquasinnick Bay and Joost Cats rode out to Nysen's Roost on the patroon's business, Jeremias was hoeing up the weeds between the high sweet burgeoning rows of corn in the stand behind the house. It was a messy proposition. The ground was wet as a sponge with the runoff from the previous night's storm, and it tugged at the hoe with a whistling suck and plop and clung to his pegleg like the grip of a dirty hand. He swatted insects, sweat dripped from his nose, there were yellow smears of mud on his face and clothing, on his pegleg and the wooden clog he wore on his left foot. It was only because it was so hot and still—even the birds were at rest till the cool of evening—that he was able to hear the shudder and whinny of the horses, and then the voices—one of them was Katrinchee's—that came to him over the fields in a sunstruck rhapsody. Staats, he thought. Or Douw.

On his way in from the field he found Squagganeek bent over an anthill with a stick, and took him by the hand. "It's *grootvader* van der Meulen," he told the boy. "Come to visit on his horse. And Uncle Douw too, I'll bet." But when he rounded the corner of the house, the boy at his side, he saw how wrong he'd been—how bitterly, painfully wrong. He'd expected an embrace from Staats, a walk with Douw, something from *moeder* Meintje's oven, and the sight of the *schout*, with his flugelhorn nose, bowed back and ugly black dab of a beard, stopped him cold. For a moment. A moment only. Then the anger took over. Trembling with it, his heart hammering and his throat gone dry, he crossed the yard, heard what the ass had to say and bent to pluck a stick of firewood from the ground.

He was so enraged—*again, the son-of-a-bitch had come to evict him again*—that he barely glanced at the second rider hovering at the edge of the trees. Until she called out, that is. Until her father unsheathed his sword and raised it above his head and she cried out in shock and horror and the keenest pitch of lamentation. Jeremias shot her a glance, her name on his lips even as the stick splintered in his hands and the force of the *schout*'s blow drove him to his knees, feeling somehow awkward and embarrassed, ashamed of his clothes and his uncombed hair, regretful of his rage, his station, his life, wanting only to hold her but holding nothing. Then there was blood in his eyes and he was on the ground.

If the sun stirred in the sky and the shadows lengthened, he was unaware of it. When he opened his eyes he could barely see for the blood that filmed them, but he knew she was there, bent over him, pressing something that smelled of her most intimate self to the side of his face, while Katrinchee sobbed somewhere in the background and Squagganeek, closer at hand, howled like a wild beast. Then it came to him: her skirts. He was bleeding, he was hurt, and she was stanching the blood with her skirts. He could see her now, the light trembling around her in an otherworldy nimbus, the coils of her hair fallen loose, her face gone dead white and her dress steeped in his wet black blood. "Neeltje?" he said, trying to shake it off and sit up.

"I'm right here," she said, appending his name in a startled whisper, "—Jeremias."

And then there was the other voice, the voice that stirred him with a thrill of hate even as he lay there flat on his back. "I'm sorry it's come to this," the *schout* said, and Jeremias could see him now too, gargantuan, all nose and broad-rimmed hat, as tall as any tree and broad enough to blot out the sun, "and I'm sorry I've struck you down. But you've got to learn respect for authority, you've got to know your place."

"Oh, *vader,* please. Can't you see he's hurt?"

The *schout* went on as if he hadn't heard her, as if she were made of air or paper. "Under the authority vested in me by the lord and proprietor of these lands, Oloffe Stephanus Van Wart, patroon," he said, his voice gone nasal in official pronouncement, "I hereby inform you, Jeremias Van Brunt, that you are now in custody of the law."

Jeremias walked the eight miles to Croton. In his filthy blood-stained clothes, with bits of grass and leaves in his hair, and the side of his face swollen to twice its size with the poultice of mud and medicinal herbs Katrinchee had applied, after the Weckquaesgeek fashion, to his open wound. His hands were bound behind his back, as if he were a thief or axe murderer, and a cord cinched around his waist connected him to the pommel of the *schout*'s saddle. It was tough going. The nag would quicken its pace unexpectedly and jerk him forward or suddenly slow to a virtual stop, causing him to stagger out to his right to avoid it, the strut digging like a goad at the stump of his leg. Another man would have complained, but not Jeremias. Though horseflies and mosquitoes made him dance with their stings, though he felt light-headed from loss of blood and sick from thirst, though the gash that leapt across his right eye, exposed the bone beneath it and opened up the flesh all the way to the hinge of his jaw felt as if it were being probed with hot needles, he never said a word. No: he just concentrated on the slow, working shift of the nag's flanks and stepped aside when the animal relieved itself.

Neeltje was up front, on her mare. Her father, in a metallic voice, had commanded her to keep as great a distance as circumstances permitted between herself and the prisoner. She'd begun to protest—"He's just a boy, *vader*: he's hurt and suffering"—but that hard cold voice clamped down on her like a steel trap. Resigned, she'd gone on ahead—ten yards or so out in front of her father—but every so often she glanced over her shoulder and gave Jeremias a look of such concentrated tenderness he felt he would collapse on the spot. Either that or go on till he'd circled the globe six times and dug a rut you could drive a wagon through.

As it turned out, he went on. Past the turnoff for Verplanck's Landing and along the river, where it was no cooler, past fields and forests he'd never before laid eyes on, through the late afternoon and into the quiet of evening. He was fixating on the mesmeric rise and fall of the nag's hooves, no longer alert enough to bother dodging the piles of dung it dropped in his path, when they rounded a bend in the road and they were there. He looked up dully. The lower manor house rose out of the fields before him, high-crowned and commanding, with a rambling long porch out front and a stone cellar beneath it that was itself half again as big as the Van Wartville house. The *schout* dismounted, freed Jeremias's hands with a rough tug at the cords that bound them, jerked open a door in the basement wall and thrust him into a cell the size of a wagon bed. The door closed on darkness.

He woke to a light rapping from the outer world, the rattle of key in lock, and then the sudden effulgence of morning as the door pulled back on its rusted hinges. A black woman, who still bore the facial cicatrices of her lorn and distant tribe, stood in the doorway. She was wearing a homespun dress, the lappet cap favored by country *vrouwen* from Gelderland to Beverwyck, and an immaculate pair of wooden clogs. "Brekkfass," she said, handing him a mug of water, a wedge of cheese and a small loaf, still warm from the oven. He saw that he was in a toolshed, the rough walls hung with wooden rakes, shovels, a moldering harness, a flail with a splintered swiple. Then the door slammed shut once more and he lay back in the straw that covered the earthen floor, chewed his breakfast and watched the sun slice through the crevice between the crude door and its stone frame.

The sun was gone by the time the door swung open again, the darkness of the cell so absolute he had to shield his eyes against the lit taper that was suddenly thrust in his face. He'd been alone with his thoughts through the interminable day, dozing fitfully and jerking awake with a start to sit up and hesitantly examine his swollen cheek or rub the butt of his leg, and over the course of so many dead hours the shock of his confrontation with the *schout* had seeped out of him. In the darkness, in the damp, in the impenetrable solitude of that strange prison, he could feel the rage gnawing at him once again. In their eyes, he was a criminal. But what had he done, really? Lay claim to a piece of land? Try to work it and survive? By what right did the *schout* claim his neat little *bouwerie*—or the patroon his estates, for that matter? The more he thought about it, the more incensed he grew. If anyone was a criminal, if anyone should be locked up, it was Joost Cats, it was Oloffe Van Wart and his fat-assed *commis* with the leather-bound accounts ledgers. They were the real criminals—the patroon and his henchmen, Their High Mightinesses of the States General, the English king himself. They were leeches, chiggers, toads; they'd got under his skin and wouldn't leave him alone till they'd sucked him dry.

When the door opened this time, he was ready. He'd actually sprung up from the ground, a rake in his hand, actually raised it above his head like a tomahawk and kicked the taper to the floor, before she called out his name in a gasp and he felt foolish all over again. "Hush," she hissed. "It's me. I bribed Ismailia and brought you this." Neeltje handed him a wooden bowl and pulled the door shut behind her. The bowl was warm and it gave off a smell of cabbage. Jeremias watched her numbly as she bent for the rush candle and held it up to illuminate her face, which was like something newly created from the void. "I hate my father," she said.

Jeremias clung to the bowl as if it were a stone at the edge of a precipice. He appreciated the sentiment, but held his peace.

"He's so, so. . . ." her voice trailed off. "Are you all right?"

He was studying the lock of pale fine hair that had worked its way out from under her cap to cling familiarly to her eyebrow. He wanted to say something significant, passionate, something like *Now that you're here, I am,* but he couldn't find the words. When he spoke, his voice sounded strange in his ears. "I'll live," he said.

She motioned him to sit and then squatted beside him as he settled back down in the straw and sipped tentatively from the bowl. "I heard them talking," she said. "My father and the patroon. They're going to leave you down here for another night to teach you a lesson, then the patroon's going to offer you tenancy on your farm."

Jeremias barely heard her. He didn't give a damn for the patroon, for the farm, for anything—anything but her. The way she talked, biting off each word like a little girl, the pout of her lips, the way her hips swelled out against the seams of her dress as she squatted there: each movement, each gesture, was a revelation. "Ja," he said, to say something. "Ja."

"Aren't you pleased?"

Pleased? To have his face slashed and his hands shackled, to be hauled off in ignominy and shut up in this hole while his sister and the boy were left to fend for themselves? Pleased? "Ja," he said finally.

"I've got to go," she said, glancing at the door.

All at once the night was charged with the chirring of insects, with doleful cries and the faint whisper of birds on the wing. Jeremias set down the bowl, edged closer to her. Just as he reached out to her, just as he took hold of her hand to pull her to him, she shook free and rose to her feet. Her eyes had narrowed suddenly and she stood cocked on one leg. "Who was that woman," she said, watching his eyes. "The one at the farm."

Woman? Farm? What was she talking about?

"She's your wife, isn't she?"

Jeremias came before the patroon the following morning. He was awakened at first light by the black woman with the strange swirling scars about her lips and nostrils. She handed him a bucket of water and a bowl of tepid corn mush, and informed him in a Dutch so crude it was like the dialogue of the beasts that he had better make himself presentable for *Mijnheer* Van Wart. When she'd gone, Jeremias slipped the crude woolen shirt over his head and gingerly laid the side of his face in the water; he held it there until the mud plaster began to dissolve. The water went cloudy, then turned the color of beef broth in a swirl of fragmented leaves, twisted stems and strange dried petals.

After a time, Jeremias sat up and tentatively explored the wound with his fingertips: a crude split ridge ran from his right eyebrow to his chin, rough ground, a topography of scab, pus and wet puddled blood. He explored it, this new grain of his metamorphosing self, ran his fingers over it again and again, till the spots of fresh blood had dried. Then he washed his hands.

It must have been around nine when the *schout* came for him. The door flung back, light surged into the room like the flood tide running up against the rocks, and there he stood, bowed over like a great black question mark against the blank page of the day. "Come *younker*," he said, "the patroon will see you now," but there was something odd in the way he said it, something hollow and uncertain.

For a moment, Jeremias was puzzled—this wasn't the *schout* he knew—but then he understood: it was the wound. The man had gone too far, and he knew it. He'd raised his hand against an unarmed and crippled boy, and here was the evidence of it etched in his victim's face. Jeremias rose from the straw and strode out of the cell, wearing the mark of the *schout*'s disgrace like a badge.

Cats escorted him around the corner to the kitchen/dairy room, where milk, butter, cheese and other foodstuffs were stored, and where the patroon's servants did most of the cooking for the household. As soon as they stepped in the door, the black woman materialized from the shadows to flay Jeremias' broad back, his shoulders and arms and the seat of his baggy pantaloons with a birch broom so stiff and unyielding it might have been cut yesterday. Then a second black—this one a slight, stoop-shouldered male with a kinked cube of hair that stood up off his head like a toque—led them up the stairs and into the family kitchen above.

This room was dominated by a big round oak-plank table, in the center of which stood a cone of sugar and a blue vase of cut flowers. A painted cupboard stood in the corner beside a heavy mahogany sideboard that must have been shipped over from the old country, and the fireplace was decorated with blue ceramic tiles depicting biblical themes like the salification of Lot's wife and the beheading of John the Baptist. Jeremias took it all in as he stood at attention just inside the basement door. The *schout,* plumed hat in hand, slumped beside him while the black knocked respectfully at the door to the parlor. A voice answered from within, and the slave silently pulled open the door and turned to them with a grin that showed off the sharp, filed points of his glistening teeth. "De patroon he see you now," he said, stepping aside with a sweep of his arm.

Jeremias glimpsed walls hung with portraits, massive blocks of dark oiled furniture, real tallow candles in silver scounces, a carpet of woven colors. As he limped forward, the *schout* at his side, a high rectangular table came into view, and he saw that it was laid out for tea, with silver service and cups of painted porcelain that might have graced the slim, smooth hands of Chinese emperors. The beauty of it, the elegance and refinement, overwhelmed him, choked him with a nostalgia as fierce and cleansing as a spoonful of horseradish. For a moment—just a moment—he was a young boy in the bosom of his parents, sitting down to Martinmas tea in the parlor of the burgomaster of Schobbejacken.

All at once he became conscious of the harsh rap of his pegleg on the floor, of his filthy shirt and pantaloons and the torn stocking that hung in tatters from his calf: he was passing through the patroon's kitchen, entering the patroon's parlor, and he began to feel very small indeed. Compared with the van der Meulens' modest little farmhouse or Jan Pieterse's dark and drafty store, the place seemed inexpressibly grand, a sultan's palace sprung up in the wilds of the new world. In truth, the house comprised but six moderate-sized rooms in its two squat stories, and it was a far cry from the burghers' houses of Amsterdam and Haarlem, let alone the great estates of the gentry, but no one who lived in a dirt-floor hovel with a thatched roof and split-log walls that dripped sap, to one who drank from wooden mugs, plucked bits of stringy rabbit from the pot with his fingers and wiped his mouth with the back of his sleeve, it was opulence itself. For all his desperation, for all his anger and resentment, Jeremias was awed by it, humbled; he felt weak and insignificant—he felt guilty; yes, guilty—and he slouched into Van Wart's parlor like a sinner slouching into the Sistine Chapel.

The patroon, a pale fleshy little man whose features seemed lost in various excrescences, was sunk deep in a settee lined with pillows, his gouty foot propped above the level of his eyes on a makeshift buttress composed of two beaver pelts, a feather duster, the family Bible and a copy of Grotius' *Inleidinge tot de Hollandsche Rechtsgeleerdheid*, all piled atop a sagging corner chair. Beside him, looking as bloated and pontifical as the next-to-biggest bullfrog in the pond, was the *commis*; in the *commis'* lap, like the Book of Doom itself, sat the accounts ledger. The moment Jeremias laid eyes on them, his humility evaporated; in its place, he felt an intoxicating rush of hatred surge through him. He didn't want to farm, care for his sister, make his fortune or wrest Neeltje away from her father—all he wanted at that moment was to snatch the *schout*'s sword from him and run it through the pasty grublike bodies of *commis* and patroon, and then lay waste to the place, gouging the furniture, shattering the crockery, dropping his pants to defecate in the silver teapot . . . but the impulse died before it could take hold of him, died stillborn, supplanted by a breathless gasp of surprise. For Jeremias suddenly realized that patroon and *commis* were not alone in the room. Seated in the corner, silent and motionless as a snake, was a man Jeremias had never seen before.

He was young, this stranger—no more than five or six years Jeremias' senior—and he was tricked out in velvet and satin like one of Their High Mightinesses Themselves. With one silk-clad leg crossed casually over the other and a smirk of invincible superiority on his face, the stranger shot Jeremias a glance of cold appraisal that ate through him like acid. For one astonished instant Jeremias locked eyes with him, and then stared down at the floor, humbled all over again. The scar seared his face, no badge now, but the mark of Cain, the brand of a criminal. He didn't look up again.

Through all that followed—through the patroon's interminable speech of admonition and reconciliation, through the *commis'* pointless pontifications and the *schout*'s terse and hushed testimony, Jeremias never uttered a word but for *ja* and *nee*. The man in the corner (who, as it turned out, was Oloffe's only son and heir, *Jongheer* Stephanus Oloffe Rombout Van Wart, newly arrived from the University of Leyden to look after his interests in the face of his father's declining health) helped himself to a clay pipe of Virginia tobacco and a glass of Portuguese wine, surveying the proceedings with the air of a man watching a pair of dung beetles struggle over a kernel of manure. He merely sat there, an ironic grin compressing his thin haughty lips, holding himself aloof from the whole business—until the moment his father spelled out the terms of Jeremias' tenancy, that is. Then he came to life like a stalking beast.

"We will, in our, er, magnanimity," the patroon intoned in a wheezy voice that bespoke ruined health and mismanaged appetites, "absorb unto ourselves the rents and damages accruing to your late, er, father's tenancy in the unfortunate year of 1663. We, er, refer of course to rent in arrears, the pilferage and wanton slaughter of one, er, rutting boar and the careless usage of our livestock, which resulted in the untimely, er, demise of two milch cows and one piebald ox."

The agent made as if to protest, but the patroon waved him silent with an impatient hand and continued. "We consider that the physical"—here he paused to suck in a great wheezing breath—"er, blemish that you've, er, received at the, er, hands of Joost Cats, is punishment enough for your trespass and willful, er, disregard for established law, and we will forego the levying of fines or remanding you to the, er, stocks, of which we have, er, none in any case." Here the patroon's voice had gone so hoarse as to carry no farther than the rasp of quill on parchment, and Jeremias had to lean forward to hear him. Coughing into his fist, the old man took a glass of port the *commis* held out to him and stared up at Jeremias out of bleary eyes. "Your rent shall be the same as your, er, father's before you, payable in stuffs and in English pounds or *seawant,* as you prefer, and it will be, er, due—"

"*Vader,*" interjected a voice from the corner of the room, and all eyes turned toward the *Jongheer,* "I beg you to reconsider your judgment."

The old man's mouth groped at the air, and Jeremias thought of a tench flung up on the cobblestones in Schobbejacken so many years before. "Your rent," the patroon began again, but faltered as his voice faded to a timbreless wheeze.

Young Van Wart was on his feet now, his hands spread wide in remonstrance. Jeremias stole a glance at him, then went back to studying the floorboards. The *Jongheer* had at some point placed atop his head an enormous, floppy-brimmed beaver hat with a two-foot plume, and it magnified his presence till he seemed to fill the entire corner of the room. "I respect your goodheartedness, *vader,*" he said, "and I agree that it will be to our benefit to settle a tenant at Nysen's Roost, but is this the man—or boy, rather—to entrust with it? Hasn't he already proven himself a criminal without respect for the law, the degenerate issue of a degenerate father?"

"Well, well, yes—" the patroon began, but his son cut him off. Regarding Jeremias with a look he might have reserved for the unhappy slug that had crawled one damp night into his glistening leathern shoe, Stephanus held up his palm and continued. "And is he capable of paying rent, this one-legged cripple in his filthy rags? Do you really think this, this . . . beggar can pay his debts, let alone feed himself and the tribe of naked half-breed savages he's sired up there in the muck?"

Jeremias was beaten. He couldn't respond, couldn't even look young Van Wart in the eye. The gulf between them—he was well-built and youthful, this *Jongheer,* handsome as the portrait of the Savior hanging in the nave of the Schobbejacken church, powerful, wealthy, educated—was unbridgeable. What *commis, schout* and the beast of the pond couldn't take from him with their accounts ledgers, rapiers and unforgiving jaws, the *Jongheer* had taken with a sneer and half a dozen stinging phrases. Jeremias hung his head. The utter contempt in the man's voice—he might have been speaking of hogs or cattle—was a thing that would be with him for life.

In the end, though, *commis* and patroon prevailed, and Jeremias was taken on as tenant with a year's grace so far as rent was concerned (and a warning that he would be driven off the property at the point of a sword if he was even a stiver short in his accounts at the end of that time), but for Jeremias it was no victory. No: he left the manor house in shame, his stomach rumbling, clothes filthy, the *schout*'s mark burning on his face and the *Jongheer*'s words charred into his heart. He didn't look back. Not even when Neeltje came to the door of her father's cottage to stand mute with her wet and glowing eyes and watch him as he limped up the road. Not even when at last she called out his name in a voice stung with hurt and incomprehension—not even then could he find it in himself to lift his eyes from the rutted road before him.

Taking stock of the situation the following morning, Jeremias understood that his options were limited. He'd just turned seventeen. He was short a leg and wore the brand of the outlaw on his face, his parents were dead, his sister's mind was like a butterfly touched by the frost, and the gaping hungry mouth of his half-breed nephew haunted his dreams. What was he going to do—bring the patroon and his smirking son to their knees by starving himself to death in the winter woods? Wearily, painfully (the stump of his leg ached as if his father were taking the saw to it at that very moment), he pushed himself up from the damp straw pallet, took a mouthful of cornmeal, and went out to his chores. He finished hoeing up the weeds, split a cord and a half of wood to take the buzz of the *Jongheer*'s disdain out of his head, and decided, between two random and otherwise unremarkable strokes of the axe, to have his nephew christened in the church and admitted to the community as a Dutchman and free citizen of the Colony of New York.

When he came to Katrinchee with the idea, she looked down at her hands. Squagganeek sat on the floor, watching him with Harmanus' eyes. "I thought we should name him after *vader*," Jeremias said.

Katrinchee wouldn't hear of it. "The guilt," she whispered, and her voice trailed off.

"Well, what about 'Wouter' then?"

She bit her lip and slowly shook her head from side to side.

Two days later, when Jeremias came in from the fields, his sister was smiling over a pan of rising dough. "I want to call him 'Jeremias,' " she said. "Or how do the Englishers have it—'Jeremy?' "

The surname was another story. On the one hand, the boy was a Van Brunt—just look at his eyes—but on the other, he wasn't. And if he were to be christened a Van Brunt, who would the Dominie list as his father? They wrestled with the problem through a blistering afternoon and a mosquito-plagued night: in the morning they agreed that the boy should be named for his natural father, who was, after all, the son of a chieftain. It was only proper. Jeremias milked his cows, then sent for Dominie Van Schaik.

It was September before the Dominie actually made it out to the farm to perform the ceremony, but neither Katrinchee nor Jeremias was much bothered by the delay. Once they'd reached their decision, it was as if the thing had already been accomplished. Now they were legitimate. They'd weathered the worst, they'd been orphaned, deserted, evicted and shunned, and now they were members of the community once more, fully sanctioned in the eyes of God, man and patroon alike.

And so things went, on through the fall and the days that slid ever more rapidly toward night, through the harvest that was less than bountiful but more than meager, through the lulling warmth of Indian summer and the cold sting of the first blighting frost. Then one afternoon, late in October, Jeremias was out on the far verge of the cornfield, burning stumps and thinking of the way the blouse clung to Neeltje's upper arms, when all at once he felt himself gripped by nameless fears and vague apprehensions. His pulse quickened, smoke stung his eyes, he could feel the scar come alive on his face. Not two days earlier, a half-plucked gobbler in his lap, his hands glutinous with feathers and his mind wandering all the way down to Croton, he'd glanced up and seen the figure of his father, clear as day, tearing across the field in his steaming nightshirt. But now, though the blood was beating in his temples and his scalp felt as if it were being manipulated by invisible fingers, though he looked over both shoulders and stared down his nose at the four corners of the field, he saw nothing.

No sooner had he gone back to his work, however, than he was startled by a voice that seemed to leap up out of the blaze before him, as if the very fire itself were speaking. "You. Who gives you the right to farm here?" rumbled the voice in very bad Dutch. Jeremias rubbed the smoke from his eyes. And saw that a man—a giant, red-bearded, dressed in skins and with a woodsman's axe flung over his shoulder—stood to the right of the burning stump. The smoke shifted, and the man took a step forward.

Jeremias could see him more clearly now. His face was as soiled as a coal miner's, he wore leggings after the Indian fashion, and the eyes stared out of his head with the exophthalmic vehemence of the eyes of the mad. A pair of coneys, still wet with blood, dangled from his belt. "Who gives you the right?" he repeated.

Backing up a step, wondering how, with his bad leg, he could possibly hope to outrun this madman, Jeremias found himself murmuring the name of his landlord and master as if it were an incantation. "Oloffe Stephanus Van Wart," he said, ". . . the patroon."

"The patroon, is it?" the madman returned, mincing his words in mockery. "And who gives him the right?"

Jeremias tried to hold the stranger's eyes while casting about for something he could use to defend himself—a stone, a root, the jawbone of an ass, anything. "Their . . . Their High Mightinesses," he stammered. "Originally, I mean. Now it's the duke of York and King Charles of the Englishers."

The madman was grinning. A flat, toneless laugh escaped his lips. "You've learned your lesson well," he said. "And what are you, then—a man to forge his own destiny or somebody's nigger slave?"

All at once the world rose up to scream in his ears, the harsh caterwauling of the hollow withered dead: all at once Jeremias understood who it was standing there before him. In desperation he snatched up a stone and crouched low, David in the shadow of Goliath. He understood that he was about to die.

"You," the madman said, laughing again. "You know who I am?"

Jeremias could barely choke out a response. His legs felt weak and his throat had gone dry. "Yes," he whispered. "You're Wolf Nysen."

Landless Gentry

MARGUERITE Mott, elder sister of Muriel, edged closer to Depeyster, scuffing the ancient peg-and-groove floor with the feet of the William and Mary side chair. Like her sister, she was a big moon-faced blonde in her mid-fifties who favored false eyelashes and cocktail dresses in colors like champagne and chartreuse. Unlike her sister, however, she worked for a living. Selling real estate. "He's rejected the bid," she said, looking up from the sheaf of papers in her lap.

"Son of a bitch." Depeyster Van Wart rose from his chair, and when he spoke again, his voice was pinched to a yelp. "You kept this strictly confidential, right? He had no idea it was me?"

Marguerite pressed her lashes together in a coy little blink and gave him a look of wide-eyed rectitude. "Like you told me," she said, "I'm bidding on behalf of a client from Connecticut."

Depeyster turned away from her in exasperation. He had an urge to pluck something up off the sideboard—an antique inkwell, a china bibelot—and fling it through the window. He was a great flinger. He'd flung Lionel trains, music boxes and croquet mallets as a boy, squash rackets, golf clubs and highball glasses as he grew older. There was actually something in his hand, some damnable piece of Indian bric-a-brac—what was it, a calumet? a tomahawk?—before he got hold of himself. He set the thing down and reached into his breast pocket for a tranquillizing pinch of cellar dust.

"So, what are you saying," he said, swinging around on her, "the place isn't for sale then—to anybody? You mean to tell me the old fart isn't hard up for cash?"

"No, he wants to sell. Word is he's trying to raise money to leave his grandson something." Marguerite paused to snap open a compact, peer into it as into a bottomless well, and dab something on the flanges of her nose. "He thinks twenty-five hundred's too low, that's all."

Of course. The son of a bitch. The hypocrite. To each according to his need, share and share alike, the crime of property and all the rest of it. Slogans, and nothing more. When it came down to it, Peletiah Crane was as venal as the next man. Twenty-five hundred an acre for a piece of property that had been worthless since the time of the red Indians, twenty-five hundred an acre for land he'd practically stolen from Depeyster's father for something like a hundredth of that. And still it wasn't enough for him. "What's he want then?"

Marguerite gave him another demure little blink and dropped her voice to soften the blow: "He did mention a figure."

"Yes?"

"Don't get excited now. Remember, we *are* bargaining with him."

"Yeah, yeah: what's he want?"

Her voice was nothing, tiny, a voice speaking from the depths of a cavern: "Thirty-five hundred."

"Thirty-five!" he echoed. "Thirty-five?" He had to turn away from her again, his hands trembling, and take another quick hit of dust. The unfairness of it all! The cheat and deception! He was no megalomaniac, no cattle baron, no land-greedy parvenu: all he wanted was a little piece of his own back.

"We could bargain him down, I'm sure of it." Marguerite's voice rose up in lusty crescendo, rich and strong, invigorated by the prospect of the deal. "All's I need is your go-ahead."

Depeyster wasn't listening. He was reflecting sadly on how far the Van Warts had fallen. His ancestors—powerful, indomitable, hawk-eyed men who tamed the land, shot bears, skinned beavers and brought industry and agronomy to the valley, men who made a *profit,* for Christ's sake—had owned half of Westchester. They'd built something unique, something glorious, and now it was finished. Eaten away, piece by piece, by blind legislators and land-hungry immigrants, by swindlers and bums and Communists. First they started carving it up into towns, then they built their roads and turnpikes, and before anyone could stop them they'd voted away the rights of the property owners and deeded the land to the tenants. *Democracy:* it was a farce. Another brand of communism. Rob the rich, screw the movers and shakers, the pioneers and risk takers and captains of industry, and let all the no-accounts vote themselves a share of somebody else's pie.

And if the politicians weren't bad enough, the crooks and confidence men were right there behind them. His great-grandfather was fleeced in the *Quedah Merchant* scheme, his grandfather lost half his fortune to touts and tipsters and the other half to thespian ladies in bustles and black stockings, and then his own father, a man with developed tastes, fell like a gored toreador among the trampling hoofs of the stockbrokers. Sure, there were ten acres left, there was the house and the business and the other interests too, but it was nothing. A mockery. The smallest shard of what had been. Landless, heirless, Depeyster Van Wart stood there in that venerable parlor, the last offshoot of a family that had ruled all the way to the Connecticut border, frustrated over a matter of fifty acres. Fifty acres. His forefathers wouldn't have pissed on fifty acres.

"What do you say? Should we split the difference with him and come in at three thousand?"

He hadn't forgotten Marguerite—she was there at his back, calculating, homing in, his woeful ally—but he was too caught up in his fugue of bitter reflection to respond. The thing that galled him above all was that the slobbering incontinent senile old pinko bastard had held his subversive rallies on the place—on land that had been in the Van Wart family from time immemorial. He'd sullied it, bloodied it, defiled it. This was land Depeyster's ancestors had fought the Indians for, and old man Crane had turned it into a picnic ground for fellow travelers. All right, yes, Depeyster had got him back for that—got him good, what with organizing the Loyalty rallies and then pressuring the school board till they forced the old fraud into early retirement—but still, even after all this time, the thought of those ragtag niggers and Jews and folksingers trampling over his property made his face go hot with rage.

"Depeyster?"

"Hm?" He turned back around again. Marguerite was leaning so far forward she looked like a sprinter crouching in the blocks.

"What do you think?"

"About what?"

"Splitting the difference. Coming in at three thousand."

What he thought was that he wouldn't pay three thousand an acre for the tip of Mount Ararat when the second flood came, what he thought was that he'd wait till the old bastard kicked off and then go after the half-wit grandson. What he said was: "Forget it."

If Marguerite was about to remonstrate with him, she never got the chance. Because at that moment the door was flung open and what appeared to be a troop of marauding gypsies invaded the cool antique confines of the parlor. Depeyster caught a glimpse of scarves and feathers and headbands, hair matted like a dog's, the stuporous troglodytic expression of the dropout, burnout and drug abuser: his daughter was home. But that wasn't the worst of it. Behind her, slouch-shouldered and gleaming as if he'd been rubbed with chicken fat, was some sort of spic with an earring and the sick dull eyes of a colicky cow, and behind *him,* speak of the devil, was the Crane kid, looking as if he'd just been hoisted up out of the Black Hole of Calcutta. "Oh," Mardi mumbled, on the defensive for once, "I thought you'd . . . uh, be at work."

What could he say? Embarrassed in his own parlor, humiliated in front of Marguerite Mott (she was gazing up at the invaders as if at some esoteric form of animal life her sister might have photographed around the Tanzanian water holes), his very hearth and home transmogrified into a hippie crash pad. He could hear the gossip already: "Yes, his daughter. Trumped up like a dope addict or streetwalker or something. And with this, this—God, I don't know *what* he was, a *Puerto Rican,* I guess—and the Crane boy, the one that dropped out of Cornell? Yes, dope is what I heard it was."

The spic gave him a toothy grin. Mardi, taking the offensive now, shot him a look of the deepest loathing and contempt, and the Crane kid slouched so low his body seemed to collapse in on itself. At that moment, all Depeyster sought was to act casual, to cover himself, brush the whole thing off as if it were just another minor aberration of the environment, on the order of the catalpa tree that dropped its pods in the swimming pool or the mosquitoes that swarmed in great whining clouds over the porch at dusk. But he couldn't. He was too wrought up. First the news about the property, and now this. He looked down and saw that he was waving his hand spasmodically, as if shooing flies. "Go away," he heard himself say. "Scat."

This was what Mardi had been waiting for: an opening, a chink in his armor, a place to drive the spikes in. Glancing over her shoulder for support, she drew herself up, squared her legs and let loose: "So this is what I get, huh? Go away? Like I'm your pet dog or something?" She allowed a fraction of a moment for her rhetoric to hit home, and then delivered the coup de grace: "I do happen to live here, you know. I mean," and here the great black-rimmed eyes filled with tears and her voice thickened with emotion, "I *am* your daughter." Pause. "Even though I know you hate me."

Behind her, the spic had stopped smiling and begun to shuffle his feet; the Crane kid, stricken with a sudden palsy of the facial muscles, was halfway out the door. Depeyster stood there, poised between grief and surcease, a sordid domestic scenario playing itself out on the Persian carpet while Marguerite Mott looked on. Would he blow up in a rage, take his daughter in his arms and comfort her, stalk out of the room and book the next flight for San Juan? He didn't know. His mind had gone numb.

And then suddenly, unaccountably, he found himself thinking of Truman's kid—Walter—and the way he'd looked propped up on his crutches in the office. His hair was longer than Depeyster would have wanted it and there was the first adolescent shadow of a mustache clinging to his upper lip, but he was a solid-looking kid, raw and big-boned, with his father's jaw and cheekbones and pale faded eyes. Mardi had mentioned him that afternoon in the kitchen. She knew him. Tried to shock her father with it, in fact. Well, he wasn't shocked. He took one look at these deadheads she was running around with and wished she *would* take up with somebody like Walter.

"All right," she was saying, and even the smallest trace of dole had faded from her voice; when she repeated the phrase half a beat later, it had all the punch of a war cry.

He didn't respond. Or if he did, it was with that same involuntary shooing motion, his hand working of its own accord. No, he wasn't a bad kid, Walter. A little confused, maybe, but then who wouldn't be, what with his crazy mother starving herself to death and his father running off with his tail between his legs—worse, running off and leaving him to grow up with a bunch of bleeding hearts and fellow travelers and the like. It was criminal. The kid had heard one side of the story all his life—the wrong side, the twisted, lying and perverted side. It was just the beginning of course, a shot in the dark, one voice raised against a howling multitude, but Depeyster had tried to straighten him out on a few things that afternoon. Beginning with his father.

Patriot, Walter had spat. What do you mean he was a patriot?

I mean he loved his country, Walter, and he fought for it too—in France and Germany, and right here in Peterskill. Tenting his fingers, Depeyster had sunk back in his chair, watching Walter's eyes. There was something there—the anger, yes, the confusion and the hurt—but something else too: Walter *wanted* to believe him. For Depeyster it was a revelation. If the child rejected the parent, if Mardi paraded around like a whore and espoused her dime-store radicalism at the dinner table to spit in her father's eye and undermine everything the community held sacred, then here was a kid who was ready to turn the other way. His parents—foster parents: Jews, Communists, the worst—had fed him hate and lies and their vicious propaganda all his life till he was ready to choke on it. He was clay. Clay to be molded.

You think the Peterskill incidents were nothing? Depeyster said. Walter just stared at him. Well, look what your Communists did four years later with the A-bomb secrets. A patriot fights that kind of business, Walter, fights it with all his heart. And that's why I say your father was a patriot.

Walter shifted his weight, leaned forward on his crutches. Yeah? And do patriots sell out their friends, their wife, their son?

Yes, Depeyster wanted to say, *if they have to.* But then he glanced down at the shiny new boot on Walter's right foot and reminded himself to go easy. Look, Walter, he said, changing tack, you don't seem to be following me. Communism doesn't work, it's as simple as that. Look at Russia today. China. Vietnam. The whole damned Iron Curtain. You want to live like that?

Walter shook his head. But that's not the point, he said.

No, of course it wasn't, but it was true, and Depeyster opened up on him anyway. He cited the Pilgrims, Brook Farm and hippie communes, deplored the fate of the kulaks, railed against the Viet Cong and pointed a finger at the face of the Worldwide Communist Conspiracy, but Walter refused to budge. Worse, he kept bringing the dialogue around to that single sore point that lay between them like a bloody stick. Whether or not communism worked wasn't the question, Walter kept insisting—the question was what had gone down on Peletiah Crane's property on that hot August evening in 1949. Depeyster dodged around the issue—not yet, not yet—vehemently asserting that he was within his rights, that everything he'd done he would do again. He looked into Walter's face and saw Truman, and at that moment he understood that he was no longer defending the vanished father—Truman was mad, he was indefensible—no: he was defending himself.

He wanted to give it to him straight, wanted to tell him just how far Morton Blum and Sasha Freeman had gone to provoke the confrontation—how he himself had been duped into responding when it would have been far better to leave it alone—wanted to ask him if he really thought a peaceful rally was worth as much to the cause as a loud and dirty riot with its front-page photographs of bloodied women, screaming children and colored men beaten till they looked like prizefighters on the losing end of a unanimous decision. But he held back. All that was for the next lesson.

Look, Depeyster had said finally, I know how you feel. I admit your father was wrong to go off and desert his family like that—and I admit he had his crazy streak too—but what he did was in the name of freedom and justice. He sacrificed himself, Walter—he was a martyr. Be proud.

But what, Walter gasped, what was it? What *did* he do?

Depeyster dropped his eyes to slip open the drawer and fortify himself with a pinch of dust, but thought better of it. He looked up before he answered. He was with us, Walter, he said, slamming the drawer home. He was with us all along.

But then the image of Walter was gone and Depeyster found himself staring into the null faces of the subversives and draft dodgers his daughter had brought home with her. Human garbage, and they were here in his house, under his roof; for all Marguerite knew, he approved of them, liked them, shared their dope and bean sprout sandwiches. "Get out," he repeated.

Through the wild frizzed fluff of her hair, Mardi was giving him a half-hateful, half-frightened look. Perhaps he'd gone too far. Yes: he could see it in her eyes. He wanted to stop himself, soften the blow, but he couldn't.

"All right," she shouted for the third time, "all right," for the fourth, "I'm leaving." There was a scurry in the hallway, the spic kid ducking out of her way, Tom Crane's hands fluttering like flushed quail, the frame-wrenching boom of the door, and then they were gone.

Depeyster glanced at Marguerite. She'd gone pale beneath the ruddy film of her makeup, her pupils were dilated and the tip of her tongue was caught between her lips. She looked as if she'd awakened from a trance. "I, um," she murmured, gathering up her things, rustling papers, reaching for her coat, "I have to be going. Appointments, appointments."

At the door, he tried to apologize for his daughter, but she waved him off. "Three thousand," she said, brightening just a bit. "You think about it."

It was late in the afternoon, and he was out back, spading up the earth around his roses, when he thought of Joanna. He'd been in the house just a moment earlier, looking for a fishing hat to keep the sun out of his eyes, and noted absently that Lula had set but a single place at the dining room table. Now, as the rich black loam of the rose bed turned beneath his spade, that solitary place setting loomed up in his mind till he saw not roots and soil but the pattern of the china, the cut of the crystal, the crease of napkin and glint of silver. It was puzzling. Mardi wouldn't be eating—probably wouldn't be home at all after the scene in the parlor—but where was Joanna? She'd left the previous morning for the Shawangunk reservation, the station wagon packed to the roof with the cast-off pedal pushers, clam-diggers and toreador pants she'd collected door to door in her biannual trouser drive. Which meant that she would spend the night at the Hiawatha Motel, as usual, and be home for dinner in the evening. As usual. And yet he was sure he'd seen just the one place.

It was something to think about as he bent to the rose bushes, mounding the earth in little pyramids at the base of the canes and tamping it down deep over the roots. He was in the act of exhuming the previous year's mulch from the trough around the Helen Traubels, when a startling thought crept into his head: she'd had an accident, that's what it was. *The* accident. The one he'd always pictured. Yawing over its oppressed springs, the station wagon had veered off one of the tricky bends of Route 17 and wound up on its roof in the icy pellucid waters of the Beaverkill; a semi had jackknifed, crushing the car like an aluminum can: Joanna was gone. Sarabande, Iceberg, Olé: he could already smell the blossoms. But no. If it were anything serious—anything fatal—Lula would have let him know.

Roses. Here it was mid-October already and he was just now getting around to preparing the beds for the hard frost to come. Not that he'd been neglecting them—he exulted in his roses, prided himself in them, wouldn't let the gardener near them—it was just that September had been glorious—Indian summer to the hilt—and he'd found himself out on the *Catherine Depeyster* nearly every afternoon. Or on the links. No, she'd had a flat, that's what it was. The engine had seized, the fan belt disintegrated, she was stuck in Olean, Elmira, Endicott. He stood, knocked the dirt from his work gloves. Little Darling, Blaze, Mister Lincoln, Saratoga: the very names gave him satisfaction. He'd finish up tomorrow, wrap the canes in burlap, manure them. But where was she? Maybe she'd left him. Vanished. Run off. As he strode up the hill to the house, a guilty little fantasy overtook him for just a moment—she was naked, that big freckle-faced dormmate of Mardi's, hovering over him and bucking like a wild animal, and he could feel his seed taking hold, could see them—his sons—marching from her hot and fertile young womb as from the mouth of some ancient cave.

Lula's face dropped when he mentioned the place setting. "Oh my blessed Jesus, it just slipped my mind." The kitchen, with its concessions to modernity—dishwasher, electric range, frost-free refrigerator—gleamed behind her like something out of a commercial for the newest wonder cleaner. She'd been pounding veal at the kitchen table when he stepped into the room. "Oh Jesus, Jesus, Jesus," she wailed, and you might have thought she'd lost her entire family in a train wreck, "I just can't figure what's come over me."

Depeyster leaned back against the radiant counter and folded his arms.

"It was one o'clock this afternoon she called. Something's come up up there, something about a protest march—here, I've got it written down." She heaved herself up from the table, a heavy woman, solid as the oaks along the drive, and snatched a scrap of paper from beneath the phone. "Here it is," she gasped, breathing hard from the effort, " 'Six Tribes Against the War.' She says not to expect her till tomorrow this time."

Six Tribes Against the War: what a joke. He let the words sit on his tongue a moment before repeating them in a tone of bitter contempt. Six Tribes Against the War. He could picture them—a bunch of unemployed half-looped overfed Indians dressed in toreador pants and carrying placards, his wife out front in curlers and beaded moccasins, marching up and down in front of the feed store in Jamestown. It would almost be funny if they weren't doing the work of the Viet Cong. And Joanna. The relief business was bad enough, but this—this was demeaning. His own wife involved in a demonstration. What next?

"Piccata tonight," Lula murmured, shuffling back to her veal.

"And Mardi?" he asked after a moment.

Lula just shrugged.

He stood there a moment longer, listening to the refrigerator start up with a wheeze and gazing out on that single accusatory plate at the dining room table. On the back wall, above the sideboard, hung a murky oil of Stephanus Van Wart, heir to the patroon and first lord of Van Wart Manor, the man who'd doubled and trebled the original holdings and then doubled and trebled them again until he owned every creek and ridge, every fern, every deer and turkey and toad and thistle between the flat gray Hudson and the Connecticut border. Depeyster glanced up at the proud smirking eyes of his ancestor and found that he'd lost his appetite. "Don't bother, Lula," he said. "I'll eat out."

When Joanna finally did get home the following evening, it was late—past ten—and Depeyster was sitting before a fire in the parlor, half-heartedly poking through a biography of General Israel Putnam, the man who'd closed his ears to all appeals for clemency and hanged Edmund Palmer for a spy on Gallows Hill in August of 1777. For the second night running, the heir to Van Wart Manor had eaten a solitary meal in a clean, well-lighted booth at the Peterskill diner, and for the second night running, he was afflicted with indigestion. He was feeling pretty low in any case—frustrated over the land business, incensed with his daughter (who still hadn't deigned to return), deeply mortified by the thought of his wife's making a public spectacle of herself, even if it was in the remotest hinterlands. And so, as he turned at the sound of the latch to confront the spectacle of his tardy wife in her ridiculous Indian costume, he gave himself over to the huffings and puffings of a fine cleansing cathartic rage. "Where the hell have you been?" he demanded, leaping to his feet and flinging the book to the floor.

Joanna was wearing the moccasins and headband she'd affected since first taking up the gauntlet in the name of Indian relief. But now, for some unfathomable reason, she'd got herself up in a ragged deerskin dress and leggings as well. The dress looked like something you'd use on the car after a heavy rain.

"No, don't tell me—it was a costume party, right? Or is this what the fashionable demonstrator is wearing these days?" The diner's stuffed peppers shot up his windpipe to immolate the cavity beneath his breastbone. He suppressed a belch.

Joanna said nothing. There was a peculiar look in her eyes, a look he recognized from the distant past. It was the look she used to give him when they were dating, when they were newlyweds, when they were a fecund young couple with a healthy fat-faced blossoming little daughter. She crossed the room to him, and he noticed that her hair was braided, Indian-fashion, with strips of birch bark. And then her hands were on his shoulders—he could smell her, woodsmoke, wild mint, a certain primordial musk of the outdoors that made his knees go weak—and she was asking him, in a lascivious whisper, if he'd missed her.

Missed her? She was pulling him toward her, hanging from his neck like a schoolgirl, pressing her lips with their faintest taste of wild onion and rose hips to his. Missed her? They hadn't had sex in fifteen years and she was asking him if he'd missed her?

Fifteen years. Over that period, sex for Depeyster had been reduced to a sad series of couplings, a spilling of seed in the desert, a succession of weekends with the Miss Egthuysens of the world or with one or another of the aggressive sun-tanned lionesses he ran into at the country club bar. But never with Joanna, never with his wife. All that had ended when she'd gathered up his lotions and unguents and aphrodisiacs and thrown them in his face, when she'd torn up his love manuals and shredded his ovulation schedules, when she'd asked him if he thought she was a prize bitch for breeding and nothing more. Mardi had been five or six at the time, entering kindergarten—or was it first grade? They'd slept in separate rooms ever since.

And now here she was, probing his palate with her tongue, pushing him back on the couch, pulling him to the floor and the rug before the fire. Was she drunk? he thought vaguely as she tugged at his trousers. She lifted her dress and he saw with a thrill that she wasn't wearing anything underneath, her breasts high and hard, not a flap or wrinkle on her, forty-three years old and supple as a coed. As she sank into him he felt transported, grateful, hopeful, his fantasy of the big freckled girl realized here on the carpet in the parlor with his own wife, and he closed his eyes and concentrated on the heir to come. Oh yes, there'd be an heir. There had to be. He'd waited so long and now . . . it was like something out of a fairy tale, The Patient Woodcutter, Sleeping Beauty awakened with a kiss. He gave himself over to the rhythm of it.

For her part, Joanna was doing what she had to do. Not that there wasn't a certain nostalgic feel to the whole exercise, not that it was particularly repulsive or anything like that. She supposed she loved him, in a way, this bloodless man, her husband. He was all right—she couldn't imagine being married to anyone else—it was just that he didn't know how to stir her, to move her in her deepest self, didn't know or care about love, romance, passion. He was cold, cold as something you'd find crawling up the riverbed waving its claws. He didn't want to make love, didn't even want to fuck—he wanted to procreate.

Well, all right. She was no Molly Bloom, but for fifteen years she'd found her romance elsewhere. And now it was necessary to do this. With her husband. Her lawful partner. Presumptive father of the child she would bear, wanted to bear.

For she hadn't been with Indians the past two days, hadn't been to the demonstration, hadn't in fact left Peterskill. Indians, no. But *an* Indian, *one* Indian, yes.

The Dunderberg Imp

IT WAS no day for a pleasure cruise. The wind was howling down out of the Canadian wilds, it was cold enough to turn back the Vikings and the sky looked dead, caught up on the mountains like a skin stretched out to dry. Walter couldn't feel his toes, and when he tried to relight the joint pinched in a vice grip between his thumb and forefinger, a sudden gust snuffed out the match. Three times in a row. Finally he gave up and flicked the thing into the water. He couldn't believe it. Halloween, and already it was cold as December.

Walter turned up the collar of his denim jacket and watched a couple of ducks huddling in the lee of the boat ramp. All around him, on trailers, on cement blocks, propped up on the cracked concrete as if awaiting a second flood, were boats. Ketches, schooners, catboats and runabouts, yawls and yachts and catamarans. And then there were the boats that would never see the water again, ancient hulks rusted through in every bolt, leprous with rot, splintered and bleached and listing on their bows as if they'd been thrown ashore in a hurricane. This was the Peterskill Marina. Three blocks from Depeyster Manufacturing and just across the tracks from the crapped-over train station and the abandoned factories made of brick so old it was the color of mud. Walter was here, at two o'clock in the afternoon, on Halloween, waiting for Mardi. What could be better? she'd said when she called. I mean, going out to the ghost ships on Halloween. Neat, huh?

Neat. That was the word she'd used. Walter spat in the water and then turned to look over his shoulder for her. There were half a dozen cars in the parking lot, but none of them seemed to contain Mardi. It was funny. Here he was going out sailing with her on a day that was like a blanket for a tombstone, and he didn't even know what kind of car she drove. He looked beyond the parking lot to the string of rust-streaked boxcars that stretched away from the station and around a corner toward the mouth of Van Wart Creek, and then up at the hills of Peterskill, a dependency of rooftops among the big ascending hummocks of trees. In the foreground, huddled in the lee of some seagoing monster with gleaming rails and curtains hung in the windows, stood his motorcycle, freshly repainted and with a new footpeg and throttle. The helmet, the one Jessica had given him, was hooked over the handlebar, and even at this distance he could make out the dull blotches where he'd scratched off the daisy decals with his penknife.

She hadn't liked it, this defacing of his birthday present, but he explained to her that daisy decals just didn't fit his image. He was no flower child—he was harder than that, colder, the nihilist and existential hero still. Then he grinned, as if to say I'm only joking, and she grinned back.

Jessica. She was at work now. His wife, who'd forgone Scripps, Miami, N.Y.U. and Mayaguez for him, was at work, counting fish larvae preserved in trays of formalin. Tom Crane had gotten her the job. Over at the nuclear power plant, the stacks and domes of which rose up from the near shoreline like the minarets and cupolas of some fantastic high-tech mosque. The larva count was part of an environmental impact study Con Ed was funding to atone for the sin of sucking up great stinking mounds of fish in their intake pipes. An old lab mate of Tom's had got him a job piloting a boat for the project two nights a week, and when a position came open, Tom thought of Jessica. She was in there now. Sniffing formalin, her eyes wet from the fumes of it.

Walter himself was out of work. Not that he didn't want to work—eventually, maybe, if the right thing came along. He just didn't feature standing up all day at a greasy whining lathe, turning out those little winged machine parts that had no use under the sun as far as he could figure (unless, as rumor had it, they were used in fragmentation bombs to grind up little children in places with names like

Duk Foo and Bu Wop). Or so he told Hesh and Lola. What he didn't tell them was that Van Wart had offered him a desk job. On the spot. No questions asked.

I like you, you know that? Van Wart had said that afternoon in the office. He'd skirted the issue of the riots for half an hour, advised Walter to read his history and assured him that wherever his father was—alive or dead—he should be proud of him. Walter, who'd taken a seat somewhere between the persecution of the kulaks and the fall of Chiang Kai-shek, had just risen to go when Van Wart made his declaration of esteem. You impress me, Van Wart said. You've got a good mind. Maybe we don't see eye to eye on politics, but that's neither here nor there. He was standing now too, clasping his hands and beaming like a haberdasher. What I'm trying to say is you've got a degree and I've got an opening for an assistant manager, $11,000 a year and all the benefits. And you can stay off that leg of yours. What do you say?

No, Walter had said, almost as a reflex, no thanks, already seeing himself in dress shirt and tie, ensconced behind a desk with the elusive Miss Egthuysen at his beck and call, Doug and all the rest of the peons cut down in a single stroke, already picturing the new Triumph, racing green, wire wheels, zero to fifty in 6.9 seconds . . . but work for Van Wart? It was inconceivable. (Never mind that he'd been doing just that for the past two and a half months—he'd been laboring in ignorance.) No, he told him. He appreciated the offer, but what with the shock of his accident and all he needed some time to recuperate before he could take a step like that.

Later, thinking it over, he wasn't sure why he'd backed off. Eleven thousand dollars was a lot of money, and Van Wart, despite his preaching, his air of condescension and his Bircherisms, despite the hatred he inspired in Tom Crane's grandfather, in Hesh and Lola and all the rest, really wasn't half bad. No ogre, certainly. No mindless, brick-throwing racist. There was a certain style about him, a polish and a toughness that made Hesh seem crude by comparison. And he believed in what he said, the conviction set deep in his eyes—too deep for lies. In fact, by the end of their little chat, Walter had begun to soften toward him. Even more: he'd begun, in an odd and somehow disturbing way, to like him.

Walter was thinking about all this, and thinking too about the consummate weirdness of the situation—married a month, and here he was sneaking down to the marina for an assignation with the ex-ogre's daughter—when he felt a tap on his shoulder. It was Mardi. In watch cap and peacoat, in deck shoes and jeans and black leather gloves, looking as if she'd just stepped off a freighter with the rest of the merchant marine. Except for her eyes. Her eyes were pinned to her head, hard and cold as marbles, the pupils shrunk to specks. "Hi," she said in a breathy voice, and then she kissed him. In greeting. But it was more than a peck on the cheek—it was a full-on osculation with a taste of her tongue in it. Walter didn't know what to do, so he kissed her back.

"All set?" she said, grinning up at him.

"Yeah," Walter said, rocking back on his good leg. "I mean, I guess so." He gestured toward the river, the sky. "You sure you want to go through with this?"

He'd seen Mardi only once since the wedding. He and Jessica and Tom Crane were sitting around the Elbow one night about two weeks back, listening to the jukebox and shooting pool, when she walked in the door with Hector. The game was elimination, it was Walter's shot, and he was keying in on Jessica's last ball while she made wisecracks, nudged the cue stick from behind and generally tried to distract, disorient and disarm him. Mardi was wearing a tie-dyed T-shirt, no sleeves, no brassiere. Walter froze. But Tom Crane, all elbows and flapping feet, with his ratty braid jogging in the breeze like the knot of hair over a horse's ass, rushed up to embrace her, pump Hector's hand in a power-to-the-people handshake and drag them over to the table. Walter exchanged greetings with Hector, nodded at Mardi and missed his shot.

Later, after a couple of pitchers of beer, more pool, innumerable treks across the expanse of dirty sawdust that covered the floor like bonemeal to urinate in the reeking rest rooms and share a surreptitious hit of whatever it was Hector had stuffed into the bowl of his pipe, everyone was feeling pretty relaxed. Jessica got up from the table and excused herself. "The ladies'," she slurred, lurching across the room like one of the wounded.

Tom had vanished and Hector was up at the bar ordering shots of tequila all around. The table, which had suddenly grown small, was littered with peanut shells, ashes, butts, plates and bottles and glasses. Walter affixed a cautious little smile to his lips. Mardi smiled back. And then, out of nowhere, she asked Walter if he was still serious about the ghost ships—she'd give him a call if he was, no problem. Walter didn't answer. Instead he posed a question of his own. "What was that business at the wedding?" he asked, trying to keep his voice steady. "You know what I mean. About my foot. I didn't like that."

She was silent a moment, and then she gave him a smile that would have melted the polar ice caps. "Don't take it so seriously, Walter," she said, peering into her drink, "I just like to shock people, that's all—see how they'll react. You know: *épater les bourgeois.*" Walter didn't know. He'd failed French.

She looked at him and laughed. "Come on, it was a joke, that's all. I'm really not as wild as I make out. Really." And then she leaned forward. "The thing I want to know is are you going with me or not?"

And now, here at the marina, hemmed in by spars and halyards and anchor chains, and breathing the very scent of the ghost of his grandfather, he was up against the wall yet again. "I don't believe you," Mardi said, and her face went numb for a moment. "Afraid of a little spray or what?" Walter shrugged, as if to say he was afraid of nothing—not cold, nor sleet, nor shadows that flit maliciously across an open roadway in the early hours of the morning. "Good," she said, grinning so wide he could see the glint of gold in her back teeth, and then he was following her through the boatyard to the dock and the slips at the far end of it.

There were only two boats in the water. The *Catherine Depeyster,* a thirty-two-foot cruising sloop with auxiliary engine and woodwork varnished to a high gleam, stood alone among the deserted slips. The other boat, a peeling, nondescript, wide-bottomed thing with a broken mast and dry rot to the water line, lay at anchor beyond it, looking as if it had been dredged up from the bottom the week before. Walter was about to join Mardi aboard the *Catherine Depeyster*—she was already fumbling through the locker for foul-weather gear—when he saw a puff of smoke rise from the stovepipe of the blistered hulk. At first he couldn't believe his eyes. But then, unmistakably, a thin gray column of smoke began to issue from the blackened pipe. He was stunned. Somebody was actually living aboard that thing, some crazed river rat who'd wake one morning to find himself under twelve feet of water. It had to be a joke. But no, the smoke was coming steadily now, flattened by the wind and blown back to him with the rich, gut-clenching scent of bacon on it. "Christ," he said, turning to Mardi, "I can't believe it."

"Can't believe what?" she said, handing him a black sou'wester as he stepped aboard.

"Over there. That piece of shit, that floating outhouse. There's somebody living on it."

"You mean Jeremy," she said.

The cold stabbed at his ears. He looked from the hulk to Mardi and back again. The wind was slowly swinging the boat around on its anchor, bringing its stern into his line of vision. "Jeremy?" he repeated, never taking his eyes from the boat.

He heard Mardi at his back. She was saying that Jeremy had been around all summer, that he fished and did odd jobs and helped out at the marina. He was a gypsy or Indian or something, and he was all right for an old guy. Walter heard her as from a great distance, the words echoing in his head as he watched the ship swing around and reveal its name, in chipped and faded letters. He felt odd all of a sudden, felt the grip of history like a noose around his neck and he didn't know why. The ship's name was the *Kitchawank*.

All right: it was cold. But once they'd left the marina and hoisted sail, once they'd felt the pulse of the river under their feet and the first icy slap of spray in their faces, it no longer mattered. Mardi, the watch cap pulled down to her eyebrows, was at the tiller, drinking coffee from a thermos and mugging as if it were June, and Walter, in rubber boots, pants and slicker, was hiking out over the rail like a kid with his first Sunfish. He hadn't been sailing since his grandfather died, hadn't even been out on the river for as long as he could remember. It awakened his blood, flooded him with memories: it was like coming home. The mountains may have been dwarfs by the standards of the Alps or Rockies—Dunderberg and Anthony's Nose were both under a thousand feet—but from here, on the water, they rose up like a dream of mountains, tall, massive and forbidding. Dead ahead lay Dunderberg, sloping back from the water like a sleeping giant, the ghost fleet nestled at its foot. To the south was Indian Point, with its power plants and estuarine biologists, with Jessica and her pickled fish; to the north, opening up like a shadowy mouth, was the entrance to the Highlands, where all the great mountains—Taurus, Storm King, Breakneck and Crow's Nest—stepped down to wade in the river.

This was the province of the Dunderberg Imp, the capricious gnome in trunk hose and sugarloaf hat who ruled the river through its most treacherous reaches, from Dunderberg to Storm King. It was he who brewed up squalls and flung thunderbolts down on the unsuspecting sloop captains of old, he who made men look foolish and strewed temptation in their paths, he who presided over Kidd's treasure and ruined any ship that came near. It was he who'd popped all the corks on Stuyvesant's kegs as old Silver Peg sailed upriver to chastise the Mohicans, he who'd lifted the nightcap from the inviolable pate of Dominie Van Schaik's wife and deposited it on the steeple of the Esopus church, forty miles distant. His laugh—the wild stuttering whinny of the deranged and irresponsible—could be heard over the keen of the wind, and his diminutive hat could be found perched placidly atop the mainmast during the fiercest gale. Not even the most hardened sea dog would dream of rounding Kidd's Point without first tacking a horseshoe to the mast and making an offering of Barbados rum to the Heer of the Dunderberg.

Or so the legend went. Walter knew it well. Knew it as he knew the story of every witch, goblin, *pukwidjinny* and wailing woman that haunted the Hudson Valley. His grandmother had seen to that. But if he'd believed it once, if there'd been a spark of the old joy in the irrational left in him, of the child who'd sat over a liverwurst sandwich and thrilled to the story of Minewa's betrayal or the legend of the headless Hessian of Sleepy Hollow, then Philosophy 451, Contemporary Philosophy with Emphasis on Death Obsession and Existentialist Thought, had extinguished it and left only the ash of cynicism behind.

Still, as the *Catherine Depeyster* cut for the base of the black mountain under a sky that was blacker still, he couldn't help thinking of the twisted little Heer of the Dunderberg. What a concept. It wasn't lousy seamanship or drunkenness or fog that had been scuttling ships in the Highlands since the time of Pieter Minuit and Wouter the Doubter, but the malicious forces of the supernatural as embodied in a leering little homunculus—the Heer of the Dunderberg, in baggy pantaloons and buckled shoes—who lived only to drive boats upon the rocks. Walter remembered his grandfather pouring two cups of rye and ginger every time he rounded Kidd's Point: one for the belly and one for the river. What's that for? Walter, twelve years old and wise in the ways of the world, had asked one day. For the Heer, his hairy grandfather had replied, smacking his lips. For luck. And then Walter, not daring to question the humorless old man, had challenged the Imp under his breath. Kill us, he whispered. Come on: I dare you. Strike us with lightning. Overturn the boat. I dare you.

The Imp had been silent that day. The sun lingered in the sky, the nets were full, they had Coke and crab cakes for dinner. Of course, the next time Walter rounded the point and rode up through the gorge of the mountains with his grandfather, thinking of baseball or a new fly rod or the way Susie Cats' pedal pushers swelled at the intersection of her thighs, the sky suddenly went dark, the wind howled down off the mountains and the engine coughed, sputtered and went dead. What the—? his grandfather had snorted, rising up over his belly to jerk the starter cord in an automatic rage. They'd just skirted West Point and entered Martyr's Reach, the most formidable of the fourteen reaches that sectioned the river from New York to Albany, a stretch of water known to generations of sailors for its treacherous winds, unpredictable currents and unforgiving shores. Just below them, two hundred and thirty feet down, lay World's End, the graveyard for sloops and steamers and cabin cruisers alike, where rotting spars groaned in a current that was like the wind and from which no body had ever been recovered, deepest hole in a river that rarely ran more than a hundred feet deep. It was here that the *Neptune* capsized in 1824, with the loss of thirty-five passengers, and here too that Captain Benjamin Hunt of the *James Coats* met his maker when the mainsheet looped around his neck in a sudden gust and severed his head. In wild weather, you could still hear his startled cry, and then, right on its heels, the chilling splash of the trunkless head. Or so the story went.

Walter's grandfather didn't like it a bit. He cursed and fiddled over the motor while the ebbing tide carried them downriver and the first few drops of rain began to pucker the surface. Take the oars! he'd roared, and Walter had obeyed without hesitation. He was scared. He'd never seen the daylight so dark. Swing it around and head for home, his grandfather snarled. Row! Walter rowed, rowed till his arms went numb and his back felt as if someone had driven hot splinters into it, but to no avail. The rain caught them just below West Point. But it wasn't just rain, it was hail too. And thunder that reverberated in the basin of the mountains like a war at sea. They wound up sitting at anchor beneath an overhang on the west bank, huddled and shivering, not daring to venture out on the open water for fear of the lightning that tore the sky apart over their heads. Two weeks later, Walter's grandfather had his stroke and toppled into the bait pen.

Now, as the mountain loomed above them, Walter pushed himself up and made his way back to where Mardi sat at the tiller.

"Having a good time?" she shouted over the wind.

He just grinned in response, rocking with the boat, and then settled down beside her and helped himself to a cup of coffee from the thermos. The coffee was good. Hot and black and tasting of Depeyster Van Wart's ten-year-old cognac. "Seen the Imp?" he said.

"Who?"

"You know, the little guy in the high hat and buckled shoes that runs around sitting on people's masts and whipping up storms and whatnot."

Mardi gave him a long slow look and a wet-lipped smile that took a moment to spread across her face. She looked good, with the cap pulled down low like that and her hair fanned out behind her in the wind. Real good. She put her free arm through his and drew him closer. "What've you been smoking?" she said.

It was Halloween, the night the dead rise from their graves and people hide behind masks, Halloween, and getting dark. Walter stood on the deck of the *Catherine Depeyster* and gazed up at the ranks of mothballed ships that rose above him on either side in great depthless fields of shadow. This time he hadn't tried to hoist himself up the anchor chain of the U.S.S. *Anima,* nor of any of the other ships either.

This time he'd been content merely to shove his hands deep in his pockets and stare up at them.

Mardi was in the cabin, sipping cognac and warming herself over the electric space heater. She'd furled the sails and started up the engine when they got in close, afraid the wind would push her into one of the big ships. Then, when they'd maneuvered their way through the picket of steel monsters and anchored amongst them, she picked up the thermos and headed for the cabin. "Come on," she said, "let's get in out of this wind," but Walter wasn't moving. Not yet, anyway. He was thinking of Jessica and feeling the stab of guilt and betrayal, knowing full well what was going to happen once he got into that cabin with Mardi. Oh, he could delay it, exercise his will, stand out here in the wind and gawk up at the ships as if they meant anything at all to him, but eventually he would follow her into the cabin. It was inevitable. Preordained. A role in a play he'd been rehearsing all his life. This was why he'd come out to the ghost ships—this, and nothing more. "Come on," she repeated, and her voice dropped to a purr.

"In a minute," he said.

The cabin door clicked shut behind him, and he never turned his head. This ship that hung over him, with its rusted anchor chain and hull streaked with bird crap, had suddenly become fascinating, riveting, a thing rare and unique in the world. He was thinking nothing. The wind bit at him. He counted off thirty seconds and was about to turn around and submit himself to the inevitable, when something—a sudden displacement of shadow, a furtive movement—caught his eye. Up there. High against the rail of the near ship.

It was almost dark. He couldn't be sure. But yes, there it was again: something was roaming around up there. A bird? A rat? He tried to keep his eyes fixed on the spot, but at some point he must have blinked involuntarily—because the next thing he knew there was an object perched on the rail, where no object had been a fraction of a second earlier. From down here, beneath the great soaring wall of the ship, it appeared to be a hat—wide of brim, high of crown, and of a fashion that had its day centuries ago, a hat the pilgrims might have worn, or Rembrandt himself. It was at that moment, as Walter stood puzzling over this shadowy apparition, that an odd flatulent sound began to insinuate itself in the niche between the slosh of the waves and the moan of the wind, a sound that brought back memories of elementary school, of playgrounds and ballfields: someone was razzing him.

Walter looked to his right, and then to his left. He looked behind him, above him, he peered over the rail, tore open the locker, searched the sky—all to no avail. The sound seemed to be coming from everywhere, from nowhere, caught up in the very woof of the air itself. The hat was still perched atop the rail of the big rotting merchantman before him, and Mardi—he could see her through the little rectangular windows—was still ensconced in the cabin. The razzing grew louder, faded, pulsed back again, and Walter began to feel an odd sensation creeping up on him, déjà vu, a sensation grown old since the day of his accident.

Sure enough, when he looked up again, the rail of the ship was crowded with ragged figures—bums, the bums he'd seen the night of the accident—each with his fingers to his nose and a vibrating tongue between his lips. And there, in the middle of them, sat their ringleader—the little guy in baggy trousers and work boots his father had called Piet. Piet's face was expressionless—as stolid as an executioner's—and the antiquated hat was now sitting atop his head like an overturned milk can. As Walter focused on him, he saw the tip of the little man's tongue emerge from between his tightly compressed lips to augment the mocking chorus with its own feathery but distinctive raspberry.

So here he was, Walter the empiricist, standing on the deck of a cruising sloop in the middle of the darkling Hudson on the eve of Allhallows, confronting a mob of jeering phantoms, and not knowing what to do next. He was seeing things. There was something the matter with him. He'd consult a shrink, have his head bandaged—anything. But for now he could think of only one thing to do, the same thing he'd done when he'd been razzed in junior high: he gave them the finger, one and all. With both hands. And he cursed them too, cursed them in a ragged raging high-pitched tone till he began to grow hoarse, his extended fingers digging at the air and feet dancing in furious rapture.

All very well and fine. But they were gone. He was cursing a deserted ship, cursing empty decks and berths unslept in for twenty years or more, cursing steel. The razzing had faded away to nothing and the only sound he could hear now was the whisper of a human voice at his back. Mardi's voice. He turned around and there she was, standing at the cabin door. The door was open, and she was naked. He saw her breasts—silken, pouting, the breasts he remembered from the night of his collision with history. He saw her navel and the fascinating swatch of hair below it, saw her feet, calves, the swell of her thighs, saw the beckoning glow of the electric coil in the darkened cabin behind her. "Walter, what are you doing?" she said in a voice that rubbed at his skin. "Don't you know I've been waiting for you?"

The blood shot from his head to his groin.

"Come on in and get warm," she whispered.

It was past seven when the *Catherine Depeyster* motored into the slip at the marina. Walter was late. He was supposed to have been at the Elbow by six-thirty, dressed in costume, to meet Jessica and Tom Crane. They were going to have a few drinks, and then go out to a party in the Colony. But Walter was late. He'd been out in the middle of the river, fucking Mardi Van Wart. The first time—there at the cabin door—he'd practically tackled her, grabbing for flesh like a satyr, a rapist, all his demons concentrated in the slot between her legs. The second time was slow, soft, it was making love. She stroked him, ran her tongue across his chest, breathed in his ear. He stroked her in return, lingered over her nipples, lifted her atop him—he even, for moments at a time, forgot about the blasted torn stump of his leg and the inert lump of plastic that terminated it. Now, as he helped her secure the boat, he didn't know what he felt. Guilt, for one thing. Guilt, and an overwhelming desire to shake hands, peck her cheek or whatever, and disappear. She'd said she was going to a party up in Poughkeepsie and that he was welcome to come along; he'd stammered that he was meeting Jessica and Tom down at the Elbow.

He watched her face as she tied off the lines and gathered up her things. It was noncommittal. He was thinking about his bike, a quick exit, thinking about what kind of excuse he was going to run Jessica and wondering what he could possibly do in the next five minutes about a costume.

Mardi straightened up and wiped her hands on the peacoat.

"Hey," she said, and her voice was husky, choked to a whisper. "It was fun. Want to do it again, sometime?"

He was about to say yes, no, maybe, when suddenly the image of the ghost ship rose up before him and he felt as if his leg—the good one—was about to buckle and drop him to the hard cold planks of the dock. He was going crazy, that's what it was. Seeing things. Hallucinating like some shit-flinger up at Matteawan.

"Hm?" she said, and she reached for his arm and leaned into him. "You had a good time, didn't you?"

It was then that he became aware of a figure standing in the shadows at the far end of the dock. He thought of muggers, trick or treaters, he thought of Jessica, he thought of his father. "Hello?" he called. "Is someone there?"

The light was bad, sky dark, a single streetlamp illuminating the dead geometry of masts and cranes at the far end of the boat yard. Walter felt Mardi go tense beside him. "Who's there?" she demanded.

A man emerged from the shadows and moved toward them, the slats of the dock groaning under his footsteps. He was big, his shoulders like something hammered on as an afterthought, he wore a flannel shirt open to the navel despite the cold, and his graying hair trailed down his back in a thick twisted coil. Walter guessed he must have been fifty-five, sixty. "That you, Mardi?" the man asked.

She dropped Walter's arm. "Jesus, Jeremy, you scared the shit out of us."

He'd reached them now, and stood grinning before them. His two front teeth were outlined in gold, and he wore a bone necklace from which a single white feather dangled. "Boo," he said in a ruined, phlegmy voice. "Trick or treat."

Mardi was grinning now too, but Walter was glum. Whatever was about to happen, he didn't want any part of it. He glanced longingly at his motorcycle, then turned back to the stranger. "I'll take the treat," Mardi said.

"Looks like you already got it," the man said, giving Walter a sick grin.

"Oh," she said, taking Walter's arm again, "oh, yeah," and she made as if to slap her brow for forgetfulness. "This is my friend—"

But the Indian—that's what he was, Walter realized with a jolt—

the Indian cut her off. "I know you," he said, searching Walter's eyes.

Walter had never laid eyes on him before. He felt his stomach drop. "You do?"

The stranger tugged at the collar of his lumberjack shirt and winced as if it were choking him. Then he spat and looked up again. "Yeah," he rasped. "Van Brunt, right?"

Walter was stunned. "But, but how—?"

"You could be two toads out of the same egg, you and your father."

"You knew my father?"

The Indian nodded, then ducked his head and spat again. "I knew him," he said. "Yeah, I knew him. He was a real piece of shit."

Mohonk, or the History of a Stab in the Back

HE WAS born on the Shawangunk reservation, Jamestown, New York, in 1909, the green-eyed son of a green-eyed father. His mother, a Seneca *ye-oh* whose bellicose forefathers had been pacified by none other than George Washington himself, had eyes as black as olives. Ignoring those black eyes and the warlike temperament that lurked behind them, Mohonk *père* followed the patrilineal custom of his own tribe, the Kitchawanks, of which he was the last known surviving member, and christened the boy Jeremy Mohonk, Jr. The boy's mother was scandalized. Her people, the warriors of the north, the survivors, claimed descent through the womb. The boy, his mother insisted, was by all rights a Seneca and a Tantaquidgeon. If he married in the clan, he'd be committing incest. But the elder Mohonk wouldn't be moved. Twice during the first month of little Jeremy's existence he took a half-strung snowshoe to the side of his wife's head, and once, after an especially vehement disputation, he chased her through the Jamestown feedlot with a dibble stick honed to the killing sharpness of a spear.

The upshot of all this was an informal knife fight between Mohonk *père* and Horace Tantaquidgeon, his wife's brother. They were scaling fish on the banks of the Conewango—yellow perch, walleyes, maskinonge—their knives glinting in the sun. Mohonk *fils*, barely able to focus his eyes, was strapped to his mother's back and gazing up into the dancing green of the trees and the stolid, unmoving sky that rose up everywhere around him, oceanic and blue. The men's hands were wet with blood, with mucus. Translucent scales clung to their forearms. There was no sound but for the rasp of the knives and the furious drone of the flies. Suddenly, and without warning, Horace Tantaquidgeon rose to his feet and sank his knife into the back of the last of the Kitchawanks but one. The knife stuck there, quivering, the blade lodged like a splinter between two ridges of the lumbar vertebrae.

For a moment, there was no reaction. The elder Mohonk, bare-chested and dressed in stained work pants, squatted over his mound of fish as before. And then all at once his eyes went cold with a new kind of knowledge, and he dropped to his buttocks, sitting upright among those hacked and dumb-staring fish that squirted out from under him as if they'd come back to life . . . but no, he wasn't just sitting, he was pitching backward from there, his legs, his gut, his bowels gone, cut loose and drifting like so many balloons puffed with helium.

The Tantaquidgeons were remorseful and penitent. Horace extracted a rumpled dollar bill from the hoard of eight he kept buried in a gourd out back of his house, walked the six miles to Frewsburg, and purchased a wheelchair from the widow of a white man who'd been crippled in the Spanish-American War. Then he wheeled it back home, all the long way up the dusty road to the reservation. And Mildred, the fractious wife, was fractious no more. Not only did she dismiss the subject of little Jeremy's descent (the boy was his father's son, a Kitchawank, one of two surviving members of the once-mighty Turtle Clan and rightful inheritor of the Kitchawank domain to the south, and that was that), but she devoted the rest of her days to the care of her husband. She prepared stewed opossum and venison, collected berries for him in season, greased his hair and diapered him like a second son. And all this was necessary, and more. For Jeremy Mohonk, son of Mohonks uncountable, last of his race but one, would never walk again.

The boy grew to manhood there on the reservation, where the light was a thing that invested the visible world with its glory, where streams met and bears roamed and the clouds held the setting sun in a grip as gentle as a mother's hand. He listened to the dew settle on the grass at night, watched the sun pull itself out of the trees in the morning, stalked game, gigged frogs, fished and climbed and swam.

He learned to read and write at the agency school, learned about Amerigo Vespucci and Christopher Columbus from a white man who wore a starched collar and whose face was like an overripe plum; at night he sat at the foot of his father's wheelchair and discovered the history of his race.

His father sat stiff in the chair, holding himself erect with arms that were eternally flexed against the numbness of his belly and bowels. The injury had made him gaunt, and he seemed to grow more attenuated day by day, year by year, as if Horace Tantaquidgeon's blade had somehow let the spirit escape like air from his body, leaving only the husk behind. Still, he told the old stories in a voice that sang, strong and true, told them with the breath of history. Jeremy was no more than four or five when he heard them the first time; he was a full-grown man of eighteen summers when he heard them the last.

His father told him how Manitou had sent his big woman to earth and how she squatted in the water that covered everything and gave birth to dry land. Undaunted by this mighty feat of parturition, she heaved herself up again and gave birth to trees and plants, and then finally to three animals: the deer, the bear and the wolf. From these, all the men of the earth are descended, and each of them—man, woman and child—has the nature of one of these beasts. There are those who are innocent and timid, like the deer; those who are brave, revengeful and just of hand, like the bear; and those who are false and bloodthirsty, like the wolf.

Wasted, his face drawn and cheeks sucked back to bone, the elder Mohonk sat beneath the stovepipe hat given him by the Tantaquidgeons as partial recompense for his injury and told his son of god and the devil, of the spirits in things, of *pukwidjinnies, neebarrawbaigs* and the imps that haunt the still and sheltered lagoons of the Hudson. Jeremy was eleven, he was twelve, fourteen. His father was dying, but the stories never stopped. In school he learned that Lincoln had freed the slaves, that the square root of four is two and that everything in the world is composed of atoms. At home he sat before the fire with his father while the spirit of the flames raised her hackles along the length of a sputtering log.

After his father's death, the last of the Kitchawanks had no reason to linger on the reservation. His mother, ancient enemy of his tribe and betrayer of his father, took another husband before the grass had gone yellow on the grave. Horace Tantaquidgeon, who'd taught him to hunt and fish and fire a clay cookpot, turned his back on him now, as if, with his father's death, the debt had been paid. And though Jeremy had stayed on to finish school with a white man's diploma, he found the doors in Jamestown shut to him. Hey, chief, people called to him on the street, where's your wigwam? Hey, you. Geronimo. No, there was nothing in Jamestown. And so it was the most natural thing in the world to bundle up his possessions—the knife that had cut his father's legs out from under him, a bearskin sleeping bag, two strips of eel jerky, a dog-eared copy of Ruttenburr's *Indian Tribes of the Hudson's River* and the notochord of a sturgeon his father had worn around his neck to remind him of the perfidy of fishes—and head east, along the Susquehanna and Delaware, then across the Catskills to that gleaming apotheosis of modern technology, the Bear Mountain Bridge, and then over the storied river to the hills of Peterskill itself.

He was almost surprised to see that those hills had houses on them, to see that the streets were paved with brick and cobblestone and lined with automobiles and telegraph poles. Battened on tales, he'd expected something different. If not dewy forests, free-running streams and open campfires, then at least a sleepy Dutch village with dogs drowsing in the streets and a noonday silence that sank into the marrow of the bones. He was sadly deluded. For Peterskill in 1927 was clanking along with the industrial revolution, stirring up dust and turning over the greenback dollar; to an Indian from the reservation it was teeming, dirty, pandemonium itself. On the other hand, it wasn't a bad place to get lost in. No one noticed an Indian on the street. No one even knew what an Indian was. They recognized Bohunks, Polacks, wops, micks, kikes and even the occasional nigger—but an Indian? Indians wore headdresses and funny underwear and lived in teepees somewhere out west.

Dressed in the work pants and faded flannel shirt he'd worn on the reservation, his hair cropped close with the blade that had stuck his father, Jeremy appeared one morning at 7:00 A.M. outside the gate of the Van Wart Foundry on Water Street, asking for work. Half an hour later he was dodging around vats of molten iron, hammer and file in hand, hacking lumps of fused residue from the castings. The first week he slept in a clump of smartweed near the mouth of Acquasinnick Creek, and he got wet twice; once he'd been paid, he took a room in a boardinghouse on the west end of Van Wart Road. From here, in the shortening evenings, on half-day Saturdays and breezy Sunday mornings, he hiked up into the hills to commune with the spirit of his ancestors.

It was on one of these hikes that he met Sasha Freeman.

Carrying nothing that would identify him to the casual observer as the innocuous footslogger and nature lover he was—no rucksack, no canteen or alpenstock, no sandwiches wrapped in butcher's paper—Jeremy made his way up Van Wart Creek one warm September afternoon, keeping off the roads and out of the way of cottages and farmhouses. He didn't want to run into any watchdogs, any fences or posted signs or inquisitive white faces. He saw enough white faces at work. In his element, in the forests that had given birth to his ancestors, he wanted to see where the deer had come down to drink, where quail nested in the grass, he wanted to see the brook trout wagging in the current and test his reflexes against the one that would make his lunch . . . it was nothing personal, but when he was outside the walls of the foundry, he wanted to see the world as it had been, and white faces were no part of it.

But it was a white face he discovered peering up at him in alarm from a clump of mountain laurel as he rounded a bend in the creek and flung himself over a fallen birch in a single gangling unconscious leap. The face was bearded, bespectacled, small-eyed and suspicious, and it was attached to the stark white body of a naked man with a book in his hand. Jeremy halted in mid-stride, every bit as surprised as the naked man stretched out there in the mountain laurel as if in his own bed, uncertain as to whether he should slink off into the undergrowth or continue on his way as if nothing were amiss. But before he could make a decision either way, the white man was on his feet, simultaneously bobbing into a pair of baggy undershorts, shouting hello and extending his hand in greeting. "Sasha Freeman," he said, pumping the Indian's hand as if he'd been expecting him all afternoon.

Jeremy gaped down at him in bewilderment. The stranger was at least a foot shorter than he, round-shouldered and slight, with the musculature of an adolescent girl and a berserk growth of coiled black hair that sprang up like a pelt on his limbs, his back, even his hands and feet. The only place he lacked hair, it seemed, was on the crown of his head, where it was thinning, though he couldn't have been more than twenty or so. "You're a fresh-air fiend too, I take it," the stranger said, squinting up into the trees.

"Sure," Jeremy mumbled, numbly shaking the proferred hand. "Fresh-air fiend. That's right." He was embarrassed, impatient, angry at this stranger for intruding on his solitude, and he was anxious to get on up the stream and explore the tributary that branched off to the left and ascended the ridge to the crown of the forest. But Sasha Freeman, with his mad toothy smile and dancing little feet, already had him by the arm, offering him a sandwich, a drink, a seat on his blanket, and for some reason—out of a desire to please, out of loneliness—Jeremy joined him.

"So what did you say your name was?" Sasha Freeman handed him half an egg salad sandwich and a tin cup of fruit punch.

"Mohonk," Jeremy said, looking away. "Jeremy Mohonk."

"Mohonk," the stranger echoed in a ruminative tone, "I don't believe I've heard that one before. Is it shortened from something?"

As a matter of fact, it was.

"From Mohewoneck," Jeremy said, staring down at his feet. "He was a great sachem of my tribe."

"Your *tribe?*" Behind the wire-rimmed spectacles that gave him the look of a startled scholar, Sasha Freeman's eyes blinked in amazement. "Then, you're . . . you're—?"

"That's right," Jeremy said, and he could feel the power growing in him as if he were a tree rooted to the earth, as if all the strength of the ancestral soil beneath him were suddenly his. He'd never spoken the words before, but he spoke them now. "I'm the last of the Kitchawanks."

It was the beginning of a friendship.

For the next two years—until the Depression descended on them and Sasha was forced to move back with his parents on the Lower East Side, until the foundry foundered and Jeremy lost his job and left the boardinghouse to reclaim his birthright from Rombout Van

Wart—they met nearly every weekend. Neither of them had a car, so Sasha would bicycle down from his grandparents' place in Kitchawank Colony, and from there they'd hike out along the river to fish the inlets or climb one of the peaks of the Highlands and camp overnight in the old way, in a wickiup made of bent and interwoven saplings. Or they'd take the train into New York for the latest Pickford, Chaplin or Fairbanks, for lectures on the people's revolution in Russia or meetings of the I.W.W.

For his part, Sasha Freeman, city kid and future novelist, who in that fall of 1927 was three months out of N.Y.U. and teaching for a gratuity at the Colony free school, felt that in Jeremy he'd found a link to an older, deeper way of knowledge. It was as if the earth had opened up and the stones begun to speak. Jeremy didn't merely teach him how to listen for the footfall of fox and deer or how to gather and boil herbs against poison ivy, impetigo and the croup, didn't merely give him the means to walk out into the woods with nothing more than the clothes on his back and survive—no, he gave him more, much more: he gave him stories. Legends. History. Leaning into a campfire on Anthony's Nose or Breakneck Ridge, snow sifting down out of the sky, Sasha Freeman learned the story of Jeremy's people, a people dispersed like his own, crowded onto reservations that were like the shtetls of Cracow, Prague, Budapest. He heard the story of Manitou's big woman, of Horace Tantaquidgeon's treachery, heard about the reservation school and the delusions of the plum-faced preceptor in the starched collar. Smoke ascended to heaven. It was spring, summer, fall again. The Indian forced up every legend, every memory, giving up his history as if it were a last testament.

Eight years later Sasha Freeman published his first book, a polemic called *Marx Among the Mohicans*. It took the redoubtable father of communism back in history, to the time of the American primitives, and allowed him to score points against the slave state of modern industrial society as contrasted with the simple communal fraternity of the Indians. So what if it sold fifty-seven copies, half of them at a meeting of the Young People's Socialist League attended by six of his cousins from Pearl Street? So what if it was printed in a basement and had a paper cover that fell to pieces if you looked at it twice? It was a beginning.

And what did Jeremy get in return? Companionship, for one thing—Sasha Freeman was the first white friend he'd ever had, and the only friend he made in Peterskill. But it went deeper than that. Jeremy too was awakened to a new way of thinking, a new way of perceiving the world that had chewed up his people as if they were lambs of the field: he became radicalized. Sasha took him to unadvertised meetings of the I.W.W., gave him *Ten Days That Shook the World* and *The Eighteenth Brumaire of Louis Bonaparte,* gave him Marx, Lenin and Trotsky, Bakunin, Kropotkin, Proudhon, Fourier. Jeremy learned that property is theft, that destruction is a kind of creation, that the insurrectionary deed is the most efficacious means of propaganda. He was beaten by hired goons outside a shoe factory in Paramus, New Jersey, hit with truncheons, billy clubs, brass knuckles and two-by-fours in the streets of Brooklyn, Queens and lower Manhattan, and it hardened him all the more. His people had never owned the land beneath their feet, but had lived on it, with it, a part of it. They hadn't bought and sold and expropriated the means of production—they'd lived in their clans, cooperating, planting and harvesting together, sharing game, manufacturing their clothes and tools from nature. Sure. And the white men—the capitalists, with their greed for pelts and timber and real estate—they changed all that forever, strangled a great and giving society, a communist society. Sasha Freeman wrote a book. Jeremy Mohonk climbed the hill to Nysen's Roost, an ancient place that spoke to him like no other, and swatted down Rombout Van Wart—the very type and symbol of the expropriator—swatted him down like a fly.

In prison he was recalcitrant, as hard and unyielding as the stones they'd stacked atop one another to build the place. Prison regulations, the guard told him the day they ushered him through the admitting gate and down the long gray corridor to the barber's chair. He'd let his hair grow out till it trailed down his back in a coil as thick as his arm, and he wore the notochord cinched around his forehead like a strip of gut. And if he'd been thin and gangling when he first met Sasha Freeman, now he was forty pounds heavier—and still growing. It took four men to hold him down while they shaved his head. They tore the notochord from his brow and swept it up with the refuse. To improve his attitude, he was given three weeks in solitary.

When the three weeks were up, he was assigned a cell on the prison block. His cellmate was a white man, a housebreaker, skin the color of raw dough and blemished all over with tattoos like grape stains. Jeremy wouldn't talk to him. Wouldn't talk to anyone—not his fellow prisoners, not the guards or trustees or the sorry fat-assed preacher who poked his head in the cell door every month or so. He hated them all as one, the race that had polluted his blood, stolen his land and locked him away, the race of money grubbers and capitalists. He was twenty years old, and for every year he'd lived he had a year to serve: twenty years, the judge had intoned, his words as harsh as the thump of his gavel. Twenty years.

During the second month, one of the guards—soft and pock-faced, an ignorant Irish from Verplanck—singled him out and taunted him with all the old sneers: chief, Hiawatha, squaw, dog eater. When Jeremy refused to respond, the Irish went further, dousing him with a pail of slops, spitting through the bars at him, waking him in the dead of night for meaningless inspections. Jeremy might as well have been deaf and mute, carved of stone. He never moved, never spoke, never expressed surprise or alarm. But one morning, early, when the lights had begun to go soft against the gray of dawn, he was there, in the shadows against the wall of his cell, waiting. The Irish was on wake-up, moving along the cellblock with a baton, rapping it on the bars to the sound of curses, groans, the thump and wheeze of men tumbling out of their beds. "Rise and shine!" he called with malicious joy, repeating it over and over as he worked his way toward Jeremy's cell, "Up and at 'em!" The Indian crouched down, motionless, as intent as if he were stalking deer or bear. And then the Irishman was there, the baton rattling the bars, his voice punishing and sadistic: "Hey, Geronimo. Hey, asshole. Roll out."

Jeremy got him by the throat, both arms thrust through the bars. They'd been working him in the quarry, and his grip was like the grip of all the Mohonks through all the generations gone down. The guard dropped the baton with a clatter, snatching desperately at the Indian's wrists. His face was a blister. Swelling. Red and swelling. Inches away. If Jeremy could only hold on long enough he'd burst it once and for all. But there was someone behind him—his cellmate, the tattooed idiot—shouting and tearing at his arms, and now there were two, three more guards, their billies raining on his hands, his wrists, the whole cellblock in an uproar. They broke his grip, finally, but he seized on the soft fat hand of one of the others and squeezed till he could feel the bones give. Then they were in the cell, they were all over him and they administered their own kind of justice.

When it was over, he got three months in solitary and two more years tacked onto his sentence.

So it was throughout his career at Sing Sing. He fought them each minute—each second—of each day. When the war came and they released muggers, second-story men and arsonists to fight the Fascists, he wouldn't yield. "You're the Fascists," he told the warden, the recruiter, the guards who stood over him in the warden's office. "The Revolution will bury you." It was the first thing anyone could remember him saying in years. The cell door clanked shut behind him.

For all his resolve, though, for all his toughness, prison finally broke him down. He knew prisoners who were executed, saw men who'd spent their entire lives behind bars, their backs stooped, faces sunk in on themselves. He was a young man still. Last of his line. His business in life was to reclaim some of what his tribe had lost, to seek out a woman of constant blood—a Shawangunk, an Oneida, even a Seneca, as his father had done—and keep the race alive. He was meant to roam the woods, to remember the old ways, to honor the sacred places—there was no one else to do it, no one among the pullulating hordes that blighted the earth like locusts. The knowledge of it mellowed him. The war years slipped past, Sing Sing was quiet, underpopulated. He stayed out of trouble. In 1946, five years short of the full term of his sentence, they set him free.

He walked out of the gate at 8:00 A.M. on a chill and windblown December morning, wearing a cheap prison-issue suit and overcoat and with the token recompense for his seventeen years' labor tucked deep in his breast pocket. By nightfall he was back at Nysen's Roost, huddled over an open fire with a can of corned beef hash and the knife he'd picked up at a pawn shop in Peterskill, a knife exactly like the one Horace Tantaquidgeon had inserted between his father's lumbar vertebrae in a time that seemed as distant as the first moment of history.

He lived there a year before anyone discovered him. He'd built himself a timber and tar-paper shack for half of what it had cost Thoreau to build his place a century earlier. Built it beneath the white oak, in the place that spoke to him, precisely where his first shack had stood so briefly twenty years before. What he didn't have—nails, an axe, plastic to stretch across the windows—he appropriated from the suburbanites who crowded the verges of his domain with their blacktop driveways and brick barbecues. When the prison suit fell away to nothing he made himself a breechclout and jacket from the hide of a doe. For cooking, he had a clay pot, shaped, tooled and fired in the way of the centuries.

The year was 1947, the season fall. Standard Crane, son of Peletiah, a sharp-nosed, round-eyed gawk of a man in his early thirties, was out hunting squirrel one morning when he blundered across the shack. Jeremy, in his stained buckskin and with the flight feathers of the red-tailed hawk braided into his hair, stepped out onto the porch and shot him a corrosive look. Puzzled, Standard dropped the muzzle of his shotgun, shoved back his cap and scratched his head. For a moment he was so disoriented, startled and surprised he could only make a series of throat-clearing noises that the Indian took to be a sort of rudimentary game call. But then, shuffling his feet, he managed to say "Good morning," and went on from there to inquire as to whether he and Jeremy were acquainted. The Indian, remembering Van Wart, said nothing. After a moment, Standard tipped his hat and wandered off down the trail.

But Standard Crane was no Van Wart. Nor was his father, Peletiah, who despite a head cold, rheumy eyes and a bad knee, hiked all the way out to the shack in twenty-five-degree weather to view this prodigy, this green-eyed Indian who was squatting on his land. Jeremy was waiting for them. On the porch. Ready for anything. But Peletiah merely greeted him with a nod of his head and invited himself to a seat on the rough-hewn step beside him. Standard, who'd served as his father's guide, hung back and grinned in embarrassment. Producing a tinfoil pouch from the inner pocket of his red-and-black plaid hunting jacket, Peletiah offered the Indian a chew, and then, in the most neighborly way imaginable, explained how he'd acquired the land from the late Rombout Van Wart.

The Indian was a tough audience. He refused the tobacco with a gesture so curt he might have been shooing flies, then made his face into a mask. Though his expression didn't reflect it, he was secretly pleased to hear that the land had passed from control of the Van Warts and deeply gratified to discover that the son of a bitch who'd put him behind bars was no longer among the living. And so he listened, as mute as the peeled logs of the porch, as the wheezy white man went on about the history of the place and circled around the question of Jeremy's identity like a mosquito looking for a patch of bare flesh. But when Jeremy cut him off in mid-sentence and began quoting Proudhon, when he insisted that property was theft and that it was his tribal right to live there beneath the hallowed oak and be damned to all thieves and expropriators, Peletiah surprised him.

Not only could this runny-eyed, pointy-nosed, skeletal old white man outquote him, he agreed with him. "On paper, I'm the owner of this land," Peletiah said, ducking his head to spit and then looking around him with a bemused little smile that barely parted his lips, "but in fact the land belongs to everyone equally, every man that walks the earth. You'll find no posted signs here."

Jeremy glanced up at the trees as if to confirm the assertion and found himself staring into the reticent eyes of the squirrel hunter. Standard slouched against a tree at least twenty feet from the cabin, and he was picking his teeth meditatively. At the mention of posted signs, he made a noise deep in his throat that was meant to convey good humor and amusement but that sounded more like the death rattle of a drowning man.

"I bought the land because I had the money when nobody else did and because I got it for a song," Peletiah was saying. "There was something about the place. I thought I'd like to build on it someday, but you know how that is. . . ." He waved his hand in dismissal. His eyes were shrewd; the little smile clung to his lips. "You want it?" he asked after a moment. "You want to camp here, swim in the creek, tramp the woods—go ahead. It's yours. More power to you."

Two years later, Peletiah extended the invitation to 20,000 like-minded people, and the field below, on the far side of Acquasinnick Creek, filled with them. That was a fine and triumphant thing, but it was the first night—the night of the aborted concert—that was the real test. No more than a hundred and fifty turned up that night, with their picnic baskets and blankets to spread out in the grass. Jeremy watched them from the trees. He had no idea that Sasha Freeman had organized the event—hadn't heard from him in twenty years—but it was a thing he could approve of, a thing he could recognize and applaud.

When the trouble started, he never hesitated. Circling the arena, a shadow among shadows, he surprised bat-toting veterans and skulking boys alike, springing from the bushes with a whoop or merely rising up before them like a wrathful demon. Most took to their heels at the sight of him, but a handful—drunker or more foolish than the rest—kept coming. It was just what he wanted. He broke noses, bloodied lips, bruised ribs—and each kick, each punch, was a debt repaid. A paunchy veteran came at him with a tire iron and he kicked him in the groin. He snatched a fence post from a man with the sunken red-flecked eyes of a pig and slapped his backside with it till he began to squeal. At some point he discovered blood on his hands and forearms, and he paused to draw a single incarnadine slash beneath each of his eyes, and then, looking fierce and aboriginal, looking like a warrior of old, he chased a pair of teenaged boys till they collapsed in tears, begging for mercy. Mercy was a thing he'd never known, but he stayed his hand, thinking of Peletiah, thinking, for once, of the repercussions. He let them go. And then, as dusk began to thicken the branches of the trees and the cries from the roadway grew more hellish and disjointed, he drifted instinctively toward the open field to the north, and there, in the gathering gloom, made the acquaintance of Truman Van Brunt.

Truman was wearing a polo shirt and a pair of baggy white trousers, and he was conferring with a big-armed man in a bloodied work shirt and what appeared to be a boy of six or seven. Though the Indian had never laid eyes on Truman before, and didn't learn his name till the following morning in Peletiah's kitchen, there was something familiar about him, something that tugged at his consciousness like a half-remembered dream. Crouched low in the bushes, Jeremy watched. And listened.

The big-armed man was wrought up, his eyes wild, his hands raking at one another as if with some uncontainable itch. He wanted to know if the man in the polo shirt would make a sacrifice for them, if he'd try to slip through the mob and get help—because if help didn't come soon, they were doomed. Truman didn't hesitate. "Sure," he said, "I'll go, but only if I can take Piet with me," and he indicated the boy. It was when the boy spoke—"Fuck, you goddamned well better take me with you"—that Jeremy recognized his mistake. He looked again. This was no boy—no, this was a man, a dwarf, his twisted little face blanched with evil, this was the *pukwidjinny* come to life. Jeremy clenched his fists. Something was wrong here, desperately wrong. Suddenly there was a shout from the direction of the arena, and the big-armed man threw a nervous glance over his shoulder. "Take him," he said, and Truman and the dwarf started across the field.

The Indian gave it a minute, till the man with the big arms had turned and jogged back toward the arena, and then he emerged from the trees and started after Truman. Silent and slow as a moving statue, bent double in his stalking crouch, he crept up on the man in the polo shirt and his undersize companion. Truman never once glanced over his shoulder. In fact, he strode through the field as if he hadn't a care in the world, as if he were strolling into a restaurant for Sunday brunch instead of going out to risk his neck among the mad dogs on the road ahead of him. The Indian, hurrying now to keep up, thought he must be insane. Either that or he was the bravest man alive.

Suddenly three figures broke from the trees at the road's edge and started for Truman and the dwarf. They wore Legionnaire's caps and dirty T-shirts. All three brandished weapons—jack handles and tire chains hastily plucked from the trunks of their cars. "Hey, nigger-lover," the one in the middle called, "come to poppa."

Jeremy sank low in the grass, ready for trouble. But there wasn't any trouble, that was the odd thing. Truman just walked right up to them and said something in a low urgent tone—something the Indian couldn't quite catch. Whatever he'd said, though, it seemed to placate them. Instead of raising their weapons, instead of flailing at him like the mad dogs and capitalist tools they were, they ducked their heads and grinned as if he'd just told the joke of the century. And then, astonishingly, one of them held a bottle out to him and Truman took a swig. "Depeyster Van Wart," Truman said, and his voice was as clear suddenly as if he were standing right there beside the Indian, "you know him?"

"Sure," came the reply.

"Is he up the road somewhere or what?"

At that moment, a dull roar rose up from the concert grounds, and all five of them—the dwarf, the Legionnaires and Truman—turned their heads. Jeremy held his breath.

"I seen him up around the bend there, up at the road into the Crane place." The man who clutched the tire chains was speaking, the dry rasp of his voice punctuated by the clank of steel on steel. "We're going to make a run at the fuckers soon as it's dark."

"Take me to him, would you?" Truman said, and the Indian, buried in the tall grass like a corpse, went cold with an apprehension that was like a stab in the back, that was like the hard-edged message his father had received from Horace Tantaquidgeon in a time past. "I've got news."

"Kikes and niggers, kikes and niggers," the dwarf sang, his voice pinched and nasal, echoing as if he'd poured himself into the bottle Truman had handed him. Then the five of them moved off through the trees that fringed the road. As soon as they were gone, Jeremy Mohonk pushed himself up from the grass. White men. They'd betrayed the Kitchawanks, the Weckquaesgeeks, the Delawares and Canarsees, and they betrayed their own kind too. It was on his lips: the taste of the shit they'd made him eat in prison. He thought of Peletiah, thought of the men he'd punished in the woods, thought of the women and children huddled around the stage with their pamphlets and picnic baskets. Thought of them all and rose up out of the weeds to trail the fink in the polo shirt.

Out on the road, all was confusion. Some of the cars parked along the shoulders had flicked on their headlights, and the pavement glittered with broken glass. In this naked white light, the Indian could see groups of men and boys hurrying in both directions, while dogs nosed about and people perched on fenders or sat in their cars as if awaiting a fireworks display or the heifer judging at the county fair. There was a smell of scorched paint on the air, of creosote and burning rubber. Somewhere a radio was playing. Jeremy squared his shoulders and emerged from the bushes between two parked cars. He sidestepped a cluster of young women passing a bottle of wine and started up the road. No one said a word to him.

The noise grew louder as he neared the entrance to the concert grounds—yelps, cries, curses, screams of drunken laughter and the roar of revving engines. Groups of men with makeshift weapons stalked past him, and boys, some as young as nine or ten, hurried up the road with sacks of stones. A blackened car lay on its side in the middle of the road up ahead, and another burned furiously behind it. He quickened his pace, craning his neck for a glimpse of the Judas in the polo shirt and his obscene little companion. A man in an overseas cap and a chest full of medals shouted something at him, an old woman in rolled-up blue jeans waved a flag in his face, there was smoke in his nostrils and the blood had dried beneath his eyes. He was about to break into a trot when he saw him, Truman, leaning in the window of a late-model Buick. In the same instant he spotted the dwarf too, propped insouciantly against the fender and leering with apparent satisfaction at the conflagration around him.

The Indian kept walking, and as he passed them, he caught a glimpse of the man behind the wheel of the Buick. He knew the face, though he'd never seen it before, knew the humorless mouth and outthrust chin, the eyes like branding irons: it was the face of the man who'd sent him to prison, the face of a Van Wart. Fighting the desire to glance over his shoulder, Jeremy felt the dwarf's eyes on him and kept going. He was about to double back—if only he could get this red-headed fink alone—when a horde of vigilantes, led by Truman's pal with the tire chains, came streaming past him.

Under cover of the diversion—all heads turned, even the dwarf's, to watch them hurry down the road toward the undefended pasture—Jeremy ducked between two cars, crouched down and waited. A moment later, Van Wart emerged from the Buick, said something to Truman and started up the road toward the barricade at the entrance to the concert grounds. Truman and his *pukwidjinny* fell into step behind him, and the Indian, after counting to ten, rose up out of the gloom to bring up the rear. He was taking a chance—the mob could fall on him any minute, his skin, his hair, his clothes like nothing they'd ever seen, like some nigger's or Communist's—but he didn't care. Hatred fueled him, and he snaked through the knots of angry men as if he were invisible.

As he approached the barricade, the crowd thickened, dark shapes moving in and out of the static glare of the headlights that flooded the narrow dirt road beyond it. This was the omphalos of confusion and strife, rage stamped on every face, voices reduced to a collective snarl, the mob shoving first one way and then the other. Jeremy almost lost his quarry here—the faces all alike, shirts and shoulders and hats, the crush of bodies—but then he spotted Van Wart conferring with a bald-headed man in an open-collared dress shirt, and just beyond him, Truman and the *pukwidjinny*. Truman was conferring with no one. He was weaving through the crowd, a man in a hurry, heading up the road and away from the whole messy business of betrayal and bigotry; the dwarf was right behind him, visible only as a sort of moving furrow in the standing field of the mob. *He's getting away,* Jeremy thought, and he surged forward, heedless, shoving vigilantes aside as if they were so many straw men. "Hey!" someone shouted at him, "Hey you!," but he never even bothered to turn his head.

By the time Jeremy managed to break free of the crowd, Truman and the drawf were a hundred yards up the road, clots of black against the richer texture of the night. They hurried past a line of stalled and battered cars on the darkened roadway, then angled off on an unpaved lane that wound through the woods in the direction of Peterskill. Jeremy broke into a run. He passed a pair of teenagers bent over a gas can in the dark, dodged a man who stood flatfooted and astonished in the middle of the road, and saw a frightened black face peering from the window of a stalled car; a moment later, still running hard, he was turning into the lane. Immediately, he saw that his luck had changed. The shouts of the crowd were muted here, the road all but deserted: this was the chance he'd been waiting for.

He came at Truman without warning, swift silent steps in the dirt, flinging himself at the shadowy form ahead of him like a linebacker going for the tackling dummy. He caught him in the small of the back—something gave: bone, cartilage, hinges that need oil—and slammed his face down in the dirt. At the moment of impact, the dwarf leapt aside with a squeal and Truman let out a gasp of surprise before the hard compacted dirt of the road sucked the breath out of him. The Indian knew then that he was going to kill this son of a bitch in the polo shirt, this back stabber, this white man, and he locked an arm around his throat and ground his face into the road. When he was done with him, he'd get up and crush the dwarf like an egg.

"Get off!" Truman choked, tearing at the Indian's arm. "Get . . . off!"

Shrill, manic, the dwarf leapt up and down in the dirt like a rodent in a cage. "Murder!" he piped. "Help! Murder!"

The Indian tightened his grip.

And so it would have gone—Truman, powerful as he was, taken by surprise, cut down and emasculated before his invisible adversary's rage, first fatality of the riots . . . so it would have gone, but for the dwarf. He screamed, and a hundred feet came running, vigilantes by the score, soreheads and rednecks and born-again racists with blood on their hands. That in itself would have been enough, but the little man was wickeder than the Indian could have guessed. He had a knife. Three inches' worth. Nothing like Horace Tantaquidgeon's gutting knife, but a knife nonetheless. And he slipped that knife from his pocket, sprung the blade with a soft evil click, and began punctuating the Indian's back. He dug a full stop first, then a colon; he slashed commas, hyphens and a single ragged exclamation point.

Half a second, that's all it took. The Indian reared up and slapped the dwarf as he might have slapped a fly, but the moment's distraction allowed Truman to wriggle free. In the next moment, he was on his feet, gasping for breath and flinging frenzied blows at his assailant, who rose up out of the darkness like a mountain in motion. Wordlessly, without so much as a grunt of effort or pain, the Indian returned the blows. With interest. "You crazy?" Truman gasped, throwing up his arms to protect himself. "You nuts or what?" Behind them, the thin white lances of flashlights and the slap of running feet.

Jeremy felt a weak fist glance off the side of his head, then another. He moved in closer. It was then that he got his first good look at the man he was about to kill. The onrushing beam of a flashlight played across the traitor's face, and again the Indian felt he somehow knew this man, knew him in some deep and tribal way. Truman must have got a good look at Jeremy too, because suddenly he dropped his hands in bewilderment. "Who the—?" he began, but it was too late for introductions. The Indian lunged for his throat and got hold of him again, both hands locked around the windpipe in an unbreakable grip, a death grip, the grip that leaves the rabbit twitching and the goose cold. Jeremy would have answered the half-formed question, would have answered Truman as he'd answered Sasha Freeman and Rombout Van Wart and anyone else who cared to know, but he never got the chance. All at once the patriots were on him, swarming over him with their sticks and tire irons and chains.

It was Sing Sing and the prison guard all over again. Jeremy held on like the swamp turtle that lent its name to his clan—pummel him, stab him, cut off his head, his grip was good to death and beyond—held on despite the wounds in his back and the fingers jerking at his wrists. Then someone brought a jack handle down across the back of his skull and he felt Truman slipping away from him. Just before he fell, desperate, guided by the turtle, he lunged forward and locked his jaws in the traitor's flesh—the ear, the right ear—and clamped down till he tasted blood.

All was quiet when he opened his eyes again, and he thought for a moment he was back in his cot listening to the crickets tick off the seconds till dawn. There were no shouts. No tires squealed, no engines roared, there were no cries of grief and rage. But he wasn't in his cot. He was laid out on his back in a ditch beside the road and his body was possessed by the demons of pain. He'd been clubbed, kicked, stabbed; his left arm was broken in two places. Lying there in the ditch, gazing up at the stars through the interstices of the trees, he listened for a moment to the chant of the crickets and let his mind touch each of his wounds. He thought of his ancestors, warriors who'd used their pain as a tool, mocking their torturers even as the blade bared the nerve. After a while, he pushed himself up and started down the road for Peletiah's place.

Jeremy Mohonk left the hills of Van Wartville six months later. The despair that had eaten at him in prison, the sense of decay and futility, drove him from his shack beneath the white oak as no man could ever have done. He returned to the reservation outside of Jamestown, looking for the mother of his twenty sons. His own mother was dead. Ten years earlier, while he was languishing beneath the stones of Sing Sing, she succumbed to a mysterious wasting disease that stole her appetite and left her looking like a corpse mummified over the centuries. Her brother, he of the perfidious knife, was hardier. Jeremy found him in a cluttered little house on the bank of the river. Snaggletoothed and wizened, with his white hair bound in a topknot and his suit of burial clothes draped over a chair in the corner, he stared at his nephew with eyes that could barely place him. As for Jeremy's coevals, the clean-limbed boys and efflorescent girls of his school days, they'd either sunk into fat so pervasive their eyes were barely visible or vanished into the world of the expropriators. Jeremy found himself a picking job—grapes at that season, apples to follow—and within the month had married a Cayuga named Alice One Bird.

She was a big woman, One Bird, with calves that swelled under the fullness of her and a broad open face that spoke of her good nature and optimism. Her two sons by a previous marriage were grown men, and though she claimed to be thirty-four, she was closer to forty. To Jeremy, her age didn't matter, so long as she was capable of bearing children, and her sons—both of them razor-eyed and tall—gave proof of that. He picked grapes, he picked apples. In the fall, he hunted. When the snow lay over the ground like a fungus and the larder was empty, he got a job as a stock boy in a supermarket in Jamestown.

A year passed. Two, three. Nothing happened. One Bird grew heavier, though she wasn't carrying a child. Jeremy was forty-three years old. He consulted a Shawangunk medicine man who'd known his father, and the old man asked him for a lock of One Bird's hair. Jeremy snipped the hair while she slept and brought it to him. With trembling fingers, the medicine man selected a hank of Jeremy's hair, clipped it close, and then rolled the two locks vigorously between his palms, as if he were trying to start a fire. After a moment he separated the strands, dropping them one by one on a sheet of newspaper. For a long while he studied their configuration in silence. "It's not you," he said finally, "it's her."

Jeremy left the next morning for Van Wartville and the tumbledown shack he'd deserted three years earlier. Save for the structure itself, there wasn't much left. The elements had taken their toll on the place, birds and rodents had used it as a dormitory and midden both, and vandals had smashed everything they couldn't carry. No matter. The Indian lived in the old way, silent and secretive, snaring rabbit and opossum, liberating what he lacked from the homes and garages and toolsheds of the wage slaves who pressed in on the property from all sides. Over the course of the ensuing years, he drifted back and forth between Peterskill and Jamestown, drawn on the one hand to his ancestral soil, and on the other to his people. One Bird always welcomed him, no matter how long he'd been gone, and he was grateful to her. Driven by natural urges, he even came to her bed now and again, but it was an exercise without hope or meaning.

The last of the Kitchawanks grew older, and as he did so, he grew increasingly embittered. The world seemed a bleak place, dominion of the people of the wolf, the bosses ascendant, the workers crushed. He was doomed. His people were doomed. Nothing mattered—not the sun in the sky, not the great Blue Rock on the verge of the Hudson or the mystic hill above Acquasinnick Creek. A decade came and went. He was in his mid-fifties—still vigorous, still powerful, still young—and he wanted to die.

Yes. And then he met Joanna Van Wart.

The Wailing Woman

THE FIRST of the Jeremy Mohonks, son of Mohonk son of Sachoes, distant ancestor of that sad radicalized jailbird whose tribe seemed destined to die with him some three centuries later, was two and a half years old and uttering his first halting words of Dutch when the shadow of Wolf Nysen fell over his world like a month of starless nights. It was October 1666, late in the afternoon of a dark graceless day that promised a premature sunset and heavy frost. Jeremy was under the kitchen table playing with sticks and dirt clods and rehearsing the words he liked best—*suycker* and *pannekoeken*—while his mother stoked the fire and stirred things into the soup. He was also watching his mother's feet as she stood at the table chopping cabbage or crossed the room to poke the fire and adjust the blackened cauldron on its armature. When he saw those feet slip into their clogs and head out the door in the direction of the woodshed, he crawled out from under the table. In the next moment he was on the *stoep,* and in the moment after that, he was gazing up at the great swirling columns of smoke that blotted the sky at the far end of the cornfield. Though he couldn't yet put it into words, he had an intuitive grasp of the situation: Uncle Jeremias was burning stumps.

Jeremy was two and a half years old, and he knew several things. He knew, for instance, that until recently his name had been Squagganeek and that he'd lived in a smoky wet hut in a smoky wet Indian village. He knew too that the wood brooding over him was home to wolves, giants, imps, ogres and witches and that he was never to leave the immediate vicinity of the house except in the company of his mother or uncle. And he knew the penalty for transgression. (No *suycker.* No *pannekoeken.* Three clean swats across the bottom and bed without supper.) Still, the shapes those columns of smoke made against the sky as they fanned out—there a butterfly, here the face of a cow—were not to be denied. Before he could think twice, he was gone. Down the steps, across the yard and out into the field with its weathered furrows and sheaves bound up like corpses.

He ran like a shorebird, stiff-kneed and quick-legged, tottering from one furrow to the next, splashing through puddles, falling flat on his face and as quickly scrambling to his feet again. When he reached the nether end of the field, he saw the stumps, a whole army of them like decapitated little men spouting smoke from their headless trunks. His uncle was nowhere to be seen. But there before him was a family of scuttling grouse, and to these he gave chase with a shout of joy. Round and round he chased them, through a funnel of smoke and a half-cleared thicket, right on up to the verge of the wood. And then he stopped. There was Jeremias, right in front of him. And another man too. A big man. A giant.

"You know who I am?" the giant roared.

His uncle knew, but he spoke so softly the boy could barely hear him. "Wolf," he said, and that was when Jeremy called out his name.

As it happened, Wolf Nysen didn't cleave Jeremias in two. Nor did he set fire to the hogpen, rape Katrinchee or devour the livestock. In fact, he merely gave Jeremias a lopsided grin, tipped the brim of his deerskin cap and slipped back into the woods. No matter: the damage was done. Just as Jeremias had taken up the yoke, just as he'd bowed his head and accepted the imprimatur of the patroon, here came this renegade to mock him and inflame all his old hate and rancor. *Who gives you the right?* The Swede's words echoed in his ears as he bent to his soup that evening, as he laid his head on the pillow that night, and when he pulled on his underwear in the morning. But that wasn't the worst of it, not by a long shot. The sequel was a steady downward slide in the fortunes of the little family at Nysen's Roost, as if the madman were indeed the evil genius of the place and they the victims of his curse.

Though they were now well-furnished (in addition to what the van der Meulens and the others had donated, the patroon, on coming to terms with his newest tenants, had sent them a wagonload of farm and household implements—on loan, of course—as well as a yoke of sway-backed oxen, a yearling calf to go with the manorial cow Oom Egthuysen had lent them, and three Hampshire shoats), nonetheless Jeremias had planted late and harvested little. The wheat, which was customarily sown in the autumn rather than the spring, had done poorly, as had his crops of rye and peas, which he'd hoped to use for winter fodder. He'd done well with Indian corn, largely because of Katrinchee's expertise, and their kitchen garden—cabbages, turnips, pumpkins and herbs—had flourished for the same reason. Still, with little grain for bread or porridge and the lion's share of the corn reserved for the stock, the menage at Nysen's Roost would be almost wholly dependent on game during the coming winter.

Problem was, the game was gone.

In the days and weeks following Wolf Nysen's visit, wildlife became increasingly scarce, almost as if the madman, like some insatiable Pied Piper, had taken the birds and beasts with him. Where Jeremias might have shot a dozen pigeons in the past, he now came back with one. Where he might have swatted gobblers from the trees and tucked them in a sack that bulged so he could barely carry it, he now found none. Ducks and geese eschewed the marshes, the deer had vanished, and bears, which tasted like pine gum and tallow anyway, had gone early to their dens. Even the squirrels and rabbits seemed to have disappeared. Of necessity, Jeremias took to the river, and for a while the river sustained them. Through November and the grim crowded days of early December, as the sun faded from the sky and the breath of the Arctic stretched a sheet of ice across Acquasinnick Bay, Katrinchee made fish balls, fish pie, fish in blankets, fried fish, boiled fish, fish with turnips and pine nuts, fish with fish. But then winter settled in in earnest, the ice stretched to the foot of Dunderberg and back and there were no more fish.

Day by day it grew colder. The well crusted over. Wolves sniffed at the door. In the woods, jays and sparrows froze to their perches, as lifeless and hard as ceramic ornaments on a Christmas tree. There was an ice storm at the New Year, followed by dropping temperatures and snow that accumulated like the sands of Egypt. When the wolves made off with one of the shoats, Jeremias moved the animals indoors.

In spite of it all, Katrinchee seemed to grow stronger by the day. She took the fish regimen in stride, put on weight, grew her hair out. For the first time in years she slept through the night. When Jeremias inventoried the corn and cut their daily ration by half, she became a genius of conservation. When the snow mounted and Jeremy took cold, when the winds blew through the house with such force as to snuff the taper on the mantelpiece, when it was dark as night though half past one by the clock, she never uttered a complaint. Not even the uncomfortable proximity of the animals could discourage her, though the shoats capered underfoot, the old cow moaned in the dark like one of the unburied dead and the oxen drooled, stank, chewed their cuds, dropped their dung and breathed their hot foul breath in her face. No, it was a small thing that undid her finally, a serendipitous discovery Jeremias made out on the front *stoep* one icebound morning toward the end of January.

What he discovered there on the porch, come to them like an answered prayer, was meat. Rich, red, life-sustaining meat. He pulled open the door to step outside and relieve himself, and blundered into the stripped and freshly dressed carcass of a doe, hanging by its hind legs from the roof of the porch. He couldn't believe it. A doe. Hanging there. And already butchered. Jeremias let out two hungry hoots of joy—Staats, it must have been Staats—and in the time it takes to draw a knife he had one haunch on the spit and the other in the pot. He was so excited his hands were trembling. He didn't notice the look on his sister's face.

When finally he did notice, the aroma of roasting venison filled the room and Katrinchee was backed up in the corner, shrunk in on herself like a spider starved in its web. "Get it out of here," she said. "Take it away."

Already the flames licked up to sear the meat; fat gilded the joint and dripped hissing into the coals. Little Jeremy stood transfixed before the fire, hands in his pants and a rhapsodic smile on his face, while Jeremias hustled around the room, hunting up the odd vegetable for the pot. The tone of his sister's voice stopped Jeremias cold. "What? What did you say?"

She was twisting the hem of her dress in both hands as if she were throttling a doll. Her hair was in her face. And her face—drawn and blanched, the eyes big with terror—was the face of a madwoman clinging to the bars in the asylum at Schobbejacken. "The smell," she murmured, her voice trailing off. In the next moment she was shrieking: "Get it out! Get it out of here!"

Jeremias could barely speak for the saliva foaming in his mouth, barely think for the knife and fork sawing away in his head, barely focus on her for the vision of the golden dripping haunch on the spit and the pretty little hoof projecting from the lip of the pot. But then he looked hard at her, and all at once he understood: it was the meat. The venison. She wanted to take it away from him. When he spoke, the words came in a rush. It was all in the past, he told her—she had to be reasonable. What were they going to eat? They were into the seed corn already. Should they kill the livestock and starve next year? "It's venison, Katrinchee. Fresh meat. Nothing more. Eat it to keep up your strength—or don't eat it if you really can't. But surely you couldn't . . . you wouldn't prevent me, your own brother . . . and what about your son?"

She just shook her head, back and forth, implacable, inconsolable, shaken with regret. She was sobbing. Biting her finger. Jeremy buried himself in her skirts; Jeremias rose from the hearth to hold her, comfort her, remonstrate with her. "No," she said, "no, no, a thousand times no," and shook her head late into the night while her brother and son sat down at the table and picked clean the least bones of the butchered doe and then cracked them with a mallet to get at the grainy rich marrow. By then, Katrinchee was beyond caring. For the second time in her short life she'd found the edge and slipped over it.

It was February. The snow fell steadily, relentlessly, mountains of it lying over the countryside in frozen blue ripples that were like the folds of a shroud. They were down to quarter rations of corn now, and even so they were decimating next year's seed. "Half a bushel of this," Jeremias would say, pounding the hard kernels to meal, "would yield a hundred next summer. But what can you do?" Katrinchee could barely lift the spoon to her mouth for guilt. She was having trouble sleeping too, the images of her father, mother, little Wouter haunting her the minute she closed her eyes. The deer hadn't come from Staats—he was having a terrible time finding meat himself, he told them a week after the second one, gutted, skinned and butchered, had appeared mysteriously on the porch. She'd known all along. Not from Staats, not from God in his heaven. It was her father, poor scalded man, who brought them . . . to punish her.

One night Jeremias woke from a dreamless sleep and felt a draft of cold air on his face. When he looked up, he saw that the door stood open, and that the hills and trees and naked snowfields had come to bed with him. Cursing, he pushed himself up and crossed the room to slam shut the door, but at the last moment something arrested him. Tracks. There were tracks—footprints—in the fresh dusting of snow on the *stoep*. Jeremias puzzled over them a moment, then eased the door shut and called to his sister in an urgent whisper. She didn't answer. When he lit the taper, he saw with a start that little Jeremy was sleeping alone. Katrinchee was gone.

This time—the first time—he found her huddled beneath the white oak. She was in her nightdress, and she'd taken a knife to her hair; strands of it lay about her in the snow like the remains of a night-blooming plant. Inside, he tried to comfort her. "It's all right," he soothed, pressing her to him. "What was it—a bad dream?"

There they were, in tableau: the animals of the manger, the sleeping child, the mutilated brother and mad sister. "A dream," she echoed, and her voice was distant, vague. Behind them, the calf bleated forlornly and the hogs grunted in their sleep. "I feel so . . . so . . ." (she meant to say "guilty," but that's not how it came out) ". . . so *hungry*."

Jeremias put her to bed, fed the fire and boiled up some milk for porridge. She lay motionless on the husk mattress, staring at the ceiling. When he brought the spoon to her lips, she pushed it away. And so the next day, and the next. He made her a stew of turnip and dried fish, baked some heavy hard bread (full of weevils, unfortunately) and gave it to her with a slab of cheese, cut the ears off one of the shoats to make her a meat broth, but she wouldn't eat. She just lay there, staring, the white parchment of her skull gleaming through the stubble of hair, her cheeks sunk in on themselves.

It was in early March, on a night that dripped from the eaves with the promise of warmth, that she wandered off again. This time she pulled the door shut behind her, and Jeremias didn't notice she was gone till first light. By then the snow had started. A wet warm drizzling snow that changed twice to rain, hovered a while on the brink of freezing, and finally, propelled by gusts blown in off the river, became a whirlwind of hard stinging pellets. By the time Jeremias had dressed the boy and started off after her, the wind was steady and the visibility no more than twenty feet.

This time there were no tracks. With the boy on his back and the pegleg skidding out from under him, Jeremias traced an ever-widening circle around the house, shouting her name into the wind. Nothing came back to him. The trees were mute, the wind threw its voice in a hundred artful ways, beads of snow rattled off his coat, his hat, his muffler. Struggling, stumbling, afraid of losing his way in the snow, afraid for Jeremy's life as well as his own, he finally turned around and hobbled back to the cabin. He tried again, early in the afternoon, getting as far as the cornfield where he'd encountered Wolf Nysen. For a moment he thought he heard her, way off in the distance, her voice raised in a doleful bone-chilling wail, but then the wind took it over from him and he couldn't be sure. He called her name, over and over, till his foot went numb and the wind drove the strength from his body. Just before dark, he put Jeremy to bed and went out again, but the snow had drifted so high he was exhausted before he reached the cornfield. "Katrinchee!" he shouted till his voice went hoarse. "Katrinchee!" But the only answer was the strange mournful cry of a great white owl beating through the storm like a lost soul.

It snowed for two days and two nights. On the morning of the third day, Jeremias fed the livestock, closed up the house and struggled through the drifts to the van der Meulens', his nephew on his back. Staats alerted the Cranes, Reinier Oothouse and the people at the upper manor house, then rode in to Jan Pieterse's to see if she'd turned up there, and if she hadn't, to locate an Indian tracker.

A party of Kitchawanks went out that afternoon, but came back empty-handed: the snow had obliterated any sign of her. If a twig had caught in her dress or a stone squirted out underfoot, the evidence was buried under three feet of snow. Jeremias despaired, but he wouldn't give up. Next morning he borrowed Staats' cart horse, and while Meintje looked after Jeremy, he and Douw poked through copses and thickets, searched and re-searched the valleys and streambeds, knocked on doors at outlying farms. They roamed as far afield as the Kitchawank village at Indian Point to the south, and the Weckquaesgeek camp at Suycker Broodt to the north. There was no trace of her.

It was Jan Pieterse who finally found her, and he wasn't looking. He was out behind the trading post one morning toward the end of the month, hauling a bucket of slops down to the Blue Rock so he could pitch them into the river, as he did every morning, the peglegged Van Brunt kid and his mad wandering shorn-headed miscegenating sister the farthest things from his mind, when something just off the path up ahead caught his eye. A swatch of blue. In a snowbank at the base of the Blue Rock, no more than a hundred feet from the store. He wondered at that swatch of blue, and set down the bucket to slash through the crusted snow and investigate. The weather had turned warmer the past few days, and his eyes had gradually gotten used to the appearance of color in what had been for some months now a world as blank as an untouched canvas. Scabs of mud had begun to break through the path he'd carved, the sky that hung low overhead like a dirty sheet had given way to the fine cerulean of a midsummer's day, pussy willows were in bloom along the Van Wartville road and tiny tight-wound buds graced box elder and sycamore. But this, this was something else. Something man-made. Something blue.

In a moment, he was standing over the spot, braced uneasily against the yielding snow on the one side and the great smooth slab of rock on the other. He was staring down at a piece of cloth projecting from the snow as if it were just the tip of something larger. He was a shopkeeper and he knew that cloth. It was blue kersey. He'd sold bolts of it to the Indians and to the farmers' wives. The Indians fashioned blankets from it. The farmers' wives liked it for aprons. And nightdresses.

Jeremias buried her beneath the white oak. Dominie Van Schaik turned up to say a few words over the grave, while the six van der Meulens, draped in black like a flock of *maes dieven,* comprised the mourners. Jeremias knelt by the grave, his lips moving as if in prayer. But he wasn't praying. He was cursing God in his heaven and all his angels, cursing St. Nicholas and the patroon and the dismal alien place that rose up around him in a Gehenna of trees, valleys and bristling hill-tops. If only they'd stayed in Schobbejacken, he kept telling himself, none of this would have happened. He knelt there, feeling sorry for Katrinchee, for his father and mother and little Wouter, feeling sorry for himself, but when finally he stood and took his place among the mourners, there was a hard cold look in his eye, the look of intransigence and invincibility he'd leveled on the *schout* time and again: he was down, but not defeated. No, never defeated.

As for Jeremy, two and a half years old, he didn't know what defeat was—or triumph either. He held back while first his uncle, then *grootvader* van der Meulen and the rest knelt at the grave. He didn't cry, didn't really comprehend the loss. What was this before him but a mound of naked dirt, no different from the furrows Jeremias turned up with the plow? Moles lived in the ground, beetles, earthworms, slugs. His mother didn't live in the ground.

Afterward, as they sat over the cider and meat pies Meintje had brought along for the funeral supper, Staats lit his pipe, let out a long sigh, and said, in an unnaturally high voice: "It's been a trying year, *younker*."

Jeremias barely heard him.

"You know, you're always welcome to come back to us."

Barent, eleven now, and with the square head and cornsilk hair of his mother, sucked noisily at a cube of venison. The younger children—Jannetje, Klaes and little Jeremy—sat hunched over their plates, silent as stones. Meintje smiled. "I've got a contract with the patroon," Jeremias said.

Staats dismissed the notion with a wave of his hand. "You can't go on without a woman," he yodeled. "You've got a boy here not three years old and nobody to look after him."

Jeremias knew his adoptive father was right, of course. There was no way he could go on farming without someone to share the work—especially with Jeremy underfoot. Jeremias may have been mulish, pertinacious, headstrong and tough, but he was no fool. The day Katrinchee disappeared, as the hopeless hours wound down and he searched the woods till his leg gave out, the germ of an idea took hold of him. There it was, in his head. A plan. Practical and romantic both: a contingency plan. "I'll get one," he said.

Staats snorted. Meintje glanced up from her plate, and even Douw, who'd been focusing every particle of his attention on the meat pie and pickled cabbage before him, paused to shoot him a questioning glance. There was a moment of silence, during which the children stopped eating to look around them as if a ghost had entered the room. Meintje was the first to catch on. "You don't mean—?"

"That's right," Jeremias said. "Neeltje Cats."

Tofu

"I FORGET, did you say you like tofu or not?"

"Sure," she said, "anything." She was huddled in a ball in the corner of Tom Crane's bed, fully clothed, in gloves, maxicoat and knit hat, sipping sour wine from a Smucker's jar. Once, maybe twice in her life, she'd been colder. She pulled the musty frigid blankets and down comforters up over her head and tried to keep her shoulders from quaking.

"Green onions?"

"Sure," came the muffled reply.

"Garlic? Soy grits? Squash? Brewer's yeast?"

Jessica's head emerged from beneath the blankets. "You ever know me to complain?" She was six feet off the ground, which was where Tom Crane had located his bed—on high, and giving onto bare rafters strewn with cobwebs, the dangling husks of dead insects, streaks of bird or bat shit, and worse. The first time she'd ever visited the cabin—summer before last, and in the company of Walter—she'd asked Tom about that. He'd been sitting by the greasy back window in his greasy Salvation Army armchair, his hair down past his shoulders even then, drinking an evil-looking concoction of powdered milk, egg yolk, lecithin, protein powder and wheat germ out of a pint glass borrowed from an Irish pub in the City. "Stop by sometime in the winter," he said, "and you won't have to ask."

Now she understood. Up here, aloft in the place of honor, she began to feel the first faint emanations from the woodstove. She held out her glass. "You mean it never warms up down there?"

Beneath her, in his tattered aviator's coat, sweat-stained thermal undershirt and zip-up boots with the jammed zippers, Tom was flinging himself around the one-room shack like the chef at Fagnoli's Pizza after a high school basketball game. Simultaneously feeding the fire, chopping onions, celery and chives, measuring out eight cups of brown rice from a grime-filled pickle jar and stirring hot oil in the bottom of a five-gallon pot so blackened it might have been a relic of the Dresden firebombing, he never missed a beat. "Down here?" he echoed, sweeping the vegetables into the depths of the cauldron with one hand while reaching up gallantly to fill her glass with the other. "On a good day—and I'm talking maybe like just twenty or twenty-five out—if I really stoke the stove, I can get the floor temp up to around fifteen." He looked thoughtful as he poured himself a second jar of the sour, viscid wine, momentarily absorbed in the question of caloric variables while the oil hissed in the pot behind him and the hole at the juncture of the stovepipe spewed smoke into the room. "Up there, I'd say it might even get up to forty or fifty on a good night."

It didn't look to be a good night. Half-past six, and already the mercury in the rusted thermometer outside the window was dipping toward the flat red hashmark that indicated no degree of temperature at all. To Tom's credit, he had managed to get the fire going seconds after stepping through the door, hurling himself at the tinder box with all the urgency of the desperate doomed *chechaquo* in the Jack London story, but as he explained between strokes of the knife on the cutting board, the place took a while to warm up. Jessica was thinking that this was an understatement in the master class, when Tom suddenly snatched up a galvanized pail and darted for the door. "You're not going back out there?" she asked in genuine horror.

The answer came in the form of a duosyllabic yelp as he fumbled with the buttons of his aviator's coat and inadvertently clanked the pail against a footlocker piled high with yellowing laundry. "Water!" he cried, hustling past her, and then the door slammed shut behind him.

Earlier that day—in the pale light of dawn, to be precise—Jessica, who'd been married for all of twelve weeks now, had complained to her husband that the car wouldn't start, and that because the car wouldn't start, she was late for work. Walter wasn't very helpful. Unemployed, unshaven, hung over from yet another late night at the Elbow, he lay inert in the center of the bed, mummy-wrapped in the quilt Grandmother Wing had given them on their wedding day. She watched the slits of his eyes crack open. The lids were about six inches thick. "Call Tom," he croaked.

Tom didn't have electricity. Tom didn't have running water. He didn't have an electric toothbrush, hair dryer or waffle iron. He didn't have a phone, either. And even if he did have one, there were no phone lines running through the woods, across Van Wart Creek and up the hill to his shack, so it wouldn't be of much use to him. Stalking back and forth in her herringbone maxicoat, gulping cold coffee and running a nervous brush through her fine blond hair, she attempted to point this out to her supine husband.

The quilt was motionless, the life presumably held in its grip, silent. After a moment she heard his breathing ease into the gentle autonomous rhythm of sleep. "Walter?" She prodded him. "Walter?"

Muffled, slurred, his words might have come from the brink of an unbridgeable gulf: "Call in sick," he murmured.

It was a temptation. The day was cold enough to exfoliate flesh, and the thought of eight hours beneath the fluorescent lights sniffing formalin was enough to make her long for the term papers, final exams and lab reports of the year before. The job had turned grim in the past few weeks, nothing but larva counts and record keeping, nothing but sitting and watching the clock—it would be March before they got out on the water again. Even Tom, who'd been hired to run the dredge on the big boat, had lately found himself hunched over a glass dish swimming with bits of weed and insect and fish larvae, breathing fumes. No: she didn't want to go to work. Especially if she had to fight Arctic blasts and a sapped battery to get there.

"You know I can't do that," she pleaded, the dregs of the coffee gone sour in her mouth. She was hoping he'd argue with her, tell her to stuff the job and come back to bed, but he was already snoring. She started up the kettle for another cup of instant, padded across the cold linoleum in her slippers and was fumbling through the cupboard for the Sanka, when she was suddenly seized with spasms of guilt. She *had* to go to work, of course she did. There was her career to think about—she knew just how good this job would look on her record when she applied to grad school again in the fall—and then, on a more prosaic level, they needed the money. Walter hadn't worked since his accident. He claimed he was weighing his options, feeling things out. Trying to deal with the trauma. He was going into teaching, sales, insurance, banking, law, he was going to go back to school, start a motorcycle repair shop, open a restaurant. Any day now. Jessica cut the flame beneath the kettle and slipped into the other room to call her father. If she was lucky, she'd catch him before he left for the train. . . .

She was lucky. As it turned out, she was only twenty minutes late, and she got to breathe formalin all through the long gray morning and the dim, slow, Hyperborean afternoon.

Tom had given her a ride home. In the dark. On the back of his ratcheting, rusty, mufflerless Suzuki 50, in wind-chill conditions that must have approximated those at Ice Station Zebra. Dancing high up off her toes, thrashing herself with clonic arms and dabbing wildly at her runny nose, she'd dashed up the steps of the cozy little Kitchawank Colony bungalow (rent: $90 a month, plus utilities) that she and Walter had chosen from among a hundred identically cozy little Kitchawank Colony bungalows, only to find that Walter was gone. Tom stood behind her, helmet in hand, the yellow scarf wrapped around the lower part of his face like a camel driver's *kaffiyeh*. "He's not here," she said, turning to him.

Tom's eyes were distant and bleary above the scarf. They took in the kitchen and living room in a single glance. "No," he said, "I guess not."

A long moment ticked by, her disappointment like some heavy weight they both suddenly had to carry—she couldn't face it, a cold night alone with defrosted enchiladas and quesadilla chips that had the taste and texture of vinyl—until Tom tugged the scarf down past his lips and asked if she wanted to come out to his place for dinner. They could leave Walter a note.

And now, here she was, clutching her legs to her chest and watching her breath crystallize before her face, a farrago of warring odors broiling up around her. There was the cold salt stink of unwashed socks and underwear, the must of mold and woodrot, the acid sting of the smoke and the unconquerable, insurmountable, savory, sweet, stomach-clenching aroma of garlic frying in the pan. She was about to spring down and give it a stir, when in came the saint of the forest, elbows flailing, water sloshing, feet beating the floor like drumsticks. He was breathing hard, and his nose was the color of tinned salmon. "Water," he gasped, setting the bucket down beside the stove, and without pausing, measuring out twenty-four cups of it for the rice. "Blood Creek," he added with a grin. "It never lets me down."

Later, after they'd each put away two heaping tin plates of gummy rice and vegetables with garlic-fried tofu and soy grits *maison,* they shared another five or six jars of wine and a joint of homegrown, listened to Bobby Blue Bland sing "Call on Me" on Tom's no-fidelity battery-powered record player, and discussed Herbert Axelrod, talking chimps and UFOs with all the passion of rabbinical students delving into the mysteries of the Cabala. Tom had left the door to the stove open, and at some point Jessica had stopped shivering long enough to climb down from the airy bed and prop herself up on a chair just beyond the range of incineration. She told Tom the story of the time Herbert Axelrod, invited to lecture at the University of San Juan, had stepped off the plane and discovered a new species of fish in a puddle just off the runway. In return, Tom told her about the Yerkes Primate Center, dolphins that could do trigonometry and the UFO he'd seen right out there on Van Wart Road. Finally, though, and inevitably, the conversation turned to Walter.

"I'm worried about him," Jessica confided.

Tom was worried too. Ever since the accident Walter had grown increasingly strange, obsessed with road signs, history and the Robeson riots, jabbering about his father as if the man existed and generally working himself into a frenzy at the Elbow every night. Even worse, he was hallucinating. Seeing his grandmother and a host of leprechauns behind every tree, seeing his mother, his father, his uncles and cousins and ancestors. All right: it must have been terrible having his foot hacked off like that, and sure, he needed time to adjust, but things were getting out of hand. "Does he tell you about seeing things?"

Jessica leaned toward him as he bent to feed the stove. "Seeing things?"

"Yeah, you know, like people? Dead people?"

She thought about this a minute, her mind numbed by the wine, the faintest queasiness spreading its fingers in her deepest gut. "His father," she said finally. "He told me once—I think it was just after the accident—that he saw his father. But I mean"—she shrugged—"maybe he did."

"Is he dead, or what?"

The wine was going to her head. Or maybe it was the pot. Or the tofu. "Who?"

"Walter's father."

She shrugged again. "Nobody knows."

It was then that they heard the thump of footsteps on the porch out front of the shack in the middle of nowhere, a sound like the rap of fleshless knuckles on the lid of a pine box, and both of them froze. "Walter," Jessica murmured in the next breath, and they relaxed. But then the door flew open and there was Mardi, in sealskin boots and a ratty raccoon coat that fell to her knees, shouting "Hey, Tom Crane, you hairy old satyr, you old man of the mountain! Have I got something for you!"

She was in, the door slammed shut behind her, and she was warming her hands over the fire and stamping her feet in a furious little seal-pounding fandango before she acknowledged Jessica's presence. "Oh," she said, the big cold coat in Jessica's face, her eyes bloated and streaked with red, "oh . . . hi."

Tom poured her a glass of wine while she shouted about the path in from the road—"Nothing but ice, like a fucking bobsled run or something"—and how she'd fallen on her ass at least six times. "See?" she said, lifting the coat to show off her buttocks in the grip of a pair of tight faded jeans that didn't show a wrinkle.

Suddenly Jessica felt as sour as the rancid wine in the pit of her stomach.

"You know what?" Mardi said, flinging off the coat to reveal a ski sweater featuring what appeared to be a band of humping reindeer, and following this with a squealing non sequitur ("Oh, what's this? Ummmmm. . . .") as she first peered into the pot and then began to pick bits of squash and tofu from it. "Hmmmmm, that's good. What is it, tofu?" She sat above them, perched on the edge of the table, jaws working, licking at her fingertips. Her hands were slim, pretty, no bigger than a child's, and she wore two or three rings on each finger. "You know what?" she repeated.

Silence. Jessica could hear the low moan and suck of the stove, the pop and wheeze of sap in the burning wood. Tom was grinning at Mardi like a hick at the sideshow. "What?" he said finally.

Mardi came up off the table in a theatrical leap and threw out her arms like a cabaret singer. "Hash!" she announced. "Blond Lebanese!" It was, she assured them, the best, the purest, the most potent, unrefined, mind-numbing, groovy and auspicious hash they'd ever partake in the glory of, and furthermore, she added with a lopsided wink, she had five grams of it for sale. Not that she wasn't tempted to keep it all for herself—just to have around, you know—nor did she usually do anything like sell drugs or anything, but it was just that she, like, needed the cash.

Jessica tried, she really did. But there was something about this girl in the raccoon coat that irritated her to the depths of her soul, that made her want to grind her teeth and howl. It wasn't just that she was crude, loudmouthed, sloppy and offensive—it went deeper than that. There was something in the very timbre of her voice, in her movements, in the way she rubbed at the touched-up mole at the corner of her mouth or drew breath through the gap between her front teeth, that unhinged Walter's sweet-tempered wife. Every word, every gesture, was a sliver driven beneath her nails.

Stoned, Mardi couldn't stop talking. She told a long, barely coherent story about seducing two of her professors at Bard, appreciated motorcycles with Tom—come spring *she* was going to get the big Honda, the 750—and dissolved in giggles over something that had happened at a concert the two of them had attended. In the middle of all this, she produced a pipe from the breast pocket of the raccoon coat, lit it, took a suction-hose drag and handed it to Tom. Resinous and rich, with an edge to it that defeated even the acid sting of the woodsmoke, the aroma of the smoldering drug filled the shack. Tom passed the pipe to Jessica.

Now when it came to hashish, Jessica was no neophyte. Hacking like a tubercular, she'd shared the occasional hookah with her college dorm mates or taken furtive hits from Walter's foil-wrapped pipe out back of the Elbow, and everything had been fine, no problem. But

Mardi's stuff took her by surprise. Especially on top of all that spoiled wine and tofu and Tom Crane's own, tight-rolled little joint. Five minutes after Mardi lit the pipe, Jessica felt as if she were sinking through the floor, great pulsing blotches of color exploding across her field of vision like the blips on a blank movie screen. The queasiness she'd felt earlier had migrated all of a sudden, from her bowels to her stomach, and it was creeping up her throat like the disembodied hand in "The Beast with Five Fingers." She was about to gag, about to leap up, throw herself through the door and spew squash, tofu, brown rice and sour white wine out into the crystallized and pristine night, when the door swung open of its own accord.

And who should be standing there, cocked on his good leg and framed by that same Arctic night, his Salvation Army greatcoat and scarf a mess of shaved leaves, burrs, twigs and other woodland refuse? Who, with his Dingo boots scuffed beyond recognition and the look of not one, not two, but falls and scrapes uncountable in his eyes? None other. It was Walter.

MacArthur coming ashore at Leyte could hardly have generated more excitement. Tom was up and across the room in two hops, slapping backs with the lost wanderer, Jessica's gorge sank momentarily and she sprang up to embrace him and peck a kiss, and Mardi, while she never moved, nonetheless allowed a big wicked lascivious smile to spread across her lips and the light of knowledge—knowledge in the narrowest and most euphemistic biblical sense—to manifest itself in her perfect, glacial, deep-set and mocking violet eyes.

All right. Questions flew. No, he hadn't eaten. Sure, he'd love some tofu. Yeah, he was at a bar down in Verplanck, shooting pool with Hector, and he hadn't realized how late it was. Uh-huh, yeah: he got the note. Probably no more than ten minutes after they'd left. Well, yeah, he got cleaned up a bit, took a shower and whatnot, and thought it might be fun on the coldest night in history to come on out and see how the saint of the forest was taking things. (This with a grin for Tom Crane, who was already at the stove, stirring the depths of the cauldron with a wild and spastic rotation of his bony arm.) And yes, he must have gone down about a hundred times on the path—damn worthless son-of-a-bitching foot kept skidding out from under him.

"Want a hit of this?" Mardi, still perched on the edge of the table, leaned toward him, her voice pinched with the effort to contain the inestimable smoke, the pipe held out to Walter like a propitiary offering.

"Sure," Walter said, touching his hand to hers, "thanks," and Jessica saw something in his eyes. "How you been, Mardi," he said, bringing the pipe to his lips, and Jessica heard something in his voice. She looked at Mardi, sitting there like a cat with a mouthful of feathers, and she looked at Walter, squinting through the smoke at Mardi, and all at once the most devastating, most heartrending and sickening thought came to her.

Mardi was talking now, her voice coming fast and hard, honed like a razor, telling Walter the same story she'd told fifteen minutes before, about the professors and her own provocative and irresistible self. And Walter, sprawled in a chair, unbuttoning his coat and passing the pipe, was listening. But no. No. She was just being paranoic, that's all. It was the hash. It always did this to her. So what if Walter wasn't home for dinner, so what if he stayed out at the Elbow half the nights of the week, so what if Mardi had preceded him by a *matter of mere minutes*—what did that prove? Oh no, she was way out of line.

For all that, though, she was on her feet in the next instant, the half-full Smucker's jar hurtling to the floor like a two-ton bomb, on her feet and out the door to the porch, where she leaned over the railing and brought up all the fire in her guts, retching so furiously, so uncontrollably and without remit or surcease, that she thought for the longest while she'd been poisoned.

Martyr's Reach

It wasn't another woman, she was sure of that. But that something was wrong, radically wrong, Christina had no doubt. She leaned back on the dog-smelling davenport her mother had fished out of the basement for her, held the steaming cup of Sanka to her lips and stared out the bungalow's yellowed windows and into the saturate dusk that gathered in the trees like a precursor of heavy weather to come. All the world was quiet. Walter was asleep already, Hesh and Lola gone out for the night. Dropping her gaze from the trees to the pine desk beneath the window (her husband's desk, with its hulking black Smith Corona and its neatly squared row of arcane little volumes with titles like *Agrarian Conflicts in Colonial New York* and *Van Wart Manor: Then and Now*), she felt a pang of sadness so acute it was like giving birth to something twisted and deformed, ugly as a lie. When she looked up again, she had to bite her ring finger to keep from crying out.

It wasn't another woman, but she almost wished it were. At least then she would know what she was up against. As things stood now, she didn't know what had gone wrong, but she had only to look into Truman's eyes to know it was bad. For the past few nights he'd been "unwinding" after work at one of the local taphouses, lurching in at midnight with wild eyes and volatile breath, distant as an alien dropped from another world into the bed beside her. Unwinding. Yes. But before that—through the whole course of that blighted summer—he'd grown so strange and self-absorbed she hardly recognized him. Each night he would drag himself back from the foundry, his face set, hardened, all the sympathy driven out of it. He'd duck away from her embrace, spin Walter in the air and pour himself a drink. Then he'd sit down at the desk, pull open his notebook and lose himself until dinner. "How was work?" she'd ask. "Okay if we have green beans again for a vegetable? Have the Martians landed yet?" Nothing. No response. He was a monk of the sacred texts, he was carved of stone. After dinner he would read his bewildered son a chapter of Diedrich Knickerbocker's *History of New York,* his voice toneless and dull, and then it was back to the books. Sometimes, even on work nights, she'd wake at one or two in the morning and there he'd be, reading, underlining, making notes, his whole being caught up in the page.

"You're working too hard," she told him.

He looked up at her like a beast surprised over its prey, the book spread open in his lap as if it were the thing he'd stalked and killed, the bloody meat he was gnawing in the refuge of his den. "Not hard enough," he growled.

At first she'd been sympathetic. She kept telling herself that there was nothing wrong, that he was under too much pressure, that was all. Working a forty-hour week, commuting to the City for his final courses in education and history, attending party meetings, maintaining the car, the yard, the house, and on top of it all trying to research and write a senior thesis in the space of ten short weeks: it was enough to put anyone off track. But as the summer progressed and he became increasingly withdrawn, unloving, single-minded and hostile, she began to realize that she was fooling herself, that the problem went deeper than she dared guess. Something outside of him, something poisonous and irrevocable, was transforming him. He was hardening himself. He was driving a wedge between them. He was slipping away from her.

It had begun in June, when Sasha Freeman and Morton Blum announced the party's plans for a rally in Peterskill and Truman had started on his final project at City College, the senior thesis. Truman chose an obscure episode of local history for his paper—Christina had never even heard of it—and he set to work with all the monomaniacal concentration of a Gibbon chronicling the decline of Rome. Suddenly there was no time for dinner with Hesh and Lola, no time for cards, a drive-in movie, no time to take Walter out on the river or to throw him a ball in the cool of the evening. There was no time for sex either. He'd work half the night, frowning in the puddle of light the lamp threw over his desk, and he'd come to bed like a man with an arrow through his back. The door would creak on its hinges, he'd take three steps and he'd fling himself forward, asleep before he hit the bed. On Saturdays and Sundays, all day, he was at the library. She tried to reason with him. "Truman," she pleaded as he jotted notes or tossed one book down to snatch up another, "you're not writing the history of Western civilization; give yourself a break, slow down. Truman!" her voice rising to a shout, "it's only a term paper!"

He never even bothered to answer.

And what was he writing? What was he killing himself over, night and day, till his wife felt like a widow and his son barely recognized him? She took a look one afternoon. One flawless sunstruck afternoon when Truman was at the plant and Walter sat smearing pea soup into his shirt. She was hauling out the kitchen trash, arms laden with two bursting bags of bones and peels and coffee grounds, when suddenly there it was, the focus of the room, the house, the city, the county, the world itself: there, in the center of his desk, lay the battered manila folder that never left his sight except when he was stretched out unconscious on the bed or punching the clock for the bosses down at the foundry. It was a magnet, a ne plus ultra and a sine qua non. She picked it up.

Inside, in a wad thick as the phone directory, were hundreds of pages of lined yellow paper covered with the jerking loops and slashes of his tiny cramped script. *Manorial Revolt: The Crane/Mohonk Conspiracy,* she read, *by Truman H. Van Brunt.* She flipped the page. "The history of Van Wart Manor is a history of oppression, betrayal and deceit, a black mark in the annals of colonial settlement. . . ." The style was wild, cliché-ridden, declamatory and passionate—hysterical, even. It was like no history she'd ever read. If she hadn't known better, she would have thought the author personally involved, the victim of some terrible injustice or false accusation. She read five pages and put it down. Was this it? Was this what had taken hold of him?

She had her answer three weeks later.

It was a Saturday afternoon, a week before the concert. The

course was done, the paper finished (at two hundred fifty-seven closely typed pages it was five times the length of any other submitted that semester), the degree awarded. They took the train back from the graduation ceremony and she pressed close to Truman in the gently swaying coach, thinking *Now. Now we can breathe.* It was late in the day when they got back to the house. Truman crossed the room and sat heavily at his desk, still dressed in cap and gown—the rented cap and gown he obstinately refused to return—the sweat seeping through the heavy black muslin in dark fists and slashing crescents. "Let's celebrate," she said. "We'll pick up Walter and we'll go out someplace for dinner—someplace nice. Just the three of us."

He was staring into the trees. He didn't look like a man who'd just crowned three years of hard work with a supreme and enduring triumph—he looked like a thief about to be led off to the gallows.

"Truman?"

He brought his face around slowly, and his eyes were strange with that shifting vacant gaze she'd come to recognize over the past few weeks. "I've got to go out," he said, glancing away again. "With Piet. I've got to help Piet with his car."

"Piet?" She threw the name back at him like a curse. "Piet?" She could see him, Piet, as pale as a hairless little grub, an ineradicable smirk on his face. "What about me? What about your son? Do you realize we haven't done anything as a family for what—months now?"

He only shrugged. His upper lip trembled, as if he were fighting back a wicked leering little smile that said *Yes, yes, I'm guilty, I'm a shit, abuse me, hate me, divorce me.* He couldn't hold her eyes.

They'd been married nearly four years—didn't that mean anything to him? What was wrong? What happened to the man she'd fallen in love with, the daredevil with the quick smile who'd flown under the Bear Mountain Bridge and swept her off her feet?

He didn't know. He was tired, that was all. He didn't want to argue.

"Look at me," she said, seizing him by the arms as he rose to go, the coarse fabric of the gown bunching under her fists. "You're seeing someone else, aren't you?" Her voice rose to a lacerating wail that filled her head till she thought it would burst. "Aren't you?"

She knew in that instant that she was wrong, and the knowledge crumpled her like a balled-up sheet of foil. It wasn't another woman. It wasn't the Crane/Mohonk conspiracy or the forty hours a week at the foundry either. She was looking into the depths of him and what she saw there was as final and irrevocable as the drop of a guillotine: he was already gone.

The paper was done, and now he had the cap and gown, artifacts of his accomplishment. He slept in them through the remainder of that week, wore them to work, fluttered into Outhouse's Tavern like the scholar-gypsy, the mortarboard raked back on his head as if it had fallen out of the sky and miraculously lighted there. She saw him in the soft light of morning as he pulled on his steel-toed boots, and she saw him silhouetted against the harsh yellow lamp in the living room as he staggered in at night: that week, that dismal fractured week that began with his commencement and ended with the concert, he didn't spend a single evening at home.

She remonstrated at dawn, pleaded at midnight, spat out her fury and despair through the small hours of the morning. He was impervious. He lay in bed, drunk, the tattered gown wound around his legs, the breath whistling through his lips. At the sound of the alarm, he started up out of bed, fumbled into his boots and staggered out the door—without coffee, without cornflakes, without a hello or goodbye. And so it went until Saturday, the day of the concert. On that mild and fateful morning, Truman was up at first light, grinning wildly at her, spouting one-liners like a desperate comedian up against an immovable audience. He whipped up a batch of pancakes, fried eggs and sausages, clowned around the kitchen for Walter with a colander on his head. Could it be all right after all? she wondered. The pancakes were on the table, Walter was giggling at his silly Daddy, Christina smiled for the first time in a week, and Truman, leering like a court jester, like a zany, like a madman pressed to the bars of his cage, tore the ragged academic gown from his back and sent it hurtling across the room and into the wastebasket in a high arcing jump shot. Then, with a wink, he disappeared into the bedroom and returned a moment later in a sparkling pristine polo shirt—a shirt she'd never seen before, a miracle of a shirt—still creased with newness and striped in glorious bands of red, white and blue.

Walter went off with his grandparents to spend the day amidst the fascinating fishes of the Hudson, while Truman and Hesh loaded the sound equipment into the back of Hesh's Plymouth and Christina made sandwiches, cookies, a thermos of iced tea. Was she humming to herself? Smiling over her private thoughts? She'd seen it in his eyes, seen that he was dead to her inside, and she didn't want to believe it. She wanted to believe that this morning of the concert was a new beginning, radiant and propitious. He was recovering, coming back to her—it *had* been the pressure after all, and now it was over. He'd got his degree, worn his robe to tatters. So what if he'd been out letting off steam? It was only natural.

Wrapping sandwiches, she thought of the concert of the year before, at the pavilion in the Colony, when they'd sat on a blanket in the grass, holding hands, Walter asleep beside them. Robeson sang "Go Down, Moses," he sang "Swing Low, Sweet Chariot" and something from Handel's "Messiah," and she slid into the cradle of Truman's arms and closed her eyes to let the great deep thrumming voice quaver on the sounding board of her body. There was no Piet then, no manila folder, no Crane/Mohonk conspiracy. There was only Truman, her husband, the man with a smile for the world, the athlete, the scholar, the party acolyte and hero—only Truman, and her.

And then the morning was gone and she was collating the pages of her pamphlets and thinking how maybe next weekend they could go up to Rhinebeck or someplace—just to get away for a couple of days. They could stay at that old inn on the river, and maybe go sailing or horseback riding. Her fingers were ink-stained. It was three o'clock, four. She was sitting by the window and listening to the radio, waiting for her husband and Hesh to get back from their last-minute conference with Sasha Freeman and Morton Blum, when she glanced up to see Hesh's Gillette-blue Plymouth swing into the driveway. She was out the door, picnic basket in one hand, A&P bag of literature in the other, before the car rolled to a stop. "Hey," she was about to call out, "I was beginning to think you forgot all about me," but she caught herself. For at that moment, with fear and loathing and a sinking sense of defeat, she saw that they were not alone. There, perched between them like a ventriloquist's dummy, his naked little hands braced against the dashboard and his face locked in a mad evil sneer of triumph, was Piet.

When she looked back on that night, the night that broke her life in two, she saw faces. Piet's face, as it was in the car, insinuated in some unspeakable way between her husband and herself. Truman's face, turned away from her, hard and unsmiling. Hesh's face: bluff, honest, opened wide to her as she slipped into the seat beside him, numb and composed for death as he lay unconscious on the scuffed pine boards of the stage while the criminals and brownshirts howled like demons in the dark. And then there were the faces of the mob itself: the rabid women thumbing their noses, eyes popping with hate; the boy who'd leaned forward to spit on the windshield; a man she recognized from the butcher shop in Peterskill who'd bared his teeth like a dog, cupped his genitals in both hands and then clasped the crook of his arm in the universal gesture of defiance and contempt. A day passed, two, three, four, a week, a month, and still she saw them. Though she struggled to escape them, though she shut her eyes fast, paced the floor, fought for sleep, those faces haunted her. They were there, ugly and undeniable, when she started up in the morning from the fitful sleep that overtook her at first light, they were there in the afternoon as she sat sobbing on the davenport, and in the maw of the night when the dark conjured its images. These were her ghosts, this her attack of history.

It began in the deeps of that first night, when the nervous phone calls had ceased and Hesh's blood had dried to a crust on the sleeve of her blouse, when she'd got to the end of the list of hospitals in the Westchester-Putnam phone book and found that none had admitted a bleeding athlete with hair the color of tarnished copper and a torn polo shirt, when she pictured him lying unconscious in a ditch or crawling home like a dog struck down on the highway. She sat by the phone, listless, the eyes sunk back in her head, willing him to call. He didn't call. The night held on, tenacious, implacable. From the back room came the arhythmic click and scrape of Walter's teeth, grinding, bone on bone. And then, caught in the window, hovering over the coleus, peering out from behind the radio console, the faces began to show themselves. Piet's face, Truman's, Hesh's, the twisted feral mug of the man from the butcher shop.

The next day Lola sat beside her through the never-ending morning, the unendurable afternoon and the starless night that fell on her like a curse. Don't worry, Lola said, her voice dabbing at the wounds, he'll turn up. He's safe, I know it. For all they knew he could have gotten away to the City with a carload of concertgoers or doubled back to Piet's place in Peterskill. He'll call, she said, any minute now. Any minute.

She was wrong. Soothing, but wrong. He didn't call. Hesh beat the bushes and Hesh found nothing. Lola wanted to know if she could get her a sleeping pill. It was 11:00 P.M. No one had seen or heard from Truman in twenty-seven hours. Scotch? Vodka? Gin?

Then it was Monday, early—seven, eight, she didn't know. Lola was standing behind the counter at the van der Meulen bakery and Hesh, his arms rough with scab and his face ripened like a fruit, was on his way to Sollovay's Auto Glass and Mirror on Houston Street. That was when he walked in. She hadn't slept in fifty hours and she was seeing faces, Walter was wound up like a dervish in his private three-year-old's dance of denial and trauma, the trash was overflowing, the larder empty, her mother rushing back from a vacation in Vermont to be with her in that bankrupt hour, and he walked in the door.

He was limping. He was drunk. There was a dark punished bruise beneath his left eye, his ear was bandaged and he was wearing the same clothes he'd worn to the concert, dirty now, torn, steeped in blood. What was there to say? We were worried sick, where were you, did they hurt you, I'm so glad, we're so glad, Walter, look, look who's come home. She was up off the davenport and rushing to him, Walter at her side, leaping to the familial embrace, tears of gratitude, Odysseus home from the wars, unfurl the banners, sound the horns, lights, camera . . . but he was numb to their touch. In the next moment he shoved past them, shielding his face like a gangster outside the courthouse, and then he was in the bedroom, the suitcase gaping open on the bed like a set of jaws.

"What are you doing?" She was on him now, tugging at his arm. "Truman, what is it? Talk to me! Truman!" Beneath her, clinging to his father's legs, Walter kept up a steady dirge, "Daddy, daddy, daddy."

Nothing could touch him. He shrugged her off as he'd shrugged off tacklers in the years of his glory, single-minded and heedless, plunging for the goal line. Books, clothes, his notes, the manuscript: the house was on fire, the woods were burning. "I'm sorry," he whispered, his lip quivering with that sick betrayer's grin—she didn't exit, Walter was invisible—and then he was on his way out the door.

Outside, the car. The Buick. They said later it was Van Wart's car, but how would she know? It was black, long, funereal. She'd never seen it before. "Truman!" She was at the door, she was on the stoop. "Talk to me!" He wouldn't talk, wouldn't even look at her. He flung the suitcase in back and sprang into the driver's seat like a hunted man, and then the car jerked into gear and lurched back down the driveway. She stood there, stricken immobile, and in that moment, through the sad slow dance of light on the windshield, she caught her final glimpse of him. Jaw set, eyes dead, he never even turned his head.

But Truman didn't leave her without a valediction of sorts. As the car swerved to the left on Kitchawank Road, presenting her with the long gleaming plane of the passenger side, Piet suddenly appeared at the open window, sprung up like a toadstool from the sunless depths of the interior. He turned to her, slow as clockwork, and lifted his pale cupped child's hand in the least and smallest wave.

Bye-bye.

When Anna Alving swung into the driveway it was just past two in the afternoon and her hands were trembling on the wheel. She'd left the rented cottage on Lake St. Catherine at seven that morning, her husband following in the second car. They stopped for lunch somewhere outside Hudson (Magnus so preoccupied with his vanishing son-in-law he barely touched his tuna on rye, and she so wrought up she had six cups of coffee with her danish) and then set off again in tandem. The Chevrolet was a racehorse compared to Magnus' creeping Nash, and though she tried to hang back and keep him in sight, by the time they reached Claverack the rear-view mirror showed nothing but blacktop. She thought about pulling over to wait for him, but the grip of emergency tightened on her, and her foot went to the floor. *Mama,* her daughter's voice came to her as it had on the phone the night before, *Mama, he's gone,* and she took the curves in a headlong rush that savaged her tires and nearly jerked the steering wheel from her hands. Now, as she pulled up to the silent bungalow, the bungalow that sat newly painted in a lattice of leaf-thrown shadow, looking placid, normal, staid, she loosened her grip on the wheel and cut the ignition. She sat there a moment, listening to the ticks and groans of the dying engine, gathering up her purse and composing her face. Then she started up the front steps.

She found Christina sunk into the davenport, shoulders bunched, legs clutched to her chest. Beside her, stretched out prone atop an avalanche of children's books, was Walter. He was asleep—mouth agape, eyelids half-closed—and she was reading to him. Oblivious. Her voice sunk to a weary monotone. "Jack Sprat could eat no fat," she read, "his wife could eat no lean."

"Christina?"

Christina looked up. In the past six hours she'd been through every fairy tale and nursery rhyme in the house. Cinderella, Snow White, Rumpelstiltskin, they all lived happily ever after. Babar, Alice, Toad of Toad Hall, life a bowl of cherries. Then there was Jack—Jack of the beanstalk, Jack of Jill, Jack the housebuilder and Jack the candlestick jumper—and Humpty Dumpty, Wee Willie Winkie and poor Cock Robin. "Have they found him yet?" her mother asked.

Slowly, reverently, as if it were part of some ritual, Christina closed the book in her lap. Her mother was standing there before her, tanned from her month on the stony shingle of Lake St. Catherine, her hair newly done and a look of permanent anguish on her face. Found him? What she wanted to know was who killed Cock Robin.

Her mother's voice came back at her: "Is he all right?'

She looked up into her mother's face, the face that had been her sun and moon, her comfort and refuge since she lay helpless in the cradle, the face that vanquished all those horrific others that infested the shadows and leered through her dreams, but all she could think of was poor Cock Robin and the birds of the air that fell a-sighing and a-sobbing when they heard the news. "They found him," she said finally.

Her mother was unconsciously clenching and unclenching her fists, there was the rumble of a second car in the driveway, Walter murmured something in his sleep. "They found him," she repeated. A car door slammed. She could hear her father's footsteps on the pavement, the stoop, she could see his anxious face through the mesh of the screen.

"Yes?" her mother said.

"Yes," she said. "He's dead."

He wasn't dead, but far better that he were. By nightfall the Alvings had heard the rumors—had heard Hesh's version, Lola's, Lorelee Shapiro's and Rose Pollack's—and Christina, stretched the length of her childhood bed like a corpse laid out for embalming, finally admitted the truth. Truman had left her. Left her unprotected at the concert, left her to agonize through two sleepless days and nights, then packed up his things and left her for good. "I can't believe it," her mother said. Her father rose from his chair. "I'll kill him," he said.

There was the second concert at the end of that week, big with triumph and pared down with defeat, and then August gave way to September, with its lingering warmth and deluded butterflies, with the fullness that yields to decay. By the time the trees turned, Christina had lost twenty-two pounds. For the first time since she was fifteen she weighed less than a hundred pounds, and her mother was concerned. "Eat," she said, "you're wasting away to nothing. Forget him. Forget him and eat. You've got to keep your strength up. Think of Walter."

She was thinking of Walter. On the first of October, while her mother was out, she met with a lawyer from Yorktown and drew up the papers giving legal guardianship to his godparents in the event of her death. As for her mother's injunctions, they were meaningless. Eat? She might as well have urged her to fly. One ate to replenish oneself, to renew cells, to build bone and muscle and fat, to live. She didn't want to live. She wasn't hungry. Meat sickened her, the smell of cooking was an anathema, fruits were vile and vegetables hateful. Milk, cereal, bread, rice, even potato latkes—they were all poison to her. Her mother would make her pudding, doughnuts, eggs Benedict, she'd appear in her room with a tray of soda crackers and broth and sit there chiding, holding the spoon to her lips as if she were a child still, but it did no good. Christina would force herself to take a swallow, if only to smooth the lines in that kind and solicitous face that hung over her, but the broth was like acid on her stomach and within the hour she'd be hunched over the toilet, gagging till the tears stood out in her eyes.

Dr. Braun, the family practitioner who'd assuaged her childhood fevers, dabbed at her chicken pox and stitched up her knee when she'd fallen from the precipitous step of the schoolbus, prescribed a sedative and felt it might do her some good to chat with Dr. Arkawy, a colleague who practiced psychiatric medicine. She didn't want to chat. She spat out the sedatives, clutched Walter and his bright hopeful books to her chest and saw faces, rabid hateful faces, Truman's the most hateful of all. By the first of November she was down to eighty-eight pounds.

They fed her intravenously at Peterskill Community Hospital but she jerked the IV from her arm whenever they left the room. She was dreaming when they moved her to the other hospital, but she smelled the river strong in her nostrils in that little space between the ambulance and the great heavy fortress door. When they pinned her arms down and started that drip of life, she could feel the water rising around her. Gray, lapping waves, nothing severe, a ripple fanning out across the broad flat surface, rocking the boat as gently as the breeze rocked the cradle of that baby high in the treetops. She was with Truman suddenly, long ago, long before Walter, the bungalow, long before the papers and the books and the party meetings that found his hand entwined in hers. Long before. They were out on the river in his father's boat, the boat that stank of fish and that was gouged across the gunwales by the friction of a thousand ropes hauling up secrets from the bottom. He'd spread a blanket for her in the bow, there was that peculiar sick-sweet smell of exhaust, the sun was high, the wind had fallen to nothing. *What's that,* she asked, *over there? That point across the river?* He sat at the tiller, grinning. *Kidd's Point,* he said, *after the pirate. That's Dunderberg behind it, and straight ahead is what they call the Horse Race.*

She felt the water swell beneath her. She looked up the river to where the mountains fell away in continents of shadow and seagulls hung in oceans of filtered light. *Above that, and around the bend,* he told her, *it's a clear channel up to West Point. Then we hit Martyr's Reach.* He knew an island there, in the middle of the river, beautiful spot, Storm King on the one side, Breakneck on the other. He was thinking maybe they'd land and have lunch there.

Lunch. Yes, lunch.

Pity was, she just wasn't hungry.

Sons and Daughters

IT WAS the morning of Neeltje's sixteenth birthday, a morning like any other: damp, dismal, curdled with the monotony of routine. There were eggs to be gathered, ducks, geese and chickens to be fed. The fire needed stoking, the porridge thickening, she could feel her fingers go stiff with the thought of the spinning, churning and milling to come. Her father was gone, off somewhere on the patroon's business and not due back till nightfall, and though it was barely light yet, her mother already sat stiffly at the flax wheel, her right arm rising and falling mechanically, her eyes fixed on the spindle. Her sisters, girls still, warmed themselves at the fire and gazed expectantly into the pot. No one so much as glanced at her as she lifted her cloak down from the hook and slipped into her clogs.

Feeling hurt and angry—she might as well have been one of the patroon's black nigger slaves for all the notice anybody took of her—Neeltje slammed out the door, crossed the yard and stopped to poke through the grass for the morning's eggs. She didn't ask much—a smile maybe, best wishes on her birthday, a hug from her mother—but what did she get? Nothing. It was her birthday, and no one cared. And why should they? She was just a pair of hands that chopped and milked and scrubbed, a back that lifted, legs that hauled. She was sixteen today, a full-grown woman, an adult, and no one knew the difference.

Absorbed in bitter reflections, she bent for eggs, her skirts already heavy with dew. Unmilked, the cows mooed emphatically from the barn, while a troop of ragged hens pecked at her heels and cocked their heads to rebuke her with their bright censorious eyes. A pall of mist breathed in off the river with a smell of sludgy bottoms, the dead and drowned, and she shivered, pulling the cloak tight around her throat. In the next moment she plucked an egg from the new grass along the fence, found two more beneath the canopy of the woodshed, and rose to dry her hands on her apron. It was then—as she straightened up, the basket caught in the crook of her arm, hands bunched in the folds of her apron—that she became aware of a movement off to her left, where the outline of the barn sank into mist. She turned her head instinctively, and there he was, cocked back on his leg, smiling faintly, watching her.

"Jeremias?" She made a question of it, her voice riding up in surprise, conscious all at once of her uncovered head, the utter plainness of her cloak and skirts, the mud that spattered her yellow peasant's clogs.

"Shhhhhh!" He held a finger to his lips and motioned her forward, before receding into the fog at the nether end of the barn. She glanced around her twice—the cows protesting, chickens squabbling, ducks and geese raising an unholy racket down by the pond—and turned to follow him.

Behind the barn, in the spill of briars and weeds and with the smell of cow dung wafting up around them, he took her hand and wished her a happy birthday (*gefeliciteerd met je verjaardag*), then dropped his voice and told her to forget the eggs.

"Forget the eggs? What do you mean?"

The mist steamed around him. The smile was gone. "I mean you won't be needing them. Not now." He opened his mouth to expand on this abrupt and rather cryptic proposition, but seemed to think better of it. He looked down at the ground. "Don't you know why I've come?"

Neeltje Cats was sixteen years old that day, as short and slight as a child, but ancient with the sagacity of her entrepreneurial and poetical ancestors, the bards and shopkeepers of Amsterdam. She knew why he'd come—would have known even if he hadn't sent old Jan the Kitchawank to tell her three separate times in the past eight months. "I know," she whispered, feeling as if, for form's sake at least, she should fall down at his feet in a swoon or something.

He'd let go of her hand in the rush of his eloquence on the subject of the eggs, and now he stood there, looking awkward, his arms hanging like empty sleeves. Frustrated, impatient, suffering, the cows bellowed. "It's all right, then?" Jeremias said finally, addressing a tree trunk twenty feet behind her.

All right? She'd been dreaming of this moment for months, lying on the rough mattress between her sprawled sisters in the dead black night, struggling to summon the image of him before she drifted off (Jeremias, the prince who would ascend the ladder of her tresses and free her from the hag's tower, who would slay dragons and crush villains for her, Jeremias of the stonemason's build and sea-green eyes). She never doubted he would come for her. She'd seen it in his eyes, seen it in the slump of his shoulders as he limped past her in his humiliation and slouched up the Peterskill road, felt it in his touch, heard it in his voice. When old Jan took her aside after delivering missives to the patroon and singing a three-note greeting to her mother from a cousin at Crom's Pond, she knew before the words had passed his lips that Jeremias Van Brunt sent his good opinion and best wishes. And she knew too when he pressed a slip of paper into her hand that it was from Jeremias and that it would open her life up for her.

Heart pounding, she'd ducked away from the family gathered around the tottering Indian and hurried out the door in the direction of the privy. When she was out of sight, when she was sure she was beyond the prying eyes of her father, her mother, her sisters, she tore open the slip of paper. Inside, she found a laboriously worked copy of Jacob Cats' paean to matrimonial ethics. She skimmed the lines, but it wasn't the poem that stirred her, it was the valediction. In the crude block letters of an unpracticed hand, Jeremias had written *Eye wll cum for u,* and then scrawled his signature across the bottom of the page in a deluge of loops and slashes. And now, as Neeltje stood there in her muddy clogs and uncombed hair, the basket of eggs clutched to her chest and the dust of sleep barely wiped from her eyes, she saw that he was as good as his word. All right? It was perfect.

"Your father doesn't think much of me," he said.

She reached up to trace the scar along the length of his cheek. "No matter," she whispered. "I do."

It took him a minute—a minute punctuated by the lowing of the cattle and suffused with the fishy reek of the river—before he moved into her arms. There was the fog, the tsk-tsking of the hens, the rank wild odor of the awakening season. When he spoke finally, his voice was thick. "Put down the basket," he said.

The basket was still lying there in the mud at four that afternoon when Joost Cats climbed down from the bony back of Donder, his purblind nag, and smoothed the seat of his sweat-soaked and tumultuous pantaloons. He'd spent the morning in Van Wartville, mediating yet another dispute between Hackaliah Crane and Reinier Oothouse—this time over the disposition of a lean, slack-bellied sow the Yankee had caught rooting up his seed onions—after which he'd hurried home with a pair of Jan Pieterse's best Ferose stockings for Neeltje on her birthday. As he led the wheezing nag into the barn, thinking of how Reinier Oothouse, in his cups, had gone down on his knees before the Yankee and pleaded for the sow's life like a father pleading for his child ("Don't kill her, don't hurt my little *Speelgoed,* she didn't mean it, never been naughty before, anything, I'll pay anything you ask"), his two youngest burst from the house, arms and legs churning, faces lit with the joy of disaster. *"Vader! Vader!"* they cried in breathless piping unison, "Neeltje's gone!"

Gone? What were they talking about? Gone? But in the next instant he saw his wife at the door, saw the look on her face and knew it was true.

Together, led by the fluttering Trijintje and intoxicated Ans, they rounded the corner of the barn to hover over the spilled basket, the tracked and muddy earth, the shattered eggs. "Was it *Indians?*" Ans shouted. "Did they kidnap her and make her their white squaw?"

Bent like a sickle and stroking his puff of chin hair, Joost tried to picture it—naked red devils slipping from the weeds to bludgeon his defenseless little Neeltje, a rough hand cuffed over her mouth, the stinking hut and moldering furs, the queue of greasy randy braves jostling at the door. . . . "When?" he murmured, turning to his wife.

Geesje Cats was a dour woman, hipless, fleshless, wasted, a woman who bore only daughters and wore her troubles at the corners of her mouth. "This morning," she said, her eyes stung with dread. "It was Trijintje—she found it, the basket. We called and called."

The mud was puckered in dumb mouths that told the *schout*

nothing. Staring down at the sad upended basket and the spill of egg yolk that seemed to claw at the earth like the fingers of a grasping hand, he relived the scenes of violence and depravity he'd encountered in his seven years as *schout,* drowned men and stabbed men floating before his eyes, women abused, bereft, violated, bones that poked through the flesh and eyes that would see no more. When he looked up he was shouting. "You searched the orchard?" he demanded. "The river? The pond? Did you inquire at the patroon's?"

Startled, shamefaced, his wife and daughters lowered their eyes. They had. Yes, *vader,* yes, *echtgenoot,* they had.

Well, then, had they gone to the de Groodts, the Coopers, the van Dincklagens? To the inn? The ferry? The pasture, the stable, van der Donk's Hill?

A light rain had begun to fall. Ans, ten years old, began to sniffle. "All right!" he shouted, "all right: I'll go to the patroon."

The patroon was supping, bent low over a plate of pickled beets, hard cheese and a shad in cream sauce he was glumly forking up as if to remark the disparity between this and Zuider Zee herring, when Joost was shown into the room. The patroon's unburdened hand was bandaged against the knife thrusts of his gout, and his face was flushed the color of a rare wine. Vrouw Van Wart, a woman given to the denial of the flesh, sat stiffly beside him, a single dry crust before her, while his brother's widow and her daughter Mariken perched on the hard bench opposite her. The *Jongheer,* in a lace collar the size of a wheel of Gouda, occupied the place of honor at the foot of the table. "My Savior in Heaven!" cried the patroon. "What is it, Cats, that couldn't keep?"

"It's my daughter, *Mijnheer:* she's disappeared."

"How's that?"

"Neeltje. My eldest. She went out for chores this morning and there's been no trace of her since."

The patroon set down his fork, plucked a loaf from the pewter dish before him, and turned it over in his hand as if it were the single telling bit of evidence left behind at the scene of the crime. Joost waited patiently as the florid little man split the loaf and slathered it with butter. "You've, er, contacted the, er, other tenants?" the patroon gasped in his dry, windless voice.

Joost was beside himself with frustration—this was no time for the niceties of leisurely inquiry. They had his daughter, the heart and soul and central joy of his existence, and he had to get her back. "It's the Kitchawanks," he blurted, "I'm sure of it. They snatched her"—here his voice broke with a sob—"snatched her as she, she—"

At the mention of Indians, the *Jongheer* was on his feet. "I told you so," he roared at his father. "Beggars in their blankets. Aborigines, criminals, vermin, filth. We should have driven them into the river twenty years ago." He crossed the room in two great strides and lifted the harquebus down from the wall.

The patroon had risen now to his gouty feet, and the ladies pressed powdered hands to their mouths. "But, er, what's this, *mijnzoon?*" the patroon wheezed in some alarm. "What are you thinking?"

"What am I thinking?" the *Jongheer* shrieked, the blood rushing to his face. "They've raped an honest man's daughter, *vader!*" The harquebus was about as wieldy as a blacksmith's anvil, and twice as heavy. He raised it over his head in a single clenched fist. "I mean to exterminate them, annihilate them, pot them like foxes, like rats, like, like—"

It was then that a knock came at the door.

The deferential head of the tattooed slave appeared between the oak door and the whitewashed wall that framed it. "A red man, *Mijnheer,*" he said in his garbled Dutch. "Says he's got a message for the *schout.*"

Before either patroon or *Jongheer* could give the command, the door flew back and old Jan stumbled into the room to exclamations of excitement from the ladies. Jan was wearing a tattered cassock, out at elbows and shoulders, and an ancient crushed caubeen with half the brim missing. His loincloth hung from his hips like a tongue, his legs were spattered with mud and his moccasins were as black as the muck in the oyster beds of the Tappan Zee. For a long moment he just stood there, swaying slightly, and blinking in the light of the candles hung around the room.

"Well, Jan," the patroon wheezed, "what is it?"

"Beer," the Indian said.

"Pompey!" Vrouw Van Wart called, and the black reappeared. "Beer for old Jan."

Pompey poured, Jan drank. The patroon looked befuddled, the *schout* anxious, the *Jongheer* enraged. Mariken, who'd been Neeltje's playmate, looked on with a face as pale and drawn as a mime's.

The old Indian set down the cup, composed himself a moment and began a slow shuffling dance around the table, all the while chanting *Ay-yah, neh-neh, Ay-yah, neh-neh.* After half a dozen repetitions, he sang his message—in three tones, and to the same beat:

Daugh-ter, sends you,
Her greet-ings, neh-neh.

And then he stopped. Stopped singing, stopped dancing. He was frozen, like a figure in a clocktower after the hour's been struck. "Spirits," he said. "Genever."

But this time, Pompey didn't have a chance to respond. Before he could so much as glance at the patroon for his approval, let alone lift the stone bottle and pour, the *Jongheer* had slammed the Indian into the wall. "Where is she?" he demanded. "Is it ransom, is that what you want? Is it?"

"Let him go," Joost said, taking Stephanus by the arm and pushing his way between them. "Jan," he said, his voice faltering, "who is it? Who's got her? Mohonk? Wappus? Wennicktanon?"

The Indian stared at his feet. There was a smear of dirt on his cheek. He was pouting like a hurt child. "No more message," he said.

"No more? You mean that's it?"

"Listen, you son of a bitch," Stephanus began, making another charge at him, but Joost held him off.

"But—but who gave you the message?"

The Indian looked around the room as if he were trying to remember. In the background, Joost could hear Vrouw Van Wart berating her husband in a terse rasping voice. "Herself," Jan said finally.

"Neeltje?"

The Indian nodded.

"Where is she? Where did she give it to you?"

This was more difficult. Joost poured Jan a pewter cup of genever while the *Jongheer* breathed fumes and the patroon and his wife and sister-in-law and niece sat in silence, as if they were at the theater.

Suddenly the Indian made a slash in the air with the flat of his hand; then he made the sign of two fingers walking.

"What?" Stephanus asked.

"Speak up, man," the patroon croaked.

It was only Joost who understood, and he held on to the knowledge for a stunned moment, as a knifed man might have held on to the haft of the blade in his belly. The Indian had made the sign of the cripple, the one with half a leg—the sign for Jeremias Van Brunt.

Next morning, before the dogs had lifted their muzzles from the nests of their forepaws or the cock had had a chance to stretch the sleep from his wings, Joost saddled a sore and reluctant Donder and set out for Nysen's Roost. He was accompanied by the *Jongheer,* who suddenly, it seemed, had taken a passionate interest in his daughter's welfare, and he carried a brace of dueling pistols the patroon had ceremoniously retrieved from a chest in the seignorial bedroom (in addition, of course, to the silver-plated rapier that had already wrought such havoc on young Van Brunt's physiognomy). The *Jongheer,* in silk doublet, French cuffs and midnight-blue cassock with matching knee breeches, had given over the unwieldy harquebus in favor of a fowling piece loaded with pigeon shot and a Florentine dirk that looked like a surgical instrument. To complete the ensemble, he wore a jeweled rapier at his side, a floppy hat surmounted by a three-foot yellow plume, and so many silver and brass buckles he actually jingled like a sack of coins as his mount picked its way up the road.

The day was typical of April in the vale of the Hudson—raw and drizzling, the earth exhaling vapor as if it were breathing its last—and they made slow progress on the slick river road. It was late in the morning when they passed the cluster of buildings that would one day become Peterskill and turned east on Van Wart's Road. The *schout,* hunched in the saddle, had little to say. As he bobbed and swayed to the nag's erratic rhythm, he focused on the image of Jeremias Van Brunt with such intensity the world was swallowed up in it. He saw the watchful cat's eyes squinted against the onslaught of the summer sun, saw the squared jaw and defiant sneer, saw the blade come down and the blood flow. And he saw Neeltje, kneeling over the fallen renegade and glaring up at him, her father, as if he were the criminal, the trespasser, the scoffer at the laws of God and man. Had she gone with him voluntarily, then? Was that it? The thought made him feel dead inside.

If Joost was uncommunicative, the *Jongheer* never noticed. He kept up a steady stream of chatter from the time they left Croton to the moment they forded the rain-swollen Van Wart Creek and Joost hushed him with a peremptory finger tapped against his lips. Stephanus, who'd expatiated on everything from the Indian problem to the poetry of van den Vondel, and who, despite the inclemency of the weather and the dead earnestness of their mission had been humming a popular ditty not five minutes before, now slipped from his mount with a stealthy look. Joost followed suit, dismounting and leading the nag behind him up the steep slick hill to Nysen's Roost. Wet branches slapped at their faces, the *Jongheer* lost his footing and rose from the ground with a stripe of mud painted the length of him, armies of gnats invaded their mouths and nostrils and darted for their eyes. They were halfway up when the drizzle changed to rain.

The house was silent. No smoke rose from the chimney, no animals chased around the yard. The rain drove down in sheets of pewter. "What do you think?" the *Jongheer* whispered. He was hunched in his cassock, water streaming from the brim of his hat.

Joost shrugged. His daughter was in there, he knew it. Defying him, betraying him, lying in the arms of that recreant, that nose thumber, that uncrackable nut. "He's taken her by force," Joost whispered. "Give him no quarter."

They approached the house warily. Joost could feel the mud tugging at his boots; the plume hung limp in his face and he flicked it back with a swipe of his dripping hand. Then he drew his rapier. He glanced over at the *Jongheer,* who did likewise, the firearms rendered useless by the damp. Water dripped from the tip of the *Jongheer*'s well-formed nose, the yellow plume clung to the back of his neck like something fished out of the river, and he wore a strangely excited look, as if he were off to a fox hunt or pigeon shoot. They were twenty feet from the door when a sudden burst of sound froze them in mid-step. Someone was inside, all right, and whoever it was was singing, the lyric as familiar as a bedtime song in old Volendam:

Good evening, Joosje,
My little box of sweetmeats,
Kiss me, we are alone . . .
. . . I call you my heart, my consolation, my treasure.
Oh! oh! how I've tricked you!

There was a giggle, and then Neeltje's husky contralto (unmistakable, no doubt about it, the *schout* knew that voice as well as he knew his own) rose up out of the patter of rain to reprise the final line—"Oh! oh! how I've tricked *you!*"—to a spanking of applause.

That was it, the breaking point, the moment that confirmed his worst fears and gravest suspicions. The *schout* was across the yard and slamming through the door before he could think, brandishing the rapier like an archangel's sword and sputtering "Sin! Sin and damnation!"

The room was dark, cold, damp as a cave; it reeked like a hog pen and the water dripped almost as persistently inside as out. Joost saw a crude table, a wall hung with kitchen implements, the cold hearth, and there, across the room, the bed. They were in it. Together. In their nightshirts still and with a mound of stinking furs piled atop them. He saw his daughter's face as a spot of white in the gloom, her mouth open to scream, eyes twisted back in her head. "Slut!" he roared. "Filth, whore, woman of Babylon! Get up out of your harlot's bed!"

The next moment was a crowded one. Everything happened at once: the half-breed child sprang up from the shadows like a cat and scurried across the room to cower behind his uncle; the smirking *Jongheer* appeared in the doorway, sword at the ready; a cookpot fell from the wall; Neeltje cried out. And Jeremias, surprised without the strut that supported him, rose up out of the bed and came at the *schout* with a prejudicial look in his eye.

No slash this time, but a thrust meant to kill: the *schout* squared himself and shot his arm forward, and so would have skewered Jeremias like a sausage and left his daughter sans husband and honor both, but for this: Jeremias slipped. Slipped and fell heavily to the floor while the tip of the rapier danced over his head like an angry hornet.

Now Joost Cats was a reasonable man, prone neither to fits of temper nor acts of violence, happier far with the role of mediator than enforcer. He'd pitied the Van Brunt boy on that chill November day when the officious and soft-bottomed ass of a *commis* had dragged him, the *schout,* out into the naked wild to evict the half-starved lad from a worthless and unlucky plot of land, had felt foolish and ashamed standing before Meintje van der Meulen's hearth with his plumed hat in hand, regretted with all his heart the brand he'd struck on the boy's face. But for all that, he wanted to kill him. He looked into his daughter's eyes and then down at this human garbage that had stolen her away, and he wanted to cut him, perforate him, pierce his heart, his liver, his lights and bladder and spleen.

If the first thrust was instinctive, the second was a liberation. Guilt, anger, fear, resentment and jealousy broke loose in him and he jabbed the hilt forward with all the punch of his uncoiled arm. Jeremias dodged it. He rolled to his right, Neeltje flashing up off the bed with her hands outspread, the *Jongheer* lunging into the room, the child howling, the rain rising to a crescendo on the roof. *"Spuyten duyvil!"* Joost cursed, and struck a third time, but again the tip of the sword betrayed him, wagging wide of the mark and burying itself in the beaten wet earth of the floor.

He was drawing himself up for the fourth and fatal thrust, when Neeltje, entering the fray, flung herself down atop Jeremias, shrieking "Kill me! Kill me!" Stooped over double, his back murdering him, reason and restraint flung to the winds, he paused only long enough to reach down his free hand and fling her roughly aside. She hated him, his own daughter, a mouthful of teeth, claws tearing at his sleeve, but no matter. The blade flashed in his hand and he thought only of the next thrust and the next and the next one after that—he'd make a pincushion of the son-of-a-bitch, a sieve, a colander!

If Joost was deranged, he was also deluded: there would be no more thrusts of the rapier. For in the confusion Jeremias had clawed his way to his feet (or rather, foot) and snatched a crude weapon from the inglenook. The weapon, known as a curiosity in those parts, was a Weckquaesgeek pogamoggan. It consisted of a flexible length of fruitwood, to the nether end of which a jagged five-pound ball of granite had been affixed by means of leather ligatures. Jeremias swung it once, catching the *schout* just behind the ear and plunging him into the rushing interstitial darkness of a dreamless sleep, and then braced himself to face the *Jongheer.*

For his part, the heir to the Van Wart patent looked like a man who's nodded off in his box at the opera only to wake and find himself at a bear baiting. In the instant the *schout* pitched forward, the smirk died on the *Jongheer's* face. This was more than he'd bargained for. This was sordid, primitive, beastly—not at all the sort of thing a lettered man should hope to experience. He tried to draw himself up and project the authority of his father, the patroon, whose rights, privileges and responsibilities would one day devolve upon himself. "Put up your weapon this instant," he demanded in a voice that sounded like someone else's, "and submit to the legally constituted authority of the patroon." His voice dropped. "You are now in my custody."

Neeltje was bent over her father now, pressing a handkerchief to his head. The child had stopped his unearthly howling and Jeremias had propped himself against the back of a chair. The club, with its freight of human hair and blood, swung idly in his hand and the scar stood out on his face. He made no answer. He turned his head and spat.

"Vader, vader," Neeltje cried. "Don't you know where you are? It's little Neeltje. It's me." The *schout* moaned. Rain drummed at the roof. "With all due respect, *Mijnheer,*" Jeremias said in a voice reined in with the effort to control it, "you may own the milch cow, the land under my feet, the house I've built with my own hands, but you don't own Neeltje. And you don't own me."

The *Jongheer* held the blade out before him as if it were a fishing pole or divining rod, as if he didn't know what to do with it. He was soaked to the skin, his clothes were filthy, ruined, the plume of authority hung limp over the brim of his hat. For all that, though, the smirk had returned to his face. "Oh yes," he said, so softly he was nearly inaudible, "oh yes, I do."

At that, Jeremias idly swung the war club to his shoulder, where the weight of the ball bowed it like the arm of a catapult. The door stood open still and the elemental scent of the land rose to his nostrils, a scent of vitality and decay, of birth and death. He looked the *Jongheer* full in the face. "Come and get me," he said.

Two weeks later, on an afternoon in May as soft and celestial as the one on which they'd first met amongst the furs and hogsheads of Jan Pieterse's trading post, Neeltje Cats and Jeremias Van Brunt were married by a subdued and solemn Dominie Van Schaik, not thirty feet from where Katrinchee lay buried. By all accounts, the feast that followed was a rousing success. Meintje van der Meulen baked for three days straight, and her husband Staats set up a pair of temporary tables big enough to accommodate every tippler and trencherman from Sint Sink to Rondout. Reinier Oothouse and Hackaliah Crane buried the hatchet for the day and drank the bride's health side by side. There was game and fish and cheese and cabbage, there were pies and puddings and stews. Drink, too: 'Sopus ale, cider and Hollands out of a stone jug. And music. What would a wedding be without it? Here came young Cadwallader Crane with a penny whistle, there Vrouw Oothouse with her prodigious bottom and a *bombas* that made use of a pig's bladder for a sound box; someone else had a lute and another a pair of varnished sticks and an overturned kettle. Mariken Van Wart came up from Croton and danced the whole afternoon with Douw van der Meulen, Staats led Meintje through half a dozen frenetic turns of "Jimmy-be-still" and old Jan the Kitchawank danced with a jug till the sun fell into the trees. Neeltje's sisters were dressed like dolls, her mother cried—whether for joy or sorrow no one could be sure—and the patroon sent Ter Dingas Bosyn, the *commis,* as his official representative. But the crowning moment of the day, as everyone agreed, was when the *schout,* dressed in funereal black and standing as tall as his affliction would allow, his head bound in a snowy bandage and with good leather boots on his feet, strode resolutely across the front yard and gave away the bride.

When Mohonk, son of Sachoes, appeared on the doorstep of the little farmhouse at Nysen's Roost some three months later, Jeremias was a changed man. Gone was the wild-eyed glare of the rebel, the underdog, the unsoothable beast, and in its place was a look that could only be described as one of contentment. Indeed, Jeremias had never known a happier time. The crops were flourishing, the deer were back, the shack had been elevated to the status of domicile through the addition of a second room, furniture both functional and pleasing to the eye and that hallmark of civilized living, a clean, planed and sanded plank floor that soared a full foot and a half above the cold dun earth below. And then there was Neeltje. She was a voice in his head, a presence that never left him even when he was adrift in the canoe or roaming the scoured hilltops with a musket borrowed from Staats; she clove to him like a second skin, each moment a melioration and a healing. She mothered Jeremy, managed the house, spun and sewed and cooked, rubbed the tightness from his shoulders, sat with him by the river while fish stirred in the shallows and the blue shadows closed over the mountains. She made peace with her father, baked as fine a *beignet* as *moeder* Meintje, arranged and rearranged the front room till it looked like a burgher's parlor in Schobbejacken. She was everything that was possible, and more. Far more: she was carrying his child.

All this the Indian saw in Jeremias' face as the door swung open. Just as quickly, he saw it fade. *"You,"* Jeremias choked. "What do *you* want?"

Mohonk was gaunter than ever, his face rucked and seamed with abuse. He was a nose, an Adam's apple, a pair of black unblinking deep-buried eyes. *"Alstublieft,"* he said, *"dank u, niet te danken."*

"Who is it?" Neeltje called from the back of the house. They'd finished supper—pea soup, bread, cheese and beer—and she was getting Jeremy ready for bed. The house had fallen dark in the gathering dusk.

Jeremias didn't answer. He stood there, letting his mood go sour. This was the man, the shit-smeared skulking savage heathen, who'd ruined his sister and then deserted her. And here he was, filthy and ragged, angular as a wading bird, standing on the doorstep with no more Dutch than he'd had four years ago. "I have nothing for you," Jeremias said, enunciating the words in the way of the pedagogue, each syllable bitten off clean and distinct. "Get out of here." It was then that he felt a movement at his side and glanced down to see Jeremy standing beside him. The boy was rapt, gazing up in wonder at this apparition in the raccoon skin coat.

"Alstublieft," Mohonk repeated, then turned his head to call out something in the Kitchawank dialect, the words like stones in his mouth.

At this, two Indians stepped out of the shadows at the corner of the house. One of them was old Jan, grinning broadly and trailing flaps of greasy deerskin and a smell of the swamp. The other was a young buck Jeremias recognized from Jan Pieterse's. The buck's face was painted, and a tomahawk decorated with the crest feathers of tanager and bunting dangled like a toy from the fingertips of his right hand. Instinctively, Jeremias reached down and pushed his nephew back into the room. "You have a message for me?" Jeremias asked, glancing from the buck to Jan.

They stopped at the front step. The buck was expressionless. Jan grinned. Mohonk hugged the coat to him as if he were cold. "Yes," old Jan said finally, "I have a message."

Neeltje had come up behind her husband now, and was pressing Jeremy to her skirts, rocking him gently back and forth. The light drained away in the west.

Jan was grinning still, as if he'd reached a height beyond the gravitational pull of simple drunkenness and passed into a realm of giddiness and light. "From him," he said, indicating Mohonk with an abrupt laugh. "From Mohonk, son of Sachoes."

The son of Sachoes never blinked. Jeremias studied him a second, then turned back to Jan. "Well?" he demanded.

Suddenly the old Kitchawank dropped his head and began to shuffle his feet. "Ay-yah, neh-neh," he chanted, "Ay-yah, neh-neh," but Mohonk cut him off. He said something in a voice as harsh and rapid as gunfire, and old Jan looked up, blinking. "He wants his son back."

If the three of them weren't so crapulous, if old Jan weren't wasted by the years, the smallpox and the curse of the burning water, if Mohonk weren't degenerate and weak and if the buck had had his senses about him, the outcome might have been different. As it was, they made a critical mistake. Jeremias, enraged by the very suggestion, drew one hand flat across the other, said "Nee" for emphasis and stepped back to shut the door on them; it was at that very moment that the young buck chose to let fly with the tomahawk. The weapon rocketed through the air with a deadly *whoosh,* only to be deflected by the edge of the door and drop harmlessly to the floor in the middle of the room. There was a moment—fleeting, the fraction of a fraction of a second—during which the Indians looked remorseful and deeply ashamed, and then they surged toward the door.

Or rather, the buck did. Mohonk insinuated his long flat-arched foot, clad in a dirty moccasin, between door and frame, while old Jan lost his balance and sat down heavily in the dirt with a grunt of surprise.

Reacting to the threat, Jeremias slammed the door on the foot of his erstwhile brother-in-law, and when it sprang back from contact with that bony appendage, he found that he was gripping the venerable pogamoggan in his right hand (Neeltje, remembering her father, had snatched it up from the inglenook and pressed it on him). The first to blunder through the door was the buck, his warpaint smeared to reveal the uncertain face of a fifteen-year-old peering out from beneath it; he caught the full force of the granite ball in the abdomen and fell gasping to the floor, where he writhed about for several minutes in imitation of an eel in a pot. Next was Mohonk, hopping on one foot while cradling the throbbing other one in both hands. Jeremias took a half-hearted swing at him, but missed, striking the wall in a storm of splinters.

It was then that things turned nasty. For Mohonk, his dignity wounded, gritted his teeth, set down the palpitating foot and drew a bone knife from the blameless folds of his raccoon skin coat. And then this same Mohonk—lover and abettor of *meisje* and squaw alike, sire of Jeremias' nephew and husband to his dear dead beloved sister—came at Jeremias with murder in his heart.

Thinking back on it, Jeremias would remember the feel of that primitive weapon in his hand, the spring of the fruitwood shaft as the ball whipped forward as if under its own volition, the deadly wet final thump that collapsed the Indian's skull like a rotten pumpkin. He remembered too the look in his nephew's eye—the boy too young to know who this gaunt toppling giant was and yet somehow connected to the moment with a look that would endure a lifetime—and then the crablike retreat of the humiliated buck and old Jan's interminable, wheezing, marrow-chilling dirge.

Mohonk, last fruit of Sachoes' loins, had been laid low.

Jeremias was sorry for it. Heartily sorry. But he'd done what any other man would have done under the circumstances: his home and family had been threatened, and he'd defended them. Afterward, shaken and penitential, he laid the body out on the table and sent for the *schout*. Hours later, old Jan, wearied by the sad drone of his own whiskey-cracked voice, set off for the Kitchawank village at Indian Point, bringer of sad tidings.

Next morning, so early the color had yet to return to the earth, Wahwahtaysee the Firefly, bent double and older by what seemed like another century, came to claim the body. Locally, from Croton all the way up to Suycker Broodt, the Indians would suffer for this attack on the white men—the *schout* would see to that, and Wahwahtaysee knew it. Her people had lived with the Mohawk, with the Dutch, with the English. Anger was futile. Reprisal meant counter reprisal, reprisal meant extermination. That was the way of the people of the wolf. Betrayal. Deceit. The open smile and the stab in the back. She wasn't bitter, only confused.

As she stood there in the dark room in that unhappy place, exuding a scent as wild and incorruptible as the spoor of the tree-dweller, the pouched one, the white beast that had lent it to her, chanting her ancient threnody and anointing her son's flesh with the unguents and resins of the gods themselves, she glanced up to see a small, dark-eyed thing in the corner of the room, a woman, a white woman, her belly hard with child. She held those dark eyes a moment, and then turned back to her dead son.

Five months later, when the snow lay crusted on the ground, Neeltje went into labor. Her mother was there to help her, and there was a Yankee midwife too. Her father, the *schout,* wasn't quite ready yet to set foot in that tainted house, and so had installed himself in the upper manor house as the guest of Vrouw Van Wart, who was once again mortifying her flesh in religious retreat. Jeremias sat before a fire in the outer room, his green-eyed nephew and adoptive father at his side, and listened to his wife's cries of anguish. "Hush," said Vrouw Cats from within. "There, there," said the midwife.

At some point the cries reached a crescendo, then fell away to a silence thick as doom. There was a rustling of skirts, the scrape of clogs on the floorboards and a new cry, thin and resilient, a cry that had to adjust itself to the novelty of throat and voicebox, lungs and air. Vrouw Cats appeared in the doorway a moment later. "It's a boy," she said.

A boy. Jeremias stood and Staats rose to embrace him. "Congratulations, *mijnzoon,*" Staats said, drawing the pipe from his lips to hold him at arm's length and gaze into his eyes. "And have you got a name yet for this prodigy?"

Jeremias felt lightheaded, giddy, felt as if he'd crossed the far boundaries of the little life he'd led up till now and entered onto a new and glorious plane of existence. "Oh, yes," he murmured. "Yes: we're going to call him Wouter."

Collision the Second

IN ANOTHER age, in a time when meat and bread came wrapped in plastic and cabbage appeared spontaneously between the kohlrabi and bok choy in the produce section of the supermarket, Walter Van Brunt found himself leaning up against a fieldstone fireplace in the house of a stranger, sipping warm Cold Duck from a wax cup and digesting a lunatic rap on the subject of Smaug the dragon's relevance to the war in Southeast Asia ("*Clearly,* man—I mean how could Tolkien make it any clearer without slapping you in the face with it?—Smaug's just a stand-in for Nixon, right?"). Walter was profoundly drunk, seminauseous, bombarded by angst and raked with regrets as with flying bullets, and he was simultaneously trying to get drunker, fend off the jerk who'd pinned him up against the fireplace and keep an eye out for Mardi. "*Fiery breath!*" shouted the jerk, who wore his hair in braids, exhaled his own fiery breath and had received his draft notice two days earlier. "And what do you think that's all about, huh?"

Walter hadn't the faintest idea. He swallowed the dregs of the Cold Duck, now flecked with bits of exfoliated wax, and felt the jerk's grip on his forearm. "Napalm, brother," the jerk whispered with a knowing shake of his head, "that's what Tolkien's talking about."

Looking fearlessly into the draftee's bloodshot eyes, Walter said he agreed with him a hundred percent, then shoved past him and made for the bathroom. On the way, he stepped over half a dozen recumbent bodies, snaked unsteadily through a maze of reeling, treacherous, arm-flailing dancers and very nearly lurched into a withered Christmas tree festooned with cigarette papers and the dangling, disconnected limbs of plastic dolls. Drums kneaded him like dough, guitars throbbed in his gut. Mardi was nowhere in sight.

It was New Year's Eve, 1968, and this was the fifth or sixth house full of strangers to which Mardi had dragged him. By way of celebration. Somewhere on the dim periphery of the evening there'd been a suburban interior and someone's gaping, tartar-toothed parents insisting they have a toddy, and then there was Mardi's father saying "You will look in on the Strangs, won't you? And the Hugleys?" and Mardi sneering "Sure, and we'll stop in at the D.A.R. quilting bee too." Then there was Cold Duck, $1.79 the bottle, Mexican pot that tasted as if it had been cured in Windex, the little striated pill Mardi had slipped him in the coffee shop where they'd stopped to get out of the cold, and houses, houses full of drunken, grinning, suspicious, long-toothed, dog-faced, silly-ass strangers. And now there was this place, with its dirty wood paneling, its unrelenting assault of Top Ten hits and its hermeneutical draftee. He didn't even know where he was exactly—somewhere out in the hind end of Tarrytown or Sleepy Hollow, he guessed. At least that's what it had looked like when Mardi, straddling the Norton and clinging to his back like a mountaineer pressed to a wind-sheared scarp, shouted "This is it!" and he'd shot right up on the lawn and skidded into the stone slab at the foot of the porch, no problem, you okay?

That was an hour ago. At least. Now he was looking for the bathroom. He fumbled into the kitchen, startling two guys in serapes and cowboy hats who were cleaning pot in a colander, and tore open the door to the broom closet. "Down the hall, man," said the near cowboy in an accent right out of western Queens.

When finally he located the bathroom, he pulled back the door to find himself staring into the steamed-up eyes of a girl with frizzy hair and a pair of blue crepe bell bottoms puddled around her ankles; she lowered herself daintily to the toilet seat and gave him a look that would have corroded metal. "Sorry," he mumbled, backing out the door like a crayfish feeling for its hole. The moment the door clicked shut, he felt a familiar grip on his arm and swung around to discover that he was standing toe-to-toe with the deluded draftee. "She's really something, huh?" the jerk said, wiping something from his hands on the sleeves of Walter's jacket.

"Who?" Walter said, knowing he should have let it drop. They were alone in the hallway. Music thumped from the direction of the living room, the Queens cowboys shared a laugh in the kitchen behind them. Walter was beginning to forget what Mardi looked like.

"My sister," the draftee said. He couldn't have been more than twenty, but with his beard and hair and the twisted maniacal leer that suddenly flamed up to disarrange his features, he might have been the ancient mariner himself, his hand fastened on the wedding guest's sleeve. "In the crapper," he added with a significant nod. "Doesn't she remind you of Galadriel, you know—the elf princess? Like when Elrond gets it on? You know who I'm talking about, right?"

No, Walter didn't know. And in any case, he'd stopped listening—perhaps, propped up against the wall with an ache in his bladder and a rushing, hissing spume of light rising like a heavy sea in his head, he even closed his eyes for a moment. He was thinking about Jessica and Tom Crane, Hector, Herbert Pompey—the people he should be with now, the people he couldn't be with. He was thinking of that bleak cold Saturday afternoon three weeks back when the sun shone pale as milk through the worn curtains in the bedroom and Jessica, booted, gloved, wrapped and muffled from her sinewy higharched feet to the glowing turned-up tip of her Anglo-Saxon nose, had bent to kiss him as he lay caught between sleep and waking. "Where to?" he'd managed.

She was going Christmas shopping. Of course.

"So early?"

She laughed. It was half-past twelve. "How do you feel about a blender?" she called from the next room. "For your aunt Katrina?" He didn't feel. His mouth was dry, he had to take a piss, and the lining of his brain seemed to have swollen overnight like dough in a pan. "I thought . . ." she murmured, and now she was talking to herself, feet beating a brisk tattoo to the door, the wheeze of the hinges, a breath of refrigerated air, and then her last words hanging suspended till the door shut softly behind her, ". . . frozen daiquiris and whatnot."

In his very next moment of consciousness he was aware of a new voice—Mardi's—projecting forcefully from the front of the house. "Hey! Anybody home? Fa-la-la-la-la! Deck the halls and all that shit!" The door slammed behind her. "Walter?"

He propped himself up on one elbow, smoothed down his mustache and pushed the hair out of his eyes. "In here," he said.

He'd been seeing Mardi three or four times a week since the afternoon of the ghost ships, and feeling bad about it too. Here he was, married less than four months, and already he was running around behind his wife's back. Worse: he was doing it while she was at work earning the money he spent on beer and cigarettes and rib-eye steak. When he let himself think about it, he felt like a shit—a real, First Class, Select, Grade A, certifiable shit. On the other hand, he was still soulless, hard and free, wasn't he? Married or not. What would Meursault have done in his situation? Fucked them both, that's what. Or neither of them. Or somebody else altogether. Sex didn't matter. Nothing mattered. He was Walter Truman Van Brunt, nihilist hero, Walter Truman Van Brunt, hard as stone.

Besides, Mardi was something he couldn't get enough of. She was dangerous, wild, unpredictable—she made him feel as if he were living on the edge, made him feel bad in the best sense of the word, like James Dean, like Belmondo in *Breathless*. While Jessica made him feel bad, period. She came home from work, stinking of formalin, her eyes red, a sack of groceries clutched to her high tight bosom while he lay sprawled on the couch amidst the refuse of the day, and she never said a word. Never asked if he'd looked for a job or made up his mind about going back to school, never reproached him for the sink full of dishes, the beer bottles set up on the coffee table like bowling pins, the haze of incinerated pot that clung to the curtains, seeped into the furniture and filmed the windows. No. She just smiled. Loved him. Went to work on the dishes with one hand and whipped up some trout amandine, fettuccine Alfredo or Texas hot chili and a vitamin-choked spinach salad with the other, all the while singing along to Judy Collins or Joni Mitchell in a high pure soprano that would have made all the angels in heaven faint with the superabundant beauty of it. And oh, did he feel bad.

He knew now that all along he'd wanted to hurt her, alienate her, test her—did she love him, did she *really* love him? No matter what?

If he was bad, if he was worthless—the worthless son of a worthless father—then he would play his role to the hilt, scourge himself with it, scourge her. He wanted her to come home with the blender for Aunt Katrina and walk into that dark connubial bedroom, her cheeks abloom with good will to men, the golden foil of the gift-wrapped packages crepitating against her chest, sacred hymns and timeless carols on her lips, and see him there, naked, thrusting away at Mardi Van Wart. He must have wanted it—else why would he have done it?

They couldn't hear the car, it was true, but the front door was unmistakable. Bang. "Walter?" Footsteps across the floor, the rustle of packages, "Walter?"

But it was Mardi too. On top of him, surging against him, pinning her mouth to his with all the frantic haste of resuscitation. She heard the door slam. She heard the footsteps and Jessica's voice—she heard them as well as he did. He moved to break away from her, to hide, run, dissemble—he was in the shower, Mardi had a headache and went in to lie down, no, that wasn't her car out front—but she wouldn't let go of him, wouldn't stop. He was inside her when Jessica came through the door. Then, only then, did Mardi look up.

Jessica's father came for her things two days later. Walter was passed out on the couch, drunk from hating himself. The door slammed and John Severum Wing, of Wing, Crouder & Wing, Investment Counsellors, was on him. "Get up, you son of a bitch," he hissed. Then he kicked the couch. John Wing, forty-eight years old, Rotarian, Little League sponsor, churchgoer, father of four, as imperturbable as a box turtle drowsing in the sun, snaked out a Hush Puppy-clad foot and shook the couch to its particle-board frame. Walter sat up. John Wing, standing over him, delivered sotto voce insults. "Sleazeball," he whispered. "Scum. Creep."

Walter had the feeling that his father-in-law would have gone on indefinitely in the same vein, plumbing the lower strata of his vocabulary, driving the spikes ever deeper, but for the sudden appearance of Jessica. For at that moment, the hair swept back from her high pale patrician brow and a Kleenex pressed to her face as if to protect her from the odor of something long dead, Jessica darted through the door and disappeared into the bedroom. In the silence that fell over them like the aftershock of an artillery barrage, Walter, sitting, and

John Wing, standing, listened to the thump and scrape of drawers flung violently open, the screech of hangers jerked hastily from the rack, the clatter of knickknacks, perfume bottles, gewgaws, curios and all the other hard-edged odds and ends of life flung carelessly together in sack and box. And they listened to something else too, a subtler sound, pitched lower, a quirk of hypothalamus and larynx: Jessica was weeping.

Walter stood. He fumbled for a cigarette.

John Wing kicked the coffee table. He kicked the wall. He launched a pillow into the kitchen as if it were a football splitting the uprights. "Answer me," he said. "How could you do it?"

Walter hated himself at that moment, oh yes indeed, and he felt bad to the bone. He lit that cigarette, let it dangle from his underlip like one of Belmondo's, and blew the smoke in John Wing's face. Then he lifted his leather jacket from the chair and sauntered out the door, shaky but somehow serene too. The door shut behind him and the wind caught him in the face. Squinting against the smoke of the cigarette, he straddled the Norton, gave it a kick that would have wrenched the leg off a John Wing, and obliterated the universe with a twist of the throttle.

But now, of course, standing there in the hallway of a strange house in the waning minutes of the old year, aching to take a piss, surrounded by strange faces and bedeviled by fools and halfwits, he had his regrets. Jessica wouldn't talk to him. (He must have called fifty times, must have sat out in front of her parents' house on the Norton fifty more till John Wing stormed out and threatened to call the police.) Tom Crane wouldn't talk to him either. Not yet, anyway. And while Hector had sat down and shared a pitcher of beer with him, he kept looking at him as if he'd developed a case of twenty-four-hour leprosy or something. Even Hesh and Lola blamed him. He'd begun to feel like a character in a country and western song, lost the most precious thing in my life, o lonesome me, and all the rest of it. Now, of course, now that he didn't have her—couldn't have her—he wanted her more than anything. Or did he?

"And Mordor," the jerk was saying, "what do you think that shit stands for, huh?"

Just then the bathroom door swung open and Galadriel strutted out, shooting Walter a withering glance and lifting her nose as if she'd stepped in dogshit. Her brother—if indeed he was her brother—was too wound up to acknowledge her. He tightened his grip on Walter's arm and leaned into him: "The good ol' U.S. of A.," he said. "That's what."

So small a pill, half the size of an aspirin, and Walter was rushing with light. Jessica. The upturned nose, the leggy leg, the martyr in the kitchen: who needed her? He had Mardi, didn't he? "Tell it to the gooks," he said, staring the jerk down. Then he was in the bathroom, bolting the door behind him.

In the mirror he saw eyes that were all pupil, a mustache in motion, hair parading around his ears. Balanced on his good foot, he flipped back the toilet seat with the toe of the other, but then missed his aim when the toilet unaccountably sprang up and danced across the room. He was zipping up when he noticed his grandmother. She was in the tub. Wearing a shower cap decorated with leaping pink, green and blue frogs. The water, soapy, dark as the Hudson, rose to her big tallowy naked breasts, which she rubbed from time to time with a washcloth. She didn't say a word till he turned to leave. "Walter?" she called, as he shot back the bolt. "You didn't forget to wash up, did you?"

Out in the hallway, there was no draftee, no draftee's sister. There were no cowboys in the kitchen. From the living room, however, there arose a clamor of shouts and razzing party horns, and when Walter got there he saw that all the strangers in the house were grinning, tossing confetti and pitching themselves deliriously into one another's arms. "Happy New Yeeah!" shouted one of the cowboys. Blazing like an angel with the light, Walter strode into the midst of them, shouldering a smooching couple out of the way and arresting the arm of a guy in mirror sunglasses who was lifting a bottle of Jack Daniel's to his lips. "Hey!" he shouted above the clatter of noisemakers and tinny horns, "you seen Mardi?"

The guy was wearing a cutoff army jacket with pink suspenders and a Mickey Mouse T-shirt. He was older, maybe twenty-six, twenty-seven. He pushed back his shades and gave Walter a baggy-eyed look. "Who?"

Walter fended off an assault from the rear—a big horse of a girl with smeared lipstick and a conical paper hat raked over her eyes like a rhino's horn came down hard on his plastic foot, belched an apology and shrieked "Happy Noooo Year!" in his face—and tried again. "Mardi Van Wart—you know, the girl I came with."

"Shit," the guy shrugged, rubbing the bottle for comfort, "I don't know nobody. I'm from New Jersey."

But the big girl was there now, lurching unsteadily before him. "Mardi?" she repeated in surprise, as if he'd asked for Jackie Kennedy or the Queen Mother. "She split."

The horns razzed in his ears. Everything was moving. He tried to control his voice. "Split?"

"Uh-huh. Must of been an hour ago. With Joey Bisordi—you know Joey, right?—and I don't know who all. For Times Square." She paused, watching Walter's face, then broke into a sloppy grin. "You know," she said, with a shake of her uncontainable hips, "Noooo Year's!"

The year was about ten minutes old when Walter fired up the Norton, swung it away from the stoop and skidded back up the lawn. He was still rushing like a comet with the light, but there was a dark place inside of him too—as dark and forbidding as the back side of the moon—and it was growing. He felt like shit. Felt like he wanted to cry. No Jessica, no Mardi, no nothing. And fuck, it was cold. He dodged a diseased-looking azalea, rattled over something that scattered under the back wheel—bricks? firewood?—and then he was out on the road.

Fine. But where was he? He passed up the first intersection and took the next instead, swinging into a long dark tunnel of stripped and twisted trees. He'd driven a mile or so, going too fast, clinging to the bends and accelerating out of them with a twist of the throttle, when he clattered across an old wooden bridge and came to a dead end. An iron chain thick as a boat hawser stretched across the mouth of the road. There were red and yellow reflectors mounted on the trees and a sign that read PRIVATE. He cursed out loud, wheeled the bike around and headed back up the road.

He was thinking that if he could find the high school he'd be all right. (Sleepy Hollow. He remembered the place from school, when he'd played forward on the Peterskill basketball team—funky showers, a gymnasium that smelled of paste wax and sweat, a big old stone and brick building just off the main drag.) It was on Route 9, that much he knew. From there it was no more than twenty minutes to Peterskill and the Elbow. He was thinking he'd drop in and have a few beers with Hector maybe, or Herbert Pompey—drown his sorrow, bewail his fate, give them his side of the story over the pool table and a shot of something that would dim the raging light in his head—when, over the roar of the bike and the stinging rush of the wind, he became aware of a noise at his back. Deep-throated, whelming, omnipresent, it came at him like the rumble of toppling mountains, the blast of the hurricane. He turned his head.

There behind him, issuing from the nowhere of the dead-end lane, was a platoon of motorcycles. Their headlights lit the night till the patchy blacktop road and the screen of naked tree trunks blazed like a stage set. Almost involuntarily, he slowed down. There must have been thirty of them, the roar growing steadily louder. He looked over his shoulder again. Was it the Disciples? The New York chapter of the Hell's Angels? But what would they be doing out here?

He didn't have long to wonder, because in the next moment they were on him, cruising, the thunder of thirty big bikes beating like a fist in his chest. As he slowed to merge with them they came up on either side and he could see them now, raked back on their choppers, colors flapping in the dead night air. Two, six, eight, twelve: he was in the eye of the hurricane. The bikes stuttered and purred, they hammered, screamed, spat fire. Fourteen, eighteen, twenty.

But wait: something was wrong. These weren't Angels—they were hoary and decrepit, leather-faced, skin on bone, their raggedy yellow beards and piss-colored locks fanned back smooth in the glare of the headlights. It was coming to him—yes, yes—like the opening motif of a recurring nightmare, when an old geek swooped in ahead of him and the legend on his jacket leapt out at him like a face in the dark. THE APOSTATES, it read, in a band of hard block letters above a winged death's head, PETERSKILL. Yes. Walter turned his head to the left and there he was—the shrunken Dutchman, the imp, the sugarloaf hat clinging to his head in defiance of wind and logic both, the crude denim colors forced down over a baggy homespun shirt he might have looted from a museum. Yes. And the imp's lips were moving: "Happy New Year, Walter," he seemed to be saying over the din.

Walter never hesitated. He jerked his head to the other side—his right side—and sure enough, his father was there, riding in tandem with him on a chopped Harley with flame decals spread like claws across the gas tank. The old man's eyes were hidden behind antiquated goggles, the slick reddish fangs of his hair beat around his head. He gave Walter his profile, then turned to face him. There was a stink of exhaust, the rush of the air, the blast of the engines and a single attenuated moment in which the whole night was suspended between them. Then Walter's father flashed a smile and repeated the dwarf's benediction—"Happy New Year, Walter." Walter couldn't resist—he could feel the smile tugging at the corner of his mouth—when all of a sudden, without warning, his father reached out and gave him a shove.

A shove.

The night was black, the road deserted. Caught in the sick slashing parabola of disaster, Walter went down again, went down for the second time. It would have been better had he gone down on his right side, nothing there but plastic and leather, after all. But he didn't. Oh, no. He went down on his left.

Part II

WORLD'S END

SIMEON: *Like his Paw.*
PETER: *Dead spit an' image!*
SIMEON: *Dog'll eat dog!*
PETER: *Ay-eh.*

—Eugene O'Neill,
Desire Under the Elms

The Hoodwinking of Sachoes

THIS time the room was painted marigold yellow, and the doctor's name was Perlmutter. Walter lay sedated in the comfortless crank-up bed while Hesh and Lola kept watch at his side and the hushed voices of the intercom whispered in his ear like the voices of the incorporeal dead. His left foot, the good one, was good no more.

As he lay there, his face as composed as a sleeping child's—not a mark on him, the hair swept back from his brow where Lola's hand had rested, his lips parted and eyelids trembling in the deeps beyond consciousness—he was assailed by dreams. But this time everything was different, this time his dreams were free of mocking fathers, sententious grandmothers and carcasses stripped to the bone. He dreamed instead of an unpeopled landscape, misted and opaque, where sky and earth seemed to meld into one and the air was like a blanket pulled over his face. When he woke, smothering, Jessica was leaning over him.

"Oh, Walter," she moaned, a low rumble of grief rising up like gas from deep inside her. "Oh, Walter." Her eyes were wet for some reason, and two sooty streaks of mascara traced the delicate flanges of her nose.

Walter looked around the room in bewilderment, looked at the gleaming instruments, the IV bag suspended above him, the empty bed in the corner and the cold gray eye of the television mounted on the wall. He gazed on the chipper yellow of the wall itself, that uplifting, breakfast-nook yellow, and closed his eyes again. Jessica's voice came to him out of the darkness. "Oh, Walter, Walter . . . I feel so bad for you."

Bad? For him? Why should she feel bad for him?

This time he didn't take her hand, press his lips to hers, fumble with the buttons of her blouse. He merely flashed open his eyes to give her a venomous look, a look of resentment and reproach, the look of the antihero on his way out the door; when he spoke, he barely moved his lips. "Go away," he murmured. "I don't need you."

Walter didn't become fully aware of his predicament until late that afternoon, when, on waking to the hellish heat of his invalid's room and a blur of snow across the window, he glanced up to see Huysterkark grinning and scraping his way into the room. Then, and only then, did he feel for his left foot—his favorite, his precious, his only foot—and understand that it was no longer a part of him. The image of the deserted landscape of his dream fused in that moment with the leering face of his father.

"Well, well, well, well," Huysterkark said, rubbing his hands together and grinning, grinning. "Mr. Van Brunt—*Walter* Van Brunt. Yes." Clamped firmly between his right arm and chest as if it were a rolled-up copy of the *Times* was the new prosthetic foot. "Well," Huysterkark beamed, drawing up a chair and crab-walking to the bed, "and how are we on this fine blizzardy afternoon?"

How were we? There was no way to answer that question. We were panicked, in the throes of despair and denial. We were angry. "You, you—" Walter sputtered. "You took my, my only—" He found himself overwhelmed by self-pity and sorrow. "Son of a bitch," he snarled, tears in his eyes. "You couldn't save it? You couldn't try?"

The question hung between them. Snow drove at the windows. *Dr. Rotifer to Emergency, Dr. Rotifer,* crackled the intercom.

"You're a very lucky young man," Huysterkark said finally, wagging his head and pressing a pensive finger to his blanched lips. His voice dropped and he extracted the foot from the nest of his underarm. "Lucky," he whispered.

Walter had been out for two days, Huysterkark informed him. When they'd got him into Emergency it was nearly dawn and he was frozen half to death. He was lucky to be alive. Lucky he hadn't lost his fingers and nose to frostbite in the bargain. Did he think the staff here was incompetent? Or apathetic? Did he understand just how mangled that foot had been—comminuted fracture, ankle joint demolished, soft tissue mashed to pulp? Did he know how Doctors Yong, Ik and Perlmutter had worked over him for two and a half hours, trying to restore circulation, set fragmented bones, reattach blood vessels and nerves? He was lucky he hadn't gone down someplace upstate or on the other side of the river—or what about in the Deep South or in Italy or Nebraska or some other godforsaken place where they didn't have Hopkins-trained physicians like Yong and Ik and Perlmutter? Did he realize just how fortunate he was?

Walter didn't realize it, no, though he tried. Though he listened to Huysterkark's voice sail through its range of expression, through the sforzando of intimidation to the allegro of thanksgiving and the bustling hearty brio of salesmanship. He could think of one thing only, and that was the unfairness of it all, the relentless, crippling, terrifying assault of history and predestination and lurking conscious fate that was aimed at him and him alone. It boiled in him till he closed his eyes and let Huysterkark do with him what he would, closed his eyes and fell back into his dream.

It was on the afternoon of the third day that Mardi showed up. She'd abandoned the raccoon skin for a black velvet cape that sculpted her shoulders and hung from her like a shroud. Underneath it she was wearing blue jeans, painted cowgirl boots and a see-through blouse in a shade of pink that glowed like Broadway on a rainy night. And beads. Eight or ten strands of them. In the doorway behind her was a guy Walter had never seen before.

There was the pain killer, the drowsy stuffiness of the room, the leaden sky with its angry black bands of cloud that stretched like bars across the window. "You poor thing," she cooed, clacking across the linoleum to bend over him in a blast of perfume and briefly insert her tongue in his mouth. He could feel the nimbus of her hair framing his face, tendrils of sensation poking through the flat dead field of his pain, and despite himself experienced the first faint stirrings of arousal. Then she was straightening up, unfastening the clasp of the cape and indicating her companion with a jerk of her head. "This is Joey," she said.

Walter's eyes cut to him like knives. Joey was in the room now, but he wasn't looking at Walter. He was looking out the window. "Joey's a musician," Mardi said.

Joey was dressed like Little Richard's wardrobe designer, in three clashing paisleys and a Tillamook-colored cravat that fell to his waist. After a moment he stole a glance at Walter, laid out flat and footless in bed, and said "What's happening, man?" without a hint of irony.

Happening? What was happening? Mutilation, that's what. Dismemberment. The reduction of the flesh, the drawing and quartering of the spirit, the metastasis of horror.

"God," Mardi said, perched on the bed now, the cape fallen open to reveal the see-through blouse and all there was to see beneath it, "if only you'd come with Joey and Richie and me the other night—down to Times Square, I mean. . . ." She didn't finish the thought. Finishing the thought would have meant admitting the inadmissible. She settled for a pronouncement on the lack of proportion in the cosmos: "It's just so bizarre."

To this point, Walter hadn't uttered a word. He wanted to utter a few, though. He wanted to give vent to the outrage percolating inside him, wanted to ask her what she meant by leaving him in a house full of strangers while she trotted off to New York with this chinless fop in the Beatle boots and cheesy necktie, wanted to ask if she loved him still, if she'd have sex with him, if she'd shut the door and pull the shades and tell Joey to go take a hike, but her eyes went strange all of a sudden and he checked himself. Her slow gaze took in the length of him stretched supine on the bed, and then she turned to look him in the face. "Does it hurt?" she murmured.

It hurt. Oh, god, did it hurt. "What do you think?" he said.

At that moment Joey let out with a whoop that might have been derisive but then again might only have been symptomatic of upper respiratory distress, and buried his face in a polka dot handkerchief the size of a prayer rug. Walter's eyes shot to him. Were his shoulders twitching? Did he find this funny, was that it?

Mardi took Walter's hand. "So now," she said, looking for a way in, "now you, uh, you won't be able to ride the bike anymore, I guess, huh?"

The bitterness welled up in him, shot through his veins like embalming fluid. Bike? He'd be lucky to walk, though Huysterkark had breezily assured him he'd be on his feet in a month, walking without support in two. Without support. He knew what it would be like, no balance, no connection, staggering down the sidewalk like a drunk walking barefoot over a bed of hot coals. He wanted to cry. And he might have, too, but for the presence of Joey and the dominion of cool. Would Lafcadio have cried? Would Meursault? "It was all you," he said suddenly, choking up despite himself. "It was you—you left me there, you bitch."

Mardi's face went cold. She dropped his hand and pushed herself up from the bed. "Don't lay it on me," she said, her voice riding up the register, a single deep groove cut between her perfect eyebrows. "It was you—drunk, stoned on your ass . . . shit, you almost killed us pulling up to the porch—or did you forget about that, huh? And if you want to know, we looked all over for you—must've traipsed through that craphole twenty times, didn't we, Joey?"

Joey was looking out the window. He said nothing.

"You fucking vampire!" Walter shrieked. "Ghoul!"

A nurse appeared in the doorway, the color drained from her face. "I'm very sorry," she said, bustling into the room, "but the patient really mustn't—"

Hostile, deliberate, with her glacial eyes and untameable hair, Mardi wheeled around on her. "Stuff it," she snarled, and the nurse backed away from her. Then she turned to Walter. "And don't you ever call me a bitch," she said, her voice sunk low in her throat, "you, you footless wonder."

This time Joey really did laugh—it was unmistakable—a high brazen bellow choked off in mid-guffaw. And then he was flashing Walter the peace sign and following Mardi's cape out the door. But that wasn't the end of it. Not quite. He paused in the doorway to look back over his shoulder and give Walter a showman's wink. "Later, bro," he said.

It all came loose right there. Walter fought off the nurse and sat up rigid, the veins in his neck purple with fury. He began to shout. Curses, jeers, nursery school taunts—anything that came into his head. He shouted like a bloody-nosed mama's boy in the middle of the playground, cried out every cunt and cocksucker and motherfucker he could muster, howled out his rage and impotence till the corridors echoed like the dayroom at the asylum, and he was shrieking and cursing and babbling still when the rough arms of the attendants pinned him to the bed and the hypodermic found its mark.

When he woke—next day? day after that?—the first thing he noticed was that the bed in the corner was occupied. The curtains were drawn, but he could see the IV stand poking out beneath them, and at the foot of the bed the folds parted to reveal a plastered limb hanging suspended over the crisp white plane of the sheets. He looked hard, as if he could somehow penetrate the curtains, curious in an idle, just-waking, bedridden sort of way—what else was there but lunch, Huysterkark and TV?—and at the same time perversely gratified: someone else was suffering too.

It wasn't until lunch—soup that was like gravy, gravy that was like soup, eight all-but-indigestible wax beans, a lump of an indefinable meatlike substance and Jello, ubiquitous Jello—that the nurse drew back the curtains to reveal his roommate and fellow sufferer. At first, Walter could barely locate him in the confusion of pillows and sheets, his view obstructed by the expansive backside of Nurse Rosenschweig, who was leaning over to minister to the new arrival's alimentary needs—good god, were his hands gone too?—but then, when the nurse straightened up, he was rewarded with his first good look at his fellow victim. A child. Shrunken, tiny, propped up in the enormous bed like a stuffed toy.

Then he looked again.

He saw a flurry of pale blanched hairy-knuckled little hands, the glint of knife and fork and, before his field of vision was occluded once again by the fearsome interposition of Nurse Rosenschweig's nates, a snatch of hair as white as a patriarch's. Peculiar child, he was thinking, reaching idly to itch at the bandage constricting his calf, when suddenly the nurse was gone and he found himself staring slack-jawed into the face of his dreams.

Piet—for Piet it was, unmistakable, unforgettable, as loathsome and arresting as a tick nestled behind a dog's ear—was inclined at a forty-five-degree angle, blithely impaling cubes of glistening emerald Jello on the tines of his fork. His nose and ears were enormous, absurdly disproportionate to his foreshortened limbs, white hair sprouted from his nostrils like frost-killed weed, his lips were slack and pouty and there was a dribble of gravy on his chin. A full five seconds thundered past before he turned to Walter. "Howdy, Chief," he said, grinning diabolically, "good chow, huh?"

Walter was lost in a chamber of horrors, a room with no exit, the dripping dark dungeon of the asylum. He was frightened. Terrified. Certain, finally, that he'd lost his mind. He turned away from the leering little homunculus and stared numbly at the slop on his tray, trying desperately to review his sins, his lips trembling in what might have been prayer if only he knew what prayer was.

"What's the matter," Piet rasped, "cat got your tongue? Hey, you: I'm talking to you."

The misery lay so heavily upon him that Walter could barely bring himself to raise his eyes. What were the five stages of dying, he was thinking, as he slowly swiveled his head: Fear, Anger, Renunciation, Acceptance and—?

Piet, hunched over his floating leg like a sorrowful gargoyle, was regarding him sympathetically now. "Don't take it so hard, kid," he said finally, "you'll get over it. You're young and strong yet, got your whole life ahead of you. Here," he was reaching out a stunted arm, at the stunted extremity of which appeared a stunted hand clasping a half-empty bowl of Jello, "you want my dessert?"

Walter's rage uncoiled with all the vehemence of a striking snake. "What do you want from me?" he spat.

The little man looked puzzled. "From you? I don't want nothin' from you—I'm offering you my dessert. I might of ate a bite or two of it, but hey, it's no big deal—I mean I'm not in here for bubonic plague or anything." He withdrew the Jello and indicated the plaster-bound foot that swayed above him. "Stubbed my toe!" he hooted, and let out a crazed choking peal of laughter.

He was chortling to himself when the nurse returned. "I just told him I . . . I . . . I stubbed my"— he couldn't go on; it was too much. He was a deflated balloon, all the air knocked out of him with the sheer debilitating hilarity of it. "My toe!" he finally bawled, subsiding into giggles.

Nurse Rosenschweig watched him patiently through all his droll contortions, her big moon face constellated with freckles, her drooping underlip coaching him on. Her only comment, once he'd delivered his punch line, was: "Well, aren't we lively today." Then she turned to Walter.

"Hey, sister!" the little man suddenly shouted, his voice twittering with mirth. "Want to dance?"

That was it. Walter had had it. "Who is this man?" he demanded. "What's he doing in here? Why in christ's name did you stick him in here with me?"

Nurse Rosenschweig was no sour fraulein, as she'd just demonstrated, but Walter's protestations made her face go hard. "You want a private room, you've got to make the proper arrangements," she said. "In advance."

"But—but who *is* this man?" Something was beginning to dawn on Walter, confused, bereft, drugged and tormented though he may have been. It went like this: if the nurse was real—walking, talking, breathing, flesh, blood and bone—and she admitted Piet's existence, then either the whole world was a hallucination or the phantom in the bed beside him was no phantom at all.

"Name's Piet Aukema," the dwarf rasped, leaning way out over the chasm between the beds to extend his hand, "and I'm pleased to meet you."

Nurse Rosenschweig fixed her withering glare on Walter, who reluctantly leaned forward to shake the proferred hand. "Walter," he mumbled, voice sticking in his throat, "Walter Van Brunt."

"There now, isn't that better?" the nurse was saying, beaming at Walter like a contented schoolmarm, when Piet suddenly dropped Walter's hand and jerked upright in bed. Slapping his forehead, he gasped "Van Brunt? Did you say Van Brunt?"

Faintly, weakly, almost imperceptibly, Walter nodded.

"I knew it, I knew it," the dwarf sang. "Soon as I laid eyes on you, I knew it."

The chill of history was descending yet again—Walter could feel it, familiar as a toothache, and he shivered inwardly.

"Sure," the dwarf said, marshaling his features into an obscene parody of amity and ingenuousness, "I knew your father."

Every time Walter opened his eyes during the course of the next three days, Piet was there, the cynosure of the room, the hospital, the universe, the first and only thing that mattered. He would wake in the morning to the little man's booming "Up and at 'em, lazybones!," jolt up from a tormented nap to see him calmly paring his nails or crunching into an apple, arouse himself from a sitcom-induced doze to watch him leaf through a pornographic magazine or hold up the centerfold with a complicitous wink. Still, Walter couldn't quite believe he wasn't hallucinating—not until Lola came to visit and recognized the wizened little runt in her first breath. "Piet?" she said, narrowing her eyes to examine him as she might have examined the ghostly figures of a faded photograph.

The dwarf perked up like a dog catching the faintest ring of silverware from the farthest corner of the kitchen. "I know you," he said, his big leathery lips twisted into the best facsimile of a smile. "Lola, isn't it?"

Lola's hands went to her hair. She fumbled with her purse, her bulky coat, and sat heavily in the visitor's chair. A change came across her face, her mouth grim, lips trembling.

"What's it been," he said, "twenty years?"

Her voice was dead. "Not long enough."

Piet went on as if he hadn't noticed, filling her in on the sliding scale of his fortunes over the past two decades. Smirking, winking, rolling his eyes, gesticulating so violently he set the traction wires atremble, the little man told her of his careers in carpentry, Off-Broadway theater (a supporting role in a short-lived musical based on Todd Browning's "Freaks"), commercial fishing, managing a bar and grill in Putnam Valley, selling doughnut makers door-to-door and Renaults, VWs and Mini-Coopers at a lot in Brewster. He chattered on for the better part of an hour, hooting at his own jokes, dropping his voice to an ominous rasp to underscore the bad times, rushing with passion as he described his loves and triumphs, going on and on, signing, guffawing and wisecracking, performing the grand symphony of his little life for an audience chained to their seats. Never once did he mention Truman.

The moment Lola left, Walter turned to him. Puffed up like a toad with the litany of his adventures, Piet regarded him slyly. "You, uh, you said you knew my father," Walter began, and then faltered.

"That's right. He was a real card, your old man."

When did you see him last? What happened to him? Is he alive?

The questions were stacked up in Walter's head like jetliners over La Guardia—Why did he leave us? What happened that night in 1949? Was he gutless? A fink? A turncoat? Was he the no-account, perfidious, two-faced, backstabbing son of a bitch everyone made him out to be?—but before he could ask the first of them, Piet was off on another jag of reminiscence.

"A card," he repeated, wagging his head in disbelief. "Did you hear about the time—?" Walter hadn't heard. Or if he had, he was going to hear it again. Waving his stumpy arms like a conductor, leering, grimacing, clucking, chortling, Piet served up the old stories. There were the pranks—flying upside down under the Bear Mountain Bridge, stealing the life-size figures from the crèche outside the Church of Our Lady of the Immaculate Conception and hoisting them up the flagpole in front of the monument on Washington Street, substituting distilled vinegar for vodka at the VFW Memorial Day picnic; there were the drinking bouts, the women, the crab boils and card games—names and places and dates that meant nothing to Walter. Finally the rasping atonal voice paused a moment, as if to collect itself—as if perhaps, at last, it had run out of stories—when Piet threw his head back on the pillow, slapped the rock-hard cast with an exclamatory palm and uttered a single astonishing proper noun, one that hadn't been uttered in Walter's presence since the death of his grandmother. "Sachoes," the dwarf said in what amounted to a prefatory sigh.

"Sachoes?" Walter flung it back at him. "What about him?"

Piet gave him a long, smirking, supremely self-satisfied look, simultaneously plumbing an ear for wax and running a gnarled hand through his hair. "That's all Truman'd talk about when I first met him back in, what?—'40, I guess it was, just before the War. Sachoes this, Sachoes that. You know, the Indian chief. Owned all this"—his hand swept the room in a gesture meant to suggest the dubious worth not only of the paltry room but of the gray landscape that fell away from the windows in a bristle of bare-crowned trees—"before us white men took it away from him, that is. Damndest thing. For a couple of months or so back then your father was all worked up about it, as though we could turn history around or something." Piet—the gargoyle, the imp—looked him full in the face. "You know the story?"

Walter knew it—one of his grandmother's stories—and suddenly he saw that neat square little house perched over the river, a night of crippling cold, his grandfather hunched hairily over the fire, plucking and jabbing at the muck-smelling length of his drift net like an old lady with her needlepoint, his grandmother busy shaping clay in a maelstrom of newspaper at the kitchen table. She was attempting something big—her major statement on trash fish, a planter in the shape of three intertwined and gaping carp. Walter was nine or ten—it was the winter Hesh and Lola had gone down to Miami over the Christmas break and left him with his grandparents. There was no TV—his grandmother mistrusted televisions as she mistrusted telephones, prying eyes and ears, conduits into which her enemies could pour their malice—but there would have been a radio. Christmas carols maybe, playing softly in the background. Cookies in the oven. Snow flying at the black impervious panes of the big bay window that looked out over the river. Gram, Walter said, tell me a story.

Her hands—big and fleshy, spotted with age—worked at the clay. She rolled out a string of it, formed an O and gave the near carp a set of lips. At first he thought she hadn't heard him, but then she began to speak, her voice barely audible over the snap of the fire, the carols, the wind in the eaves: It was the winter after they'd buried Minewa, and Sachoes, great sachem of the Kitchawanks, was in despair. Smeared with otter fat against the cold, wrapped in the fur of Konoh, the bear, he stared glumly into the fire while the wind flapped the thatch of elm bark and basswood strips till he could have sworn all the geese in the world were beating around his head.

Despair? Walter asked. What's that?

Soon enough, growled his hairy grandfather, looking up from his torn drift net, you'll find out. Soon enough.

Walter's grandmother gave her husband an impatient look, etched a triad of scales under the gill plate of the middle carp, and turned to Walter. He was sad, Walter, she said. He'd lost hope. Fizzled out. Given up. He sat there in the longhouse with Wahwahtaysee, with Matekanis and Witapanoxwe, his elder sons, and Mohonk, the lanky, flat-footed boy who was to disappoint his mother so, and poked at the embers of tobacco and red dogwood bark in the bowl of his pipe. When morning came, Jan Pieterse would be at the door, bearing gifts.

A pair of yellow-eyed dogs, kettles harder than stone, knives, scissors, axes, blankets, nuggets of colored glass that made even the most highly polished disk of *wampumpeak* look like just another pebble. Gifts, yes: but no gift comes without a price.

When Jan Pieterse came amongst them some six years before, the Kitchawanks were amazed not only by the limitless supply of well-made and bewitching objects he brought with him for trade, but also by the persistence and subtlety of his haggling, by the stream of graceless and mangled Mohican words that never stopped dribbling from his lips. "Composed of Mouth" is what they called him, and they came to him in all their strength and dignity to trade skins for these fine wares with which he'd loaded his little sloop to the gunwales. But it wasn't just beaver pelts he wanted, no—it was the land itself. It was the Blue Rock and the land that lay around it. Sachoes, as chief and elder statesman, came forward to negotiate with him.

And what did Sachoes get for his people in exchange for the land on which Composed of Mouth set up the boxy inhospitable fortress of his trading post? Things. Possessions. Objects of envy and covetousness. Axes whose handles broke and whose blades went dull, jars that shattered, scissors that locked at the joint with rust and the gleaming insuperable coins that introduced theft and murder to the village of bark huts on Acquasinnick Bay. And where were these things now? All gone their own careless way—even the blankets eaten up by some mysterious corruption from within—while the beaver that helped buy them were as scarce as hairs on a Mohawk's head. Composed of Mouth was no fool. He had the land. Incorruptible and eternal.

In the early days, Jan Pieterse came to them. But now they came to Jan Pieterse. Wasted by the English pox, sick with drink, starved with a winter severe beyond the recall of old Gaindowana, eldest man of the tribe, they'd crept like dogs in the humiliation of their need to the big barred door of Composed of Mouth's trading post and begged him to remember the land they'd given him. They wanted cloth, food, things of iron, things of beauty—to their everlasting shame, they wanted rum. Sure, Composed of Mouth told them, certainly, of course and why not? Credit, he said, in his barker's patois, a Dutch term festering deep in a felicitous Mohican sentence, Credit for all, and especially for you, my reverend friend, my dear, dear, dear Sachoes.

Nothing for nothing, Walter's grandmother said, giving the far carp a round and staring eye with a swirl of her little finger. The old chief owed that canny Dutchman, and he knew it.

Well, Jan Pieterse, so the story goes, had a friend. Two friends. They were the Van Wart brothers, Oloffe and Lubbertus. Oloffe, who had influence in the Company, was granted a patroonship by Their High Mightinesses that encompassed not only all the Kitchawanks' tribal lands, but those of the Sint Sinks and Weckquaesgeeks as well. It was already carved up and mapped out, plenty for him and his brother and half the population of the Netherlands too. All he had to do was satisfy the original owners, who, as everybody in Haarlem knew, were a bunch of naked, illiterate, drink-besotted and disease-ridden beggars who couldn't add up their fingers and toes, let alone survey the land and read the fine print of your basic, binding, inviolate and ironclad contract. Jan Pieterse, an adept in Indian ways, was to be his go-between. For a fee, of course.

Now Sachoes didn't know anything of this—couldn't begin to imagine the polders and dikes and cobbled streets, the factories, breweries and cozy pristine parlors of that distant and legendary Dutch homeland—but he did know that come morning, with its pale streaks of Arctic light, Composed of Mouth would be on his hut step, with the great mustachioed and bloat-bellied patroon-chief in tow, and that the patroon-chief was hungry to own what no man had a right to own: the imperishable land beneath his feet. But what could the old chief do? Deer were dropping dead in the woods, their stomachs stuffed with bark; snowdrifts buried the village; Mother Corn was comatose till spring; and the people wanted everything the trader put up for sale. If he didn't deal with Jan Pieterse, then Wasamapah, his bitterest rival for control of the tribe, a man who understood credit, spoke with the wind and leaped tall trees in a single bound, would. And Manitou help the old chief if he let Composed of Mouth and the patroon-chief cheat him.

But cheat him they did, Walter's grandmother said, rising with a groan to rinse her hands at the sink in the kitchen. And do you know how they managed it? she asked over her shoulder.

Walter was nine years old. Or maybe ten. He didn't know much. Uh-uh, he said.

She shuffled back into the room, a big gray-haired woman in a print dress, rubbing her thumb over the tips of her first two fingers. Vigorish, she said, that's how.

When Sachoes sat down in his hut the following morning with Composed of Mouth and the patroon-chief and his brother, Wasamapah sat down beside him. And rightfully so. For Wasamapah was the memory of the tribe. As each term of a treaty was struck, he would carefully select a polished fragment of clam, mussel or oyster shell from the pile spread out in the dirt before him, and string it on a piece of rawhide. Each article, each proviso, amendment and codicil had its own distinctive signifier; afterward, when the dust had settled over the mountain of exchanged gifts, when the *kinnikinnick* had been smoked and the *yokeag* and doe's tongue eaten, Wasamapah would convene the council of elders and repeat for them, over and over, the significance of each buffed and rounded shell.

And so it was this time. Sachoes put on his most inflexible face, the patroon-chief tugged uneasily at the joints of his puffed-up fingers, Composed of Mouth talked till he was hoarse, Wasamapah strung shells. With dignity, with stateliness and a serenity that belied his unease, Sachoes accepted the gifts, made his demands on behalf of the tribe and grudgingly gave ground in the face of Composed of Mouth's verbal onslaught. Then they passed a pipe and feasted, the patroon-chief eating sparingly of the cornmeal and tongue and plentifully of the Dutch stuffs—stinking cheeses, rock-hard loaves, salted this and pickled that—that he'd brought along. The new dogs took care of the scraps.

As he smoked, as he gnawed at the foul-smelling cheeses and chewed the tongue, Sachoes felt elated. In addition to the heap of gifts piled up outside the longhouse and distributed throughout the tribe, he'd bargained for barrels of meal, for blankets and bolts of cloth, for beads by the hundredweight and sturdy iron plows and adzes and cookpots. Even better, the patroon-chief's brother had been persuaded to give up the gold ring that encircled his little finger, Jan Pieterse threw in a gilt-edged mirror and a keg of black powder, and in the crowning moment of the negotiations, the patroon-chief himself presented Sachoes with a great floppy-brimmed sugarloaf hat that trailed a plume half as long as his arm. And best of all, Sachoes had given up practically nothing in return—a little plot of land that ran north from the Blue Rock to the Twice Gnarled Tree, south only as far as Deer Run and east to the Brook That Speaks. Nothing! He could walk the length and breadth of it three times over in an afternoon. Finally, finally he'd bested them. Yes, he thought, pulling at the ceremonial pipe and inwardly gloating, what a deal!

But alas, his elation was short-lived. For Wasamapah, eager to make the old chief look bad and with the patroon's note for two thousand guilders stuffed in his moccasin, had surreptitiously added three jagged bruise-colored shells to the treaty string, shells that extended the boundaries of the patroon's purchase till they encompassed every last verst, morgen and acre of the Kitchawank's homeland. Where Sachoes had heard the Twice Gnarled Tree, Wasamapah, so he claimed, had heard the Twice Gnarled Tree Struck Twice by Lightning. And where Sachoes had agreed to Near Deer Run as the southern boundary, Wasamapah had registered Far Deer Run, another matter altogether; so too with the Brook That Speaks, which Wasamapah had recorded as the Brook That Speaks in Winter. When Wasamapah told over the treaty shells for the council of elders, outrage crept into the worn and weary faces of that august body, the light of recrimination flickered in their ancient eyes.

Six months later, Sachoes was dead. Unable to eat, to sleep, unable to stand or sit or lie flat in his robes, the old chief ate himself up with grief over what he'd done. Or rather, what Jan Pieterse, Oloffe Van Wart and Wasamapah had done to him. Not a brave in the tribe sided with him—he was senile, doddering, a woman in a breechclout, and he'd dealt away the soul of his tribe for a few baubles, for dogs that had run off, a white man's hat that mouldered away to nothing, for food that had been eaten and beads that hid themselves in the grass. He was done. Finished. Wasamapah, stern, righteous, unforgiving, a man of sudden wealth and confidant of the great patroon-chief who now held dominion over them, stepped in to replace him. Outcast, hunched with grief, a traitor to his own tribe, Sachoes fell away to nothing, his life as tenuous as the fluff that clings to the dandelion. Wahwahtaysee tried to protect him, but it was no use. One day, in the middle of the strangely pale and wintry summer that succeeded the patroon's coup, the wind blew. Blew hard. Blew a regular gale. And that was the end of Sachoes.

"Yeah, Sachoes," Piet sighed, and Walter started and looked around him as if he were waking to a nightmare. "Got taken by one of his own, wasn't that the story?" The imp was leering at him now, showing acres of gum at the edges of his grin, his eyes recessed in twin sinkholes of wrinkle. "Betrayed, fucked over, stabbed in the back. Right?"

Walter only stared.

And then Piet leaned way out over the abyss between the beds, his face still squinched in that unholy leer, and hit Walter with everything he had: "So what do you hear from your old man?"

What does he hear? The question choked him with bitterness—he could barely get the words out. "I haven't heard from him. At all. Not since—since I was eleven." He looked down at the floor. "I don't even know if he's still alive."

The dwarf fell back into himself with surprise—or feigned surprise. His eyebrows shot up. He fanned himself with a quick hand. "Eleven? Shit. I got a card from him just—when?—shit, must of been a week before my accident."

The whole of Walter's being was caught up in the sudden hammering of his heart. "Where?" he blurted. "Where is he?"

"He's teaching," Piet said, and let a beat go by. "In Barrow."

"Barrow?"

"Point Barrow." Pause, grin, lick lips. "You know: like in Alaska?"

Next morning, Piet was gone. Walter woke to the clatter of the day-shift nurse and the furtive tones of desperation and bewilderment that trickled down the corridor to him, and saw that the bed in the corner was made up as if it had never been occupied. After breakfast, Lola appeared with the big dusty clothbound atlas from the bookshelf in the front room, and Walter barely had time to graze her cheek before snatching it from her hands. "Barrow, Barrow, Barrow," he muttered to himself, flipping impatiently through the pages and then scanning the jagged, glaciated outline of the big bleak mysterious state as if he were seeing it for the first time. He found Anchorage, Kenai, Spenard and Seward. He found the Aleutians, the Talkeetna Mountains, Fairbanks, the Kuskokwim Range. But no Barrow. He had to consult the index for Barrow—G-1—and follow his finger to the top of the map. There it was, Barrow, the northernmost city in the world. Barrow, where windchill took the temperature down to a hundred below and night reigned unbroken for three months of the year.

Lola, looking on with a bemused smile, had a question for him: "Why the sudden interest in Alaska—thinking of doing some seal hunting?"

He looked up as if he'd forgotten she was there. "There was a thing on TV about it last night," he said, flashing his winning smile. "Sounds cool."

"Cool?"

They laughed together. But the minute she left he got an outside line and phoned a travel agent in Croton. Round-trip from Kennedy to Anchorage/Fairbanks alone was $600, plus tax, and service from Fairbanks to Barrow was spotty at best, and could cost another hundred on top of that, not to mention cabs, food and hotel. Where was he going to get that kind of money?

This time, when Walter was discharged from the hospital to continue his recuperation at home, it was not the sweet-smelling champagne-toting Jessica who came to retrieve him; this time Walter departed those depressing tangerine and avocado hallways in the company of his adoptive mother, haunted more than ever by ghosts of the past. Lola drove: white hair, skin tanned to leather, the turquoise earrings she'd picked up in New Mexico. The Volvo ratcheted and wheezed. Did he want a monster burger? she wanted to know. With pickle, relish, mayonnaise, mustard and three-star chili sauce? Or did he just want to go straight home and rest? No, he told her, he didn't want a monster burger, though the food in the hospital had been crap—tasteless, overcooked and heavy on the Jello end of the scale—but he didn't want to go home either.

Where to, then—Fagnoli's? For pizza?

No. He didn't think so. What he really wanted was to go to Depeyster Manufacturing. On Water Street.

Depeyster—?

Uh-huh. He had to see about a job.

But he'd just got out of the hospital. Couldn't it wait a few days?

It couldn't.

Walter didn't bother with the entrance marked EMPLOYEES ONLY—he had Lola park out front, and he swung through the big double doors that gave onto the carpeted vestibule of the inner sanctum, fluid as a gymnast on his crutches, all his weight on his arms and what was now, by default, his good leg. He didn't bother with Miss Egthuysen either, clumping down the hall as if he owned it, pausing half a moment to knock at the frosted-glass door of executive office #7, and then, without waiting for a response, pushing his way in.

"Walter?" Van Wart gasped, getting up from his desk. "But I thought . . . I mean, my daughter told me —"

But Walter had no time for explanations. He leaned forward, the padded supports of the crutches cutting like knives into the pits of his arms, and waved his hand in dismissal. "When do I start?" he said.

Open House

ALL RIGHT, he was thinking, so maybe the place did need a new coat of paint, and perhaps the wisteria was lifting the slate off the stepped gables out front, and yes, the window frames were gouged, the roof leaked and the interior, big as it was, had grown too small for the clutter of ancestral furnishings, but for his money Van Wart Manor was still the best-kept place of its kind in the Hudson Valley, bar none. Sure, there were the museums—Philipsburg Manor, Sunnyside, the lower Van Wart house itself—but they were soulless, husks of houses, uninhabited, ghostly, useless. Even worse were the private restorations like the Terboss place in Fishkill or the Kent house in Yorktown, owned and occupied by strangers, parvenues, interlopers with names like Brophy, Righetti, Mastafiak. Talk about tradition—it went all the way back to some tramp steamer out of Palermo in 1933. It was a joke, that's all. A bad joke.

Depeyster Van Wart stood in the loam of his rose garden at the base of the great sloping manorial lawn and gazed up at the house with a rush of proprietary pride, secure in his heritage, in his position, and now, with the unhoped-for miracle of Joanna's news, secure in his future too. No parvenu he—he was born here, in the master bedroom on the second floor, between the Chippendale chest-on-chest and the Duncan Phyfe wardrobe. His father had been born here too, in the shadow of that same wardrobe, and his father before him. For better than three hundred years, none but Van Warts had trod those peg-and-groove floors, none but Van Warts had mounted the groaning staircases or crouched in the ancestral dirt of the hoariest and bottommost cellar. And now, at long last, he knew in his heart that none of it would ever change, that Van Warts and Van Warts alone would walk those venerable corridors into the golden, limitless, insuperable future.

For Joanna was pregnant. Forty-three-year-old Joanna, bride of his youth, mother of his daughter, lover of unguents and creams and the cuisines of Naples, Languedoc and the Fiji Islands, champion of the dispossessed, stranger to his bed and purveyor of rags, Joanna was pregnant. After fifteen years of desperate longing, recrimination, rancor and despair, she'd come to him and he'd responded, simple as that. He'd risen to the occasion, impregnated her, knocked her up, got her with child. But not just *a* child, not just *any* child—a male child. What else could it be?

He remembered the cruel disappointment that had followed on the heels of that intoxicating, primal, woodsy tryst before the fireplace last fall—*Honey,* she'd said to him a scant month later, *darling, I think I'm going to have a baby.* A baby? He could barely speak for astonishment. Had his prayers been answered, his hopes exhumed? A baby? Was it true? Was he really going to have one more shot at it?

The answer was as unequivocal as the flow of blood: no, he wasn't. It was a false alarm. She was late with her period, that was all, and he fell into a despair more profound than he'd ever known. But then, just after the New Year, she came to him again. And then again. She was frenzied, urgent, wild, her skin darkened with smears of some reddish pigment, a smell of swamps and cookfires and bitter uncultivated berries caught in the heavy braids of her hair, buckskin against naked flesh. He was John Smith and she was Pocahontas, untamed, feverish, coupling as if to preserve their very lives. Who was she, this stranger beneath him with the musky smell and the faraway look in her eyes? He didn't care. He mounted her, penetrated her, spilled his seed deep within her. Blissfully. Gratefully. Thinking: this Indian business isn't so bad after all.

Then there was the second alarum, the trip to the doctor, the test, the examination, the indubitability of the result: Joanna was pregnant. So what if she was mad as a hatter? So what if she shied away from him even more violently than before and redoubled her visits to the reservation? So what if she humiliated him at the market in her paints and leggings and all the rest? She was pregnant, and Van Wart Manor would have its heir.

And so it was that on this particular day—this day of days—as he clipped roses for the big cut-glass vases stationed strategically throughout the house for the delectation of the sightseers and history buffs who would any moment now begin to arrive with appropriately awed and respectful faces, Depeyster felt supreme, expansive, beyond hurt, felt like Solomon awaiting the morning's petitioners. It was June, his wife was pregnant, the sun shone down on him in all its benedictory splendor, and the house—the ancient, peerless, stately, inestimable house—was open to the public and looking good.

"Did you hear about Peletiah Crane?"

Marguerite Mott, in a huddle with her sister Muriel, balanced a white bone china cup on its saucer and looked up expectantly at her host. It was late in the afternoon, and a small band of the historically curious, eyes glazed after an exhaustive three-hour tour of the house and grounds that left no shingle undefined or nook unplumbed, was gathered for refreshments in the front parlor. Lula, in white apron and cap, had just served tea and a very old but distinctly musty sherry, and set out a platter of stale soda crackers and tinned pâté, and the group, which consisted of two nuns, a legal secretary from Briarcliff, a self-educated auto mechanic and the withered octogenarian treasurer of the Hopewell Junction Historical Society, as well as young Walter Van Brunt, LeClerc and Ginny Outhouse and, not least, the redoubtable Mott sisters, fell upon these humble offerings like wanderers come in off the desert.

Marguerite's question caught the twelfth heir in the middle of a complex architectural dissertation on how the present house had managed to grow up over the generations from the modest parlor in which they now stood. Buoyant, with the energy and animation of a man half his age, Depeyster had driven the octogenarian and the legal secretary up against the Nunns, Clark & Co. rosewood piano in the corner, urging them to appreciate the thickness and solidity of the wall behind it. "Built from native fieldstone and oyster-shell mortar, all the way back in 1650," he said. "We've painted it, glazed it, repaired the mortar, of course—go ahead, feel it—but that's it, the original wall put up by Oloffe and Lubbertus Van Wart three hundred and nineteen years ago." Depeyster had been talking for three hours, and he wasn't about to stop now—not as long as anyone was still standing. "The patroon settled in Croton, at the lower house—you know, the *museum*—and he built this one for his brother, but after Lubbertus passed on he alternated between the two houses. Ironically, the lower house went out of the family just after the Revolution—but that's another story—while this one has been continuously occupied by Van Warts since the day —" he suddenly broke off and turned to Marguerite. "What did you say?"

"Peletiah. Did you hear about Peletiah?"

In that moment, secretary and treasurer were forgotten, and Depeyster felt his heart leap up. "He's dead?" he yelped, barely able to contain himself.

The auto mechanic was watching him; LeClerc and Walter, who'd had their heads together, looked up inquisitively.

"No," Marguerite whispered, pursing her lips and giving him a quick closer's wink, "not yet." She let the moment hang over him, huge with significance, and then delivered the clincher: "He's had a stroke."

He didn't want to seem too anxious—the legal secretary was glancing around her uneasily, afraid to set her cup down, and the old boy from Hopewell Junction looked as if he were about to have a stroke himself—and so he counted to three before he spoke: "Is it . . . serious?"

Marguerite's smile was tight, the white-frosted lips pressed firmly together, the foundation at the corners of her eyes barely breached. It was a realtor's smile, and it spoke of quiet triumph, of the thorny deal at long last closed. "He can't walk," she said. "Can't talk or eat. He keeps slipping in and out of it."

"Yes," Muriel said, interposing her glazed face between them, "it looks bad."

Looks bad. The words stirred him, gladdened him, filled him with vengeful joy. So the old long-nosed land-grubbing pinko bastard was finally slipping over the edge, finally letting go . . . and now it was the grandson—the pothead—who would take charge of things. It was too perfect. Thirty-five hundred an acre—ha! He'd get it for half that, a quarter—he'd get it for the price of another fix or trip or whatever it was the kid doped himself up on . . . yes, and then he'd find himself a horse, a Kentucky Walker like his father used to have, old blood lines, blaze on the forehead; he'd refurbish the stables, lean on the town board to erect one of those horse-crossing signs up the road at the entrance to the place, and then, with his son up in front of him, he'd ride out over the property first thing every morning, sun like fire on the creek, the crush of hickory nuts underfoot, a roast on the table. . . .

Unfortunately, the grand and triumphal procession of his thoughts suddenly pulled up lame. For there, outside the window, in full Indian drag and shouldering a bundle the size and shape of a buffalo's head, was Joanna. Back. Early. Hauling garbage out of the station wagon in full view of the legal secretary and the wheezing old ass from Hopewell Junction. But what was she doing home already? he thought in rising panic. Wasn't she supposed to be up in Jamestown overseeing the canned succotash drive or some such thing? Suddenly he was moving, nodding his way out of range of the Mott sisters' waxen smiles, shaking off the auto mechanic's query about BTUs and heating costs, trying desperately to head her off.

He was too late.

The parlor door eased open and there she was, in fringed buckskin and plastic beads, her skin darkened to the color of mountain burgundy. "Oh," she faltered, glancing around the room in confusion and finally settling on her husband, "I saw all the cars . . . but it just—it's open house, then—is that it?"

Silence gripped the room like fear.

The nuns looked bewildered, the secretary appalled; Ginny Outhouse smiled tentatively. It was Lula, coming forward with the tray of pâté and crackers, who broke the spell. "Want some canopies, Mizz Van Wart?" she said. "You must be half-starved after that drive."

"Thank you, Lula, no," Joanna said, dropping the bundle to the floor with a clatter, "I had some—some dried meat on the way down."

By now, Depeyster had moved forward stiffly to greet her. Muriel had begun to gush small talk ("How *are* you dear, so good to see you again, you're looking fit, still rescuing the Indians I see"), and the murmur of conversation had resumed among the others.

Depeyster was mortified. LeClerc and Ginny were old friends—they knew of Joanna's growing eccentricity, and it was nothing. Or almost nothing. And Walter was his protegé, no problem there. But these others, the Mott sisters and these strangers—what must they think? And then it came to him. He'd take them aside, one by one, that's what he'd do, and explain that his wife's getup was part of the spirit of the open house, touching base with the aboriginal inhabitants of the Valley in a spontaneous bit of historical improvisation and all that—cute, wasn't it?

The thought calmed him, and he was turning to the shorter of the nuns with an anecdote on his lips, when the door flew open and Mardi, the wayward daughter, burst into the room. "Hello, hello, everyone!" she shouted, "isn't it a fantastic day?" She was wearing an imitation leopard-skin bikini that showed more of her than her father cared to know about, and her skin was nearly as red as her mother's with overexposure to the sun. She went straight for the sherry decanter, downed a glass, made a sour face, then downed another.

It was too much, it was impossible.

Depeyster turned away from the horror of the scene, fumbling for a pinch of cellar dust to sprinkle over his tea, the mechanic at his elbow, nuns agape, the legal secretary gathering up her things to go. "Oh, hi, LeClerc," he heard his daughter say in a voice as false and unctuous as an insurance salesman's. "Must be a bear to heat this place," the mechanic opined.

Next thing he knew, Mardi was leading Walter out of the room—"Come on," she purred, "I want to show you something upstairs"—the nuns were thanking him for a lovely afternoon, Joanna had thrown open her satchel in the middle of the Turkish rug and was offering Indian pottery for sale, and LeClerc and Ginny were talking about dinner. "How about that Italian place in Somers?" Ginny said. "Or the Chinese in Yorktown?"

And then he was standing at the front door, numbly shaking hands with the mechanic, who'd laid out five dollars apiece for a pair of unglazed Indian ashtrays that looked like a failed kindergarten project (what were they supposed to be, anyway—fish?). "Mind if I take a look at the plumbing on my way out?" The mechanic—he was a young man, bald as an egg—gave him a warm, almost saintly look.

"I'd really like to see what you did with the pipes and those three-foot walls."

"Or that steak and lobster joint in Amawalk? What do you think, Dipe?" LeClerc said, pulling him away from the mechanic.

What did he think? The Mott sisters were covering their retreat with a desperate barrage of clichés and insincerities, the old boy from Hopewell Junction announced in a clarion voice that he was going to need help getting to the bathroom, and the legal secretary left without a word. Dazed, defeated, traumatized, he couldn't say what he thought. The day was in ruins.

For Walter, on the other hand, the day had just begun.

He'd been sitting there with LeClerc Outhouse, uncomfortable in his seersucker suit and throat-constricting tie, his lower legs aching from the rigors of the estate tour, discussing, without candor and with little conviction, the moral imperative of the U.S. presence in Indo-China and the crying need to bomb the gooks into submission with everything we had. And now, here he was, following Mardi's compelling backside up the stairs and into the dark, enticing, black-lit refuge of her room. She was talking trivialities, chattering—Did he know that Hector had joined the marines? Or that Herbert Pompey landed a gig with the *La Mancha* road company? Or that Joey's band broke up? She wasn't seeing Joey any more, did he know that?

They were in her room now, and she turned to look at him as she delivered this last line. The walls were painted black, the shades drawn. Behind her, a poster of Jimi Hendrix, his face contorted with the ecstasy of feedback, glowed wickedly under the black light. Walter gave her a cynical smile and eased himself down on the bed.

Actually, he didn't know that Hector had joined the marines or that Herbert was going on the road—he hadn't set foot in the Elbow since he left the hospital. And as for Joey, the only emotion that might have stirred in him had he heard that the band hadn't merely broken up but burst open and fallen to pieces in unidentifiable fragments would have been joy. Mardi had hurt him. Cut him to the quick. Touched him where Meursault could never have been touched. And he was all the better for it. Stronger. Harder and more dispassionate than ever, cut adrift from his anchors—from Jessica, from Tom, from

Mardi and Hesh and Lola—the lone wolf, the lonesome cowboy, the single champion and seeker after the truth. Love? It was shit.

No. He hadn't seen Mardi, Tom, Jessica—any of them. He'd been seeing Miss Egthuysen, though. Twenty-seven years old, slit skirts, lips like butterflies. And he'd been seeing Depeyster. A lot. Learning the business, learning history. He'd moved out of the clapboard bungalow in Kitchawank Colony and taken his own place—a vine-covered guesthouse behind the big old place overlooking the creek in Van Wartville. And the Norton was gone too. He drove an MGA now, sleek, throaty and fast.

Mardi pulled the door closed. Her hair was in her face, the flat flawless plane of her belly showed a bruise of sunburn, a gold chain clasped her ankle. She crossed the floor to drop the needle on a record, and the room opened up with a cataract of drums and a thin manic drone of guitar. Walter was still smiling when she turned to him again. "What did you want to show me?" he said.

She padded back across the room, a paradigm of flesh—Walter thought about his ancestors and how inflamed the mere sight of an ankle would get them—and held out a tightly closed fist. "This," she said, uncurling her fingers to reveal a fat yellow joint. She waited half a beat, then unfastened her halter and wriggled out of the leopard-skin panties. "And this," she whispered.

In de Pekel Zitten*

WELL, yes, here were a Van Wart and a Van Brunt fornicating in historic surroundings, but it had taken them centuries to arrive at so democratic a juncture. At one time, such a thing would have been unthinkable. Unspeakable. As absurd as the coupling of lions and toads or pigs and fishes. In the early days, when Jeremias Van Brunt was chafing under the terms of his indenture, when the patroon's authority went uncontested and those that worked his land were little higher on the social scale than Russian serfs, the closest a Van Brunt had come to a Van Wart was the pogamoggan incident, in which the aforementioned Jeremias had threatened to open up the side of the *Jongheer*'s head for him.

At that time, the incident seemed a serious challenge to manorial prerogatives—almost an insurrectionary act—but over the years, all that had been forgotten. Or at least covered over with a shovel or two of dirt, like a corpse hastily buried. Absorbed in looking after his burgeoning family and staving off the anarchic forces of nature that threatened at any moment to overwhelm the farm and thrust him back into the desperate penury he'd known after the death of his parents, Jeremias barely gave a passing thought to his landlord. In fact, the only time he called to mind the man who held sway over him and by whose sufferance he earned his daily bread and raised the roof over his head was in November of each year, when the annual quitrent was due.

* Literally "sitting in the pickle."

For weeks in advance of the date he would storm and rage and fulminate about the inequity of it all, and the old contumacious fire-breathing spirit arose like a phoenix from the ashes of his contentment. "I'll move!" he'd shout. "Rather than pay that parasitic fat-assed son of a bitch a single penny I'll pack up every last stick of furniture, every last cup and saucer and plate, and go back to Schobbejacken." And every year Neeltje and the children would plead and beg and remonstrate with him, and on the fifteenth, when Ter Dingas Bosyn wheeled up in the patroon's wagon, Jeremias would lock himself in the back room with a bottle of rum and let his wife count out the coins, the pots of butter, the pecks of wheat and the four fat pullets the patroon demanded as his yearly due. When he emerged the following day, red-eyed and subdued, he'd limp wordlessly out into the yard to repair the barn door or put a new wall in the henhouse where the porcupines had chewed their way through it.

And for his part, Stephanus, who'd succeeded his father as patroon after the pestilence of '68 carried the old man off in a fit of wheezing, was too busy maneuvering his way around the Governor's Council of Ten (of which he was the guiding light), managing the shipping business he'd inherited from his father and raising his own family to worry about an ignorant dirt clod on a distant and negligible plot of land. It was enough that said dirt clod paid his annual rent—a fact duly registered in the *commis'* accounts ledger for the given year. Beyond that, Jeremias could go to the devil and back for all Stephanus Van Wart cared.

All well and good. For twelve years Van Warts and Van Brunts went their own way, and slowly, gradually, the wounds began to heal and a truce settled over the valley.

But scratch a scab, however feebly, and it will bleed.

So it was that in the summer of 1679, just after Jeremias' thirtieth birthday, Neeltje's father, the redoubtable *schout,* paid a visit to the farm at Nysen's Roost with a message from the patroon. Joost arrived late in the afternoon, having spent the better part of the day making the rounds of the neighboring farms. At fifty, he was more bowed than ever, so badly contorted he looked as if he were balancing his head on his breastbone, and the nag he rode was as bony, swaybacked and ill-tempered as its predecessor, the little-lamented *Donder.*

He'd long since reconciled himself to his fiery son-in-law (though every time he glanced at the pogamoggan on its hook beside the hearth his left temple throbbed and his ears began to sing), and when Neeltje begged him to spend the night, he agreed.

It was at dinner—or rather, after dinner, when Neeltje served seed cakes and a fragrant steaming caudle of cinnamon and wine—that Joost gave them the news. The whole family was gathered around the big rustic table, which Neeltje had set with the veiny china and Zutphen glassware she'd inherited on the death of her mother. Jeremias—shaggy, mustachioed, huge and hatless—pushed back his chair with a sigh and lighted his pipe. Beside him, in a long tapering row on the bench that grew shorter every year, sat the boys: nephew Jeremy, with his wild look and tarry hair, now nearly fifteen and so tight-lipped he would have exasperated the stones themselves; Wouter, eleven and a half and a dead ringer for his father; and then Harmanus and Staats, eight and six respectively. The girls—each as slight and dark-eyed and pretty as her mother—sat on the far side of the table, ranged beside their grandfather. Geesje, who was nine, got up to help her mother. Agatha and Gertruyd were four and two. They were waiting for seed cake.

"You know, *younker,*" Joost said, tamping tobacco in the bowl of a clay pipe half as long as his arm, "I'm up here on the patroon's business."

"Oh?" said Jeremias, as indifferent as he might have been to news of the emperor of China, "and what might that be?"

"Not much," Joost managed, between great lip-smacking sucks at the stem of the pipe, "not much. Road building, is all."

Jeremias said nothing. Geesje cleared away the children's pewter bowls and the remains of the milk soup. Erect and unfathomable, Jeremy Mohonk exchanged a look with Wouter. "Road building?" Neeltje echoed, setting down the bowl of spiced wine.

"Hm-hm," returned her father, sucking and puffing as vigorously as if he'd been plunged into the icy waters of Acquasinnick Creek. "He's going to be here at the upper house for the rest of the summer. With a carpenter from New York. He's planning to fix up the house where it's got run-down and I guess he couldn't persuade his brother to come out from Haarlem and take it over, but he's got Lubbertus' boy of an age now to move in and start a family. . . ."

"And what's it to me?" Jeremias asked, puffing now himself and sending up a bitter black cloud of smoke.

"Well, that's just it, you see—that's what I've been going around to the tenants for. The patroon wants —"

Jeremias cut him off. "There is no patroon—this is an English colony now."

Puffing, waving his hand impatiently to concede the point, Joost lifted his head up off his breastbone and went on: "Patroon, landlord—what's the difference? Anyway, he's calling on all the tenants to give him five days' work with their teams—he wants to widen the road from Jan Pieterse's to the upper house and then on out to the new farms at Crom's Pond. There's a post road to go through here one day, and *Mijnheer* wants to be sure it won't pass him by."

Jeremias set down his pipe and dipped a cup of wine. "I won't do it," he said.

"Won't do it?" Joost's eyes hardened. He watched the angry scar on his son-in-law's cheek as it flushed with blood and then went dead white again. "You've got no choice," he said. "It's in your contract."

"Screw the contract."

Here it was, all over again. Jeremias would never learn, never accept it, not if you locked him up in that cell for a hundred years. But this time, Joost wouldn't rise to the bait. This time things were different. This time the renegade sat there across the table from him, husband to his daughter, father to his grandchildren. "But the patroon—" Joost began, controlling himself, trying to reason with him.

He was wasting his breath.

Jeremias' fist hit the table with a shock that set the china jumping and so startled little Gertruyd that she burst into tears. "Screw the patroon," he snarled.

Wouter sat silently through his father's outburst, his head bowed, his eyes on the platter of seed cakes in the middle of the table. "Jeremias," his mother reproved in the soft, chastening voice Wouter knew so well, "you know it's your duty. Why fight it?"

The words were barely out of her mouth before his father turned on her, as Wouter knew he would, the stubborn disputatious tones of the old man's voice riding up the scale to explode in a thunderous tirade against the patroon, the lord governor, rents, taxes, stony soil, wood rot, white ants, earwigs and anything else that came to mind. As his father cocked himself toward her and his mother took an involuntary step away from the table, Wouter made a quick snatch at the seed cakes, secreted a fistful in his shirt and nodded at Jeremy. "Wouter took all the cakes!" howled little Harmanus, but in the heat of the moment, no one noticed. As the two accomplices ducked away from the table and slipped out the door, grandfather Cats was raising his voice too, urging everyone to calm down, to please calm down!

Neither Wouter nor Jeremy uttered a word as they felt their way down the path to Acquasinnick Creek in the gloom of dusk. They'd been up and down the trail so many times the figure approached infinitude, and though it was barely light enough to see, they knew every dip, drop-off, pothole and rib of stone as if they'd carved them themselves. In less than five minutes they were sitting on the high undercut bank of the creek, listening to the suck and pop of rising trout and the flatulent complaint of the bullfrog. Wouter had made off with six cakes. He handed three to his cousin.

For a long while they merely chewed, the water dodging the rocks at their feet in rhythmic wash, mosquitoes cutting the air, crickets chirruping. Wouter broke the silence. "Damned if I'm going to bust my back for the patroon," he said in a sort of ruminative, octave-shattering yelp. He was at that stage in his life when his father was a small deity, reverenced and wise, incapable of error, the very oracle of truth and decision. If Jeremias told him that geese knew algebra and the creek flowed backward, he'd never doubt it, all appearances to the contrary.

Jeremy said nothing. Which wasn't unusual, since he rarely spoke, even if directly addressed. He was tall, dark, with the spidery limbs and prominent Adam's apple of his late progenitor, and though he knew Dutch and English both, he declined to use either, communicating in gurgles, grunts and belches, or in an elaborate sign language of his own device.

"You know *vader* won't do it," Wouter said, reaching out to snatch a firefly from the air and smear its phosphorescence in a greenish streak across his forearm. "He's no slave."

Night was deepening around them. There was a splash downstream, from the direction of the bridge. Jeremy said nothing.

"It'll be us, you know," Wouter said. "*Vader* won't do it, and then *moeder* and *grootvader* Cats'll make us do it. Just like the wood. Remember?"

The wood. Yes. Jeremy remembered. When the rent came due last November and Jeremias retreated, muttering, to the back room, it wasn't just the pounds and pence, the butter, wheat and pullets the patroon demanded, but two fathoms of firewood to boot. *No son of mine,* Jeremias had blustered, *or nephew either* . . . but his voice had trailed off, and he'd taken a pull at the bottle and staggered out into the yard to be alone with his indignation and his rage. Neeltje, *moeder* Neeltje, had seen to it that Wouter, Harmanus and Jeremy cut and split the patroon's wood for him. The three of them—Harmanus was only eight and not much good—worked through two bitterly cold afternoons, and then had to hitch up the oxcart and drive out to the upper manor house with the firewood to warm the patroon's crazy skeletal old mother, who'd been living there ever since the old patroon kicked off. That was in November, when the wood needed cutting. Now it was July, and the road needed widening.

"Well I'm not going to do it," Wouter growled. "No matter what *moeder* says."

Though he heartily concurred, still Jeremy said nothing.

A long moment passed, the night sounds of the forest crepitating around them, the water spilling ever louder over the stones at their feet. Wouter tossed a handful of pebbles into the black swirling water, then pushed himself up. "What are we going to do?" he said. "I mean, if the patroon comes."

Jeremy's reply was so guttural, so strangled, so full of clicks and grunts and pauses, that no one but Wouter, his bosom companion and bedmate, would have known what he said. But Wouter heard him as clearly as if he'd spoken the purest King's English—or stadtholder's Dutch—and in the darkness he smiled with the comfort of it. What his cousin had said, in his arcane and contorted way, was this: "The patroon come, we fix him."

Inevitably, like frost in its season, like corn blight or bread mold, like the crow that arrives to feast on the dead ox or the fly that hovers over the pan of rising dough, the patroon came. He came by sloop, to the landing at Jan Pieterse's Kill, and he brought with him his wife,

Hester Lovelace (who was, by happy coincidence, niece to the most powerful man in New York, his honor the lord governor), his four children, three rooms of furniture, two crates of crockery, a spinet and several somber family portraits meant to enliven the dreary atmosphere of the upper house. Pompey II, now eighteen and the only male issue of the union between the late patroon's domestic slaves, Ismailia and Pompey the First, rode shotgun over the crates, stores and furniture. His sister Calpurnia, a light-skinned girl with something of the old patroon in the crook of her nose and the odd, almost spastic skew of her limbs, kept *Mijnheer*'s three young boys from drowning themselves and saw to the tonsorial needs of Saskia, the patroon's ethereal ten-year-old daughter.

Stephanus was met at the Blue Rock by a fatter, older and considerably richer Jan Pieterse, and by a delegation of slow-moving, baggy-breeched farmers with chaff in their hair and clay pipes in their pockets. His factotum, an unctuous, incessantly twitching whipsnake of a man by the name of Aelbregt van den Post, took charge of the unloading of the sloop and the concurrent loading of the two wagons that stood ready to receive the patroon and his effects. Summoning all his sinewy energy, van den Post, who was said to have survived a shipwreck off Cape Ann by clinging to a spar and eating jellyfish for three weeks, flung himself into the task like a desperate man. He skittered up and down the big slab of rock, shouting orders to the sloop's torpid crew, handing *Mijnheer*'s wife down from the gangplank and up into the wagon, steadying the horses, cuffing the hapless carpenter for lagging behind with his tools, castigating Pompey, chiding the children and managing, in the intervals, to bow and scrape at *Mijnheer*'s heels like a fawning spaniel. When all was ready, the patroon and his family went ahead in the light wagon, Pompey at the reins. Van den Post and the carpenter, hunched over a pair of evil-smelling oxen on the rough plank seat of the overladen farm wagon, brought up the rear.

The patroon was anxious to get to the house. He'd paid a visit during the spring and was shocked by the general decline of the place, the millstones ground to dust, the farms run down, the house itself sagging into the earth like a ship listing at sea. Mismanagement was what it was. That, and his own preoccupation elsewhere. How could he expect his tenants to advance at more than a crawl if there was no one to crack the whip over them?

Well, all that was about to change.

He planned to live at the upper house himself till the weather turned, tightening the reins on his tenants and putting things in order so he could install his dunderhead of a cousin in the place without having to worry about its falling to wrack and ruin. In a decade's time he'd want the house for Rombout, his eldest boy, and when he passed on himself, the lower house—and the Cats farm—would go to Oloffe, his middle son, and Pieter, the youngest. But for now he was here with his family to live beneath the roof of the fine old stone house his father and uncle had raised not thirty years ago, and he meant to put all his energy into it. Old Ter Dingas Bosyn, the *commis,* would look after the lower house and the goods due in from Rotterdam at the end of the month, and he had Cats to see to things in Croton as well. And then, of course, it wasn't as if he were going into exile on a desert isle or anything—the lower house was no more than half a day's ride, if something should come up.

It took him a week to get settled. His mother, who'd been living there alone, was cold and irascible, and he spent the first several days trying to disabuse her of the notion that he'd come to turn her out to her martyrdom among the beasts of the wilderness. Then there was Vrouw van Bilevelt, the housekeeper, who took every suggestion as a personal affront, regarded Pompey and Calpurnia as cannibals in Dutch clothing, and fought bitterly over every cup, saucer and stick of furniture Hester brought into the house. And finally, there was the sticky question of the de Vries. It was they—Gerrit Jacobzoon de Vries, his wife and two cretinous sons—who'd managed the farm all these years—and managed it badly. On the very first night, after a dinner of stewed eel and cabbage charred into the pan out of spite by a murderous-looking Vrouw van Bilevelt, Stephanus summoned Gerrit de Vries to the front parlor. He began by saying how much he appreciated the long and honorable service Gerrit had given him and his father before him, sketched in his plans for the upper house and mill, and ended by offering him a new farm out beyond the van der Meulens' place, on the same terms he'd offer any prospective tenant—a stake in building materials, livestock and farm machinery, all improvements descending to the patroon, quitrent due in November.

De Vries was struck dumb. His face flushed; he turned his hat over in his rough hands. Finally, in his peasant's Dutch, he managed to stammer, "You—you mean, start all over again?"

Mijnheer nodded.

The rest was simple. De Vries spat at his feet and the patroon had van den Post show him to the door. The following morning, after thirteen years at the upper house, the de Vries were gone.

Once all that had been settled, the patroon set van den Post to work on the farm and ordered the carpenter to begin reroofing the house and hauling stone to frame the two-story addition that would more than double the size of the place. Then he turned his thoughts to road building. And widening.

It was on a fine hot August morning, while the blackberries ripened in the woods, the corn grew sweet in the fields and the crabs crawled right up out of the bay and into the pot, that the patroon called on his tenants to give him the labor that was his due. By eight o'clock they were there, gathered in front of the house with their carts and teams, their axes and shovels and harrows. The patroon, dressed in flowing rhinegrave breeches and a sleeveless silk jerkin, and mounted on the sleek Narragansett pacer the *schout* had brought up from Croton for him, acknowledged each of them with a lordly nod of his head—first the van der Meulens, old Staats and his son, Douw, who leased his own farm now; next the Cranes and Ten Haers and Reinier Oothouse's boy, who'd taken over after the delirium tremens softened his father's brain; and finally, the Lents, the Robideaus, the Mussers and Sturdivants.

All told, there were nearly two hundred people living on the Van Wart estate, upper and lower manors combined, but the majority of these were gathered along the Hudson in Croton and sprinkled inland along the Croton River. Up here, on the northern verge of Stephanus' estate, there were only ten farms under cultivation, and a total, at last count, of fifty-nine souls—excluding, of course, the ragged band of Kitchawanks at Indian Point and the twenty-six free subjects of the Crown who lived at Pieterse's Kill, on plots the trader had sold them for fifty times what he'd paid for them. Ten farms. That was four more than there'd been in his father's time, but in the *Jongheer*'s eyes it was nothing. Not even a start.

He'd been buying up land to the east from a degenerate tribe of the Connecticuts, and to the south from the Sint Sinks. And by skillful recruitment among the dazed and seasick immigrants who staggered ashore at the Battery with little more than the wind at their backs and stuffed-up noses, he'd managed to find tenants for nearly all the choice Croton plots—and he would find more, a hundred more, to domesticate the wild lands up here. What he wanted was nothing less than to amass the biggest estate in the Colony, a manor that would make the great estates of Europe look like so many vegetable patches. It had become his obsession, his overmastering desire, the one thing that made him forget the paved streets, the quiet taverns, the music, art and society of Leyden and Amsterdam. He looked out over the sun-burnished faces of the farmers who'd come to build him a road—a road that would bring swarms of beholden peasants up from the river to fell the trees, fire the stumps and plow up the ground—and for the briefest moment he saw it all as it would one day be, the hills rolling with wheat, onions sprouting from the marshes, pumpkins and cabbages and crookneck squash piled up like riches, like gold. . . .

But then one of the farmers cleared his throat and spoke up, and the picture was gone. It was Robideau, a bitter, leathery Frenchman who'd lost an ear in a calamitous brawl outside the Ramapo tavern, which mysteriously burnt to the ground a week later. Robideau sat high up on the hard plank seat of his wagon, his close-set eyes gleaming, the whip lazily flicking at the flies that settled on the blistered rumps of his oxen. "And what about Van Brunt," he said. "The pegleg. Where's he?"

Van Brunt? For a moment the patroon was confused, having so successfully suppressed the memory of that ancient and unseemly confrontation that he'd forgotten Jeremias existed. But in the next moment he was back in that miserable hovel, the *schout* laid out on the hard dirt floor, Jeremias Van Brunt defying him, challenging him with a crude aboriginal weapon, and slim pretty dark-eyed little Neeltje regarding him from her bed of sin. *You don't own Neeltje,* Jeremias said. *And you don't own me.*

"It is because he's married to the *schout*'s daughter—is that why he gets special treatment?"

Van Brunt. Yes: where in hell was he? Stephanus turned to the *schout,* who'd come up from Croton the previous evening to oversee the road work. "Well?" he said.

Cats was bowed nearly to the ground as he shuffled forward to make his excuses. "I don't know where he is, *Mijnheer,*" he said in a voice so halting and reluctant he seemed to gag on each word. "I've informed him, and—and he said he would come."

"Oh, he did, did he?" The patroon leaned forward in his saddle, the great billowing folds of his breeches engulfing his stockings, his buckled pumps and the stirrups too. "That's very generous of him." And then, straightening up again so that he towered over the *schout* like an equestrian monument come to life, he cursed so vilely and emphatically that young Johannes Musser snatched a hand to his mouth and Mistress Sturdivant, the stoutest woman in Van Wartwyck, fainted dead away. "I want him here within the hour," he said, speaking through clenched teeth. "Understand?"

The day was half gone, and the patroon in a rage approaching apoplectic closure, when finally the Van Wart wagon, drawn by a pair of gaunt, toothless and half-lame oxen, appeared around the bend and made for the work crew at a somnolent pace. Joost Cats, leading his nag and listing so far forward it looked as if he were about to plunge face down in the dirt, limped beside it. The patroon glanced up angrily, then turned to the first farmer at hand—young Oothouse—and began an earnest chat about manure or dried shad or some such nonsense; he wasn't about to give Van Brunt the satisfaction of thinking that he, Stephanus Oloffe Rombout Van Wart, landowner, patroon, shipping magnate and member of the Governor's Council, could experience even the slightest anxiety over the whereabouts of so insignificant a creature as he.

The crew—men and women both, including a revived Mistress Sturdivant—had cleared and graded the outside lane in front of the patroon's house, and were now taking their *de noen* break. They lounged in the shade, appropriating a round from one of the felled trees for a table, chewing hard black bread, cold bacon and cheese. One of them—Robideau, from the look of his stockings and shoes—was snoring blissfully beneath a blackberry bush, a soiled white handkerchief spread over his face. As the patroon listened to young Oothouse apotheosize dung, he was aware of every creaking revolution of the wagon wheels behind him, of every snort and wheeze of the winded old oxen. Finally, with an excruciating shriek of the axles, the wagon ground to a halt at his back.

Lifting his nose, and turning around with all the imperious dignity he could muster, the patroon was prepared to be mollified, Van Brunt's very presence—however reluctant, however tardy—proof positive that yes, he did own him, just as he owned all the rest of these sorry soil grubbers, his word the law, eviction and banishment his prerogatives. He turned, but what he saw wasn't at all what he expected. This wasn't Van Brunt hunched over the reins—this was a boy, a half-breed, with the soupy staring eyes of the mentally deficient. And beside him another boy, younger, weaker, thinner, the sort of boy you'd send out to gather nuts, not build roads.

"I'm—I'm—" Cats was trying to say something. The patroon speared him with a savage glance. "—I'm sorry, but my son-in-law, I mean, Farmer Van Brunt, is, uh, indisposed, and he, uh, sent, his, uh—"

"Silence!" the patroon exploded. "I ordered you," he roared, advancing on the shrinking *schout* in the great boatlike mules he wore over his pumps to protect them from the dirt of the road, "to bring him here, did I not!?"

"Yes, *Mijnheer,*" the *schout* said, whipping off his hat and working it in his hands. He was staring at his feet. "But instead because he, he was ill—"

It was then that the boy spoke up—the smaller one, the white boy. His voice was as high and shrill and discordant as a badly played piccolo. "That's not it at all, *grootvader,*" he said, working himself up. He turned to face the patroon, as bold as a thief. "He won't come, that's all. Said he's busy. Said he's paid his rent. Said he's as good a man as you."

The patroon said nothing. He turned his back on them, shuffled over to the pacer, kicked off the mules and swung himself into the saddle. Then he motioned to young Oothouse. "You," he growled, "go fetch *Heer* van den Post." Everyone—even Mistress Sturdivant, who'd been addressing herself to a shepherd's pie the size of a football—turned to watch him go. No one moved, and no one said a word, till he returned.

Young Oothouse, an indolent young man given to fat and a

measured pace, jogged all the way, and he was red-faced and running with sweat when he appeared around the bend in the road, van den Post loping easily at his side. In the next moment, van den Post stood before the patroon, gazing up steadily at him from beneath the brim of his steeple hat. "Yes, *Mijnheer?*" he said, barely winded.

From his eminence atop the horse, the patroon spoke, his voice cold and brittle. "Aelbregt, you will remove from *Heer* Cats the plumed hat and silver-plated rapier that are the perquisites of his office—they now belong to you." And then, addressing Joost, who stood there in a daze as van den Post took the rapier from him, *"Heer* Cats, you will oversee the roadwork this afternoon, and then return to your farm."

Still, no one said a word, but shock was written on every face. Why, Joost Cats had been *schout* as long as anyone could remember, and to have him removed just like that—it was unheard of, impossible.

A moment later, grinning like a shark, van den Post stood before his patroon in silver-plumed hat and rapier, awaiting his further instructions.

"Heer schout," Stephanus said, raising his voice so that all could hear him, "you will take these two young renegades," indicating Wouter and Jeremy Mohonk, "and confine them in the root cellar at the house on a charge of impertinence and sedition."

This brought a murmur of protest from the farmers, particularly from Staats van der Meulen, who stood up angrily amidst the crumbs of his lunch. Someone sneezed and one of the oxen broke wind. Robideau's snores sawed away at the motionless air. No one dared to speak up.

"And when that's done, I want you to ride out to Nysen's Roost and inform the tenant there, one Jeremias Van Brunt"—here the patroon paused to look menacingly on the faces gathered beneath the trees—"that his lease is hereby terminated. You understand?"

Van den Post practically writhed with delight. "Ja," he said, licking his lips. "Do we evict him tonight?"

In his anger, in his wrath and resentment, Stephanus very nearly said yes. But then his pragmatic side spoke to him and he relented, thinking of the crops in the field. "November," he said finally. "After he's paid his rent."

Grand Union

HALF an inch taller, ten pounds gaunter, his sunken cheeks buried beneath the weedy untamed beard of the prophet or madman, Tom Crane, self-proclaimed hero of the people and saint of the forest, made his way down the cool umbrageous aisles of the Peterskill Grand Union, blithely pushing a shopping cart before him. It was high summer, and he was dressed for the season in huaraches, a pair of striped bell-bottoms big enough to picnic on, a tie-dyed T-shirt that featured a series of dilating archery targets in three shades of magenta, and various scarves and headbands and dangling superfluous strips of leather, the whole of it overlaid with a gypsy jangle of beads, rings, Cocopah god's eyes, pewter peace signs, Black Power buttons and feathers. In contrast, the cart itself appeared almost spartan. It was wonderfully free of the specious glittering boxes of the newest improved wonder product shoved down the throat of the consumer by those running dogs of the profit mongers, the ad execs of Madison Avenue. The saint of the forest wasn't about to be taken in by frills and false promises; he went only for the basics—the unrefrigerated, plain-wrapped, vegetarian basics, that is.

Back at the shack, where rodents whispered in the eaves and delicate iridescent flies settled on unwashed plates, the larder was bare; though his vegetable garden was producing all the kohlrabi, bok choy and beet tops he could want, he was out of staples—out of pinto beans, brown rice, yeast powder and soy grits. He was out of soap and Sterno, hyssop and teriyaki. He'd awakened that morning to marmiteless toast, watery thrice-used tea leaves, to gruel bereft of condensed milk, and felt he'd procrastinated long enough. And so here he was, shopping. Whistling along with a peppy version of "Seventy-six Trombones" rendered on glockenspiel and cowbell, startling watery-eyed widows in the meat department, squeezing grapefruit, trotting up and down the aisles jingling like a turnstile and exuding the peculiar odor of rotting leaves that seemed to follow him everywhere, as happy a soul as you could find between Peterskill and Verplanck.

Happy? Yes. For he was no longer the horny celibate monkish saint he'd been for so long—things were different now, radically different: now he had a roommate. A soulmate. A love to share his vegetable medley and mung bean casserole and hang his socks out on the line where the sun peeked through the sylvan umbrella to warm the mossy banks of Blood Creek. It was this love that made him blissful, rapturous, silly even, this love that made him want to cut capers in the parking lot like Herbert Pompey sailing across the stage in *La Mancha* or kiss old Mrs. Fagnoli as she dragged herself from the car at the post office. Tom Crane had passed from sainthood to ecstasy.

He was happy on other counts too. For one thing, he'd failed his draft physical for the third straight time. Too skinny. He'd fasted the whole month of June (no way he was going to be a tool of the capitalist oppressors and take up arms against his revolutionary brothers in Vietnam) and staggered off the Selective Service scale at six foot two, a hundred and twenty-three pounds. Now he wouldn't have to skulk off to Canada or Sweden or go through the trouble of faking a suicide. And to compound the joy, on the very day he'd failed his physical, the bees came into his life. Forty hives. Put up for sale by some decrepit old bankrupt redneck in Hopewell Junction for a pittance, a fraction of what they were worth. Tom had them now. Bees. What a concept: they did all the work, and he collected the profit. It was like the goose that laid the golden eggs. All he had to do was gather the stuff, strain it, pour it into the old mason jars he'd found in his grandfather's basement, and sell it by the roadside, each jar decorated with a twenty-five-cents-the-gross lick 'em and stick 'em label that read TOM CRANE'S GOLD in Jessica's handsomest script.

And then, as if all this bounty of bliss weren't enough, there was the *Arcadia*.

Since he'd left Cornell, he'd led an aimless, commitmentless, dirtbagging, pot-growing, goat-turd-mulching sort of existence, drifting from one placid scene to the next, like a water chestnut before it puts down roots. The *Arcadia* gave him an anchor for those roots. If there was a God, and He had come down from the portals of heaven to sort through all the world's employments and enthusiasms in order to match Tom Crane up with his true, his only, his quintessential métier, the *Arcadia* would have been it.

The first he'd heard of it was at the April meeting of the Manitou-on-Hudson Marshwort Preservationists' League. The speaker that evening was a tiny, bearded, lectern-thumping apologist for the Arcadia Foundation who, between thumps, gave a brief history of the fledgling organization, fulminated against the polluters and despoilers of the river, distributed membership applications and passed the hat (a porkpie cap, actually) for donations. What's more, he showed slides of the *Arcadia* itself, sprung full-blown from Will Connell's imagination.

It seemed that Will, the crusty radical folksinger and friend of the earth whose voice had rung loud and clear over Peletiah Crane's cow pasture on that infamous day back in 1949, had had a dream. A vision. One that involved gentle breezes, halcyon days, sails and rigging and teakwood decks. He'd been reading a dog-eared old tome (*Under Sail on Hudson's River,* by Preservation Crane, New York, 1879) that hearkened back to the days when the river was crowded with the low-bellied, broad-beamed Dutch sloops rendered obsolete by the steam engine, and suddenly the *Arcadia* rode up out of the misty recesses of some old chantey lodged in his brain. That very afternoon he strapped the mandolin to his back and hitchhiked down to the Scarsdale home of Sol and Frieda Lowenstein.

The Lowensteins were Communists who'd weathered the McCarthy era to make a killing in the recording industry. They were longtime friends and champions of Will and his music, known for their generosity in support of worthy causes. Will plunked himself down on the white linen couch in the Lowenstein drawing room, picked a song or two on the mandolin and wondered aloud why there were no big old work sloops on the Hudson anymore, the kind you saw in dim oil paintings and daguerreotypes in bars with names like

"The Ship 'N' Shore" and "The Spouter Inn." You know, he said, the kind of big, quiet, white-sailed ship that would make people feel good about the river, and he showed them some pictures from Preservation Crane's book. Sol and Frieda didn't know, but they were willing to put up a piece of the money to find out. The result was the Arcadia Foundation, eight hundred and sixty-two strong, a nonprofit, tax-deductible organization dedicated to cleaning up the river, saving the short-nosed sturgeon, the osprey and the marshwort, and the *Arcadia* itself, all one hundred and six feet of her, a working replica of the sloops of old that would run up and down the river spreading the good news. The launching, from a shipyard in Maine, was scheduled for the Fourth of July.

Tom was electrified. It was as if all the disparate pieces of his life had come together in this one inspired moment. Here was something he could get behind, a slogan, a banner, a raison d'être: Save the River! Hail, Arcadia! Power to the People! Here was a way to protest the war, assert his extraterrestrial/vegetarian/nonviolent hippie credo, stick a thorn in the side of the establishment and clean up the river all in one blow. It was too perfect. The Will Connell connection went all the way back to the early days of the struggle that had consecrated the ground on which the shack stood, and the ecology thing tied up the loose ends of his job at Con Ed—with his experience, with his savvy and know-how, he could step aboard the *Arcadia* as a crew member, maybe even captain it! The fluorescent lights sizzled overhead, the little man raised his fist aloft in exhortation and all at once Tom pictured himself at the helm, champion of the lowly perch and sucker, foe to the polluters, the robber barons, the warmongers and orphan makers, the glorious high-masted ship cutting upriver like the great Ark itself, bastion of righteousness, goodness and light.

He joined that night. The next morning he quit his two-day-a-week job at Con Ed (no more formalin sniffing for him!) and gunned the Packard all the way up to South Bristol, Maine, where he found the *Arcadia* and volunteered his services as carpenter, fitter, pot scrubber and gofer. He was aboard for the launching, crewed on the trip down from New England, and in two weeks—was it only two weeks?—he'd be going aboard for a month as second mate.

Too much, too much, too much. The thought of it—all of it,

love, freedom, bees and the sloop—had him capering around the Grand Union like a fool in motley. In fact, he was juggling two oranges and an avocado, watching his hands and gradually expanding the perimeter of his arc, when he looked up and saw Walter standing there before him.

It was a shock. His mood evaporated, his concentration broke. One of the oranges skewed off to the right and vanished in a bin of bean sprouts; the other landed at his feet with a sick thump. Walter caught the avocado.

The saint let out a gasp, mumbled two or three nonsensical phrases along the lines of "Hi are you, how?" and inadvertently jerked the cart over the little toes of his right foot.

Walter said nothing. He merely stood there, smiling faintly, the sagacious professor with an awkward student. He was dressed, to Tom's amazement, in wingtip shoes, Arrow shirt, light tan summer suit and clocked tie. He was suntanned, handsome, big, standing up straight and tall on his inert feet like a man who'd never known the violence of the surgeon's blade. "Tom Crane," he said finally, grinning wider to show off his strong white teeth, "so how the hell are you? Still living up in the shack?"

Tom was fine. And yes, he was still living in the shack. And though he didn't look it—and didn't feel it—he was glad to see Walter. Or so he heard himself saying, the words dropping from his mouth as though he were a grinning little wooden dummy and someone else was doing the talking: "I'm glad to see you."

"Me too," Walter said. "It's been a while."

The two considered the weightiness of this observation for a moment, while strangely silent shoppers glided past them, each affixed to his or her own cart. Tom stooped for the smashed orange, and was surreptitiously reinserting it in the display pyramid, when Walter caught him with the question he'd been dreading: "Seen Jessica lately?"

Now, while the aforementioned love that had played so big a part in transforming Tom Crane's life has not, to this juncture, been named, her identity should come as no surprise. That love, of course, was Jessica. For whom else had the saint silently yearned all his miserable life—or for years, anyway? Whom else had he dreamed of marrying even as Walter slipped the ring on her finger and the sky outside the shack grew as dark and turbulent as his own tempestuous feelings? Who else had sat between him and Walter at the movies while he burned to take her hand, kiss her throat, blow in her ear? Could he begin to count the times he'd sat transfixed with lust as she'd tried on clothes in a dress shop, licked at a double scoop of Bavarian fudge chocolate swirl ice cream or read aloud to him from *Franny and Zooey* or *The Dharma Bums* in her soft, hesitant, little-girl voice? Or the times he'd envisioned the sweet, tapering, blond-pussied length of her stretched out beside him in his musty hermit's bed?

Jessica. Yes, Jessica.

Hurt, bewildered, disoriented, subject to sudden attacks of snuffling and nose-blowing, knee-knocking and sulks, she'd come to him, her dear old platonic friend, for comfort. And he'd plied her with fried okra and brown rice with shredded carrots and pine nuts, with the peace of a winter's night, a spring morning, the everlasting and restorative midsummer's eves at the cabin, with birds, fireflies, the trill of lovesick toads, the timeless tranquility that holds beyond the range of streetlights and paved roads. What could he say? One thing led to another. Love bloomed.

Walter was crazy. Walter was crippled. Walter was gloomy, angry, self-destructive. In his bliss, in his jealously guarded happiness, the saint of the forest forgot all about his old friend and boon companion. Walter had gone over to the other side now—working *with* that fascist Van Wart, not just for him—and it wasn't as if he hadn't rejected her, after all. Humiliated her, kicked her aside like a piece of trash. No, Tom Crane didn't feel any guilt, not a shred of it. Why should he? Of course, for all that, as he stood there puzzling over Walter's tight-cropped hair with the razor-slash part and vanishing sideburns, he couldn't help but think of Jessica, stuffing underwear, sheets and filth-stiffened jeans into the washer at the laundromat next door—or, more particularly, of the fact that she was due to join him any minute now.

"J-Jessica?" he stammered in response to Walter's query. "Yes. No. I mean, I quit that Con Ed gig, did I tell you?"

Walter's smile faded. There was something of it in his eyes still, but now his lips were pursed and the lines of his forehead lifted in surprise.

"You know, with Jessica? At Indian Point?"

"No, I didn't know," Walter murmured, turning aside to sift through a basket of plums, the dark bruised fruit like strange coin in his hand, "—I just . . . wondered . . . you know, if she's okay and all."

The saint of the forest threw a nervous glance up the aisle, past the checkout counters, the slouching boxboys and impatient housewives, to the automatic door. It was just an ordinary supermarket door—one way in, one way out—but suddenly it had taken on a new and hellish aspect.

"So you don't see much of her anymore either, huh?" Walter said, dropping a handful of plums into a plastic bag. Tom noticed that he was bracing himself against the cart now, using it as an old woman with fused hips might use an aluminum walker.

"Well, no, I wouldn't say that. . . ." He took a deep breath. What the hell, he thought, might as well tell him—he'll find out sooner or later anyway. "What I mean is, uh"—but then, why spoil a beautiful afternoon?—"actually, you know, I think I left my wallet in the car and I think I better, um, well—"

But it was too late.

Here she was, Jessica, sweeping through the door like a poster come to life, like Miss America stepping over the prostrate forms of the second, third and fourth runners up, the light in her hair, her flawless posture, her golden knees. He saw the soft anticipatory smile on her lips, watched the graceful sweep of her head as she scanned the aisles for him, then the full flower of her smile as she spotted him and waved. He didn't wave back—he could barely bob his head and force his lips back over his gums in a paralyzed grin. His shoulders seemed to be sinking into his chest.

Walter hadn't looked up yet. He was fumbling with a recalcitrant bunch of bananas, a little unsteady on his feet, waiting for the sequel to what Tom had been saying about his wallet. Jessica was halfway down the aisle, caught between the eggplant and summer squash, when she recognized him. Tom saw her face go numb, then suffuse with blood. There was confusion—no, outright panic—in her eyes, and she faltered, nearly stumbling over a pudgy six-year-old from whose mouth a Sugar Daddy protruded like a second tongue. Tom tried to warn her off with his eyes.

And then Walter looked at Tom, and saw that Tom was looking at someone else.

"Jessica!" Tom shouted, trying to inject as much surprise into his tone as he could. "We were—we were just talking about you!"

Walter was rigid. He gripped the cart so hard his knuckles turned white, and he cradled the bananas as if they were alive. Jessica was on them now, awkward, too tall, gangling, her legs and arms naked, the shell top too bright, the cloisonné earrings scorching her ears. "Yeah," Walter murmured, looking down at the floor and then up into her eyes, "we were. Really." And then, in an undertone: "Hi."

"What a coincidence, huh?" Tom yelped, slapping his hands together for emphasis. "God," he said, "God, you're looking good, Jessica. Isn't she, Van?" and he trailed off with a strained laugh.

Jessica had regained her composure. She moved toward Tom, erect and commanding, hair floating at her shoulders, neck arched, mouth set, and slipped an arm around his waist. "We're living together, Walter," she said. "Tom and I. Up at the shack."

In that moment Tom felt as small and mean as a saint ever felt. He watched Walter's face—the face of his oldest and closest friend—as it struggled for control, and he felt like a liar, a traitor, he felt like a scorpion in a boot. Jessica gripped him tighter. She was leaning into him now with virtually her full weight (which, by latest reckoning, was six pounds greater than his), and he found himself in the uncomfortable position of having to strain toward her to keep from tumbling backward into the onions. She had spoken decisively, bluntly, treading wide of emotion, but now her lower lip was trembling and her eyes were bright with fluid.

Walter's face had initially registered the shock of seeing her, and then, as she came up to them, he uttered his heavy-lidded and sheepish greeting, with all its conciliatory freight, and he'd looked open, hopeful, truly and ingenuously pleased. Now, as her words sank in, his expression hardened, all the emotion chiseled away, until at last he wore the perfect unassailable mask of the outcast, the cold of eye and hard of heart, the man who feels nothing. He began to say something, but caught himself.

"It's been so long," Jessica said, softening. "We—Tom and I—thought about you, wondered how you were coming along"—and here she glanced down at his feet—"and we would have called, really, but I didn't know how you felt about it, I mean, after that last time in the hospital and all. . . ." She trailed off, her voice catching in her throat.

Walter was silent. Tom couldn't look him in the eye; he tried to think about pleasant things, good things, things of the earth. Like his goat, his cabbage, his bees. "You and Tom," Walter said finally, as if trying out the words for the first time; "you and Tom," he repeated, and his tone had turned venomous.

Tom could feel Jessica go tense beside him; she shifted her weight suddenly and he had to snatch at the cart to keep his balance. "Yeah, that's right," she said, cold fury in her voice. "Tom and me. You have any objections?"

A version of "Love Me Do," for bicycle horn and chorus, droned through hidden speakers. An elderly man, guiding his cart with the broad beam of his fallen abdomen, maneuvered his way between them and began sifting through the onions as if he were panning for gold. "Hey, Ray!" the manager barked at an invisible stockboy, "get the lead out of your pants, will ya?"

As Tom feared, Walter did have objections. He vented them nonverbally at first, clutching the cart with both hands and hammering it with his invulnerable foot till it shuddered, and then he waxed sarcastic. And rhetorical. "Objections?" he sneered. "Who, me? I'm only your husband—why should I object if you're fucking my best friend?"

The onion sifter turned to look at them. Tom felt like an interloper. Or worse: he felt like a Lothario, a snake in the grass, and envisioned Walter's hands at his throat, Walter's fist in his face, Walter's hundred and ninety footless pounds hurtling at him over the basket laden with soy grits and rice. Jessica suddenly let go of him, snatching her arm from around his waist and holding up a single searing finger: "You walked out on me," she said between her teeth, each syllable edged with an inchoate sob.

"You walked out on me," Walter shot back. Puffed with rage, big as cueballs, his eyes swept from Jessica to Tom and back again.

Out of the corner of his eye, Tom saw the old onion sifter jam his hands to his hips as if to say "Enough, already!" The saint, agitated enough as it was, swiveled his head to give the old fart his fiercest "fuck off" look (which admittedly wasn't all that fierce), and when he turned back to Jessica she was stamping her feet like a flamenco dancer warming up to the beat, and tears glistened on her face. "I don't have to take this, this"—her voice went over the top in a breathy squeak—"this shit!"

Walter stepped back then, calmly, gravely, and gave them all—Tom, Jessica, the old man with the bag of onions and the half-dozen housewives who'd lingered over the Swiss chard to eavesdrop—a look of supreme contempt. Then he nodded his head fifteen or twenty times, as if to concede the point, and wobbled out behind his cart, shuffling unsteadily down the aisle till he rounded the corner by the condiments and disappeared.

Jessica didn't take it lightly. She felt around her for a moment as if she were blind, dabbed a damp wrist to her eyes and bolted for the exit without a word. She was sobbing when Tom, who'd left the cart behind and dashed out after her, reached the car. She sobbed as he drove, sobbed as she pressed the duffel bag crammed with still-wet laundry to her chest and made her way down the steep path from the road, through the pasture, across the footbridge and up the hill to the shack. She sobbed as Tom boiled up the last of the old rice and threw together a Bibb lettuce and zucchini salad from the garden, and she sobbed as they sat in the gathering darkness sharing a forlorn joint and two jelly jars of sour wine.

By nightfall, she'd wound down from a sporadic mewl and whimper to the regular heaving of long, stuttering, world-weary sighs. The saint of the forest was gentle, tender, awkward and clumsy. He clowned for her, joked that she should take salt tabs to replenish that vital mineral she'd extruded by the shaker-full and even (partly by design, partly by accident) fell backward over the porch railing and into the big washtub full of dirty dishwater. This last brought a rueful smile to her lips, and he poured it on, standing on his hands, balancing a broom on his nose and all the rest. She laughed. Her eyes cleared. They went to bed.

The bony saint made love to her that night, a soft, therapeutic love, and he was as careful and tentative in his lovemaking as if it were the first time. After she fell asleep, he lay there beside her in the darkness, the day's events replaying themselves over and over in his head. He winced when he thought of his own falseness and cowardice, of the role Walter's sudden appearance had thrust him into, but when he thought of Jessica, he was afraid.

He reached out to touch her, to stroke her sleeping arm, as if to reassure himself she was still there. It was the picture of her disconsolate eyes and tortured mouth, of her runny nose and quaking shoulders, that got him. She wasn't his, she was Walter's—why else would she act like that?

Sad to the core, jealous, fearful, the would-be saint lay there in the darkness with his hurt and his regret. They made such a great pair, he and Jessica—into fish, the Hudson, goats and bees and home-pressed cider. They did. Of course they did. And as he thought of all the things they had in common, he began to feel better. Certainly she had feelings for Walter—they'd been through a heavy thing together—but she had feelings for him too. He knew it, and she knew it. They fit together. They were made for each other. Theirs was such a—and the joke sprang into his head like an anodyne, like a cold compress applied to a fresh bruise—such a grand union.

A Question of Balance

COOLLY, methodically, step by scrupulous step, Walter went through the motions of his biweekly trip to the supermarket as if nothing had happened. Was he out of dental floss, or no? Planter's peanuts? Salt-water taffy? Onions? He deliberated over the pasta—linguine, vermicelli or shells?—tapped the watermelons, rejected the Pancho Villa Authentic Mexican TV dinner (enchilada, rice, beans and salsa verde, with a dollop of baked custard on the side) in favor of the I Ching (egg roll, pork fried rice, Canton strudel and fortune cookie). Never lifting his head, never peering around the corners or gazing up the aisles, he examined each product as if he'd never seen its like before, as if each individual package were a wonder on the order of bleeding statues or extraterrestrial life.

He may have looked cool, but beneath the broad-cut lapels and flared waist of his beige Bertinelli suit, he was seething. And sweating. His armpits were wet—Right Guard, was he out of Right Guard?—water coursed down his back inside the Arrow shirt and pasted it to his skin, his crotch was clammy. As he stood at the checkout stand staring hostilely at the herd of cud-chewing checkout girls, pregnant housewives, yammering children and pimply boxboys, he wanted to scream out, hit something, slam his fist into the counter till the skin opened up to reveal the naked bones of his hand, cracked and white and hurt to the marrow. Tom Crane and Jessica. It couldn't be true. It wasn't. They were kidding him—it was a joke, that's what it was.

He bowed his head and tried to concentrate on a wad of soiled paper balled up beneath the candy display. He counted to twenty. Finally, when he could stand it no longer, he lifted his head and glanced furtively around him. One quick look: to the right, to the left, then face forward and out the window to scan the lot for her car.

They were gone.

Son of a bitch. He wanted to tear the place apart, wanted to kill her, kill him. "Hey, shake it up there, will you," he heard himself snarl, the checker, the woman ahead of him, the stringy looking boxboy all suddenly gone white in the face, "you think I got all day here?"

Outside, the first thing he did—even before he loaded the perishables into the trunk of the MG or stripped off his damp jacket and rolled up the sleeves—was trundle angrily on up to the liquor store on the far side of the laundromat and buy himself a pint of Old Inver House. He didn't usually drink in the afternoon—even on a Saturday afternoon—and he hadn't been drunk, or stoned either, since New Year's and the occasion of his second dire miscue in the face of history. But this was different. This was a situation that called for meliorative measures, for a dampening and allaying of the spirit, for loss of control. He dropped the groceries in the trunk and eased into the driver's seat. Right then and there, though the top was down and everyone could see him, he cracked the Scotch and took a long burning hit of it. And then another. He glared at a beefy armed old woman who looked suspiciously like his grandmother, tossed the bottle cap over his shoulder, jammed the pint between his legs and took off in a smokescreen of exhaust, laying down rubber as if he were flaying flesh.

The bottle was half-gone and he was hurtling up the Mohican Parkway, concentrating on pinning the obstinate little white needle on a speck of dust mired between the 8 and the 0, when he thought of Miss Egthuysen—of Laura. If he was now the very model of the disaffected hero, cut off from friends, wife and family (the last two times he'd stopped in for dinner with Hesh and Lola he'd wound up in a shouting match over his relationship with Depeyster Van Wart), cut off from feeling itself, well, at least he had Laura. As a consolation of sorts. If Meursault had his Marie ("A moment later she asked me if I loved her. I said that sort of question had no meaning, really; but

I supposed I didn't"), Walter had his Laura. And that was something. Especially at a time like this.

He might have paused to reflect on the turmoil of his feelings, to wonder why, when ostensibly he couldn't have given a shit what Jessica, Tom Crane, Mardi or the pope in Rome himself did or didn't do, he felt so bitter and desperate all of a sudden. But he didn't pause. The trees beat past him, endless lashings of green, the wind tore at his hair and the image of Miss Egthuysen loomed up out of his fevered brain. He saw her stretched out naked on the black velvet couch in her living room, her lips puckered in a kissy pout, hands masking her breasts, her private hair so blonde it might have been white. Suddenly the onrushing breeze went sweet with the scent of the vanilla extract she dabbed behind her ears, on her wrists and ankles and between her breasts (extra-thick shakes, napoleons, Boston cream pie, that's what he thought of when he closed his eyes and plunged into the creamy aromatic core of her), and he hit the brakes so hard the car fishtailed a hundred yards up the parkway. In the next instant he was humping over a grassy divider—no one coming either way, thank god—and peeling out on the far side of the road, headed south.

The bottle was two-thirds gone and the day's second disappointment on him as he jabbed angrily at what for a moment had become the glowing little omphalos of Miss Egthuysen's existence, the door buzzer. He listened, first with anticipation, then with impatience, and finally with despair shading into rage, as the harsh trill of the buzzer sounded in the cluttered hallway he knew so well. There was no answer. He felt defeated. Put out. Abused. The bitch, he muttered, throwing himself down heavily on the front steps and peering into the aperture of the bottle like a jeweler examining a rare stone. As luck would have it, he was sitting in a puddle of something resinous and sticky, something that was even then irreparably transforming the hue of his beige slacks, but he was too far gone to notice.

Overwhelmed with drunken gloom, Walter tilted the bottle back and drank, pausing only to level his eyes on the pinched censorious features of Laura's landlady, Mrs. Deering, who was regarding him with loathing from behind the sunstruck front window of the apartment next door. Walter momentarily lowered the bottle to fix her with a look so vehement, so bestial, slack-jawed and irresponsible, that she backed away from the window as if from the sight of some half-wit abusing himself in the street. Keeping her eyes on him all the way, she disappeared into the fastness of her apartment, no doubt to telephone the sheriff, the state police and the local barracks of the National Guard. Okay, fine. What did Walter care? What were they going to do to him—string him up by his feet? He had a bitter laugh at the thought, but it only served to intensify his gloom. The fact was that the confectionery comforts of Miss Egthuysen were not available to him, and his bottle was nearly empty. Yes, and his wife was living with his best friend, he himself was crippled, unloved and doomed by the scourge of history, and all those letters he'd addressed to Truman Van Brunt, c/o General Delivery, Barrow, Alaska, had vanished as if into the snowy wasteland itself, pale missives overwhelmed by white.

Cursing, he took hold of the rusty wrought-iron railing and pulled himself to his feet. He stood there a moment, swaying like a sapling in a storm, glaring angrily at Mrs. Deering's window as if challenging her to show herself again. Then he killed the bottle, dropped it in the bushes and wiped his hands on his shirt. A kid on a bicycle—eight, nine years old, red hair, freckles—came tearing down the sidewalk as he lurched for the car, and it was all Walter could do to avoid him. Unfortunately, the concentration and force of will expended in this tricky maneuver left him vulnerable to other obstacles. Like the fire hydrant. In the next instant, the kid was gone, Mrs. Deering's head had reappeared in the window, and Walter was reclining face down on the lawn.

Back in the car, he examined the grass stains on the knees of his once-beige trousers and the suspicious smear at the base of his clocked tie. What next? he muttered angrily, jerking the tie from his neck and flinging it into the street. It took him a while to fit the key into the little silver slot of the ignition, which kept dodging away from him and bobbing back again, like a float with a nibbling fish beneath it, but at last he succeeded, firing up the car with a vibraphonic rattle of the valve lifters. He looked around him for a moment, the world gone suddenly strange, his face tingling as if a swarm of tiny hairy-legged creatures were trapped beneath the skin and struggling to get out. Then he slammed the car into gear and took off with a screech Mrs. Deering would never forget.

Before he knew it, he was on Van Wart Road. Heading west.

That is, heading in the direction of several significant landmarks. Tom Crane's hubcap, for one. Van Wart Manor, for another. And for yet another, the hellish, mysterious, realigned and reinforced historical marker that had launched him on this trail of tears in the first place.

And where was he going?

Not until he'd come within a cigarette's length of sideswiping a van full of fist-waving teenagers at Cats' Corners, not until he'd lumbered through the wicked *S* curve that followed, not until he slowed at Tom Crane's elm to bore his eyes into the back of the car pulled up on the shoulder beneath it, did it become clear to him: he was going to Van Wart Manor. For Mardi. The MG rolled to a halt and he gazed ruefully at the hubcap leering at him from the bole of the elm—*I'm home, yes,* it seemed to mock, *and so is she*—until a station wagon roared past him in the outside lane, horn blaring, and he came to his senses. He jerked the wheel and lurched away from that declamatory hubcap, intent on Van Wart Manor and the solace of Mardi, but almost as soon as he hit the gas—gravel flying, tires protesting, Jessica's Bug falling away to his right—he was stabbing for the brake. Violently. Desperately.

There before him, strung out across the road and down the shoulder as far as he could see, was a line of people. Picnickers. The men in hats and baggy pants, the women in culottes and sandals and ankle socks, their arms laden with baskets, children, lawn chairs, newspapers to spread out on the ground. He was headed right for them, their cries of alarm terrible in his ears, people scattering like dominoes, a single woman—pamphlets tucked under her arm, a toddler at her side—frozen in his path, and his foot, his impotent alien foot, only now finding the brake. There was a scream, a blizzard of paper, his own face, his mother's, and then they were gone and he was wrestling with the wheel, all the way out on the far side of the road.

He wasn't aiming for it, didn't mean it—he was drunk, freaked out, hallucinating—but there it was. The marker. Dead ahead of him. By the time he reached it, he couldn't have been doing more than twenty, battling to keep out of the ditch, billows of dust rocketing up behind him—on the wrong side of the road, for christ's sake! Still, he did hit it, dead on, the bumper of the MG like the prow of an icebreaker, cryptic Cranes and unfathomable Mohonks flung to the winds, metal grinding on metal. In the next instant he was in control again, swerving back across the road just in time to thread the stone pillars and make the hard cut into the long stately sweeping drive of Van Wart Manor.

Here, peace reigned. The world was static, tranquil, timeless, bathed in the enduring glow of privilege and prosperity. There were no phantasms here, no signs of class strife, of grasping immigrants, trade unionists, workers, Communists and malcontents, no indication that the world had changed at all in the past three hundred years. Walter gazed out on the spreading maples, the flagstone paths, the spill of the lawns and the soft pastel patterns of the roses against the lush backdrop of the woods, and he felt the panic subside. Everything was all right. Really. He was just a little drunk, that was all.

As he swung around the parabola of the driveway and approached the house itself, he saw that there were three cars pulled up at the curb in front: Dipe's Mercedes, Joanna's station wagon and Mardi's Fiat. He was a little sloppy with the wheel—almost nodded off while shifting into reverse, in fact—but managed to wedge himself in between the station wagon and Fiat without hitting anything. So far as he could tell, that is. He was standing woozily in front of the MG, inspecting the bumper where the sign had raked it, when he heard the front door slam and looked up to see Joanna coming down the steps toward him.

She was dressed in moccasins and leggings, in fringed buckskin spotted with grease or ink or something, and her skin had a weird rufous cast to it, the color of old brick. Bits of feathers and seashells and whatnot dangled from her hair, which was knotted and tangled and so slick with grease she must have shampooed with salad oil. She had a box with her. A big cardboard supermarket box that bore the logo of a detergent guaranteed to brighten your shirts and socks and your mornings too. The box was overladen and she was balancing it on the apex of her swollen abdomen, waddling a bit, her lips molded in a beatific smile.

"Hi," Walter said, straightening up and rubbing his hands together, as if crouching down in her driveway were the most natural thing in the world for him to have been doing. "Just, uh, checking to see if the beast was leaking oil again, you know?" he slurred, making it a question, an excuse and a plea all rolled in one.

Joanna acted as if she hadn't heard him. Just kept coming, waddling, embracing the big box full of—what was it, dolls? "Hi," Walter repeated, as she drew even with him, "need a hand with that?"

Now, for the first time, her eyes seemed to focus on him. "Oh, hi," she said, her voice as tranquil and steady as if she'd been expecting him, "you startled me." Her eyes were Mardi's, but all the ice was melted from them. She didn't look startled at all. In fact, if Walter didn't know better, he would have guessed she was stoned. "Yes," she said, dumping the box in his arms, "please."

Walter took the box. Inside were dolls. Or rather, parts of dolls: heads, limbless torsos, the odd arm or leg with its molded sock and shoe affixed. Each of them—each face, limb, set of buttocks, belly and chest—had been slathered with some sort of paint or polish that made it look rusty, flesh gone the color of rakes left out in the rain. Walter clutched the box to his chest while Joanna fumbled through her rabbit-skin purse for the keys to the station wagon's rear door.

It seemed to take her forever. Walter began to feel uncomfortable, standing there beneath the unwavering August sun in his stained pants and sweaty shirt, staring drunkenly into the heap of dismembered limbs, frozen smiles and madly winking eyes, and so he said, "For the Indians?" just to say something.

She took the box from him, gave him a look that made him wonder if she really had recognized him after all, then slid the box into the back of the wagon and slammed the door. "Of course," she said, turning away from him to make her way to the front of the car, "who else is there?"

Next it was Lula.

She knew him now, of course, knew him well—he was the friend of her nephew Herbert and one of Mr. Van Wart's executives. And a very special friend of Mardi too. She greeted him at the door with a smile that showed all the fillings in her teeth. "You look like you been run down in the street," she said.

Walter gave her a sloppy grin and found himself in the anteroom, glancing first up the staircase to where the door to Mardi's lair lay masked in shadow, and then to his left, where the comforting gloom of the old parlor was steeped in muted sunlight.

"Mardi's upstairs," Lula said, giving him a sly look, "and Mr.

Van Wart's out back someplace—poking around in the barn, I think. Which one you want?"

Walter was aiming for nonchalance, but the Scotch was drilling holes in his head and his feet seemed to have called in sick. He took hold of the banister for support. "I guess I came to see Mardi," he said.

Only now did he notice that Lula was clutching her purse, and that a little white straw hat floated atop the typhoon of her hair. "I'm on my way out the door," she said, "but I'll give her a hoot." Her voice rose in stentorian summons, practiced, assured and familiar all at once—"Mardi!" she called, "Mardi! Somebody here to see you!"—and then she gave him another great wide lickerish grin and ducked out the door.

There was a moment of restive silence, as if the old house were caught in that briefest hiatus between one breath and another, and then Mardi's voice—querulous, world-weary, so shot through with boredom it was almost a whine—came back to him: "Well, who is it—Rick?" Silence. Then her voice again, faint, muffled, as if she'd already lost interest and turned away, "So send him up already."

Walter was not Rick. Walter did not in fact know who Rick was, nor did he much care. Shakily, unsteadily, he lifted the stones of his feet, gripping the banister as if it were a lifeline, and mounted the stairs. At the top, Mardi's door, first one on the right. The door stood slightly ajar, a garish poster of a band Walter had never heard of crudely affixed to the face of it. He hesitated a moment, staring into the hungry shameless eyes of the band's members, trying out the ponderous flat-footed syllables of their esoteric name on his tongue, wondering if he should knock. The booze decided for him. He pushed his way in.

The room was as dark as any cave, a low moan of bass and guitar caught in the far speaker, Mardi, in the light from the door, hunkered over an ashtray in the middle of the bed. She was wearing a T-shirt and panties, nothing more. "Rick?" she said, squinting against the invasion of light.

"No," Walter murmured, feeling immeasurably weary, vastly drunk, "it's me, Walter."

The light fell across her face, the wild teased bush of her hair. She lifted a hand to shield her eyes. "Oh, fuck," she spat, "shut the door, will you? The top of my head feels like it's about to lift off."

Walter stepped inside and shut the door. It took a moment for his eyes to adjust to the dark, a moment during which the plaint of bass and guitar was amplified by the addition of a muddy quavering vocal track—some guy who sounded as if he were singing through his socks. From the bottom of a sewer. In hell. "Nice music," Walter said. "Who is it—the guys on the door?"

Mardi didn't answer. Her cigarette—or no, it was a joint; he could smell it—glowed in the dark.

He started for the bed, thinking to ease himself down on it, maybe take a hit of the joint, help her off with her T-shirt, forget himself for a space. But he didn't quite make it. Something immovable—the beveled edge of her bureau?—caught him in the groin, and his foot came down hard on something else, something frangible, that gave way with a splintering crack.

Still Mardi said nothing.

"You got a headache?" he said, struggling for balance, bending low to reach for the near corner of the mattress, "is that it?" And then, mercifully, he was sinking into the mattress, off his feet at last and so close to her he could feel the heat of her body, smell her hair, her sweat, the least maddening essence of her secret self.

"I'm waiting for Rick," she said, and her voice was strange, distant, as if it weren't really plugged in. "Rick," she repeated, in a murmur. And then: "I'm stoned, really stoned. I'm tripping. Seeing things. Scary things."

Walter pondered this revelation for a minute, then confessed that he wasn't feeling so hot himself. This, he hoped, would be the prelude to some meliorative embraces and consolatory sex, but his hopes were immediately dashed when she sprang up from the bed as if she'd been stung, stalked across the room and flung the door open. Her face was twisted with fury and the cold hard irises of her eyes contracted round the pinpoints of her pupils. "Get out!" she shouted, her voice rising to a shriek with the punch of the adverb.

The term "flipping out" came to him, but he didn't know whether it properly applied to Mardi or himself. In any case, he got up off the bed with alacrity, envisioning a vindictive Depeyster taking the stairs two at a time to see what his most trusted employee was doing to his half-dressed and hysterical daughter in the darkness of her room. As he staggered toward her, though, all the hurts and dislocations of the day began to fester in him, and he stopped short to demand an explanation along the lines of *I thought we were friends* and *what about last month when we . . . and then we. . . ?*

"No," she said, trembling in her T-shirt, nipples hard, navel exposed, legs strong and naked and brown, "never again. Not with you."

They were face to face now, inches apart. He looked down at her: a tic had invaded the right side of her face, her lips were parted and dry. All of a sudden he was seized with an urge to choke her, throttle her, knead that perfect throat till all the tightness went out of it, till she dropped from his hands limp as a fish slapped against the gunwale. But in the same instant she shouted "You're just like him!" and the accusation caught him off balance.

"Like who?" he sputtered, wondering what she was talking about, how he'd managed to put his foot in it in the space of two minutes, and even, for a second there, wondering who he was. He watched her closely, drunk but wary. She was swaying on her feet. He was swaying on his feet. Her breath was hot in his face.

"My father!" she shrieked, lunging into him to pound her balled hands on the drum of his chest. He tried to snatch at her wrists, but she was too quick for him. "Look at you," she snarled, pushing away from him so violently he nearly lurched backward over the railing and plunged to the unforgiving peg-and-groove floor below. "Look at you, in your faggoty suit and fucking crew cut—what do you think you are, some kind of Shriner or something?"

"Mardi?" Depeyster's voice echoed from the rear of the house. "That you?"

She stood poised in the doorway, drilling Walter with a look that tore through the last tattered rags of his self-esteem. "I'll tell you what you are," she said, lowering her voice as a bull lowers its horns for goring, "you're a fascist just like him. A fascist," she repeated, lingering over the hiss of it as if she were Adam discovering the names of things—fink, pig, narc, fascist—and slammed the door for punctuation.

Terrific, Walter thought, standing there in the empty hallway. He was footless, fatherless, loveless, his wife was living with his best friend and the woman he'd left her for probably felt better about Mussolini than she did about him. And on top of it all, he was sick to his stomach, his head ached and he'd nearly ripped the bumper off his car. What next?

Walter braced himself against the banister and turned to peer down the well of the staircase. Below him, at the foot of the stairs, in an old pair of chinos and a faded blue shirt that brought out the color in his eyes, stood Depeyster Van Wart—Dipe—his boss and mentor. Depeyster was working something in his hands—a harness or bridle, it looked like—and he wore a puzzled expression. "Walter?" he said.

Walter started down the stairs. He was forcing a smile, though the muscles of his face seemed dead and he felt as if he were either going to pass out cold or break down and sob—hard, soulless and free though he may have been. All things considered, he did pretty well. When he reached the last step, leering like a child molester, he held out his hand and boomed "Hi, Dipe," as if he were greeting him from the far side of Yankee Stadium.

They stood a moment at the foot of the stairs, Walter losing all control of his face, the lord of the manor dropping the bridle—yes, bridle it was—to lift a hand and scratch the back of his head. "Did I hear Mardi?" he asked.

"Uh-huh," Walter said, but before he could enlarge on this curt and wholly inadequate reply, Depeyster cut him off with a low whistle. "Jesus," he said, "you look like hell, you know that?"

Later, over successive cups of coffee in the ancient cavernous kitchen that gleamed with the anachronisms of dishwasher, toaster, refrigerator and oven, Walter experienced the release of confession. He told Depeyster of Jessica and Tom, of his hallucination on the road, the defeat in his heart and his crazy confrontation with Mardi. Hunched over the bridle with a rag soaked in neat's-foot oil, Depeyster listened, glancing up from time to time, his aristocratic features composed, priestly, supremely disinterested. He offered the encouragement of the occasional interrogatory grunt or interjection, heard him out and chose sides without hesitation. "I hate to say it, Walter"—he spoke in clean, clipped, incisive tones—"but your wife sounds like she's gone off the deep end. I mean, what can you expect from a woman who could move into a shack that hasn't even got electricity, let alone running water—and with a doped-up screwball like that Crane kid, yet. Is that stable or what?"

No, of course it wasn't. It was irrational, stupid, a mistake. Walter shrugged.

"You made a mistake, Walter, forget it. We all make mistakes. And as for Mardi—well, maybe that's for the best too." Depeyster gave him a long look. "I admit it, Walter, I hoped that maybe you and her, well. . . ." He broke off with a sigh. "I hate to say this about my own daughter, but you're worth ten of her."

Walter blew the steam from his fifth cup of coffee and toyed with a wedge of peach cobbler. He was feeling better, the nausea held temporarily in check, his despair tempered in absolution. And he was feeling something else too, a sense that his moment of triumph and decision was hovering just in front of him: his life had come to a point of crisis, and now, he thought, still drunk but infused with a sort of alcoholic rapture, he was on the verge of release. "You know all those letters I wrote to my father?" he asked suddenly. "In Barrow?"

If Depeyster was caught off guard by the abrupt turn in the dialogue, he didn't show it. He leaned back in the chair, dropping the bridle on the newspaper he'd spread out on the table. "Yeah," he said, "what about them?"

"They never came back." Walter paused to let this sink in.

"So you think he's there, then, huh?"

"Uh-huh. And I want to go find out." Walter raised the cup to his lips, but in his excitement put it down without drinking. "I've been saving my money. I'm going to fly up there."

"Walter, listen," Depeyster began, "that's terrific, that's great—but have you really thought about it? What if he's not there and you waste all that time and money for nothing? How you going to feel then? Or what if he won't see you? Or if he's changed? You remember his problem with alcohol. What if he's a drunk in the gutter? Look, I don't want to discourage you, but don't you think if he wanted to see you he would have answered your letters? It's been what—eleven, twelve years? A lot can happen in that time, Walter."

Walter was listening—Dipe was only trying to protect him, he knew that. And he was grateful to him. But he had to go. He hadn't told Depeyster about the marker—he'd never have believed it was an accident—but the fact was that it was gone: blasted, obliterated, wiped out. There was nothing here that had a hold on him any more—not Hesh, not Dipe, not Mardi, Jessica, Tom Crane or Laura Egthuysen. The marker had started the whole sick cycle and now he'd completed it—the Van Wartville stage of it, anyway. There was nothing left now but to go find his father and bury the ghosts forever.

"I think you're crazy," Depeyster was saying. "You're a strong smart young man, Walter, with a lot of good qualities and personal attractiveness. You've had some bad luck—terrible, rotten luck—but I say forget the past and look ahead of you. With what you've got you can go a long way—and I don't just mean in my business, but in any business you want." Depeyster pushed back the chair and went to the stove. "More coffee?"

Walter shook his head.

"You sure? You feel all right to drive?" Depeyster poured himself a cup and crossed the room to sit back down at the table. Outside the window, a solid unbroken monolith of shadow fell from the house to engulf the lawn and the rose garden at the foot of it. "I'm paying you a good salary, Walter—damn good, for a kid of your age," Depeyster said finally. "And you're worth every penny of it. Stick with me. It can only go up."

Walter pushed himself up from the table. "I got to go, Dipe," he said, a fearful sense of urgency on him, of things closing in.

At the front door, he turned to shake hands with him, so charged with emotion he felt as if he were leaving that moment for the penumbral wastes of the north, felt like a daredevil climbing into his barrel on the icy lip of Niagara. "Thanks, Dipe," he said, nearly choking up, "thanks for listening and, you know, for the advice and all."

"My pleasure, Walter," Depeyster said, grinning his aristocratic grin. "Be careful now, huh?"

Walter dropped his hand, and then, in the rush of his good feeling, said, "One other thing, Dipe—I'm going to need two weeks off. . . . I mean, if it's not going to be a problem or anything."

In that instant Depeyster's face went cold. The look he gave Walter was the same look Hesh put on when he was challenged or disappointed. Confused, growing hot, already knowing the answer from the set of that face, Walter suddenly thought of the last time he'd seen Hesh, nearly a month ago. It was during dinner—Walter's favorite, borscht, lamb chops and potato latkes, with sauerkraut and homemade apple sauce and lettuce from the garden—and Walter had mentioned his father—Truman—and Hesh had made some deprecatory remark. *Well, you may hate him,* Walter blurted, *but Depeyster says—*

At the very mention of Depeyster's name Hesh had exploded, leaping up from his chair to pound his fist on the table, leaning over to rage in Walter's face like a barking dog. *Depeyster says,* he mocked. *Who the hell you think it was that raised you, huh? The bum that left you an orphan? This, this robber baron, this crook that puts all these ideas in your head—is he the one? What right does he have?*

Hesh, Lola was at his side now, her slim blue-veined hand on the rock of his forearm, trying to restrain him, but he shook her off. Walter sat frozen in his chair.

Hesh rose up to his full height, his bald head flushed and his nose as red as the borscht in the bowl before him. His voice dropped an octave as he struggled to control it. *When I got you that job at Depeyster Manufacturing it was through Jack Schwartz because I know him from all my life and I thought you could use some experience of the real world and maybe some money in your pockets . . . but this, this is crazy. The man is a monster, Walter, don't you know that? A Nazi, a union buster. Depeyster this, Depeyster that. It was him that ruined your father, Walter. Know it. On the grave of your mother, know it.*

The same look. Depeyster leveled it on him now. "Walter, you know this is our busy season. We've got six thousand aximaxes and three thousand muffins to ship to Westinghouse by the end of the month. Orders are coming in by the truckload. And then that guy just quit in the paint room, didn't he?"

Walter may have been fatherless, but everybody seemed to want the job. "You won't let me go, then?"

"Walter, Walter," Depeyster said, and again his arm went around his shoulder, "I'm just trying to look out for you. Listen, if you really want to go, can't it wait a little? Two months, how's that? I'll give you your time off in two months, in the fall, when things slow down at the plant and you've had some time to think about it—what do you say?"

Walter said nothing. He broke away, and trying to muster all the dignity he could, what with his rumpled shirt, crapped-over pants and the first sharp stab of a crippling hangover shooting through his brain, he shuffled down the steps of the porch.

"Walter," Depeyster called at his back. "Hey, come on, look at me."

Walter turned when he reached the MG, and despite himself gave his boss and mentor a rueful smile.

"Hey, I didn't tell you the good news!" Depeyster shouted as Walter turned the engine over. Walter waited, the car shuddering beneath him, as Depeyster sprang down the steps and leaned over the passenger side. He still had the bridle in his hand, and now he held it up in triumph, like a hunter with a brace of pheasant. "I'm buying a horse!" he sang, and the evening seemed to rise up around him in all its promise, the golden glow of the setting sun illuminating his grinning face as if this were the final frame of a movie with a happy ending.

As for Walter, he made it home without incident—no scrapes with history, no shadows springing up out of the blacktop, no ghosts or mirages or other tricks of the eye. He pulled into the driveway of his lonely little rented place, cut the engine and sat a moment as the air balled up around him. Sitting there, he gradually became aware that there was something wrong with this air he'd dragged in with him—it was tainted, rotten, the rank, foul air of the fish market or dump. It was then that he remembered the groceries.

He lifted the lid of the trunk, and there they were: strewn cans, wilted lettuce, fractured eggs, deliquescing meat. It was too much for him. The smell of corruption rose up out of the hot enclosure to stagger him, ram one fist into his belly and another down his throat. He lost his balance and fell to his knees, mercifully, before the Old Inver House, the coffee and peach cobbler and whatever it was he'd had for breakfast began to come up. For the longest time he knelt there, bent over this acrid little puddle of spew. From a distance, you might have thought he was praying.

Between a Rock and a Hard Place

In THAT distant and humid summer of 1679, when the patroon came to Van Wartville to widen roads and improve his property, and Jeremias Van Brunt brazenly defied him, the *Jongheer* saw that defiance for what it was: yet another insolent blow struck against the very system of civilized government itself. Not half a mile from the cow pasture in which the Peterskill riots would one day unfold, and not much farther than that to where Walter knelt cathartically in the driveway of his rented cottage, Stephanus took his stand. If this ignorant, unwashed, violent, one-legged clod could challenge him, what would prevent a reprobate like Robideau or a subtle snake like Crane from doing the same? There were no two ways about it: if he were to give an inch, if he showed the slightest hint of indecision or trace of flexibility, the whole edifice of the manor would come crashing down around his ears. And how would that sit with his plans to build an estate that would make Versailles look like a cabbage patch?

And so, in high dudgeon, the patroon demoted Joost Cats, incarcerated Van Brunt's half-breed nephew and incontinent son, and sent word to the shirker that his tenancy was terminated come November. Then he ordered the carpenter to cease work on the roof and begin constructing a set of public stocks. Abuzz with gossip, scandalized and not a little afraid for themselves, the common folk—the Cranes and Sturdivants and van der Meulens and all the rest—took up their tools and went back to work. Scythes rose and dropped, trees fell, dust rose and deerflies hovered over redolent *paltroks* and sweaty brows. But they worked with one eye only, the other fixed firmly on the road ahead of them—the road that branched off to Nysen's Roost.

It was late in the afternoon—past four, by Staats' reckoning—when two figures appeared in the distance. Van den Post was one of them, unmistakable in his new, high-crowned, silver-plumed hat and with the gleam of the rapier electric at his side, but the other—well, it wasn't Jeremias. No way. This figure was smaller, far smaller, and slighter too. And there was no trace either of the wide-slung, irregular gait peculiar to the man who'd lost a leg in early youth and communicated with the ground through a length of oak ever since. To a man—and woman—the workers paused to lean on the hafts of their rakes and shovels, steady their teams or lower their scythes. And then all at once, as the figures drew closer, a whisper raced through the crowd. "It's Neeltje!" someone exclaimed, and the rest took it up.

They had to send a boy to fetch Stephanus, who'd retired to the house for refreshment. In the meantime, Neeltje, pale and trembling, fell into her father's arms, while Staats and Douw kept the others back to give them room. Van den Post, with a triumphant leer, swaggered through the crowd to prop one dusty boot up on a log and help himself to a cup of cider from the keg the patroon had provided for the enjoyment of his tenants. He took a long drink, spat the dregs in the dirt and wiped his mouth with the back of his sleeve, and then, with studied insolence, pulled out his pipe and had himself a smoke.

Neeltje's face was wet. "*Vader,*" she cried, "what are we going to do? He's . . . he's evicted us and taken the boys and still Jeremias won't come."

Bent over double, looking twice his already considerable age, the former *schout* had no ready answer. Silently cursing the day Jeremias Van Brunt had come into their lives, he pressed his daughter to him, clinging to her as if he were caught in a torrent and about to go under.

"He can't just . . . he's got no right . . . after all these years, to just—" Staats sputtered. "We'll fight it, that's what we'll do."

But now Robideau was there, insinuating his hard, leathery face between them. "What do you mean, he's got no right?" he rasped. "The patroon's word is law, and every one of us knows it. There's nobody here that didn't sign his lease with his wits about him, and I'll be damned to know why *Mijnheer* shouldn't evict the son of a bitch when I've got to break my back out here in the sun while Mr. High-and-Mighty sits home with a bowl of punch."

There was a rumble of assent from the crowd, but Staats, loyal as a bulldog, turned on Robideau and warned him to stay out of it.

That was all the Frenchman needed. He took a step forward and gave Staats a shove that sent him reeling back into Neeltje and her father. "Fuck off, cheese-eater," he hissed.

The obscenity was too much for the virginal ears of Goody Sturdivant, and for the second time that day she let out a doleful whoop and fainted, pitching face forward into the dust with a cyclonic rush of air. In the same instant, Douw and Cadwallader Crane stepped between the antagonists. "Calm down, *vader,*" Douw pleaded, "this isn't doing anyone any good," while on his end, the scrawny loose-limbed young Crane held fast to the bucking Frenchman with a pair of arms so long and attenuated they might have been hemp ropes wound twice around him. "Let me go!" Robideau grunted, dancing in place and uttering a string of oaths that might have embarrassed a sailor. "Let me go, damn you!"

Thus it was that faces were hot, the crowd bunched and Mistress Sturdivant stretched out in the dirt like a sick cow when the patroon drew up on his pacer, a look of the severest condemnation quivering in his fine nostrils. "What in the name of God is going on here?" he demanded, and instantly the scuffling stopped. Neeltje looked up out of her tear-stained face, Meintje van der Meulen bent to assist poor Mistress Sturdivant, Robideau backed away from Cadwallader Crane and glared angrily about him. No one said a word.

The patroon scanned the crowd from on high, his eyes finally coming to rest on van den Post. "Aelbregt," he snapped, "can you tell me what's going on?"

Stepping forward with a bow, a wide malicious grin flapping the wings of his beard, van den Post said, "With pleasure, *Mijnheer*. It seems that Van Brunt's criminality has infected his neighbors. Farmer van der Meulen, for instance—"

"Enough!" Stephanus cast a withering glance out over the lowered heads of the farmers and their wives and progeny, then turned back to van den Post. "I want to know one thing only: where is he?"

"With all respect, *Mijnheer,* he would not come," van den Post replied. "Had you given the order to employ force," he continued, grinning the grin of a man who could survive indefinitely on jellyfish and saltwater, "I assure you he would be standing before you now."

It was then that Neeltje came forward, desperately pushing her way through the ranks of her neighbors, her face spread open like a book. "*Mijnheer,* please," she begged, "the farm is all we have, we've been good tenants and we've improved the place ten times over for you—just this year we cleared a full morgen along Blood Creek and put in rye for fodder and a crop of peas on top of it. . . ."

Stephanus was in no mood to hear appeals to sympathy or reason. He was a powerful man, an educated man, a man of taste and refinement. He looked at Neeltje in her humble clothes, still pretty after all these years, and saw her as she was in that filthy bed with her sluttish mouth and the hair in her eyes, a picture no gentleman should have to carry around with him, and he gritted his teeth. When finally he spoke, he had to struggle to contain his voice; he drew himself up, staring down like a centaur over the powerful sculpted shoulder of the mount that was one with him. "The half-breed and the other one, the loudmouthed boy, are in our custody," he said, barely moving his lips. "Tomorrow, when my man has completed work on the stocks, they will commence their punishment." Here he paused to let his words build toward the final pronouncement. "And, I assure you, *huis vrouw,* they will sit in those stocks until such time as your husband comes to this house and goes down at my feet to beg—yes, beg—for the privilege of serving me."

There were mice in the root cellar, rats, slugs and other lowly things that throve in the absence of light. It was as black as the farthest wheeling reaches of a sunless universe, eternal midnight, and it was damp, dripping wet as the bottom of a deep and lonely grave. Wouter didn't like it. He was eleven and a half years old, and his imagination festooned the invisible ceiling with the leering faces of the imps, demiurges and savage gods that people the quiet places of the valley, with the bloody visage of old Dame Hobby, who'd been scalped and left for dead by a renegade Sint Sink, with Wolf Nysen's flaming beard and butcher's eyes. Huddled close to his cousin, for comfort and warmth both, he took it as long as he could, which is to say about three and a half minutes after van den Post dragged the heavy timber pallet over their heads, and then confessed that he was frightened. They were seated at the bottom of a four-foot-deep pit dug into the earth of the cellar floor, and the hatch above it was secured by the weight of three hogsheads of ale. "I'm scared, Jeremy," Wouter said, his voice a thin squeak in that unfathomable dark.

Characteristically, Jeremy said nothing.

"*Vader* says they buried the old patroon's brother just out there, in back of the house . . . what if, if he's still, you know—like a ghost? He could come through the dirt and—"

Jeremy grunted. This was followed by a series of sounds emanating from deep in the hollow of his throat: clicks, chirps, gurgles, the muffled signifiers of a private system of speech. What he said was, "You open your hole, they dump us in this one."

Wouter couldn't deny the truth of the assertion, but it gave him small comfort. The seat of his pantaloons was soaked through and his crotch began to itch. If anything, the darkness was deeper than it had been a moment before. He edged closer to his cousin. "I'm scared," he said.

Later—how much later he couldn't say—a medley of homely sounds manifested themselves in the void beyond their cell, and then there was the quick tattoo of footsteps on the pallet above them, followed by the quavering tones of a dry and withered voice. "Here, boy," the voice wheezed, "put those barrels back where they belong and lift that pallet this instant." Light shone down from above, faint and diffuse. Barrels rumbled over their heads. "This is simply intolerable," the voice went on in Dutch, falling off to a nagging murmur, "treating half-grown boys like hardened criminals. . . ."

When the pallet edged back a foot or two, they stood on cramped legs to poke their heads from the hole like a pair of groundhogs at the mouth of their burrow. Above them, peering into the pit as keenly as they were peering out of it, stood the patroon's stooped and ancient mother, shrouded in black and holding a tallow candle out in front of her like a talisman; beside her, the light leaping from his eyes, was a slave not much older than Jeremy, and what Wouter, in his confusion, at first mistook for an angel of Elysium. But then the angel giggled, and for the moment the spell was broken. "Come up out of there this instant," the old woman scolded, as if they'd locked themselves up in that foul airless hole for the sheer irresistible joy of it.

Wouter glanced at Jeremy. His cousin's stony profile showed nothing, but the fist of his Adam's apple rose and fell twice in rapid succession. Then, cool as the patroon himself, Jeremy stepped lightly from the pit and stood before the little group gathered in that larger cellar with its kegs of ale and cider, its firkins of butter, its buckets of milk and wheels of cheese set high off the floor on rude wooden racks. Wouter was scared and disoriented, images of the grave rising up again to play tricks with his eyes: old Vrouw Van Wart could have been a ghoul wrapped in her winding sheet, the slave some tarry servant of the devil and the girl—well, the girl was clearly a heavenly intercessor come down to do battle for his soul. "Out!" the old woman suddenly squawked, seizing his ear in a ferocious grip, and then he too was up and arisen from the tomb.

The old woman gave him a reproachful look, her jaw set, lips faintly trembling. "Don't you understand Dutch?" she demanded.

Shamefaced, on the verge of tears, Wouter was trying to stammer a reply when the girl began tittering again. He stole a quick glance at her—the broad, full-lipped grin, eyes that overwhelmed him, the abundance of her hair beneath the cap that perched like a butterfly on the crown of her head—and looked down at his feet. He didn't know it at the time, but this was to be his introduction to Saskia Van Wart.

"No matter," the old woman wheezed, softening a bit. Then she turned to the slave. "You, Pompey," she said, recovering her voice, "take them into the kitchen and see that they're fed. And then I want you to put some straw down here in the corner for them," indicating a space along the wall, "—and don't you give me that look. I don't care what my son says—until he banishes me to the woods I'm still mistress of this house."

The next morning, early, the jellyfish man came for them.

Van den Post was wearing *grootvader* Cats' plumed hat and rapier, and a discomfiting emotion lit his eyes and played at the corners of his mouth. "Up," he barked, kicking at them as they lay in the straw, and Wouter saw it in his face—the look of a boy with a sharp stick and a cornered rabbit.

He led them out of the penumbral gloom of the storage cellar, through the bright and vivid lower kitchen with its paradisiac aromas, its sour-looking cook and glowing hearth, and then out into the explosion of light that was the morning and the world all around them. Shielding his eyes and blinking, half-asleep yet, Wouter hurried to keep up with the *schout:* he didn't see the stocks until he was on them.

Pine. White and fresh and with a smell of resin to it. Four footholes under the lower cross bar, four wristholes beneath the upper. Behind the frame, a bench. Or no, it was just a log, crudely trimmed, rough with bark and bole, so green it must have been standing yesterday.

At first Wouter didn't understand. But as van den Post lifted the crossbar, a taut smile fixed on his lips, Wouter's emotions got the better of him. He wanted to protest—what had they done? He'd only talked, spoken up to the patroon, told the truth. They hadn't stolen anything or hurt anybody. It was only words. But he couldn't protest: he was too frightened. All at once he felt as if he were choking. Strangling. The air wouldn't pass his throat, there was something heavy in his chest, and it was rising, rising, ready to burst—

It was then that Jeremy made his break.

One moment he was standing there beside Wouter, gazing with his sullen green eyes on the contraption before him, and the next he was streaking across the cornfield like a white-tailed deer with the bloody mark of the catamount on its rump. Jeremy was a wicked runner, as quick and lank and fleet of foot as the intrepid chieftains he counted among his ancestors. This was Mohonk's son, after all, and though Mohonk may have been a degenerate, a miscegenator and a disgrace to his tribe, he was nonetheless as much a familiar to these hills and valleys as the bears, wolves and salamanders themselves, and a runner of the very first water. And so, kicking up his heels, flailing his bony legs and pumping his bony arms, Jeremy Mohonk—son of Mohonk son of Sachoes—called up the spirit of his ancestors and beat a path for the sanctuary of the woods.

What he hadn't figured on was the tenacity of van den Post, the eater of jellyfish. Without a thought for Wouter, the hyperkinetic *schout* threw off hat and rapier and lit out after Jeremy like a hound. They were twenty paces apart at the outset, and twenty paces apart they remained, as first the Indian, then the *schout,* disappeared into the woods at the far verge of the field.

Wouter looked around him. The sun was climbing over the ridge behind him now, pulling back the shadows as if drinking them up. He watched a flock of blackbirds—*maes dieven*—settle back down in the corn where Jeremy and van den Post had cut their swath through it, and then he looked down at the plumed hat and rapier lying in the wet grass. Somewhere a cow was lowing.

Wouter didn't know what to do. He was afraid. Afraid of the cellar, afraid of the stocks and their cruel chafing grasp, afraid of van den Post and the patroon. What he wanted more than anything was to go home and bury himself in his father's arms, ask him to explain it all to him once again—he wasn't sure he had it right anymore. He'd stood up to the patroon, defended his father, made his stand, and what had he got for it? Pain and abuse, a pinched ear, wet pants and moldy bread. He looked down the hill, past the great house and out to the road that lay quiet before it. Fifteen minutes. He could be home in fifteen minutes, hugging his *moeder,* watching the light flash in his *vader*'s eyes when he found out what they'd done to him. . . .

But no. If he ran, they'd come for him. He could see them already: a dozen armed men, the strange black among them, come with dogs and shouts, with hot pitch and feathers, their torches lighting the night. What'd he do? one of them would holler as they held him down, and another, grim as death, would answer in a voice edged with outrage: Why, he bearded the patroon, the little snipe, that's what he did.

Biting his lips to fight back the tears, Wouter Van Brunt, eleven and a half years old and as full of regrets as any septuagenarian, slouched around the white pine frame, sat himself down on the rough log behind it and stuck his feet out straight before him. Slowly, deliberately, giving it all his concentration, he eased down the crossbar until it clamped firm around his ankles. Then he went to work on his hands.

He was still there when his father came for him.

Up the dusty road, through the gauntlet of his neighbors with their bent backs and anxious faces, his shoulders thrown back, powerful arms laid bare, Jeremias never faltered. He lashed out with the wooden strut as if it were a weapon, striding with such brisk determination he might have been marching off to war, and he didn't stop to say a word to anyone, not even Staats or Douw. Everyone looked up, of course, but they couldn't see his face, which was hidden beneath the turned-down brim of his hat. One-two, one-two, his arms swung out at his sides, and he was moving so fast he was almost through them when Staats flung down his shovel and started after him.

The act was contagious. One by one the farmers threw down their tools and silently followed Jeremias up the drive to the house—even Robideau, though he was the last. By the time Jeremias had reached the meadow in front of the house, the whole neighborhood—Cranes and Oothouses, van der Meulens, Mussers and all the rest—was behind him. No one said a word, but there was fear and expectancy on every face.

The patroon had ordered the stocks erected midway up the ridge behind the house, where they would be convenient to the immediate discharge of any sentence he might pass down, and yet not so close as to discommode him with any noise, odor or other unpleasant contingency that might arise as a result. To get to them, one had to circumnavigate the kitchen garden and cross a meadow of pasturage, beyond which lay a cornfield and the woods into which cousin Mohonk and van den Post had vanished. Jeremias was in a hurry. He did not circumnavigate the kitchen garden, but instead trod right through it, intent only on the tiny distant figure imprisoned in the cruel machine on the slope above. He trampled parsnips, beets and succory, rent the leaves of lettuce, leeks and cresses, crushed cucumbers and burst tomatoes. In their agitation, the others followed him.

They were close enough to see that only half the contraption was occupied and to see too that it was the younger boy who occupied it, when the three riders, barely settled in their saddles, shot out from the rear of the barn to intercept them. Jeremias kept going. And his neighbors, aware of the riders bearing down on them, aware of the patroon's certain displeasure and of the wrong they were doing, followed. If you'd stopped any one of them—even Robideau or Goody Sturdivant—and asked him why, he couldn't have told you. It was in the air. It was electric. It was the will of the mob.

The riders cut them off no more than thirty feet from the stocks. Clods flew, the horses beat the ground with iron hoofs. "Halt!" bellowed the patroon. They looked up into his face and saw murder there. His mount wheeled and stamped while he fought to level his late father's dueling pistols—one in each hand—on the crowd. Beside him, clinging like a leech to a dappled mare, was van den Post, the recovered rapier held high and naked to the sun, and beside him, the third rider, a stranger no taller in the saddle than a boy of eight, his wizened face set in a smirk, a musket clenched in his gnarled little fist. Now normally, at the very least, they would have remarked the arrival of this stranger—of any stranger, but particularly of such an ill-favored and lean-fleshed little radish as this one—but there wasn't time to think, let alone gossip.

"The next man that moves dies by this hand!" roared the patroon.

They stopped. All of them. To a man, woman and child. Except for Jeremias, that is. He never broke stride, never wavered. He marched straight for the patroon as if he didn't see him, his eyes fixed on the stricken face of his son. "Halt!" the patroon commanded in a voice that lost itself in the effort, and almost simultaneously, he fired.

There was a shout from the crowd, while Wouter, impotent, unheeded, eleven and a half years old, cried out in a voice of dole—and for the third time in two days, Mistress Sturdivant fell. Hugely. Thunderously. With all the dramatic moment of a Phaedra or Niobe. Suddenly, all was confusion: women shrieked, men dove for cover, young Billy Sturdivant flung himself atop his mother's supine hulk and the patroon ducked his head like a man guilty of the ultimate solecism. As it turned out, however, Goody Sturdivant wasn't hit. Nor, for that matter, was Jeremias. The ball kicked up a divot at the blameless instep of Cadwallader Crane's well-oiled boot and buried itself harmlessly among the grubs and worms.

Jeremias kept walking. He brushed past the patroon's horse, moving like a somnambulist, and threw himself on the stocks. Before the enraged patroon could steady the second pistol, Jeremias had thrown back the lock and lifted the crossbar from his son's wrists. He'd just taken hold of the lower bar when the patroon fired again.

Wouter was to remember that moment for the rest of his life. He cried out a second time, kicking wildly though his legs were held fast, no horror to approach it, no nightmare or trauma, and watched his father's hands lock on the crossbar. Watched them lock. Freeze. As if his father had suddenly turned to stone. Was he hit? Was he dead?

The day was still, suspended on the cusp of the afternoon, breathing down the silence of the ages. No one moved. No one spoke. Then, the kindness of a breeze. It came up from the river with a smell of the mud flats on it—Wouter could feel it in his hair—and it lifted the hat from his father's head.

Someone gasped, and Jeremias turned his head slowly toward them, toward the white-faced patroon and the men and women pressing their hands to their mouths. Ever so slowly he straightened up and began to move forward—a step, two steps, three—until he stood in the shadow of that powerful man aloft in the fluttering breeches, and it was then that Wouter noticed the change in his face. *Vader* wore an expression he didn't recognize—this was his father, and yet it wasn't, as if at the moment the shot rang out some ghost or demon had taken possession of his soul. The look on that face—it wasn't fear or resignation, but a look of defeat, utter and abject defeat—hurt Wouter more than all the stocks and patroons in the world could have begun to. And then, before he could react, *vader* was down on his knees and begging the patroon's forgiveness in a tearful croak.

Wouter wanted to turn away, but he couldn't. The shot had missed, his father was all right, a moment earlier he'd been flooded with redemptive joy. Now that joy turned to disbelief, to shock, to a deep and abiding shame. Everything his father had told him, every word, was a lie.

"I beg you," Jeremias sobbed, broken at long last, broken like a horse or mule, "I beg you to let me . . ." and his voice faded away to nothing, "to let me serve you."

The patroon's face was impassive. He looked down at the smoking pistols as if they'd appeared spontaneously, through some act of bewitchment. It took him a moment, but then he dropped them to the ground and swung down from his mount. Behind him, the dwarf cocked his musket and van den Post glared at the subdued mob as if daring them to make a move.

"And to stay, to please let us stay," Jeremias went on, the thunder of his voice reduced to a whine, a snivel. "We've worked the farm all our lives, it's the only thing we have, and you must, I beg you, I'm sorry, I didn't think. . . ."

Stephanus didn't answer. He took a step forward, his face recovered now, the magnificent nostrils alive with disdain, and held out his foot, as if expecting the ultimate obeisance. "Who owns you?" he asked, his balance perfect, voice inflexible.

"You," Jeremias croaked, staring at the gleaming shoe as if transfixed.

"And who owns your wife, your son, your half-breed bastard?"

To a soul, the tenants leaned forward to hear the reply. Jeremias Van Brunt, the wild-eyed, the proud, the vain, heir to mad Harmanus and madder Nysen, was about to deny his manhood. His voice was a whisper. "You," he said.

"Good." The patroon straightened up, and in the same instant he dropped his foot to the ground and drove it up again into Jeremias' face. The force of the blow snapped back the petitioner's head and sent him sprawling, his mouth bright with blood. "I don't want your service," the patroon hissed. And then, motioning to van den Post, who had dismounted and stood beside him now with drawn rapier, he completed the thought: "I want your blood."

As it turned out, no further blood was drawn that afternoon, but Jeremias was made to exchange places with his son, and sat there in the stocks, day and night, for the better part of a week. It was a painful week. His back was on fire, his legs numb, his wrists and ankle rubbed raw where his exhausted frame tugged them into the pine, mosquitoes bloated his face, agues settled in his joints. Staats and Douw stood watch over him, lest any enemy—man or beast—take advantage of him, and both Neeltje and *moeder* Meintje brought him food and drink. The other neighbors, even Robideau, stayed away. In the old country, when a man sat in the stocks, his enemies would gather to jeer and pelt him with stones, offal, dead cats, rats and spoiled fish. But here, the neighbors were indifferent. They held no grudge against Jeremias, and though most felt he'd got what he deserved—"Too proud is what he is," Goody Sturdivant was heard to observe, "too proud by half"—there was also a current of sympathy for him, though it may have been weak and intermittent. Somewhere, deep within them, they too resented the young patroon in his fancy clothes, and for a moment, trampling his garden, gathered behind their one-legged champion, it had come, like an embarrassment, to the surface.

Jeremias suffered, yes, the merciless sun in his face, the chill morning dew poking at his bones, but his inward suffering was worse by far. He was nothing, he knew that now. He was a peasant, a slave, a servant like his father and mother before him. All he'd worked for, all he'd built, all his dignity and toughness, were nothing. The patroon had showed him that. And here he'd preached to his sons, played the big man, the boaster—and for what? To crawl on his knees to Van Wart? For the rest of his miserable life he would be the mere husk of a man, no better than Oothouse or Robideau or any of them—and he knew it.

Wouter knew it too.

When they released him, when van den Post sauntered up to throw back the bars that pinioned him, he didn't fall into grandfather van der Meulen's arms or run home to where his mother sat stricken over a mound of flax and grandfather Cats anxiously paced the *stoep*—no, he took off like a sprinter, like a dog with a pair of sticks tied to its tail, streaking across the field and through the standing corn, hightailing it for the gap in the trees where his cousin had disappeared in the shock of dawn. He didn't look back. When he reached the tree line he kept going—a hundred yards, two—and then collapsed in the bushes, wishing only that he might die on the spot, that the earth would open up and swallow him or the sky turn to stone. Distraught, betrayed—how could his father have sunk so low? how could he have done this to him?—he looked blindly around him for some weapon, some stone he could swallow or stick that would poke out his sorry eyes.

How long he lay there, he didn't know. When he regained his senses, all was quiet in those terrible fields behind him, and the pall of evening had fallen over the woods. Somewhere a woodpecker knocked at a decimated tree, a lonely random tapping that haunted him with its persistence. He got up slowly, shakily, as if the ground had shifted beneath his feet, and looked around him in bewilderment. There were no leaves, no trees, no hills, rocks, glades or streams, there was only the image of his father kneeling before the icon of the patroon. He heard the beggar's whine of his father's voice, saw the blood on his lips. Why? he asked himself. Why hadn't *vader* risen up to choke the life out of that self-important dandy in the fancy pumps and silk doublet? Why hadn't he burned his barn, scattered his livestock and run howling for the woods like Wolf Nysen? Why hadn't he packed up and started over in New York, Connecticut, Long Island or Pavonia? Why, when all was said and done, hadn't he gone out to work on the road crew in the first place?

Because he was a coward, that's why. Because he was a fool.

Suddenly, with the night creeping around him, Wouter was seized with a fearful urgency: he had to find Jeremy. Jeremy was the one. Jeremy was his hope and salvation. It was Jeremy who'd stood up to them, Jeremy alone—you didn't see him sitting in the patroon's stocks, you didn't see him working the patroon's road. An hour after their race for the woods, the jellyfish eater had come back empty-handed, his face and forearms scored from the embrace of briar and bramble, his breeches muddied to the crotch, shirt torn and stockings down around his ankles. And Jeremy? He was out there somewhere among the trees, no man's prisoner, no man's servant.

"Jeremy!" Wouter called, slashing through a sea of mountain laurel, nearly choked with excitement, "Jeremy!" He'd find him—any minute now, at the cave or down by the creek—and then they'd run off together. Just the two of them. Across the river, to a place where they could live alone, hunting and fishing, far from patroons, *schouts*, rents, stocks and all the rest—far from *vader*. "Jeremy!" he called, as the owl took wing and night drove down the day, "Jeremy!"

What he couldn't know was that his dark and elusive cousin was so far out of earshot even a salvo from one of His Majesty's men o' war wouldn't have reached him. Van den Post—indefatigable, unshakable, crazed, intransigent, his limbs oiled and fluid, curses spewing from his lips—had chased his quarry up hill and down dale, through brake and briar, swamp, creek and esker. But Jeremy had seen those cuffs of pine, those gaps cut in the unyielding wood to receive him, and he was desperate. Taking the air in measured breaths, churning his legs and beating his arms, he flew through the woods like a sprite, leading van den Post under fallen trees, along ankle-turning streambeds and up slopes that would have prostrated a mountain goat. But he wasn't fleeing blindly: all along he had a plan.

He knew these woods as no adult did—as no jellyfish eater could ever hope to know them—and he was heading for the maze of swamps the Kitchawanks called *Neknanninipake,* That Has No End. It was a place of darkness at noon, of floating islands and hummocks of grass surrounded by muck that tugged you down till it took hold of you by the groin and refused to let go. It was a place Jeremy Mohonk knew as well as any snake or frog. It was a place where even the jellyfish eater would be powerless.

When he reached the fringes of the swamp—skunk cabbage, black slime to the ankles—Jeremy's heart leapt up. By the time he'd reached the heavy stuff, springing lightly from hummock to hummock, van den Post was out of sight, floundering in the slop and cursing like a virtuoso. Five minutes later there was no sound behind him but the *brak-brak* of the frogs and the homely call of the warbler flitting through the thatch of the trees. But he didn't stop. He traversed the swamp, dried his clothes and kept on going—going north, to a place he knew only in dimmest memory, a place his forgotten mother had gone for refuge when his forgotten father had turned his back on her. He didn't know where the camp was, knew the Weckquaesgeeks only as a ragged, scarred and bandaged lot that twice a year crowded the *stoep* at Jan Pieterse's, and knew only the haziest outlines of his parents' story, but somehow something led him to the camp at Suycker Broodt.

It was late. Dogs barked at him. Cook fires glowed in the wilderness of trees. Three braves, not much older than he, confronted him. Sentinels of that hapless and clumsy tribe, one was missing a hand, another was bereft of an ear and the third limped on a fused ankle. They regarded him in silence till the rest of their kith and kin shoved in around him. "What do you want?" One-Hand demanded in his trading-post Dutch, and Jeremy, scorner of the language of words, said nothing. One-Hand repeated the question, and still Jeremy said nothing. When finally, in frustration, the brave reached for his knife, Jeremy realized that even if he'd wanted to answer the question, even if the words were available to him, he couldn't. What did he want? He had no idea.

But then an old woman shuffled forward and cocked her head to regard him with eyes as opaque as a winter storm. She walked around him twice and then peered again into his face, so close he could smell the hide she'd been chewing with the stumps of her worn molars. "Squagganeek," she said, and turned her head to spit.

After a moment, one of the others took it up, an old man so wrinkled and dirty he might have been dug from the ground for the occasion. "Squagganeek," he rasped, and then, like children with a new plaything, they all tried it out, repeating the phrase over and over in a soft, caressing, rhythmic chant.

Wouter didn't find him that evening, or the next either. Even in the depths of his fright and disillusionment, of his despair and denial, he couldn't have imagined that it would be another eighteen months before he would lay eyes on his cousin again. He did go home eventually, for lack of anything better to do—home to his mother. She tended to his chafed wrists and ankles, fed him, put him to bed. In time, he healed. Or rather, part of him did. His cousin was gone and he missed him as he would have missed a limb wrenched from his body. And his father—he had no father. Sure, the man who sat heavily in the birch rocker or cut and baled hay shirtless in the field looked like his father, but he wasn't. He was an imposter. A spineless man, a man without definition or spirit, a man who floated through his days like a jellyfish at sea, waiting only for some survivor to snatch him up and consume him.

Such Sweet Sorrow

THE FOOTING was bad—very bad, treacherous even—and it was all Walter could do to ease himself down the path step by step, clinging like a mountaineer to an extended lifeline of low-hanging branches, willowy saplings and flimsy shrubs that whipped away from him like catapults and left a gummy residue in the palm of his hand. It had rained the night before, and the path was slipperier than an eel's back—or belly, for that matter. And the leaves didn't help any. Wads of them, yellow, red, orange, the dingy brown of crumbling newsprint, all glued wet to the ground and to each other, too. If there were times when the business of life made him forget that he stood upright only through the intercession of two lumps of molded plastic, this wasn't one of them.

Still, he didn't bother asking himself why, on this day before his departure for Fairbanks, Nome and Points North, on this thirty-first day of October, on this Halloween, he was fighting his way down the slope to the infamous pasture that gave onto the bridge that in turn gave onto the path up to Tom Crane's cramped and goat-stinking shack. Especially when the question would have been complicated by the fact, duly noted and painstakingly observed over the course of the past several weeks, that while at this hour of any given day the salutatory hubcap remained in place, the Packard—Tom Crane's Packard—was gone. And the corollary to that fact, that the Bug—Jessica's Bug—sat idly, invitingly, provocatively even, on the shoulder beneath it.

But no, he didn't question himself, didn't think. There was no reason to. Ever since that cleansing afternoon in mid-August, that afternoon of the Grand Union, he'd entered on a new and intoxicating phase of his life, one in which he acted rather than considered, one in which he accepted his demons for what they were and let his impulses take him where they would. He was leaving for Barrow in the morning. Jessica was home alone. In the cabin. Cut off from the world. Isolated. Without water, electricity, indoor plumbing, without a telephone. He was paying her a visit, that was all.

But these feet!

Damn, and now he was on his ass. In the mud. Some leafy crap in his face, the whole woods stinking of mold and rot, of leaves gone bad and some defunct squirrel or skunk quietly turning to mulch under a bush. Furious, he grabbed hold of a branch and jerked himself to his feet. The seat of his new Levi's was soaked through, and his lumberjacket—the one he'd bought to wear beneath the big down parka in Alaska—was so festooned with dangling bits of twig and leaf he might just as well have used it to line the bottom of his trash can. He beat angrily at his clothes, snatched some catkins from his hair and struggled down the relentless grade to the pasture below.

Here the going was easier. Walking straight ahead, walking on a flat—that he'd mastered. It was the up and down that gave him trouble. He brushed at his clothes as he walked, stepping aside to dodge the occasional cow pie, the new hiking boots with the supergrip tread no more connected to him than the dead appendages that filled them. It was a low-hung day, raw and opaque, and he was just coming up on the bridge when he spotted something moving in the trees along the creek. He gritted his teeth, expecting some further collision, some parting gift of history. He squinted. The haze shifted. It was only a cow.

Moooo.

Going up was a little better, though the path was just as slick. Somehow it was easier to wedge his feet into the dirt here, and there seemed to be more rock, ribs of it washed clean by the runoff of a thousand storms. He snatched at branches, a mountaineer still, and hoisted himself up. Soon he was passing through Tom's garden, with its wet glowing pumpkins and the brown stalks of all the rest, and then he sideskirted a clutch of beehives to emerge in the little clearing beneath the big naked oak.

There it was, the cabin, in all its ramshackle glory—but was she home, that was the question. Just because her car was out front was no guarantee. What if she'd gone someplace with Tom? What if she was out gathering nuts or acorns or dried flowers? Or washing her undies, taking a shower, painting her pretty toenails in her parents' spacious and well-appointed bathroom? What if she was even then breezing up and down the rarefied aisles of the Peterskill Grand Union? The possibility that he'd find the place empty had haunted him all the way down the path from the road, across the field and up the ridge to the cabin. But now, even before he fastened on the smeared windows or glanced at the porch, he knew he had her—the smoke gave her away. He smelled it first, then lifted his eyes to the rust-eaten stovepipe and there it was, smoke, pale wisps of it against a sky that was like smoke itself.

Suddenly confident, elated even, he started across the yard, the place just as he remembered it: a few scattered stumps, honeysuckle fallen back from the house in frost-killed clumps, rusted machinery poking its bones from the subsiding bushes. The porch, as usual, was cluttered with everything that wouldn't fit in the house but was too valuable yet to toss to the elements, and then there was the venerable old wood of the shack itself, aged to the color of silver fox, no lick of paint ever wasted on its parched and blistered hide. As he mounted the steps, a pair of bandy-legged goats stuck out their necks to peer at him around the far corner of the house, and a cat—brindled, with a patch of white over one eye—shot between his legs and vanished in the litter along the path. And then all at once he could feel Jessica moving across the floorboards inside—the same boards that supported him outside the door. Or at least he thought he could. What the hell. He forced his face into a smile and rapped twice. On the door. With his knuckles.

Dead silence.

Frozen silence.

Silence both watchful and tense.

He tried again, *tap-tap,* and then thought to make use of his voice: "Jessica?"

Now she *was* moving, he could feel her, could hear her, moving across the floor with a pinch and squeak of the dry boards beneath her, beneath him. One, two, three, four, the door swung open—stove going, bed made, jars of this and that on the shelf—and she was standing there before him.

"Walter," she said, as if identifying a suspect in a police lineup. He saw the surprise and consternation on her face, and he grinned harder. She was wearing jeans, a pair of men's high-top sneakers and a cable-knit sweater. Her hair hung loose, and bangs—folksingers' bangs, newly cut—concealed the high white patrician swell of her brow. She looked good. Better than good. She looked like the girl he'd married.

"I was just passing by," he joked, "and thought I'd stop in to say hello, I mean, goodbye—"

Still she stood there, the door poised on its hinges, and for a second he thought she was going to slam it in his face, send him packing, boot him out like a fast-talking door-to-door salesman with a vacuum cleaner strapped to his back. But then her face changed, she stepped back, and, perhaps a little too brightly, said: "Well, why don't you come in out of the cold, at least?"

And then he was in.

As soon as she shut the door, though, confusion took hold of them both—they were in a cell, a box, a cave, there was nowhere to go, they didn't know what to do with their hands, where to cast their eyes, where to sit or stand or what to say. His back was to the door. She was there, two feet from him, her face as white as it was the time they'd carved a sun-warmed melon in a Catskill meadow and the knife had slipped and gashed her palm. Her head was bowed, her hands clasped in front of her. Was this an awkward moment? You bet.

It was Jessica who recovered first. She turned, brushed past him and bent briskly to relieve the room's sole armchair of its burden of hats, jackets, dope pipes, cheese graters, paperback books and other impedimenta, at the same time echoing what he'd said at the door: "Goodbye? What do you mean—are you moving or something?"

And so he was able to settle into the vacant armchair and tell her of his impending journey to the heart of the polar night, to joke about mushers and mukluks and ask, in mock earnestness, if she knew a good dog he could take along to warm his hands in. "But seriously," he went on, encouraged by her laugh, "you don't have to worry about me—I'm no tenderfoot. I mean, I know my Jack London cold, and there's no way I'm going to try humping from my motel room to the bar without spitting first."

"Spitting?"

He glanced over his shoulder as if revealing a closely guarded secret, and then leaned forward. "Uh-huh," he said, dropping his voice. "If your spit freezes before it hits the ground, you go back to bed and wait till spring."

Laughing, she offered him a glass of wine—the same vinegary stuff Tom Crane had been fermenting in the corner for the past two years—and settled down at the table beneath the window to string beads and listen. He took it as a good sign that she poured herself a glass too.

"You know," he said suddenly, "there was this guy in the hospital, in the bed next to me . . . a midget, I guess he was. Or a dwarf. I always forget the difference."

"Midgets look like little children," she said, drawing the shape with her hands. "Everything in proportion."

"Well, this guy was a dwarf then. He was old. And his head was huge, big ears and nose and all that." He paused. "His name was Piet. He knew my father."

She snuck a look at him, then turned back to her work, tugging at a coil of monofilament with her teeth.

"He's the one who told me he was in Alaska."

"So that's it," she said, turning to him. "Your father."

Walter chafed the glass between his palms as if he were trying to warm them. He smiled, staring down at the floor. "Well, it's not exactly the time of year for a vacation up there, you know. I mean, people are losing their noses, earlobes frozen solid, toes dropping like leaves—"

Again she laughed—an old laugh, a laugh that gave him hope.

He looked up, no smile now. "I'm hoping to track him down. See him. Talk to him. He *is* my father, after all, you know?" And then he was telling her about the letters he'd written—sometimes two or three a day—trying to catch up eleven years in a couple of months. "I told him it was okay, let bygones be bygones, I just wanted to see him. 'Dear Dad.' I actually wrote 'Dear Dad' at the top of the page."

He drank off the wine and set the glass down on a carton of old magazines. She was turned away from him, in profile, stringing her beads as if there were nothing else in the world. He watched her a moment, her lips pouted in concentration, and knew she was faking it. She was listening. She was trembling. On fire. He knew it. "Listen," he said, shifting gears all of a sudden. "I never told you how hurt I was that day in the Grand Union. But I was. I wanted to cry." His voice was locked deep in his throat.

She looked up at him then, her eyes soft, a little wet maybe, but she let it drop. It was almost as if she hadn't heard him—one moment he was pouring out his heart to her and the next she was off on a jag of disconnected chatter. She talked about the war, protest marches, the environment—there was untreated sewage being pumped into the river, could he believe that? And then ten miles downstream people were drinking that very same water—incredible, wasn't it?

Incredible. Yes. He gave her a soulful, seductive look—or what he thought was a soulful, seductive look—and settled in to hear all about it. They were on their third glass of wine when she brought up the *Arcadia.*

To this point, her litany of industrial wrongs, her enumeration of threatened marshes and polluted coves, her wide-eyed assertion that so-and-so had said such-and-such and that the something-or-other levels were a thousand times the maximum allowable by law, had only managed to lull him into a state of quiet contentment. He was half-listening, watching her hands, her hair, her eyes. But now, all of a sudden, he perked up his ears.

The *Arcadia.* It was a boat, a sloop, built on an old model. He hadn't seen it yet, but he'd heard about it. Heard plenty. Dipe and his VFW cronies were up in arms about it—*It's the riots all over again, Walter,* Depeyster had told him one night, *we taught them a lesson twenty years ago in that cow pasture down the road and now it's as if it never happened.* As far as Walter was concerned, it was no big deal—who cared if there was one hulk more or less on the tired old river?—but at least he had some perspective on it. It was Will Connell's connection to the thing that burned Dipe and LeClerc and the others, that much was clear. The very name was a bugbear, a red flag, a gauntlet flung down at their feet—Robeson was dead, but Connell was still going strong, vindicated by the backlash against the McCarthy witch hunts, a survivor and a hero. And here he was parading up and down the river in a boat the size of a concert hall (*Can you believe it, Walter,* Depeyster had asked, his voice lit with outrage, *to put together this, this floating circus as a front for his Communistic horseshit . . . clean water, my ass. All he cares about is waving the Viet Cong flag on the steps of the Capitol Building . . .*), here he was laughing in the faces of the very people who'd turned out to shut him and Robeson down twenty years back.

Rednecks. That's how Walter had always thought of them—how he'd been taught to think of them—but now that he actually knew Dipe, now that he'd worked with him, sat in his living room, drunk his Scotch, confided in him, he saw that there was a lot more to it than he'd imagined. Hesh and Lola and his mother's parents had forced their version on him, and wasn't that propaganda? Hadn't they given him one side of the story only? Hadn't they told him all his life that his father was no good, a traitor, a fink, a broken man? They were wrong about the Soviets, after all—they knew in their hearts they were. Here they'd bought the party line as if it were carved in stone, and then Stalin rotted away from within, and where were they? Freedom? Dignity? The Workers' Paradise? Russia had been a morgue, a slave camp, and the party the ultimate oppressor.

They were gullible—Hesh, Lola, his own sad and wistful mother and her parents before her. They were dreamers, reformers, idealists, they were followers, they were victims. And all along they thought they were the champions of the weak and downtrodden, thought they could blunt the viciousness of the world by holding hands and singing and waving placards, when in truth they themselves were the weak and downtrodden. They were deluded. Unhard, unsoulless, unfree. They were dreamers. Like Tom Crane. Like Jessica. He was leaving for Alaska in the morning and he was going to find his father there and his father was going to tell him how it was. Traitor? Walter didn't think so. Not anymore.

"You didn't know we were founding members?" Jessica said, and he was looking right through her. "Tom and me? Tom even crewed down from Maine on her maiden voyage."

He hadn't known. But he could have guessed. Of course, he thought, hardening all of a sudden, Jessica and Tom Crane, Tom

Crane and Jessica. The two of them, out on the river, clasped together in their sanctimonious bunk, waving their I'm-Cleaner-Than-You banners on the deck and chanting for peace and love and hope, crowing for the spider monkeys and the harp seals, for Angel Falls and the ozone layer and all the rest of the soft-brained shit of the world. Suddenly he pushed back the chair and stood. "Did you hear me before?" he asked, and there was no trace of humor in his voice now, no humility, no passion even. "When I said how much you mean to me?"

She bowed her head. The stove snapped, a bird shot past the window. "I heard you," she whispered.

He took a step forward and reached for her—for her shoulders, her hair. He could feel the heat of the stove on his left side, saw the dreary woods through the smeared window, felt himself go hard with the first touch of her. She was still sitting, slumped in the chair, a welter of beads, elastic thread, fishing line and sewing needles spread out across the table before her, and though he pressed her to him, she didn't respond. He petted her hair, but she turned her head away and let her arms fall limp at her sides. It was then that he felt it, a tremor that began deep inside her, a wave that rose against the tug of gravity to fill her chest to bursting and settle finally, trembling, in her shoulders: she was crying.

"What's the matter?" he said, and his voice should have been soft, tender, solicitous, but it wasn't. It sounded false in his ears, sounded harsh and impatient, sounded like a demand.

She was sniffling, catching her breath at the crux of a sob. "No, Walter," she breathed, looking away from him still, as limp as one of the dead, "I can't."

He had his hands on the sweater now, and he was pressing his lips to the part of her hair. "You're my wife," he said. "You love me." Or no, he'd got that wrong. "I love you," he said.

"No!" she protested with sudden vehemence, turning on him with a face that was like a mask, like someone else's, like something she'd put on for a costume party, for Halloween, and then she seized both his arms just above the elbow and tried to push him away. "No!" she repeated, and all at once he could see her as if through a zoom lens, the tiny capillaries of her eyes gorged with blood, droplets of moisture trapped in her lashes that were thick as fingers, the nostrils of her turned-up nose dilated and huge, red as an animal's. "It's over, Walter," she said. "Tom. I'm with Tom now."

Tom. The name came at him out of nowhere, out of another universe, and he barely heard it. Victims. Dreamers. He fought down her arms and jerked at the sweater like a clumsy magician trying to pull the tablecloth out from under a service for eight. She cried out. Flailed her arms. Fell back against the table. Beads scattered, falling to the floor like heavy rain, like the drumbeat of the polluters marching off to war. He tugged the sweater up, bunched it in an angry knot beneath her chin and lifted her from the chair, pinning her groin to the edge of the table with the weight of his own. He went for her mouth, but she turned away from him; he went for her breasts, but she hung on to the sweater with both hands. Finally, he went for her jeans.

She cried the whole time, but she clung to him. And he leaned into her and felt her tongue and when she stiffened against him she held fast to him as if he were her life and her all. When it was over he pulled back from her and the look in her eyes frightened him. She looked whipped, wounded, like a dog that's been fed and beaten at the same time. Was that a bruise under her left eye? Was that blood on her lip? He didn't know what to say—he'd run out of words. In silence he zipped up, buttoned his jacket; in silence he backed away from her and felt for the door.

Slowly, tentatively, as if he were facing down a wild beast that might spring at him if he glanced away for even an instant, he turned the knob behind him. It was then that she let herself fall to the floor, lifeless as a doll. She lay there, motionless, her head cradled in her arms, the jeans down around her ankles. He couldn't hear her sobs now, but the balled white length of her was trembling with them, that much he could see.

It was his last picture of her.

Coming down the hill was nothing. He seemed to skate on his feet and each time he lost his balance a stiff young sapling sprang up for him to latch hold of. He squeezed his mind as he might have squeezed a blister, and purged himself of the image of her. By the time he reached the bridge he was in Barrow, with its unfathomable shadows, its hard edges, its geometry of ice. He saw his father there, and his father was healthy and vigorous, the man who'd taken him to the trestle to plumb the murky river for crabs, the man who'd stood up to Sasha Freeman and Morton Blum and all the rest. *Walter,* his father said, *it's been a long time,* and he held out his arms.

Costumes

SHE WAS a good-looking woman, a beauty, what with her expensive teeth, her full proud bosom, the flat abdomen that had grown round only once to contain the swell of life. He liked her eyes too, eyes that were like the marbles he'd won as a boy, the palest cloud of violet in a prism of glass, and he liked the way she looked at him when he was telling her things. He told her about Manitou's big woman or Mishemokwa the bear-spirit or about his father and Horace Tantaquidgeon, and she leaned forward, her lips parted, brow furrowed, eyes so intent she might have been listening to the oracle, to the father of nations, to Manitou himself. But what he liked best of all about her was that she was a white woman, the wife of the son of his ancient enemy—that was too perfect.

He'd first met her up there, in Jamestown. What was it—four, five years ago? He was tired of the shack, tired of carrying the burden of his hopeless race, tired of solitude, and he'd gone north to pick apples and shoot duck for a couple of weeks—till Thanksgiving, maybe. Till the lakes froze and the ducks were gone, anyway. It was November, the Tuesday before Turkey Day, and he was sitting out on One Bird's porch with a rag, a can of 3-In-One oil and One Bird's hoary single-shot Remington. He'd used it the day before to bring down a pair of canvasbacks and a pintail, and he'd cleaned and oiled it after supper. He wasn't really cleaning it now—he was just stroking the barrel with a rag soaked in oil, just to have something to do with his hands. The day was clear, breezy, with a scent of the tundra on the wind.

The station wagon—it was a Chevy, brand-new, white, with that fake wood business along the side—surprised him. It came around the corner by Dick Fourtrier's place, muscling its way over the washboard dirt and the potholes, and then slowed in front of One Bird's, jerking to a halt finally just down the road. On came the back-up lights, and the wagon lumbered back till it was even with him. He saw a head bob in the window, saw the wind tug at the exhaust. The morning locked itself up in silence. Then the driver's door fell open and there she was, Joanna, the charity lady, coming around the side of the car in her leather pumps, her cashmere sweater and pleated skirt, coming up the flagstone path with its hackles of stiff yellow weed, coming to the house that needed paint, coming to him.

"Hello," she said when she was halfway up the walk, and her smile gave back the glory of all those years of six-month checkups and all those miles of dental floss well-plied.

He was stoic, he was tough, he was an ex-con, a survivor, a man who lived off the land, a communist. His own teeth were rotten as a hyena's and he was wearing work pants, a flannel shirt and a vest that had once been sky blue in color but was now smeared with grease, blood, steak sauce, the leavings of rabbit, pheasant, fish. He watched her with cold green eyes and he said nothing.

She stopped at the foot of the porch, her smile just the smallest bit strained, and she clasped her slim hands together and began twisting a ring round her finger—a diamond, of the type that proclaimed her the property of another man. "Hi," she said, reiterating the greeting, as if he might not have heard her the first time, "can you tell me where I might find the social hall?"

The social hall. He wanted to sneer at her, shock her, hurt her, wanted to tell her she could look for it up her ass for all he cared, but he didn't. There was something about her—he couldn't say what—that set her apart from the others, those blue-haired old loons with their ratty blankets and their bibles and the rest of their do-goody claptrap, and it frightened him. Just a bit. Or maybe it wasn't fright exactly—it was more of a frisson, a jolt. He just couldn't picture her waving a placard (Save the Poor Ignorant Downtrodden Native American!) with the rest of them or slipping into a cheery barbecue apron and serving up flapjacks and sausage links at one of those horrific charity breakfasts.

She was a good-looking woman, of course—young, too—but that wasn't it. There was something else here, something deeper, something that was coming to him like a gift, like a birthday cake with all the candles aglow. He didn't know what. Not yet. It was enough to know it was there.

Since he'd said nothing, merely dug into her with those insolent eyes and dropped the barrel of the gun between his legs, rubbing it up and down as suggestively as he could, she went on, her voice a little jumpy, talking too fast now: "It's my first time. Here, I mean. I'm from downstate, in Westchester, and Harriet Moore—she's a friend of my cousin from Skaneateles—well, to make a long story short," tossing her hair to indicate the wagon behind her, "I've got a load of stuff that we collected in the Peterskill area—cranberries, canned peaches and yellow beans, and—and gravy mix—for the, for you, I mean—no, I mean for your people and . . ." she trailed off in confusion, the green gaze too much for her.

He stopped rubbing. A wedge of geese called out from half a mile up. She glanced over her shoulder to where the car sat at the curb, still running, the door flung open wide, and then turned back to him: "So can you tell me where it is?"

For the first time, he spoke: "Where what is?"

"The social hall."

He set the gun down on the newspaper spread out to protect the weathered boards of the porch, then rose from his chair to tower over her. And then he grinned, rotten teeth and all. "Sure," he said, coming down off the steps to stand there and catch the scent of her, "sure I know where it is. I'll take you there myself."

He had sex with her that night, after she'd unloaded her dusty cans of succotash and anchovy paste and whatever other garbage the good wives of Peterskill had found cluttering the dark recesses of their cupboards, sex that necessarily involved some damage to underwear that looked as if it had just come off the shelf at Bloomingdale's. He tore it from her on the bed of her sanitized room at the Hiawatha Motel, where everything—chairs, bureau, mirror frame, even the TV cabinet—was constructed of Lincoln Logs, painstakingly fit, glued and shellacked by reservation squaws for fifty cents an hour. It was a decor designed to give you that woodsy feeling, that half-naked, tomahawk-thumping, mugwump-in-his-lodgehouse sort of feeling. In Jeremy, however, it produced a very different feeling. One that made him want to tear the underwear from charity ladies.

Joanna surprised him, though. He'd expected prim, he'd expected blushing and beautiful, the averted eye and the trembling flesh. But she wasn't like that at all. She was hungry, needful, more savage than he. Once he'd heard her name, once he'd unraveled the threads of her identity—"*Van Wart?*" No, it can't be? Depeyster Van Wart, son of the old man, old Rombout?"—he knew he'd have her, that it was destined to be, that this was the gift wrapped specially for him, and he knew that he would humiliate her, ravage her, fill her right up to the back of the throat with all the bitterness of his fifty-five bleak and hopeless years. But she surprised him. The more brutal he was, the more she liked it. She came at him, lashing, lacerating, leaving marks on his back, and the whole thing turned on him. He backed off. Gave in. Fell, for the first time in his life, in love.

He waited for her, every other week, for the station wagon laden with rhinestone-encrusted handbags, golf clubs, Caldor sneakers, with wood-etching sets, men's overcoats, galoshes, and took her directly from the social hall to the motel. He never confessed to her how much he hated the place, how much he resented it. But after a month or two, after he'd overstayed his welcome at One Bird's, and Christmas and New Year's had come and gone, he told her that the Hiawatha Motel made him sick. But it wasn't just the motel, it was the whole godforsaken, fenced-in, roped-off disease of the reservation itself. It was One Bird. The Tantaquidgeons. The whole thing. It stank.

They were walking the banks of the Conewango after making love, she in the fringed buckskin jacket and leggings he'd given her for Christmas, he in his work pants and flannel shirt and the new down vest she'd given him in return, and she stopped him with a tug of her arm. "What do you mean?" she asked.

"I mean it's time for a change. I'm going back to Peterskill."

Her face went strange for a moment, and he could see that she was trying to fit the idea into her scheme of things, trying to place her wild aboriginal lover in the tranquil picture of her Peterskill, alongside her husband, her daughter, the big galleon of a house that rode the sea of all those perfect lawns in an unbroken chain of perfect days. Then she shrugged. Reached her face up to his and kissed him. "Fine with me," she said. "I'll be able to see you all the more."

And so he packed up his things—underwear, socks, moccasins, the rude garments he'd fashioned from hides and that he wore only on his native soil, Ruttenburr's book, the gutting knife—while One Bird offered her opinion of the charity lady with the glass eyes, and then he climbed into the station wagon beside Joanna and rode in comfort over the creeks and hills he'd crossed on foot for the first time so many years before. He gazed out the window on the Allegheny, the Cohocton and the Susquehanna rivers, on the timber-lined mounds of the Catskills, on the plunging dark drop of the Hudson's gorge. Then they were over the Bear Mountain Bridge, through the outskirts of Peterskill and heading east on Van Wart Road, and he felt like Hannibal coming into Rome, like a conquering hero, like a man who would never again know defeat.

Joanna coasted right on by the big house on the ridge, past the historical marker that had his name on it—Jeremy Mohonk, the woeful, the ancient, cut down for his trespasses against the almighty patroon—and pulled off on the shoulder across from the path that ran down into the pasture below. "Later," he told her, and he slipped like a ghost into the ranks of the trees, invisible the moment he turned away from her.

She came to him in that cheerless shack, and she brought him food, books, magazines, she brought him blankets, kerosene for his lamp, cooking utensils, dishes, fine linen napkins that bore the Van Wart monogram. Life was good suddenly and he embraced it like a man risen from the dead. He trapped and hunted, he visited with Peletiah Crane and his gangling grandson, he sat by the stove on a cold afternoon and turned the pages of a book. And he waited, patient as a mogul, for Joanna.

A year went by, and then another. In the spring of the third year, things began to change. As winter let go and the sap began to flow in the trees, as he sat mesmerized by the trill of the toads or watched the May flies swarm to the surface of the creek, the old ache came back to him, the ache that could never be salved. What was he doing? What was he thinking? She was a good-looking woman, Joanna Van Wart, but he was the last of the Kitchawanks and she was mother to everything he despised.

"Throw it away," he told her when she came to the door of the cabin that afternoon, beautiful in shorts and halter top and with her hair the color of all the leaves in the fall.

"Throw what away?"

"Your diaphragm," he said. "The pill. Whatever it is that comes between us."

"You mean —?"

"That's right," he said.

He wanted a son. Not the son One Bird could never give him, nor the infinitude of sons he'd spilled in his hand in the dark hole of Sing Sing—that was impossible. He would settle for another sort of son, a son who had less of the Kitchawank in him and more of the people of the wolf. This son would be no blessing, no purveyor of grace or redemption. This son would be his revenge.

At first she thought she'd leave Depeyster for him, that's how strongly she felt. She really did. Jeremy was a kind of god to her. He made love to her, rough and tender at the same time, and it was as if the earth itself had become flesh and entered her, as if Zeus—or no, some dark Indian god, some brooding son of Manitou—had come down from his mountaintop to take a mortal woman. He was nearly twenty years older than she, and his life was a legend. He was her mentor, her father, her lover. He was all and everything. She wanted him inside her. She wanted to celebrate him, worship him, she wanted to lie against him and listen to his ragged voice become the pulse of her heart as he sifted through the old stories as if fingering jewels.

Was she obsessed? Besotted? Swept away? Was she a sex-starved middle-aged charity lady in a string of pearls who went wet in the crotch at the thought of him, who wanted to hump like a dog, like a squaw, like an Indian princess with an itch that wouldn't go away?

Yes. Oh, yes.

She sat at the dinner table with her passionless husband and her vacant daughter while a black woman bent over the hereditary Delftware with a medallion of veal or a morsel of lobster and she wanted to touch herself, wanted to get up from the table and take to the woods howling like a bitch in heat. Lady Chatterley? She was a nun compared to Joanna Van Wart.

Of course, all things have their season, and all things must come to an end.

Looking back, she saw now that the beginning of the end was as clearly delineated as a chapter in a book. It came on that spring afternoon two and a half years back, just before he left the cabin for good, the afternoon he told her to throw away her diaphragm and give him a child. That was life. That was nature. That was how it was supposed to be.

The only problem was that he'd turned strange on her. They came together, flesh to flesh, invigorated by a new sense of purpose and hope of fulfillment, ecstatic once again, and it lasted a week. If that. Next thing she knew, he was gone. She came to the cabin early, to surprise him, and he wasn't there. He's fishing, she thought, he's checking his traps and he's lost track of the time, and she settled in to wait for him. It was a long wait. For he'd gone back to Jamestown, back to One Bird.

After a week—an interminable week, an eternal week, a week during which she neither slept nor ate and haunted the cabin like one of the unappeased spirits that were said to brood over the place in never-ending torment—she loaded up the station wagon with eighteen cartons of Happy Face potholders and came looking for him. She found him on One Bird's porch, shirtless, a necklace of polished bone dangling from his throat, the terrible freight of his years caught in the saraband of his scars, in the sullen slump of his shoulders, in the reptilian gaze of his eyes. He was cleaning fish and his hands were wet with blood. He looked as savage in that moment as any of his savage ancestors. But no more so than One Bird, all two hundred fifty pounds of her, who sat glaring at his side.

Joanna was unimpressed. She jerked the station wagon to a halt out front, flung open the door and tore up the path like an avenging demon. She was wearing the leggings, the jacket, the rawhide shift, and she'd darkened her skin with bloodroot till it was the color of a penny scooped from the gutter. Half a dozen strides and she was on him, her nails sunk like talons in the meat of his arm, and then she was leading him down the steps and around the corner of the house, oblivious to the unbroken skein of One Bird's threats and insults. When she got him out back, out behind the drooping clothesline hung with One Bird's gently undulating sheets and massive underdrawers, she flogged him with the sharp edge of her tongue. She began with the bloodcurdling philippic she'd rehearsed all the lonely way up Route 17, and ended with a rhetorical question delivered in a shriek so keen it would have driven eagles from their kill: "Just what the hell do you think you're doing? Huh?"

He was twice her size, and he looked down on her out of the green slits of his eyes. "Cleaning perch," he said.

She gave it a minute, rocking back on the balls of her feet, and then she lashed out and slapped him. Hard. So hard the tips of her fingers went numb.

Just as quickly, and with twice the force, he slapped her back.

"You bastard," she hissed, her stony eyes wet with the sting of his blow. "You're leaving me, is that it? To live up here with that—that fat old woman?"

He said nothing, but he was wearing a little smile now. One Bird's great innocent bloomers floated on the breeze.

"You're not sleeping with her," she said. "Don't tell me that."

He didn't tell her anything. The smile spread.

"Because if you are . . ." she trailed off. "Jeremy," she whispered, so softly, so passionately she might have been praying. "Jeremy."

He took her hands. "I want to fuck you," he said, "so bad."

Later, after he'd led her away from the dumb show of those billowing bloomers and they'd wound up making love in a clump of milkweed behind Dick Fourtrier's place, he answered her question. "I'm thinking things over, that's what I'm doing," he said.

"What things?"

"Boats."

"Boats?" she echoed, as bewildered as if he'd said "pomeranians," "sputniks" or "saxophones."

Boats. He was giving up the cabin—at least until their son was born, and by the way, was she, uh—? No? Well, they'd keep trying. Anyway, what he wanted was a change of scene. All of this ancestral soil business was beginning to wear on him—he could feel the spirits of Sachoes and the first doomed Jeremy Mohonk pressing in on him, and he needed a break, something different, did she know what he meant? He thought he'd like to live on a boat—off his feet, off the land that was draining him day by day of the little strength he had left. He'd seen a ketch for sale at the Peterskill marina. He needed fifteen hundred dollars.

She didn't like it, didn't like it a bit. For one thing, her husband had a boat at the marina, and how could she visit Jeremy there without arousing suspicion? And for another, Indians didn't live on boats. They lived in longhouses, in lodges and wickiups and tar-paper shacks, they lived on land. And why in God's name would he want to spoil the setup they already had? The way it was, she could visit him any time the spirit moved her—through the woods, direct to his bed, a fifteen-minute walk that got her juices flowing and put the sparkle back in her eyes. No, she didn't like it, but she gave him the money all the same. And now, in the grimmest month of her life, in the penultimate month of her pregnancy, in the dismal, disastrous October of a year of riots in the streets, assassinations and men on the moon, now, after two years of trysts in the secret swaying darkness of that damp and fishy boat, she knew why he'd done it—to get away from her, that's why. To mock her. To punish her.

It was an old story, a sad story, and it went like this: three weeks ago, gravid, swollen with his child, weighed down by this alien presence within her and yet lighter than air too, she went to him, full of the future, wanting only to hold him, touch him, rock with him in the cramped bunk of the *Kitchawank* as it rode the translucent skin of the river. As usual, she parked in the lot of Fagnoli's restaurant and took a cab to the marina, and as usual, she found him below decks, reading. (He was going through two or three books a day—anything from Marcuse, Malcolm X or Mao Tse Tung to James Fenimore Cooper and the fantasies of Vonnegut, Tolkien or Salmón.) On this particular day—she remembered it distinctly—he was reading a paperback with a cover that featured a busty half-clad woman cowering before a liver-colored reptilian creature with teeth like nail files and an unmistakable genital bulge in the crotch of his silver jumpsuit. "Hello," she said softly, ducking low to avoid the insidious beam on which she'd cracked her head a hundred times in the past.

He didn't return her greeting. And when she made as if to squeeze in beside him on the bunk—stooped awkwardly, the baby swinging like a pendulum—he didn't move. She felt the boat lurch beneath her and she sat heavily on the edge of the bunk across from him, a distance of perhaps three feet in those cramped quarters. For a long while she just sat there, glowing, beaming at him, drinking in the sight of him, and then, when she felt she wanted him so badly she couldn't take it another second, she broke the silence with a soft amiable inquiry: "Good book?"

He didn't answer. Didn't even so much as grunt.

Another moment passed. The air coming down the gangway was cool, salt, smelling of the mélange of things that ran through the river's veins—fish, of course, and seaweed. But other things too, things that weren't so pleasant. Or natural. Who was it had told her they were dumping sewage upriver? She peered out the grimy porthole behind Jeremy and pictured the gray chop awash with human excrement, with toilet paper and sanitary napkins, and all at once she felt depressed. "Jeremy," she said suddenly, and the words were out of her mouth before she could stop them. "I'm going to leave Depeyster."

For the first time, he looked at her. The hooded eyes she knew so well lifted themselves from the page and focused their green squint on hers.

"I don't care what he thinks or my parents or the neighbors or anyone else either. Even if he won't give me a divorce. What I mean is, I want to be with you"—she reached out to squeeze his hand—"always." Now it was said, now it was out in the open and there was no turning back.

It was a subject he'd avoided. Strenuously. Assiduously. Even, it seemed to her, fearfully. Yes, he assured her, he wanted her to have his child. Yes, he wanted to live out on the river for a while, fishing, crabbing, doing odd jobs around the marina to pick up the little he needed to get by—a dollar here and there for used paperbacks, a carton of eggs, the occasional soft drink. And yes, he loved her (though the question really didn't have any meaning, did it?). But she was another man's wife and things were fine the way they were. Besides, he couldn't see the future at all. Not yet, anyway, not yet.

But now it was out in the open and there was no turning back:

she was going to leave Depeyster for him. "I could live here on the boat with you," she went on, staring at the floor, the words coming in a spate, "and we could go upriver and dock at Manitou or Garrison or Cold Spring. Or maybe on the other side of the river—at Highland Falls or Middle Hope. I have some money, my own money, a trust fund my mother's father set up for me when I was a girl, and I've never touched it, you know, thinking that someday—" but she couldn't go on, because now, suddenly, unconsciously, she was looking into his face.

And his face was terrible. No longer the face of the stoic who could have posed for the frieze on the back of a nickel, nor even of the strange charismatic man who'd led her across the threshold of the bright little room at the Hiawatha Motel or taught her to slip through the woods like the ghost of a deer, it was the face of the raider, the avenger, the face beneath the raised tomahawk. He sat up. Shoved himself violently from the bunk and stooped over her, his back, shoulders, neck melding with the dark low rafters. "I don't want you," he said. "I don't want your half-breed bastard, or your quarter-breed either."

His face was in hers. She could smell the fish on his breath, the sweat dried in the armpit of his shirt. "Destroyer," he hissed. "Usurper. She-wolf. Charity Lady." He pursed his lips, almost as if he were about to kiss her, and held her with his fierce unstinting gaze. "I spit on you."

The next morning, the *Kitchawank* was gone.

Depeyster's voice—"Joanna! Joanna, get that, will you?"—came to her as if from another dimension, as if she were trying to conduct her life on the cold floor of the river and the current drove all the words down. "Joanna!"

It was the door. Children were at the door—she could see them through the window—dressed as witches, ghosts, imps, Indian braves, Indian princesses. A jack-o'-lantern leered from the corner, where her husband, who couldn't have loved the tradition more were he a child himself, had set out a bowl of candy corn and Hershey's Kisses. Numbly she rose from the chair, fought the tug of the current, and fumbled to open the door. Their voices piped around her, swallowed her up, and their ugly little paws clutched at the contents of the bowl she'd somehow managed to lift from the table and prop against the swell of her belly. Then they were gone and she was struggling upstream to sink ponderously into the waiting chair.

"Joanna? Sweetheart?"

She turned in the direction of his voice, and there he was, in silk hose and knee breeches, in a square-skirted coat with stupendous brass buttons, in buckled shoes and sugarloaf hat. "How do I look?" he said, adjusting the brim of his hat in the mirror over the mantelpiece.

How did he look? He looked like a refugee from one of Rembrandt's group portraits, like a colonist, a pioneer, like the patroon who'd wrested the place from the Indians. He looked, down to the smallest detail, exactly as he looked each year for LeClerc Outhouse's Halloween party. There was one year, a long time back, when he was still young and adventurous, that he'd dressed as Pieter Stuyvesant, pegleg and all, but ever after he'd been the patroon. After all, he told her, why fool with perfection? "You look fine," she said, the words trailing from her mouth as if encapsulated in the little bubbles they used in the funny papers.

She was turning away, already falling back into the depths, when he surprised her. Awakened her. Crossed the room to resuscitate her, to lift her, fathom by fathom, from the depths. It began with the percussive release of a cork, and the touch of a cold long-stemmed glass. "A toast," he proposed, and he was right there at her side, his voice as clear as if it were only air that separated them after all.

She looked up at him, numb, stiff as a corpse, all the weight of all those tons of water pressing down on her, and fought to lift her glass. "A toast," she repeated.

He was beaming, grinning, crossing his eyes and licking his lips with the sheer crazy joy of it, and he bent to take her free hand and hold it till he had her full and undivided attention. When he spoke, he dropped his voice to parody the deep unctuous tones of Wendell Abercrombie, the Episcopalian minister. "To the memory of Peletiah Crane," he said, holding his glass aloft as if it were a chalice.

So deep down was she, it took her a moment before she understood. "You mean, he's . . . he's dead?"

"Yes, yes, yes!" he crowed, and she thought he was going to kick up his heels and caper around the room like a goat. "Tonight. This afternoon. Just after dark."

She couldn't help herself. She looked at his face, his costume, the empty glass in his hand, and felt herself coming up for air. She didn't stop to think about the propriety of it—this sudden joy at the news of the death of a fellow creature—because something was happening to her face, something that hadn't happened in so long it was a novelty: she was smiling. There she was, giving back the joy and triumph on her husband's face, her dimples showing, the light rising in her eyes.

"Marguerite just called," he added, and then, in his excitement, he was down on his knees before her, sweeping off the antique hat and pressing his cheek to the bulge of her stomach. "Joanna, Joanna," he murmured, "I can't tell you how much this means to me, the baby, the property, the whole beautiful thing that's happening to us. . . ." Under the circumstances, it was the most natural thing in the world to do, and she wasn't even aware she was doing it: she took his face in her hands, held him to her, and bent to touch her lips to the crown of his head.

They finished the champagne. He sat at her feet, rocking back and forth over his glass, all the while chattering on about breeds and temperaments, about saddles, riding clothes and whether she thought they'd be able to find a good part-time groom and maybe a riding teacher too—for the boy, he meant. He was so ebullient, so full of the moment, not even Mardi could dampen his mood. She paraded down the hallway in her kitten costume (half a dozen mascara whiskers, a tail of twisted pipe cleaners and a leather corset so low-cut in front and pinched in the rear she couldn't have worn it to the beach), and Joanna watched her pause at the front door, begging for a confrontation, but Dipe wouldn't have it. He turned away as if he didn't recognize her and went on with what he was saying even as the door slammed behind him. "Listen, Joanna," he said, "I know this isn't really your cup of tea and I know you've passed on it the last couple of years, but do you think you might want to come with me tonight?" And before she could answer, before she could think, he was running on, as if to forestall her objections: "You don't even have to change if you don't want to—you can go like this, like Pocahontas, like an

Indian princess, and to hell with them. Your outfit'll go great with this," he laughed, plucking at the collar of the museum piece he was wearing.

It was then that she finally caught her breath, then that she felt herself shaking it off once and for all, coming up, up, till she broke free and filled her lungs to surfeit with the sweet, light, superabundant air. "No," she said, her voice soft, yet steady, "I think I'll change."

Van Wartwyck, Sleeping and Waking

FOLLOWING the events of that tumultuous summer of 1679, the summer that saw Joost Cats demoted, the adolescent Mohonk driven over the edge of the known world and Jeremias Van Brunt put once and forever in his place, the drowsy backwater of Van Wartwyck fell into a deep and profound slumber. Leaves turned color, just as they were supposed to, and fell from the trees; ponds froze over and the snow came, as usual, and then receded again. Cows calved and goats kidded, the earth spread its legs to receive the annual offering of seed, crops grew tall through the mellow months of summer and fell to scythe and mathook in the fall. Old Cobus Musser passed quietly out of this world and into the next one cold winter's eve as he sat smoking before the fire, but no one outside the immediate family heard of it till spring, and by then it didn't seem to matter all that much; Mistress Sturdivant found herself pregnant, but to her everlasting sorrow gave birth to a stillborn girl with a birthmark in the shape of a bat over the left breast, a tragedy she ascribed to the fright she'd taken on that terrible day at the patroon's the previous summer; and Douw van der Meulen netted a one-eyed sturgeon longer than a Kitchawank canoe and so heavy it took three men to carry it. Still, discounting the carcass of the big fish itself, that was about it for the gossips to chew on through the long somnolent year that followed on the heels of that tantalizing summer.

It wasn't until the winter of the following year, the winter of '80–'81, that the community had occasion to rouse itself, if ever so briefly, from its torpor. That occasion was the arrival of the new patroon (i.e., the patroon's cousin, Lubbertus' boy Adriaen, with his napiform head and fat wet lips) and the coincident return of the green-eyed half-breed with his blushing Weckquaesgeek bride and quarter-breed son. Now, while Adriaen Van Wart wasn't exactly patroon—Stephanus had long since bought out his cousin's share of the estate—he wasn't simply a caretaker either, as Gerrit de Vries had been before him. What he was, apparently, was a place marker, a pawn or knight or rook occupying a strategic square until the grand master chose either to sacrifice him or put him into play. What he was, beyond that, was a corpulent, slow-moving, baggy-breeched scion of the lesser Van Warts, born in the year of his father's death and raised by his nervous, repatriated aunt in Haarlem (where his mother thought he would get a superior education and aspire to the directorship of the family brewery, but where in fact he became an adept only in the quaffing rather than malting of beer), who had now, enticed by his influential cousin, returned to the New World to make his fortune. What he was, was fat, eighteen, unmarried and stupid. His mother was dead, his sister Mariken living with her husband in Hoboken. Cousin Stephanus was all he had to hold onto, God and St. Nicholas preserve him.

And Jeremy?

Not yet seventeen, he was a married man, according to the rites and customs of the Weckquaesgeeks, and the father of a nine-month-old boy. He was healthy too, clean of limb and sharp of eye, and the native cuisine seemed to have agreed with him—he'd filled out through the chest and shoulders, and where before the sticks of his legs had merely melted into his torso, there was now the rounded definition of an unmistakable pair of buttocks. It seemed, however, that in his absence he'd totally lost the power of speech. What had begun as a predilection for taciturnity, or rather a disinclination toward noun, verb, conjunction, modifier or preposition, had developed into something aberrant during his sojourn among the Weckquaesgeeks. Perhaps it was tiggered by some particularly caustic memory of his earliest days among that star-crossed tribe, days that suffered his mother's dereliction and his own unending torment at the hands of his uniformly dark-eyed playmates. Or perhaps the cause was physical, something linked to the pathology of the brain, a failure of the speech centers, an aphasia. Who could say? Certainly not the good squaws and shamans of the Weckquaesgeeks, who had all they could do to stanch the flow of blood from the deluge of accidents that daily befell their clumsy constituency and barely noticed that the rehabilitated Squagganeek didn't have much to say for himself. And most certainly not a physician such as the learned Huysterkarkus, who, if he'd been consulted, would no doubt have prescribed bleeding, cautery, emetics, purgatives and fen leeches, applied in random order.

At any rate, even if Jeremy had lost the power of speech, his prodigious return, coupled with the arrival of Adriaen Van Wart, gave the tongue waggers plenty of fodder over the next several months: *To think that after all this time, and who didn't know but that he was dead and disemboweled by the wild beasts and didn't he have it coming to him, running off from the law like that? to think he'd show up on his uncle's doorstep nice as you please, as if he'd been out for a stroll around the neighborhood or something. And with a woman at his side, no older than a child really, swaddled in greasy skins and stinking like the kitchen midden, and his own little half-breed bastard bound up in one of those papoosey baskets—or no, it'd be a quarter-breed, wouldn't it? Couldn't talk though, not a word. Goody Sturdivant says he'd forgot his Dutch and his English both, living up there amongst the heathens (like his mother before him, and wasn't that a sad case?), taking part in their lewd and ungodly rites and who knows what all. Mary Robideau says they cut his tongue out, the savages, but who knows what's true and what isn't these days? And did you get a load of the patroon's cousin—the one that's going to sit by his big fat bachelor self up in the grand house? Yes, yes, that's what I heard too—Geertje Ten Haer dressed her daughter up like a tart, the little one, not fifteen yet—shameless, isn't it?—and came calling the very day the young bucket of lard moved his bags in. Oh, I know it, I know it. . . .*

And so it went, till Adriaen was settled in, the silent Jeremy and his equally silent wife became fixtures at Nysen's Roost, and the incestuous little community of Van Wartwyck could doze off again.

To Wouter, the fact of his cousin's return was miraculous enough, but that he had a place to return to was even more miraculous. The autumn of their impending doom came and went and still the Van Brunts were in possession of the five-morgen farm at Nysen's Roost. On November 15 old Ter Dingas Bosyn wheeled up in the wagon and collected the quitrent, which *vader,* obsequious as a lapdog, counted out and loaded up himself. The patroon had moved his family back down to Croton as soon as the first frost put the trees to bed for the winter, and he took his *schout,* the jellyfish eater, with him. And that was that. No eviction. Another year rolled by and again *vader* paid his rent without demur and again the globular old *commis* accepted it and made his precise notation in the depths of his accounts book. Wouter, who'd expected the worst—who'd expected to be driven from his home while his mother and sisters wrung their hands and his father fawned and begged and licked the patroon's boots—was puzzled. He'd been dreading the day, dreading the patroon's sneer, the dwarf's evil stare and stunted grasp, the cold naked steel of the rapier that had once laid his father's face open, but the day never came.

Word had it that the patroon had relented. Geesje Cats had gone down on her knees to the patroon's mother, and the crabbed old woman, that eschewer of pleasure and comfort both, had interceded in the Van Brunts' behalf. Or so they said. And then too, Wouter remembered a week in late October of that fateful year when Barent van der Meulen came to keep him and the other children company while *moeder* and *vader* hitched up the wagon and drove down to stay with *grootvader* Cats in Croton. No one knew what went on then, but Cadwallader Crane, who'd got it from his father, claimed that Neeltje and Jeremias had petitioned the patroon indefatigably, haunting his garden, crying out their fealty day and night, even going so far as to kneel to him and kiss his gloved hand as he sauntered to the stable for his daily exercise—all in the hope that they might convince him to change his mind.

However it was, the whole thing revolted Wouter. He almost wished the patroon had come and chased them off his lands, wished that they could have gone west and started over, lived as beggars on the streets of Manhattan, hacked their hair and scarified themselves to live naked among the Indians. At least then his father might have come back to life. As it was now, he was a slave, a gelding, a sot who lived only to serve his betters. He worked the fields, anesthetized, from dawn till dusk, whitewashed the house, cleared acreage, put up stone fences—and all for the patroon, for the profit and increase of the man by whose magnanimity he drew breath from the air, water from the ground and bread from the oven. After that horrific day in the patroon's back lot, he shied away from Wouter, always his favorite, and fell into a sort of trance, like an ass harnessed to the wheel of a gristmill. He was a husk of his former self, a man of straw, and his son—his eldest, the joy of his life, the boy who'd made an icon of him—regarded him with contempt, with pity, with the unassuageable hurt of the betrayed.

Wouter turned twelve in the bleakness of that first winter, thirteen in the second. It was the most hopeless period of his life. He'd lost his father, lost the cousin who was a brother to him, lost his own identity as son to the man who defied the patroon. For the longest while, he couldn't eat. No matter what his mother served him—pancakes, cookies, the most savory roast or meaty stew—the very smell of it made him sick, his throat constricted and his stomach seized. He lost weight. Wandered the woods like a ghost. Found himself sobbing inexplicably. If it weren't for Cadwallader Crane, he might have gone off the deep end of his grief, like his Aunt Katrinchee before him.

Young Cadwallader, who had attained the physical age of twenty by the first of those miserable winters, was the last-born and least quick-witted of that scholarly and grallatorial clan presided over by the ancient Yankee intellectual, Hackaliah Crane. For some fifteen years, the elder Crane had maintained Van Wartwyck's sole institution of learning, known among the wags at Jan Pieterse's as Crane's Kitchen School, in reference to its venue. Each winter, when the crops were harvested and stowed away in attic and loft, when the days grew short and the weather wicked, Hackaliah gathered his six, eight or ten reluctant scholars in the kitchen of the rambling stone house he'd built with his own blistered hands, and lectured them in the mysteries of conning the letters of the alphabet and doing simple sums, throwing in a smattering of Suetonius, Tacitus and Herodotus for good measure. He held his sessions because he had a calling, because it was the purpose and office of his life to keep the lamp of learning lit and to pass it on from hand to hand, even on the wild and darkling shores of the New World. But, of course, it wasn't solely a labor of love—

there was a small matter of recompense. And the Yankee preceptor, notorious skinflint that he was, exacted his basket of apples or onions, his string of cucumbers dried for seed, his bundle of combed flax or his turkey gobbler battened on corn as if it were tithed him—and woe to the unsuspecting scholar who was remiss with his payment. It was in this rudimentary seat of learning that Wouter, over the desolation of the months, gradually began to attach himself to Cadwallader Crane.

In happier days, Jeremy had expertly mimicked the younger Crane's erratic gait and the darting, birdlike movements of his scrawny neck and misshapen head, while Wouter had done an inspired impersonation of his laryngeal squawk of greeting and the tepid washed-out drone with which he read from slate or hornbook, but now, in his loneliness, Wouter felt strangely drawn to him. He was ridiculous, yes, five years older than Tommy Sturdivant, the next oldest student in the class, unable to master his lessons though he'd been through them five hundred times, the bane of his venerable father's existence and a sore trial to his mother's love. But he was interesting too, in his own way, as Wouter would soon discover.

One forbidding January afternoon, when Wouter lingered after lessons were over, Cadwallader took him around back of the house to the woodshed and produced, from a hidden corner, a board on which he'd tacked a brilliant spangle of moths and butterflies caught in hovering flight. Wouter was dumbstruck. Chocolate and gold, chrome blue, yellow, orange and red: there, in the dim confines of the winterbound shed, the breath of summer touched him.

Astonished, Wouter turned to look at his friend and saw something in Cadwallader's eyes he'd never recognized before. The habitual glaze of stupefaction was gone, replaced by a look at once alert, wise, confident, proud, the look of the patriarch showing off his progeny, the artist his canvases, the hunter his string of ducks. And then, miracle of miracles, Cadwallader, the lesser Crane, the hopeless scholar, the beardless boy-man who couldn't get out of the way of his own feet, began to discourse on the life and habits of these same moths and butterflies, speaking with what almost approached animation of worms and caterpillars and the metamorphosis of one thing into another. "This one, do you see this one?" he asked, pointing to a butterfly the color of tropical fruit, with regular spots of white set in a sepia band. Wouter nodded. "He was a milkweed worm, with horns and a hundred ugly feet, just last summer. I kept him in a stone jar till he changed." Wouter felt the wonder open up like a flower inside of him, and he lingered in that comfortless shed till he couldn't feel his feet and the light finally failed.

In the coming weeks, the awkward enthusiast—now bounding over a precipice to pluck a wisp of moss from between two ice-bound boulders, now shimmying up a decayed trunk to retrieve a two-year-old woodpecker's nest—opened up the visible world in a way Wouter had never dreamed possible. Oh, Wouter knew the woods well enough, but he knew them as any white man knew them, as a place to pick berries, hunt quail, bring down squirrels with a sling. But Cadwallader knew them as a naturalist, as a genius, a spirit, a revealer of mysteries. And so Wouter followed him through the stripped bleak woods to gaze on a slit of barren earth in the midst of a snowbank where Cadwallader assured him a black bear was sleeping out the winter, or to listen as he pulled apart a handful of wolf droppings to speculate on the beast's recent diet (rabbit, principally, judging from the lean withered turds bound up in cream-colored hair and flecked with tiny fragments of bone).

"See that?" Cadwallader asked him one day, indicating the frozen hindquarters of a porcupine wedged in the crotch of a tree. "When the sun warms it in spring, that meat will give rise to new life." "Life?" Wouter questioned. And there, on the lesser Crane's thin lips and hairless cheeks, crouched a smile all ready to pounce. "Blowflies," he said.

Though there was eight years difference in their ages, the friendship was not so one-sided as one might imagine. For his part, Cadwallader, long an object of contempt and denigration, was happy to have anyone take him seriously, particularly someone who could share in his private enthusiasm for the underpinnings of nature, for worms, caterpillars, slugs and the humble nuggets of excrement he so patiently scrutinized. Wouter suited him perfectly. No rock of maturity himself—any other man of twenty would have had his own farm and family already—he found the Van Brunt boy his equal in so many ways, a natural leader, really, persuasive, agile, curious, but not so much his equal as to challenge him seriously. As for Wouter, his fascination with the scholar's son was a distraction from the emptiness he felt, and he knew it. Cadwallader, absorbing though he may have been in his own skewed way, made a poor substitute for Jeremy—and for the lapsed father who worked the farm like an encumbered spirit, an old man at thirty. Thus, like all incidental friends, they came together out of mutual need and because each propped up the other in some unspoken way. Cadwallader sought out Wouter, and Wouter sought out Cadwallader. And before long, the scholar's unscholarly son became a regular guest at Nysen's Roost, staying to supper and taking Jeremy's spot at the table, occasionally even spending the night when the weather was rough or the company too stimulating.

The company, yes. Though Jeremias faded into the background as if he were fashioned from the stuff of clouds, Neeltje was busy with her spinning or sweeping or washing up and the younger children, confined to the house throughout the endless winter, hissed, squabbled and caterwauled like aborigines, the young long-nosed Yankee nature lover found the company irresistible. Ah, but it wasn't Wouter, either, who moved him, though he liked him well enough and would claim him as his closest friend till nearly the time of his death—no, it was Geesje. Little Geesje. Named after her grandmother, inheritor of her mother's fathomless eyes and rebellious ways, ten years old the day he first stepped through the door.

They played cards through those long winter evenings—Cadwallader hunched over his knees like a singing cricket, Wouter with a ferocious zeal to win that sometimes astounded even him, and Geesje, her legs drawn up beneath her, the cards masking her sly child's face, playing with an insouciance that belied a will to win every bit as ferocious as her brother's. They skated on the pond where Jeremias had long ago lost his foot to the swamp turtle. They played at big ball, I spy, flick-fingers, hunt-the-slipper and quoits, the gangling, awkward scholar's son as eager and excited as the children he was playing with. By the time the second winter came around, the winter of Adriaen Van Wart's ascension and Jeremy's return, Wouter began to understand that it was no longer for him that Cadwallader Crane came to the house.

If Wouter felt betrayed, he didn't show it. He played just as hard, followed his long-legged companion just as often through copse and bower, bog and bramble, lingered as usual in the Crane woodshed to marvel over a set of fossilized horse's teeth or a pipefish preserved in pickling brine. But inwardly he felt as if he'd been knocked off balance again, shoved from behind just as he'd begun to regain his footing. Disoriented, uneasy, thirteen years old and set adrift once again, he went to the door one raw February night and found his cousin standing there in a blanket of sleet, and in the grace of a single moment he felt redeemed: Jeremy was back.

But redemption doesn't come so easily.

Even as he embraced him, even as he shouted out his cousin's name in triumph and heard the household rouse behind him, he knew something was wrong. It wasn't the Indian getup—the ragged bearskin, the string of *seawant,* the notochord cinched around his cousin's brow—or the fierce primordial reek of him either. Nor was it the strategic emplacement of bone, sinew and flesh that had transformed him from boy to man. It wasn't that at all. It was ice. His cousin was made of ice. Wouter embraced him and felt nothing. Cried out his name and saw that his eyes were glazed and impenetrable, hard as the surface of the pond. In confusion he let go of him as the doorway filled with jostling children, with *moeder*'s smile and *vader*'s lifted eyebrows and fallen lip. Jeremy merely stood there, rigid as stone, and for a terrible moment Wouter thought he was hurt—he'd been gouged, stabbed, they'd cut out his tongue and he'd come home to die, that's what it was. But then Jeremy stepped back into the shadows and there, in his place, stood a squaw.

A girl, that is. A female. Calves, thighs, bosom. Wrapped up in deerskin, otter and mink, her hair greased and queued, mouth set in a pout. And in her arms, an infant. Wouter was stunned. He looked up into the shadowy features of his cousin and saw nothing. He looked at the girl and saw the quiet triumph of her eyes. And then he looked at the infant, its face as smooth and serene as the Christ child's. "In, in," *moeder* was piping, "it's no night for visiting on the *stoep,*" and all at once Wouter became conscious of the sleet pelting his face, of the dank subterranean breath of the wind and the restlessness of the night. Then the squaw brushed past him and the infant, dark as cherrywood and not half the size of a suckling pig, opened its eyes. Its eyes were green.

A moment later Jeremy was sitting in the inglenook, mechanically spooning porridge into the dark slot of his mouth, while the girl crouched on the floor beside him, the baby at her breast. Where had he been? the children asked. Why was he dressed like that? Was he an Indian now? *Moeder*'s voice was tender. She hoped he was home to stay, and his wife too—was this his wife? She was welcome, more than welcome, and what was her name? *Vader* wanted to know the obvious: was this his child? Wouter said nothing. He felt as if the floor were buckling under him, he felt jealous and betrayed. He looked from Jeremy to the girl and tried to imagine what it was between them, what it meant and why his cousin wouldn't look him in the eye.

For his part, Jeremy couldn't begin to fathom their questions, though he felt for them and loved them and was glad in his heart to be back. Their voices came at him like the rumble of the foraging bear, like the soliloquies of the jays and the clatter of the brook outside the door, rising and falling on an emotional tide, a song without words. Dutch words, English, the markers and signifiers of the Weckquaesgeek and Kitchawank dialects he'd once known—all was confusion. He knew things now as Adam must have known them that first day, as presences, as truths and facts, tangible to touch, sight, smell, taste and hearing. Words had no meaning.

His wife had no name—or no name that he knew. Nor his son either. He looked shyly at Wouter and he knew him, and he knew Jeremias, Neeltje, Geesje and the other children. But to summon their names was beyond him. He knew, in an immediate and concrete way, in the way of enzymes churning in the gut or blood surging through the veins, that Jeremias had killed his father, that the jellyfish eater had wanted to lock him up in his infernal machine, that the people of the wolf were ravening unchecked over the face of the earth. He knew too that Jeremias had raised him as his own and that Wouter was his brother and that his place was both here and among the Weckquaesgeeks at the same time. He knew that he was grateful for the food and for the fire. But he couldn't tell them. Not even with his eyes.

In the morning, Jeremy went out beyond the last deadened tufts of the farthest, stoniest pasture and built himself a wigwam. By late afternoon, he'd covered the ground with a mat of sticks, on which he meticulously arranged an assortment of moldering furs. Then he got a cookfire going and moved in the girl and the baby. Over the years to come, as he fell into the old ways with Wouter, as he bearded the patroon and lived off his land without once breaking the ground, as he watched the pestilence take two of his daughters and scar his son, he rebuilt, remodeled and expanded the crude bark domicile he'd erected that morning, but he never left it. Never again. Not until they came for him, that is.

As for Wouter, his cousin's return devastated him. Here was yet another stab in the back, another wedge driven between him and the savior he so desperately needed. First it was Cadwallader and Geesje, now Jeremy and this moon-faced girl with the pendulous teats and the green-eyed little monkey who clung to them. He was hurt and confused. What was it about his spindly-legged little sister that could so captivate Cadwallader? What did Jeremy see in an evil-smelling little squaw? Wouter didn't know. Though he was awash with hormones and driven by indefinable urges, though he ducked away from the fields to spy on Saskia Van Wart as she romped with her brothers on the lawn at the upper house, though he ached in the groin to think about her and woke from tangled dreams to a bed mysteriously wet, he still didn't know. All he knew was that he was hurt. And angry.

In time, as he began to reforge his relationship with Jeremy, as he worked around the inescapable conclusion that Cadwallader Crane cared more for his little sister than he did for him, he recovered. Or at least outwardly he did. He was fourteen and thought he was in love with a girl from Jan Pieterse's Kill by the name of Salvation Brown; he was fifteen and followed Saskia Van Wart around like a tomcat with the scent on him; he was sixteen and stood best man when Cadwallader Crane took his sister's hand in marriage. It all passed—the death of his father's spirit, the renunciation of Cadwallader Crane, the blow he'd received from his cousin on that sleet-struck night when the squaw stepped between them. He grew into his manhood, and to look at him you'd never know the depth of his hurt, never guess that he was as crippled in his way as his father before him.

Van Wartwyck slumbered again. The decade of the eighties, which had begun so promisingly, petered out in the unimpeachable dullness of the quotidian. Nothing happened. Or at least nothing scandalous or violent or shocking. No one died even. Each spring the crops came up, the weather held—not too wet, not too dry—and the harvests got better by the year. On a still night you could hear the gossips snoring.

It was Jeremias Van Brunt, so long the catalyst for ferment and upheaval, who woke them up again. He didn't know it at the time, nor would he live to see it, but he unwittingly set in motion a series of events that would plunge the community into darkness, rouse the tongue waggers as if their very sheets and counterpanes had been set ablaze, and culminate finally in the last tragic issue of his youthful rebellion.

It began on a day of unforgiving wind and flagging temperature, a blustery afternoon at the very end of October 1692, some three years after that crafty Dutchman, William of Orange, had been proclaimed king of England and all her colonies. Shouldering a battered matchlock that had once belonged to his father and with a crude flax bag cinched at his waist, Jeremias left the cabin just after the noon meal and slouched off into the woods to commune with his favorite chestnut tree. Though this was to be a nutting expedition and nothing more, he carried the gun because one never knew what one might encounter in those haunted woods.

He worked his way arduously down the path from the cabin, snatching at trees and bushes to brake his descent, driving his pegleg into the compacted earth like a piton into rock, the wind hissing in his face and threatening in gusts to take his hat. Thumping across the bridge and wading into the marshy hollow that lay between Acquasinnick Creek and Van Wart's Road, he startled a pair of ravens from their perch in a crippled elm. Up they rose, like tatters from the Dominie's funereal gown, bickering and complaining in their graceless tones. Jeremias went on, a little more circumspectly than usual—the sight of a raven never brought anyone an excess of good luck, so far as he knew—until he was halfway across the marsh and the crown of the chestnut came into view in the near distance, shouldering its way above the lesser trees that surrounded it. It was then that he flushed the unlucky birds again, this time from the ground—or rather from a weedy hummock choked with vines and a blaze of blood-red sumac that seemed to float up out of the puddled expanse of the marsh like some sort of strange haunted craft.

Jeremias was curious. He tugged at his boot, straightened the brim of his hat, and slogged off to investigate, thinking he might find the buck he'd wounded two days back, holed up and breathing its last. Or maybe the remains of the pig that had mysteriously disappeared just after the leaves turned. The birds were on to something, that much was sure, and he meant to find out what.

He parted the vines, hacked at the sumac with the butt of the gun, paused twice to disentangle the sack from the scrub that seized it like fingers. And then he spotted something in the tangle ahead, a glint of iron in the pale cold sunlight. Puzzled, he bent for it, and then caught himself. The smell—it hit him suddenly, pitilessly—and it should have warned him off. Too late. He was stooping for an axehead, and the axehead was attached to a crude oaken handle. And the handle was caught, with all the rigor of mortis, in the grip of a hand, a human hand, a hand that was attached to a wrist, an arm, a shoulder. There before him, laid out in the sumac like the giant fallen from the clouds in a fairy tale, was the man who'd given Blood Creek its name. The eyes were sunk into the face, raw where the birds had been at them, the beard was a nest for field mice, the arms idle, the hair touched with the frost of age. He'd looked into that face once before, so long ago he could barely remember it, but the terror, the humiliation, the mockery, these he remembered as if they were imprinted on his soul.

It took all five of them—Jeremias, his three sons and his nephew Jeremy—to haul the body, massive and preternaturally heavy even in death, out of the marsh and up to the road, where with a concerted effort they were able to load it into the wagon. Jeremias laid out the body himself, helped by the cold snap, which mercifully kept the odor down. If he'd thought to charge admission to the wake, he would have been a rich man. For the news of Wolf Nysen's death—the death that confirmed his life—spread through the community like the flu. Within an hour after Jeremias had stretched the fallen giant out on his bier, the curious, the incredulous, the vindicated and the faithful had gathered to stand hushed over this legend in the flesh, this rumor made concrete. They came to marvel over him, to measure him from crown to toe, to count the hairs of his beard, examine his teeth, to reach out a trembling finger and touch him, just once, as they might have touched the forsaken Christ pulled down from the cross or the

Wild Boy of Saardam, who'd cooked and eaten his own mother and then hung himself from the spire outside the drapers' guild.

They came from Crom's Pond, from Croton, from Tarry Town and Rondout, from the island of the Manhattoes and the distant Puritan fastnesses of Connecticut and Rhode Island. Ter Dingas Bosyn showed up, Adriaen Van Wart, a wizened old cooper from Pavonia who claimed to have known Nysen in his youth. On the second day, Stephanus himself rode up from Croton, with van den Post and the dwarf, and a delegation of somber, black-cloaked advisors to Colonel Benjamin Fletcher, the new governor of the Colony and His Majesty William III's loftiest representative on the continent. By the third day, the Indians had begun to pour in—maimed Weckquaesgeeks, painted Nochpeems, even a Huron, before whom all the others gave way as if to the devil himself—and after them, the oddballs and cranks from outlying farms and forgotten villages, women who claimed they could transform themselves into beasts and had the beards and talons to prove it, men who boasted that they'd eaten dog and lived as outlaws all their lives, a boy from Neversink whose tongue had been cut out by the Mohawk and who said a prayer over the body that consisted entirely of three syllables, "ab-ab-ab," repeated endlessly. It was on the evening of the third day that Jeremias put an end to the circus and laid the giant to rest. Beneath the white oak. Just as if he'd been a member of the family.

Well, this stirred the gossips up, sure enough. *I told you, I told you a thousand times that mad murthering Swede was a fact, didn't I? Didn't I tell you he nearly scared the life out of Maria Ten Haer that time down by the creek and can you believe this unholy fool burying the devil right there in the ground where he put his own sister and father too?*

Worse, far worse, was the sequel. For the death of Wolf Nysen—bogey, renegade, scapegoat, the monster who'd taken on all the sins of the community and worn them in his solitude like a hairshirt—was the death of peace itself. In the months that followed, the accumulated miseries of a decade rained down upon the heads of Van Wartwyck's humble farmers, and the grave opened its maw like some awakening beast at the end of a long season's fast.

Under the circumstances, perhaps it was only appropriate that

Jeremias was the first to go. What happened to him, so they said, was the Lord's retribution for his unholy alliance with the outlaw Nysen and for his early sins against the patroon and the constituted authorities, against the king himself, if you came down to it. What happened to him was by way of just deserts.

Two weeks after he'd laid Nysen to rest, Jeremias was dead, a victim of his father's affliction. No sooner had the shovel tamped the Swede's grave and the mourners and curiosity seekers gone on their way, than Jeremias felt the first preternatural pangs of hunger. It was a hunger like nothing he'd ever felt, a hunger that snatched him up and dominated him, made him its creature, its slave, its victim. He wasn't merely hungry—he was ravenous, starved, voracious, as empty as a well that went down to China without giving up a drop of water. He came in after the funeral, and though for so long now he'd been invisible in his own house, he shoved in between his hulking sons and lashed into the olipotrigo Neeltje had made for the funeral supper as if he hadn't eaten in a week. When it was gone, he scraped the pot.

In the morning, before the family was up, he managed to devour the six loaves his good wife had baked for the week, a pot of cheese, a string of thirty-six smoked trout the boys had caught in the course of three days' fishing, half a dozen eggs—raw, shells and all—and an enormous trencher of hashed venison with prunes, grapes and treacle. When Neeltje awoke at first light, she found him passed out in the larder, his face an oleaginous smear of egg, grease and molasses, a half-eaten turnip clutched like a weapon in his hand. She didn't know what was wrong, but she knew it was bad.

Staats van der Meulen knew, and Meintje too. Though Wouter scoffed and Neeltje protested, Staats made them pin Jeremias to the bed and bind him ankle and wrist. Unfortunately, by the time Staats had got there, the damage was already done. The family's winter provisions were half-exhausted, three of the animals—including an ox and her calf—were gone, and Jeremias was bloated like a cow that's got into a field of mustard. "Soup!" he cried from his pallet. "Meat! Bread! Fish!" For the first few days his voice was a roar, as savage as any beast's, then it softened to a bray and finally, near the end, to a piteous bleat of entreaty. "Food," he whimpered, and outside the wind stood still in the trees. "I'm, I'm"—his voice a croak now, fading, falling away to nothing—"starrrr-ving."

Neeltje sat by his side the whole time, sponging his brow, spoon-feeding him broth and porridge, but it was no use. Though she begged grain from the van der Meulens, though she plucked hens she would need for eggs, though she fed him two, three, four times what any man could hold, the flesh seemed to fall from his bones. By the end of the first week his jowls were gone, his stomach had shrunk to a layer of skin thin as parchment and the bones of his wrists rattled like dice in a cup. Then his hair began to fall out, his chest collapsed, his legs withered and his good foot shrank into itself till she couldn't tell it from the stump of the other. Midway through the second week she could stand it no longer, and when her sons left to hunt meat, she slipped in and cut his bonds.

Slowly, painfully, like one waking from the dead, Jeremias—or what was left of him—rose to a sitting position, threw back the blankets and swung his legs to the floor. Then he stood, shakily, and made for the kitchen. Neeltje watched in horrified silence. He ignored the decimated larder, bypassed the dried fruits, the strings of onions, cucumbers and peppers suspended from the rafters, and staggered out the door. "Jeremias!" she called, "Jeremias, where are you going?" He didn't answer. It was only after he'd crossed the yard and swung back the door of the barn that she saw the butcher's knife in his hand.

There was nothing she could do. The boys were God knew where, desperately beating the bushes for grouse, coney, squirrel, anything to replace the meat their wild-eyed father had squandered; her own father was all the way down in Croton and so enfeebled by age he barely responded to his own name any more; Geesje was with her husband; and she'd sent Agatha and Gertruyd to the van der Meulens, so as to spare them the sight of their father's decline. "Jeremias!" she cried as the door blew shut behind him. The sky was dead. The wind spat in her face. She hesitated a moment, then turned back to the house, bolted the door behind her and knelt down to pray.

He was already cold when they found him. He'd gone for the pigs first, but apparently they'd been too quick for him. Rumor, the old sow, had two long gashes in her side and one of the shoats was dragging a leg half-severed at the hock. The milch cows, confined in their stalls, were less fortunate. Two of the yearlings had been eviscerated—one partially butchered and gnawed as it lay dying—and Patience had had her throat cut. The boys found her like that, the black stain of her blood like a blanket thrown over the earthen floor, and Jeremias, his teeth locked in her hide, pinned beneath her. It was the fifteenth of the month, rent day. But Jeremias Van Brunt, former rebel, longtime ghost, spiritual brother to Wolf Nysen and sad inheritor of his father's strange affliction, would pay rent no more. They buried him the next day beneath the white oak, and thought they'd seen the end of it.

It was only the beginning.

Next to go was old *vader* van der Muelen, who went rigid with the stroke as he was splitting wood, and from whose hands the axe had to be pried before the Dominie could commit him to the frozen earth. He was followed shortly by his stalwart wife, that merciful and strong-willed woman who'd been a second mother to Jeremias Van Brunt and whose apple *beignet* and cherry tarts were small tastes of heaven. The cause of death was unknown, but the gossips, stirred up like a nest of snakes, attributed it variously to witchcraft, toads under the house and tuberous roots taken with wine. Then, in a single horrific week in January, the two Robideau girls broke through the ice while skating on Van Wart's Pond and vanished into the black waters below, Goody Sturdivant choked to death on a wad of turkey breast big as a fist and old Reinier Oothouse got away from his wife, drank half a gallon of Barbados rum, saw the devil and tried to climb Anthony's Nose in his underwear. They found him clinging frozen to a rock high above the river, pressed to the unyielding stone like a monstrous blotch of lichen.

The community was still reeling from the grip of catastrophe when the Indians came down with the French disease and brought it to the settlements. All the children under five died in their beds and word came from Croton that old *vader* Cats had succumbed and that a whole host of people who didn't even know they were alive had passed on too. It was blackest February and just after Cadwallader Crane's Geesje had expired in childbirth that the goodmen and goodwives of Van Wartwyck, led by the stooped and aged Dominie Van Schaik, marched up to Nysen's Roost and hacked open the grave of the monster who'd lurked through their dreams and now threatened to destroy their waking lives too. The Swede was unchanged, frozen hard, the black earth clinging to him like a second skin. Huddled in his cloak and shouting prayers in three languages, the Dominie ordered a pyre built and they set fire to the corpse and let it burn, warming their hands over the leaping flames and standing watch till the faggots were coals and the coals ashes.

Spring came late that year, but when it came the community breathed a sigh of relief. *It's over,* the gossips said, whispering among themselves for fear of jinxing it, for fear of goblins, imps and evil geniuses, and it seemed they were right. Staats van der Meulen's middle son, Barent, took up his father's plow and worked the family farm with all the vigor and determination of youth, and Wouter Van Brunt, twenty-five years old and for better than a decade now the real soul of Nysen's Roost, filled his father's shoes as if they'd been made for him. The weather turned mild in mid-March, the breezes wafting up from Virginia with just the right measure of sweetness and humidity. Tulips bloomed. Trees budded. Douw van der Meulen's wife bore him triplets the first of May, the cattle bred and increased and there wasn't a single two-headed calf born the length and breadth of the valley, so far as anyone knew, and the pigs had litters of twelve and fourteen (but never thirteen, no) and to a one the piglets emerged with three comely twists to their tails. It looked as if finally the world had slipped back into its groove.

But there was one more jolt yet to come, and it was beyond the scope or reckoning of any of the humble farmers and honest bumpkins of Van Wartwyck or Croton. It had to do with letters patent, with William III, that distant and august monarch, and with Stephanus Van Wart, no mere patroon any longer, but Lord of the newly chartered Van Wart Manor. It looked forward to the near future when the power of the Van Warts would encompass the whole of northern Westchester. And it looked back to the day when Oloffe Van Wart had brought a disgruntled herring fisherman to the New World to clear land and farm for him, working its inscrutable way through Jeremias' rebellion, Wouter's disillusionment and the death of Wolf Nysen. Though no one yet knew it, the final cataclysm was at hand, the last dance between Van Warts and Van Brunts, the moment that would ignite the tongue waggers like no other and then pull the blankets over Van Wartwyck for a snooze that would last two and a half centuries.

On the one side, there was Stephanus Van Wart, now one of the two or three wealthiest men in the Colony, First Lord of the Manor, confidant of the governor, and his minions, van den Post and the impenetrable dwarf. On the other, there was Cadwallader Crane, lover of humble worm and soaring butterfly, bereaved widower, unscholarly scholar, a boy caught in a man's jerky body. And there was Jeremy Mohonk, savage and speechless, the feral half-breed with the Dutchman's eyes. And finally, inevitably, borne down under the grudging weight of history and circumstance, there was Wouter Van Brunt.

Barrow

WALTER might as well have flown on to Tokyo or Yakutsk—it couldn't have taken any longer, what with fog delays, connecting flights that ran every third day and the sleepless night he spent in the Fairbanks airport waiting for the red-eyed maniac who would fly him, an oil company engineer and a case of Stroh's Iron City Beer to Fort Yukon, Prudhoe Bay and Barrow in a four-seat Cessna that had been stripped right down to the bare metal by weather he didn't want to think about. The oil company man—bearded, in huge green boots that looked like waders and a parka that could have fit the Michelin Man—took the rear seat and Walter sat next to the pilot. It was November third, nine-thirty in the morning, and it was just barely light. By two, the oil man assured him, it would be deepest night again. Walter looked down. He saw ice, snow, the desolation of hills and valleys without roads, without houses, without people. Dead ahead, pink with the reflection of the low sun at their backs, was the jagged dentition of the Brooks Range, the northernmost mountain range on earth.

The Cessna dipped and trembled. The blast of the engine was like a bombardment that never ended. It was cold to the point of death. Walter gazed out on emptiness until exhaustion began to catch up with him. Half-dozing, he focused on the disconcerting little notice taped to the grimy plastic glovebox: THIS AIRCRAFT FOR SALE, it read in shaky upper-case letters, $10,500, TALK TO RAY. Talk to Ray, he thought, and then he was asleep.

He woke with a jolt as they set down in Fort Yukon, where the case of beer was deplaning. Ray grinned like a deviate and shouted something Walter didn't catch as they taxied up to a grim-looking little shack to refuel; the oil man got out to stretch his legs, though it was something like twenty-seven below with a good wind, and Walter nodded off again. From Fort Yukon it was up over the Brooks Range and into darkness. The oil man got off at a place called Deadhorse, where, he assured Walter, there was enough oil to float Saudi Arabia out to sea. And then it was Ray and Walter, hurtling through endless night, on the way to Barrow, three hundred and thirty miles above the Arctic Circle, the northernmost city in America, the end of the line.

When the lights of Barrow came into view across the blank page of the tundra, Ray turned to Walter and shouted something. "What?" Walter shouted back, distracted by uncertainty, his stomach sinking and the nausea rising in his throat—Here? he was thinking, my father lives *here?*

"Your foot," Ray shouted. "I saw you having some trouble there when we were boarding back at Fairbanks. Lost one of your pegs, huh?"

Lost one of his pegs. Walter gazed out on the approaching lights and saw the image of his father, and all at once the roar of the plane became the roar of that ghostly flotilla of choppers in the doomed Sleepy Hollow night. Lost one of his pegs. And how.

"No," Walter hollered, snatching at the handgrip as a gust rocked the plane, "lost both of 'em."

Ray shouted something into the teeth of the wind as Walter trudged across the fractured skating rink of the airstrip. Walter couldn't hear him, couldn't even tell from the tone whether the man with whom he'd just risked his life in a rickety, worn-out, 10,500-dollar for-sale aircraft was blessing him, warning him or mocking him. "Good luck," "Look out!" and "So long, sucker," all sound pretty much the same when the temperature is down around forty below, the wind is tearing in off the frozen ocean with nothing to stop it for god knows how many thousand miles and you've got the drawstrings of the fur-lined hood of your parka tightened to the point of asphyxiation. Without turning around, Walter raised an arm in acknowledgment. And promptly fell face first on the jagged ice. When he pushed himself up, Ray was gone.

Ahead lay the six frozen blocks of wooden shacks that comprised the metropolis of Barrow, population three thousand, nine-tenths of whom, Ray had told him, were Eskimos. Eskimos who hated honkies. Who spat on them, pissed on them, cut them to pieces with the glittering sharp knives of their hooded eyes. Walter tottered forward, toward the lights, his suitcase throwing him off balance, the ragged uneven knobs of ice punching at his feet like the bumpers of a giant pinball machine. He'd never been so cold in his life, not even swimming in Van Wart Creek in October or jogging off to Philosophy 451 at the state university, where it sometimes got down to twenty below. No Exit, he thought. The Sickness Unto Death. Barrow. They'd got it all wrong, he thought, some cartographer's mistake. Barren was more like it. He kept going, fell twice more, and began to regret his Jack London jokes. This was serious business.

Five minutes later he was staggering up the main drag—the only drag—of Barrow, last home and refuge of Truman Van Brunt. Or so he hoped. If the airstrip was deserted, the street was pretty lively, considering the temperature. Snowmobiles shrieked and sputtered around him, racing up and down the street; dogs that looked like wolves—or were they wolves?—fought and snarled and careened around in packs; hooded figures trudged by in the shadows. Walter's hand, the one that gripped the suitcase, had gone numb despite his thermal mittens, and he thought grimly that at least he didn't have to worry about his feet. No problem there. No sir.

The wind was keen and getting keener. The hairs inside his nostrils were made of crystal and his lungs felt as if they'd been quick-frozen. He'd stumbled past three blocks of windowless shacks already, most of them with chunks of some sort of frozen meat, bloody naked ribs and whatnot, strung up on the roof out of reach of the dogs, and still no sign of a hotel, bar or restaurant. There were only three blocks more to go, and then what? He was thinking he might go on trudging up and down that icy dark forbidding street until he curled up in a ball and froze through like a side of beef, doomed like the heedless tenderfoot in the Jack London story, when finally, up on the left, he spotted an Olympia Beer sign, red neon, white script, glowing like a mirage in the desert, and below it, a hand-painted sign that read "Northern Lights Café." Shaken, desperate, shivering so hard he thought he'd dislocate his shoulders, he fumbled in the door.

For a minute, he thought he'd found nirvana. Lights. Warmth. A Formica counter, stools, booths, people, a wedge of apple pie in a smudged glass case, a jukebox surmounted by a glowing neon rainbow. But wait a minute, what was this? The place smelled, stank like a latrine. Of vomit, superheated piss, rancid grease, stale beer. And it was filled to capacity. With Eskimos. Eskimos. He'd never seen an Eskimo in his life, except in books and on TV—or maybe that was only Anthony Quinn in mukluks on a backlot in Burbank. Well, here they were, slouching, standing, sitting, snoozing, drinking, scratching their privates, looking as if they'd been dumped out of a sack. Their eyes—wicked, black, sunk deep beneath the slits of their lids—were on him. Their hair was greasy, their teeth rotten, their faces expressionless. To a one—he couldn't tell if they were man or woman, boy or girl—they were dressed in animal skins. Walter dropped his suitcase in the corner and shuffled up to the counter, where an electric heater glowed red.

There was no one behind the counter, but there were dirty plates and beer bottles on the tables, and a couple of the Eskimos were bent over plates of french fries and what looked like burgers. No one said a word. Walter began to feel conspicuous. Began to feel awkward. He cleared his throat. Shuffled his feet. Stared down at the floor. Once, when he was sixteen, he and Tom Crane had taken Lola's car down to the City, to an address they didn't know—a Hundred Thirtieth or Fortieth Street, something like that—because Tom had seen an ad for cheap jazz albums at a Hearns department store. It was the first time Walter had been in Harlem. On the street, that is. In the hour he spent there, he saw only two white faces—his own, reflected in the grimy window of the department stores, and Tom's. It was an odd feeling, a feeling of alienation, of displacement—even, almost, of shame for his whiteness. For that hour, he wanted desperately, with all his heart, to be black. Beyond that, nothing happened. They bought their records, climbed into the car and drove back to the suburbs, where every face was white. It was a lesson, he realized that. An experience. Something everyone should go through.

Somehow, he'd never felt the need to repeat it.

How long had he been standing here—a minute, five minutes, an hour? This was worse, far worse, than Harlem. He'd never seen an Eskimo before in his life. And now he was surrounded by them. It was like being on another planet or something. He was afraid to look up. He was beginning to feel that anything was better than this—even freezing to death on the streets or being torn to pieces by the wolf dogs or run down by drunken snowmobilers, when the swinging doors to the kitchen flew open and an extravagantly blonde, heavily made-up, rail-thin woman of Lola's age hustled into the room, six long-necked beers in one hand and a steaming plate of something in the other. "Be with you in a minute, hon," she said, and eased past him, arms held high.

The waitress seemed to have broken the spell. She served the beers and the plate of something, and the place came back to life. A murmur of low, mumbled conversation started up. An old man, his face as dead and leathery as the face of a shrunken head Walter had once seen in a museum, pushed past him with a seething glare and practically fell atop the jukebox. And then a teenager—yes, he could distinguish them now—tried to catch his eye and Walter looked timidly away. But now the waitress was there, and Walter looked into her tired gray eyes and thought for just an instant he was back in Peterskill. "What'll it be, honey?" she asked him.

The old man struggled with a quarter at the jukebox, dropped it to the floor and let out a low heartfelt curse, the gist of which Walter didn't quite catch—a malediction involving seals, kayaks and somebody's mother, no doubt. Or on second thought, had he said something about honkies? Honkie sons of bitches?

"Uh," Walter fumbled, tearing frantically at the parka's drawstring, "um, uh . . . coffee," he finally squeaked.

Without ceremony the waitress turned to the nearest Eskimo, said "Charley," and jerked her neck. Scowling, the man got up from his stool and lurched across the room, a bottle of beer in his hand.

"But, I—" Walter protested.

"Sit," the waitress said.

Walter sat.

He was on his second cup of coffee and had begun to detect signs of life in his fingertips, when the old man at the jukebox finally managed to locate the quarter and feed it into the slot. There was a mechanical buzz, succeeded by the plop of the record dropping, and then Bing Crosby was singing "White Christmas," crooning to the grim, silent, drunken men in their animal skins, crooning to the grease, the forlorn-looking wedge of apple pie, the shacks, the ice sheet, the heaps of frozen dogshit in the streets, crooning to Walter about white Christmases he used to know . . .

Was this a joke? A dig? Walter was afraid to look around him.

"Refill?" the waitress asked, poised above him with a steaming Pyrex pot.

"Uh, no, no thanks," Walter stammered, putting his hand over the cup for emphasis, "but, uh, maybe you could help me—?"

The waitress gave him a big lipsticky smile. "Yes? You looking for someone?"

"Maybe you don't know him. I mean, maybe he doesn't even live here any more. Truman Van Brunt?"

But for Bing Crosby, the place went quiet. The waitress' smile was gone. "What do you want with him?"

"I'm"—he couldn't say it, couldn't spit out the words—"I'm his son."

"His son? He never had a son. What are you talking about?"

Nothing could have prepared him for that moment. It hit him like a shove from behind, like something immovable along the side of the road. He was devastated. He wanted to dig a hole in the dirty linoleum at his feet and bury himself till the world slid closer to the sun and palm trees sprouted outside the window. *He never had a son.* For this he'd come four thousand miles.

The waitress' mouth was a tight slash of suspicion. The Eskimos were silent, watching him, the indifference in their eyes replaced all at once by a look of cruel amusement, as if now the fun were about to begin, as if Walter—big and white and with his dirty red hair and freakish eyes and feet that didn't work—had come to town as part of some sideshow. And Bing, Bing was going on with it, warbling about days being merry and bright—

"Hey, dude." The young Eskimo who'd tried to catch his eye earlier was standing beside him. Walter looked up into the broad smooth face and hesitant eyes of a kid of fourteen or so. "Mr. Van

Brunt, he lives up there," jerking his thumb, "third house on the left, got a old car broke down out front."

Numb, Walter rose to his feet, fought to tug a crumpled dollar from his pocket, and dropped it on the counter beside his cup. He was hot, burning up inside the heavy parka, and he felt lightheaded. He bent to pick up his suitcase, then turned back to the kid and ducked his head in acknowledgment. "Thanks," he said.

"Hey, no sweat, dude," the kid said, grinning to show off the blackened nubs of his teeth, "he's my teacher."

It was four in the afternoon and black as midnight. In two weeks the sun would set on Barrow for the final time—till January 23 of next year, that is. Walter had read about it in *A Guide to Alaska: Last American Frontier,* while he swatted mosquitoes in the lush backyard of his cottage in Van Wartville. Now he was here. On the steps of the Northern Lights Café, gazing up the dim street to where a '49 Buick sat up on blocks in front of an unremarkable, low-roofed shack no different from any of the others, except for the dearth of caribou carcasses frozen to the roof. His father's house. Here, in the far frozen hind end of nowhere.

Walter started across the street, the wind at his back, suitcase tugging at his arm. "Look out, asshole!" shouted a kamikaze on a snow machine as he shot past, engine screaming, treads churning up ice, and as Walter lurched out of the way he found himself in the middle of a pack of snarling dogs contending for a lump of offal frozen to the ice between his feet. Barrow. The sweat was freezing to his skin, his fingers were numb, and fourteen blood-crazed wolf dogs were tearing themselves to pieces at his feet. He'd been in town for something like half an hour and already he'd had it. In a sudden rage he struck out viciously at the dogs, swinging his suitcase like a mace and shouting curses till the wind sucked his voice away, and then he staggered up the berm of frozen garbage and dogshit that rose up like a prison wall in front of his father's house. Fifty yards. That's all it was from the café to his father's doorstep, but they were the hardest fifty yards of his life. *He never had a son.* Four thousand miles to hear that little bulletin from the lips of a stranger, a hag in a baggy sweater and two tons of makeup. God, that hurt. Even if he was hard, soulless and free.

Walter hesitated on the icy doorstep. He felt like some poor abused orphan out of a Dickens story—what was he going to say? What was he going to call him, even—Dad? Father? Pater? He was weary, dejected, chilled to the marrow. The wind screamed. There was something like slush caught in the corners of his eyes. And then suddenly it didn't matter—the son of a bitch never had a son anyway, right?—and Walter was pounding on the weather-bleached door for all he was worth. "Hey!" he bawled. "Open up! Anybody in there?" Boom, boom, boom. "Open up, goddammit!"

Nothing. No movement. No response. He might as well have been pounding on the door of his own tomb. His father didn't want him, he wasn't home, he didn't exist. Walter knew then that he was going to die right there on the doorstep, frozen hard like one of the grotesque carcasses on the roof next door. That would show him, he thought bitterly. His son, his only son, the son he'd denied and deserted, frozen on his doorstep like so much meat. And then, all at once, the rage and frustration and self-pity building in him till he couldn't help himself, he threw back his head and shrieked like an animal caught in a trap, all the trauma of a lifetime—all the ghosts and visions, the tearing of flesh and the wounds that never healed—all of it focused in the naked shattering plaint that rose from his belly to startle the wolf dogs and silence the wind: "Dad!" he sobbed. "Dad!" The wind choked him, the cold drove at him. "Daddy, Daddy, Daddy!"

It was then that the door fell back and there he was, Truman Van Brunt, blinking at the darkness, the ice, at Walter. "What?" he said. "What did you call me?"

"Dad," Walter said, and he wanted to fling his arms around him. He wanted to. He did. As much as he'd ever wanted anything. But he couldn't move.

Forty below. With wind. Truman stood there with the door open, still big, still vigorous, the deep red fangs of his hair shot through with dirty bolts of gray and beating furiously around his head, a look of absolute bewilderment on his face, as if he'd awakened from one dream to find himself in the midst of another. "Walter?" he said.

Inside, the place was meticulously tidy, almost monastic. Two rooms. Woodstove in the corner of the front one, bookshelves lining three walls, kitchenette against the other, a glimpse of a tightly made bed and night table in the back room, more books. The books had titles like *Agrarian Conflict: Van Wart and Livingston Manors; County Records, North Riding; Under Sail on Hudson's River; Folk Medicine of the Delaware; A History of the Indian Tribes of Hudson's River.* Up against the stove, so close it might have been kindling, was a desk piled high with papers and surmounted by the dark hump of a big black ancient typewriter. Under the desk, a case of Fleischmann's gin. There was no running water.

His father had filled two mugs with hot lemonade and gin before he could even get his parka off, and now Walter sat there in a patched easy chair, cradling the hot cup in his insensate hands and silently reading off book titles. Truman straddled a wooden chair opposite him. The stove snapped. Outside, there was the sound of the Arctic wind, persistent as static. Walter didn't know what to say. Here he was, at long last, face to face with his father, and he didn't know what to say.

"So you found me, huh?" Truman said finally. His voice was thick, slow with alcohol. He didn't exactly seem overjoyed.

"Uh-huh," Walter said after a moment, staring into his cup. "Didn't you get my letters?"

His father grunted. "Letters? Shit, yeah—I got your letters." He pushed himself up from the chair and lumbered into the back room, a big square-shouldered man with the sad vague air of a traveler lost in a city of strangers. There was nothing, absolutely nothing, wrong with his legs. Or feet. A moment later he thumped back into the room with a cardboard box and dropped it in Walter's lap.

Inside were the letters: Walter's hopeful script, the postmarks, the canceled stamps. There they were. Every one of them. And not a one had been opened.

He never had a son. Walter looked up from the box and into his father's glassy stare. They hadn't touched at the door, hadn't even shaken hands.

"How'd you know where to find me?" Truman asked suddenly.

"Piet. Piet told me."

"Pete? What do you mean 'Pete'? Pete who?" The old man wore a full beard, red as Eric the Conqueror's, gone gray now about the mouth. His hair was long, drawn back in a ponytail. He was scowling.

Walter felt the gin like antifreeze in his veins. "I forget his name.

A little guy—you know, your friend from all those years ago, when . . ." He didn't know how to put it. "Lola told me about him, about the riots and how—"

"You mean Piet Aukema? The dwarf?"

Walter nodded.

"Shit. I haven't seen him in twenty years—how the hell would he know where I was?"

Walter's stomach sank. He felt history squeezing him like a vise. "I met him in the hospital," he said, as if the fact would somehow corroborate his story. "He told me he just got a letter from you. From Barrow. Said you were teaching."

"Well, he's a goddamned liar!" Truman roared, lurching to his feet, his face puffed with sudden rage. He looked around him wildly, as if he were about to fling his cup against the wall or rip the stove up off the floor or something, but then he waved his hand in dismissal and sat down again. "Ah, piss on it," he murmured, and looked Walter hard in the eye. "Hey, I'm glad to see you anyway," he suddenly boomed, a bit too heartily, as if he were trying to convince himself. "You're a good-looking kid, you know that?"

Walter might have thrown it back at him—*What the hell do you know about it?*—and he would have been justified, too, but he didn't. Instead he gave him a shy smile and looked back down into his cup. It was the closest they'd come.

But then the old man surprised him again. "There's nothing wrong with you, is there—physically, I mean? You weren't limping when you walked in here or anything, were you?"

Walter's eyes leapt at him.

"I mean, it's none of my business. . . . I just . . . it's easy to get a touch of frostbite up here, you know." He shrugged his shoulders, then threw back his head to drain his cup.

"You mean you don't know?" Walter looked at him and saw the ghost ships, the dark lane opening up before him with its patches of ice clinging like scabs to the blacktop. He was incredulous. He was indignant. He was angry.

Truman looked uneasy. Now it was his turn to glance away. "How the hell would I know," he mumbled. "Listen, I'm sorry—I left all that behind. I haven't been much of a father, I admit. . . ."

"But, but what about that night—?" Walter couldn't finish, it was all a hallucination, of course it was, he'd known that all along. The man sitting before him now was a hallucination, a stranger, the vacant terminus of a hopeless quest.

"I told you I'm sorry, for christ's sake," Truman snapped, raising his voice. He pushed himself up from the chair and crossed the room to the stove. Walter watched him fill his cup from the kettle perched atop it. "Another toddy?" the old man peered at him over his shoulder, his voice softening.

Walter waved him off, then struggled to his feet. "All right,' he said, thinking, *the letters, the letters, he never even bothered to open them,* "I know you don't give two shits about me and I know you want to get this over with, so I'm going to tell you why I came all the way up here into the ass-end of nowhere to find you. I'm going to tell you everything, I'm going to tell you what it feels like to lose your feet—yes, both of them—and I'm going to tell you about Depeyster Van Wart." His heart was hammering. This was it. Finally. The end. "And then," he said, "I want some answers."

Truman shrugged. Grinned. Lifted his mug as if to offer a silent toast, and then drained it in a gulp. He brought the bottle of gin back to the chair with him, sat down and filled his cup, nothing to dilute it this time. His expression was strange—sheepish and belligerent at the same time, the look of the schoolyard bully hauled up in front of the principal. "So go ahead," he said, the gin at his lips, "tell me." He nodded at the door, the blackness, the unbroken tundra and the icy sea that lay beyond it. "We've got all night."

Walter told him. With a vengeance. Told him how, when he was twelve, he waited through the summer for him, and then waited again the next summer and the next. Told him how hurt he'd felt, how tainted and unwanted, how culpable. And how he got over it. Told him how Hesh and Lola had nurtured him, sent him to college, how he'd found a soft and sweet girl and married her. And then, when the first bottle was empty and the gin burned like acid in his veins, he told him of his visions, of the poison that infested him, of how he'd skewered Jessica with his bitterness and run up against the ghost of his father till his feet were ground to pulp. He talked, and Truman listened, till long after the sun should have set and the cows come home. But there were no cows. And there was no sun.

Walter was disoriented. He peered through the iced-over window and saw the deep of night. He hadn't eaten in god knew how many hours and the drink was getting to him. He fell heavily into the chair and glanced up at his father. Truman was slouched over, his head lolling sloppily on the prop of his hand, his eyes weary and red. And it came to Walter then that they were sparring, that was all, and that for all the exhilaration he'd felt in laying out his wrongs, it was only the first round.

"Dad?" he said, and the word felt strange on his tongue. "You awake?"

The old man lurched up as if from a bad dream. "Huh?" he said, instinctively feeling for the bottle. And then: "Oh. Oh, it's you." Outside, the wind held steady. Unforgiving, relentless, eternal. "All right," he said, rousing himself. "You've had it tough, I admit it. But think of me." He leaned forward, the massive shoulders and great brazen head. "Think of me," he whispered. "You think I live up here because it's a winter wonderland, the great vacation paradise, the Tahiti of the North or some shit? It's penance, Walter. Penance."

He rose, stretched, then shuffled back to reach under the desk and fish out another bottle. Walter watched him crack the seal with a practiced twist of his hand, pour out a full cup and then proffer the bottle. Walter was going to say no, going to lay his palm over the rim of the cup as he'd done in the café, but he didn't. This was a marathon, a contest, the title bout. He held out his cup.

"You get tired," Truman said, "you sleep over there, by the stove. I've got a sleeping bag, and you can take the cushions off the couch." He sat again, arching his back against the hard wooden slats of the chair. He took a long sip from the cup and then walked the chair across the floor till he was so close to Walter he might have been bandaging a wound. "Now," he said, his voice a hard harsh rumble of phlegm, "now you listen to *my* story."

Truman's Story

"No matter what they tell you, I loved her. I did."

The old man drained his cup, flung it aside and lifted the bottle to his lips. He didn't offer Walter any. "Your mother, I mean," he said, wiping his mouth with the back of his sleeve. "She was something. You probably don't remember her much, but she was so—what do you call it?—earnest, you know? Idealistic. She really bought all that Bolshevik crap, really thought Russia was the workers' paradise and Joe Stalin everybody's wise old uncle." There was a single lamp burning, brass stand, paper shade, on the desk behind him; the shadows softened his features. "She was like Major Barbara or something. I'd never met anybody like her."

Walter sat there transfixed, the rasping voice and the everlasting night holding him as if by spell or incantation. His mother, she of the soulful eyes, was right there before him. He could almost smell the potato pancakes.

"But you've been married, right? What was her name?"

"Jessica." The name was an ache. Jessica and his mother.

"Right," the old man said, his voice gravelly and deep, ruined by drink and nights that never end. "Well, you know how it is, then—"

"No," Walter snapped, suddenly belligerent. "How is it?"

"I mean, once the first glow dies and all that—"

Walter jumped on him. "You mean you screwed her over. From the beginning. You married her so you could destroy her." He tried to get up, but his feet were numb. "Sure I remember her. I remember her dead too. And I remember the day you left her—in that car out there, right? Depeyster Van Wart's car, isn't it?"

"Bullshit, Walter. Bullshit. You remember what Hesh taught you to remember." The old man's voice was steady—he wasn't debating, he was narrating. The pain of it, the pain that made him hide out in the hind end of the world, was up on a shelf in a little bottle with a tight cap. Like smelling salts. "Don't give me that self-righteous look, you little shit—you want to know hurt, you listen to me. I did it. Yes. I'm a fink, I'm a backstabber. I murdered my wife, set up my friends. That's right, I'll tell you that right off. So don't argue with me, you little son of a bitch. Just listen."

The temperature had gone up high under the old man's voice, and for the second time in as many hours he looked as if he were about to lurch up and tear the place apart. Walter sat frozen, so close he could smell the stink of the gin on his father's breath. "If you want to get beyond all that, I mean. And you do, right? Or you wouldn't have come all the way up here."

Numb, Walter nodded.

"Okay," the old man said, "okay," and the calm had returned to his voice. He was wearing mukluks and a bulky wool sweater with reindeer dancing across the front of it, and when he leaned forward, his hair and beard touched with gray, he looked like some scored and haunted figure out of an old Bergman movie, the pale oracle of the north. "Let me start at the beginning," he said, "with Depeyster."

Truman had met him in England during the war—they were both G2, Army Intelligence, and they'd struck an immediate chord on discovering they both hailed from the Peterskill area. Depeyster was a smart guy, good-looking, tough—and a pretty good ball player too. Basketball, that is. They shot some hoop with a couple of other guys once in a while when they were off duty. But then Depeyster got another assignment and they drifted apart. The important thing was that Truman met Christina—and married her—before he ever laid eyes on Depeyster Van Wart again. And that was the truth.

"But you joined the party," Walter said, "—I mean, that's what Lola—"

"Oh, fuck," Truman spat, a savage crease cut into his forehead. He pushed himself up from the chair and paced the little room. Outside, the wolf dogs set up a howl. "Yeah. Okay. I joined the party. But maybe it was because I was in love with your mother, ever think of that? Maybe it was because she had some influence over me and maybe because, in a way, I wanted to believe that happy horseshit about the oppressed worker and the greed of the capitalists and all the rest of it—hey, my father was a fisherman, you know. But who was right, huh? Khrushchev comes along and denounces Stalin and everybody in the Colony shits blood. You got to put things in perspective, Walter." He paused at his desk, picked up a sheaf of paper covered in a close black typescript, then set it down again. Instead he shook a cigarette—a Camel—from the pack that lay beside it, and raised a lighter to it. Walter could see that his hands were shaking, for all his bravado.

"So then, what—we're married a year, two years—and Depeyster comes back into the picture. *After,* Walter," he said, something like a plea in his eyes for the first time, "*after* I met your mother and married her, I run into him in the store at Cats' Corners out there, we're going on a picnic, your mother and me and Hesh and Lola, and I stop in for a beer and pack of smokes on a Sunday afternoon, and there he is." He paused, took another drink from the neck of the bottle. "There's a lot of factors here, things you know nothing about. Don't be so quick to judge."

Walter found that he was gripping the arms of the chair as if he were afraid he would topple out of it, as if he were high up on a Ferris wheel in a wind like the wind outside the door. "I told you," he said, "I work for him. He's all right. Really, he is. He says Hesh and Lola are wrong. Says you're a patriot."

Truman let out a bitter laugh, the pale swampy green of his eyes obscured in smoke, the massive torso swaying ever so slightly with the effect of the alcohol and maybe the emotional charge too. "Patriot," he repeated, his face contorted as if he'd bitten into something rotten. "Patriot," he spat, and then he stretched himself out on the floor in front of the stove and fell asleep, the lit cigarette still jammed between his fingers.

In the morning—if you could call it morning—the old man was guarded, frazzled, hung over and furious, as communicative as a stone. At some point, deep in the folds of that interminable night, Walter had heard him stagger up from the floor, pour himself a drink and dial the phone. "I'm not coming in today," he growled into the receiver. There was a pause. "Yeah, that's right. I'm sick." Another pause. "Let 'em read the Constitution—better yet, have them copy it out." Click.

Now it was light—or rather there was a noticeable softening of the darkness that pressed up against the windows—and there was a smell of bacon, strong as life, mixed in with a subtler smell, a mnemonic smell, a cruel and heartless smell: potato pancakes. Walter lurched up out of the sleeping bag as if it were on fire, living flesh in a house of ghosts. The dogs howled. It must have been about noon.

Truman served him bacon, eggs over easy, potato pancakes—"Like your mother used to make," he said out of a pouchy, expressionless face, and then he said nothing more till the sun flickered out an hour later. "Gone dark," he said suddenly out of the silence. "Cocktail hour," he said with a sloppy grin. "Story time."

There was more gin. Endless gin. Gin that flowed like blood from the gashes under a middleweight's eyes. Not yet two in the afternoon and Walter was reeling. Slouched in the easy chair, his limbs gone plastic and light, so light they seemed detached from his body, Walter cradled a glass of industrial-strength gin and listened to his father tell out history like an Indian *sachem* telling out beads.

"Depeyster," the old man rumbled by way of introduction, "I was talking about Depeyster Van Wart, wasn't I?"

Walter nodded. This is what he'd come to hear.

Truman ducked his head, stuck a thick finger in his drink—gin and gin—and sucked it. "Maybe I misled you a little last night," he said. "About that day when I ran into him at the store. It was an accident on my part, I swear it was, but not on his. No. Nothing he ever does is by accident."

Walter fought down his fear, his anger, fought down the urge to challenge him, and sank deeper into the chair, sipping gin that tasted like cleaning fluid, while the old man went on.

It was funny, he said, the way Depeyster suddenly came back into his life. After that day at Cats' Corners, he began to see more and more of him, even as he fell into the routine of Colony life, attending the lectures and concerts, even as he joined the association and then the party. Depeyster was everywhere. He was getting a new muffler at Skip's garage when Truman took the car in for shocks and brake pads, he was hunkered over a drink at the Yorktown Tavern when Truman stopped in with one of the guys after work, he was in Genung's buying drapes, at Offenbacher's with a bag of kaiser rolls. He was everywhere. But especially, he was on the train.

Two days a week, when the 4:30 whistle blew at the plant, Truman picked up his lunchbox, pulled an old army rucksack out from under the iron work bench and walked the six blocks down to the train station. He was studying American history at City College, studying sociology, transcendentalism, American labor movements, the causes and effects of the War of Independence, and he chewed a sandwich, sipped coffee and read his texts on the seventy-five-minute ride into New York. One evening he looked up from his books and there was Depeyster, tanned and easy, in a business suit and with a briefcase under his arm. He had business in town, he said, though what sort of business he might have had at six o'clock at night Truman never thought to ask.

After that, Truman saw him frequently on the train, sometimes alone, sometines in the company of LeClerc Outhouse. They made a good group. Van Wart, of course, came from the old family, and he was a real repository of local history, not to mention a Yale B.A., class of '40. LeClerc collected artifacts from the Revolutionary War, most of which he'd dug up himself, and he knew more about the fight for New York than Truman's professor. They talked history, current events, they talked politics. LeClerc and Depeyster were hard-line Republicans, of course, Dewey men, and they saw Communists everywhere. In China, Korea, Turkey, in the incumbent's administration. And, of course, in Kitchawank Colony. Truman found himself in the position of defending the Left, defending Roosevelt and the New Deal, defending the Colony, his wife and father-in-law and Hesh and Lola. He didn't do very well at it.

And why not? Maybe because he was confused himself.

"What did you mean," Walter asked, interrupting him, "about Dipe never doing anything by accident? You mean he came after you? Purposely?"

The old man leaned back in that Essene chair, that hard untenable rack of a chair, and leveled a contemptuous look on him. "Don't be a jerk, Walter—of course he did. Some of those guys we knew in G2 stayed on after the war and wound up in some pretty high places. Depeyster kept in touch."

"So you were a spy," Walter said, and the emotion was gone from his voice.

Truman sat up, cleared his throat and turned his head to spit on the floor. For a long moment he fiddled with the rubber band that held his hair in place. "If you want to call it that," he said. "They convinced me. Made me see the light. Them and Piet."

"But—" Walter was defeated, his last hope a fading contrail in a leaden sky. The rumor was truth. His father was shit. "But how could you?" he insisted, angry in his defeat and loud in his anger. "I mean how could anybody convince you—words, how could words convince you—to, to screw over your friends, your own wife, your"—it still stuck in his throat—"your son?"

"I was right, that's how. I did what I did for a higher principle." The old man spoke as if he had no problem with it, as if it hadn't destroyed his life, taken his family, made him into a drunk and an exile. "There might have been people like Norman Thomas around, people like your mother, but there were also devious little shits like Sasha Freeman and Morton Blum, who set us all up, traitors and crazies like Greenglass, Rosenberg, Hiss, who just wanted to kill everything we had in this country—and they were right there in the Colony too. Still are."

"But your own wife—I mean, don't you have a conscience? How could you do it?"

The old man was silent a moment, regarding him fixedly over the lip of the bottle. When he spoke, his voice was so soft Walter could barely hear him: "How could you?"

"What? What do you mean?"

"Your wife—what's her name?"

"Jessica."

"Jessica. You lost it with her, didn't you? You fucked her over, didn't you? And for some reason you can't even name." Truman's voice came on again, caustic, harsh, a snarl that overrode the wind. "And what about Depeyster Van Wart—'Dipe,' as you call him. He's your man now, isn't he? Screw Hesh. Fuck the old man. Dipe's the one. He's more your father than I am."

The old man's eyes were bright with malice. "Walter," he whispered. "Hey, Walter: you're already halfway there."

Walter suddenly felt weak, terminally exhausted, felt as if he were going down for the count. It was all he could do to rise shakily from the chair. "Bathroom," he murmured, and staggered toward the back room. He tried to walk tall, tried to throw back his shoulders and tough it out, but he hadn't gone five steps before his feet got tangled and he slammed into the doorframe.

Bang. End of Round Two.

For a long while Walter knelt over a bucket in the frigid closet that served the old man for a bathroom, his insides heaving, the sweet-sour stench of his own guts overpowering him. There was another smell there too, the smell of his father, of his father's shit, and it made his stomach clench again and again. His father's shit. Shit in a bucket. Christina and Jessica. Truman and Walter.

There was a barrel of water in the kitchenette. Walter cupped his hands and splashed some on his face. He put his mouth to the tap and drank. Outside, the night went on. The old man, rock-still in his chair, meditatively sipped his drink. Walter shivered. The place was cold, though Truman had stoked the stove with coal till the iron door glowed on its hinges. Walter crossed the room, picked his parka up from the floor and shrugged into it.

"Going someplace?" the old man said, faintly mocking.

Walter didn't answer. He plucked his cup from the arm of the chair and held it out for the old man to fill, glaring so hard Truman had to look away. Then he shook a Camel from the old man's pack, lit it and settled back in the chair. It would go three rounds, he could see that now. Then he could take the plane back to Van Wartville and he'd be free of his ghosts forever—*Father? What father? He never had a father*—damaged, but free. There was another possibility, of course. That the old man would triumph. Lay him out. Crush him. And then he'd board that plane with his tail between his legs and go on home to a life scrambled like a plate of eggs, pursued and haunted till he died.

"You'd do it again," Walter said finally, jabbing, probing, "you were right, a patriot, and my mother, Hesh and Lola, Paul Robeson himself, they were the traitors."

Truman brooded over the bottle. He said nothing.

"They got what was coming to them, right?"

Silence. The wind. The snow machines. Muffled shouts. Dogs.

"The children too. I could have been there that day, your own son. What about the children playing in front of the stage—did they deserve it too? Do patriots beat the shit out of Communists' children? Do they?" Walter was reviving, coming alive again, so hot for the fight he forgot which side he was on. Let him refute that, he thought. Let him convince me. And then I can rest.

Truman rose with a sigh, stirred his drink vaguely and then crossed the room to where his own coat—animal skin, just like the Eskimos'—hung from a peg. He took down the hat that hung above it, a Sergeant-Preston-of-the-Yukon sort of affair, leather and fur, with earflaps pinned up like wings, and dropped it on his head. He circled the chair twice, as if reluctant to sit, and then, mashing the hat down low over his eyes, he eased himself down again. "You want black-and-white," he sighed. "Good guys and bad guys. You want simple."

" 'I was right,' you said. 'I loved her,' you said. So which was it?"

The old man ignored the question. Then he looked up suddenly and held Walter's eyes. "I didn't know she was going to die, Walter. It was a divorce, you know, that's how I saw it. Happens every day."

"You twisted the knife," Walter said.

"I was young, confused. Like you. We didn't shack up in those days, you know, we got married. I loved her. I loved Marx and Engels and the Socialist revolution. Three and a half years, Walter—it's a long time. It can be, anyway. I changed, all right? Is that a crime? Like you, like you, Walter.

"Your mother was a saint, yeah. Selfless. Good. Righteous. Those eyes of her. But maybe too good, too pure, you know what I mean? Maybe she made me feel like shit in comparison, made me feel like hurting her—just a little, maybe. Like your Jessica, right? Am I right? Goody-good?"

"You're a son of a bitch," Walter said.

Truman smiled. "So are you."

There was a silence. Then Truman went on. He'd been wrong to hurt her so deeply, he said, he knew it, and this life was his penance, this talk his act of contrition. He should have just left, got out. He should have warned her. But for a year and a half he'd been meeting secretly with Depeyster, LeClerc and the others—vets, like himself—and he'd fed them information. It was no big deal—minutes of the association, who said what at party meetings—nothing, really, and he didn't take a cent for it. Didn't want it. He'd turned around, one hundred eighty degrees, and he believed in his heart that he was right.

Sure it hurt him. He drank more, stayed away from the house, looked into Christina's martyred eyes and felt like a criminal, like shit, like the two-faced Judas he was. "But you know, Walter," he said, "sometimes it feels good to feel like shit, you know what I mean? It's a need, almost. Something in the blood."

The week that preceded the concert was the worst of his life. The end was coming and he knew it. He was out every night, drunk. Piet was with him then, and that helped. Piet was there with a joke, with an arm around the shoulder. Funny little guy. "What should I do, Piet?" Truman asked him. "Do it," Piet said. "Stick it to 'em. Jews, Commies, niggers. The world's gone rotten like an apple." There was money this time. Money to get away and start over, sort things out. Someplace. Anyplace. Barrow, even. He wasn't supposed to take the car—permanently, that is. But when it was all over, he hated Depeyster more than he hated Sasha Freeman and the Worldwide Communist Conspiracy. For making him hate himself. So he kept it. Drove the shit out of it. Seven, eight years, up here and back. Till it gave out. Till there was no reason to go back.

The funny thing was, it was all in vain.

Sasha Freeman and Morton Blum and whoever controlled them were one step ahead of Depeyster all along. "You want to talk expediency," Truman growled, "you want to talk cynicism, Freeman and Blum, those sons of bitches had a corner on the market."

Truman was supposed to let the boys in at some point so they could break things up—really tan the asses of Robeson and Connell and all the rest of the nigger lovers, teach them a lesson they'd never forget: *Wake Up, America: Peterskill Did!* That's how Depeyster saw it. That was the plan. Truman would help the cause and he'd get a thousand dollars to bail himself out of his life and start someplace else. But it all backfired, of course. If Sasha Freeman had been there he would have let the animals in himself. Gladly. It was his idea all along to stir thing up till they were good and hot, work in a little slaughter of the innocents with some broken bones and bloody noses thrown in for good measure and get a bunch of pictures of women in blood-stained skirts into the newspapers. And if some poor coon got lynched, so much the better. A peaceful sing-along? What the hell good was that?

"You tell me, Walter," the old man said, leaning into him, "who the bad guys were."

Walter had no answer. He looked away from his father's eyes, and then back again.

Truman was fingering his right ear. The lobe was deformed, shriveled back on itself like the inner fold of a sun-dried apricot. Walter knew that ear well. Shrapnel, the old man had said when he took Walter down to the trestle to catch crabs, Walter eight, nine, ten years old. "That's how this happened," Truman said suddenly, no act of contrition if not entire, if not heartfelt and complete.

"You always told me it was the war."

The old man shook his head. "That night. It's my Judas mark. The weirdest thing, too." His eyes were squinted against the smoke of his fiftieth Camel, his face struck with something like wonder. Or puzzlement. "It was over and we were gone, Piet and me, out of the mob and up one of those back roads to where we'd left the car, when this maniac comes flying out of the bushes and takes me down from behind. I'm pretty strong in those days, pretty big. This guy is bigger. He doesn't say a word, just starts beating the shit out of me—trying to kill me. And I mean kill. Weirdest thing . . ."

"Yeah?" Walter prompted.

"He was an Indian. Like you see on TV—or out in New Mexico." Pause. "Or out the window here. Stank like a septic tank, greased up, feathers in his hair, the whole schmeer. He would have killed me, Walter—and maybe he should of—except for Piet. Piet got him off me. Stabbed him with his penknife. Then a bunch of guys jumped on him, five or six or more, I don't know. But the guy wanted me—just me—and I'll never know why. They had his hands, so he bit me. Like an animal. He went down, Walter, and he took a piece of me with him."

Walter leaned back in the chair. He knew it all now, the fight was over, and where had it got him? His father was nothing, neither hero nor criminal, he was just a man, weak, venal, confused, impaled on the past, wounded beyond any hope of recovery. But so what? What did it mean? The imp. Piet. The waking nightmares and the hallucinations, a life lived out on feet that were dead, the marker, Tom Crane, Jessica. *You're already halfway there,* the old man had said. Was that it? Following in his father's footsteps? History come home to roost?

"Crazy, huh?" the old man said.

"What?"

"My ear. The Indian."

Walter nodded absently. And then, as if correcting for that nod, he snarled, "Tell you the truth, who cares? I don't want to know about some crazy Indian biting your ear, I want to know why, why you did it." Walter pushed himself up from the chair and he could feel his face twisting toward some explosive show of emotion, tears or rage or desperation. "The whole thing—Piet, Depeyster, you were confused—it's all just excuses. Words. Facts." He found to his surprise that he was shouting. "I want to know why, why in your heart, why. You hear me: why?"

The old man's face was cold, implacable, hard as stone. Suddenly Walter felt frightened, felt he'd gone too far—over the edge and into the abyss. He took a step back as his father, exuding gin from his very pores and with the savage skin hat raked down over eyes that shone with malice, rose from his chair to deliver one final blow, the knockout punch.

No, Walter thought, it isn't over yet.

"You're a real masochist, kid," Truman hissed. "You want it all, don't you? And you push till you get it. Okay," he said, turning his back on him and lumbering toward the big oak desk that dominated the room.

"This is it," he said, looking over his shoulder and hefting a manuscript, and in that moment he looked just as Walter had pictured him in his waking dreams; in that moment he was the ghost on the ship, the joker in the hospital room, the annihilator on the motorcycle. Walter felt something seize him then, something that would never let go. It was tightening its grip, yes, he could feel it, terrible and familiar, when the old man turned on him again. "Walter," he said, "you listening?"

He couldn't speak. There were pine needles in his throat, wads of fur. He was mute, he was gagging.

"So you're into Colonial history, huh? Done a little reading, huh? About Peterskill?" The words dangled like a hangman's noose. "What I want to ask you is this: you ever run across a reference to Cadwallader Crane?"

He was dead. He knew it.

"Or maybe Jeremy Mohonk?"

Gallows Hill

THE MANUSCRIPT lay in his lap, dead weight. It was massive, ponderous, like the Sunday *Times* on Labor Day weekend, like a Russian novel, like the Bible. Six inches high, typed space and a half on legal-sized sheets, better than a thousand pages. Walter glanced at the title page in stupefaction: *Colonial Shame: Betrayal and Death in Van Wartville, the First Revolt,* by Truman H. Van Brunt. Was this it? Was this why he'd destroyed his wife, deserted his son and hid himself so far out on the frozen tip of the continent even the polar bears couldn't find him?

Betrayal and death. Colonial shame. He was crazy as a loon.

Fighting back his dread, Walter thumbed through the pages, read over the title again with a slow studied movement of his lips. It was only words, only history. What was he afraid of? Cadwallader Crane. Jeremy Mohonk. A marker along the side of the road—passed it by a thousand times. He'd never even bothered to read it.

But Truman had.

At the moment Truman was in the kitchenette, his back to Walter, spreading butter and Gulden's mustard on slices of white bread. He had about him an air of unconcern, as if showing his alienated son the work of his mad wasted life was an everyday occurrence, but Walter could see from the way he too briskly lathered the bread and then clumsily poured himself a tall gin and lemonade that he was wrought up. The old man suddenly darted a glance over his shoulder. "Hungry?" he asked.

"No," Walter answered, his stomach still clenched in anticipation of some terrible withering revelation, his father the phantom come to life, the book of the dead spread open in his lap. "No, I don't think so."

"Sure? I'm making sandwiches—spam and onions." He held up an onion as if it were a jar of beluga caviar or pickled truffles. "You're going to need something on your stomach."

Was this a threat? A warning?

"No," Walter said, "thank you, no," and he flipped back the page and began to read:

> Feudalism in the U.S.A., land of the free, home of the brave, the few over the many, lords and ladies set up over the common people, English corruption (and Dutch before it) throttling American innocence. Hard to believe? Think back to a time before the Revolution (the bourgeois revolution of 1777, that is), when patroons and manor lords reared their ugly heads over Negro slaves, indentured servants and tenant farmers who could not even be sure of passing on the fruit of their labors to their own children. . . .

This was the introduction—thirty-five, forty, fifty pages of it. Van Wartville. 1693. An uprising. A revolt against Stephanus Rombout Van Wart, First Lord of the Manor. Walter tried to scan it, plowing through, looking for the meat, the essence, the key, but there was too much of it, the whole mad tome nothing more than a sustained rant. He flipped to the last page of the introduction:

> . . . and it looked forward to a time not so long ago when an unchecked populace ran amok on that very same hallowed ground and those who would undermine our precious democracy nearly held sway. We refer, of course, to the Peterskill (more properly, Van Wartville) Riots of 1949, the treatment of which, in their fatal connection to that first doomed revolt, will occupy the later chapters of this work. . . .

Was that it? The old man manipulating history to justify himself? He skipped to the bottom of the page:

> We purpose here to examine a truth that resides in the blood, a shame that leaps over generations, an ignominy and infamy that lives on in spirit, though no text dares to present it. We, in this history, are the first to—

"Pretty fascinating, huh?" The old man was hovering over him, drink in one hand, an indented sandwich in the other.

Walter looked up warily. "Jeremy Mohonk. Cadwallader Crane. Where are they?"

"They're in there," Truman said, waving his sandwich at the mountain of paper, "they get hung. But you knew that already. What you want to know is how. And why." He paused to address the sandwich, and then, easing himself back down on the chair, he said, in a kind of sigh, "First public execution on the Van Wartville books."

Walter was indignant. "You mean you expect me to read this—all of it?" The weight of it alone was putting him through the floor. He couldn't read ten pages of it, not if it promised eternal life, revealed the secret names of God and gave him his feet back. Suddenly he felt tired, immeasurably weary. The sky was black. How long had he been here? What time was it?

"No," Truman said after a while, "I don't expect you to read it. Not now, anyway." He paused to lick a smear of mustard from the corner of his mouth. "But you wanted answers and I'm going to give them to you. Twenty years I been working on this book," and he leaned over to tap the manuscript with a thick proprietary finger, "and you can sit home in Peterskill and read it when it's published. But now, since you asked—since you especially asked—I'm going to tell you what it's about. All of it. No stone unturned." There was a grin on his face, but it wasn't a comforting grin—more like the smirk of the torturer as he applies the hot iron. "And I'm going to tell you what it means to both of us, Walter, you and me both.

"Hey," he said, reaching out that same hand to take Walter by the arm, the affectionate squeeze, first bodily contact between them, "we are father and son, right?"

The old man had edged the chair closer. His voice was the only thing in the room, and the room was the only place in the universe. There was no longer any sound of dogs—not so much as a whimper. The snow machines had fallen silent. Even the wind seemed to have lost its breath. Uneasy, wishing he'd let it go, Walter sat rigid in his chair, submitting himself to his father's harsh rasping voice as to a dose of bitter medicine.

It was the fall of 1693. A time before historical markers, Norton Commandos, Nehru shirts and supermarkets, a time so distant only the reach of history could touch it. Wouter Van Brunt, ancestor of a legion of Van Brunts to come, was getting ready to take his wagon down to the upper house to settle his quitrent and enjoy a day of dancing and feasting. He was twenty-five years old and he'd buried his father a year ago to the day. In the back of the wagon there were two fathoms of split firewood, two bushels of hulled wheat, four fat pullets and twenty-five pounds of butter in clay crocks. The five hundred guilders—or rather, its equivalent in English pounds—had already been paid out at Van Wart's mill in value of wheat, barley, rye and peas for sale downriver. Wouter's mother would ride beside him in the wagon. His brother Staats, who worked the farm with him, would walk, as would his sisters Agatha and Gertruyd, now eighteen and sixteen respectively, and as pretty-footed and nubile as any girls in the county. Brother Harmanus was no longer living at home, having left one morning before light to seek his fortune in the great burgeoning metropolis of New York, a city of some 10,000 souls. Sister Geesje was dead.

Cadwallader Crane was also planning to attend the festivities, though he wouldn't be paying his rent. Things had gone sour on him since Geesje's death, and he just didn't have it. The butter he was able to churn had turned rancid (and in any case it was closer to five pounds than twenty-five), some mysterious agent of the wild had got into his henhouse and carried off the lot of his poultry, and his fields, broken by his doleful plow and seeded by his lugubrious hand, hadn't yielded enough to bother taking to the mill. Of cash, he had none. But firewood! Firewood he'd cut and delivered with a vengeance. Six, eight, ten fathoms, he'd filled the young lord's woodshed to the top of its canted ceiling and then built a tower of wood beside it that could have warmed all the hearths of Van Wartville right on through the winter and into the blaze of July.

What he was hoping, as he loped down the road from his farm on the birdlike sticks of his legs, was that the plethora of his firewood might make up for his dearth of coin and the inadequacy of his produce. His heart was like a stone, of course, and he wore a suit of black clothes, as befits a widower in mourning, and he was determined not to enjoy himself. He wouldn't lift his eyes to admire the way the petticoats peeked out from beneath the skirts of Salvation Oothouse (née Brown), nor gaze on the resplendent face and figure of Saskia Van Wart either, if she was there. No, he would just take his long face up to the refreshment table—keeping an eye out for old Ter Dingas Bosyn and his damnable accounts ledger—and drink up Van Wart's wine and gorge on Van Wart's food till he swelled up like a garter snake with a whole family of frogs inside.

As for Jeremy Mohonk, the third principal player in the mortal drama about to unfold, he didn't pay rent, hadn't ever paid rent and never would. He lived on a seedy corner of his late uncle's farm amid a tangle of pumpkin vines and corn stalks, in the bark hut he'd erected on a cold winter's day back in '81, and he claimed that corner as ancestral land. He was a Kitchawank, after all, or half a one, and he was married to a Weckquaesgeek woman. A woman who'd borne him three sons and three daughters, of whom, unfortunately, only the first son and last daughter had survived infancy. On this particular day—November 15, 1693, the day of Van Wart's first annual harvest feast—he was sitting before the fire in his hut, smoking *kinnikinnick* and carefully stripping the skin from his winter bear, a great fat sow he'd shot practically on the doorstep when he went out to make his morning water. He smoked and plied his quick sharp knife. His wife, whatever her name was, busied herself over a pot of corn mush, the smell of which touched the pit of his belly with tiny fingers of anticipation. He was content. For the Van Warts and their party, he had about as much use as he had for words.

Wouter and his mother were among the first to arrive at the upper house, where long plank tables had been set up in the yard around a great deep pit of coals, into which a pair of spitted suckling pigs dripped their sweet combustible juices. Five huge covered pots—of olipotrigo, pea and prune soup flavored with ginger, minced ox tongue with green apples and other aromatic delicacies—crouched around the pigs as if standing watch. The tables were heaped with corn, cabbage, pumpkin and squash, and there were kegs of wine, beer and cider. "Very nice," Neeltje admitted as her son helped her down from the wagon and her daughters joined her to compose themselves for their grand entrance, such as it was.

The day was overcast and cold, hardly the sort of day for an outdoor gathering, but the patroon—or rather, lord of the manor, as he was now called—had decided to make a grand public occasion of the paying of the rents, rather than the private and often onerous affair it had been for so many years. He would give back his tenants a small portion of what they gave him, he reasoned, and it would help keep them happy with their lot—and besides, it would save him the time and trouble of sending his agent around to collect. And so, no matter that the sky looked as if it had been dredged up from the bottom of the river and it was cold enough to put a crust on a flagon of cider left out to stand, there would be fiddling, merrymaking and feasting at both upper and lower houses on this august day.

Nor was this the only innovation. Since the summer, when William and Mary, acting through the offices of their Royal Governor, had chartered Van Wart Manor and consolidated all Stephanus' patent purchases with the original estate left him by his father, several other changes had come to Van Wartville as well. There was the alteration of the place name, the Dutch "wyck" subsumed in the English "ville." A millpond was created and a sawmill erected upstream from the gristmill. Three new farms were cleared and tenanted by red-nosed, horse-toothed, Yankee religious fanatics. And finally, most surprising of all, Van Wart evicted his cousin Adriaen from the upper house, replacing him with his own eldest son, Rombout. Adriaen, like Gerrit de Vries before him, had been sent packing without so much as a thank you, and this provoked a storm of unfavorable comment among the tenants and their sharp-tongued wives. Sluggish, inoffensive, perhaps even a little soft in the head, Adriaen had been well-liked. Rombout, on the other hand, was like his father.

At any rate, by three in the afternoon, the entire community had gathered at the upper house to unload their wagons, fill their bellies with the patroon's good port, smoke their long pipes and dance, flirt, gossip and drink till long after the sun faded in the west. There were Sturdivants, Lents, Robideaus, Mussers, van der Meulens, Cranes,

Oothouses, Ten Haers and Van Brunts, as well as the three new families, with their pinched and stingy faces and sackcloth clothes, and the odd Strang or Brown wandered up from Pieterse's Kill. Jan Pieterse himself turned out, though he was older now than Methuselah, fat as four hogs and deaf as a post, and Saskia Van Wart, still unmarried at the advanced age of twenty-four, came down from the parlor, where she'd been visiting with her brother, to dance a spirited galliard with her latest suitor, a puny English fop in canions and leather pumps. And throughout the day, old Ter Dingas Bosyn, who was older even than Jan Pieterse—so old he'd lost his fat and shriveled away till he was nothing more than a pair of hands and a head—sat in the lower kitchen, beside the fireplace, his accounts ledger spread open on the table before him and a coinbox at his side. One by one, the heads of the families bowed their way through the low door to stand before him and watch as his arthritic finger pinned their names to the page.

It was growing dark and the party was about to break up, when Pompey II, who'd been assisting the *commis* with his inventory, found Cadwallader Crane slumped over the olipotrigo pot and led him into old Bosyn's presence. Cadwallader, towering with drink and dilated like an anaconda with the patroon's food, belched twice and began to offer the withered *commis* a whole string of excuses for not having made his rent. He'd got past the death of Geesje and was unsuccessfully fighting back his tears while describing the lamentable and mysterious sacking of his henhouse, when he saw that the old man was holding up a shrunken monkeylike paw in a gesture of forbearance. "Enough," the *commis* rasped. Then he wheezed, sighed, studied his books a moment, took a pinch of snuff, sneezed into a silk handkerchief with some very pretty embroidery work along the border, and said: "No need for . . . *huffff*, excuses. The lord of the manor, seeing that you've lost your wife and have no . . . *hummmm*, issue, has decided to terminate your lease forthwith." The *commis* turned his head away quickly and spat or perhaps puked into the handkerchief with a prodigious dredging of his throat and trumpeting of his nose, after which he wiped his watering eyes on the sleeve of his jacket. "You have two days," he announced finally, "before the new tenants take over."

And then it was Wouter's turn.

Just as he was getting set to leave, lifting his mother and sisters into the now-empty wagon, his belly full and head light with cider and beer, he felt Pompey's deferential hand at his elbow. "Old Misser Bosyn, sir, he want a word with you."

Puzzled, wondering if somehow the old geezer had miscounted his produce or shortchanged him at the mill, he followed the slave into the warm and redolent kitchen. "I'm on my way out, Bosyn, got *moeder* and the girls waiting in the wagon," he said in Dutch. "What's the problem?"

The problem was that the lord of the manor was reviewing his leases with an eye to more profitable management. Wouter's farm, along with one other, had been reassigned.

"Reassigned?" Wouter echoed in astonishment.

The old man grunted. "The lease was in your father's name, not yours."

Wouter began to protest, but the words stuck in his throat.

"Two days," the *commis* croaked. "Take the increase of the stock over what *Mijnheer* allowed your father, pack up your personal belongings, if there be any such, and vacate the premises for the new tenants." He paused, drew a watch from his waistcoat pocket and consulted it, as if it could plot the course of those honest, hopeful, industrious newcomers. "They'll be here Tuesday noon. On the sloop up from New York.

"And oh yes," he added, "the Indian, or half-breed or whatever he is, he goes too."

Wouter was too thunderstruck to reply. He merely turned his back, ducked through the open door and climbed into the wagon. His mother and sisters were chattering about the party, about who danced with whom and did you see so-and-so in that ridiculous getup, but he didn't hear them. He was eleven years old, the boy who sat himself in the stocks, the boy who'd seen his father broken and humiliated and felt the shame of it beating like poison through his veins. The horses lifted their feet and set them down again, the wagon swayed and creaked, trees melted into darkness. "Is there anything the matter?" his mother asked. He shook his head.

He unhitched the wagon and stabled the horses in a state of shock. He hadn't said a word to his mother—or sisters—and his brother had stayed on at the party with John Robideau and some of the other young bucks. For all they knew, the world was still in its track, they'd acquitted themselves of their obligations to the landlord for another year and the farm at Nysen's Roost would go down through the generations from father to son. It was a joke, a bad joke. He was rubbing down the horses, barely able to control his hands for the rage building in them, when he heard the doorlatch behind him.

It was Cadwallader Crane. The widower, the naturalist, his sad and sorry brother-in-law. Cadwallader's coat and hat were dusted with the fine pellets of snow that had begun to sift down out of the pale night sky. His eyes were red. "I've been evicted," he said, his voice quavering. "From the farm my father . . . helped me . . . set up for, for"—he began to blubber—"for Geesje."

"I'll be damned," Wouter said, and he never guessed how prophetic the expression might prove.

Five minutes later they were in cousin Jeremy's hut, warming themselves over the fire and passing a bottle of Dutch courage. Wouter pressed the bottle to his lips, handed it to his brother-in-law and leaned forward to give Jeremy the bad news. Gesturing, pantomiming, running through a stock of facial expressions that would have made a thespian proud, he told him what the *commis* had said and what it meant for all of them. Jeremy's wife looked on solemnly, the baby in her arms. Young Jeremy, twelve years old now and with the eyes of a Van Brunt, quietly ran his fingers over the teeth of the bear his father had killed that morning. Jeremy said nothing. But then he hadn't said anything in fourteen years.

"I say we go back up there," Wouter took the bottle back and waved it like a weapon, "and let the scum know how we feel."

Cadwallader's eyes were muddy, his voice lost somewhere in the pit of his stomach. "Yeah," he wheezed, "yeah, let 'em know how we feel."

Wouter turned to his cousin. "Jeremy?"

Jeremy gave him a look that needed no interpretation.

Next thing they knew, they were standing on the lawn outside the upper house, gazing up at the parade of bright, candle-lit windows. The snow was falling harder now and they were thoroughly drunk—drunk beyond reason or responsibility. The party had long since broken up, but three hardy souls were still hunkered over the open fire, gnawing bones and making doubly sure the cider and beer kegs were properly drained. Wouter recognized his brother and John Robideau. Coming closer, he saw that the third member of the group was Tommy Sturdivant.

The three conspirators, who hadn't as yet decided what they were conspiring to do, joined the others around the fire. Someone threw on a few extra logs from the mountain of wood stacked around the patroon's woodshed, and their faces flared diabolically—or perhaps only drunkenly. The news—the shocking, heartless, arbitrary news—went around the little circle in the time it took the gin to make a single pass. Tommy Sturdivant said it was a damn shame. The flames leapt. John Robideau agreed. Staats, who was more directly affected, cursed the patroon and his mealy-mouthed son in a voice loud enough to be heard in the house. Wouter seconded his brother with an enraged whoop, the like of which hadn't been heard in the valley since the Indian hostilities of '45, and then—no one knew quite how it happened, least of all Wouter—the bottle left his hand, described a graceful parabola through the drift of the falling snow, and took out the leaded glass window in the parlor. This was immediately succeeded by a shriek from inside the house, and then a general uproar punctuated by cries of terror and confusion.

Pompey was the first out the door, followed closely by young Rombout and the English fop who'd been making love to Saskia. The fop lost his footing on the slick doorstep and went down on his overbite, and Pompey, recognizing the glitter of abandonment in the eyes of the little group around the fire, pulled up short. But Rombout, in his leather pumps and silk hose, came on. "Drunkards!" he screeched, slowing to what might have been a dignified, if hurried, walk if it weren't for the outrage jerking at his limbs. "I knew it, I knew it!" he exploded, stalking up to Wouter. "Nothing's good enough for you . . . you rabble. Now this, eh? Well, you'll pay, damn your hide, you'll pay!"

Rombout Van Wart was twenty-one years old and he wore his hair in ringlets. He wasn't old enough to grow a beard, and his voice had a hollow gargling catch to it, as if he were trying to speak and swallow a glass of water at the same time.

"We've already paid," Wouter said, gesturing with a sweep of his arm at the woodshed, the cellar, the henhouse.

"Yeah," Cadwallader jeered, suddenly interposing his long sallow face between them, "and we've come"—here he was interrupted by a fit of hiccoughs and had to pound his breastbone before he could recover himself—"we've come," he repeated, "to tell you and your father to go fuck yourselves." And then he stooped down, as calmly as if he were picking wildflowers or assaying the sinuous path of the earthworm, and plucked a fist-sized fragment of brick from the gathering snow. Straightening up, he let his gangling arm drop behind him, paused to give Rombout a look of drunken bravado and then heaved the brick through the upper bedroom window.

The English fop was just getting to his feet. Pompey had vanished in the shadows. A howl of outrage arose from the upper bedroom (with some satisfaction, Wouter recognized the bristling voice of old Ter Dingas Bosyn) and the faces of the women could be seen at the door.

Everything hung in the balance.

Worlds. Generations.

"You, you—" Rombout sputtered. Struck dumb by rage, he raised his hand as if to box the transgressor's impertinent ears, and Cadwallader shrank bank from the anticipated blow. The blow never came. For Jeremy Mohonk, his lank ancestral frame fleshed out with the solid Dutch brawn of the Van Brunts, struck him a stunning warrior's thump just over the left temple and laid him out cold. From then on, no one was quite sure what happened or how, though certain moments did tend to stand out.

There was Saskia's scream (or somebody's, some female's, that is. It might have come from Vrouw van Bilevelt or Rombout's young wife, or even, for that matter, from that aged and decrepit relic, Vrouw Van Wart. Somehow, though, Wouter liked to think of it as Saskia's scream). And under cover of that scream, there was the fop's judicious retreat, followed by the icy crash of the third and fourth windows. Then, too, there was the fire. Somehow it got away from the safe and cheery confines of the roasting pit and into the hayloft of the barn, a distance of perhaps two hundred feet. And, of course, given the hour and the meteorological conditions, there was the ensuing conflagration that climaxed with a roar of shattering timber. And finally, there was the long, cold night spent by a bitter and headachy Rombout, who gathered his family about him in the cellar of the windowless and snowswept house while the plaint of singed ungulates echoed in his throbbing ears.

By noon the following day, Stephanus himself was in Van Wartville, accompanied by his *schout*, the bellicose dwarf and a posse comitatus composed of eight baggy-breeched, pipe-puffing, weather-beaten farmers from Croton. To a man, the farmers were mounted on ponderous, thick-limbed plow horses and they were armed with scythes and mathooks, as if they were going haying rather than pursuing a dangerous and degraded lot of seditionists and barn burners. Most of them, owing to the season, had runny noses, and they all wore great floppy-brimmed elephantine hats that hid their faces, banished their heads and drooped down over their shoulders like parasols.

Stephanus posted a reward of one hundred English pounds for the capture of any of the malefactors, and instructed his carpenter to erect a gallows at the top of the ridge behind the house, a place ever after known as Gallows Hill. Within the hour, he had Tommy Sturdivant, John Robideau and Staats Van Brunt lined up in front of him and pleading their innocence. He gave them each five minutes to defend themselves, and then, with respect to the ancient rights of court baron and court leet invested in him by His Royal Majesty, King William III, he administered justice as he saw fit. Each was stripped to the waist and given twenty lashes and then ordered to sit in the stocks for three days, the foul weather notwithstanding. The gallows he reserved for the ringleaders: Crane, Mohonk and Wouter Van Brunt.

Unfortunately, that infamous trio was nowhere to be found. Though he searched the farms of both the elder and young Cranes, though he personally razed the half-breed's shack at Nysen's Roost and oversaw the eviction of Neeltje and her daughters, though he scoured the miserable stinking huts of the Weckquaesgeeks at Suycker Broodt and the Kitchawanks at Indian Point, Stephanus could discover no trace of them. After three days of boarding his troops at the upper house (true Dutch and Yankee trenchermen, for whom a side of venison was little more than an hors d'oeuvre), the first lord of the manor retired to Croton, leaving van den Post and the dwarf behind to pursue the search and see to the completion of the gallows and the construction of a new barn. The reward was raised to two hundred fifty pounds sterling, a sum for which half the farmers in the valley would have given up their own mothers.

The fugitives held out for nearly six weeks. Once the barn caught fire, they understood, drunk as they were, that things had gotten out of hand and that Van Wart and the jellyfish eater would pursue them to the ends of the earth. Staats, John Robideau and Tommy Sturdivant were guilty of nothing more than stamping their feet and shouting, but the others—Wouter, Jeremy and Cadwallader—were in deep. Wouter had started it all, Cadwallader had broken windows in full sight of everyone present and Jeremy had assaulted the eldest son of the lord of the manor. And then there was the more serious question of the fire. It wasn't Jeremy, it wasn't Cadwallader, it wasn't any of the three lesser offenders who'd carried the flaming brand into the barn: it was Wouter. Seized suddenly with the fury of his father, he'd snatched up the torch and raced across the yard like an Olympian to toss it high into the rafters of the barn. When it caught and the barn went up, when Wouter felt the madness rise to a crescendo in his chest and then fall again to nothing, he'd taken his brother by the sleeve and admonished him to go home and look after *moeder*. Then he rounded up Jeremy and Cadwallader and fled.

They hid themselves in a cave not half a mile from the scene of the crime, and there they lived like cavemen. They were cold. Hungry. Snowed in. They built meager fires for fear of detection, they ate acorns, chewed roots, trapped the occasional skunk or squirrel. They might have gone to Neeltje for help, but the dwarf kept a perpetual watch on the cramped hovel in Pieterse's Kill into which she'd moved with Staats and her daughters and Jeremy's wife and children. And then too there was van den Post to contend with. He was indefatigable—and mad with a thirst for revenge against Jeremy Mohonk, who'd escaped him once before. He'd found himself an Indian tracker to sniff them out, a fierce and mercenary Mohawk who wore a belt of scalps and would as soon cut a throat as squat down and relieve himself or skin a hare for supper. They had no choice but to lie low.

Jeremy brooded. Cadwallader hunched himself up like a praying mantis and sobbed for days on end. And Wouter—Wouter began to feel as he had on that terrible afternoon when he sat himself down in the stocks and dropped the crossbar on his own feet.

One night, when the others were asleep, he slipped out of the cave and made his way through the nagging branches and crusted snow to the upper house. He was wasted, his lungs ached with the cold and the clothes hung from him in tatters. The house was dark, the yard deserted. He saw that the windows had been replaced and that a crude unpainted and unroofed structure stood where the old barn had been. It was too dark to see the gallows on the hill.

He was thinking of his father as he knocked at the door, thinking of the fallen hero, the coward who'd been a traitor to his son and to himself too. He knocked again. Heard voices and movement from within and saw his father, mad and broken, lying beneath the cow in the barn. Rombout answered the door with a candle in one hand, a cocked pistol in the other.

"I want to turn myself in," Wouter said. He dropped to his knees. "I beg for your mercy."

Rombout shouted something over his shoulder. Wouter could detect movement in the background, a hurry and scuffle of feet, and then the pale face of the unattainable Saskia floated into view amidst the shadows. He dropped his eyes. "It was the half-breed," he said. "He set fire to the barn, he was the one. And Cadwallader too. They made me go along with them."

"On your feet," Rombout gargled, backing away from him with the gun. "Inside."

Wouter lifted his hands to show that they were empty. A gust of air fluttered his rags as he rose to his feet. "Spare me," he whispered, "and I'll lead you to them."

The execution took place on the first of January. The half-breed, Jeremy Mohonk, offered no defense when he came before the first lord of the manor to meet his accusers, and his co-defendant, Cadwallader Crane, was thought to be wandering in his mind. No one contradicted the testimony of Wouter Van Brunt.

In his wisdom, in his clemency and forbearance, the first lord of the manor waived the capital charges against Wouter Van Brunt. Van Brunt was lashed, branded for a criminal on the right side of his throat and banished forever from Van Wart lands. After wandering for some years he returned to live in Pieterse's Kill with his mother, where he took up the trade of fisherman, eventually married and had three sons. He died, after a long illness, at the age of seventy-three.

As for Jeremy Mohonk and Cadwallader Crane, they were convicted of high treason and armed rebellion against the authority of the Crown (the brick constituting, for Stephanus' purposes, a potentially lethal weapon—lethal, in any case, to manorial windows). Their sentence read as follows: "We decree that the Prisoners shall be drawn on a Hurdle to the Place for Execution, and then shall be hanged by the Neck, and then shall be cut down alive, and their Entrails and Privy members shall be cut from their Bodies, and shall be burned in their Sight, and their Heads shall be cut off, and their Bodies shall be divided into four Parts, and shall be disposed of at the King's Pleasure."

Whether or not it was fully complied with is not recorded.

When the old man had finished, the sky was growing light beyond the windows for the second time since Walter had arrived in Barrow. Mad—certainly, definitively and inarguably mad—Truman had dwelt obsessively on each smallest detail of his story, puffing and fulminating as if he were trying the case himself. Cadwallader Crane, Jeremy Mohonk. Walter knew it all now. Finally, he knew it all.

"You know what 'Wouter' translates to in English?" Truman asked him with a leer.

Walter shrugged. He was beaten. Down for the count and out.

" 'Walter,' that's what," the old man snarled as if it were a curse. "I named my own son after one of the biggest scumbags that ever lived—my ancestor, Walter, your ancestor—and I didn't even know it till I was a grown man in college, till I went to Professor Aaronson and told him I wanted to write about Van Wartville and the illustrious Van Brunts." He was on his feet now. Pacing. "Fate!" he shouted suddenly. "Doom! History! Don't you see?"

Walter didn't see, didn't want to see. "You can't be serious," he said. "You mean this is the big secret, this is why you screwed us all over—because of some forgotten shit that went down hundreds of years ago?" He was incredulous. He was enraged. He was frightened. "You're crazy," he murmured, trembling as he said it, the marker looming up on his right—Cadwallader Crane, Jeremy Mohonk—the pale green walls of the hospital closing in on him, Huysterkark with the plastic foot in his lap. . . .

Suddenly Walter was out of the chair, stuffing things into his suitcase, the door, the door, thinking only to run, to get away, fight himself out of the nightmare and start again, back in Peterskill, in Manhattan, Fiji, anywhere but here, anything but this. . . .

"What's the hurry?" Truman asked with a laugh. "You're not leaving already? All this way to see your dear old dad and you stay what, two days?"

"You're crazy!" Walter shouted. "Nuts. Apeshit." He was spitting out the words, out of control, the suitcase clutched tight in his hand. "I hate you," he said. "Die," he said.

He jerked open the door and the wind caught him by the throat. The sick pale light played off the torn ribs on the roof next door. His father stood there in the shadows of his box at the end of the world. He wasn't grinning, he wasn't jeering. He seemed small suddenly, tiny, shrunken, wasted, no bigger than a dwarf. "No use fighting it," he said.

The wind came up, the dogs went mad.

"It's in the blood, Walter. It's in the bones."

Hail, Arcadia!

SHE WAS one hundred and six feet long, from her taffrail to the tip of her carved bowsprit, and her mainmast—of Douglas fir, a towering single tree—rose one hundred and eight glorious feet above the deck. When the mainsail was raised, the jib flying and the topsail fluttering against the sky, she carried more sail than any other ship on the East Coast, better than four thousand square feet of it, and she plied the Sound or glided across the Hudson like a great silent vision out of the past.

Tom Crane loved her. Loved her unreservedly. Loved her right down to the burnished cleats on the caprail and the discolored frying pans that hung above the woodstove in the galley. He even somehow managed to love the cracked plastic buckets stationed beneath the wooden seats of the head. He swabbed the decks as they swayed beneath his feet, and loved them; he split wood for the stove and loved the cloven pieces, loved the hatchet, loved the hoary oak block with its ancient grid of gouges and scars. The sound of the wind in the sails made him rhapsodic, dizzy, as drunk with the pulse of the universe as Walt Whitman himself, and when he took hold of the smooth varnished grip of the tiller and the river tugged back at him like something alive, he felt a power he'd never known. And there was more, much more—he loved the cramped bunks, the dampness of his clothes when he slipped into them in the morning, the feel of the cold decks beneath his bare feet. And the smells too—of woodsmoke, salt air, rotting fish, the good rich human macrobiotic smell of the head, the incense of the new raw wood of the cabin, garlic frying in the galley, someone's open beer, clean laundry, dirty laundry, the funky sachet of life at sea.

It amazed him afresh every time he thought of it, but he was saint of the forest no longer. He was a seaman, a tar, a swab, Holy Man of the Hudson, no hermit but a communer with his mates, admired and appreciated for his clowning, his beard, the soft and soulful Blues harp he mouthed in his bunk at night, Jessica curled beside him. The *Arcadia*. It was a boon. A miracle. As amazing to Tom as the first Land Rover must have been to the aborigines of the Outback. Just think: a floating shack! A floating shack christened in and dedicated to all the great hippie ideals—to long hair and vegetarianism, astrology, the snail darter, Peace Now, satori, folk music and goat turd mulching. And, surreptitiously, to pot, hash and acid too. The original month aboard—September—had turned to two, and then Halloween came and went and it was November, and Tom Crane had risen through the ranks to the office of full-time second mate. Holy Man of the Hudson. He liked it. Liked the ring of it.

And the shack? The summer's crop? The goat? The bees? Well, he'd get back to them someday. For now, the exigencies of the seafaring life made it impossible to keep the place up, and so he'd padlocked the door, sold the goat, abandoned his late squash and pumpkins to the frost and left the bees to fend for themselves. Since the funeral, he and Jessica had quietly moved their things into his grandfather's roomy, gloomy, eighteenth-century farmhouse with all its gleaming appurtenances of modernity, with its dishwasher, its toaster, its TV, its paved driveway and carpeted halls. It all seemed a bit too—well, bourgeois—for him, but Jessica, with her frantic schedule, liked the convenience of it. She'd been accepted at N.Y.U. in marine biology, and what with the commute and her part-time job at Con Ed, she was running around like a madwoman. After the shack, she suddenly realized how much she liked running water, frost-free refrigerators, reading lamps and thermostats.

He knew he was being selfish, deserting her like that. But they'd discussed it, and she'd given him her blessing—everybody's got to do their own thing, after all. And it wasn't as if they didn't see each other—she joined him whenever she could, even if it was just to study a couple of hours in the main cabin or lie beside him and close her eyes as the river gently rocked the bunk. Besides, she'd soon have him back full-time—for the winter at least. It was mid-November, and this was the *Arcadia*'s last sail of the year. From now till April he'd be home every day, shuffling around in his grandfather's fur-lined slippers in the morning and whipping her up a batch of tofu-carrot delight in the electric skillet when she came in at night. Of course, Tom would gladly have stayed out all winter, breaking ice on the water barrel and beating his hands on the tiller to keep them from stiffening up—hell, he'd even hang an albatross around his neck if he thought it'd do any good—but the business of the *Arcadia* was to educate people about the river, and it was kind of hard to get their attention when the temperature dipped to nineteen degrees and the icy gray dishwater of the spume swatted them in the face with every dip of the bow. And so, they were on their way upriver to put into port at Poughkeepsie for the winter; two days hence, the ex-saint of the forest would bum a ride back to Van Wartville and drydock himself till spring in his grandfather's snug, oil-heated den.

But for now—for this thumping, glorious, wind-scoured moment—he was sailing. Beating upriver against a strong head wind, standing proud and runny-nosed at the helm while the captain, first mate and bosun sat around the coffeepot below. Jessica was below too, elbows braced on the big square dining table in the main cabin, boning up on the morphology of the polychaete worm as the pale silk of her hair fell forward to trickle over her ears and mask her face. He looked out over the gray chop of the river—not another boat in sight—and he looked down through the spattered glass and into the cabin. The deck moved beneath his feet. The captain drank coffee. Jessica studied.

They were just rounding Dunderberg and heading into the Race, Manitou Mountain and Anthony's Nose looming up on the right, Bear Mountain rising on the left. They'd left Haverstraw at noon, and were scheduled to dock at Garrison for the night. Normally, they'd be in within the hour, but the wind was steady in their faces and the tide was slack. There was no telling when they'd get there. Tom studied the sky, and saw that it looked bad. He sniffed the breeze and smelled snow. Shit, he thought, of all days.

But then he brightened. Snow or no snow, they *were* on their way to a party. Dockside at Garrison. And it couldn't start till they got there. Awash in light, he took in the mountains, the plane of the river, the soar and dip of the gulls, he filled his lungs, savored the spray. A party, he thought, working the image over in his mind until he could taste the food and hear the music. But it wasn't just another party, it was a foot-stomping, finger-waving, do-si-doing, year's end blowout for all the members and friends of the *Arcadia*, replete with a mini concert from the guru himself, Will Connell, and the Tucker, Tanner and Turner Bluegrass Band. They'd set up a big circus tent with electric heaters right down on the green, and there would be square dancing, there would be beer, a bonfire, hot food and hotter drinks. It was a big day. A great day. Her inaugural year was over, and the *Arcadia* was coming home to roost.

The sky darkened. The chop got rough. Sleet began to drive down, pins and needles whipped by the wind. And the wind—suddenly it was playing tricks, blowing steady across the bow one minute, puffing from the stern the next and then all at once shearing across the port side in a sudden gust that whipped the boom halfway around and nearly jerked the tiller from the numbed hands of the scrawny ex-saint. There were eight crew members aboard, and all eight of them—plus Jessica—got into the act before it was over.

With the first lurch of that great deadly boom, Barr Aiken, the *Arcadia*'s captain and a man for whom Tom would gladly plunge into raging seas or fight off the Coast Guard single-handed—just let him give the word—shot across the cabin and up the gangway like a hurdler coming out of the blocks. He called for all hands, relieved Tom at the helm and in half a minute had everybody scrambling to reef the sails. Thirty-five years old, a sallow and weather-beaten native of Seal Harbor, Maine, with a hangdog look and eyes that always focused in the distance, the captain was a man of few and soft-spoken words. He pronounced his name Baaaa, like a forlorn sheep.

Now, the wind dancing and the sleet in their teeth, he spoke so softly he might have been whispering, yet his every word was as distinct as if he'd been screaming to the roots of his hair. Down came the jib. The mainsail was reefed again. Everyone held on as he jibed and began tacking from point to point across the narrow neck of the

Race. It was business as usual, no problem, only a little more exciting maybe with the way the wind was kicking up. Tom almost fainted from happiness when the captain handed the tiller back to him.

"Must be the Imp," Barr observed, folding his arms and spreading his feet for balance. He spoke in his characteristic whisper, and there was something like a smile hovering around the lower part of his face.

Tom looked around him. The mountains were shaggy with denuded trees, their great puffed cheeks bristling with stubble. The sky was black over Dunderberg, blacker ahead. "Uh huh," Tom said, and found that he was whispering too.

It was almost five, the sleet had changed to a pasty wet snow and the party was in full swing when they motored into the dock at Garrison. A purist, Barr had kept her under sail as long as he could, but with the unpredictable wind he'd given up any notion of sailing in, and started the engines five hundred yards out.

The decks were slick and anything that stood upright, including the crew, trailed a beard of snow. Ahead, the dock was white, and beyond it the ground lay pale and ghostly under an inch of snow. There was the scent of food on the cold air, distant strains of music. Hunched and bony, the ex-saint of the forest stood in the bow, holding Jessica's hand and watching as the lights rode toward them across the water. "Well I'll be damned," he said, "if they didn't start without us."

By seven o'clock Tom had gone through three soyburgers, an egg salad sandwich, two falafel delights, a bowl of meatless chili, six or seven beers (he'd lost count) and maybe just one too many hits of Fred the bosun's miracle weed, puffed stealthily in the lee of the tent. Winded, he'd just sat down after a spate of fancy gangly-legged do-si-doing and swinging his partner, and he was beginning to feel a little vague about his surroundings. Those are the walls of the tent, he said to himself, gaping up from his hard wooden seat as if he were tarred to it, and those the big electric heaters. Outside, in the dark, is the dock. And next to the dock is the sloop. Yes. And down deep, tucked way up under the taffrail in the innermost recess of the main cabin, is my bunk. Into which I can fall at any moment. Suddenly he blinked his eyes rapidly and jerked up with a start. He was babbling. Only seven o'clock and he was babbling.

He was giving some thought to extricating himself from the oozing tarpit of his chair and maybe bellying up to the food table for just one more soyburger with tomato, lettuce, ketchup and onions, when he was assailed by a familiar, probing, cat's purr of a voice and found himself staring up into a face so familiar he knew it as well as his own.

The purr rose to a yowl. "Tom Crane, you horny old dirtbagging sex fiend, don't you recognize me? Wake up!" A familiar hand was on his elbow, shaking it like a stick. And now that familiar face was peering into his, so close it was distorted, big hard purple eyes, ambrosial breath, lips he could chew: Mardi.

"Mardi?" he said, and a flood of emotions coursed through him, beginning with a thunderbolt of lust that stirred his saintly prick and ending with something very like the fear that gives way to panic. He was suddenly lucid, poised on the edge of his chair like a debutante and scanning the dance floor for Jessica. If she should see him talking to . . . sitting beside . . . christ, breathing the same air in the same tent . . .

"Hey, you okay or what? T.C.? It's me, Mardi, okay?" She waved her mittened hands in his face. She was wearing some sort of fur hat pulled down to her eyes and a raccoon coat over a flesh-colored body stocking. And boots. Red, blue, yellow and orange frilled and spangled high-heeled cowgirl boots. "Anybody home?" She rapped playfully at his forehead.

"Uh—" he was stalling, scheming, caught between lust and panic, wondering how he was going to keep himself from bolting out of the tent like a purse snatcher. "Um," he said, somewhat redundantly, "um, I was thinking. Want to step outside a minute and have a hit of some miracle weed with me and Fred the bosun?"

She put her hands to her hips and smiled out of the corner of her mouth. "Ever know me to refuse?"

And then he was outside, the chill air revivifying him, a cold whisper of snow on his face. Mardi trooped along beside him, her coat open and sweeping across the ground, her breasts snug in spandex. "Isn't this a trip?!" she said, whirling twice and throwing her hands out to the sky. There was snow in her hair. Across the river, to the north, the lights of West Point were dim and diffuse, as distant as stars fallen to earth.

"Yeah," he said, throwing his head back and spreading his arms, remembering the excitement of waking as a boy to a world redeemed by snow, remembering the big console radio in his grandfather's living room and the measured, patient voice of the announcer as he read off the list of school closings. "It is, it really is." And suddenly the torpor was gone—indigestion, that's all it was, indigestion—and he was whirling with her, cutting capers, swinging her by the arm and do-si-doing like a double-jointed hog farmer from Arkansas. Then he slipped. Then she slipped. And then they went down together, helpless with laughter.

"Pssssst," called a voice from the shadows. "Tom?"

It was Fred. The bosun. He was conferring over a joint with Bernard, the first mate, and Rick, the engineer. They were being discreet.

Unfortunately, discretion was not one of Mardi's strong points.

The first thing she said—or rather shouted—when they joined the nervous little group hunkered over the glowing joint was: "Hey, what are you guys—hiding? You think pot's illegal or something?"

She was met by stony looks and a furtive rustling of anxious feet. There were plenty of people out to kill the *Arcadia*—the same chicken-necked, VFW-loving, flag-waving, anti-Communist warmongers who'd beat the shit out of everybody twenty years ago in Peterskill—and a drug bust would be heaven come to earth for them. Tom could envision the headline in the *Daily News*, in block letters left over from Pearl Harbor: POT SHIP SCUTTLED; GOV ASKS POT SHIP BAN. That was all they needed. People mistrusted them already, what with the Will Connell connection and the fact that the crew was composed exclusively of longhairs in Grateful Dead T-shirts with FREE HUEY! and MAKE LOVE, NOT WAR buttons pinned over their nipples. The first time they'd docked at Peterskill there'd been a bunch of jerks waiting for them with signs that read WAKE UP, AMERICA: PETERSKILL DID!, and at Cold Spring a troop of big-armed women in what looked like nurses' uniforms had showed up to wave flags as if they had a patent on them.

"It's a sacrament," Mardi said. "A religious rite." She was trying to be funny, trying to be hip and bubbly and trying to act more stoned than she was. "It's, it's—"

"Barr Aiken catches us with this shit, we can hang it up," Bernard drily observed. In a whisper.

Fred was a little guy with a Gabby Hayes beard, bandy legs and the upper body of a weight lifter. He loved puns, and couldn't resist one now. "Barr catches us, our ass is grass."

Rick tittered. "He'll keelhaul us."

"Make you walk the plank, hey, right?" Mardi said, getting into the spirit of it. For some strange reason, probably having to do with the moon shot, UFOs and the accoustic quality of the snow-laden air, her voice seemed to boom out across the water as if she were leading cheers through a megaphone. Someone handed her the joint. She inhaled, and was quiet.

For a time, they were all quiet. The joint went around, became a roach, vanished. The snow anointed them. Beards turned white, Mardi's hair got wilder. The music fell away and started up again with a skitter of fiddle and a thump of bass. Fred produced a second joint and the little group giggled conspiratorially.

It was at some point after that—at what point or what time it was or how long they'd been there, Tom couldn't say—that Mardi took him aside and told him he was an idiot for living with that bitch Walter was married to, and Tom—ex-saint, apprentice holy man and red-hot lover—found himself defending his one and only. The snow was falling faster and his head was light. Rick and Bernard were engaged in a heated debate over the approach to some island in the Lesser Antilles and Fred the bosun was unsuccessfully trying to shift the conversation back to the time he'd heroically climbed the shrouds in a thunderstorm to free the fouled mainsail and how he'd slipped and fallen and cut his arm in six places.

" 'Bitch'? What are you talking about?" Tom protested. "She's like the calmest, most copacetic—"

"She's skinny."

Tom's hair was wet. His beard was wet. His denim jacket and the hooded sweatshirt beneath it were wet. He began to feel the chill, and the vagueness was coming over him again. Jessica was probably looking for him that very minute. "Skinny?"

"She has no tits. She dresses like somebody's mother or something."

Before Tom could respond, Mardi took hold of his arm and lowered her voice. "You used to like me," she said.

It was undeniable. He used to like her. Still did. Liked her that very minute, in fact. Had half a mind to—but no, he loved Jessica. Always had. Shared his house with her, his soy grits, his toothbrush, his bunk aboard the *Arcadia.*

"What's wrong with me?" Mardi was leaning into him now and her hands, mittenless and hot, had somehow found their way up under his shirt.

"Nothing," he said, breathing into her face.

Then she smiled, pushed him away, pulled him back again and gave him a kiss so quick she might have been counting coup. "Listen," she said, breathless, warm, smelling of soap, perfume, herbs, wildflowers, incense, "I've got to run."

She was five steps away from him, already swallowed up in a swirl of snow, when she turned around. "Oh, yeah," she said. "There's something else. I shouldn't tell you cause I'm mad at you, but you're too cute, right? Listen: watch out for my old man."

The snow was a blanket. The vagueness was a blanket. He tried to lift it from his head. "Huh?"

"My father. You know him. He hates you." She waved her hand at the tent, the dock, the dim tall mast of the *Arcadia.* "All of you."

If he hadn't had to take a leak so bad—all that beer and all—he would have run into Jessica a lot sooner. She *was* looking for him. And she passed the very spot where Rick, Bernard and Fred were conducting their huddled rant, but Tom had vacated it to drift off into the storm and christen the breast of the new-fallen snow. Problem was, he got turned around somehow and the snow was falling so fast he couldn't for the life of him figure out exactly where he was. The band was on a break, apparently, so the music was no help, and even the noise of the party itself seemed muted and omnipresent. Was it over there, where those lights were? Or was that the train station?

All he wanted, really, after he'd zipped up and plunged off into the gloom, was to find Jessica and crawl back to his bunk and the comfort of his ptarmigan-down sleeping bag, the one that could keep a man toasty and warm out on the tip of the ice sheet. But which way to go? And Jee-sus! it was cold. Shouldn't have stayed out so long. Shouldn't have smoked so much. Or drunk so much. He belched. His hair had begun to freeze, trailing down his neck in ringlets of ice.

He started toward the lights, but when he was halfway there he realized that they were, after all, the old-fashioned hooded lamps of the railway station. Which meant that, if he turned around one hundred and eighty degrees and marched off toward those lights glimmering behind him, he'd reach the tent. Three minutes' effort, punctuated by a series of desperate arm-flailing slaloms across the slick earth, proved him wrong. He was under a light, all right, but it illuminated a false storefront that carried the legend YONKERS over it. Well that stumped him for a minute, but then the vagueness let go long enough for him to remember *Hello, Dolly,* and how the crew that filmed it had put up all sorts of gingerbread facades over the weathered old buildings to evoke the spirit of Yonkers in some bygone era. He stared stupidly at the sign for a moment, thinking *Yonkers? The spirit of Yonkers?* Yonkers was a derelict place of rotten wharves, blasted tenements and a river that looked like somebody's toilet—that *was* somebody's toilet. And this place, Garrison, had about as much spirit as Disneyland.

God, this snow was something. He couldn't see the nose in front of his face. (He was attempting the experiment, looking cross-eyed at the index finger and thumb of his cold and wet right hand, which were tugging at the cold and wet tip of his nose, when a pair of headlights swept across him.) Ah, so, here he was. In front of the antique shop. And down there, yes, the barn-red duplex with the Hollywood front, and around the corner, the green and the tent. He was on his way now, oh yes, stepping out with real confidence, when he spotted something that caught him up short. Somebody up ahead. Slipping around the corner. He knew that walk. That tottering, footshorn, awkward, big-shouldered walk. "Walter?" he called. "Van?"

No answer.

A car started up behind him, then another farther up the street. Two girls in knit hats rounded the corner, arm in arm, and then an older couple, in matching London Fog raincoats. When Tom got to the corner, he found the tent, found the party, found about a hundred people milling around over goodbyes and plastic cups of beer. A moment later, he even found Jessica.

"I was worried," she said, "where were you? God, you're soaked. You must be freezing."

"I, uh, had too much. . . . Took a walk, you know. Try to clear my head."

Onstage, the band had been joined by Will Connell for an encore. Will's goatee was flecked with white. He was thin and hunched, his face like something out of an old painting. He made a few cracks about the weather and then started strumming his banjo like an egg-beater salesman. After a while he set it aside in favor of the guitar and launched into "We Shall Overcome."

"You're shivering," Jessica said.

He was. He didn't deny it.

"Let's go," she whispered, and her hand closed over his.

When they got back to the sloop, everyone was gathered around the woodstove in the tiny galley, eating cookies and drinking hot chocolate. Tom stripped down right there, hugging the stove. He drank chocolate, munched cookies, cracked jokes with his mates. He didn't worry about Mardi or the worrisome fact that he'd failed to mention her to Jessica. He didn't worry about Mardi's father or Walter either. (Had he really seen him? he wondered ever so briefly between sips of hot chocolate. But no, he must have been dreaming.) He didn't worry about tomorrow's sail or the icy decks or his yellowed underwear. He merely yawned. A great, yodeling, jaw-cracking yawn of utter peace and satiation, and then he shrugged into his longjohns and climbed into the ptarmigan-down bag, his lady love at his side. He lay there a moment, breathing in the atmosphere of quiet joy and repletion that closed gently over the cabin, and then he shut his eyes.

The bunk was snug. The river rocked them. The snow fell.

World's End

It was one of those pressed-glass lamps with a hand-painted shade, ancient, no doubt, and priceless, and Walter was staring into it as if into a crystal ball. He was sitting hunched over his knees on a loveseat in the front parlor of the museum Dipe called home, clutching a tumbler of single-malt Scotch that had probably been distilled before he was born and trying to smoke a menthol cigarette in a properly nihilistic way. He'd been back from Barrow just over a week now, and he was feeling very peculiar all of a sudden, feeling light-headed and a bit nauseous. His groin ached, he was wet under the arms and the arch of his right foot began to itch so furiously he was actually reaching for it before he caught himself. It was funny—or no, it wasn't funny at all—but it was almost as if he were bracing himself for another attack of history.

Dipe sat on the couch across from him, sipping at his Scotch and furrowing his handsome brow at LeClerc Outhouse and a stranger in trench coat and black leather gloves. The stranger, whose name Walter hadn't caught, wore his hair in a crewcut so severe his scalp shone through like a reflector. He didn't unbutton his trench coat and he didn't remove his gloves. "It's a shame," the stranger said, slowly shaking his head, "it really is. And nobody seems to care."

LeClerc, who always seemed to have a suntan, even in winter, and whose favorite expression was "damn straight," said, "Damn straight."

Dipe leaned back in his chair with a sigh. He glanced at Walter, then back at LeClerc and the man in the trench coat. "Well, I tried.

Nobody can say I didn't." He sipped Scotch, and sighed into it. The others made consoling and affirmative noises: yes, he'd tried, they knew that. "If it wasn't for the damn weather—" He waved his hand at the ceiling in futility.

"Damn straight," LeClerc said.

Depeyster set his glass down and the stranger finished the thought for him, "—they'd never have got that floating circus within half a mile of Garrison."

"Damn straight," LeClerc said.

"Snow," Depeyster grunted, and from the tone of his grunt you would have thought shit was dropping from the trees.

The conversation had been going on along these lines for the better part of an hour. Walter had come home with Depeyster after work and had stayed for supper with Joanna, LeClerc and the grim-looking stranger, who'd kept his gloves on even while buttering his bread. Mardi's seat was vacant. Walter couldn't taste his food. It had been snowing—unseasonably, unreasonably—since three.

The principal theme of the evening was the *Arcadia,* and Dipe's thwarted effort to organize a rally against its landing at Garrison, "or, for shit's sake, anywhere else on this side of the river." The centerpiece of the rally was to have been a flotilla from the Peterskill Yacht Club—everything from cabin cruisers to dinghies—that would track north with banners and flags, harass the *Arcadia* and then block access to the Garrison dock through sheer force of numbers. The only problem was the weather. Dipe had taken Walter down to the marina at lunch, and only three boat owners had showed up. The rest were presumably discouraged by gale winds and predictions of two to four inches of snow that were later updated to as much as a foot.

"Apathy," Depeyster growled. "Nobody gives a good goddamn."

"Damn straight," LeClerc said.

The stranger nodded.

"If I was twenty years younger," Depeyster said, glancing at Walter again.

"It's a shame," the stranger said in a doleful whisper, and whether he was referring to Depeyster's age or the Communist-inspired, anti-American, long-haired hippie outrage being perpetrated that very moment and not five miles from his tumbler of Scotch, wasn't clear.

Walter didn't wait for clarification. All at once he was assailed by the most racking, god-awful stomach pains he'd ever known. He jerked upright, then leaned forward to set his tumbler down on a coffee table older than coffee itself. The pain hit him again. He snubbed his cigarette with a shaking hand. "You all right?" Dipe asked him.

"I'm"—he stood, wincing—"I think I'm . . . hungry, that's all."

"Hungry?" echoed LeClerc. "After a meal like that?"

Lula had served stuffed pork chops, mashed potatoes and canned asparagus, with homemade apple pie, ice cream and coffee for dessert. Walter hadn't felt much like eating, but he'd done justice to it anyway, putting away a modest portion, if not exactly polishing his plate. But now, as the words escaped his lips, he realized that the sudden pains, these volcanic contractions and dilations that felt as if they would split him open, were hunger pains. And that he was hungry. But not just hungry. Ravenous, starved, mad—killing mad—for the scent and texture and taste of food.

Dipe laughed. "He's a growing boy. You remember growing, right, LeClerc?" This was a reference to LeClerc's ballooning gut. The stranger laughed. Or rather snickered. The gloom lifted momentarily.

"Go on into the kitchen, Walter," Dipe was saying. "Stick your head in the refrigerator, go through the cupboards—you're welcome to anything I've got, you know that."

Walter was already in the hallway when the stranger called out, "Bring me back some peanuts or something, will you?"

The first think he saw on opening the refrigerator door was a six-pack of Budweiser. He didn't want beer, not exactly, but he popped one and drained it anyway. Beside the beer were the remains of the apple pie—nearly half of it, in fact—still in its baking dish. Walter made short work of it. In the meat compartment he found half a pound of pastrami, a rock-hard fragment of Parmesan and six thin pink slices of roast beef in an Offenbacher's bag. Before he knew what he was doing, he had the whole mess in his mouth and was washing it down with another beer. He was reaching for the glossy bright can of whipped cream, thinking to squirt some of it down his throat, when Mardi walked in on him.

"Oh, uh, hi," he said, guiltily closing the refrigerator door. He held a beer in one hand, and, somehow, a jar of marinated artichoke hearts had appeared in the other.

"What's happening?" Mardi said, laconic, her eyes wide and amused, yet a bit blunted too. She was wearing a flesh-colored body stocking, no brassiere, cowgirl boots. Her raccoon coat and woolen scarf were thrown over one arm. She reeked of pot. "Pigging out, huh?"

Walter set the beer down to unscrew the lid of the jar. He fished out a couple of artichoke hearts with his fingers and wedged them in his mouth, dabbing with the back of his hand at the oil dribbling down his chin. "I'm hungry," he said simply.

"Why don't you just move in?" she said in a breathy whisper. "Take my room." She opened the refrigerator and took a beer herself.

From across the house came the rumble of lamentation and the muffled but unmistakable tones of LeClerc Outhouse affirming an unheard proposition: "Damn straight!"

Walter couldn't help himself. He finished the artichoke hearts—there were only about twelve of them—and, still chewing, tilted back the jar and drank off the thick, herb-flavored olive oil in which they'd been preserved.

Mardi pulled the short-necked bottle from her lips and gave him a look of mock horror. "Disgusting," she said.

Walter shrugged, and went for the crullers in the bread box.

She watched him eat a moment, then asked him how Alaska was.

"You know," he said between mouthfuls, "cold."

There was a silence. The voices from the parlor became more animated. Joanna, hugely pregnant Joanna, passed by in the hallway in a silk dressing gown. Her skin was white, her hair upswept in a conventional coif. She wasn't even wearing moccasins.

"What's going on in there," Mardi asked, indicating the parlor with a jerk of her head, "—they plotting something or what?"

Walter shrugged. He was considering the half loaf of thin-sliced whole wheat bread he'd found beside the crullers. Peanut butter? he was thinking. Or pimento cream cheese?

Suddenly Mardi had hold of his arm and she was leaning into him, brushing his cheek with her own. "Want to go upstairs for a quickie?" she breathed, and for a minute, just a minute, he stopped chewing. But then she pushed away from him with a laugh—"Had you, didn't I? Huh? Admit it."

He looked from the loaf in his hand to her breasts, her lovely, familiar breasts, the upturned nipples so well delineated she might just as well have forgone the body stocking. The hunger—the hunger of the gut, anyway—began to subside.

Mardi was grinning, poised to dodge away from him like a kid with a swiped cap or notebook. "Only kidding," she said. "Hey, I'm on my way out the door."

Walter managed to summon a "where to?" look, though at the moment he couldn't have cared less.

"Garrison," she said, "where else?" And then she was gone.

Walter stood there a long moment, listening to the voices drifting in from the parlor, listening to Dipe Van Wart, his employer, his mentor, his best and only friend. Dipe Van Wart, who'd molded his father into a piece of shit. He thought about that a moment longer, and thought about Hesh and Lola, Tom Crane, Jessica, the late lamented Peletiah, Sasha Freeman, Morton Blum, Rose Pollack. They were pieces of shit too. All of them. He was alone. He was hard, soulless and free. He was Meursault shooting the Arab. He could do anything, anything he wanted.

He put the bread back in the bread box and poured the rest of his beer down the drain. His coat was in the parlor, but he wouldn't need it. He didn't feel like going back in there now, and besides, it wasn't cold—not when you've just come back from Barrow, anyway. He leaned against the counter and focused on the clock over the stove, forcing himself to wait until the second hand had circled it twice. *It's in the blood, Walter,* he heard his father say. And then he crossed the kitchen and slipped out the back door.

The night assaulted him with silence. He stumped through the snow, fighting for balance, and caught himself on the fender of the car. When he fired up the engine and flicked on the lights, he could see the dark rectangle where Mardi's car had been drawn up to the curb, and then the long trailing runners of her tire tracks sloping gracefully down the drive. And when he got to the bottom of the drive he saw that the tracks veered left, toward Garrison.

He could have turned right and gone home to bed.

But he didn't.

Fifteen minutes later he was pulling into the commuter lot on the dim far fringes of the Garrison station. The lot was unpaved and untended, a dusty Sonoran expanse of sharp-edged rock and brittle weed. Tonight it was white, smooth, perfect. Cars lined the single street in front of the station and there were another fifty or so in the lot, but they were close in, beneath the station lights. Walter chose to go beyond them, to blaze his own path. He wanted to be inconspicuous.

The MG had good traction, but he could feel the wheels slipping out from under him. Hidden obstacles were giving him a roller coaster ride, the visibility was about the same whether he had his eyes open or not and the rear end seemed to have a will of its own: before he knew it he was sunk in a crater deep enough to swallow a school bus. Furious, he gunned the accelerator. The rear wheels whined, the chassis shuddered beneath him. He slammed it into reverse, gunned it, rammed it back into first, gunned it again. Nothing. He kept at it for maybe ten minutes, gaining an inch on one run to lose it on the next.

Shit. He pounded the wheel in frustration. He didn't even know why he'd come—it wasn't to see Tom and Jessica, that was for shit sure, or Mardi either. In fact, he didn't want to see anyone, or be seen either. And now he was stuck. Like an idiot. Enraged, he popped the clutch and gunned it again, and then he slammed his fist into the dash so hard he went through the odometer lens and slashed his knuckles. He was sucking at the wound and cursing, so frustrated he could cry, when someone rapped at the windshield.

A muffled figure stood there in the snow. Walter rolled down the window and saw a second muffled figure lurking behind the first. "Need help?" A guy with shaggy wet hair and a beard stuck his head in the window. For a moment Walter panicked, thinking it was Tom Crane, but then he recovered himself. "Yeah. Son of a bitch. There's a pit or something here, feels like."

"We'll push," the guy said. "Hit it when I yell."

Walter left the window down. Snow drifted in to melt against the side of his face. It was warm, really it was. He was wondering how it could possibly be snowing when it was so balmy, when he heard a yell from behind and hit the accelerator. The car went up the hump, hesitated, and then a new impetus from the rear put it over the top and he was sailing out across the lot. He didn't stop till he'd reached the far side, all the way across, under the lowering cover of the trees. When he climbed out, his benefactors were gone.

He still didn't know why he'd come, or what he was going to do, but he thought for starters he'd maybe just cross the lot and poke his head in at the tent. He wasn't sure Jessica would be there, but he knew she and Tom were really into this sloop thing—that much she'd told him herself—and he guessed she would be. Tom too, of course. Maybe he'd just have a beer, hang out in the back. He didn't really want to talk to her—not after what had happened in the cabin. But a beer. Maybe he'd just have a beer.

Easier said than done.

The going was tough—as tough as it had been in Barrow, though not as icy—and he went down twice on his knees before he reached the railway platform. His jacket—wool blend, black and gray herringbone, one hundred and twenty-five bucks—was wet through already, ruined no doubt, and the tie had tightened like a noose around his neck. He began to regret not going back for his coat. For a long moment he stood hunched on the platform, sucking at the gash between his knuckles. Then he drifted off toward the music.

He was shivering by the time he ducked inside, and despite himself, he made his way toward the nearest of the heaters. He was surprised at how many people had turned out—a couple of hundred, at least. There looked to be half that many out on the dance floor alone—four big double rows of square dancers, going at it like refugees from the harvest hoedown in Hog's Back, Tennessee. The beer was good—Schaeffer, on tap—but after his eating attack Walter felt filled up right to the back of his throat and he could only sip at it. He didn't recognize a single face in the crowd.

He was still wondering what he was doing there and beginning to feel less than inconspicuous in his short hair, sports coat and tie, when he caught a glimpse of Jessica. She was out on the dance floor, in the middle of the throng, swinging from somebody's arm, he couldn't see whose. Wedging his way between a pair of middle-aged characters with white ponytails and mustard-colored sweatshirts that featured reproductions of the *Arcadia* listing beneath the swell of their middle-aged bellies, he got a better look. She was wearing an old-fashioned calico dress with ruffles and peaked shoulders, her hair was in braids and there was a smile of pure pleasure on her lips. He didn't recognize the guy she was dancing with, but it wasn't Tom Crane. He fell back away from the heater and into the shadows, suddenly agitated. He felt his face twist up and he flung his beer violently to the ground. The next minute he was outside again.

The snow seemed heavier now and a wind had come up to make it dance and drift. It seemed colder too. Walter crossed in front of the tent and made his way into a deep fold of shadow behind the duplex that fronted the street. There he propped himself up against the wall, lit a cigarette with hands that had already begun to tremble and watched. He watched the party wind down and begin to break up. He watched people slap backs, gesture at the sky, heard them call out to one another in hearty, beery voices, watched them troop off, heads bowed, toward the cars parked along the street and in the commuter lot beyond it. He watched an elderly couple in matching London Fog raincoats hump up the hill past him and he watched Tom Crane, gangling like a great pinched spider, his denim jacket so sodden it practically pulled him down, stagger through the mob and into the tent. He watched Mardi too—leaving with a guy in serape, boots and sombrero who looked as if he were on his way to a costume party. He watched all this, and still he didn't know why he'd come. Then Will Connell was singing "We Shall Overcome," cars were cranking over like the start of the Gran Prix, and Tom and Jessica, arms entwined, sauntered out of the tent.

Like lovers.

Like lovers in a dream.

Walter watched as they turned away from the crowd and made their way toward the dock—and the sloop. And then he understood: they had the romance of the storm, the romance of the do-gooders and marshwort preservers, of the longhairs and other-cheek turners, the romance of peace and brotherhood and equality, and they were taking their weary righteous souls to bed in the romance of the sloop. All at once he knew why he'd come. All at once he knew.

It took them an hour to settle down. At least. Equipment loaders, garbage haulers, stragglers and kibitzers, all of them milling around the front of the tent as if they'd just stepped out of an Off-Broadway theater. Walter, chilled through now, fumbled his way back to the MG—the snow so furious he could barely find it—to huddle over the heater and give them time. He smoked. Listened to the radio. Felt the jacket pinch around his shoulders and pull back from his wrists as the moisture began to steam out of it. An hour. The windshield was gone, his footprints erased. He concentrated on the eerie spatulate light of the station and crossed the lot for the third time that night.

The ship was dark, the marina deserted. He stood there on the snow-covered dock, breathing hard, the musty, damp, polluted breath of the river in his face, the sloop rising above him like an ancient presence, like some privateer dredged up from the bottom, like some ghost ship. Creaking, whispering, moaning with a hundred tongues, she rode out away from the dock on the pull of the flood tide, and the dock moaned with her. Three lines held her. Three lines, that was all. One aft, one amidships, one at the stern. Three lines, looped over the pilings. Walter was no stranger to boats, to cleats and half-hitches and the dark tug of the river. He knew what he was doing. He rubbed his hands together to work the stiffness out of them, and then he reached for the stern line.

"I wouldn't do it, Walter," sang a voice behind him.

He didn't even have to turn around. "Go home, gram," he whispered. "Leave me alone."

"It's in the bones," his father said, and there he was, big-headed and crude, the snow screening his face like a muffler. He was bent over the piling amidships, tugging at the line.

"Leave it!" Walter shouted, startled by the sound of his own voice, and he stalked up the dock and right through the old man as if he weren't there. "Leave it," he muttered, clomping around the piling like a puppet on a string, "this is for me to do, this is for me." He lifted his hand to his mouth, sucked at the dark blood frozen to his knuckles. And then, in a rage, he jerked the line from the piling and dropped it in the river.

He straightened up. Laughter. He heard laughter. Were they laughing at him, was that it? His mouth hardened. He squinted into the driving snow. Up ahead, in the shadows, he saw movement, a scurry of pathetic little legs and deformed feet, dwarfish hands fussing over the aft line. There was a splash, muted by the snow and the distance, and then the sloop swung free like the needle of a compass until it fixed on the open river, held now only by the single rigid line at its stern.

It took him a moment. A long moment. He moved back down the dock and stood there over that last frail line, and the line became a ribbon, the bow on a little pony Parilla motorbike, just tug it—tug it once—and it falls free. He jerked his head around. Nothing. No father, no grandmother, no ghosts. Only snow. What had he wanted—to go aboard, climb into the bunk with them, save the marshwort and become a good guy, an idealist, one of the true and unwavering? Is that what it was? The thought was so bitter he laughed aloud. Then he pulled the ribbon.

The moment held—perfect balance, utter silence, the slow grace of gathering movement—and then off she went, all one hundred six feet and thirteen tons of her, pulling away from him like a figure in a dream. She followed her nose and the flood tide and she drifted out across the invisible river, dead on for Gees Point and the black haunted immemorial depths of World's End. He watched till the snow closed over her, and then he turned away.

He was trembling—with cold, with fear, with excitement and relief—and he thought of the car. Almost wistfully, he looked once more out into the night, out over his shoulder and into the slashing strokes of the snow and the void beyond, and then he turned to go. But the dock was slick and his feet betrayed him. Before he could take a step, the hard white surface of the dock was rushing up to meet him and he hit it with a boom that seemed to thunder through the night. And then the unexpected happened, the unaccountable, the little thing that pumped him full of dread: a light went on. A light. Out there at the end of the dock, thirty feet from him, a sudden violation of the night, the river, the storm. He lay there, his heart hammering, and heard movement from below: heavy, muffled sounds.

And then he saw it—the low shadow of a boat drawn up on the other side of the dock, a second light gone on now, much closer. He pushed himself up, choked with panic, and his feet slid out from under him again. "Hey," a voice called out, and it was right beside him. There was a man on the boat, a man with a flashlight, and as the boat materialized from the shadows, Walter went numb. He knew it. He knew that boat. He did. Peterskill Marina. Halloween. The floating outhouse with the bum aboard, the Indian—what had Mardi called him?

Jeremy. She'd called him Jeremy.

Suddenly he was on his feet and running—scrambling, flailing, staggering, pitching headlong into the night—the voice raking him from behind. "Hey," it called, and it was the bay of a hound. "Hey, what's going on?"

Walter didn't know how many times he'd fallen by the time he reached the end of the dock and broke right along the tracks, his jacket torn and heavy with snow, the strap of his left foot twisted loose. He kept going, whipping himself on, expecting to hear the Indian's footsteps behind him, expecting the madman to leap out of the gloom and throw himself at him, lock onto his throat, his ear. . . .

The snow came at him like a judgment. He went down again and this time he couldn't get up—he was winded, out of shape, he was a cripple. There was a stitch in his side. His lungs burned. He gagged. And then it was coming up, all of it, beer, pastrami, artichoke hearts, crullers, the stuffed pork chops and canned asparagus. The heat of it rose in his face and he pushed himself away from it, sprawling in the snow like a dead man.

Later, when the cold made him move, his fingers refused to work. The prosthesis was loose—both of them were—and he couldn't pull the straps. When finally he stood, he couldn't feel the ground. He could feel his bleeding knuckles, could feel the tightness in his chest, but he couldn't feel the earth beneath his feet. And that was bad, very bad. Because the earth was covered with snow and the snow was mounting and everything seemed like something else. He knew he had to get to the car. But which way was the car? Had he crossed the tracks? And where was the station? Where were the lights?

He started off in what must have been the right direction—it must have been—but he couldn't feel the ground, and he fell. The cold had begun to sting now, the cold that was eighty degrees warmer than Barrow's, and he pushed himself up. Carefully, methodically, putting one foot in front of the other and lifting his arms high for balance, he started off again. Counting steps—three, four, five, and where was the car?—but he went down like a block of wood. He got back up and almost immediately pitched forward again. And again. Finally, he began to crawl.

It was while he was crawling, his hands and knees gone dead as his feet, that he heard the first tentative whimper. He paused. His mind was fuzzy and he was tired. He'd forgotten where he was, what he'd done, where he was going, why he'd come. And then there it was again. The whimper rose to a sob, a cry, a plaint of protest and lament. And finally, shattering and disconsolate, beyond hope or redemption, it rose to a wail.

Heir Apparent

THERE was no reason to have come in at all, really. Orders were traditionally slow this time of year, and even if they weren't, even if another world war broke out and they had to cook aluminum and cast aximaxes around the clock, they wouldn't have needed him anyway—except maybe to sign the paychecks every other week. He was superfluous, and no one knew it better than he. Olaffson, the production manager, could have handled ten times the volume without even switching his brain on, and the kid they'd found to replace Walter in sales and advertising was a natural. Or so they told him. Actually, he hadn't even met the kid yet.

But Depeyster liked the office. He liked to stretch out for a nap on the leather couch in the corner or cogitate over a paperback thriller in the rich spill of light from the brass desk lamp with the green glass shade. He liked the smell of the desk, liked the sound of the electric pencil sharpener and the way the big walnut chair tilted with the small of his back and glided across the carpet on its smooth silent casters. In the afternoons, he liked taking a two-hour lunch or slipping off to play a round of golf with LeClerc Outhouse—or, when the weather permitted, sailing up to Cold Spring for a Beefeater's martini, straight up, at Gus' Antique Bar. Best of all, though, he liked to get out of the house, liked to feel productive, useful, liked to feel he'd put in his day like anybody else.

Now, idly fanning the pages of a magazine and sitting over a cup of stone-cold coffee, he lifted his gaze to the window and the parking lot beyond, and saw that it was raining. Again. It seemed as if it had rained every day now since that freak snowstorm two weeks back. The plow had left a snowbank five feet high at the far end of the lot, and now there was nothing left of it but a broken ridge of dirty ice. All at once he had a terrible premonition: the rain would turn to sleet, the roads would ice up like a bobsled run and he'd be stuck here, away from home, and there'd be no way to get Joanna to the hospital.

He jerked open the drawer and fumbled with the phone book. "Weather service," he muttered to himself, "weather service, weather service," and he paged through the book and muttered until he gave it up and had Miss Egthuysen dial for him. Bland and indifferent, the recorded voice came over the wire with a crackle of static: "Rain ending late this afternoon, temperatures in the mid to high thirties, slight chance of overnight freezing in outlying areas."

In the next moment he was pacing around the desk, half-frantic with worry, fighting the temptation to call home again. He'd called not five minutes before and Lula, in her laconic way, had done her best to reassure him. Everything was fine, she told him. Joanna was resting. She didn't think she should be disturbed.

"Her water hasn't broken yet, has it?" he asked, just to hear his own voice.

"Nope."

There was a silence over the line. He was waiting for details, an update on Joanna's condition, today was the day, didn't she know that for christ's sake? Didn't she know that Dr. Brillinger had called it, right down to the very day—to *this* very day? The only reason he'd come into the office in the first place was because Joanna said he was making her nervous poking his head in the door every other minute. Pale to the roots of her hair, she'd squeezed his hand and asked him if he wouldn't feel better at the office, the diner, a movie—anything to make the time pass for him. Just leave a number, that's all. She'd call him. Not to worry, she'd call.

"Nope," Lula had repeated, and he began to feel foolish.

"You'll call me," he said. "The minute anything happens, right?"

Lula's voice was deep and rich and slow. "Uh huh, Misser Van Wart, soon's anything happen."

"I'm at the office," he said.

"Um-hm."

"Okay, then," he said. And then, for lack of anything better to do with it, he'd dropped the receiver back in its cradle.

No, he couldn't call again. Not already. He'd wait half an hour—or no, fifteen minutes. God, he was jittery. He looked out at the rain again, trying to mesmerize himself, clear his brain, but all he could think of was ice. His hands were trembling as he reached into his breast pocket for the envelope of cellar dust, dipped a wet finger in it and rubbed the fine ancient dirt over his front teeth and gums as if it were a drug. He prodded it with the tip of his tongue, rolled it luxuriously against his palate, worked it over his molars and ground it between his teeth. He closed his eyes and tasted his boyhood, tasted his father, his mother, tasted security. He was a boy, hidden in the cool, forgiving depths of the cellar, and the cellar was the soul of him, avatar of Van Warts past and Van Warts to come, and he felt its peace wash over him till he forgot the world existed beyond it.

And then the phone rang. And he jumped for it.

"Yes?" he gasped. "Yes?"

Miss Egthuysen's airy voice came back at him. "Marguerite Mott on line two."

Marguerite Mott. It took him a moment. The tang of the cellar dust began to fade and the familiar contours of his office came back to him. Yes. All right. He would talk to her. He punched the button.

"Dipe?" Her voice was a distant crowing.

"Yes? Marguerite?"

"We've got it."

He was at a loss. Got what? Had Joanna delivered already? He had a sudden vision of Marguerite, in her champagne cocktail dress and white pumps, holding the baby by its feet as if it were something she'd pounced on in the bushes. "Huh?" he said.

"The property," she cried. "Peletiah's place."

All at once it began to take hold of him, flowering in his brain like a whole long double row of Helen Traubels opening their sweet compacted buds in a single unstoppable moment. The property. The Crane property. Desecrated by Communists and fellow travelers, lost to the Van Warts nearly his whole life—the fifty wild undeveloped and untrammeled wooded acres that were his link to the glorious past and the very cornerstone and foundation of the triumphant future.

And she was telling him that now, at long last, it was his. "How much?" he asked.

Marguerite gave a little laugh. "You won't believe it."

He waited, the smile growing on his face. "Try me."

"Sixty-two and a half."

"Sixty—?" he repeated.

"Dipe!" she crowed. "That's twelve-fifty an acre! Twelve-fifty!"

He was stunned. He was speechless. Twelve-fifty an acre. It was half what he'd offered the old long-nosed son of a bitch—twenty-two fifty less than what he'd been asking. "I knew it," he said. "I knew it. Peletiah's grave isn't even cold yet and already the kid needs money—what's he going to do, buy a truckload of pot or something?"

"It's not pot, Dipe"—she cleared her throat—"but the catch is he's going to need the money right away."

"No problem." Christ, he practically had the ten percent down in his pocket, and Charlie Strang down at County Trust would write him a note for six times sixty thousand. Without even blinking. "I knew it," he repeated, crowing himself now. "So what was it? Gambling? Women? What the hell does that little shit need with sixty thousand?"

Marguerite paused for dramatic effect, then lowered her voice. "Listen, he didn't want to tell me—not at first. But you know how I am, right?"

He knew. She'd probably taken out her false teeth and gummed him into submission.

"It was that boat. The ecology thing? You know, the one that had that accident in the paper two weeks ago or so?"

"The *Arcadia*."

"Yeah. Well listen, I mean I don't know much about it, but apparently it was pretty well beat up—Sissy Sturdivant says there was this hole you could drive a Volkswagen through in the bottom of it and god only knows how much water damage. . . ."

The light of perfect understanding settled on him and Depeyster found himself grinning. He anticipated her: "So he's going to put up his own money for repairs, right?"

"Uh huh. That's what he says." She paused. "He's a weird kid, you know—and I don't just mean the way he dresses. It's almost as if there's something not right with him, know what I mean?"

Hallelujah and amen. There was something not right with his daughter too—with half the kids in the country—and he could have curled the ends of her wig with what he knew about it, but he didn't answer. He was savoring the rich irony of the whole thing—his money going to repair the *Arcadia*—and then, in the next instant, he was thinking about Walter, about the funeral and the cold driving rain that fell without remit as they lowered him into the ground. Tom Crane was there, looking half-drowned, and a tall, flat-chested blonde with a ski-slope nose who must have been Walter's wife. Mardi showed up too, though she wouldn't deign to come with her father—or be seen with him either. She stood off on the far side of the group gathered around the open grave, huddled under a torn beach umbrella with a ragtag crew of hippies—the spic she ran around with and a nigger kid dressed up like the Fool in *King Lear*. There was no minister, no service. Hesh Sollovay read something—some atheistic hogwash that gave everybody about as much comfort as the rain did—and that was that. No ashes to ashes, no dust to dust. Just dump the poor kid in the ground and forget it.

They said he'd been dead twelve hours or more by the time they found him. It was late in the afternoon, when the storm was already on its way out to sea and everybody was busy digging out. Eighteen inches had fallen, and it had drifted to three and four times that. No one thought a thing of the buried car, and if it hadn't been for a couple of sixth-graders building a snow fort, they might not have found him at all—at least until the rain cut the drifts down. The plant was closed, the schools were closed, everything was closed, and all anybody could talk about that afternoon was the *Arcadia* gone aground at Gees Point and how the police were looking into reports of sabotage. Depeyster and LeClerc and one or two of the others were actually celebrating the sad and untimely demise of that noble craft with a good fire and a bottle of Piper-Heidsieck when the call came about Walter. No one made the connection. Not at first. But Depeyster knew what had happened, knew just as certainly as if he'd been there himself. Walter had done it, done it for him.

Depeyster had wanted to cry. Standing there in the hallway, the cold black receiver in his hand, LeClerc and the others gaping at him from the parlor, he felt stricken. Walter had sacrificed himself. For him. For America. To strike a blow at the dirty little kikes and atheists who'd poisoned his childhood and somehow got a stranglehold on the whole great suffering country. It was a tragedy. It really was. It was Sophocles. It was Shakespeare. And the kid was, was—he was a hero, that's what he was. A patriot. He'd wanted to cry, he really had, thinking of the waste, thinking of Walter's sad and doomed life and the sad doomed life of his father before him, and he felt something high in his throat that might have been the beginning of it and something in his chest too. But he wasn't in the habit of crying. Hadn't cried probably since he was a child. The moment passed.

"Dipe?" Marguerite was still on the line.

"Hm?"

"You there?"

"Sorry," he said. "I went blank there for a minute."

"I was saying, do you want me to go ahead with it?"

Of course he wanted her to go ahead with it. He wanted it more than he'd ever wanted anything in his life. Except for a son. His son. Due today. "Yeah, sure," he said, glancing at his watch. Fifteen minutes. Maybe Joanna had been trying to get through, maybe he'd missed her, maybe—"Listen, Marguerite, you take care of it. Got to go. 'Bye."

And then he was dialing home.

The rain had stopped. The roads were clear. Depeyster Van Wart, twelfth heir to Van Wart Manor and the imminent acquirer of fifty pristine ancestral acres marred only by a single flimsy ramshackle structure the wind might have blown down on a good day, paced the worn gray carpet of the Peterskill Community Hospital's maternity ward. Joanna was somewhere inside, beyond the big double swinging doors, strapped down and sedated. There was a problem with the delivery, that much he knew, that much Flo Dietz—Nurse Dietz—had told him as she flew through the door on one of her hundred errands to god knew where. The baby—his baby, his son—was in the wrong position. His head wasn't where it was supposed to be and they couldn't seem to turn him around. They were going to have to do a C-section.

Depeyster sat. He stood. He looked out the window. He rubbed dirt on his gums. Every time the double doors swung open he looked up. He saw corridors, gurneys, nurses in scrub suits and masks, and he heard sobs and shrieks that would have made a torturer wince. There was no sign of Joanna. Or of Dr. Brillinger. He tried to occupy his mind with other things, tried to think about the property and the satisfaction he'd have in leveling that tumbledown shack and how he'd ride with his son in the first light of morning, before breakfast, when the world was still and their breath hung on the air, but it didn't work. The intercom would crackle, the doors would fly open, and he was undeniably, interminably and irrevocably there, in the hospital, watching the second hand trace its way around the great ugly institutional clock and staring at the pale green walls as if at the interior of a prison cell. He ducked his head. He felt as if he were going to throw up.

Later, much later, so much later he was sure Joanna had died on the operating table, sure his son was a fantasy, already dead and pickled in a jar as a curiosity for some half-baked obstetrical surgeon who'd got his training in Puerto Rico and barely knew which end the baby was supposed to come out of, Flo Deitz slipped up behind him in her noiseless, thick-soled nurse's shoes and tapped him on the shoulder. He jerked around, startled. Flo was standing beside Dr. Brillinger and a man he didn't recognize. The man he didn't recognize was wearing a scrub gown and rubber gloves and he was so spattered with blood he might have been butchering hogs. But he was smiling. Dr. Brillinger was smiling. Flo was smiling. "Dr. Perlmutter," Dr. Brillinger said, indicating the bloody man with a nod of his head.

"Congratulations," Dr. Perlmutter said in a voice too small to be hearty, "you're the father of a healthy boy."

"Nine pounds, six ounces," Flo Deitz said, as if it mattered.

Dr. Perlmutter snapped the glove from his right hand and held the bare hand out for Depeyster to shake. "Joanna's fine," Dr. Brillinger said in a fruity whisper. Numb, Depeyster shook. Relieved, Depeyster shook. All around. He even shook Flo's hand.

"This way," Flo was saying, already whispering off in her silent shoes.

Depeyster nodded at Drs. Brillinger and Perlmutter and followed her down a corridor to his right. She walked briskly—amazingly so for a pigeon-toed, middle-aged woman who couldn't have stood more than five feet tall—and he had to hurry to keep up. The corridor ended abruptly at a door that read NO ADMITTANCE, but Flo was already gliding down another corridor perpendicular to it, her brisk short legs as quick and purposeful as a long-distance runner's. When Depeyster caught up to her, she was standing before a window, or rather a panel of glass that gave onto the room beyond. "The nursery," she said. "There he is."

It had been what—twenty, twenty-one years? How old was Mardi?—and he could barely contain himself. His heart was pounding as if he'd just sprinted up ten flights of stairs and the hair at his temples was damp with sweat. He pressed his face to the window.

Babies. They all looked alike. There were four of them, hunched like little red-faced monkeys in their baskets, hand-lettered name tags identifying their parentage: Cappolupo, O'Reilly, Nelson, Van Brunt. "Where?" he said.

Flo Deitz gave him an odd look. "There," she said, "right there in front. Van Brunt."

He looked, but he didn't see. This? he thought, something like panic, like denial, rising in his throat. There it was—there *he* was—his son, swaddled in white linen like the others, but big, too big, and with a brushstroke of tarry black hair on his head. And there was something wrong with his skin too—he was dark, coppery almost, as if he'd been sunburned or something. "Is there anything . . . wrong with him?" he stammered. "I mean, his skin—?"

Flo was smiling at him, beaming at him.

"Is that some kind of, of afterbirth or something?"

"He's darling," she said.

He looked again. And at that moment, as if already there were some psychic link between them, the baby waved its arms and snapped open its eyes. It was a revelation. A shock. Depeyster's eyes were gray, as were his father's before him, and Joanna's the purest, regal shade of violet. The baby's eyes were as green as a cat's.

For a long while, Depeyster stood there in the hallway. He stood there long after Nurse Deitz had left him and gone home to her supper, long after the other proud fathers had come and gone, so long in fact that the janitor had to mop around him. He watched the baby sleep, studied its hair, the flutter of its eyelids and the clenching of its tiny fists as it drifted from one unfathomable dream to another. All sorts of things passed through Depeyster's mind, things that unsettled him, made him hurt in the pit of his stomach and feel as empty as he'd ever felt.

He was a strong man, single-minded and tough, a man who dwelt in history and felt the pulse of generations beating in his blood. He had those thoughts, those unsettling thoughts, just once, just then, and he dismissed them, never to have them again. When at long last he turned away from the window, there was a smile on his lips. And he held that smile as he strode down the corridor, across the lobby and through the heavy front door. He was outside, on the steps, the cool sweet air in his face and the stars spread out overhead like a benediction, when it came to him. *Rombout,* he thought, caught up in the sudden whelming grip of inspiration, he would call him *Rombout. . . .*

After his father.